S Par

CW00537127

Penguin Books
Awakenings

Pramoedya Ananta Toer was born in Blora, a small town in
central Java, Indonesia, in 1925. Some of his early works were
written while in a Dutch colonial prison during 1947–49. His
major works, a series of four novels – *This Earth of Mankind,
Child of All Nations, Footsteps* and *Glass House* – emerged from
a period as a political prisoner, without trial, from 1965–79 on
eastern Indonesia's Buru Island. The first two books of the series
published were banned by the Indonesian government in 1981,
despite having become best-sellers in Indonesia. Pramoedya also
completed several other works during his imprisonment. Since
1981 Pramoedya has edited and revised collections of early Malay
writings.

Among Pramoedya's other works are *Story from Blora,
Corruption, The Fugitive, The Sparks of the Revolution, Dawn,
Not an All Night Fair, On the Banks of the Bekasi River* and
Guerilla Family, many of which have been translated into several
languages.

Max Lane, the translator, was Second Secretary in the Australian
Embassy in Jakarta from April 1980 until recalled in September
1981 because of his translation of Pramoedya's works. As well as
translating the other three novels of this series, he is also working
on a book surveying contemporary society and politics in
Indonesia, and editing a quarterly magazine on Indonesian
affairs called *Inside Indonesia*. He has previously translated works
by Indonesian dramatist, W. S. Rendra, including *The Struggle
of the Naga Tribe*.

Awakenings

Awakenings combines *This Earth of Mankind* and
Child of All Nations, the first two novels of a
quartet by Pramoedya Ananta Toer

Pramoedya Ananta Toer

Translated and introduced by Max Lane

> '*Han, indeed this is nothing new.*
> *This narrow path has been trod many a time*
> *already, it's only that this time the journey*
> *is one to mark the way.*'
> *P.A.T.*

Penguin Books

Penguin Books Australia Ltd
487 Maroondah Highway, PO Box 257
Ringwood, Victoria 3134, Australia
Penguin Books Ltd
Harmondsworth, Middlesex, England
Viking Penguin, A Division of Penguin Books USA Inc
375 Hudson Street, New York, New York 10014, USA
Penguin Books Canada Limited
10 Alcorn Avenue, Toronto, Ontario, Canada M4V 1E4
Penguin Books (NZ) Ltd
182-190 Wairau Road, Auckland 10, New Zealand

This Earth of Mankind
First published in Indonesia by Hasta Mitra Publishing House,
Jakarta, 1980
Published by Penguin Books Australia, 1982, reprinted 1982
Revised 1991
Child of All Nations
First published in Indonesia by Hasta Mitra Publishing House,
Jakarta, 1980
Published by Penguin Books Australia, 1984
This combined edition published 1991 by Penguin Books Australia
10 9 8 7 6 5 4 3 2 1
Copyright © Pramoedya Ananta Toer, 1975
English language copyright © Max Lane, 1990

All rights reserved. Without limiting the rights under copyright
reserved above, no part of this publication may be reproduced, stored
in or introduced into a retrieval system, or transmitted, in any form
or by any means (electronic, mechanical, photocopying, recording or
otherwise), without the prior written permission of both the copyright
owner and the above publisher of this book.

Typeset in 8¼ pt Plantin by Midland Typesetters,
Maryborough 3465, Victoria, Australia
Made and printed in Australia by Australian Print Group,
Maryborough 3465, Victoria, Australia

National Library of Australia
Cataloguing-in-Publication data:

Toer, Pramoedya Ananta, 1925–
[Bumi manusia. English]. Awakenings.

ISBN 0 14 013420 4.
I. Toer, Pramoedya Ananta, 1925–   . [Anak semua bangsa.
English]. II. Title. III. Title: Awakenings. IV. Title:
[Anak semua bangsa. English].

899.22132

Introduction

During the first six or seven years on Buru Island, prisoners were not allowed reading material, except for a few religious texts. To be found with illicitly obtained material could result in severe punishment. One prisoner while out working in the fields came across a piece of torn newspaper. It had been used to wrap nails in and was full of holes. When the prison guards found the newspaper on him they took him away to the cell block. Three days later his body was found floating in a nearby river, his hands bound behind his back.

Pramoedya Ananta Toer's commitment to literature has clearly survived this hostility to the printed word. Of Javanese descent, he has been writing since the armed struggle for Indonesian independence which broke out in 1945. Many of his early works were written while languishing in a Dutch prison. He was captured by the Dutch Colonial Army during its attack on Jakarta in 1947, two years after the Revolutionary War started, and was released in 1949. After Indonesia's independence, Pramoedya began an active life in the literary world, producing several novels and many short stories. In the late fifties, he began his serious study of history and lectured in history and journalism at universities and academies in Jakarta. In the sixties he entered the polemics on the role of literature in society. He was a leading member of the People's Cultural Institute, many of whose members were close to the Indonesian Communist Party. Pramoedya himself was not a member and did not write in the Party's daily newspaper, but rather became the Cultural Editor for another independent newspaper, *Bintang Timur* (the *Eastern Star*), which reprinted many early writings of the pioneers of Indonesian fiction and journalism.

Pramoedya's interest in history continued to flourish and the *Eastern Star* published many of his articles about the period of Indonesia's national awakening. A part of this historical work included carrying out the research and contemplating the framework for a series of historical novels about the birth of national consciousness in Indonesia. The period to be covered was the turn of the century, 1890–1920. With the help of many of his students, a great deal of work was done and material collected.

Then, in September 1965, a coup attempt took place in Indonesia. Disorder and confusion occurred in Jakarta and throughout the country. The Indonesian army took control to restore order, but in the process almost all centre, left-wing and progressive political groups suffered persecution. The coup attempt was blamed on the Indonesian Communist Party. Along with thousands of others, Pramoedya was arrested (though even after 14 years in goal, never tried). His library, including all his notes and the results of his research, was burnt on the spot. In 1962 the Sukarno Government banned his history of the role of Chinese in Indonesia; in 1966, with the rise of Indonesian McCarthyism, a blanket ban was placed on all his earlier books – a ban that has never been revoked.

It was only eight years later that he was able to begin to put down on paper what had been lost in 1965. Pramoedya had already, each day before roll-call, presented an oral version of the novels – to ensure, he says, that the story would not be lost if the chance to produce a manuscript never arrived. In 1975, after two years' writing from memory, he finished his series of novels.

This Earth of Mankind was published in Jakarta as *Bumi Manusia*, a year after Pramoedya's release from Buru Island concentration camp in 1979. Soon after, its sequel *Anak Semua Bangsa (Child of All Nations)* was published. Both novels became best-sellers in Indonesia, as reviewers hailed Pramoedya's return to the nation's literary life. However, in May 1981 both books were banned in Indonesia. The Government accused the books of surreptitiously spreading 'Marxism-Leninism' – surreptitious because, they claimed, the author's great literary dexterity made it impossible to identify actual examples of this 'Marxism-Leninism'. Later in the year students from the University of Indonesia were arrested and expelled when they invited Pramoedya to speak on campus. One of the publishers of Pramoedya's books, Mr Yusuf Isak, was imprisoned for over three months, without being charged. Pramoedya himself and Hasyim Rahmam, Yusuf's partner in the publishing house Hasta Mitra, were repeatedly interrogated. Despite this perseeution, Hasta Mitra intend to publish further works by Pramoedya.

In its letter to the Prosecutor General calling for a revocation of the ban on *This Earth of Mankind*, the Jakarta Legal Aid Institute reminded the authorities that it was no longer rational to try to isolate Indonesia from so-called 'foreign ideologies'. This was because free exchanges of ideas came automatically with the social intercourse between nations, the international coming and going of reading materials, the progress in communications technology and the coming together of persons in the world's cultural centres. Such exchanges keep the world dynamic, generating pressures for change and demands for debate everywhere. They did so to no less an extent one hundred years ago in the colonies of all the European imperial powers.

Consider Surabaya in 1898, the place and year when *This Earth of Mankind* begins. The port of Surabaya was an old town that grew up around a major harbour. On the ships frequenting the port were the famed products of the Spice Islands – the spices that originally attracted Europeans to the East Indies. There were also goods from all parts of Asia, machinery and products from nearly every country of Europe, as well as other natural products like rubber, coffee, sugar and also minerals, all heading back to Europe. The same products left southwards in ships supplying the colonies soon to form Australia, while ships returned, bringing, among other things, dairy cattle for Java's dairy industry.

The ships also carried people – Dutch officials, businessmen and adventurers from all over Europe, seeking their fortunes and perhaps ending up in the Dutch Colonial Army, or prison. Arabs, Indians and Chinese were also always in port; many had long settled in Java. All these people brought with them aspects of the life of their own countries: their politics, their ideas on religion, philosophy and morality, their prejudices and their hatreds, and sometimes, their imagination and foresight.

Many of these ideas and ways of thinking came in other forms – books, for example. The narrator of our novel says, as he introduces his story, that of all the wonders of science, that at which he marvelled most was printing, especially the printing of photographs. Books, newspapers, magazines, pamphlets were circulating everywhere; and soon there would be the international telegraph service.

This dynamising environment was no small problem for the government of the Dutch East Indies. That government presided over a colony, the exploitation of whose resources made one of the smallest countries of Europe, Holland, one of its richest. This exploitation needed a special condition for its continuation: the maintenance of an attitude of acceptance on the part of the colonised and the governed. The colonisers' determination was that the native people, especially the toiling classes, of the Netherlands Indies should remain for ever submerged in a 'culture' of silence. This made exploitation easier and gave some Dutch their reason to exhibit the traditional colonial feelings of cultural arrogance and superiority.

The characters of *This Earth of Mankind* are set amid the tensions and contradictions created by the colliding of the liberating aspects of the expansion of capitalist industry and its technology on the one hand with the power of the colonial state on the other. In the centre is the novel's narrator – Minke, an eighteen-year-old Native Javanese youth. He is the only Native in the Dutch High School in Surabaya. His attendance there points immediately to an outstanding success in primary school and, at least equally importantly, strong backing from an important Dutch or Native official, in Minke's case his grandparents.

His grandparents symbolise the third element in the world that the novel presents. This is the world of Java itself, or, more specifically, the world of those who for so long had dominated Java. Minke's mother, whom he refers to as *Bunda* (a soft, respectful and loving term, inadequately translated in the text as Mother) and Minke's father, whom Minke only ever knew as a title, 'Father', are feudal Java's delegates in the novel. Through Minke's relations with his family, we are brought back to the ways of thinking and acting that the modern world and colonial power faced when dealing with Java's feudal rulers. To the ways and ideas of Minke's father and mother, the forces of the imperialist economy pay no heed, while those of the colonial state seek only to manipulate them. But as his mother consistently reminds him, a Javanese must eventually come to terms with his own identity.

There are many more revelations for the reader about life in Java during this period. The reader may note for example the constant references to the language used by the characters: Javanese, Dutch, Malay, Madurese, High Javanese. The use of language in this period was an important indicator of a person's social caste. Dutch, of course, was the language of the governing caste; Javanese, the Native language of the Javanese, and Madurese, the Native language of Madura (an island off Java). Malay was the language of inter-racial, or rather inter-caste communication (as many elite Javanese could speak Dutch), as well as the language of many Eurasians. Indeed, in situations where the caste order needed to be emphasised, Natives were forbidden to use Dutch. Not only did colonialism install Dutch as the supreme caste language of Java, it helped reinforce and even exaggerate caste distinctions in the Native languages themselves, especially Javanese. The Javanese language already operated on at least three different levels, each used according to whom one was speaking. This feudal stratification was given extra force as Javanese feudal notables, devoid of real political power in the face of the Dutch cannon and Dutch capital, channelled their oppressive energies into culture, something which Dutch cannon and capital were, in turn, frequently ready to buttress. The egalitarian and colloquial Javanese that was used in the palaces and royal houses of Java actually died out in this period. Only the masses of peasants and other toilers retained such an egalitarian Javanese.

The reader will also note that the terms 'Native', 'Mixed-Blood' and 'Pure' are capitalised. This is because they do not simply identify the racial origin of the persons involved, but manifest how, even in everyday life, racial caste dominated all of Netherlands Indies society. These categories were eventually given legal status. In the tragic story that unfolds through *This Earth of Mankind*, the true non-racial origins of this caste system – namely the whim of colonial power and colonist – are exposed.

But this is not a tale of revenge or hatred. Its spirit is not that of a simple denunciation. Pramoedya Ananta Toer set out to recreate the past through the telling of a story and the evocation of an atmosphere. He has recreated – no, he has actually brought to life in the first person – the real ego of his main character, *a new historical personality in the process of being forged, by history itself*. It is Minke, his psyche, his predicament, that is able to bring such a huge kaleidoscope of characters and stories together and engross the reader in the process. The figure of Minke himself is announcing the coming of something that would envelop everybody, that would leave no part of society free of turmoil: a revolutionary future, the awakening of a people.

Among the many complex interrelated themes of political, cultural and social life in the Indies, Pramoedya describes the emergence of a bourgeois from a feudal culture; the demands for rights of indigenous language and culture; the divisions amongst the colonialists over their treatment of the Natives; the intervention of Dutch colonial capitalism into the Javanese countryside; and the humiliation of the Javanese nobility in their dependence on Dutch officialdom. Most importantly, he writes of the development of those energies that would galvanise the Indonesian people into finally standing up and throwing off the yoke of colonial domination.

These themes are brought to life by the richly drawn characters in *This Earth of Mankind*, many of whom reappear in *Child of All Nations*: Nyai, Minke and Annelies; Ah Tjong, the corrupt Chinese brothel owner who murders Meneer Mellema, Nyai's Dutch master; Robert Mellema, his and Nyai's son who imitates his father's Pure-Blood Dutchness, and hates Natives; Robert Suurhof, Minke's Dutch rival from school; Magda Peters, the liberal Dutch teacher expelled from the Indies; Jean Marais, the one-legged Frenchman, painter and veteran of the colonial war in Aceh; Mr de la Croix, the liberal but interfering Dutch district officer and his two socially-conscious daughters; Maiko, the Japanese prostitute used by both father and son Mellema; Robert Jan Dapperste (alias Panji Darman), the Native boy adopted by a Dutch preacher; Maarten Nijman, the editor of the powerful Dutch newspaper published in the Indies, the *Soerabaisch Niews*; Kommer, the exuberant Eurasian editor of a popular Malay-language newspaper; Dr Martinet, a representative of Dutch science and education at its best; Darsam, the tough fighter and right-hand man of Nyai; Mr Lelliobuttockx, the cowed Dutch accountant; the mysterious Fatso, shadowing Minke everywhere; Minke's authoritarian, aristocratic father and his gentle and Javanese-educated mother; as well as a host of minor characters.

While *This Earth of Mankind* saw the battle to defend Annelies brought to a climax, the struggles of Nyai and Minke continue in *Child of All Nations*. The fate of Nyai's 'first child', the business, is not resolved. But more fundamental is the fate of Minke. With Annelies seemingly lost, how will he deal with the lessons he learned in the course of that battle? His environment has been completely changed; no longer is it limited to his school, his old boarding house, Nyai's home and Jan Marais's gallery. Minke has been drawn into the vortex of colonial society and must now confront all its harsh implications.

In *Child of All Nations*, Minke has become part of the vanguard that would change the face of the East Indies. Like iron on the anvil, he is beaten into shape by the forces of change operating in the early twentieth century. It is not only a time of change for the Indies: China is awakening – a phenomenon Minke has to face personally; Japan is aroused and is soon to defeat Russia in war; the Filipino people have created, even if only briefly, the first Asian republic. At home he is confronted by things he had never dreamed of. Most importantly, he becomes involved with representatives of his own people: the peasants. There are certainly new lessons to learn and greater challenges to come in *Child of All Nations*.

Now these two novels are available in one volume – *Awakenings*.

Translator's note

To preserve something of the rich texture of cultures, languages, forms of address, dialects, beliefs and meilieus of the Indies, I have retained numerous Malay, Javanese and Dutch terms.

These are italicised throughout, except for very common terms, which are italicised only the first time they appear. If explanations or translations are required, they can be found in the Glossary at the back of this book. The Glossary also contains some English words or acronyms that may not be familiar to the English-speaking reader. The explanations given have been kept to the minimum. A richly rewarding project that awaits scholars of Indonesian history is the preparation of a detailed guide to all the historical and cultural material contained in Pramoedya's tetralogy. For this edition the previously published English translation of *This Earth of Mankind* has been revised.

The production of such a complex translation is not easy. The contributions made by Elizabeth Flann to the editing of *This Earth of Mankind*, and Susanna Rodell and Jackie Yowell at Penguin Australia to the editing of *Child of All Nations* have been very important.

Here I must thank Anna Nurfia Lane, Kerry and Carolyn Groves and especially Dr Geoff Blunden. Also Blanche d'Alpuget for her suggestions for improving the difficult beginning to the book.

I am grateful to Professor A. H. Johns of the Australian National University for providing facilities, including an office, while I was working on this translation. I must also thank those concerned in Indonesia for their continuing friendship, which has been a cable that has kept the energy of my commitment to Indonesia flowing here in Australia.

Max Lane
Canberra, 1990

This Earth of Mankind

1

People called me: Minke.

My own name . . . for the time being I need not tell. Not because I'm crazy for mystery. I've thought about it quite a lot: I don't really yet need to reveal who I am before the eyes of others.

In the beginning I wrote these short notes during a period of mourning: she had left me, who could tell if for a while only or for ever? (At the time I didn't know how things would turn out.) That eternally harassing, tantalising future! Mystery! We shall all eventually arrive there – willing or unwilling, with all our soul and body. And too often it proves to be a great despot. And so, in the end, I arrived too. Whether it be a kind or a cruel god, is, of course, its own affair: humanity too often claps with just one hand.

Thirteen years later I read and studied these short notes over again, I merged them together with dreams, imaginings. Naturally they became different from the original. Different? Ah! But that doesn't matter! And here is how they turned out.

2

I was still very young, just the age of a corn plant, yet I had already experienced modern learning and science: they had bestowed upon me a blessing whose beauty was beyond description.

The Director of my school once told my class: your teachers have given you a very broad general knowledge, much broader than that received by students of the same level in many of the European countries.

Naturally this breast of mine swelled. I'd never been to Europe. So I did not know if the Director was telling the truth or not. But because it pleased me, I decided to believe him. And, further, all my teachers had been born in Europe, and educated there. It didn't feel right that I should distrust my teachers. My parents had entrusted me to them. Among the educated European and Indo communities, they were considered to be the best teachers in all of the Netherlands Indies. So I was obliged to trust them.

This science and learning, which I had been taught at school and whose manifestation in life I had witnessed all around me, meant that I was rather different from the general run of my countrymen. I don't know whether this violated my being as a Javanese or not. And that's how it was that I, a Javanese, liked to make notes, because of my European training. One day they would be of use to me, as they are now.

One of the products of science at which I never stopped marvelling was printing, especially zyncography. Imagine, people can reproduce tens of thousands of copies of any photo in just one day. Pictures of landscapes, big and important people, new machines, American skyscrapers, everything and from all over the world – now I could see them for myself upon these printed sheets of paper. How deprived had the generation before me been – a generation that had been satisfied with the accumulation of its own footsteps in the lanes of its villages. I was truly grateful to every single person and indeed to all those people who had worked so tirelessly to give birth to these new wonders. Five years ago there were no printed pictures, only block and lithographic prints, which gave very poor representations of reality.

Reports from Europe and America brought word of the latest discoveries. Their awesomeness rivalled the magical powers of the gods and knights, my ancestors in the *wayang*. Trains – carriages without horses, without cattle, without buffalo – had been witnessed now for over ten years by my country-men. And astonishment still remains in their hearts even today. Batavia –Surabaya can be traversed in only three days! And they're predicting it will soon take only a day and a night! A day and night! A long train of carriages as big as houses, full of goods, and people too, all pulled by water power alone! If I had ever been so lucky as to meet Stephenson, I would have made him an offering of a wreath of flowers, all of orchids. A network of railway tracks splintered my island, Java. The trains' billowing smoke coloured the sky of my homeland with black lines, which faded and faded into nothing-ness. It was as if the world no longer knew distance – it too had been abolished by the telegram. Power was no longer the monopoly of the elephant and the rhinoceros. They had been replaced by small man-made things: nuts, screws and bolts.

And over there in Europe, people had begun making even smaller machines, with even greater power, or at least with the same power as steam-engines. Indeed not with steam. With oil. There were also vague reports saying that a German had made a vehicle that worked by electricity. Oh *Allah*, and I couldn't really understand what electricity was.

The forces of nature were beginning to be changed by man so as to be put to his service. People were even planning to fly like *Gatotkaca*, like Icarus. One of my teachers had said: just a little while longer, just a little while, and humankind will no longer have to force their bones and squeeze out their sweat for so little result. Machines would replace all and every kind of work. People will have nothing to do except enjoy themselves. You are fortunate indeed, my students, he said, to be able to witness the beginning of the modern era here in the Indies.

Modern! How quickly that word had surged forward and multiplied itself like bacteria throughout the world. (At least, that is what people were saying.) So allow me also to use this word, even though I still don't truly fathom its meaning.

In short, in this modern era, tens of thousands of copies of any photo could be reproduced each day. And the important thing was: there was one of these photos that I looked at more often than any other: of a maiden, beautiful, rich, powerful, glorious, one who possessed everything, the beloved of the gods.

Rumours, furtively whispered among my school friends: even the richest bankers in the world have no chance of courting her. Handsome and manly nobility scramble head over heels just to be noticed. Just to be noticed!

Whenever I had nothing to do, I would gaze at her face while supposing: Oh, how would it be! How would it be! And how high, too, was her station. And how far away she was, nearly twenty thousand kilometres from where I was: Surabaya. One month's sail by boat, encompassing two oceans, five straits and one canal. Even then there'd be no certainty of being able to meet

3

her. I didn't dare speak my feelings to a single soul. They would have laughed at me and called me mad.

At the post offices, so rumour also whispered, a letter was occasionally received proposing marriage to the maiden who lived so far away and so high above. None ever reached its destination. Even if I had been mad enough to try, it would have been just the same: the post officials would have only kept the letter for themselves.

And that beloved of the gods was the same age as me: eighteen. We were both born in the same year: 1880. Only one figure shaped like a stick, the others roundish, like miscast marbles. The day and the month were also the same: 31 August. If there were any differences, they were only the hour and sex. My parents never noted down the time of my birth. And I didn't know the hour of her birth. Difference in sex? I was a male, she was a female. As to that bewildering difference in time: when my island was blanketed in the darkness of night, her land was lit with sunshine. When her country was embraced by the blackness of night, my island shone brightly under the equatorial sun.

My teacher, Magda Peters, forbade us to believe in astrology. It was nonsense, she said. Thomas Aquinas, she said, once saw two people who were born in the same year, in the same month, on the same day and at the same hour, even in the same place. A joke played by astrology. The one became a great landowner, and the other: his slave!

And indeed I don't believe in it. How could anyone believe in it? It has never lit the way for humanity's progress in science and in learning. And all it demands of us is that we submit to its predictions. There is nothing else we can do, except to throw it into the pig's slops bucket. Once I had my fortune told, just for fun. My horoscope was turned over and over. The fortune-teller opened her mouth. She had two gold teeth: if Sir is patient, you will surely meet the maiden . . . So I just prefer to trust my intellect. Even with the patience-of-all-mankind, I would never meet her.

I prefer to put my trust in scientific understanding, in reason. With these at least, there are certainties that can be grasped.

Without knocking on the door of my rented room, Robert Suurhof – I won't use his real name here – entered. He found me crouched over the picture of that maiden, that beloved of the gods. He burst out laughing; my eyes grew moist, I was so embarrassed. His shout was even more impudent:

'Oho, oh *philogynist*, lady-killer, our crocodile! What is the good of dreaming over the moon?'

I could have thrown him out. But instead: 'Oh . . . you never know?!'

Let me tell you about him: he was my school-friend from *HBS*, HBS

Street, Surabaya. He was taller than me. In his body ran Native blood. Who knows how many drops or clots.

'Forget her,' he said. His voice had a coaxing, groaning note in it. Then: 'There is a goddess here too in Surabaya. Beautiful beyond comparison, easily equal to this picture. It's only a picture anyway.'

And he mocked me, I, the one who had defined beauty, and he quoted my definition back at me: Bone structure and body proportion must be in balance. And with fine, soft skin. She must have eyes that shine and lips that are *clever at whispering*.'

'You've added *"clever at whispering"*.'

'Yes, then if she curses you, you won't hear.'

'Tsss, tsss,' I offered him silence.

He gave me a look. 'If you are a real man, a true philogynist, come with me there. I want to see what you do, whether you're indeed as manly as you say you are.'

'I've still got a lot of work to do.'

'You're afraid even before you descend into the arena,' he accused.

That offended me. I knew that the HBS brain inside the head of Robert Suurhof was only clever at insulting, belittling, disparaging, and working evil on people. He thought he knew my weakness: I had no European blood in my body.

'It's on!' I answered. That was several weeks ago, at the beginning of the new school year.

And now all of Java was celebrating, perhaps also the whole of the Netherlands Indies. The tricolour fluttered joyously everywhere: that one-and-only maiden, Goddess of Beauty, Beloved of the Gods, was now ascending the throne. She now was my Queen. I was her subject. Exactly like Miss Magda Peters's story of Thomas Aquinas. She was Her Majesty Wilhelmina. Date, month, and year of birth had given the astrologer the opportunity to raise her to become a queen and to cast me down to become her subject. And my Queen would never know that I had walked this earth.

7 September 1898. *Legi* Friday. This was in the Indies. Over there in Holland: 6 September 1898. *Kliwon* Thursday.

All the school had gone crazy celebrating the coronation: competitions, performances, exhibitions of all those skills and abilities studied by Europeans – soccer, acrobatics, and softball. And none of this interested me. I didn't like sport.

The world around me was bustling. The cannons were booming. Parades and hymns of praise. My heart was empty, tormented. So I went, as usual, to my next-door neighbour and business partner, Jean Marais. Jean was a Frenchman and had only one leg. But his story comes later. He greeted me in French, forcing me too to use his language.

'*Ca va*, Jean, I have some work for you. One sitting-room suite,' I gave him a drawing of what the customer wanted.

'Master Minke!' came a call from next door.

Sticking my head out the window I saw Mrs Telinga waving to me.

'Jean, I'm going. She may be serving cake.'

At home I found no cake. Only Robert Suurhof.

'*Ayoh!*', he said. 'We'll go now.'

A new model buggy, a *karper*, was waiting for us at the front gate. We climbed aboard; the horses began to move; the coachman was an old Javanese.

'The rent for this must surely be more expensive than for any other,' I said in Dutch.

'No fooling, Minke, this is no ordinary buggy, no cheap *kretek*, it's got springs – perhaps the first in Surabaya. Its springs probably cost more than the rest of the buggy put together.'

'I can believe you, Rob. Come on tell me, where are we going?'

He replied in his insolent, mysterious way:

'A place to which every youth dreams of receiving an invitation. Because of the angel that lives there, Minke. Listen, I've had the good luck to be invited by her older brother. Nobody has ever got an invitation, except this one,' he pointed to himself with his thumb. 'Listen, coincidently her brother is also called Robert . . .'

'There are a lot of children called Robert now . . .' He took no notice of me and continued:

'. . . We met at a soccer match. And now I am invited to lunch, to eat bull calves. That is what interests me most,' he glanced slyly at me.

'Bull calves?' I did not understand.

'Veal, to eat veal. That's my problem. Your problem,' he made a noise with his lips, his eyes sharply examined mine, 'is that little sister of Robert's I want to see how far this masculine charm of yours gets you, you philogynist.'

The steel frame of the *karper*'s wheels rattled on as it ground along the stone road of Kranggan Street, to Blauran, in the direction of Wonokromo.

'Come on, sing *veni, vidi, vici* – I came, I saw, I conquered,' he prompted me to join in between the rattle of the wheels. 'Ha-ha, you've gone pale now. He no longer believes in his own virility. Ha! Ha!'

'Why don't you take it all for yourself. Veal and this goddess?'

'I? Ha! Ha! For me – only a goddess with Pure European blood!' So the goddess we were about to visit was an Indo girl, a Mixed-Blood, Indisch. Robert Suurhof – I remind you once again, I'm not using his real name – was also an Indo. When his mama, also an Indo, was about to give birth, his father, also an Indo, rushed her to Perak Harbour, boarded the ship *Van Heemskerck*, which was tied up in port, so she had the child there, and: he not only became a Dutch subject but a Dutch citizen as well. So he thought anyway. But I found out later that to be born on board a Dutch

6

ship had no legal consequences whatever. And: perhaps his behaviour was similar to that of the Jews with Roman citizenship. He held himself to be different from his own brothers and sisters. He did not look upon himself as an Indo. If he had been born only one kilometre from that ship, maybe on the docks of Perak, perhaps on a Madurese *sampan*, and obtained Madurese citizenship, his behaviour would have been a bit different. At least I began to understand why he carried on about not being interested in Indo girls. Under the illusion he was actually a Dutch citizen he strove to act as one for the sake of his grandchildren's future. He hoped that, in the future, he'd have a position and salary higher than that of an Indo, let alone a Native.

It was a very beautiful morning. The blue sky was clear, cloudless. Young life breathed nothing but pleasure. I was succeeding in all that I was doing. I was doing well in my studies. And I had an unworried heart and clear emotions. And she who had ascended the throne? That was all over. All the decorations on the buildings and gateways were for her. All the official gatherings were also for her. Beloved of the gods! Heavenly Goddess! And now Suurhof wanted to make fun of me in front of this other earthly girl whom he also wanted me to conquer.

I did not even notice all the village people walking to town. The yellow-stone road went straight to Wonokromo. Houses, dry-fields, wet paddy-fields, trees enclosed in bamboo lattice along the road, clumps of forest washed with silver rays of sunshine, all of it, all flew past gaily. And, far away in the distance, indistinctly visible, were the mountains, standing silent in their arrogance, like a reclining ascetic turned to stone.

'So we're off to a party in clothes like this?'

'No, I just told you, I'm only going to eat, you to conquer.'

'Where are we going?'

'Direct to target.'

'Rob?' I boxed his shoulder because of my curiosity. 'Come on, tell me.' And still he would not say.

'Don't make such a sour face! If you prove your virility,' he smacked his lips, 'I will respect you more than I do my own teacher. If you fail, look out, all your life you will be the butt of my jokes. Remember that well, Minke.'

'You're mocking me.'

'No. One day, Minke, you'll become a *bupati*. Perhaps you'll get a regency where the land is arid. I'll pray that you get a fertile one. If this goddess were to be beside you as your *raden ayu*, ah! all the *bupatis* of Java would be in a high fever because of their envy.'

'Who said I shall become a *bupati*?'

'Me. And I shall continue my education in Holland. I shall become an engineer. Then we'll meet again. I shall visit you with my wife. Do you know what will be the first question I ask you?'

'You're dreaming. I will never become a *bupati*.'

'Listen, first I will ask: Heh, philogynist, lady-killer, crocodile, where is your harem?'

'It seems you still look upon me as an uncivilised Javanese.'

'What Javanese, and a *bupati* too, is not but a crocodile on land?'

'I'm not going to be a *bupati*.'

He laughed at me scornfully. And the buggy still didn't stop, and with time we moved further and further away from Surabaya. I had been offended. Actually, I was too easily offended, and my feelings too easily hurt. Rob did not care. Indeed he had once said: the only way a wealthy and powerful Javanese could prove that he did not intend to have a harem was for him to marry a European, Pure or Eurasian. Then there could never be any co-wives or concubines.

The *karper* entered Wonokromo district.

Look to the left, Rob suggested.

A Chinese-style house with a big yard, well-kept and with a hedge. The front doors and windows were closed. It was painted red all over. I didn't think it was at all attractive. And we all knew whose house it was and what it was! A pleasure-house, a brothel, owned by *Babah* Ah Tjong. -

But the buggy kept on going.

'Keep looking to the left.'

For about one hundred or one hundred and fifty metres past the pleasure-house the land was empty. Then there stood a two-storied timber house, also with extensive grounds. Standing behind the wooden fence was a big sign with the words: *Boerderij Buitenzorg*—Buitenzorg Agricultural Company.

And everyone who lives in Surabaya and Wonokromo, I thought, knew: that was the house of the wealthy Mr Mellema – Herman Mellema. Everyone thought of that house as Mellema's private palace, even if it was only from teak. Its grey, wooden-shingle roof was already visible from quite a distance away. Its doors and windows stood wide open. Not like Ah Tjong's pleasure-house. There was no verandah. In its place there was an expansive and broad awning overhanging the wooden stairs, which were also wide, wider than the front door.

But that's all that anyone knew, his name: Mr Mellema. People would see him once or twice only, or once and then never again. But everyone talked about his concubine: *Nyai* Ontosoroh. People admired her very much. She was handsome, in her thirties, and she managed the whole of this great agricultural firm. People called her Ontosoroh, a Javanese pronunciation of *Buitenzorg*.

The family and its business was guarded by a Madurese fighter, Darsam, and his men. No one dared to call in on that timber palace.

I sat up, startled.

The buggy suddenly turned, passed through the gate, passed the *Boerderij*

Buitenzorg sign, and headed directly to the house's front steps. I shuddered. Darsam, whom I had never seen, appeared in my mind's eye. Just a moustache; nothing but a moustache, a fist and a giant sickle. I had never heard of anyone receiving an invitation from this eerie and sinister palace.

'Here?'

Robert just spat.

An Indo-Eurasian youth opened the glass door, and came down the steps to greet Suurhof. He appeared to be about my age. He looked European, except he had brown skin. He was tall, well-built, sturdy.

'Hi, Rob!'

'Oho, Rob!' greeted Suurhof. 'I've brought my friend. It's okay, isn't it? You don't mind, do you?'

He didn't greet me. I was just a Native. He looked at me piercingly. I started to become anxious. I knew we were beginning a new round in a game. If he refused to receive me, Suurhof would laugh, and wait for me to crawl back to the main road, driven away by Darsam. He hadn't yet refused, hadn't yet expelled me. With just one movement of his lips, I could be driven out – God!, where must I hide my face? But no, suddenly he smiled and held out his hand:

'Robert Mellema,' he introduced himself.

'Minke', I responded.

He still held my hand, waiting for me to give my family name. He raised his eyebrows. I understood: he thought I was not, or not yet, legally acknowledged by my father. Without a family name, an Indo is considered beneath contempt, like a Native. And I was indeed a Native. But no, he didn't demand my family name.

'Pleased to meet you: come on in.'

We went up the steps. His sharp glance did nothing to dispel my suspicions.

But suddenly a new mood replaced suspicion: in front of us stood a girl, white-skinned, refined, European face, hair and eyes of a Native. And those eyes, those shining eyes! ('Like a pair of day-time stars,' I called them in my notes.) If this was the girl Suurhof meant he was right: not only could she rival the Queen, she triumphed over her. And she was alive, flesh and blood, not just a picture.

'Annelies Mellema,' she held out her hand to me, then to Suurhof.

The voice that came from her lips left an impression that I was never to forget for the rest of my life.

The four of us sat on a rattan settee. Robert Suurhof and Robert Mellema were soon engrossed in talk about soccer. I felt awkward about joining in. I had never liked soccer. My eyes began to poke around the big drawing room: the furniture, the ceiling, the dangling crystal, candle chandelier, hanging gas lights with their copper piping (I couldn't work out where the main gas tank was), a picture of Queen Emma, who had just abdicated, hanging on the wall in a heavy wooden frame. Being a trader in furniture, just one dip into these surroundings with my eyes told me that they were nothing but the most expensive, made by master craftsmen. The carpet under the settee was decorated with a motif I'd never come across before. And for the umpteenth time my gaze ended resting on Annelies's face.

'Why are you so quiet?' Annelies asked. She addressed me in familiar Dutch.

Once again I gazed at her face. I hardly dared look into her eyes. Surely she would be repulsed by me. I had no family name and I was a Native too. All I could do was smile – and once again I forced myself to look away, towards the furniture. And:

'Everything is so beautiful here.'

'You like it here?'

'Very much,' and once again I looked at her.

Truly: in the middle of all this sumptuousness she appeared grand, a part of it all but outshining all these rich and beautiful things.

'Why do you hide your family name?' she asked.

'I haven't hidden it,' I answered, and I began to become anxious again. 'Do I really need tell?' I glanced over at Robert Suurhof. Before I could look away, he let fly his own glance.

'Of course you do,' Annelies said. 'Otherwise people will think you're not acknowledged by your father.'

'I don't have a family name. Truly I have none.' I answered gamely.

'Oh!' she exclaimed slowly. 'Forgive me.' She was silent for a moment. 'That's quite all right,' she then said.

'I'm not an Indo,' I added in a defensive tone.

'Oh!' she exclaimed once again. 'No?'

It felt as if a drum was pounding in my heart. So she knew: I was a Native. I could be thrown out at any moment. I could feel the glances of Robert Suurhof examining those parts of my body which were not covered up. Yes, like a vulture examining a candidate carcass. When I looked up I saw Robert Mellema stabbing at Annelies with his eyes: At that moment he turned to me, his lips becoming a thin, straight line. Oh Lord, what will happen to me? Must I be thrown out like a dog from this beautiful house, accompanied by the cascading laughter of Robert Suurhof? His eyes were knifing at my neck. The Mellema boy hadn't even blinked.

For a moment my vision blurred. All I could see was Annelies's white gown, without a face, without limbs.

And then I began to realise: it had been Suurhof's intention all along to humiliate me here in someone else's house. And now all I could do was to wait for the expulsion to explode.

A moment more and Darsam, the fighter, would be called and ordered to throw me out onto the street.

All of a sudden I heard the shrill laughter of Annelies and this crazed heart of mine felt as if it no longer beat. Slowly I lifted my eyes towards her. Her teeth gleamed, visible, more beautifully white than any I had ever seen. Ahoy! Oh philogynist! Even in a situation like this you can still admire and praise beauty.

'It's all right to be a Native,' she said, still laughing.

Now Robert Mellema's look was directed at his little sister, and Annelies, challenging him, looked him straight in the face. Her brother looked away.

What sort of drama was all this? Robert Suurhof did not say anything. Neither did Robert Mellema. Were the two youths in league to force me to apologise? Only because I had no family name and was a Native as well. Why should I! No! I would not.

'Being Native is good too,' Annelies said earnestly. 'My mother is a Native. Native Javanese. You are my guest, Minke,' her voice had the tone of an order.

Only then could I breathe freely again.

'Thank you.'

'It seems that you don't like soccer. I don't either. Let's sit somewhere else.' She stood up and showed me the way, putting out her hand; in that sweet, spoiled way of hers. She wanted me to take her by the hand.

I stood up, and excused myself, nodding to her brother and Suurhof. Their eyes followed us. Annelies glanced back with an apologetic smile to the guest she left behind.

We crossed that broad drawing room. My knees almost gave way. I could feel the glances of the two youths stabbing into my back. We went into the back parlour, which was even more sumptuously furnished.

Here, too, all the walls were made from light-brown, varnished teak. In the corner there was a dining suite, consisting of one table and six chairs. Close by there were stairs leading upstairs. Small tables stood on guard, night and day, in each of the other three corners. Vases of European porcelain stood upon each one.

Seeing my eyes fixed upon the display cabinet, she took me over to it. The cabinet stood against the wall opposite the dining table. In it were displayed art objects – I'd never seen such things before.

'I am not carrying the keys with me,' said Annelies. 'That's the one I like best.' She pointed to a small, bronze statue. 'Mama says it's an Egyptian Empress,' she thought for a moment, 'if I'm not mistaken her name is Nefertiti.'

Whatever the name of the figurine, I was amazed that a Native, and a concubine too, knew the name of an Egyptian Empress.

There was also a Balinese carving of Erlangga, riding on the back of a *garuda*. Unlike the others, it was not made from *sawoh* wood, but from some other kind that I had never come across before.

11

On the first shelf there was a row of little ceramic masks, picturing all sorts of animal faces.

'These are the masks from the story of *Sie You Chie*,' she explained. 'Have you heard the story?'

'Not yet.'

'One day I'll tell it to you. Would you like that?'

The question sounded so inviting it drowned out all the sumptuousness, and the differences that existed between us.

'Very much so.'

'Then you'd definitely like to come here again.'

'An honour.'

There were no great clam shells sitting at the feet of the small tables such as I had seen in the *bupati* buildings. There was a phonograph on a low table with a small wheel on each of its four legs. The lower section of the phonograph was used as a place to store music. The table itself was overly carved. It must have been made to order.

'Why are you silent?' she asked again. 'You're still at school?'

'A school friend of Robert Suurhof.'

'It looks like my brother is really proud to have him as a friend, an HBS student. Now I too have a friend who is an HBS student. You!' Suddenly she turned round towards the back door and called: 'Mama! Over here! Mama, we have a guest.'

And soon after, a Native woman entered, wearing a *kain*, a white blouse embellished with expensive lace, perhaps the famous Dutch lace made in Naarden as we had been told about in ELS. She was wearing black velvet slippers embroidered with silver thread. Her neat attire, her clear face, her motherly smile, and her very simple adornments made a deep impression on me. She looked lovely and young, her skin was smooth and light-coloured like the fruit called *langsat*. So this was what she looked like, this *Nyai* Ontosoroh who was talked about by so many people, whose name was on the lips of everyone in Wonokromo and Surabaya, the *nyai* in control of the *Boerderij Buitenzorg*.

'Yes, Annelies, who is your guest?' I was even more startled, for she spoke in Dutch.

'An HBS student, Mama.'

'Oh yes? Is it true?' Nyai asked me. Her Dutch was good, with correct school pronunciation.

And I hesitated. Should I offer my hand as to a European woman, or should I treat he as a Native woman – and ignore her? But it was, on the contrary, she who first offered her hand. I was dumbfounded, and clumsily accepted her grip. This was not Native custom: European! If that's how they do things here, then I, of course, will offer mine first.

12

'Annelies' guests are my guests too,' she said. Her Dutch was so fluent. 'How must I call you? Sir? *Sinyo*? But you're not Indo . . .'

'Not Indo . . .' What should I call her, Nyai or Madam?

'Are you really an HBS student?' she asked, smiling affably.

'Yes, really . . .'

'People call me Nyai Ontosoroh. They can't pronounce *Buitenzorg*. Sinyo appears to hesitate to call me that. Everyone does. Don't be reluctant.'

I didn't answer. And it seemed she forgave my awkwardness.

'If Sinyo is an HBS student, Sinyo is no doubt the son of a *bupati*. *Bupati* of what district, Nyo?'

'No, Ny, Ny . . .'

'Sinyo is so reluctant to call me by my name. Well, then, call me Mama, like Annelies – that is if you don't feel insulted, Sinyo.'

'Yes, Minke,' the daughter added. 'Mama's right. Call her Mama.'

'I'm not the son of any *bupati*, Mama,' and with the use of the new name, my awkwardness, the differences between her and me, even her strangeness, abruptly disappeared.

'Then you must be the son of a *patih*,' Nyai Ontosoroh continued.

'Not the son of a *patih* either, Mama.'

'Very well. But I am so pleased that Annelies has a friend to visit her. Hey Ann! Look after him properly, this guest of yours.'

'Of course, Mama,' she answered gaily, now that she had her mother's blessing.

Nyai Ontosoroh left us. I was amazed that this Native woman could speak Dutch so well, but also was so relaxed with a male guest. Where was she educated? And why was she only a *nyai*, a concubine? And who educated her to be so free, just like a European woman? What had been a sinister, eerie place, was changing into a castle of puzzles.

'I'm glad I have a guest,' Annelies became gayer, knowing her mother had no objections. 'No one has ever visited me. People are afraid to come here. Even my old school friends.'

'Where did you go to school?'

'ELS, I didn't finish, I didn't even get to fourth class.'

'Why didn't you go on?'

Annelies bit her finger, and looked at me:

'There was an accident,' she answered, and did not go on. Suddenly she asked: 'You're Moslem?'

'Why?'

'So that you don't eat pork.'

I nodded.

A maid served chocolate milk and cakes. And the servant didn't come cringing in as she would have before Native masters. She walked in and stood gaping at me in amazement. That would never be allowed by a Native master:

a servant must bow down, bow and scrape continuously. And how beautiful is life when one doesn't have to cringe before others.

'My guest is Moslem,' said Annelies in Javanese to her servant. 'Tell them out the back not to let pork touch the other food.' Then she quickly turned to me and asked, 'Why are you so silent?'

'Don't you know?' I asked in return. 'Because I never dreamed I'd ever come face to face with such a beautiful goddess as this." She was silent and stared at me with her day-star eyes. I regretted having said it. Hesitantly and slowly she asked:

'Who do you mean by this goddess?'

'You', I whispered, and the look on her face changed. She tilted her head. Her eyes opened wide.

'Me? You're saying I'm beautiful?'

I became more daring, insisting:

'Without rival.'

'Mama!' exclaimed Annelies and turned round to the back door. Disaster! I exclaimed no less loudly than her – but in my heart, of course. The girl went to the back door. She was going to take the matter to Nyai. Crazy child! Such a contrast with her beauty. And she's going to complain: Minke's being impertinent. Indeed this house is a place of misfortune. No, no, not misfortune. Whatever happens now, it will all be of my own doing.

Nyai appeared at the door and walked towards me.

My heart started to pound again. Perhaps I had done wrong. Punish this impudent-mouthed one, but don't shame me in front of Robert Suurhof.

'What's the matter now, Ann? Has she started an argument, Nyo?'

'No, we weren't arguing,' the girl flashed, then she complained in that sweet, spoiled manner of hers, 'Mama,' her hand pointed to me. 'Imagine, Mama, how could Minke say I was beautiful?'

Nyai stared at me. Her head was tilted a little. She looked at her daughter. In a whisper, with her two hands placed on Annelies's shoulders, she said:

'You know I've often said that you're beautiful? And extraordinarily beautiful? There's no doubt you're beautiful, Ann. Sinyo is not wrong.'

'Oh, Mama!' Annelies's face reddened.

Now Nyai sat down on the chair beside me. She said quickly:

'I'm glad you've come, Nyo. She's never mixed properly like other Indo children. She hasn't become an Indo, Nyo.'

'I'm not an Indo,' the girl contradicted. 'Don't want to be an Indo. I only want to be like Mama.'

I was even more amazed. What was going on in this family?

'Nyo, you heard it for yourself: she'd rather be a Native. why is Sinyo silent? Perhaps you're offended I'm only calling you: Nyo or Sinyo? Without any title?'

'No, Mama, no,' I answered hastily.

14

'You look confused.'

Who wouldn't have been confused? Nyai Ontosoroh was behaving as if I was someone who had known her for a long time, but who had forgotten her. It was as if she had given birth to me herself and was closer to me than Mother, even though she looked younger than Mother.

I awaited expectantly for Nyai's anger to explode because of my crazy compliments. But she was not angry. Exactly like Mother, who also had never been angry with me. My soul's ear heard a warning too: beware, don't equate her with Mother. She is just a *nyai*, living in sin, giving birth to illegitimate children, low in moral character, selling honour to live easily and in luxury . . . And I couldn't say she was ignorant. Her Dutch was fluent, and polite: her attitude towards her daughter was refined, and wise, and open, not like that of Native mothers: she behaved just like an educated European woman.

'The trouble is, Ann,' Nyai added, 'you don't mix, you only want to be close to Mama; you're nineteen.' But suddenly, her words were then directed at me, 'Nyo, do you usually compliment girls in this way?'

The question flashed at me like lightning. Seeing this as a good omen, I was encouraged to parry like lightning, carefully.

'If a girl is indeed beautiful, there isn't anything bad in saying so, is there?'

'A European or a Native girl?'

'How is it possible to compliment Native girls? It's impossible even to get close, Mama. European girls, of course.'

'Does Sinyo dare do such a thing?'

'We're taught to state our feelings honestly.'

'So you are game enough to compliment European girls to their face?'

'Yes, Mama, my teachers teach European civilisation.'

'How do they respond to your compliments? Abuse?'

'No, Mama. There is nobody who doesn't like being complimented, my teacher says. If some one gets insulted because of a compliment, they say, it's a sign of a dishonest heart.'

'So how do these European girls answer?'

'Their answer, Mama, is: thaank you.'

'Like in the books?'

She reads European books, this Nyai.

'Ah, Ann, answer: thaank you.'

Just like a Native girl, she blushed with embarrassment. She didn't say anything.

'And how about Indo girls?' asked Nyai.

'If they've received a good European education, they behave just the same, Mama.'

'If they haven't?'

'If not, and especially if they're in a bad mood, they abuse you.'

15

'Sinyo is often abused?'

I knew then: I was blushing. She smiled, and turned to her daughter:

'You heard it yourself, Ann. Come on, say thankyou. Hmmm, wait a minute. Nyo, say it again, this compliment of yours, so I can hear it too.'

Now I became really embarrassed. What sort of person was I dealing with? She was so clever at capturing and seizing my mind in her hands.

'I'm not allowed to hear?' she asked, looking at my face. 'All right.'

And again she left us. Annelies and I followed her with our eyes until she disappeared behind the door. And we gazed at each other like two children, equally startled. I burst into uncontrollable laughter. She bit her lip and looked away.

What sort of family was this? Robert Mellema with his frightening, stabbing glances. Annelies Mellema, so childlike. Nyai Ontosoroh, so clever at capturing and seizing control of people's minds, that even I lost my judgement, and forgot that she was only a concubine. And what about Mr Mellema, owner of all this abundant wealth?

'Where is your father?' I asked.

Annelies frowned.

'You don't need to know. What for? Even I have no desire to know. Even Mama doesn't want to know.'

'Why?' I asked.

'Do you like to listen to music?'

'Not now.'

And so the conversation dragged on until lunch was served. Robert Mellema, Robert Suurhof, Annelies and I, sat surrounding the table. A young servant, female, stood near the door awaiting orders. Suurhof sat beside his friend and every now and then stole a glance at me and Annelies. Mama sat at the head of the table.

There was much more food than we could have eaten. The main dish was veal, a food I tasted then for the first time in my life.

Annelies sat beside me and served me, as if I were some European master or a very respected Indo.

Nyai ate calmly like a genuine European woman who had graduated from an English boarding school.

I earnestly examined the position of the spoons and forks, the use of the soup ladle and the knives, carving forks, and also the elaborate dinner service. It was all perfect. The white steel knife seemed not to have been sharpened on stone but on a steel grinding wheel, so there were no scratches. From everything I had read, even the position of the serviettes and the finger bowls, and the position of the glasses in their silver cases could not be faulted.

Robert Suurhof ate greedily as if he had not seen food for the last three days. I was hesitant even though hungry. Annelies hardly ate anything, only because of the attention she paid to serving me and me alone.

16

When Nyai stopped eating, naturally I did too, and so did Annelies. Robert Suurhof continued eating and seemed to completely ignore Nyai. And I realised I had not heard the woman speak to her son even once.

'Minke,' Nyai said, 'is it true people can now make ice? Ice that is really cold, as the books say?'

'It's true, Mama, at least according to the newspapers.'

Suurhof swallowed, while glaring at me.

'I only want to know if the newspaper reports are true.'

'It seems everything will be able to be made by man, Mama,' I answered, though in my heart I was more amazed that somebody could doubt a newspaper report.

'Everything? Impossible,' she replied.

The conversation stopped abruptly. Robert Mellema invited his friend to go outside. They stood and left without taking leave of the Native woman.

'Forgive my friend, Mama.'

She smiled, nodded to me, stood up, then left too. The servant cleared the table.

'Mama must continue her work in the office,' Annelies explained. 'After lunch like this, I have work to do, but out the back.'

'What do you do?'

'Come on, join me.'

'What about my friend?'

'No need for you to worry yourself. My brother will invite him to go off hunting. He always goes hunting birds or squirrels with his air gun after lunch.'

'Why must it be after lunch?'

'The birds and squirrels are also full and sleepy, they're not so quick. Come on, come along.'

I walked behind her like a child following after his mother. And if she hadn't been beautiful, how would that have otherwise been possible? Oh! Philogynist!

Passing through the back door we entered an area containing steel-hooped wooden barrels. On top of the largest one there was a churning machine. The smell of cow's milk filled the room. People worked without making any sound, as if they were dumb. Now and then they wiped their bodies with a piece of cloth. Each wore a white headband. All wore white shirts with the sleeves rolled up to about ten centimetres above their elbows. Not all of them were men. Some were women; you could tell from the *batik kains* below their white shirts. Women working in a business. Wearing calico shirts too! Village women wearing coats! And not in their own kitchens! Were they wearing a breast-cloth too under their calico shirts?

One by one I looked them over. They only paid attention to me for a moment.

Annelies approached them each in turn, and they greeted her, without speaking, just with a sign. That was the first time I knew this beautiful child-like girl was also a supervisor, who must be paid heed to by her workers, male and female.

I was dumbfounded to see women leaving their kitchens in their homes, wearing work-clothes, seeking a living in someone else's business, mixing with men! Was this also a sign of the modern era in the Indies?

'You're amazed to see women working?'

I nodded.

'They wear the same uniforms here as workers in Holland, but we can only give them calico.'

She pulled me by the hand and took me out into an open compound, the area for drying produce. Several people were working, turning over soya beans, young corn, peas and peanuts. As soon as we arrived, they all stopped work and greeted us by nodding and lifting up their hands. They all wore bamboo farmer's hats.

Annelies clapped her hands and held up two fingers to somebody. A moment later a child worker came up with two bamboo hats. Annelies put one on my head, and wore one herself. And we walked several hundred metres along a path laid with river gravel.

'There are big celebrations on at the moment,' I said. 'Why aren't they given a holiday?'

'They can holiday if they like. Mama and I never holiday. They're day-labourers.'

Along the path, up in front of us, quite far away, I could see the two Roberts, each with a rifle slung over his shoulder.

'What work is it you do?' I asked.

'Everything, except the office work. Mama does that herself.'

So Nyai Ontosoroh does office work. What sort of office work can she do?

'Administration?' I asked groping around.

'Everything. The books, trading, correspondence, banking . . .'

I stopped in my steps. Annelies also. I stared at her with a look of disbelief. She pulled at my hand and we walked on again towards a row of cattle pens. I already could smell the stench of their dung. It was only because a beautiful girl was taking me that I did not run to avoid it, indeed I even went into the pens themselves. Only once in all my life. Truly.

The row of pens was very long. In each one there were people busy looking after the feed and drink for the dairy cows. The smell of cow-dung and of rotten grass made the atmosphere foetid, and I had to withstand the urge to vomit.

Lifting up the edge of her satin dress, Annelies went up to several cows and patted them on the forehead, talked to them in a whisper, even laughed

18

too. I observed her from a distance. She had such easy manners entering the pens and talking with the cows, and in a satin gown like that!

Here too there were women workers. They were sweeping, rinsing down the pen floors, and scrubbing them with a very long-handled brush. They all seemed surprised to see me there.

Annelies walked along by the shelves, and I walked along opposite her. She stopped. I saw her talk with a worker, and they both glanced at me, as if sharing a secret.

Another worker, stooped over in deference, walked out in front of me carrying two empty zinc buckets. Her face was pretty. Like the others she wore a breast cloth and *kain*, barefooted, wet, dirty, with her toes trumpeting outwards. Her breasts were firm and full and by themselves attracted attention. She bowed, glanced up at me from under her forehead and smiled invitingly.

'Greetings, Sinyo!' she addressed me freely, softly and enticingly.

I'd never met a Native girl so free as that, greeting a man she had never met before. She stopped in front of me, and asked in Malay:

'Checking up on things, Nyo?'

'Yes,' I said.

Suddenly Annelies was behind me. 'How many buckets a day are you getting from your cows, Sis Minem?' Now she used Javanese.

'The usual, Non,' Minem replied in High Javanese.

Annelies appeared impatient.

'I can still collect more milk than any of them,' she said when we went outside. 'I don't think you like cows. Let's go to the stables, if you like; or to the fields.'

I had never been to a field. There is nothing interesting there. Yet I still followed her.

'Or do you like riding?'

'Ride a horse?' I cried. 'You ride horses?'

This child-like girl who had never graduated from primary school suddenly stood revealed as a person of extraordinary character: not only was she such an efficient manager, but she could ride horses and could get more milk from her cows than any of the other workers.

'Of course. How else could you keep check on fields as large as these?'

We came to a field that had just been harvested. Peanuts. The harvest could be seen heaped on the ground everywhere. There were also piles of peanut stems and plants being carted off for cattle fodder.

'The land here is very good; it can produce three tonnes dry weight of peanuts per hectare. If we hadn't proved it ourselves maybe people would never have believed it,' Annelies said. 'Good land. First-class quality. Profitable. Even the leaves and stems are good for fertiliser and for cattle fodder.'

19

It seems that she could read my thoughts: who cares if it's two or five tonnes a hectare? I heard her voice: 'You're not interested. Let's race the horses. Agree?'

Before I could answer, she pulled my hand. I was dragged along as she ran. I could hear her breathing and then panting heavily. She took me into a big, broad shed that turned out to contain coaches, carriages, waggons and buggies. Saddles, with all sorts of stirrups, hung along the walls. Most of the building was empty.

Seeing my amazement at finding a carriage stable as big as a Regency building, she laughed, then pointed to a carriage adorned with shining brass and with carbide lights.

'Have you ever seen such a beautiful buggy?'

'Never, never,' I answered as I approached the vehicle.

Annelies pulled me along again. We entered into a long, wide stable. There were only three horses inside. Now it was the stench of horses permeating the air and colliding with my sense of smell. She approached a grey-coloured horse and embraced the animal's neck and whispered something in its ear, calling it *Bawuk*.

Bawuk neighed lightly as if laughing in response. Then Annelies stroked the horse's forehead and it grinned, showing its mighty teeth.

Annelies laughed gaily, in cascading tones.

Then, in a serious voice, after whispering while embracing Bawuk's neck, she glanced at me, 'We have a guest. That's him. His name is Minke. An alias: It is not a Javanese name, nor Islamic, not even Christian, I reckon. An alias. Do you believe his name is Minke?'

And once again the horse neighed in response.

'*Nah!*' she said, then to me: 'She said that of course your name is an alias.'

They were plotting. I was their target. And the other two horses joined in neighing, looking at me with their big, unblinking eyes. Accusingly.

'Let's go outside,' I said but she went over to the other two horses and stroked each of their backs, only then did she say to me: 'Come on.'

'You smell of horses,' I said.

She only laughed.

'Apparently it doesn't worry you.'

'It's not really important,' she answered grumpily. 'Bawuk has been treated that way ever since she was small. Mama would be angry if I didn't love her. You must be grateful to everything that gives you life, says Mama, even if it's only a horse.'

I didn't annoy her again about the stench.

'Why don't you believe my name is Minke?'

Her eyes shone with disbelief, accusing, alleging.

It was, of course, not my idea that my name be, or that people should call me, Minke. I too had been amazed by how it had happened. It is a bit of an involved story. It started when I was still at ELS and did not know a word of Dutch. Mr Ben Rooseboom, my very first teacher, was always cross with me. I could never answer his questions. I always ended up bawling. Yet every day a servant escorted me to that hated school.

I was stuck in first class for two years. Mr Rooseboom remained cross with me and I remained scared of him. But by the time the new school year arrived, my Dutch was somewhat better. My friends had all gone up to second class. I stayed in first class. I was seated between two Dutch girls, who were always making trouble and annoying me. On one occasion, one of the girls who sat beside me, Vera, pinched my thigh as hard as she could, as a way of getting acquainted. And I? I screamed in pain.

Mr Rooseboom's eyes popped out frighteningly, and he yelled:

'Quiet you, monk . . . *Minke!*'

From that day, everyone in the class called me Minke, the one and only Native. My teachers followed suit. Then my friends from all the other classes. Also from outside school.

I once asked my elder brother what did 'Minke' mean? He didn't know. He even ordered me to ask Mr Rooseboom himself. I didn't dare. My grandfather didn't know Dutch. He couldn't even read or write Latin script. He only knew Javanese, written and spoken. His view was that Minke should be my permanent name: it was a sign of respect from a good and wise teacher. So my real name was almost lost.

I always believed that the name meant something unpleasant. The day my teacher spoke that word '*Minke*', his eyes popped out like cow's eyes. His eyebrows jumped off his broad face. And the ruler in his hand fell to the desk. Goodness and wisdom? Far from it.

I could not find the word in the Dutch dictionary.

Then I entered the HBS, Surabaya. My teachers there did not know what it meant either. Unlike us Javanese they would never make a guess based just on feelings. One even quoted to me from some Englishman: What's in a name? (It was a long time before I could remember the Englishman's name.)

Then we began English lessons. Six months passed and I came across a word similar in pronunciation and spelling with my name. I began to think back over it: eyes popping out and eyebrows ready to disengage from his broad face: for sure he was insulting me. And I remembered how Mr Rooseboom hesitated in saying the name. Fearfully I dared to guess: perhaps he intended to insult me by calling me monkey.

And I've never told anyone what I thought, not even Annelies.

'Minke is a good name,' said Annelies. Then: 'Let's visit the villages. There are four villages on our land. All the family heads work for us.'

All along the road the villagers acknowledged us with respect. They called the girl *Non* or *Noni*.

'How many hectares do you have?' I asked.

'One hundred and eighty.'

One hundred and eighty! I couldn't even imagine how vast that was. And she continued:

'That's the paddy and fields. It doesn't include the forests.'

Forests! She owns forests. Crazy. She owns forests! What for?

'For the firewood,' she added.

'Perhaps you own swamps too?'

'Yes. There are two small swamps.'

'What about mountains?' I asked. 'Mountains?'

'You're teasing me,' she pinched me.

'Volcanoes, no doubt, so you can catch their flames if they erupt, just like the gods.'

'*Iiih!*' she pinched again.

'What's all that growing over there?' I asked, pointing to a marshy area a few metres away.

'Only reeds. Haven't you ever seen that kind of reed?'

'Let's go over there,' I said.

'No,' she answered firmly and hunched her shoulders. Her head shuddered visibly.

'You're scared of that place.'

She took my hand and hers felt cold. All of a sudden her eyes became nervous and she tried to tear them away as quickly as possible from the marshes. Her lips were pale. I glanced behind. She pulled my hand and whispered nervously:

'Don't pay any attention. Come on, walk a little faster.'

We entered another village, then left it and entered yet another. It was the same everywhere: little, stark-naked children playing everywhere, most with snot hanging from their noses. There were also a few who licked it off. In the shady places, women in late pregnancy sat sewing while carrying their youngest children in a *kain* sling, or two or three women sat in a row looking for head lice.

Several women stopped Annelies and wanted to talk with her, asking for help. And this extraordinary girl, like a mother, affably attended to them all.

She loved her horses because they gave life to her and so it was also with her people. She appeared so grand among the villagers, her people. More grand perhaps than the maiden I had so often dreamed of and who now, in great pomp, had taken her place on the throne, to govern the Indies, Surinam, the Antilles and the Netherlands itself. Even Annelies' skin was finer and more radiant. And Annelies could be approached.

As soon as she finished attending to her people's demands, we continued our walk. Vast nature and a clear, cloudless sky enveloped us. It was scorching hot. It was at that moment I whispered to her these words:

'Have you seen a picture of the Queen?'

'Naturally. She's gorgeous!'

'Yes. You're not wrong.'

'Why do you ask?'

'You're more beautiful than her.'

She stopped walking, just to look at me, and:

'Thaank you, Minke,' she answered, embarrassed.

The road became hotter and more still. I jumped over a drain just to see if she would jump or not. She picked up her long dress as high as she could and jumped. I caught her hand, I pulled her close and kissed her upon the cheek. She looked startled, her eyes wide open, examining me.

And I kissed her once again. This time I felt how her skin was smooth like velvet.

'The most beautiful girl I have ever met,' I whispered with all my heart's honesty.

She didn't answer, and she didn't say thank you either. She signalled we should go home. She walked along silently all the way. Then a presentiment came upon me: you are going to get nothing but trouble from these actions of yours, Minke. If she complains to Darsam, you'll be beaten up before you can even bark.

She walked with her head bowed. I realised only then that her sandals had been left on the other side of the drain. And soon I felt ashamed for pretending not to notice.

'Your sandals have been left behind, Ann.'

She didn't care. Didn't answer. Didn't look back. She increased her pace.

Quickly I moved up beside her:

'Are you angry, Ann? Angry at me?'

She continued to keep her silence.

The timber palace was visible far away high above the roofs of the other buildings. I could see Nyai watching us from an upstairs window. Annelies, who was walking with her head down, did not know the eyes upstairs followed us until the roofs of the godowns blocked Nyai's view.

We entered the house and sat once again on the front-parlour settee. Annelies sat quietly, leaving frozen all my questions. All of a sudden she leapt up, and went into another room. As I sat there in my chair, I became more and more anxious. She is going to complain to Nyai for sure. I'll get my just deserts now. But no, I will not run.

It wasn't long after that she came out again, carrying a big paper bundle. She placed the object upon the table. She said coldly.

'It's late. Rest. That door,' she pointed to the back, at a door, 'is your room. In this bundle there are sandals, a towel and pyjamas. You can bathe there. I still have work to do.'

Before going, she went to the door, which she had just pointed out, opened it and invited me to enter.

And gently she pushed me inside, closed the door from outside and so I was left alone behind it.

These small and big tensions had made me very tired. My fears about the consequences of my impertinence continued to worry me. Though I didn't think I had really done anything wrong. What was it that I had done wrong? Any young man would have behaved the same in the presence of such an extraordinarily beautiful maiden? Didn't my biology teacher say . . . Ah, to the devil with biology!

Entering the bathroom was another experience again: another kind of luxury. The walls were lined with mirrors at least three millimetres thick. The floor was made of cream porcelain tiles. I had never seen such a big, clean and beautiful bathroom. Even a *bupati*'s home would not be equipped with such a bathroom. The bluish water in the porcelain-lined bathtub called out to me to submerge myself in it. And wherever your eyes were directed, it was always yourself that you saw: front, behind, sides, everything.

The bluish clear cool water washed away my anxieties and fears.

And if ever I am rich, I thought, I will build luxury like this. Nothing less than this.

Mama offered me a chair in the parlour. She sat down beside me and tried to start up a discussion about business and trade. It was soon revealed that I knew nothing about these things. She was acquainted with many European terms that I didn't know. Sometimes she would explain them to me just like a teacher. And how clearly this Nyai could explain things!

'Sinyo is interested in business and trade,' she said afterwards, as if I had understood everything. 'That's very unusual for a Javanese, especially the son of an important official. Or perhaps Sinyo has plans to become a trader or a businessman?'

'I am already trying my hand at business, Mama.'

'Sinyo? The son of a *bupati*? What sort of business?'

'Perhaps also because I'm not the son of a *bupati*,' I replied.

'What business are you in?'

'Top-class furniture, Mama,' I began my propaganda, 'the latest styles and models from Europe. I go to meet the ships bringing newcomers from Europe. I also visit the houses of the parents of my school friends.'

'And Sinyo's progress at school? You're not left behind?'

'Never, Mama.'

'Interesting. For me, all those who really endeavour are always interesting. Does Sinyo own his own furniture workshop? How many tradesmen?'

'No, I only sell the furniture. I carry pictures with me.'

'So you came here to sell furniture? Let's see your pictures.'

'No. I came here without bringing anything. But, if Mama feels it necessary, I will bring them another time: wardrobes, for example, as in the palaces of Austria or France or England – renaissance, baroque, rococo, Victorian . . .'

She listened to me carefully. Twice I heard her smack her lips, I don't know if in praise or as an insult. Then she said slowly:

'Happy are they who eat from the products of their own sweat, obtain pleasure from their own endeavours and advance because of their own experiences.'

The tones sounded as if they had come out of the chest of a priest in a *wayang* performance. Then she called out:

'Fantastic!' She was looking up at the head of the stairs. 'Ah!'

Down those stairs descended the angel Annelies, in a *batik kain*, a laced *kabaya*. Her *sanggul* was a bit too high, revealing her long white neck. Her neck, arms, ears and bosom were decorated with a pattern of green-white emerald, pearls and diamonds. (Really I didn't know which were diamonds and which were the others, what was real and what was fake.)

I was entranced. She must have been more beautiful and arresting than Jaka Tarub's angel in the legends of *Babad Tanah Jawi*. She was grinning all over as if embarrassed. The adornments she was wearing were somewhat or indeed definitely overdone, too extravagant. And I knew she had dressed up for me and me alone.

And for a countenance and presence as beautiful as that, there was no need for any adornment. Naked too, she would remain beautiful. How foolish of us to think that the beauty bestowed by the gods did not always triumph over the inventions of humans. With all those adornments from the sea and the land she looked alien. While the clothes, which she was not used to wearing, made her movements like those of a wooden doll. Everything about her seemed somehow pretentious. But it didn't matter, what is beautiful stays beautiful. It was up to me to cleverly ignore her extravagances.

'She has dressed up for you, Nyo!' whispered Nyai.

Annelies walked up to us while still smiling and perhaps with a *thaank you* readied in her heart. But before I could get in my compliment, Nyai got in first:

'From whom did you learn to dress up and adorn yourself like that?'

'Ah, Mama!' she exclaimed prodding her mother's shoulder and glancing at me with her big eyes. She was blushing.

I was embarrassed to be listening to such a conversation between mother and daughter: too intimate to be heard by a stranger. Yet near Mama I felt I ought to be resolute. I had to leave behind an impression of being a man who was resolute, interesting, dashing, an unappeased conqueror of the Goddess of Beauty. In front of the Queen I think I would have also had to exhibit the same attitude. That is the cock's plumage, the deer's antlers, the symbol of virility.

I knew what was proper, I did not involve myself in the affairs of mother and daughter.

'See, Ann, Sinyo was ready to go home. It's fortunate we stopped him. Otherwise, he would have really missed out on something!'

'Ah, Mama!' Annelies said again, in her sweet, spoiled manner and prodded her mother. Her eyes glanced at me.

'Well, what about it, Nyo? Why are you silent? Have your forgotten your own custom?'

'Too beautiful, Mama. What words are appropriate for beauty's beauty?'

'Yes,' added Nyai, 'fit to become Queen of the Indies, isn't she, Nyo?' and she turned to me.

The relationship between mother and daughter seemed strange to me. Maybe it was the result of the illegitimate marriage and birth. Perhaps this is the atmosphere in the homes of all *nyai*s. Perhaps even among modern families in Europe today and among Indies Natives far in the future. Or perhaps it wasn't right – but abnormal. Yet I liked it. And luckily the mutual praising finally ended without having led anywhere.

The day got darker. Mama talked on. Annelies and I just listened. There were too many new things, which my teachers had never mentioned that proceeded from her lips. Remarkable. And, I was still not allowed to go home, although:

'*Dokar*?' she said, 'Out the back, there are many *dokar*. If you like you can even go home in a *grobak*.'

A young boy began to light the gas lamps. I still did not know where the mains was located.

The servants began to prepare the dining table.

The two Roberts were summoned into the back parlour. So dinner began in silence.

Another servant entered the front room, closing the door. The back-parlour light, covered by a milk-white glass shade, shone dimly. No one said a word. Eyes just moved about from plate to bowl, from bowl to dish. The sound of spoons, forks and knives clinked as they touched the plates.

Nyai lifted up her head. The front door could be heard opening; without any knock, without announcement. I looked up at Nyai. Her eyes radiated vigilance towards the front room.

Robert Mellema glanced in the same direction. His eyes shone with pleasure and his lips had a satisfied smile. I also wanted to glance behind, to where their looks were directed. I held back my desire, it wasn't polite; not gentlemanly. So I glanced at Annelies. Her head bowed down, her eyeballs raised high, clearly she was straining her ears.

Deliberately, I stopped my spoon in mid-air and focussed my hearing on the area behind me. Shoes walking, scraping along the floor. As time passed they became clearer. Closer. Nyai stopped eating. Robert Suurhof did not put the food in his mouth: he put the spoon and fork down on his plate. What I heard: the steps coming closer, drowning out the tick-tock of the pendulum clock.

Robert Mellema continued eating as if nothing was happening.

Finally Annelies, who was sitting beside me, also glanced behind. She blinked open her eyes, startled. Her spoon dropped with a clang to the floor. I tried to pick it up. A servant came running and took it. Then she quickly got out of the way. Annelies stood up as if she wanted to confront this new arrival, who was getting closer.

I placed my spoon and fork on the plate, followed Annelies's example, stood up and turned around.

Nyai also stood in readiness.

The arrival's shadow, sprayed out by the front-room lamps, became longer and longer. The dragging shoe steps became clearer and clearer. Then a European man emerged – tall, big, fat, too fat. His clothes were rumpled and his hair in a mess, who knows if really white or grey.

He looked in our direction. Stopped a moment.

'Your father?' I whispered to Annelies.

'Yes,' almost inaudible.

Looking straight at me, Mr Mellema, dragging his shoes, walked towards me. Towards me. He stopped in front of me. His eyebrows were bushy, almost white, and his face was frozen like chalk. For a moment my eyes fell to his shoes which were dusty, unlaced. Then I remembered what my teachers had taught me: look those who want to talk to you in the eyes. Quickly, I lifted my eyes and offered my greetings:

'Good evening, Mr Mellema,' in Dutch and in a quite polite tone.

He growled like a cat. His unironed clothes were loose on his body. His hair, uncombed and thin, covered his forehead, ears.

'Who gave you permission to come here, monkey!' He hissed his sentence in Bazaar Malay, awkwardly and, in accord with its contents, crudely.

Behind me Robert Mellema ahemmed. Then I heard Annelies holding back a sob. Robert Suurhof put his shoes into action and stood up also to extend his greetings. But the ogre in front of me paid him no heed.

I admit it: my body shook, although only a little. In such a situation I could only await words from Nyai. I could expect nothing from anyone else. It was going to be a disaster for me if she stayed silent. And indeed she was silent.

'Yuh think, boy, cause yuh wear European clothes, mix with Europeans and can speak a little Dutch yuh then become a European? Yuh still a monkey!'

'Shut up!' shouted Nyai loudly in Dutch. 'He is my guest.'

Mr Mellema's eyes dully shifted to his concubine. And must something happen because of this uninvited Native?

'*Nyai!*' said Mr Mellema.

'A mad European is the same as a mad Native!' Her eyes burnt with hatred and disgust. 'You have no rights in this house. You know where your room is,' the *nyai* pointed to a door. And her pointed finger was clawed.

Mr Mellema still stood in front of me, hesitant.

'Do I need to call Darsam?' she threatened.

The tall-big-fat man was confused; he growled in answer. He turned his body, walked, dragging his feet, to a door next to the room I had just occupied, and disappeared behind it.

'Rob,' Robert Mellema said to his guest. 'Let's go outside. It's too hot in here.'

They went out together, without excusing themselves to Nyai.

'Trash!' Nyai cursed.

Annelies was sobbing.

'Be quiet, Ann. Forgive us, Minke, Nyo. Sit down again. Don't make a din, Ann. Sit down in your chair.'

We both sat down again. Annelies covered her face with a silk handkerchief. And Nyai, still kept an eye on the just-closed door.

'No need to be ashamed in front of Sinyo,' Nyai said without looking at us, still in a rage. 'And you, Nyo, you may never forget this. I'm not ashamed. Sinyo shouldn't be shocked or feel ashamed either. Don't be angry. I've done exactly what I had to. Just pretend that he doesn't exist, Nyo. Once I was indeed his faithful *nyai*, his loyal companion. Now he is only worthless garbage. All he is good for now is shaming his own descendants. That is your father, Ann.'

Satisfied after her abuse, she sat down again. She didn't resume her dinner. The look on her face was hard and sharp. Calmly, I looked at her. What sort of woman was this?

'If I wasn't hard like that, Nyo – forgive me that I must offer a defence for myself in my humiliation – what would become of all this? His children . . . his business . . . we would be reduced to destitution. So I do not regret acting this way in front of you, Nyo.' She lowered her voice as if pleading with me, 'Don't think me insolent and rude, Nyo,' she said, continuing in her beautiful Dutch. 'It is all for his own good. I treat him the way he wants. This is what he wants. It is the Europeans themselves who have taught me to act this way, Minke, the Europeans themselves,' her voice pleaded with me to believe. 'Not at school, but in life.'

I was silent. I nailed every one of her words into my memory: not in school, in life! Don't think me insolent and rude! Europeans themselves have taught me this . . .

Nyai stood up, walked slowly towards the window. And behind the door she pulled a cord that ended in a bunch of tassels. In the distance a bell could be indistinctly heard ringing. The servant girl who had just vanished reappeared. Nyai ordered her to take away the food. I still didn't know what I was supposed to do.

'Go home now, Nyo,' she said.

'Yes, Mama, it's better I go home.'

She walked up to me. Her eyes returned to their original motherly gentleness.

'Ann,' she said still more softly, 'let your guest go home now. Wipe away those tears.'

'Forgive us, Minke,' Annelies whispered, holding her sobs back.

'It's nothing, Ann.'

'When holiday time arrives later, come and spend the vacation here, Nyo. Don't hesitate. Nothing will happen. What do you think? Agree? Now Sinyo must go home. Darsam will escort you in the *dokar*.'

She walked again to the door and pulled that cord. Then she sat back down in her seat. She was amazing: this *nyai*: the people and everything around her were indeed in her grip, and I, myself, too. From what school had she graduated that she appeared so educated, intelligent. And she was able to look to the needs of several people at once, with a different manner for each. And if she did graduate from a school, how was she able to accept her situation as a *nyai*? I couldn't understand any of this.

A Madurese man arrived. He was about one metre sixty high, he was approaching forty; shirt and pants all black, and a *destar* on his head. A short machete was fastened at his waist. His moustache was twirled up high, pitch-black and thick.

Nyai gave him an order in Madurese. I didn't catch all of what it meant. She was probably ordering that I be escorted safely home in a *dokar*.

Darsam stood straight. He didn't speak. He looked at me with searching eyes – as if he wanted to memorise my face – without blinking.

'The Young Master is my guest, is Miss Annelies' guest,' said Nyai in Javanese. 'Take him home. Don't let anything happen on the way. Be careful!' Apparently this was only a translation of the earlier Madurese.

Darsam raised his hand, without speaking, and left.

'Sinyo, Minke,' Nyai complained, 'Annelies has no friends. She is happy that Sinyo came here. You, of course, don't have a lot of time. I know that. Even so, try to come here often. You don't need worry about Mr Mellema. I will look after him. If Sinyo would like, we would be very happy for you to live here. You could be taken to school each day by buggy. That's if Sinyo would like.'

Such a strange and frightening house and family! It's no wonder they have such a sinister reputation. And I answered:

'Let me think about it first, Mama. Thank you for such a generous invitation.'

'Don't refuse us,' Annelies said. There was rebuke in her voice.

'Yes, Nyo, think about it. If you have no objections, Annelies will look after it all. Isn't that so Ann?'

Annelies nodded in agreement.

The carriage could be heard coming along beside the house. We walked to the front area of the house and found Robert Suurhof and Robert Mellema sitting silently looking out at the darkness. The carriage stopped in front of the steps. Suurhof and I went down the steps and boarded the carriage.

'Good night everybody, and thank you very much, Mama, Ann, Rob!' I said.

And the carriage began to move.

'Stop!' ordered Mama. The carriage stopped. 'Sinyo Minke! Come down here first.'

Like a slave I was caught in her grip. Without stopping to think for a moment, I climbed out and approached the steps; Nyai descended one step and so did Annelies, and Nyai said slowly into my ears:

'Annelies has told me, Nyo – don't be afraid – is it true, you kissed her?'

Even a flash of lightning would not have startled me so greatly. Anxiety creeped and crawled its way through my body, down to my feet, and my feet tripped.

'Is it true?' she insisted. Seeing I couldn't answer, she pulled Annelies and drew her to me. Then, 'Nah, so it's true. Now Minke, kiss Annelies in front of me. So that I may know that my daughter does not lie.'

I shuddered. Yet I could not resist her command. And I kissed Annelies on the cheek.

'I'm proud, Nyo, that it's you who kissed her. Go home now.'

I was unable to say a word all the way home. I felt as if Nyai had cast a spell over my mind. Annelies was indeed gloriously beautiful. Yet her clever mother subdued people so they would bow down to her will.

Robert Suurhof didn't speak either.

And the carriage rattled as it went on grinding the street pebbles. The carriage's carbide light relentlessly split open the darkness. Our carriage was the only one on the road that night. It appeared that everyone had streamed into Surabaya to celebrate the coronation of the maiden Wilhelmina.

Darsam escorted me to my boarding-house in Kranggan. He stayed until he saw me enter the house before he left to escort Suurhof home.

'*Ai-ai*, Master Minke!' Mrs Telinga, my talkative old landlady called out. 'So Young Master doesn't eat at home any more? I've just put a letter in your room. I see that you still haven't read the earlier letters either. The envelopes haven't even been opened. Remember Young Master, those letters were written, were given stamps, and were sent to be read. Who knows if there may be something important in them? They all seem to come from the town of B—. Eh, Young Master, what about it? Tomorrow there'll be no shopping money left, eh.'

I gave over a *talen* to the garrulous, good-hearted woman. She said thank you over and over again, as usual, without it needing to come from her heart.

There was hot chocolate milk ready for me in my room. I drank it down quickly. I took off my shoes and shirt, jumped onto the bed and started to reflect upon all that had happened. But my eyes fell upon the portrait of the goddess, near the oil lamp on the wall. I got out of bed, studied it well, then turned it over. And I climbed back into bed.

I pushed aside the Surabaya and Betawi papers, which were, as usual, placed on my pillow. It had become my custom to read the papers before sleeping. I don't know why but I liked to seek out reports about Japan. It pleased me to find out that their youth were being sent to England and America to study. You could say I was a Japan-watcher. But now there was something more interesting – that strange and wealthy family: Nyai, with her power to grip hold of people's hearts as if she were a sorceress; Annelies Mellema who was beautiful, child-like, yet was experienced and able in managing workers; Robert Mellema with his sharp glances, who cared about nothing except soccer, not even his own mother; Mr Mellema, as big as an elephant, sullen, but powerless over his own concubine. Each like a character in a play. What sort of family was this? And myself? I too was powerless before Nyai. Even as I turned over on the bed her voice still called: Annelies has no friends! She is happy Sinyo has come here. You, of course, don't have much time. Even so, try to come here often . . . we would be very happy if you were to stay here . . .

It felt like I had only been asleep a little while when there was a commotion outside the house. I lit the oil lamp in my room. Five o'clock in the morning.

'There is a package. For Young Master Minke,' I heard a man's voice, 'milk, cheese and butter. There is also a letter from Nyai Ontosoroh herself.'

3

Life went on as usual. It was, perhaps, only I who changed. *Boerderij Buitenzorg* in Wonokromo continued calling, summoning me, every day, every hour. Was I the victim of black magic? I knew many Pure and Indo-European girls. Why was it only Annelies I saw before me? And why did the voice of Nyai not want to go from my soul's ear? Minke, Sinyo Minke, when are you coming?

I was confused.

Every day I left for school with little May Marais. I would walk hand in hand with her as far as her school at ELS, Simpang. Then I walked on by myself to my school in HBS Street. I closely observed every carriage driver that passed by me, just in case it was Darsam. And whenever a carriage wanted to pass me from behind, I had to look around. It was as if I had some business with every carriage that passed.

At school, Annelies also hovered before me continuously. And over and over again came Nyai's voice. When are you coming? She has got all dressed up for you. When are you coming?

Robert Suurhof never bothered me with anything about Wonokromo. He avoided me. He refused to honour his promise to respect my success with Annelies. And I somehow felt as if I was separated from reality by some grey veil. Everything was unclear; all uncertain feelings. All my schoolfriends, Pure European or Indo, male and female, it was as if they had all changed. And they too saw changes in me. Yes, I was no longer the same easy-to-get-on-with and affable Minke.

On my way home from school, I went straight to Jean Marais' workshop. He was, as usual, absorbed in his drawings, sketches or in some design he was preparing. That day I didn't want to go straight back to my lodgings. I didn't feel like going down to the harbour either. I didn't want to go to the auction-paper office to write up advertising texts. I had no inclination to write any serious journalism either. I certainly had no desire to go visiting my friends' homes to try to sell furniture or seek orders for portraits.

No, I didn't feel like doing anything. All my body wanted to do was lie in bed turning over and over while I remembered Annelies. Only Annelies, that child-like maiden.

Mrs Telinga never tired of asking to hear the story of my visit to *Boerderij Buitenzorg*, only afterwards to have me listen to her coarse, repetitious insults: 'Young Master, Young Master, of course Young Master likes the daughter; but it's her mother who has the great lust. Everybody, of course, says her daughter is beautiful. No one dares go there. Young Master is very lucky. But remember this about Nyai, lest Young Master be gobbled up by her!'

Not only Mrs Telinga and I knew, but it felt as if the whole world knew, that such indeed was the moral level of the families of *nyais*: low, dirty, without culture, moved only by lust. They were the families of prostitutes; they were people without character, destined to sink into nothingness leaving no trace. But did this popular judgement hold for *Nyai* Ontosoroh? This was what was confusing me. No, she wasn't like that. Or was I just a careless observer? Maybe I just didn't want to know. All social classes had passed judgement on the *nyai*; also all races: Native, European, Chinese, Arab. How could I, just one person, say *no*. Her order that I kiss Annelies, wasn't that a sign of her low morals? Perhaps. Yet Mrs Telinga's insults offended something inside me. Perhaps it was because I was fantasizing. During the last few days I had been trying to convince myself that what had taken place between Annelies and myself was just a normal event in the life of a young man and a young woman. It happens to people from all walks of life: kings, traders, religious leaders, farmers, workers, even the gods in heaven. True. But an invisible finger pointed accusingly at me and said: the trouble is you're trying to justify your own fantasies.

And so that afternoon I found myself compelled to go and ask Jean Marais. I could not yet hope for a really serious conversation with him, although his Malay was getting better every day. He didn't know Dutch. That was the difficulty. His Malay was limited. My French was pretty hopeless. He resisted learning Dutch with all his might, even though he had fought in Aceh with the Dutch Colonial Army for more than four years. His Dutch was confined to military terms.

But he was my oldest friend, my companion in business. It was only proper that I ask him.

The workmen were finishing off furniture ordered by someone called Ah Tjong. I suspected that it was the one who owned the pleasure-house next door to Nyai Ontosoroh's. Because the order was for European-style furniture, the Chinese hadn't gone to a Chinese carpenter. I had received the order through someone else.

Jean was playing with his pencil, making a sketch for his next picture. 'I want to disturb you, Jean,' I said and sat on the chair at the drawing table. He lifted up his face and looked at me. 'Do you know the meaning of *sihir*?'

He shook his head.

'*Guna-guna*?' I asked.

'Yes – black magic – so I have heard anyway. The Negroes practice it, people say. That's if I have heard properly.'

I began to tell him of my situation, about being under a spell, and about the popular view of the *nyais* in general, and of Nyai Ontosoroh in particular.

He put down his pencil on top of the drawing paper, stared at me, and tried to capture and understand each of my words. Then, calmly and in a mixture of several languages:

'You're in trouble, Minke. You've fallen in love.'

'No, Jean. I am not in love. She is certainly an attractive, enchanting girl: but in love, no.'

'I understand. You're really in trouble, it's serious when you can't tell somebody they've fallen in love. Listen, Minke, your young blood wants to have her for yourself, and you're afraid of what people will say.' He laughed slowly. You must pay heed to and respect what people think if they are correct. If they're wrong, why pay them any heed? You're educated, Minke. An educated person must learn to act justly, beginning, first of all, with his thoughts, then later in his deeds. That is what it means to be educated. Go and visit this family two, or maybe three more times. Then you might be able to judge for yourself if Nyai and her family deserve their bad reputation.'

'So you think I should go back?'

'I think you should find out for yourself if what people say is fair or not. To go along with unfair gossip is wrong. You might find you're judging a family that is perhaps better than the judge himself.'

'Jean, I've been asked to go and stay there.'

'Take up the offer. Only don't forget your studies. You don't really need to chase after new orders any more. Look, there are still five portraits that have to be finished. And this,' he patted his sketch paper, 'I'm going to paint something I've long dreamed of doing.'

I pulled across the sketching paper in front of him. The picture immediately made me forget my own problems. A Netherlands Indies soldier – it was obvious from his bamboo hat and his sword – was thrusting his foot down onto the stomach of an Acehnese fighter. The soldier was pushing his bayonet down towards the bosom of his victim. And the bayonet pressed onto the black shirt, and from under the shirt emerged the breast of a young woman. The eyes of the woman were wide open. Her hair fell in bunches over the fallen bamboo leaves. Her left hand was resisting as she tried to rise. Her right hand powerlessly held a dagger. Above them both, like an umbrella, was a cluster of bamboo bent down by the attack of a strong wind. It was as if only those two lived: one who was to kill and one who was to be killed.

'But this is so vicious, Jean. You like to talk about beauty. Where is the beauty in viciousness, Jean?' He sucked on his cigarette. Then:

'It's not easy to explain, Minke. This picture is very personal, not intended for public display. Its beauty is in the memories it records.' He was silent, and I realised:

'So you are the soldier, Jean? You've carried out such barbarity as this?' He shook his head. 'You killed this young woman?' He shook his head again. 'So you freed her?' He nodded. 'She must have been grateful to you.'

'She was not grateful, Minke. She asked me to kill her. She was ashamed that she had been sullied by the touch of an infidel.'

He answered, dispiritedly, and as if his words were not directed at me, but at his own past which was now far beyond his reach.

'And now she is dead. Her younger brother sneaked into the camp and stabbed her in her side with a poison-tipped dagger. She died immediately. Her killer then himself died, hearing his own cries: "To hell with you infidel, follower of the infidels!" '

'Why did her brother stab her?' Already I'd forgotten all about my own troubles.

'Her brother had continued fighting for his country, for his beliefs. His sister had surrendered. There was nobody there when she died, Minke. Her child was being taken for a walk at the time. Her husband was away on duty.'

'So this woman lived amongst the soldiers? As a prisoner? As a prisoner until she had a child?'

'At first she was a prisoner. Then later, no longer,' he answered quickly.

'So she married?'

'No. She didn't marry.'

'And the child that was out walking with the neighbour, where did it come from?'

'That child was the baby she gave me, my own child, Minke.'

'Jean!'

'Yes, Minke, don't tell this story to May.'

All of a sudden I was overcome by emotion. I ran to find May who was safely asleep on a wooden divan, without a sheet. I picked her up and I kissed her. She was startled and looked at me with wide-open eyes. She didn't say a thing.

'May! May!' I cried to her, to myself, and I carried her out and found Jean Marais again. 'Jean, this is your child. this is that baby, Jean. You're not lying to me, Jean? You're lying to me, aren't you?'

The Frenchman, his chin now resting on his hand, was gazing outside the house away into the distance. He didn't want to repeat his story. He didn't want to answer. And I remembered how often he'd spoken of his love for his wife.

'That's why you advise me to go to Wonokromo?' I asked.

'Love is beautiful, Minke, very, very beautiful, but perhaps disaster follows on behind. You must dare face its consequences.'

35

The child prattled. 'Will we go for a walk, Papa?' and when he said they would go after she had bathed, she ran merrily off. I said:

'Jean, I'm not sure I love this Wonokromo girl.'

'Perhaps you don't or at least don't yet love this girl. It's not up to me to determine that. And also there is no love that appears suddenly out of the blue, because love is a child of culture, not a stone dropped from heaven. You must test yourself, your own heart. This girl may like you. It's clear, from what you've told me, that her mother is very fond of you. Fond of you after the first meeting. I don't believe in black magic. Perhaps it exists, but I don't need to believe in it, because it can only be common where life is still at a very simple level of civilisation. Moreover you've said Nyai does all types of office work. Someone like that is not going to believe in black magic. She will believe more in strength of character. Only people without any character practise black magic. Nyai knows what she needs. Perhaps she realises how lonely her daughter is.'

'Do you want to take May for a walk this afternoon?'

'You never take her!' I replied. 'She wants to go walking with you.'

'Not yet, Minke. Pity on her. People will stare at us both. One day she will hear someone say: Look at the lame, stumped Dutchman and his child! No, Minke. She mustn't have her young soul scarred by some unnecessary hurt, especially not one caused by her own father's deformity. She should love me and look upon me as the father who loves her, without regard to the voices and views of others.'

I had never seen him talk so much. I had never seen him so depressed. What was happening inside him? Perhaps he was longing for his past, lost and no longer within his reach? Or for the country where he was born, brought up and saw the sun for the first time? A country that he doesn't dare return to because he's without one leg and has a daughter born in a foreign country? Or is he longing to create a painting that will force his country to acknowledge his greatness as an artist?

'You have never had any time for pity, Jean,' I rebuked him.

'You're right, Minke. As I've told you before, pity is the feeling of well-intentioned people who are unable to act. Pity is only a luxury, or a weakness. It is those who are able to carry out their good intentions who deserve praise. I can't, Minke. The more I reflect on it the more beautiful that word 'pity' sounds here in these Indies, though not in Europe.'

He sounded even more gloomy.

'This is not the Jean I know,' I chided him. 'I'm worried about you. You don't seem to be yourself, Jean.'

'Thanks for caring, Minke. You're becoming sharper every day.'

May came in. As soon as she found out her father wouldn't be taking her, the look on her face changed.

'Go with Uncle Minke, May. It's a pity but I still have work that I must finish. Don't frown like that, darling.'

I took the little French-Acehnese, Mixed-Blood girl by the hand and left the house.

'Papa never wants to walk with me,' she complained in Dutch, 'he doesn't believe I'm strong enough to lead him, Uncle. I'm able to make sure he doesn't fall down.'

'Of course you're strong enough, May. He'll take you another time.'

I took her to Koblen field, and she began to forget her disappointment. We sat on the grass and watched the kites battling each other. She began to prattle in Javanese mixed with Dutch, sometimes also French. I didn't pay any attention. I just said 'yes' to everything. My own thoughts were still confused, under attack from several directions: The Mellema family, the Marais family, the changing attitude of my schoolfriends towards me, and my own changing feelings. Some kites broke loose, and whirled around the sky aimlessly . . .

May pulled at my hand, and pointed at a patch of clouds on the horizon.

'You love your father, May?'

She looked at me with amazed eyes. I saw Jean Marais in her face. I could not find the smallest trace of the face of the young woman sprawled out under the bamboo, threatened by the bayonet. This was perhaps what Jean looked like as a child. And this little Marais does not know at all who her father really is.

Jean, so he said himself, once studied at the Sorbonne. He never told me in what department or to what level. Commanded by the voice of his own heart, he abandoned lectures and poured all his strength into painting. He lived in the Latin Quarter in Paris, and hawked his paintings on the street pavements. His works always sold well, but never caught the society's attention or that of the Parisian critics. While hawking his paintings, he also did carvings on the street pavement too. Five years passed. He still didn't get anywhere. He was bored with his surroundings – with the mobs of sight-seers who watched him make African statues or other carvings; with Paris; with his own society; with Europe. He longed for something new, that might fill life's barrenness. He left Europe, went to Morocco, Libya, Algeria and Egypt. He still didn't find that something he sought after but could not identify: he never felt satisfied; he was always anxious and agitated. He still couldn't create the painting of which he dreamed. He left Africa. By the time he arrived in the Indies, his money had run out. The only road open to him was to join the Dutch Indies Army. He joined, underwent training for several months, and departed for the front in Aceh. In his army unit too he lived within himself, having almost no contact with anyone except through the orders he received in Dutch. And he was unwilling to learn that language.

May Marais did not know, or did not yet know, any of this.

37

I can paint and be a soldier too, Jean Marais resolved. The Indies Natives are very simple. They will never win any war. How can daggers and spears defeat rifles and cannons? he thought. He was sent to Aceh as a private first-class. The commander of his platoon, Corporal Bastian Telinga, was an Indo-European. If he hadn't been a Pure, he would certainly never have got higher than private, second-class. Jean lived amongst the other Pure Europeans, who spoke no Dutch: Swiss, Germans, Swedes, Belgians, Russians, Hungarians, Rumanians, Portuguese, Spaniards, Italians – from almost all the nations of Europe – the discarded rubbish from their own countries. They were people who had given up hope, or bandits on the run, or people running from debts, or bankrupt because of gambling and speculation – adventurers all. And none of them was less than a private, first-class. Second-class was reserved for Indos and Natives – generally Javanese from Purworejo.

Why mainly Natives from Purworejo? I once asked. They, Jean said, are a very calm people, with very strong nerves. That's why the army chose them to fight the Acehnese, who are as tough and hard as steel, men of action, and able to instil terror in most people. Perseverance and stamina were absolutely essential to withstand the onslaughts of the Javanese.

He soon had to admit that his initial views about the Natives' ability to wage war turned out to be wrong. The Acehnese had great ability; it was only their weapons that were inadequate; they also had very good organisation. On the other hand he also acknowledged the Dutch army's outstanding ability in selecting personnel.

Jean also once admitted to me he had been wrong to say that dagger, spear, and Acehnese bamboo trap, would not be able to face up to rifle and cannon. The Acehnese waged war in their own special way. Using the local environment, all their abilities, and their beliefs, they were able to destroy much of the strength of the Colonial Army. He was, he added, astounded by this. They fought to defend what they regarded as their rights, mindless of death. Everybody, even the children! Even when defeated they fought back. They fought back, Minke, with all their abilities and all their inabilities.

He once told me another story in that mixture of languages of his. The Acehnese defences had been pushed far into the interior and to the south, to the region of Takengon. An Acehnese commander, Tjoet Ali, had lost a lot of his men and his territory, yet the morale of his men was still high – a secret Jean could not fathom. They kept fighting, not only resisting the army, but resisting their own decline as well. The army's communications links were their easy targets: bridges, roads, telegraph lines, trains and railways; then came the drinking water which they poisoned, surprise attacks, bamboo traps, ambushes, surprise stabbings, running amok in the barracks . . .

The Dutch generals almost gave up. The Dutch were only ever able to destroy the children, the grandmothers and grandfathers, the ill, the pregnant women. And these helpless people, Minke, Jean said, felt fortunate if they died at the hands of the army. Jean's superiors spread rumours that the casualties amongst the European soldiers never reached the three thousand that they did in the Java War; but everyone was still afraid with every square of land that they stepped upon.

And Jean Marais began to learn to admire and love these noble-heroic Natives, with their strong character and personality. For twenty-seven years they had waged war, confronting the most powerful weaponry of the age, a product of the science and the experience of the whole of European civilisation.

Love is beautiful, Minke, very, very beautiful, he had said. But he never told me how he came to love the enemy he captured or how she may have come to love him, and to give him a beloved child, May – now sitting in my lap prattling.

I stroked her hair. For how many months was your mother able to feed you from her breasts, sweet one? You have lost something that nothing and no one will ever replace!

'Look over there, Uncle,' she called out in Dutch, 'above those clouds, kites shouldn't be like crabs!'

'Yes, crabs shouldn't be flying in the sky. The clouds are getting darker, May, let's go home.

Jean Marais was still crouched over his drawing-table. He looked up when we entered. May quickly went to him and prattled to him about the crab kites over the clouds. Jean nodded attentively. I moved around and about looking at the finished pictures that tomorrow or the day after I'd have to deliver to customers.

Jean would never have been able to satisfy their argumentativeness. There is always something they wanted changed more to their own liking. And that was my job – a heavy job certainly – to convince them: the artist is a great French painter, and that alone is enough to guarantee the eternal appeal of the work, to make it more eternal than the customers themselves. If it's changed, that eternal appeal will be destroyed and it will become an ordinary chemical snapshot. The most determined querulousness came from the female customers. It's lucky I had been able to learn a lot from listening to Jean: women prefer to serve the present and are afraid of age; they are in the grip of dreams about their fragile youth and want to hang eternally to the youth of their dreams. Age is truly an oppression for women. You must reply to their arguments in kind: this painting will make an excellent inheritance for Madam's children, not just for Madam. (Luckily our women customers aren't all sterile.) Usually my argumentativeness wins out. If not, well, I'm forced to make threats: well, if Madam doesn't like it, I'll pay it off myself and hang it in my room. Usually this threat arouses their curiosity. They quickly answer: what for? And I answer: if it becomes my property there are no obstacles to stop me doing anything I like to it. Doing what for example? Yes, well I could give it a moustache . . . (but I've never actually said that). In short, until now I've never been defeated, especially after I realised women look upon argumentativeness as a measure of one's shrewdness.

'It's getting late, Jean, I'm off home . . .'

I climbed over the hedge into the front yard of my boarding-house. Darsam had long been waiting for me with a letter.

'Young Master,' he offered his respects, then he spoke in Javanese, 'Nyai awaits a reply. Darsam will wait, Young Master.'

The letter reported: the family at Wonokromo was waiting for me: Annelies had fallen into daydreaming, did not want to eat, much of her work was unfinished, and incorrectly done. 'Sinyo Minke, how grateful would I be, a mother with so much to do, if Sinyo would consider her difficulties. Annelies is my only helper. I cannot handle all the work by myself. I'm worried about Annelies' health. It would mean so much to us both. Come and visit, Nyo, even if only for a little while. One or two hours would be enough. Though we hope very much that Sinyo will want to stay with us. Lastly, let me express our unbounded gratitude for Sinyo's co-operation.'

The letter was written in correct and proper Dutch. There was no way it could have been written by an inexperienced primary school graduate. I thought it might have been written by somebody else. At least I knew it was not written by Robert Mellema. But who cares who wrote it? It gave me courage, gave me back my character: if I was in their grip, they were also in mine. In each other's grip, if you couldn't actually say under each other's spell. A wise mother, naturally emanating authority like Nyai, is needed by every child, and a maiden whose beauty is beyond compare, is needed by every youth. See, I thought: they need me in order to save their family and their business. So I was pretty remarkable too, heh? *Aduh!* how many arguments could I now assemble to justify myself in my actions.

Good. I will go.

4

Nyai's letter certainly didn't exaggerate. Annelies looked gaunt. She greeted me on the house's front steps. Her eyes shone, bringing her face to life again which had been so pale when she had shook my hand.

Robert Mellema wasn't to be seen. And I didn't ask after him.

Nyai emerged from the doorway at the side of the front parlour.

'You've come at last, Nyo. Annelies had to wait so long for you. Look after your friend, Ann; I've still a lot of work, Nyo.'

I was able to steal a glance into the room next to the front parlour. It turned out to be nothing other than the business office. Nyai closed the door, and disappeared behind it.

There arose that same feeling I had experienced the first time I came here: foreboding. Something strange could happen at any moment. Be careful, this heart of mine reminded me. Be vigilant. As before, now too, a voice asked me: why are you so stupid as to come here? Why don't you go home to your own family if you're tired of boarding? Or find somewhere else to board? Why do you follow the pull of this forbidding house, without resisting, but rather surrendering unconditionally?

Annelies took me into the room where I had stayed last time. Darsam lifted down my suitcases and bags from the buggy and brought them into the room.

'Let me put your clothes into the wardrobe,' said the girl.

I handed over the suitcase keys and she began to busy herself. She lined up the books on the table, the clothes went into the wardrobe. Then she unpacked my bag. Darsam put the empty suitcase and bag on top of the wardrobe. And Annelies now fixed up the row of books so they looked like a column of soldiers.

'*Mas!*' That was the first time she called me thus – a call that made my heart pound, making me feel as if I was in the midst of a Javanese family. 'Here are three letters. You haven't read them yet. Why don't you read them?'

It felt as if everyone was demanding I read the letters I received.

'Three letters, Mas, all from B—.'

'Yes, I'll read them later.'

She brought them over to me, saying:

'Read them. They might be important.'

She went to open the outside door. And I put the letters on the pillow. I followed after her. In front of us opened up a beautiful garden, not big, you could almost say tiny, with a pool and a few white geese chatting away – like in pictures. A stone bench stood at the edge of the pool.

'Come on,' Annelies took me outside, along a cement path hemmed in on either side by the green lawn.

We sat down on the stone bench. Annelies was still holding my hand.

'Does Mas prefer I speak Javanese?'

No, I didn't want to oppress her with a language that would force her to position herself according to the complicated Javanese social order.

'Dutch is fine,' I said.

'We had to wait so long for you.'

'I had a lot of schoolwork, Ann; I must pass.'

'Mas will surely pass.'

'Thank you. Next year I must graduate. Ann, I think of you all the time.'

She looked at me with a glowing face and pushed her body closer to mine.

'Don't lie,' she said.

'Who would ever lie to you? No.'

'Is it true?'

'Of course. Of course.'

I held her around the waist and heard her panting. Oh Allah, You have given me the most beautiful maiden in the world. My heart raced too.

'Where is Robert?' I asked in an attempt to tranquillise my heart.

'Why ask that? Even Mama never asks where he is.'

Ah, there is something the matter here. And I didn't feel it was right for me to interfere.

'Mama feels she can't do all her work any more, Mas,' she bowed her head and her voice contained sorrow. 'These days I have to carry out all her duties.'

I observed her pale, candle-like lips.

'He doesn't like Mama. He doesn't like me either. He's hardly ever at home. He hates everything Native, except the pleasure he can get from them. It's like he's not Mama's first-born son, not my brother. He's like a stranger who has wandered off the road, into our house.'

She obviously thought a lot about her brother, and thought about him with compassion – and she was still so young.

'I haven't seen Mr Mellema either,' I said, looking for something else to talk about.

'Papa? Are you still afraid of him? Forgive that horrible night. You shouldn't think about him any more. Papa has become such a stranger. Sometimes he only comes home once a week, but then leaves again the same day. Sometimes he sleeps awhile, then vanishes, I don't know to where. That's why Mama and I have to look after everything now.'

What sort of family was this? Two women, mother and daughter, working silently away to maintain a family and a business as big as this?

'Where does Mr Mellema work?'

'Don't pay any attention to him, I beg you, Mas. No one knows where he works. He never speaks, it's like he's mute. And we never ask. No one talks with him. This has been going on for five years now. It feels that's how it's been for as long as I can remember. He used to be so good and so friendly. Every day he put aside time to play with us. All of a sudden, when I was in fourth class at ELS, everything changed. The business closed down for several days. Red-eyed, Mama came to the school to pick me up, to take me away from school forever. Beginning that day I've had to help Mama with her work in the business. Papa never appeared again, except for a few minutes every one or two weeks. Since then, Mama has never spoken to him, or wanted to answer his questions . . .'

An unhappy story.

'Was Robert also taken out of school?' I asked, turning the conversation.

'When I was taken out of school he was in seventh class – no, he wasn't taken out.'

'Where did he continue his schooling afterwards?'

'He passed that year, but didn't want to go on. He didn't want to work. Soccer and hunting and horse-riding. That's all he was interested in.'

'Why doesn't he help Mama?'

'He hates Natives, except the pleasure they give, says Mama. For him there would be nothing greater than to become a European and for all Natives to bow down to him. Mama refuses to bow down. He wants to control the whole business. Everyone would have to work for him, including Mama and me.'

'He looks on you as a Native too?' I asked cautiously.

'I *am* a Native, Mas,' she answered without hesitation. 'You're surprised? Yes, I could call myself an Indo. I love and believe in Mama, Mas, and Mama is a Native.'

A puzzling family indeed, each member playing their part in some fearful play.

Annelies kept on talking and I just listened.

'If that's what you want, easy, Robert, said Mama. You're an adult now. When your papa dies, go to a lawyer, perhaps you could get control over the whole business. Mama also said: But you must remember, you still have a step-brother from a legitimate marriage, an engineer called Maurits Mellema, and you would never be able to stand up to a Pure European. You are only a Mixed-Blood. If you really want to own and run this company properly, learn to work like Annelies. You can't even govern workers; because you have never worked yourself.'

'Look at the swan, Ann, white, like cotton-wool,' I wanted to change the conversation. But she kept on talking. 'Why are you telling me all your family secrets?'

'Because you are our first guest in five years. Our guest, a family guest. There have been some visitors but they've all been business contacts. There was one man, a family guest, but he was our doctor. So you're our first real guest. And you're so close to us, so good to Mama and also to me,' her voice faded into quietness, no longer childlike. 'See, I'm ready to tell you everything, Mas. And you mustn't feel restrained about anything here either. You'll be the good friend of us both,' She became very sentimental: 'Everything I own is yours, Mas. You are free to do as you wish in this house.'

How lonely were the hearts of this girl and her mother in the midst of this abundant wealth.

'Rest now. I want to do some work.'

She stood, ready to leave. She looked at me for a moment, hesitated, kissed me on my cheek, then quickly walked away leaving me by myself, alone . . .

How long had she been saving up all her feelings? Now it was I who became the receptacle into which they overflowed.

I could hear the racket from the rice factory from where I was sitting. And the sounds of the milk carts coming and going. The bang and clatter of the buffalo carts as they took things to and from the warehouse. The threatening pounding as peanuts were broken from their shells; the noise of workers joking.

I entered the room, opened up my notebook and began writing about this strange and frightening family that, by sheer accident, had now involved me too in its affairs. Who knows, I thought, some day in the future I may be able to produce stories like 'When the Roses Wilt', the remarkable serial by Hertog Lamoye? Yes, who knows? So far I've only written advertisements and short articles for the auction papers. Who could tell? With my own by-line and read by the public? Who could tell?

I wrote down all of Annelies's words. And what about Darsam, the fighter? I still did not know much about him. With which of this forbidding family's three factions did he side? Wasn't he precisely the closest danger to all three? Danger? Is there really any danger? If there is, then I too must be under threat? If it's true there is danger, why am I staying here? Isn't it better I leave?

The knock on the door startled me. Nyai was standing in front of me.

'We can't tell you how happy we are that Sinyo was prepared to come. See, Nyo, she is beginning to work again, she has got back her earlier liveliness. Sinyo's arrival is not only helping the company, but more importantly, Annelies. She loves Sinyo. She needs your attention. Forgive my frankness, Minke.'

'Yes, Mama,' I answered respectfully, more respectfully, it felt, than to my own mother. And I felt again her black magic gripping hold of me.

'All right, stay here for the time being. I will set aside buggy and driver for Sinyo's use.'

'Thank you, Mama.'

'So Sinyo is willing to stay here? Why are you quiet? Yes, yes, think it over first. Anyway, Sinyo's here now.'

'Yes, Mama,' and her hold on me made itself felt even more.

'Good, Rest. Even if a bit late, there's no harm in me congratulating you on doing so well at school.'

And so I became a new member of this family. Noting, however, that I must remain vigilant, especially towards Darsam. I will not get too close to him. On the contrary I must always be polite towards him. There's no doubt that Robert will hate me as a worthless Native. Mr Herman Mellema will, for sure, spit abuse at me whenever the opportunity arises. In short I must be vigilant – vigilance is the price to be paid for the happiness of being close to Annelies Mellema. And what can be obtained in this life without payment? Everything must be paid for, or redeemed, even the shortest happiness.

Robert didn't appear at dinner time. Nor did the shadows and scraping strides of Mr Mellema.

'Minke, Nyo,' Nyai begun, 'If you like to work and strive, you'll be happy here with us. We also will feel safer with a man around the house. I mean, a man who can be relied upon.'

'Thank you, Mama. That is all good and very pleasing, although I still must give it some thought first,' and I told them about the situation of Jean Marais's family and how they still needed my services.

'That is good,' said Nyai, 'It's proper that people have friends, friendships without self-interest. Without friends, life is too lonely . . .' Her words were directed more at herself. Suddenly: 'Nah! Ann, Sinyo Minke is now *close to you*. Look well. He is already close to you. Is there anything else you want?'

'Ah, Mama,' Annelies murmured as she glanced across at me.

'Ah Mama! Ah Mama! That's all you can ever say. Come on, speak now, while I can hear too.'

Annelies glanced at me again and her face was scarlet. Nyai smiled happily. Then she stared at me, and said:

'So, Nyo, this one here . . . is like a little child. And what about yourself Nyo, what do you have to say now you're close to Annelies?'

Now it was my turn to be embarrassed into silence. And there was certainly no way I would be calling out 'Ah-Mama' like Annelies. This woman thought quickly and sharply, able to reach straight into people's hearts, as if it was easy for her to know what lived inside people's breasts. Perhaps there lay the power with which she held people in her grasp, and bewitched them from afar. Let alone from nearby.

'Why are you both silent like kittens caught out in the rain?' she laughed, pleased at her own turn of phrase.

Indeed this was no ordinary *nyai*. She faced me, an HBS student, without any feeling of inferiority. She had the courage to state her opinion. She was aware of her own strength of character.

We passed away the night listening to Austrian waltzes on the phonograph. Mama read a book. I don't know what book. Annelies sat near me without talking. My own thoughts wandered to thinking about May Marais. She'd be happy here, I thought. She liked listening to European music. There was no phonograph at home, nor in my lodgings.

I began to tell them about the little girl who had lost her mother. And the fate of that mother. And the goodness of Jean Marais. And his wisdom. And his simplicity.

Nyai stopped reading, put the book down in her lap and listened to my story.

I continued my story about Jean Marais. One day he heard that his platoon had received orders to attack a village at Blang Kejeren. They departed early and arrived at the village around nine in the morning. Already, some distance from the village, they had let off shots into the air to frighten away opposition, so no battle would be necessary. They fired into the air again while resting under the shade of some trees. A while later they set off again, ready to enter the village. Yes, the village was already empty. The platoon entered without coming up against any opposition. No one could be found. Not even a baby. They started going into the houses and smashing up whatever they could.

The people had become impoverished during the twenty years of war. There was nothing the soldiers could take as souvenirs. Corporal Telinga ordered that all the houses be burnt. Precisely at that moment the Acehnese came into view in the distance, like columns of ants, men and women. They all wore black. They shouted in all sorts of voices calling to Allah. Then, all of a sudden, a group of young men appeared out of nowhere and attacked. They ran amok with their daggers. No one knew from where they came. The rifles had no ammunition left. And the black ants in the distance were getting closer. Picking up its wounded, Telinga's platoon rushed from the village. Jean Marais was caught in a bamboo trap. A sharp wooden spike pierced his leg. Telinga was also caught in a trap, but it wasn't so serious. They pulled the wooden spike out of Jean's leg, and he fainted. They ran and ran and ran. No one could be sure what else the Acehnese had planned. A new band of attackers could appear suddenly at any moment. All they could do was run and run. And take the wounded who could travel. Fifteen days later it was clear that Jean Marais was infected with gangrene at the base of his knee. Several months earlier he had lost his lover, now he was to lose a leg, cut off above the knee.

'Bring the child here,' said Nyai. 'Annelies would like very much to have a little sister. Wouldn't you, Ann? Oh, no, you don't need a little sister, you've got Minke now.'

'Ah, Mama,' she exclaimed, embarrassed.

And I wasn't anything less than embarrassed either. That was my last chance. I'd tried to build up myself before this remarkable woman as a man with character, as somebody whole. Every time she spoke, my efforts were brought to nothing. My individuality was being hidden by her shadow. And I knew: this could not be allowed to go on forever.

'Mama, permit me to ask,' I started my effort to escape from her shadow, 'Mama graduated from which school?'

'School?' she tilted her head as if spying on the sky, clearing her memory. 'As far as I can remember I've never gone to school.'

'How's that possible? Mama speaks, reads, and maybe also writes Dutch. How is that possible without schooling?'

'Why not? Life can give everything to whomever tries to understand and is willing to receive new knowledge.'

Her answer truly startled me. Such words had never been spoken by my teachers.

So that night I found it difficult to sleep. My thoughts worked hard trying to understand this woman. Outsiders viewed her as only a *nyai*, a concubine. Or people respected her only because of her wealth. I saw her from yet another angle: from all that she was capable of doing, from everything she said. I think Jean Marais was right: you must first of all think justly. Don't sit in judgement over others when you don't know the truth of the matter.

There are many outstanding women. But I have met Nyai Ontosoroh. According to Jean Marais' stories, Acehnese women used to descend into the battlefield to fight the Indies Army, ready to die beside their men. So too in Bali. In my own birthplace women peasants worked side by side the men in the paddy fields. Yet none of these was like Mama – she knew more than just the world of her own village.

And all my school-friends knew too that there was another outstanding Native woman, a maiden, a year older than me. She was the daughter of the *Bupati* of J—, the first Native woman to write in Dutch. Her writing had even been published in literary magazines in Betawi. She was seventeen when her first writings were published. Writing in a language other than her mother tongue! Half of my friends denied the accuracy of these reports. How was it possible that a Native, a girl to boot, only an ELS graduate, could write and articulate her opinions in the European manner, let alone have them published in a scholarly magazine?* But I believed it and must believe it; it was something that strengthened my belief that I too could do what she had done. Hadn't I already proved that I could do it? Even if still just initial attempts and in a very small way? It was indeed her example that stimulated me to write. And now I was coming to know this older woman. She didn't write articles but she was expert in seizing people in her grasp. She runs a big, European-type firm! She confronts her own eldest son, controls her master Herman Mellema, trains her youngest daughter to be a future administrator, Annelies Mellema – the beautiful maiden of whom all men dream.

I would study this strange and frightening family. And one day I'd write.

---

* Undoubtedly the famed author, Raden Ajeng Kartini, 1879-1904.

5

I could not restrain my curiosity to know who this extraordinary Nyai Ontosoroh really was. It was only several months later that I found out from Annelies the story about her mother. After re-ordering, it came out as follows:

You must surely remember your first visit here, Mas? Who could forget it? Certainly not me. Not in all my life. You trembled as you kissed me in front of Mama. I trembled too. If I hadn't been dragged away by Mama I'd still be standing benumbed on the steps. Then the *dokar* tugged you away from me.

Your kiss felt hot on my cheeks. I ran to my room and examined my face in the mirror. Nothing had changed. There had been no chilli paste with dinner that night, just a little pepper. Why were my cheeks so hot? I scrubbed and I rubbed. They were still hot. Wherever I sent my eyes off wandering they always ended up colliding with yours.

Had I gone mad? Why was it always you that appeared, Mas? Why did I suddenly feel this loss after you went away?

I changed into my night clothes and put out the candles, got into bed. But the darkness only made your face clearer. I wanted to hold your hand as I had that afternoon. But your hands were not there. I turned onto my left side, then onto my right, but I still couldn't sleep, hour after hour. I felt there was a pair of hands within my breast whose fingers were tickling me, agitating me. I felt I needed to act. But what? I didn't know. I threw off the blanket and *guling*. I left the room.

I charged into Mama's room without knocking. As usual, she hadn't gone to bed. She was sitting at her table, reading. She looked at me, closed the book, and I caught a glimpse of the title, *Nyai Dasima*.

'What's the book, Mama?'

She put the object into the cabinet.

'Why aren't you asleep?'

'I want to sleep with Mama tonight.'

'A girl old as you, and still wanting to sleep with your mother?'

'Let me, Ma.'

'Over there, climb up first!'

49

I got into the bed. Mama went downstairs to check the doors and windows. Then she came up again, locked the door, pulled down the mosquito net, and put out the candle. Pitch black in the room.

Near her I felt more calm, full of impatient hope, waiting for her words about you, Mas.

'Well, Annelies,' she began, 'why are you afraid to sleep by yourself? – aren't you grown up by now?'

'Mama, has Mama ever been happy?'

'Even if for only a moment and only a little, everyone has been happy, Ann.'

'Are you happy now, Mama?'

'I don't know about now. All there is now is worry. It has nothing to do with the happiness you're asking about. What does it matter if I am happy or not? It's you I worry about. I want to see you happy . . .'

I embraced Mama and I kissed her in the darkness. She was always so good to me. I believed there was no one better.

'Do you love Mama, Ann?'

This question, spoken for the first time, brought tears to my eyes, Mas. She had always seemed so hard.

'Yes, Mama wants to see you happy always. Not ever to feel the pain that I once did. I don't want you to suffer the loneliness I suffer now: without acquaintances, without friends, let alone really close friends. Why all of a sudden do you bring up *happiness*?'

'Don't ask me, Ma, tell me the story.'

'Ann, Annelies, perhaps you don't feel it, but I've been deliberately harsh with you so that you would develop the ability to work, so in the future you won't have to be dependent on your husband, if – yes, may it never happen – in case your husband turns out like your father.'

I knew Mama had lost all her respect for Papa. I understood how she felt so I never asked about it. And indeed I wasn't hoping to hear talk about that. I wanted to know if she had ever felt the way I was feeling at that moment.

'When did Mama feel very, very happy?'

'There were many such years after I was with Mr Mellema, your father.'

'Then, Ma?'

'Do you remember when I took you from school? That was when our happiness ended. You're grown up now, it's time you knew. It's best you know what really happened. I've been meaning to tell you for several weeks now. The opportunity has never arisen. Are you sleepy?'

'I'm listening, Ma.'

'Your father once said, earlier, when you were very, very small: a mother must pass on to her daughter everything she will need to know . . .'

'In those days . . .'

'Yes, Ann, in those days I respected every word that came from your Papa, I remembered them well, I made them my beacons. Then he changed, and became the opposite of everything he had ever taught me.'

'Ma, Papa was clever then, Ma?'

'Not only clever, but kind. It was he who taught me everything about farming, business, looking after the livestock, the office work. At first I was taught to speak Malay, then to read and write, then after that, Dutch. Your Papa not only taught me, but then also patiently tested everything he'd taught. He made me speak in Dutch with him. Then he taught me to deal with the bank, lawyers, about trade practices, everything that I've now begun to teach you.'

'Why did Papa change so much, Ma?'

'There was a reason, Ann. Something happened. Just that once, then he lost all his goodness, his cleverness, his intelligence, his skills. Broken, Ann, destroyed in an instant. He became someone else, an animal that could no longer recognise his own children or his wife.'

Mama didn't continue her story. It was as if the tale was an omen about my future, Mas. The world became more and more still. All that could be heard was our own breathing. Probably, if Mama had not been so hard towards Papa – so Mama told me again and again – who knows what might have happened to me. Perhaps something far, far worse than I could ever imagine.

'At the time it happened I thought of taking him to a mental hospital. But I hesitated, Ann. What would people think about you later, Ann? If your father was proven to be mad and was declared by the law as "under tutelage"? His business, his wealth and his family would be under the control of an executor appointed by a court of law. Your Mama, just a Native, would have no rights over anything, and would not be able to do a thing for her child, you, Ann. All our back-breaking efforts, with never a holiday, would have been in vain. And my giving birth to you, Ann, would have been in vain too, because the law would not acknowledge my motherhood, only because I'm a Native and was not legally married. You understand?'

'Mama!' I whispered. I'd never dreamed the troubles she faced had been so great.

'Even permission for you to marry would not come from me, but from that executor – neither kith or kin. By taking your Papa to a mental hospital, by involving the courts, the condition of your Papa would become public knowledge, the public would . . . you, Ann, your fate then, Ann. No!'

'But why would I suffer, Ma?'

'Don't you understand? What would happen to you if everybody knew that you were the daughter of a crazy man? How would we behave in front of everybody?'

I hid my head in her armpit, like a chick.

51

'His madness was not hereditary,' she said to assure me. 'He became so because of a misfortune. But people may not understand that, and you could be thought to have the same lineage.' I became scared. 'That's why I've let him be. I know where he's hiding. As long as no one else knows.'

Slowly my own problem was pushed aside by my pity for Papa.

'Let me, Ma, let me look after Papa.'

'He doesn't know you.'

'But he's my Papa, Ma.'

'Sst! Pity is only for those who are conscious of their condition. You need pity, not him – the child of someone like him. Ann, you must understand: he is no longer a human being. The closer you are to him, the more your life is threatened by ruin. He's become an animal who can no longer tell between good and evil. He's no longer capable of any service to his fellow human beings. It's over, don't ask about him again.'

I put to sleep my desire to know more. Whenever Mama was serious like that, it wasn't wise to press her further. I wasn't acquainted with any other mothers and children. Both of us had no friends, no comrades. Life as an employer dealing with workers, and as a business person dealing with customers, surrounded by people with no concerns besides business, had left me incapable of making comparisons. I didn't know how other Indos lived. Mama not only didn't allow me to mix socially, but did not ever leave me the time that would have made it possible. Mama was the only greatness and power that I knew.

'You must understand, don't forget it for as long as you live, the two of us must strive with all our might to make sure no one ever knows that you are the child of a man who has lost his mind,' Mama closed the matter.

We were both silent. I didn't know what she was thinking about or imagining. Within my breast those fingers began tickling again. I couldn't stand it. She still hadn't spoken about you, Mas. Did she approve of you or not, Mas? Or were you just to be considered another new factor in the business?

It felt as if the darkness did not exist. Only you existed. Nothing besides you! So I had to bring to an end this unpleasant story of Mama's. Then:

'Mama, tell me how you met and then how it was when you lived with Papa.'

'All right, Ann. But don't be shocked. You are a spoiled and happy child compared with your Mama when she was younger. All right, I'll tell you.'

And she began the story:

I had an elder brother: Paiman. He was born on the market day of Paing, so he was named with the first syllable *Pai*. I was three years younger, and named: Sanikem. My father changed his name to Sastrotomo after he was married. The neighbours used to say the name meant: the fore-most scribe.

People said that my father was very industrious. He was respected as the only person in the village who could read and write; the sort of reading and writing used in offices. But he wasn't satisfied with just being a clerk. He dreamt of a higher post, even though the job he held was quite a respected one. He no longer needed to hoe the ground or plough or labour, or plant or harvest sugar cane.

My father had many younger brothers and sisters as well as cousins. As a clerk he had great difficulty in getting them jobs at the factory. A higher post would have made it easier, and also it would have raised him up higher in the eyes of the world. Especially as he wanted his relations to be able to work in the factory as something more than just labourers and coolies. At the very least they should be foremen. You didn't need a blood relative as a clerk to get jobs as coolies – anybody could get a job as a coolie as long as the foreman agreed.

He worked diligently and became even more diligent. For more than ten years. But still no promotion though his salary and commission rose every year. So he tried every other way: *dukuns*, magic formulae, went on rice-fasts, Monday and Thursday fasts. Still no result.

He dreamed of becoming paymaster: cashier, holder of the cash of the Tulangan sugar factory, in Sidoarjo. And who did not have business with the factory paymaster? There were the cane foremen. They came to receive their money and leave their thumb print. If the foreman refused to accept a toll on the coolies' wages, he could withhold the foreman's gang's weekly wages. As paymaster he would be a big man in Tulangan. Merchants would bow down in respect. The Pure and Mixed-Blood *tuans* would greet him in Malay. The stroke of his pen meant money! He would be counted as among the powerful in the factory. People would listen to his words: 'Sit down on the bench there' in order to receive their money from his hands.

Pathetic. These dreams did not bring him a rise in position, respect or esteem. On the contrary, they brought hatred and disgust. And the position of paymaster remained hanging in limbo far away. His crawling behaviour, which often harmed his friends, caused him to be cut off from society. He was isolated in the middle of his own world. But he didn't care. He was indeed hard-hearted. His trust in the generosity and protection of the white-skinned *tuans* could not be broken. People were sickened to see the things he did to get the Dutch *tuans* to come to his house. One or two did turn up and he served them with everything that pleased them.

But the post of paymaster still did not come his way.

He even went as far as using a *dukun* and ascetic practices to cast a spell on the Tuan Administrator, the *Tuan Besar Kuasa*, the 'Great, Powerful Tuan', to come to the house. Also to no avail. On the other hand, he often visited the *Tuan*'s house. Not to see the official on some business. But to help with the work out the back! Tuan Administrator never took any notice.

I too was revolted by all this. Sometimes I would watch my father and feel moved. His whole body and soul wrestled with that dream. How he humiliated himself and his dignity. But I didn't dare say anything. Sometimes I did pray that he would stop his shameful behaviour. The neighbours often said: it was better and indeed best to ask of Allah, for how great anyway was mankind's power; but it was undignified to beg from the white people. I did not pray that he obtain his post – but rather that he be able to shake himself free from his shameful behaviour. At that time I would not have been able to explain all this. It was something I just felt inside me. But all my prayers were to no avail.

Tuan Besar Kuasa was a bachelor, as was usually the case with newly arrived Pures. He was, perhaps, older than my father, Sastrotomo, the clerk. People said my father once tried to offer him a woman. He not only rejected the offer and refused to say thank you but abused father and threatened to sack him. After that my father became the object of public ridicule. My mother quickly lost weight as she listened to people's taunts: 'Maybe he'll end up offering his own daughter.' They meant me.

You must certainly be able to imagine how suffocating life became after that. From that time on I never dared leave the house. My eyes were always looking uncontrollably to the front room to see if there was a white-skinned guest. Thanks be to God, there never was.

Unlike the other Dutch men, Tuan Besar Kuasa didn't like participating in the *tayub* dance festivities. Every Sunday he went to Sidoardjo for devotions at the Protestant church. At seven in the morning he could be seen on a horse or in a carriage. I myself once saw him from afar.

Ever since I turned thirteen I was kept at home, and was only acquainted with the kitchen, back parlour and my own room. All my friends had already married. Only when a neighbour or relative visited us, did I ever feel that I was free of the house as I had been in my childhood. I wasn't even allowed to sit in the *pendopo*. Not even to step onto its floor.

When the factory stopped work and the employees and workers went home, I often watched from inside as someone would walk back and forth all the time glancing at our house. Of course, all our lady guests said I was beautiful, the flower of Tulangan, the blossom of Sidoardjo. And if I looked at myself in the mirror, I found no reason not to agree with their flattery. My father was a handsome man. My mother – I never knew her name – was a pretty woman and knew how to look after her body. Actually my father should properly have had two or three wives, especially as he owned land that was rented by the factory and other land worked by tenants. But he didn't. He felt it was enough to have one wife who was beautiful. His only other dream was to become the paymaster, factory cashier, the most respected Native, for the rest of his life.

That was how things were, Ann.

By the time I reached fourteen, people already considered me an old maid. I'd already began having periods two years earlier. Father had some special plan for me. Even though people hated him, proposals of marriage to me came in often. All were refused. From my room I heard it happen several times. Unlike other Native women my mother had no say in any of this. Father decided everything. My mother did once ask what sort of son-in-law was it that he was hoping for. He didn't answer.

No, Ann, I'm not going to be like my father and decide what sort of son-in-law I must have. You choose; I only advise. But that was my situation, Ann, the situation of all young girls then – they could do nothing else but wait for a man to take them from the house, to who knows where, who knows as wife number what, first or fourth. My father and my father alone determined everything. You were lucky indeed if you turned out to be the first and only wife. And that was an extraordinary unusual thing in a factory area. There was more. The girl never need know beforehand whether the man would be young or old. And once married, the girl had to serve this man, whom she had never met before, with all her body and soul, all her life, until she died or until he became bored and got rid of her. There was no other way, no choice. He could be a criminal, a drunkard and gambler. No girl would know until after she became his wife. You were lucky if the one who came was a good man.

One night, the Tuan Administrator, Tuan Besar Kuasa, came to the house. I was on edge. My father was rushing hither and thither giving orders to mother and me to do this and that, and then cancelling them with still other orders. He ordered me to put on my best clothes and once or twice came in to watch me putting on my make-up. I was indeed suspicious, maybe the people's whisperings were true. My mother was even more suspicious. Nothing had really happened yet, and she was already crying and sobbing in a corner of the kitchen, silent in a thousand tongues.

My father, clerk Sastrotomo, ordered me to come out and serve strong coffee and milk, and cakes. My father had, of course, already given orders: make the coffee strong.

I came out carrying a tray. The coffee and cakes were on it. I didn't know what Tuan Besar Kuasa's face was like. It was not proper for a well-mannered girl to lift up her eyes and face towards a male guest who was not known well to the family. Especially if he was white. I kept my head down, placing the tray's items on the table. Even so, his trousers were visible; they were made from white drill cloth. And his shoes: big, long. A sign that the man was tall and big.

I felt the eyes of Tuan Besar Kuasa pierce my hands and my neck.

'This is my daughter, Tuan Besar Kuasa,' my father said in Malay.

'It's time she had in-laws,' responded the guest. His voice was big, heavy and deep, as if it emanated from his whole chest. No Javanese had a voice like that.

I withdrew again to await new orders. And no orders came. And then the Tuan Besar Kuasa left with father. Who knows to where.

Three days later, after lunch, midday Sunday, father called me. He sat with mother in the central room. I kneeled in front of him.

'Don't, Pa, don't,' Mother protested.

'Kem, Ikem,' Father began. 'Put all your possessions and clothes into your mother's suitcase. Dress yourself well, neatly, attractively.'

Ah, how many questions attacked my heart! I must carry out all my parents' orders, especially Father's. I could hear my mother protest and pro-test, but father took no notice. I packed all my clothes and possessions. My clothes could have been considered expensive and numerous, compared to those of other girls, so I had looked after them well. I had more than six *batiks*. Among them were some I had made myself.

And I came out carrying the old, brown case, with its dents here and there. Father and mother were still sitting in the same place. Mother refused to change clothes. Then all three of us left in the *dokar* that was waiting in front of the house.

Once on the vehicle, father spoke, his voice clear and free of hesitation:

'Look at your home, Ikem. From today this is no longer your home.'

I had to be able to understand his meaning. I heard Mother sobbing. I was indeed being expelled from my home. I also wept.

The *dokar* stopped in front of Tuan Besar Kuasa's house. We all got down. That was the first time Father did anything for me: he carried my case.

I didn't dare look around me. Yet I felt there were thousands of pairs of eyes staring at us in amazement.

I just stood there at the top of the steps of that stone house. My thoughts and feelings only added to my burden, sucking everything from my body. All that was left of my body was its skin. So in the end I was being brought here. Truly, Ann, I was ashamed to have as a father, Sastrotomo, the clerk. He was not fit to be my father. But I was still his daughter, and there was nothing I could do. Neither the tears nor the tongue of my mother could prevent the disaster. Let alone I, who neither understood nor owned this world. I did not even possess my own body.

Tuan Besar Kuasa came out. He smiled happily and his eyes were bright. And I heard his voice. In a foreign sign-language he invited us to come up. In a flash it became clearer to me just how big and tall his body was. Perhaps three times as heavy as Father. His face was reddish. His nose protruded very much, enough at once for three or four Javanese. The skin on his arms was coarse like iguana's skin, and was thick with yellow hair.

I gnashed my teeth, bowed my head down further. His arms were as big as my legs.

So it was true that I was to be surrendered to this white, iguana-skinned giant. I must be strong, I whispered to myself. No one is going to help you! All the devils and demons had encircled me.

For the first time in my life, at the invitation of Tuan Besar Kuasa, I sat on a chair the same height as Father. Before the three of us: Tuan Besar Kuasa. He spoke in Malay. I could catch only a few words. During the conversation everything felt as if it were surging and then falling again like in the ocean. I could not find a moment of peace. Tuan Besar Kuasa took out an envelope from his pocket and handed it to father. And from his pocket too he took out a piece of paper with writing on it and father put his signature to it. Afterwards I found out, the envelope contained 25 *guilders*, representing father's surrender of me to him, along with the promise that father would be made cashier after first successfully completing a two-year trial period.

So, Ann, that was the simple ritual whereby a child was sold by her own father, clerk Sastrotomo. And who was it who was sold: I, myself, Sanikem. From that moment on I lost all respect and esteem for my father – for anyone who has ever sold their own children. For whatever purpose or reason.

I kept my head bowed down, knowing that no one would be able to take up my cause. In this world only father and mother held power. If father was as he was, if mother could not defend me, what could anyone else do?

Father's final words:

'Ikem, you must not leave this house without the permission of Tuan Besar Kuasa. You may not return home without his permission and without my permission.'

I did not look at his face as he spoke those words. I kept my head bowed.

Father and Mother went home in the same *dokar*. I was left on the chair, bathing in my own tears, shaking and not knowing what I must do. The world seemed dark. Looking up from under my bowed forehead, my vision blurred, I could still see Tuan Besar Kuasa as he entered the house after having farewelled my parents. He picked up my suitcase and took it into a room. He came out from the room and approached me. He pulled my hand ordering me to stand. I trembled. It wasn't that I didn't want to stand up, or that I was rebelling against an order. I didn't have the strength to stand. My *kain* was soaking. My two legs trembled so badly it was as if my bones and sinews had come loose from their joints. He picked me up as if I were an old *guling* and carried me in his arms into the room, and put me down on a beautiful and clean bed, powerless. I was not able even to sit. I rolled over, perhaps I fainted. But my eyes could still vaguely make out the view in the room. Tuan Besar Kuasa opened my keyless suitcase and put my clothes into a big wardrobe. He wiped the suitcase with a cloth and put it inside the bottom section.

He returned to me, where I had rolled over prostrate on the bed.

'Don't be afraid,' he said in Malay. His voice was low like thunder. His breath blew in my face.

I closed my eyes tightly. What was this giant going to do to me? It turned out he picked me up and carried me around the room like a wooden doll. He took no notice of my wet *kain*. His lips touched my cheeks and my lips. I could hear his breath which blew so hard into my ears. I dared not cry. I dared not move. My whole body was soaked in a cold sweat.

He stood me on the tiles. He caught me again when he saw I stooped, about to collapse. He picked me up again and hugged me and kissed me. I can still remember his words, though I didn't then understand their intent:

'Darling, my darling, my doll, darling, darling.'

He threw me up and caught me on his hip. He rocked me, and that way I got back some of my strength. He stood me up again on the floor. I swayed and he guarded me with his hand so I would not fall. I still swayed, falling headlong onto the edge of the bed.

He strode towards me, and opened my lips with his fingers. With signs he ordered me to brush my teeth. He walked me to the back of the house, to the bathroom. That was the first time I saw a toothbrush and how to use it. He waited on me until I had finished, and my gums hurt all over.

Again, with signs, he ordered me to bathe and to scrub myself with scented soap. I carried out all his orders as if they were from my own parents. He waited for me outside the bathroom with sandals in his hands. He put the sandals on my feet. Very, very big – the first sandals I ever wore in my life – made from leather, heavy.

He carried me inside the house, to the room. He sat me in front of a mirror. He rubbed my hair until it was dry with a thick cloth, which I found out later was called a towel, then he put oil on it – its scent was so fragrant. I didn't know what kind of oil it was. And it was he too who combed my hair, as if I couldn't. He tried to set my hair in a bun, but he couldn't and he let me finish it.

Then he instructed me to change clothes, and he observed all my movements. I felt I had no soul anymore, like a *wayang* puppet in the hands of the puppet-master. After I had finished dressing, he powdered my face. Then he put a little lipstick on my lips. He took me out of the room. He called his two maid-servants.

'Look after my *nyai* well!'

And such was my first day as a *nyai*, Ann. And it turned out that his caring and friendly actions drove away some of my fears.

After giving the orders to his servants, Tuan Besar Kuasa left. Who knows to where. The two women babbled about how lucky I was to be taken as a *nyai*. No, I may not and did not want to say anything. I didn't know this house and its customs. Of course there was in my heart the wish to run.

But from whom could I seek protection? Then what would I do? I didn't dare. I was in the hands of someone very powerful, more powerful than Father, than all the Natives in Tulangan.

They prepared food and drinks for me. Every second moment they knocked on the door offering this and suggesting I take that. I was silently mute, just sitting on the floor, not daring to touch anything in the room. My eyes were open, but I was afraid to look. Perhaps this was death in life.

That night Tuan came. I heard the steps of his shoes as they came nearer. He came straight into the room. I shuddered. The lamp, which the servants had lit earlier in the evening, threw the light onto his clothes, all white and dazzling. He came up to me. He picked up my body from the floor, put it on the bed and laid it down there. It seemed I dared not even breathe, afraid that I might enrage him.

I don't know how long that mountain of flesh was with me. I fainted, Annelies. I didn't know any longer what was happening.

As soon as I regained consciousness, I knew I was no longer the Sanikem of the previous day. I'd become a real *nyai*. Later I found out the name of that Tuan Besar Kuasa: Herman Mellema. Your Papa, Ann, your true Papa. And the name Sanikem disappeared forever.

You're already asleep, not yet? Not yet?

Why am I telling you this story, Ann? Because I don't want to see my child go through such accursed experiences as these. You must marry properly. Marry someone like you, of your own will. You, my child, you must not be treated like a piece of livestock. My child may not be sold to anyone, no matter at what price. Mama will make sure that such a thing does not happen to you. I will fight to preserve the dignity of my child. My mother was incapable of defending me, so she was not fit to be my mother. My father sold me like the offspring of a horse; he wasn't fit to be my father. I don't have any parents.

Life as a *nyai* is very, very difficult. A *nyai* is just a bought slave, whose duty is only to satisfy her master. In everything! Then, on the other hand, she has to be ready at any moment for the possibility that her master, her *tuan*, will become bored with her. And she may be kicked out with all her children, her own children, unhonoured by Native society because they were born outside wedlock.

I swore in my heart: I would never look upon my home or my parents again. I did not even care to remember them. I never wanted to think about that humiliating event again. They had made me into a *nyai* like this. So I must become a *nyai*, a bought slave, a good *nyai*, the very best *nyai*. I studied everything possible about my master's wants: cleanliness, Malay, making the bed, ordering the house, cooking European food. Yes, Ann, I would have revenge upon my own parents. I had to prove to them, that whatever they had done to me, I would be more worthy of respect than them, even if only as a *nyai*.

Ann, I lived for one year in the house of Tuan Besar Kuasa, Herman Mellema. I never went out, was never taken anywhere or met any guests. What would have been the point anyway? I myself was ashamed to meet the outside world. Especially acquaintances, neighbours. I was even ashamed to have parents. I ordered all the servants to go. I did all the housework myself. There were to be no witnesses to my life as a *nyai*. There were to be no reports about me: a degraded woman, without value, no real will of her own.

Clerk Sastrotomo came to visit several times. I refused to receive him. Once his wife came. I wasn't even prepared to look at her. Mr Mellema never chided me for my behaviour. On the contrary, he was very satisfied with everything I did. It appeared he was very pleased with how I liked to learn. Ann, your Papa cared for me very much. But all that could not mend my wounded pride and self-respect. Your Papa remained a stranger to me. And indeed your Mama never made herself dependent on him. I always looked upon him as someone I did not really know, who could leave home for the Netherlands at any moment, leaving me, and forgetting everything about Tulangan. Indeed, I prepared myself precisely for that eventuality. If Tuan Besar Kuasa went away, I had to be able not to return to the house of Sastrotomo. Mama learnt to be thrifty, Ann, to save. Your Papa never asked how I used the shopping money. He himself used to buy the monthly provisions in Sidoardjo or Surabaya.

Within a year I had saved more than a hundred *guilders*. If one day Mr Mellema went home, or got rid of me, I'd have capital to take to Surabaya and would be able to trade in whatever I liked.

After I'd lived with Mr Mellema a year, your Papa's contract expired. He didn't extend it. Ever since he arrived in Tulangan, he had kept dairy cattle from Australia and I was taught how to look after them. In the evening I was taught to read and write, to speak and to put together Dutch sentences.

We moved to Surabaya. Mr Mellema bought a large piece of land in Wonokromo, our place here now, Ann. But it wasn't as busy as this then, still bush and patches of new jungle. The cattle were moved here.

At that time I began to feel glad, happy. He always paid attention to me, asked my opinion, invited me to discuss everything with him. Gradually I came to feel I was equal to him. I was no longer ashamed if I had to meet with old acquaintances. Everything that I had learnt and done during that year had returned my self-respect to me. But my outlook was still the same: I readied myself to be no longer dependent on anyone. Of course, it was going too far for a Javanese woman to speak about self-respect, especially one as young as I was then. It was your Papa who taught me, Ann. It was much later that I was able to truly feel the meaning of that self-respect.

Father also visited us at our new address several times, but I still refused to meet him.

'Meet your father,' Mr Mellema ordered, 'no matter what, he's still your father.'

'I did indeed have a father, once, not any more. If he wasn't Tuan's guest, I would have already thrown him out. It'd be better to leave here than meet him.'

'If you went, what would happen to me? What about the cattle? There'd be nobody to look after them.'

'There are many people who you can hire to look after them.'

'Those cows only know you.'

So it was that I began to understand that in reality I was not at all dependent on Mr Mellema. On the contrary, he was dependent on me. So I then began to take a role in making decisions on all matters. He never rejected this. He never forced me to do anything, except for study. In this matter, he was a hard but good teacher. I was an obedient and good pupil. I knew everything he was teaching me would, one day, be of use to me and my children if he went home to the Netherlands.

Tuan never pressured me about Sastrotomo again. Several times that clerk passed on messages through Tuan, that if I was unwilling to meet him, then could I write him a letter. I never responded to any of this. I never wrote even one or two lines to him. Even though I could now write well, both in Malay and Dutch. Sastrotomo wrote again and again. I never read any of his letters; I just sent them back.

Then, once, mother and father came to Wonokromo. Tuan was uneasy, perhaps embarrassed, because I still refused to meet them. The guests, according to Tuan, had kept pressing to meet me. Mother had cried. Through Tuan, I said:

'Consider me your egg that has fallen from the egg racks. Broken. It's not the egg's fault.'

With that, all business between my parents and me was over.

Why are you squeezing my arm, Ann? I've brought you up to be a business woman and merchant. You should not be sentimental. Our world is one of profit and loss. You don't agree with your Mama's attitude, do you? Hmmm, even fowls, and the hen most of all of course, defend their chicks, even against the eagle in the sky. It was only proper that my parents received fitting punishment. You too may take that attitude towards Mama one day. But later, when you're capable of standing on your own feet.

Tuan then imported more cattle. Also from Australia. The work increased. Workers had to be hired. Tuan began to hand over all the work within the business to me. At first I was afraid to give the workers orders. Tuan guided me. He said: Their employer is their livelihood. You are the master of their livelihood! Then, under his supervision, I began to dare to give orders. He remained a hard and wise teacher. No, he never hit me. Had he done so just once, my bones would have shattered. As difficult as it was, I was slowly able to do what he wished.

Tuan himself spent most of his time away looking for customers. Our business began to flourish.

At that time Darsam arrived, an unemployed hobo. But he loved to work. He would do anything that was given to him. One night, after a knife fight, he caught a thief. The thief died. Yes, there was a court case, but he was freed. Since then I have put my trust in him, I've made him my right-hand man. In the meantime Tuan spent less and less time at home.

Mama almost forget to tell you this too, Ann. It was Tuan who taught me how to dress properly, to choose matching colours. He liked to wait upon me while I put on my make-up. On those occasions he would say:

'You must always be beautiful, Nyai. A crumpled face and untidy clothes also reflect a crumpled and untidy business. No one will trust you.'

See how I fulfilled all his desires? How I satisfied all his needs? I was always neat and tidy. Sometimes I even put on make-up before sleeping. To be attractive and beautiful is truly better than being crumpled, Ann. Remember that, Ann. And nothing bad is attractive. If I was a man, I'd tell my friends that any woman who was unable to look after her own beauty was not worth marrying; 'she can't do anything, she can't even look after her own skin,' I would say.

Tuan said:

'You are not allowed to chew betel nut, that way your teeth will stay gleaming white.'

And I never chewed betel nut.

Ann, almost every month books and magazines arrived from the Netherlands. Tuan liked to read. I don't know why you're not like your father, especially when I like to read too. None of this reading material was in Malay. Let alone Javanese. When the work was finished, at twilight, we'd sit in front of our hut, a bamboo hut, Ann – we didn't have this beautiful house then – and he would order me to read. Also newspapers. He listened to my reading, correcting me when wrong, explaining the meaning of words I didn't understand. So it went every day until eventually I was taught how to use a dictionary by myself. I was only a bought slave. I had to do everything as he wished. Every day. Then he gave me a quota of reading. Books, Ann. I had to finish them and retell their contents.

Yes, Ann, as time went on, the old Sanikem began to disappear. Mama grew up into a new person with a new vision and new views. I no longer felt like the slave who was sold years before in Tulangan. I felt as if I no longer had a past. Sometimes I asked myself: had I become a Dutch woman with brown skin? I didn't dare answer, even though I saw the backwardness of the Natives around me. I didn't mix very much with Europeans, except with your Papa.

I once asked him were European women taught as I was now being taught. Do you know how he answered?

'You are far more capable than the average European woman, especially the Mixed-Bloods.'

Ah, how happy I was with him, Ann! How clever he was at flattering me and encouraging me. I was ready to surrender my whole body and soul to him. If my life was to be short, I wanted to die in his arms, Ann. I knew my decision to cut off my links with the past was right. He was exactly as taught by the Javanese: teacher of men, teacher of gods. Perhaps to prove what he said, he subscribed to some women's magazines from the Netherlands for me.

Then Robert was born. Four years later, you, Ann. The business got bigger. Our land grew larger. We were able to buy some wild forest at the edge of our land. All was bought in my name. There were no rice paddy or other fields yet. After the business became very large, Tuan began to pay me for my labour, also for the years that had already gone by. With that money I bought a rice mill and other plant and equipment. Since then the business was no longer the property of Mr Mellema as my master, but also my property. Then I received a share of five years' profit, five thousand *guilders*. Tuan obliged me to save it in a bank under my own name. By then we had named the business *Boerderij Buitenzorg*. And because I carried out all its affairs, people who had dealings with me called me Nyai Ontosoroh, Nyai Buitenzorg.

Asleep yet? Not yet? Good.

After following the women's magazines for a long time and carrying out much of what they taught, I repeated my question to Tuan:

'Am I like a Dutch woman yet?'

Your Papa only laughed broadly, and:

'It's impossible for you to be like a Dutch woman. And it's not necessary either. It's enough that you are as you are now. Even thus, you're cleverer and better than all of them. All of them!' He laughed expansively again.

Of course he was exaggerating. But I was pleased, and happy. At least, I was not below them. It pleased me to hear his praises. He never criticised, there was nothing but praise. He never ignored my questions; they were always answered. I became more confident, more daring.

Then Ann, then this happiness was horribly shaken, rocking the foundations of my life. One day Tuan and I went to Court to acknowledge Robert and you as the children of Mr Mellema. In the beginning I thought that with such acknowledgement my children would receive legal recognition as legitimate children. But it wasn't so, Ann. Your elder brother and you continued to be considered illegitimate, but now you were recognised as the children of Mr Mellema and could use his name. The Court's decision meant that the law no longer recognised you as my children, you weren't my children any longer, thought it was I who gave birth to you. Since that day, both of you, according to the law, were the children of Mr Mellema alone. According to the law, Ann, Dutch law in these Indies. Don't be mistaken. You're still my child. Only then did I realise how evil the law was. You obtained a father, but lost a mother.

Following that, Ann, Tuan wanted you both to be baptised. I didn't go with you to church. You all returned home quickly. The priest refused to baptise you. Your Papa became gloomy.

'These children have the right to a father,' said Tuan. 'Why don't they have the right to receive the absolution of Christ?'

I didn't understand such matters, and was silent. Afterwards I found out that you could only become legitimate if we married in a Civil Registry Office. You could then be baptised, so I began to press your Papa that we marry. I urged and urged. Your Papa, who had been depressed over those last few days, all of a sudden became angry. The first time he'd ever been angry in all those years. He didn't answer. And he never explained the reasons either. So, according to the law, you are still illegitimate children. And you've never been baptised either.

I didn't try again, Ann. I had to be happy with things as they were. No one would ever call me Mrs. The title Nyai would follow me forever, for all my life. It didn't matter as long as you both had a respected father, who could be relied upon, who could be trusted, who had honour. Especially as that acknowledgement meant a lot in your own society. My own interests need not concern anyone, as long as you both obtained what was rightfully yours. My interests? I could look after them myself. Ah, you're asleep.

'No, Ma,' I denied.

I still awaited her words about you, Mas. At another time, when another opportunity arose, perhaps she would not talk as much as this. So I had to be patient until she turned to talking about our relationship, Mas.

So I asked, leading her on:

'So Mama eventually loved Papa too.'

'I don't know what the meaning of love is. He carried out his responsibilities, so too did I. That was enough for us both. If, in the end, he did go home to the Netherlands I would not have tried to stop him, not only because I had no right to do so, but because we owed each other nothing. He could leave anytime he liked. I felt strong with everything I'd learnt, and I'd obtained, everything I owned and could do. Anyway, Mama was just a concubine who he'd bought once from my parents. My savings amounted to more than ten thousand *guilders*, Ann.'

'Mama never visited the family in Tulangan?'

'I had no family in Tulangan. Only in Wonokromo. My brother Paiman

64

visited me several times and I would receive him. He came to ask for help. It was always the same. The last time he came was to report; Sastrotomo died in a cholera epidemic along with all the others. His wife had died earlier, who knows of what.'

'Perhaps it'd be better if we visited there, Ma?'

'No, It's better the way it is now. Let the past be severed from the present. The wounds to my pride and self-respect still haven't healed. If I remember how I was so humiliatingly sold . . . I'm not able to forgive the greed of Sastrotomo and the weakness of his wife. Once in their lives people must take a stand. If not, they will never become anything.'

'You're too hard, Mama, too hard.'

'And what would become of you if I wasn't ready to be hard? Hard towards everybody. In this, let me be the only victim, I've already accepted my fate as a slave. You're the one who is too weak, Ann, showing pity where it's out of place . . .'

And Mama still hadn't talked about you. It seemed that Mama had never loved Papa so I was embarrassed to talk about it, Mas. Papa remained a stranger to Mama. While you, Mas, why were you so close to me now? Mas, and why did I always want to be near you?

'Then the second blow fell, Ann,' Mama continued. 'And the wound was never to heal . . .'

The government decided to repair and upgrade Tanjung Perak harbour. A team of harbour engineers was brought out from the Netherlands. At that time our dairy business was expanding well. Every month there were more and more requests for regular deliveries. The whole DPM, the Dutch oil company, was ordering from us. All of a sudden, like a thunderbolt, disaster crashed down. A thunderbolt of disaster.

(Mama went downstairs to drink. The room was dark. No one was listening to us in that upstairs room. It was a still night. The tick-tock of the pendulum clock could be faintly heard coming from the living room through the open door. And that sound disappeared when Mama came back and closed the door.)

There was a young engineer in that team of experts. I first read his name in the newspaper: Engineer Maurits Mellema. A little of his life story was presented. He was a hard-headed engineer. Already in his short career he had proved his great ability, it said.

Perhaps he's your Papa's family, I thought. I didn't want anybody else mixing in our lives that had become so calm, stable and happy. Our business must not be touched by anyone. So I hid the paper before your Papa was able to read it. I said it hadn't arrived, perhaps the delivery man was sick. He didn't ask further about it.

Three months later, Mama went on, after you and Robert had left for school, a guest arrived in a big, beautiful government carriage, pulled by two horses. Your Papa was working out the back. Mama was working in the office.

The government carriage stopped at the front steps. I left the office to greet it. Perhaps some government office needed dairy products. I saw a young European alight from inside. He was dressed all in white. His coat was white, closed, the coat of a marine officer. He wore a marine cap, but there were no marks of rank on his sleeves or shoulders. His body was straight and his chest broad. He unhesitatingly knocked on the door several times. His face was identical to Mr Mellema's. The silver buttons on his shirt gleamed with pictures of anchors.

In bad Malay, he spoke abruptly and arrogantly, in a manner I felt straight away to be impudent and opposed to the European politeness I knew:

'Where's Tuan Mellema,' he asked without a question-mark.

'Tuan who?' I asked, offended.

'I only need to meet Tuan Mellema,' he said more roughly than before.

I felt again like a *nyai* without the right to be respected in my own home. As if I wasn't a shareholder in this big business. Perhaps he thought I was sponging on Mr Mellema. Without my help my master would never have been able to build this house, Ann: This guest did not have the right to act so arrogantly.

I did not invite him to sit down and left him standing. I ordered somebody to fetch Tuan.

Your father taught me never to read a letter or listen to a conversation with which one had no business. But this once I was suspicious. I left the door between the office and the front room open a little. I had to know who he was and what it was he wanted.

The young man was still standing when Tuan came. Through the gap left by the open door I saw your Papa stand nailed to the floor.

'Maurits!' Tuan greeted him, 'you're already so dashing.'

At once I knew this was Engineer Maurits Mellema, the member of the team of harbour construction experts at Tanjung Perak.

He didn't answer respectfully, Ann, but, corrected your Papa arrogantly: 'En-gin-eer Maurits Mellema, Mr Mellema!'

Your Papa looked taken aback at receiving the correction. The guest still stood there. Your Papa invited him to sit down, but he didn't respond, neither did he sit.

You must listen to this story well, Ann, you must not forget it. Not only because your grandchildren must know, but because his arrival was the source of all your and my difficulties today. And the business's.

The young Dutch guest said:

'I didn't come here to sit down in this chair. There is something more important than sitting. Listen, Mr Mellema! My mother, Mrs Amelia

Mellema-Hammers, after you left in such a cowardly manner, had to work breaking her back to sustain me, to educate me, until I graduated as an engineer. I and Mrs Mellema-Hammers had resolved to no longer hope for your return, Mr Mellema. As far as we were concerned, you had disappeared, swallowed up by the earth. We sought after no reports of your whereabouts.'

Through the gap in the door, the side of your Papa's face was visible. He raised his hands. His lips moved but no voice came out of his mouth. His cheeks trembled uncontrollably. then his hands fell, dropping.

Ann, Engineer Mellema spoke like this:

'You, Sir, left behind the accusation that Mrs Amelia Mellema-Hammers had been unfaithful. I, her son, share her feelings of humiliation. You never brought this matter to court. You never gave my mother the opportunity to defend herself and her honour. Who knows to whom else you have passed on or told your dirty accusations. By coincidence I'm now serving in Surabaya, Mr Mellema. By coincidence also I read in an auction paper an advertisement offering dairy goods and milk produced by *Boerderij Buitenzorg* and there below was displayed your name. I hired a detective to find out who you were. Yes, H. Mellema was Herman Mellema, the husband of my mother. Mrs Amelia Mellema-Hammers could have married again and lived happily. But you, Sir, left the matter hanging.'

'She could have gone to the court any time she liked if she wanted a divorce,' answered your Papa very weakly, frightened of his own son who'd become so wild.

'Why should it be Mrs Mellema-Hammers when it was you who made the accusations? If you really believe my mother was unfaithful, why don't you, Sir, file for divorce right now.'

'If it had been me that took the case to court, your mother would have lost all her rights over my dairy business in Holland.'

'Don't give us all these ifs and buts, Mr Mellema. The fact is that you never took the case to court. Mellema-Hammers became the victim of your ifs and buts.'

'If your mother had not objected to opening up the scandal to the public, I would have done something long ago, and without your advice.'

'In those days my mother could not afford to hire lawyers. Now her son is ready and able; yes, even to hire the most expensive. You can open the case. You're also rich enough to hire them, and wealthy enough to pay alimony.'

Nah! Ann, it was now clear, Engineer Mellema was none other than your Papa's only legitimate son from his legitimate wife. He came as an aggressor to ruin our lives.

I trembled as I heard all this. Clerk Sastrotomo and his wife were never allowed to disturb my children's lives; neither was Paiman. Nor would a change in attitude by Mr Mellema, should he ever change – or even a change by any one of my children. The family and business had to remain as they were. Now there came your step-brother who didn't want just to disturb our lives. He came attacking, aiming to ruin everything.

Up until that time I didn't say anything. Unable to bear hearing what was being said I came out to cool down the atmosphere. Naturally I had to help Tuan.

'The detective gave me a very detailed and trustworthy account of things,' he continued ignoring my presence. 'I know what is in every room of this house, how many workers you have, how many cattle, how many tonnes of paddy and other crops you get from your fields, how much is your annual income, how much is in your bank account. And the most fantastic thing in all this concerns the foundation of your way of life, Mr Mellema, you who accused Mrs Amelia Mellema-Hammers of unfaithfulness. What's the reality now? Legally you, Sir, are still the husband of my mother. But you have gone ahead and taken a Native woman as your bed-mate, not for one or two days, but for years! Night and day. Without a legitimate marriage. You, Sir, have been responsible for the birth of two *bastard* children!'

On hearing that, my blood rose to my head. My lips trembled, dried. My teeth gnashed. I stepped slowly towards him and was ready to claw at his face. He had insulted all that I had secured, looked after and striven after; and I had loved all this time.

'Words that are only fit to be heard in the house of Mellema-Hammers and her son!' I retorted in Dutch.

He wasn't even prepared to look at me, Ann. To him I was no more than a piece of firewood. As far as he was concerned I had committed sin with his father and his father had committed sin with me. Perhaps it was his right and the right of the whole world to make such a judgement. But that your Papa and I had cheated on this woman Amelia, whom I'd never known, and her child . . . that was the climax of his vulgar impudence. And it was happening in the house we ourselves had worked for and built, in our own house . . .

'You have no right to talk about my family,' I roared in Dutch.

'I have no business with you, *nyai*,' he answered in Malay, pronounced very coarsely and stiffly. He refused to look at me again.

'This is my house. You can speak like that out on the street, not here.'

I signalled to your father that he should go, but he didn't understand. Meanwhile this impudent man continued to ignore me. Your Papa just stood there open-mouthed, like somebody who'd lost his senses. And it turned out later that indeed he had lost his mind.

'Mr Mellema,' he spoke again in Dutch, still ignoring me. 'Even if you married this *nyai*, this concubine, in a legal marriage, she is still not Christian. She's an unbeliever! And even if she was Christian, you, Sir, are still more rotten than Amelia Mellema-Hammers, more rotten than all the rottenness you accused my mother of. You, Sir, have committed a blood sin, a crime against blood! Mixing Christian European blood with coloured, Native, unbeliever's blood! A sin never to be forgiven!'

'Go!' I roared. He still ignored me. 'Disturbing people's homes. You say you're an engineer, but you have no manners at all.'

He still ignored me. I moved forward a step and he moved back half a step, as if to show his disgust at being approached by a Native.

'Mr Mellema, you now know who you really are.'

He turned his back on us, descended the steps, got into the carriage. He did not glance back or say another word.

Your Papa still stood nailed to the floor, in a state of stupefaction.

'So this is the child you had with your legal wife,' I shouted at Tuan. 'So this is the European civilisation about which you've been teaching me all these years? You've been glorifying to the heavens? Night and day? Checking into peoples' private lives and homes, insulting them, so as to come and blackmail them? Blackmail? What else if not to blackmail? Why else does one investigate the affairs of other people?'

Ann, Tuan didn't hear my roaring. His eyeballs moved, but he gazed unblinking at the main road. I shouted at him again. He still didn't hear. Several workers came running up wanting to know what had happened. When they saw me berating Tuan so furiously, they all ran away.

I pulled at him and I scratched his chest. He was silent, and he didn't feel anything. But the hurt in my heart went amok, striking out looking for a target. I didn't know what he was thinking. Perhaps he was remembering his wife. How my heart hurt, Ann, especially because he didn't want to know about the hurt I was suffering in this bosom of mine.

Tired of pulling and scratching, I began to cry, I collapsed; sitting down exhausted, like old clothes dropped on a chair. I lay down my face on the table. My face was wet.

When would my humiliation end? Must everyone be allowed to hurt me? Must I curse my dead parents, who sold me to become a *nyai*? I had never cursed them, Ann. Couldn't he understand, an educated person, an engineer, that he had not only humiliated me but also my children? Must my children become a rubbish bin, a place for insults to be flung? And why didn't my master, Mr Herman Mellema, tall and big, broad chested, hairy and with mighty muscles, have any strength to defend his life-friend, the mother of his own children? What's the use of a man like that? He wasn't just my teacher, but the father of my children, my god? What was the use of his knowledge and learning? What was the use of his being a European respected by all Natives? What was the use of him being my master and my teacher at once, and my god, if he wasn't even able to defend himself?

From that moment on, Ann, my respect for him vanished. His teachings about self-respect and honour had become a kingdom within me. He was no better than Sastrotomo and his wife. If that was all he was able to do when faced with such a little test as this, then even without him I could still look after my children, could still do everything myself. How my heart hurt, Ann; it's impossible that I could ever feel a greater hurt as long as I live.

When I lifted my head, I saw him still standing there without blinking, stupefied, looking out towards the main road. Did he look at me, his life-friend and foremost helper? No, he didn't. He coughed, took a step, very slowly. He called out slowly, as if afraid of being heard by the devils and demons:

'Maurits! Maurits!'

He walked down the stairs, crossed the front yard. When he reached the main road, he turned right, towards Surabaya. He was not wearing shoes, he was in field clothes, wearing sandals.

Your Papa didn't come home that day. I didn't care. I was still preoccupied attending to my pain. He didn't return home that night either. The next morning – still no sign. Three days and nights, Ann. During all that time the tears drenching my pillow were to no avail.

Darsam looked after everything. On the third day, he summoned up the courage to knock on the door. It was you, Ann, who opened the door and brought him upstairs. I never dreamed he'd dare come up. My hurt and sadness at once exploded into anger: How dare he come upstairs! Then it came to me, perhaps he thought there was something more important than my hurt and sadness. The door wasn't locked. It was you, Ann, who opened it. Perhaps you've forgotten it all now. That was the first and last time he came upstairs.

Darsam spoke like this:

'Nyai, except for the reading and writing, Darsam has looked after everything,' he spoke in Madurese. I didn't answer. I wasn't thinking about the business. I was still lying on the bed, hugging my pillow. 'Nyai shouldn't worry. Everything is fixed. You can trust Darsam, Nyai.'

And it turned out, he could indeed be trusted.

On the fourth day I went out from the house and garden. I took you from school. This business, the fruit of our efforts, must not collapse, must not be wasted. It was everything; upon it, our lives rode. It was my first child, Ann, your eldest brother, this business.

Having finished telling her story, Mama wept and sobbed, feeling over again the pain of her humiliation, a humiliation she could neither answer nor revenge. After the crying died away, she resumed:

You know yourself how many people – fifteen – I dismissed. It was they who had sold information to Maurits for one or two *talen*. Perhaps they weren't even paid anything. And I must ask your forgiveness too, Ann. Your Papa and I had agreed to send you to school in Europe, where you could study to be a teacher. I felt I sinned greatly when I took you from school.

I've forced you to work so hard, long before you were old enough, to work every day, without holidays, without friend or comrade, because you mustn't have any, for the business's sake. I have made you learn to be a good employer. And employers may not become friends with their employees. You mustn't be influenced by them. What can one do, Ann?

After the arrival of Engineer Mellema, tremendous changes occurred. I knew about Papa without anyone telling me. On the seventh day he returned. The strange thing was that he wore clean clothes, and new shoes. That was in the evening, after the work day was over. Mama, I and Robert were sitting at the front of the house. And Papa came.

'Don't speak to him. Don't greet him,' Mama ordered.

The closer Papa came the more visible was his pale, cleanly shaven face. His hair was now parted in the middle. The odour of hair oil, never used at home, excited our nostrils. Also the smell of strong drink mixed with spices. He passed us without a remark or a glance, went up the steps, disappeared inside.

Suddenly Robert stood up, and with eyes popping out stared at Mama and frowned angrily:

'My Papa is not a Native!' he ran calling after Papa.

I looked at Mama. And Mama was looking at me, she said slowly:

'If you like, you may follow your brother's example.'

'No, Mama,' I exclaimed and I hugged her neck. 'I only follow Mama, I'm a Native too like Mama.'

Nah! Mas, that's our true situation. I don't know if you're going to despise us like Robert, my brother, and Engineer Maurits, my step-brother.

Who knows what Papa did in the house. We didn't know. All the rooms upstairs and downstairs were locked.

About a quarter of an hour later he came out again. This time he looked at Mama and me. He offered no greeting. Behind him followed Robert. Papa left the yard again, descended to the main road and disappeared. Robert came back to the house with a gloomy face, disappointed because Papa had ignored him.

I've hardly ever seen Papa since that event five years ago. Sometimes he would appear, not saying anything, and then go again, not saying anything. Mama refused to look for him or look after him. Mama forbade me too to look for him. We were even forbidden to talk about him. Papa's portraits were taken down from the walls by Darsam and Mama ordered that they be burnt in the yard in front of the whole household and all the workers. Perhaps that was how Mama let go of her feelings of revenge.

At first Robert was just silent. Only after Papa's portraits were burnt did he protest. He ran inside the house, took down Mama's portraits and burnt them himself in the kitchen.

'He can join his father,' Mama said to Darsam.

And the fighter passed on Mama's words to Robert, adding:

'Whoever dares disturb Nyai and Noni, I don't care if it's you yourself, Sinyo Robert, he will die under my machete. Sinyo can try if he likes, now, tomorrow or whenever. And if Sinyo tries to find Tuan . . .'

Two months after all this, Robert graduated from ELS. He never reported it to Mama, and Mama didn't care either. He wandered about everywhere. A silent enmity has continued between Mama and Robert till this day. Five years.

At first Robert sold anything he could lay his hands on, from the godown, kitchen, house, office. He kept the money for himself. Mama got rid of every worker who took orders from him to steal. Then Mama forbade Robert from entering anywhere other than his own room and the dining room.

Five years passed, Mas. Five years. And there appeared two guests: Robert Suurhof for my brother, and Minke for me and Mama. Yes, you, Mas, no one else but you . . .

6

Five days I had been living in that luxurious house at Wonokromo. And: Robert Mellema invited me to his room.

I entered vigilantly. There was more furniture there than in my room. There was a desk with a glass top. Underneath the glass top there was a big picture of a freighter, the *Caribou*, a ship flying the English flag.

He seemed friendly. His eyes were wild, a bit red. His clothes were clean and smelled of cheap perfume. His hair shone with pomade cream and was parted on the left. He was a handsome youth, tall-bodied, agile, fit, strong, polite, and looked as if he was always thinking. It was only his brown, marble-like eyes with their stealthy glances and his curled-up lips that really put me on edge. With just the two of us there I felt very uneasy.

'Minke,' he began, 'it looks as if you like living here? You're a school-friend of Robert Suurhof, aren't you? In the same class at the HBS?' I nodded suspiciously.

We sat on chairs, facing each other.

'I should have gone to HBS too, and would have already graduated by now.'

'Why didn't you go on?'

'That was Mama's responsibility, and Mama didn't do it.'

'Pity. Perhaps you never asked her.'

'No need to ask. It was her responsibility.'

'Maybe Mama thought you didn't want to go on.'

'There's no use in supposing about fate, Minke. This is my situation now. I'm outdone by you, Minke, you, just a Native – an HBS student. Eh, what's the point of talking about school?' He was silent a moment, examining me with his chocolate, marble-like eyes. 'I want to ask how come you're staying here? It seems you like it here too? Because of Annelies?'

'Yes, Rob, because your sister is here. Also because I was asked.'

He ahemmed as I scanned his face.

'You've got objections perhaps?' I asked.

'You like my sister?' he asked in return.

'Yes.'

'What a pity you're only a Native.'

'It's a crime to be a Native?'

He ahemmed once again, looking for words. His eyes wandered outside the window. I took the chance to check out his room more closely.

His bed had no mosquito-net. In a hole in the floor there stood a bottle with the remnants of a mosquito coil in its neck. Around the bottle were scattered, shattered ashes. The room hadn't been swept yet.

I stopped inspecting the hole when I heard his voice again:

'This house is too quiet for me,' he said. 'Do you like playing chess perhaps?'

'Unfortunately no, Rob.'

'Yes, a pity. Do you hunt? Let's go hunting.'

'I am sorry, Rob, but I need the time to study. Actually, I like hunting too. Perhaps some other time?'

'Good, another time,' he looked piecingly into my eyes. I knew there was a threat in that look. He dropped the palm of his right hand to his thigh. 'How about if we go for a walk?'

'It's a pity, Rob, but I have to study.'

We were both silent for quite a while. He stood up and put aright the position of the door. My eyes groped around seeking something to talk about while remaining ever vigilant, ready for every possibility. The window caught my attention. If he suddenly attacked me, that's where I'd run and jump out. Especially as below it there was a bench without any flowerpots.

Upon the other chair, the one Robert wasn't sitting on, lay a squashed, folded-up magazine. It looked as if it had been used as a prop for a cupboard or table-leg.

'You don't have anything to read?' I asked. He sat in his chair again and answered with a voiceless laugh. His teeth were white, well looked after and gleaming.

'You mean by something to read, that paper?' his eyes pointed to the folded-up magazine. 'I've had a look through it.'

He picked it up and gave it to me. At that moment I was unsure if he wasn't about to do something. His eyes pierced my heart and I shivered. It was a magazine. Its cover was damaged, yet I could still read part of its name: *Indi . . .**

'A magazine for lazy people,' he said sharply. 'Read it if you like. Take it.'

From the paper and ink, you could tell it was a recent edition.

'What do you want to be when you've graduated from HBS?' he suddenly asked. 'Robert Suurhof says you'll be a *bupati*.'

'It's not true. I don't want to be an official. I prefer being free, as I am now. And anyway, who'd make me a *bupati*? And you yourself, Rob?' I asked in return.

* *Indische Gids*, a scholarly historical journal.

74

'I don't like this house. I don't like this country either. Too hot. I like the snow better. This country is too hot. I'll go home to Europe. Sail. Travel the world. Immediately I board my first ship, I'll tattoo my chest and arms.'

'That'd be great,' I said, 'I'd like to see other countries too.'

'The same. So we could sail around the world together. You and me, Minke. We could make a plan, yes? It's a pity you're a Native. Look at the picture of this ship. A friend gave it to me,' his spirits picked up. 'He was a sailor on the *Caribou*. I met him by coincidence at Tanjung Perak. Spoke a lot, mainly about Canada. I was ready to join him. He wouldn't let me: "What's the point in you becoming a sailor. You're the son of a wealthy man. Stay at home. You could buy your own ship if you wanted to." ' He gazed at me with dreaming eyes. 'That was two years ago. And he's never put in at Perak again. Hasn't sent any letters either. Perhaps he's drowned.'

'Maybe Mama won't allow you to go,' I said. 'Who'll look after this big business.'

'Huh,' he hissed. 'I'm an adult, with the right to decide for myself. But I'm still unsure. I don't know why.'

'It's better you talk it over with Mama first.' He shook his head. 'Or with Papa,' I suggested.

'A pity,' he sighed deeply.

'I've never seen you talk with Mama. Perhaps it'd be all right if I told her?'

'No. Thank you. I hear from Suurhof you're a bit of a crocodile.'

I felt my face pound as my blood galloped through my veins. I knew at once: I'd got to his sensitive spot. Now his true intentions were being revealed.

'Everyone has been judged good or bad by a third party at some time or other. Equally, on the other hand, everyone has passed judgement on other people too. I have. You have. Suurhof has,' I said.

'Me? No,' he answered firmly. 'I've never cared about what other people say or do. Especially not about what people say of you. And even less so about what they say of me. But Suurhof said: be careful of that filthy Native Minke, a "goat-class crocodile".'

'He's right, everybody has a duty to be careful. Suurhof too. Nor am I any less careful of you, Rob.'

'Look, I've never dreamed of sleeping in another person's house because of a woman. Even if I had been invited.'

'I've already told you, I like your sister. Mama asked me to stay here.'

'Good. As long as you know it wasn't me that invited you.'

'I fully understand, Rob. I 've still got Mama's letter.'

'Let me read it.'

'It's for me, Rob, not for you. A pity.'

As time went on, his attitude and his voice increasingly evinced enmity. He was trying to frighten me.

'I don't know if you will marry my sister in the end or not. It seems Mama and Annelies like you. Even so, you must remember, I'm the male and the eldest child in this family.'

He ahemmed and carefully scratched his head, afraid of messing up his hair.

'I know, you also know, all the people here are against me. Everyone ignores me. All this is *not* without its cause. Now you arrive. You're with them no doubt. I stand alone here. It's best you never forget what a person standing alone can do,' he said threateningly, with smiling lips.

'Yes, Rob, and don't forget your own words either, because they're directed at yourself as well.' His eyes now dreamily gazed at me as he took the measure of my strength, and I followed his example, also smiling. I followed all his movements. At the slightest indication of a suspicious move, hup, I'd be up and out the window. He would no longer find me in the room.

'Good,' he said nodding. 'And don't you forget either, you're only a Native.'

'Oh, I'll certainly always remember that, Rob. Don't worry. Don't you forget either, in your veins runs Native blood too. I'm indeed not an Indo, not a Mixed-Blood European; but while I'm studying at European schools, there's European knowledge and learning inside me too, if it's European things that you value so much.'

'You're clever, Minke, fit to be an HBS student.'

That short conversation felt as if it had gone on tensely for hours. Then I realised it had lasted only ten minutes. Luckily Annelies called from outside, and I excused myself.

Catching me entirely by surprise, Robert, still sitting, said calmly:

'Go, your *nyai* is looking for you.'

I stopped at the door and looked at him in astonishment. He only smiled.

'She's your sister, Rob. You shouldn't talk like that. I too have my honour . . .'

Annelies hurriedly pulled me away to the back room as if something important had occurred there. We sat on the thick-cushioned sofa. The cover had a floral pattern on a cream base. She clung to me and whispered.

'Don't see too much of Robert. Let alone go into his room. I worry. Each day he changes more. Twice now Mama has refused to pay his debts, Mas.'

'Do you have to be enemies with your own brother?'

'It's not that. He must work to earn his living. He could if he wanted to. But he doesn't want to.'

'Yes, but why must you two be enemies.'

'It doesn't come from my side. Mama is right in everything. He doesn't want to acknowledge that Mama is right just because she is a Native. So what must I do?'

I didn't press her further. But I thought to myself then: What was that handsome youth getting from this family? From his mother nothing, from his father nothing. Let alone his sister. Neither sympathy, nor love. I come to his home, and he's jealous of me. It's only natural.

'Why don't you try to be the peace-maker, Ann?'

'What for? He's gone too far, made me curse him.'

'Curse him? You've cursed him?'

'I don't want to even look at his face. Before I was still prepared to be good to him. Now, for as long as I live – never. Never, Mas.'

I regretted having tried to interfere. And her face, which all of a sudden reddened, showing her anger.

Nyai joined us. She had a copy of the *Surabaya Daily News* in her hand. She pointed out to me a short story 'Een Buitengewoon Gewoone Nyai die Ik ken' (An Extraordinary Ordinary Nyai that I Knew).

'Have you read this story, Nyo?'

'Yes, Ma, at school.'

'I think I recognise the person described in this story.'

Perhaps I went pale on hearing her words. Although the title had been changed, that was my own writing, my first short story published in other than an auction paper. A few words and sentences had been improved, but it was still my work. The material wasn't from Annelies, but my own im-aginings based on Mama's day-to-day reality.

'Who's the author, Ma?' I asked pretending.

'Max Tollenaar. Is it true you only write advertisements?'

Before the conversation became involved I quickly confessed:

'Yes, I wrote it, Ma.'

'I thought so. You're indeed clever, Nyo. Not one in a hundred people can write like that. Though if you mean me in that story . . .'

'I based my imaginings on Mama,' I answered attacking quickly.

'I see. It's not surprising then that there are a lot of incorrect things in it. As a story it's indeed good, Nyo. Let's hope you become a writer, like Victor Hugo.'

And I was embarrassed to ask who Victor Hugo was. And she could praise the strengths of a story. When did she ever study story-writing? Or is it all just pretence?

'Have you read Francis? G. Francis?'

I felt truly at a loss. I'd never heard of him either.

'It seems Sinyo never reads Malay.'

'Malay books, Ma? Are there such things?'

'It's a pity you don't know. He's written many Malay books. I think he's a Pure or a Mixed-Blood, not a Native. It would be a real pity, Nyo, if you never read any of his books.'

She spoke still more about the world of fiction. And the more she spoke, the more I doubted her. She might be just parading everything ever taught to her by Herman Mellema. My teachers taught us quite a lot about Dutch language and literature. They had never touched on the things that she was discussing. And my favourite teacher, Miss Magda Peters, must know more than any *nyai*. This *nyai* was even trying to talk about literary language as well!

'Francis, Nyo, he wrote *Nyai Dasima*, a really European-style novel. But in Malay. I've got the book, perhaps you'd like to study it.'

I just mechanically replied 'yes'. What did she know about the literary world? And why did she want to read stories, interfere in the affairs of the imaginary characters of the world of writers, even commenting on the language they used, while under her own eyes her own son Robert was neglected? It gave me cause to have doubts.

As if she could read my thoughts, she asked:

'Perhaps you want to write about Robert too.'

'Why, Ma?'

'Because of your youth. You'll want to write, of course, about the people you know around you. That interest you. That excite your sympathy or anti-pathy. I think Rob will attract your attention, for sure.'

Luckily that rather unpleasant conversation was soon followed by dinner. Robert didn't join us. Both Mama and Annelies were not surprised, neither did they enquire after him. The servant didn't ask any questions either.

In the middle of dinner I was about to pass on Robert's desire to become a sailor, to go home to Europe. At that moment Nyai spoke instead:

'Write, Nyo, always about humanity, humanity's life, not humanity's death. Yes, whether it's animals, ogres or gods or ghosts that you present. There's nothing more difficult to understand than humanity. That's why there is no end to the telling of stories on this earth. Every day there are more. I don't know a lot about this myself. But once I read something that said, more or less, the following: do not underestimate the human being, who sometimes appears so simple; even with sight as sharp as an eagle, a mind a sharp as a shaving knife, senses more powerful than the gods, hearing that can catch the music and the lamentations of life, your knowledge of humanity will never be total.' Mama had stopped eating altogether. The spoon with its load still hovered in mid-air under her chin. 'It's true that during the last ten years I've read more fiction. It's as if every book is concerned with people's efforts and strivings to escape or overcome some difficulty. Stories about happy things are never interesting. They are not stories about people and their lives, but about heaven, and clearly do not take place on this earth of ours.'

Mama resumed eating. I concentrated all my attention in order to catch every one of her words. At that time she was really an unofficial teacher whose lessons were delivered officially enough.

After dinner she resumed:

'Because of all this, you are no doubt interested in Robert. He always seeks out trouble and then can't get out of it. I think, if I'm not wrong, that's what's called tragic. The same as his father. Perhaps through your writings – if he was willing to read them – he could see himself as in a mirror. Perhaps he could change his ways. Who knows? Only, I ask, before you publish them, let me see them first. Of course that's if you don't mind. You never know but that there might be some false impressions or assumptions that could be avoided.'

As it happened I was indeed working on a piece about Robert. Nyai's warning rather startled me. It was if her eagle-eyes saw my every move. I also felt that she was invading my privacy as a story-teller. The publication of my first story had raised my spirits. But the enthusiasm that success had generated could not now spur on my writings about Robert. Mama, with her eagle eyes, had blocked that progress in the middle of its journey.

The discussion at dinner made me submerge myself in reflections. It was clear that she had read a great deal. Probably Mr Herman Mellema was a truly wise and patient teacher. Nyai was a good pupil, and she had the ability to develop herself, after having obtained some capital in the form of understanding from her master. What I can't obtain from school, I will harvest in the midst of this concubine's family. Who would ever have guessed? Perhaps, too, she does understand Robert Mellema better than I can. What she had said about the Native-hating youth pointed to a deep compassion for her eldest child.

I still didn't know much about that tall youth. Perhaps he too read a lot like his mother. The magazine he gave me turned out to be no ordinary magazine. It could have come from Mama's library, or have been taken from the postman and not handed over to Mama. Maybe, too, he hadn't finished reading it either. I don't know for sure. All the articles in it were about the Netherlands Indies. One amongst them was about Japan's relations – whether they were limited or extensive – with the Indies.

That article greatly enriched my notes about Japan – a country that had been discussed very much during those preceding few months. None of my schoolfriends had paid any attention to that country even though it had been touched upon in discussions at school. My friends still did not consider Japan as worthy of discussion. They off-handedly equated Japan with the prostitutes who filled up the Japan Garden, and with the little cafés, restaurants and barber shops, with the hawker and his goods. None of these reflected in any way the factory challenging modern science and learning that was Japan.

In one discussion, when my teacher, Mr Lastendienst, tried to get the students interested, most just chatted lazily to each other. He said that Japan was also experiencing a resurgence in the field of science. Kitasato had discovered the plague bacteria, Shiga had discovered dysentery bacteria – and in that manner Japan, too, had been of service to humanity. He compared it with the Dutch nation's contribution to civilisation. Seeing that I was fully engaged in the subject and was taking notes Mr Lastendienst asked me in an accusing tone of voice: Eh, Minke, the Javanese delegate in this room, what has your nation contributed to humanity? I would not have been alone in getting such a start to hear that sudden question; in all likelihood all the gods in the *wayang* chest of the puppet-master would have exhausted their energy just to answer. So the best way of getting out of my difficulty was to utter the following sentence: Yes, Mr Lastendienst, I can't answer at this time. And my teacher reacted to this with a sweet smile – very sweet.

That's just a little from my notes about Japan. Now with the articles in the magazine Robert gave me, my notes had been supplemented by quite a deal of extra information. About the current developments in Japan and the struggle over its defence strategy. I didn't understand much about those things. Precisely because of that I noted it all down. At the very least it would be excellent material for use in a school discussion.

It said there had been competition between the Japanese army and navy. A maritime defence strategy was then chosen. And the army, with its centuries-old samurai tradition, was dissatisfied.

And the Indies itself? In the article it said: the Netherlands Indies has no navy, only an army. Japan is made up of islands. The Netherlands Indies is just a great string of them. Why does Japan emphasise naval defence while the Indies emphasises the land? Isn't the problem of defence (against the outside) the same? Didn't the Indies fall into the hands of the English a hundred years ago precisely because of the weakness of the Indies Navy? Why hasn't that lesson been learnt?

I also found out from that magazine: the Netherlands Indies had no navy. The warships that sailed back and forth in Indies waters did not belong to the Netherlands Indies but to the Kingdom of the Netherlands. Governor-General Daendels had made Surabaya a naval base in a period when he had not a single ship! Almost a hundred years later still no one gave any thought to the Indies having its own navy. The honourable gentlemen in charge put their trust in the British naval defences of Singapore and the American naval defences of the Philippines.

The article speculated about war with Japan. In what kind of position would the Indies be with its undefended waterways? While the Royal Dutch Navy only irregularly carried out patrols? Could not the experience of 1811, when the Indies fell into British hands, be repeated, once again, to Holland's loss?

I don't know whether Robert ever read and studied the article. Seeing he wanted to travel the world as a sailor perhaps he had read it. And as

80

someone who believed in European superiority, he would no doubt put his faith in the white race. The article also said: Japan was trying to imitate, on the seas, the English. And the writer warned people that they should stop insulting the Japanese by calling them imitating monkeys. At the beginning of all growth, everything imitates. All of us, when we were children, also only imitated. But children grow up, and begin their own development . . .

And the same theme occurred in a conversation between Jean Marais and Telinga that I once overheard, and I noted it down like this:

Jean Marais: roles shift, from one generation to another, from one nation to another. Previously, coloured peoples conquered the white peoples. Now the white peoples conquered the coloured peoples.

Telinga: the whites had never been beaten in three centuries by coloureds. Three centuries! Indeed it could happen that one white people could conquer another white people. But a coloured people could never conquer whites. Not in the next five centuries. Not ever.

And Robert wanted to become a sailor, a European. He dreamt of sailing on the *Caribou*, under the flag of England – a country of no great size, with a sun that never set . . .

7

It felt as if I hadn't been asleep for long. Nervous knocking on the door jolted me awake.

'Minke, wake up.' It was Nyai's voice.

I found Mama standing in front of the door, carrying a candle. Her hair was a bit of a mess. In the morning darkness the tick-tock of the pendulum clock reigned over the room.

'What's the time, Ma?'

'Four. Someone is looking for you.'

A person was sitting on the settee in the gloom. The closer Mama's candle came, the clearer the person became: a police agent! He stood up out of respect, then immediately spoke in Malay but with a Javanese accent:

'Tuan Minke?'

'Yes.'

'I have an order to take Tuan with me. Straight away.' He held out a letter. What he said was true. It was a summons from the Police Station at B—, approved by the Police Station at Surabaya. My name was clearly stated there. Mama too had read it.

'What have you been up to, Nyo?' she asked.

'Not a thing,' I answered nervously. Yet I began to have doubts about my own actions. I searched and searched my memory, I lined up everything I'd done over the last week. I repeated: 'Not a thing, Ma.'

Annelies came. She wore a long black velvet gown. Her hair was a mess. She was still bleary-eyed.

Mama approached me:

'The agent hasn't said what you've been charged with. It's not in the summons either.' And to the police agent: 'He has the right to know what is the matter.'

'I have no such orders, Nyai. If it is not stated clearly in the summons, then indeed no one may know, or yet know about it, including the person involved.'

'It can't be done like that,' I retorted, 'I'm a *Raden Mas*, I can't be treated in this way,' and I waited for an answer. Seeing that he didn't know how he should answer, I resumed, 'I have *forum privilegiatum**.'

---

* The right to be tried under the same law as Europeans.

'No one can deny that, Tuan Raden Mas Minke.'

'Why are you doing things in this manner?'

'My orders are only to fetch Tuan. Even the person who issued the orders would not know anything more, Tuan Raden Mas,' he said defending himself. 'Please get ready, Tuan. We must leave quickly. We must be at our destination by five o'clock.'

'Mas, why do they want to take you?' asked Annelies, afraid. I sensed a shiver in her voice.

'He won't say,' I answered briefly.

'Ann, fix Minke's clothes and bring them here,' ordered Nyai, 'Who knows how long they will detain him. He can bathe and breakfast first, can't he?'

'Of course, Nyai, there's still a little time.'

He allowed half an hour.

I found Robert watching the event from his room at the back. A yawn was his only greeting. Once in the bathroom, I began to mull over the possibilities: Robert is the cause of this trouble, passing on false and fanciful reports. He didn't appear for dinner last night or the night before. One by one his threats came back to me. All right, if it's true you are the one who has caused all this disturbance, I will never forget you, Rob.

On my return to the front room I found coffee and cakes ready. The police agent was enjoying his breakfast. He looked more polite after receiving his food. And he didn't appear to have any personal enmity towards us. On the contrary, he chatted to us, all the time laughing:

'Nothing bad is going to happen, Nyai,' he said finally, 'Tuan Raden Mass Minke will return, at the very latest, within the next two weeks.'

'It's not a matter of two weeks or a month. He's been arrested in my house. I have a right to know what it's all about,' pressed Nyai.

'Really, I don't know. Forgive me. That's why I'm fetching him so early in the morning, Nyai, so no one will know.'

'So no one will know? How? You had to meet with my watchman before getting to see me, didn't you?'

'Then arrange so that your watchman doesn't talk.'

'You can't do this to me,' said Mama, 'I'm going to ask the Police Station for an explanation.'

'That's a good idea. Nyai will get an explanation quickly. And for sure it will be a truthful one.'

Annelies, who was standing holding my suitcase, approached me, unable to speak. She put the suitcase and bag down. She grabbed hold of my hand and held it. Her hand trembled.

'Breakfast first, Tuan Raden Mas,' the agent reminded me. 'Maybe there won't be any breakfast as good as this at the Police Station. No? Then let's leave now.'

'I'll be back soon, Ann, Mama. There must be some mistake. Believe me.'
And Annelies wouldn't let go of my hand.

The police agent picked up my things and carried them outside. Annelies gripped my hand tightly as I followed the agent out. I kissed her on the cheek and freed myself of her hold. And she still didn't speak.

'Hopefully all will be well, Nyo,' Nyai prayed. 'That's enough now, Ann; pray for his safety.'

The *dokar* that awaited us proved not to be a police carriage but a hired one. We climbed aboard and left in the direction of Surabaya. The agent was taking me to B—. And in the early morning dark I conjured up in my mind all the buildings I'd ever seen in B—. Which one among them was our destination? The police station? The gaol? An inn? It didn't even occur to me to think of private houses.

Our *dokar* made up the only traffic on the road. Oil waggons, which usually started moving out of the DPM refinery at dawn, twenty or thirty in a row, were not yet to be seen. One or two people were carting vegetables on their backs for sale in Surabaya. And the agent kept his mouth closed as if he'd never, in all his life, learnt to speak.

Maybe it was true that Robert had slandered me. But why was B— our destination?

Our oil lamps were reluctant to pierce the darkness of the misty, early morning. It was as if only I, the agent, the driver, and the horse, were alive upon that road. And I imagined Annelies crying unconsoled. And Nyai confused, concerned that my arrest would give her business a bad name. And Robert Mellema would have reason to cackle: See! isn't it true what Suurhof said?

The *dokar* took us to the Surabaya Police Station. I was invited to sit down and wait in the reception room. I wanted very much to ask questions about my case. But I got the impression that in the misty, early morning air no one was in the mood to give explanations. So I didn't ask. And the *dokar* still waited in front of the police station. The agent just left me there alone with no orders.

It was a long time. The sun still hadn't risen. And when it did rise, it was unable to expel the mist. Those grey particles of water reigned over everything, even the inside of my lungs. The traffic in front of the Police Station was beginning to get busy: carriages, carts, pedestrians, hawkers, workers. And I still sat alone in the waiting-room. Finally, at a quarter to nine, the agent appeared. He looked as if he'd had an hour's sleep and had had a hot bath. He looked fresh. On the other hand, I felt weary, exhausted by waiting. And, still I had no chance to enquire.

'Let's go, Tuan Raden Mas,' he invited, in a friendly manner.

We climbed back aboard the *dokar*, and headed off to the railway station. Once again it was he who carried my bags, and unloaded them and escorted me to the ticket window. He pushed a letter inside and obtained two tickets – first class. This was not the time for the express train. Uh! we were travelling on a slow train too. Yes, it was true, we climbed aboard that boring train carriage, on the western line. I'd never been on a train such as this. I always went by express if there was one. Except, yes, except from B— to my own town T—.

The agent returned to his state of muteness. I sat next to the window. He sat facing me.

There were just a few passengers in the carriage. Besides the two of us, there were three European men and a Chinese man. They all seemed bored. At the first stop two passengers got off, including the Chinese man. No new passengers came aboard.

I'd travelled that distance dozens of times. So there was nothing in the sights along the journey that interested me. In B— I usually stayed at an inn until the next morning when I would continue the journey on to T—. This time I wouldn't be heading towards my usual inn. Most probably I would end up at the Police Station.

The view became more and more dreary: barren land, sometimes grey, sometimes a whitish-yellow. I fell asleep with a hungry stomach. Whatever was going to happen, let it. Ah! This earth of mankind. Sometimes a tobacco plantation would appear, shrink and disappear, swept away in the train's acceleration. Appear again, shrink again, disappear again. And paddy fields and paddy fields and paddy fields, unirrigated, planted with crops, but no rice, almost ready to be harvested. And the train crawled on slowly, spouting forth thick black and dusty and sparking smoke. Why wasn't it England that controlled all this? Why Holland? And Japan? What about Japan?

The touch of the agent's hand woke me. Laid out beside me were the things he'd brought with him: the wrapping cloth was opened out as a kind of table-cloth. On top: fried rice shining with oil, adorned by a fried egg and fried chicken, plus a spoon and fork, all in a banana-leaf container. Perhaps it had been specially prepared for me. An agent would think twice about serving food like this for himself – it was too sumptuous. A white bottle containing chocolate milk – a drink not yet widely known by Natives – stood beside the banana-leaf container.

And that gloomy town, B—, finally, as the time approached five o'clock in the afternoon, appeared before our eyes. The agent still didn't speak. But again he carried my bags. And I didn't stop him. What was the significance of a police agent, first-class, compared with an HBS student? At the most he might have been able to read and write a little Javanese and Malay.

A *dokar* took us away from the station. To where? I knew those white, rocky streets that were such an eye-sore. Not to the hotel, not to my regular inn. Also not to the B— Police Station.

The town square looked deserted with its brownish grass carpet, balding and tattered in places. Where was I being taken? The hired carriage headed for the *bupati*'s residence and stopped a distance from its stone gate. What was the link between my case and the *Bupati* of B—? My mind began groping around madly.

And the agent alighted first, looking after my bags as before.

'Please,' he said suddenly in high Javanese.

I accompanied him into the Regency Office situated diagonally across from the *bupati*'s residence. An office deserted of wall ornaments, devoid of appropriate furniture, without a single occupant. All the furniture was rough, from teak, and unvarnished, with the appearance of not having been measured for need and without any plan of use, just thrown together. Coming from the luxurious house in Wonokromo into this room was like making a visit to a produce godown. It was, you might say, just slightly more luxurious than Annelies's chicken-coop. This, presumably, was the interrogation room. Just some tables, a few chairs, and some long benches. Over the other side, there were shelves on which were piles of papers and several books. There were no instruments of torture. Just ink bottles on all the tables.

The agent left me by myself again. And for the second time I waited, and waited. The sun had set. He still didn't appear. The grand mosque's drum began its beating, followed by that sad call of the *azan*. The street lanterns were being lit by the lampmen. The office became darker. And those demonic mosquitoes, they ganged up, and attacked the room's only occupant. The insolence! I swore. Is this how people treat a *Raden Mas* and an HBS student too? An educated person with blood of the kings of Java running in him?

And I could feel my clothes sticking to my body. And my body was starting to be afflicted by the odour of sweat. I'd never experienced such maltreatment as this.

'A thousand pardons, Ndoro Raden Mas,' the agent invited me to leave the mosquito-filled, dark office. 'Allow your servant to escort you to the *pendopo*.'

Once again he carried my bags.

So I'm being brought before the *Bupati* of B—! 'God!' what's it all about? And must I, an HBS student, cringe in front of him and – at the end of every one of my sentences, pay obeisance to someone I don't even know? As I walked along the path to the *pendopo*, already lit up by four lamps, I felt like crying. What's the point in studying European science and learning, mixing with Europeans, if in the end one has to cringe anyway, slide along like a snail, and worship some little king who is probably illiterate to boot. 'God, God!' To have audience with a *bupati* is the same as being ready to be an object of humiliation without being able to defend oneself. I'd never forced anyone to act like that towards me. Why did I have to do so for others? Thundering damnation!

Ah, see, it's true? The agent was already inviting me – the impudence – to take off my shoes and socks. The beginning of a great tyranny. Some supernatural power forced me to follow his orders. The floor felt cold under my bare soles. He signalled me, and I went, step by step, to the top. He pointed out to me the place where I must sit, eyes towards the floor, before a rocking chair. One of my teachers had once said: the rocking chair is the most beautiful thing left behind by the Dutch East Indies Company after its bankruptcy. *Aduhai!* rocking chair, you will be a witness to how I must humiliate myself in order to glorify some *bupati* I don't even know. Damn! What would my friends say if they saw me travelling on my knees like this, like someone without thighs, crawling towards the relic of the Company at the time it approached bankruptcy? – that unmoving chair near the wall in the *pendopo*?

'Yes, walk on your knees, Ndoro Raden Mas,' the agent was herding a buffalo into a mud-hole.

And I covered the almost ten metres distance while swearing in three languages.

And to my left and right there were spread out clam-shell ornaments. And the floor shone from the rays of light from four oil lamps. Truly, my friends would ridicule me to their full satisfaction if they could see this play, where a human being, who normally walks on his two whole legs, on his own feet, now has to walk with only half his legs, aided by his two hands. *Ya Allah!* you, my ancestors, you; what is the reason you created customs that would so humiliate your own descendants? You never once gave it any thought, you, my ancestors who indulged in these excesses! Your descendants could have been honoured without such humiliation! Shallow misfortune! How could you bring yourself to leave such customs as an inheritance?

I stopped in front of the rocking-chair. I sat, legs tucked under, and eyes towards the floor, as custom decreed. All I could see was a low, carved bench and on top of it, a foot-rest cushion of black velvet. The same as Annelies' gown earlier that morning.

Good, now I had sat down cross-legged before that damned rocking-chair. What business did I have with the *Bupati* of B—? None. Neither kith nor kin, not an acquaintance, let alone a friend. And for how much longer would this oppression and humiliation continue? Waiting and waiting while being oppressed and humiliated in this way?

I heard the creaking of a swing door as it opened. Then, as the seconds passed, the sound of footsteps made by leather slippers became clearer. And I remembered the scraping footsteps of Mr Mellema on that other frightening night. From where I was seated, the striding slippers slowly began to come into view. Above them a pair of clean legs. Still further above a widely pleated *batik* sarong.

I raised my hands clasped in obeisance as I had seen the court employees do before my grandfather, and my grandmother, and my parents at *lebaran* time. And I did not now withdraw my pose until the *bupati* had sat himself comfortably in his place. In making such obeisance it felt as if all the learning and science I had studied year after year was lost. Lost was the beauty of the world as promised by science's progress. Lost was the enthusiasm of my teachers in greeting the bright future of humanity. And who knows how many times I'd have to make such obeisances that night. Obeisance – the lauding of ancestors and persons of authority by humbling and abasing oneself! Level with the ground if possible! Uh! I will not allow my descendants to go through such degradation.

This person, the *Bupati* of B—, ahemmed. Then slowly he sat down on the rocking-chair, kicking off his slippers behind the foot bench and placed his honourable feet on the velvet cushion. The chair began to rock a little. Damn! How slowly time passed. Some object, by my reckoning fairly long, gently tapped upon my uncovered head. How insolent was this being that I must honour. And every tap I must greet with a sign of grateful obeisance.

After five taps, the object was withdrawn, and was now hung beside the *bupati*'s chair: a horse-whip made from a bull's genitals, with a shaft of thin, choice leather.

'You!' he addressed me weakly, hoarsely.

'Yes, I, My Master, Honoured Lord Bupati,' said my mouth, and like a machine my hands were raised in obeisance for the umpteenth time and my heart cursed for I don't know how many times now.

'You! Why have you only come now?' his voice now emerged more clearly from his throat which was suffering the end of a bout of influenza.

It felt as if I had heard that voice before. It was also his cold which prevented me from recalling the voice easily. No, no, it could not be him! Impossible! No! I still didn't know what this was all about. So I kept silent.

'The Honoured Government does not run a postal service for nothing – capable of getting my letters safely to you at the proper and exact address . . .'

Yes, it was his voice. Impossible! It couldn't be! Impossible: I was just guessing.

'Why are you silent? Now that your schooling is so advanced, is it that you feel humiliated to have to read my letters?'

Yes, it was his voice! I raised my hands in obeisance once again, deliberately lifting my head a little and taking a peep. *Ya Allah!* it was indeed him.

'Father!' I cried, 'forgive me, your servant.'

'Answer! you feel humiliated to have to reply to my letters?'

'A thousand pardons, my Father: no.'

'Your Mother's letter, and why didn't you answer that either?'

'My Father, a thousand pardons . . .'

'And the letter from your elder brother?'

'Forgive me, my Father, a thousand pardons, I was not there, I'm no longer at that address, forgive me, a thousand pardons.'

'So you were educated as high as a coconut tree to learn to deceive?'

'A thousand pardons, my Father.'

'You think we're all blind, ignorant of the date you moved to Wonokromo? And do not know that you took with you all our letters still unread?'

The horse-whip from bull's genitals swayed to and fro. The hairs on my back crawled ready to receive the whip as it fell upon me, as a rebellious horse.

'Do you still need to be humiliated in public with this whip?'

'Humiliate me with the horse whip in public,' I answered recklessly, unable to stand such tyranny. 'But it would be an honour if that order were to come from a father,' I continued, still more recklessly. And I would show the same attitude as Mama did to Robert, Herman Mellema, Sastrotomo and his wife.

'Crocodile!' he hissed angrily. 'I took you out of the ELS at T— for the same reason. As young as that! The higher your schooling, the more you turn into a crocodile! Bored of playing around with girls of your own age you're now holing up in a *nyai*'s nest. What do you want to become of yourself?'

I kept silent. Only my heart roared in anger: so you insult me thus, blood of kings! Husband of my mother! Good, I will not answer. Come on, keep going, continue, blood of the kings of Java! Yesterday you were just an irrigation official. Now all of a sudden you are a *bupati*, a little king. Strike me with your whip, king, you who knows not that science and learning have opened a new era on this earth of mankind!

'Prepared by your grandfather to be a *bupati*, to be honoured by all people, the cleverest child in the family . . . the cleverest in the town . . . yes, God, what will become of this child!'

Good, come on, continue, little king!

'The only grounds for forgiving you are because you've passed and went up a class.'

I can go on up to eleventh class! I roared inside my breast, offended. Come on, let fly with all your ignorance, little king.

'Don't you think it's dangerous to hole up with a *nyai*? If her master goes into a rage and you're shot dead by him, or perhaps attacked with a dagger, or a sword, or a kitchen knife, or strangled . . . how will it be? The papers will announce who you are, who your parents are. What sort of shame will you bring upon your parents? If you haven't thought things through as far as that . . .'

Like Mama, I was ready to leave all my family, I roared louder, a family that burdens me with nothing but bonds that enslave! Come on, continue, continue, blood of the kings of Java! Continue! I too can explode.

'Haven't you read in the papers, tomorrow night your father is celebrating his appointment as a *bupati*? *Bupati* of B—? Mr Assistant Resident of B—, Mr Resident of Surabaya, Mr Controller and all the neighboring *bupatis* will be present. Is it possible an HBS student doesn't read the newspapers? If not, is it possible nobody else told you about it? Your *nyai*, can't she read the papers for you.'

Indeed the civil service reports were something that never attracted my interest: appointments, dismissals, transfers, pensions. Nothing to do with me! The world of *priyayi* bureaucracy was not my world. Who cared if the devil was appointed smallpox official or was sacked dishonourably because of embezzlement? My world was not rank and position, wages and embezzlement. My world was this earth of mankind and its problems.

'Listen, you, renegade!' he ordered, like a newly-important official whose spirits were now aroused. 'You've become absent-minded, looking after someone else's *nyai*. You've forgotten your parents, your duties as a child. Perhaps you're indeed ready to take a wife. All right, another time we'll discuss it. Now there is another matter. Pay attention. Tomorrow night you will act as interpreter. Don't shame me and the family in public, before the Resident, Assistant Resident, Controller and neighbouring *bupatis*.'

'Yes, my Father.'

'You're able and ready to be interpreter?'

'Able and ready, my Father.'

'Ah, that's better; once in a while please your parents' hearts. I'd begin to worry that Mr Controller would be carrying out that task. Imagine how it would look at a party to celebrate my appointment, with all the important officials as witnesses, if there was a son missing? When should they start becoming acquainted with you? This will be the best opportunity. It's a pity you're such a renegade. Perhaps you don't understand that your parents are clearing the way to a high position for you. You, a son, glorified as the cleverest in the family. Or perhaps you're more inclined towards the *nyai* than towards rank?'

'Yes, my Father.'

'This is how your road to high rank will be clear.'

'Yes, my Father.'

'There, go to your mother. You indeed did not intend to return home. It was so shameful, having to ask the assistance of My Assistant Resident. You're happy, aren't you, being arrested like an unpractised thief? No sense of shame at all. Go kneel before your Mother though I know you're resolved to forget her. Sever your relations with that *nyai* who doesn't know when she's already well off!'

Naturally, I did not answer. I just gave the sign of obeisance again. Then: walking on half legs, assisted by my hands, I crawled off, carrying the burden of my indignation on my back, like a snail. Destination: the place I had taken off my shoes and socks, the place where this accursed experience began. There were no Natives in the *bupati*'s building wearing shoes. With my shoes in my hands I walked alongside the *pendopo*, entering the inner courtyard. The gloomy lanterns showed the way to the kitchen. I collapsed into a broken-down lounge chair, ignoring the things I was carrying.

Someone came to have a look. I pretended not to notice. I was served a cup of black coffee. I gulped it all down.

If my elder brother hadn't turned up, perhaps I would have fallen asleep. Putting on a vicious countenance, he spoke to me in Dutch:

'It seems you've forgotten politeness too, and so have not gone quickly to kneel before Mother?'

I rose and accompanied him, a SIBA student, a future Netherlands Indies civil servant. He kept frowning as if he was the guardian whose job it was to ensure the sky wouldn't fall in and smash up the earth. Because his Dutch was limited, he resumed in Javanese his lecture about how I was a child who no longer knew proper custom. I, of course, didn't respond. We entered the *bupati*'s building, passing by several doors. Finally, in front of one door, he said:

'Enter there, you!'

I knocked slowly on the door. I didn't know whose room it was, but opened it and entered. Mother was sitting in front of the mirror combing her hair. A tall oil lamp stood on a stand beside her.

'Mother, forgive me,' I said braying, kneeling down before her and kissing her knees. I don't know why my heart was seized so suddenly by this longing for my mother.

'So you have come home at last, *Gus*. Thank God you're safe,' she lifted up my chin, looked into my face, as if I was a four-year-old child. And her soft, loving voice moved me. My eyes overflowed with tears. This was my mother, just as before, my own mother.

'This is Mother's wayward child,' I submitted hoarsely.

'You're a man now. Your moustache is beginning to come through. People say you like a rich and beautiful *nyai*,' and before I could deny this, she continued, 'it's up to you, if you indeed like her and she likes you. You're an adult now. You're no doubt ready to shoulder the consequences and responsibilities and not run like a criminal.' She took a breath and stroked my cheek as if I was a baby. '*Gus*, they say you are doing very well at school. Thanks be to God. It amazes me sometimes how your schooling can go so well while you're in the power of that *nyai*. Or perhaps you're truly very clever? Yes, yes, that's a male for you; all men are cats pretending to be rabbits. As rabbits they eat all the leaves, as cats they eat all the meat. All right, Gus, you must do well at school, keep advancing.'

See, Mother didn't fault me. I did not have to deny anything.

'Men, Gus, they love to eat. Who knows if leaves or if meat? That's all right: providing you understand, Gus, the more you advance at school does not mean the more you can eat other people's food. You must be able to recognise limits. That's not too hard to understand, is it? If people don't recognise such limits, God will make them realise in His own way.'

Ah, Mother, how many pearl-like words have you soldered into my being.

'You're still silent, Gus. What are you going to report to your mother? My waiting is not going to be in vain, is it?'

'Next year I will graduate, Mother.'

'Thanks be to God, Gus. Parents can only pray. Why have you only come now? Your father was so worried, Gus, angry every day because of you. Your father was appointed *bupati* very, very suddenly. No one guessed it would be so fast. You, one day, will reach the same heights. You surely must be able to. Your father only knows Javanese, you know Dutch; you are an HBS student. Your father only went to a Basic People's School. You have mixed widely with the Dutch. Your father hasn't. You will surely become a *bupati* one day.'

'No, Mother, I don't want to become a *bupati*.'

'No? Strange. Yes, as you wish. So what do you want to become? If you graduate you can become whatever you want, of course.'

'I only want to become a free human being, not given orders, not giving orders, Mother.'

'Ha? Will there be a time like that, Gus? This is the first I've heard of it.'

When I was a little boy, I used to tell her excitedly about what my school teachers had said. This time too. About Miss Magda Peters, whose stories were so interesting: about the French Revolution, its meaning, its basic principles. Mother only laughed, not refuting anything. Just as when I was a little child.

'Uh! you're so dirty, smell of sweat. Bathe, and with hot water! It's already so late. Rest. Tomorrow you'll be working hard. You know your duties tomorrow?'

I was not yet acquainted with the building. I went into the room prepared for me. An oil lamp was alight inside. It appeared that my brother was also in that room. He was sitting reading by the table-lamp. I passed by to get my things ready. And my brother, who always exercised his rights as the first-born, did not lift his head at all, as if I did not exist on this earth. Was he trying to impress me with his diligence as a student?

I ahemmed. He still showed no reaction. I glanced at what he was reading. Not printing: handwriting! And I became suspicious when I looked at the book's cover. Only I owned a book with a beautiful cover, hand-made by

Jean Marais. Slowly I moved up behind him. I was not wrong: my diary. I seized it from him and I became enraged:

'Don't touch this! Who gave you the right to open it? You! Is this what your school has taught you?'

He stood up, staring at me wide-eyed.

'Indeed you are no longer Javanese.'

'What's the use of being Javanese if only to have one's rights violated? Perhaps you don't understand that notes like that are very personal? Haven't your teachers taught you about ethics and individual rights?'

My brother was silent, observing me in a powerless anger.

'Or is this indeed the practice given to trainee officials? Fiddling in other people's affairs and violating the rights of anybody they like? Aren't you taught the new civilisation? Modern civilisation? You want to become a king who can do as he pleases, like your ancestors' kings?'

My resentment and anger had spilled out.

'And is this what the new civilisation means? To insult people?? To insult government officials? You yourself will become one!' he defended himself.

'A government official? The person you're facing now will never become one.'

'Come on, I'll take you to Father, and you can tell him that yourself.'

'Not only tell him, with or without you, but I'm quite able even to leave behind this whole family. And you! You touch things violating my rights and don't know you should apologise. Have you never been to school? Or have you indeed never been taught civilised behaviour?'

'Shut up! If I'd never been to school, I'd have already ordered you to crawl and pay obeisance to me.'

'Only a buffalo-brain would think that way about me. Illiterate.'

And Mother entered, intervening:

'You meet for the first time in two years . . . why do you have to carry on like village children?'

'I'll fight anyone at all who violates my individual rights, Mother, let alone just a brother.'

'Mother, he has admitted all his evil doing in his diary. I was going to present it to Father. He was afraid and went amok.'

'You're not yet an official with the right to sell your brother just to obtain some praise,' said mother. 'It's not certain that you are any better than he.'

I picked up my things.

'It's better I return to Surabaya, Mother.'

'No! You have received a task from your father.'

'He can do it,' I said, looking at my brother.

'Your brother is not an HBS student.'

'If I am needed, why am I treated like this?'

Mother ordered my brother to another room. After he had left, she resumed:

'You're indeed no longer Javanese. Educated by the Dutch you've become Dutch, a brown Dutchman, acting this way. Perhaps you've become a Christian.'

'Ah, Mother, don't go on so. I'm still the same son as before.'

'My son of the past wasn't a rebel like this.'

'Your son didn't know right and wrong then. I only rebel against that which is wrong, Mother.'

'That is the sign you're no longer Javanese, not paying heed to those older, those with greater right to your respect, those who have more power.'

'Ah, Mother, don't punish me this way. I respect what is nearest to what is right.'

'Javanese bow down in submission to those older, more powerful; this is a way to achieve nobility of character. People must have the courage to surrender, Gus. Perhaps you no longer know that song either?'

'I still remember, Mother. I still read the Javanese books. But those are the misguided songs of misguided Javanese. Those who have the courage to surrender are stamped and trodden upon, Mother.'

'*Gus!*'

'Mother, I've studied at Dutch schools for over ten years now in order to find out all this. Is it proper that Mother punish me now I've found out?'

'You've mixed too much with the Dutch. So now you don't like to mix with your own people, even your own family, not even with your father. You won't answer our letters. Perhaps you don't even like me any more.'

'Oh, forgive me, Mother.' Her words had struck me sharply. I dropped to the ground, kneeling before her and embraced her legs. 'Don't speak like that, Mother. Don't punish me more than my errors deserve. I only know of what Javanese are ignorant, because such knowledge belongs to the Europeans, and because I indeed have learnt from them.'

She twisted my ear, then knelt down, whispering:

'Mother doesn't punish you. You've discovered your own way. I will not obstruct you, and will not call you back. Travel along the road you hold to be best. But don't hurt your parents, and those you consider don't know all that you know.'

'I've never intended to hurt anyone, Mother.'

'Ah, Gus, this is perhaps the fate of a woman. She suffers pain when giving birth, then suffers pain again because of her child's actions.'

'Please! for Mother to feel pain because of my actions is only an excessive luxury. Didn't Mother always tell me to study hard and well? I've done that to the full. Now Mother finds fault with me.' And as if I were still a little child she caressed my hair and cheeks.

'When I was pregnant with you, I dreamt that someone I didn't know

94

came and gave me a dagger. Since then I've known, Gus; the child in my womb held a sharp weapon. Be careful in using it, Gus. Don't you yourself become its victim . . .'

Since early morning people had been preparing the place for the reception to celebrate my father's appointment. The news was that the best and most beautiful dancers in all the residency had been hired for the occasion. Father had brought the best *gamelan* of pure bronze from T—, my grandmother's *gamelan*, which was always wrapped in red velvet when not being used. Every year it was not only tuned, but bathed in flower water.

With the *gamelan* came an expert tuner. My father wanted not only the *gamelan* itself, but the harmony too, to be pure East Javanese. So since morning, the *pendopo* had been buzzing with the sounds of people filing things into tune.

The administrative work of the *bupati*'s office stopped altogether. Everyone was helping Mr Niccolo Moreno, a well-known decorator brought in from Surabaya. He brought with him a big chest of decoration utensils the like of which I had never seen before. And it was then that I first realised: arranging decorations and ornamentations was a skill all of its own. Mr Niccolo Moreno came on the recommendation of Mr Assistant Resident B—, approved of and guaranteed by Mr Resident Surabaya.

That morning I too had to meet him. With his own hands he took my measurements, as if he wanted to make me some clothes. Then he let me go.

He had turned the *pendopo* into an arena whose focus was the portrait of Queen Wilhelmina, that beautiful maiden I had once dreamed after – brought from Surabaya, the work of a German artist named Hüssenfeld. I still admired her beauty.

The tricolours were hung everywhere, singly or in twos. Tricolour ribbon also streamed out from the portrait to all parts of the *pendopo*, and would later captivate the audience with its authority. The *pendopo*'s columns were painted with some new kind of paint, made from flour, that dried within two hours. Banyan tree leaves and greenish-yellow coconut fronds in traditional colour harmonies transformed the dry, barren walls into something refreshing, and impelled people to enjoy them with their sight. So eyes were swayed by the play of the flowers' colours; yellow, blue, red, white and purple – a saturating beauty – flowers that in day-to-day life stuck separately and silently out along fences.

The big night in my Father's life arrived. The *gamelan* had already been rumbling softly and slowly for some time. Mr Niccolo Moreno was busy in my room: dressing up and adorning me! Who would have ever guessed that I, already now an adult, would be dressed up by somebody else? A white person too! As if I was a maiden about to ascend the wedding throne!

All the time he was dressing me, he spoke in a strange-sounding, mono-tone Dutch, as if it came out of the chest of a Native. He obviously wasn't Dutch. According to his story: he often dressed and adorned the *bupatis*, including my father tonight, and the sultans of Sumatra and Borneo. He'd designed many of their clothes, and even now was often summoned by them. He said also: the costumes of the guards of the kings of Java were also designed by him.

Silently I listened to his stories, neither affirming nor refuting them, although I didn't believe them fully either.

He had dressed me in an embroidered vest, stiff, as if made from tortoise-shell. I could never have bent over in it. The stiff leather collar tended to dissuade my neck from turning around. Indeed the intent was that my body should be straight and stiff, not turning around frequently, eyes straight ahead like a true 'gentleman'. Then a *batik* sarong with a silver belt. The style in which the *batik* was worn truly brought out that dashing East Javanese character. That's what Father no doubt wanted. I suffered all this like a young maiden. A *blangkon* headdress, a mixture of East Javanese and Madurese styles, something entirely new, Niccolo Moreno's own creation, was placed upon my head. Then came a *keris* inlaid with jewels. Then a black outer upper garment like a coat with a cut at the back so the people could admire the beauty of my *keris*. A bow-tie made my neck, usually active as guiding my eyes to its targets, feel as if it was being snared. Hot perspiration began to soak my back and chest.

In the mirror I found myself looking like a victorious knight out of the *Panji* stories. From under my shirt protuded velvet cloth embroidered with gold thread.

I was clearly a descendant of the knights of Java so I too was a knight of Java. But why was it a non-Javanese that was making me so dashing? And handsome? Why a European? Perhaps an Italian? Already since *Amangkurat I* in the 1600s, the clothes of the kings of Java had been designed and made by Europeans, said Mr Niccolo Moreno. I'm sorry, but your people only wore blankets before we came. Below, above, on the head, only a blanket! His words truly hurt!

Whether his story was true or not, in the mirror I did look dashing and handsome. Perhaps people would say later: 'a true Javanese costume', for-getting all the European elements in the blouse, collar, tie, and even forgetting the lasting and velvet made in England.

I considered my clothes and my appearance to be a product of mankind's earth at the end of the nineteenth century; the time of the birth of the modern era. And I truly felt: Java and all its people were a not-too-important corner of this earth of mankind. The town of Twente in Holland now wove for the Javanese, and chose the material too. Village-woven cloth was left now only

96

to the villagers. The Javanese were left with only *batik*-making. And this one body of mine – still the original!

Mr Moreno went. And I sat down. When I became aware of the sounds of the East Javanese *gamelan*, which would cradle this evening's atmosphere, I awoke from my reflections, looked in the mirror again and smiled with satisfaction – every satisfaction. In accord with custom, I would be Father's and Mother's escort as they entered the reception. My brother would lead the way, while my sisters had no public function. They would be busy out the back.

The guests had all arrived. Father and Mother proceeded forth. My brother was in front, I behind them. As soon as we entered the reception area in the *pendopo*, the Assistant Resident of B— came up, because that was the program.

All stood in respect. Mr Assistant Resident walked straight to Father, offered his respects, bowed to Mother, shook hands with my brother and me. Only then did he sit beside Father. The *gamelan* played *Kebo Giro*, a song of welcome, flaring-up and filling the reception area and people's hearts. And the *pendopo* was packed with people, their faces shining with pleasure and the light of the gas lamps. Behind them in the compound, on woven mats, sat rows of village heads and village officials.

The Master of Ceremonies, the *Patih* of B—, opened the program. After a moment's hesitation, the *gamelan* became silent as if controlled by some supernatural power.

The Dutch national anthem, 'Wilhelmus', was sung. People stood. Very few joined in singing. Most, of course, couldn't. Only one or two Natives. The others just stood gazing, perhaps swearing at that strange and aggravating melody.

Mr Assistant Resident B—, as the representative of Mr Resident Surabaya, began to speak. Mr Controller Willem Ende came forward ready to interpret in Javanese. Mr Assistant Resident shook his head and waved his hand in interdictment against it. He indicated that I be interpreter.

For a moment I was nervous, but in a second I regained my character. No, they are no better than you! And that voice gave me courage. Carry out this task in the same way as you take on your exams!

I came to the front, forgot to bow and stand with my hands clasped before me, according to Javanese custom. I felt as if in front of class. Wherever my eyes wandered they collided with the eyes of the *bupatis*. Perhaps they were admiring this Javanese knight in his half-Javanese, half-European clothes. Or perhaps they were indulging their antipathy towards me because of my not showing respect towards them.

Mr Assistant Resident finished his speech. I too finished putting it into Javanese. He shook hands with Father. And now it was Father's turn to speak. He didn't know Dutch, and that was still better than the other *bupatis* who were illiterate. He spoke in Javanese and I put it into Dutch. Now I delivered it in a totally European manner directed at Mr Assistant Resident B— and the Europeans in attendance. I saw Mr Assistant Resident nodding, and observing me as if it were I myself who was giving the speech, or perhaps he was enjoying my act as a monkey in the middle of a crowd. Father's speech ended and so too did my translation. The senior officials stood up and congratulated Father, Mother, my brother and me.

When Mr Assistant Resident congratulated me he felt he had to praise my Dutch:

'Very good,' then in Malay, 'Tuan Bupati, Tuan must indeed be happy to have such a son as this. Not only his Dutch, but more importantly his attitude.' Then he resumed in Dutch, 'You are an HBS student, yes? Can you come to my house tomorrow afternoon at five o'clock?'

'With pleasure, Sir,'

'You will be picked up in a carriage.'

The congratulations did not take long. The village dignitaries didn't normally shake hands with the *bupati*. So Father's hand was saved from the one thousand and two hundred or so hands of the village officials. They stayed seated on their mats out in the compound.

The *gamelan* resumed its tumultuous din. A full-bodied dancer entered the arena, as if flying, carrying a tray, upon which was a sash. Carrying the silver tray, she made her way directly to the Assistant Resident. And the white official rose from his chair, took the sash and draped it over his shoulder.

People cheered, clapped in agreement. He nodded to Father, asking permission to open the *tayub* dance. Then he nodded to the crowd. Unhesitatingly he stepped forward, partnered by the dancer, and moved into the centre of the gathering to the crowd's applause and cheering. And he danced, his two fingers holding the corners of the sash, and at every beat of the gong he jerked his head in rhythm with the gong. And before him that full-bodied, pretty, eye-catching woman danced provocatively.

A few minutes later another dancer entered running, also gloriously pretty. With a silver tray in her hand, and as if flying, she entered the arena carrying liquor in a crystal glass. She took up a position beside the Assistant Resident and joined in dancing.

The official stopped dancing, stood up straight in front of the new dancer. He took the crystal glass and swallowed down three-quarters of its contents. The glass with the remaining quarter he placed upon the lips of his dancemate, who drained it down only after trying to resist while still dancing. Then she bowed down her head in extreme embarrassment.

The gathering cheered in glee. The village chiefs and officials stood and contributed to the hubbub.

'Drink it, sweetie! Drink, *hoséééééé*!'

That handsome dancer with bare, firm, shining, *langsat* skin took the glass from the official's hands and placed it on the silver tray.

Mr Assistant Resident nodded with pleasure, clapping gleefully, and laughed. Then he returned to his chair.

Now another dancer came and offered the sash to Father. And he danced with her beautifully. And that dance too ended with liquor from a silver tray.

Following this, the Assistant Resident went home. The *bupatis* too then went home, one by one, each in his own grand carriage. The village chiefs, district officers, police constables, charged the *pendopo*, and the *tayub* continued until morning with the shout of *hoséééé* after every swallow of liquor.

I only found out the next morning that in my bag there was a small bundle of silver coins. Wrapped in paper, with Annelies's writing: 'Don't let us go for long without hearing news from you. Annelies.'

The money totalled fifteen *guilders*, enough for a village family to live for ten months, even twenty months if their daily budget was really kept at two and a half cents a day.

That morning I set off to the post office. The postmaster, I don't know his name, an Indo, shook my hand and praised my Dutch at the previous night's reception as being very excellent and exact. All the office employees stopped working just to listen to our conversation and to take in what I looked like.

'We would be very proud if you would work here; you are an HBS student, yes?'

'I only want to send a telegram,' I answered.

'There's no bad news, I hope?'

'No.'

The postmaster attended to me himself and gave me the form. He invited me to sit at a table, and I began to write, then I handed the form back to him. Once again he attended to it himself.

'If you have the opportunity, perhaps we could invite you to dinner?'

It appeared that the Assistant Resident's invitation had become big news in B—. It could be predicted that all the officials, white and brown, would be sending me invitations. So, all of a sudden, I'd become a prince without a principality. How tremendous, an HBS student! in his last year! in the middle of an illiterate society. They will all be out to indulge me. If the Assistant Resident has started inviting you, naturally you are without flaw, everything you do is right, there is nothing you would ever do that could be said to have violated Javanese custom.

That prediction didn't have long to wait before it was verified. As I left that small office I surveyed the whole area. Everyone bowed in respect. Perhaps among them there were some already sizing me up for their son-in-law or a brother-in-law. 'Imagine: an HBS student.' And it was true. On arrival back at home I found several letters had already arrived, all written in Javanese script: invitations!

I knew not one of the people inviting me. My guess remained the same: they were all thinking of themselves as my future parents – or brothers-in-law. 'Imagine: the son of a *bupati*, himself considered to be a future *bupati*, an HBS student, final-year. As young as that and he's already been noticed by an Assistant Resident. He even defeated the Controller!' B—! ah, a grey corner on this earth of mankind! I spent the whole morning writing apologetic replies: I am unable to accept your invitation, because I must quickly return to Surabaya.

And that afternoon the promised carriage arrived to pick me up. I wore European clothes, as was my usual way in Surabaya, even though Mother didn't approve.

It seemed that the news about my invitation had spread throughout all B—. People needed to see me cover that short distance between the *bupati* buiding and the assistant-residency building. Unfamiliar faces, in neat Javanese dress, but with naked feet, bowed in respect. Those wearing hats over their *blangkon* headdress needed to raise them.

The carriage took me straight to the back of the assistant-residency building, stopping at the veranda.

The Assistant Resident rose from his garden chair, so too did the two maidens beside him. He got in his greeting first.

'This is my eldest daughter,' he introduced her, 'Sarah. This is my youngest daugher, Miriam. Both are HBS graduates. The youngest went to the same school as you, before you, though, of course. Well, excuse me, I have some unexpected work to do,' and he went.

So this was what the honoured invitation rocking B— was all about. I'm introduced to his daughters and then he goes.

Probably Sarah and Miriam were older than me. And every HBS student knew with certainty: seniors seek every opportunity to put on airs, to strike a pose, to insult and to topple upside-down any poor junior.

You be careful now, Minke. See, Sarah is starting:

'Is Miriam's Dutch language and literature teacher, Mr Mähler, still teaching? That crazy, talkative one?'

'He's been replaced by Miss Magda Peters,' I answered.

'No doubt more talkative still and with only a kitchen vocabulary,' she followed on.

'Do you know for sure that she is a Miss?' asked Miriam.

'Everyone calls her Miss.'

And Miriam giggled. Then Sarah too. Truly, I didn't know what they were laughing about.

I answered hot-headedly and recklessly:

'I think she has more than just a kitchen vocabulary. She is my cleverest teacher, the one of whom I'm most fond.'

Now they both laughed, giggling, while covering their mouths with a handkerchief. I was confused, not knowing what was so funny. For a moment I saw shining glances coming from my left and right.

'Fond of a teacher?' teased Miriam. 'There has never been a Dutch language and literature teacher who people have liked. Castor oil dispensers, all of them. What do you get from her?'

'She can cleverly explain the eighties style and compare it with the contemporary style.'

'*Wah, wah!*' cried Sarah. 'It that's the case, try declaiming one of Kloos' poems, so we can see if your teacher really is so great.'

'She is clever in explaining the sociological and psychological background of the works of the eighties,' I continued.

'Very interesting.'

'What do you mean by psychological and social background?'

Sarah and Miriam burst into a fit of giggling again.

Now I was beginning to become annoyed with their fits of giggling. I moved across to the Assistant Resident's chair to avoid their glances. Now I faced them directly. And they came over as Pure-Blooded girls who were adroit and not at all unattractive. Yet a junior could never relax his vigilance with seniors.

'If you do indeed require an explanation of that,' I continued, putting on a serious countenance, 'we would need to look at actual literary texts.'

Seeing me get more and more into a corner, their giggling escalated and they glanced at each other knowingly.

'Come on, when has there been a Dutch language and literature teacher talk about social and psychological background? It sounds a lot of hot air to me! What does she want to become, this Miss Magda Peters? At the most she'd be able to present the Eighties Generation writers who barked at the sky destroyed by the factory smoke, the fields blasted by the din of traffic, under assault by roads and railway lines,' Miriam, who was more aggressive, attacked. 'If she wants to discuss social background she shouldn't be talking about that sentimental Generation, she would be talking about Multatuli . . . and the Indies!'

'Yes, that's when you're really talking about noble literature, where mud has fostered the growth of the water lily.'

'She's also spoken about Multatuli,' I answered resolutely.

'Ah, come on, how could Multatuli be discussed in school? Stick to the truth. He has never been mentioned in any textbook.' Miriam continued her attack.

'Miriam's right,' Sarah confirmed. 'If one wants to talk about social background, Multatuli is indeed a typical example,' then she glanced at her sister.

'Miss Magda Peters not only put Multatuli forward as a typical example. She went as far as to elucidate his writings.'

'Elucidate them!' cried Sarah disbelievingly. 'An HBS teacher in the Indies elucidating Multatuli! Could that happen in the next ten years, Miriam?' and Miriam shook her head in disbelief. 'Or have you changed your textbooks?'

'No.'

'Your teacher is truly puffed-up. You're only her pupil,' Sarah tormented me.

'No.'

'Your teacher is really daring. If what you say is true; she could get into trouble,' Miriam began to get serious.

'Why?'

'How simple you are. So you don't know. And you need to and indeed are obliged to know.' Miriam continued. 'Because if what you say about your teacher, if it's true, maybe she is from the radical group.'

'There's nothing wrong with the radicals, is there? They're bringing progress to the Indies?' By this time I felt really stupid.

'But good doesn't necessarily mean right, or it might not yet be appropriate. It could come at the wrong time and place!' pressed Miriam.

Sarah ahemmed. She didn't speak.

'Come on, tell us which of his writings she is enthusiastic about?'

They were becoming more and more annoying. And a junior, I don't know who started the rule, must always show respect. So:

'The main work is of course: *Max Havelaar* or *De Koffieveilingen der Nederlandsche Handelsmaatschappij* (The Coffee Auctions of the Netherlands Trading Company).'

'And who do you think Multatuli is?' now Sarah was launching an assault on me.

'Who? Eduard Douwes Dekker.'

'Excellent. You must also know of the other Douwes Dekker. That's obligatory,' Sarah continued her attack.

This mad senior was getting worse and worse. And why was she attacking me like this, glancing at her sister too, lips trembling as she held back her laughter? They're playing out a drama, playing around with a Native slave. There were going too far. There was only one Douwes Dekker known to history.

'So you don't know,' Sarah insulted. 'Or you're in doubt?'

Miriam burst into a fit of uncontrolled giggling.

Very well, I would confront this satanic conspiracy. And so this was the value of the honoured and sensational invitation from the Assistant Resident. Very well, because I didn't know I answered as reasonably as possible:

'I only know of Eduard Douwes Dekker whose pen-name is Multatuli. If there is any other Douwes Dekker I truly don't know of him.'

'Indeed there is,' Sarah resumed again. Miriam hid her face in a silk handkerchief. 'But more importantly, who is he? Don't be confused, don't go pale,' she teased. 'You know, don't you, you're just pretending not to know.'

'I truly don't know,' I answered restlessly.

'Then your teacher Miss Magda Peters, whom you so greatly praise, has insufficient general knowledge. Listen, and remember not to shame your seniors. Don't forget this. The other Douwes Dekker, who is more important than Multatuli, is a youth . . .'

'He's still a youth?'

'Of course he's still a youth. He's on board a ship. Or perhaps he's already in South Africa, fighting with the Dutch against the British. Have you heard of him?'

'No. What has he written?' I asked humbly.

'He's still a youth. So he can, of course, be forgiven if he hasn't yet written anything,' answered Sarah, then she too giggled.

'So why should I know about him?' I protested. 'People become known because of their works?' Now I was getting the chance to defend myself. 'Hundreds of millions of people on this earth have not produced works that would have made them famous, so they are not famous.'

'Actually he's produced a lot of writings too. But there's only one reader. Here she is, that most faithful of all readers: Miriam de la Croix. He is her boyfriend, understand?'

The hide! I swore in my heart. What have I got to do with him if he's only Miriam's boyfriend? These two misses wouldn't know who Annelies Mellema was either. I'd bet on it!

'Come on, Mir, tell us about your boyfriend,' coaxed Sarah in high spirits.

'No. It's not anything to do with our guest. Let's talk about something else,' Miriam refused. 'You're a pure Native, aren't you Minke?' I was silent, not answering, I felt that, without knocking, they were about to open the door of humiliation. 'A Native who has obtained European education. Very good. And you already know so much about Europe. Perhaps you don't know as much about your own country. Perhaps. True? I'm not wrong, am I?'

The humiliation has now begun, I thought.

'Your ancestors,' Miriam de la Croix continued, 'I'm sorry, it's not my intention to insult anyone - your ancestors, generation after generation, have believed that thunder is the explosion caused by the angels trying to capture the devil. It's so, yes? Why are you silent? Are you ashamed of your own ancestors' beliefs?'

Sarah de la Croix had stopped laughing. She put on a serious face, and observed me as if I was some mysterious animal.

'There's no need to single out my ancestors,' I answered her, 'your European and Dutch ancestors in prehistoric times were no less ignorant.'

'Ah,' Sarah intervened, 'just as I suspected. You two are going to fight about your ancestors.'

'Yes, we're like cattle, Minke,' Miriam continued. 'Fight at our first meeting, but be friends afterwards, perhaps forever. That's right, yes?'

A very adroit girl! My suspicions began to subside.

'My ancestors may have been more stupid than your ancestors, Minke. Your ancestors were building paddy fields and irrigation when mine were still living in caves. But that's not what we want to discuss. Look, at school you're taught: thunder is only the clash of positive and negative clouds. Benjamin Franklin is now even able to build a lightning rod. Yes? While your ancestors have a beautiful legend – the story that I have heard – about Ki Ageng Sela who was able to capture the thunder and then lock it up in a chicken coop.'

Sarah burst into laughter. Miriam became even more serious, observing my face as twilight reached its climax, then she let fly her puzzle:

'I believe you can accept the teachings about positive and negative clouds. Because you need the marks to pass. But be honest, do you believe in the truth of this explanation?'

Now I knew: she was testing my inner character. Yes, a real test. To be frank, I'd never asked myself such a question. Everything had just seemed to flow smoothly requiring no questioning.

Now Sarah interfered:

'Of course I believe that you know and have mastered this natural science lesson. But now the problem is: do you believe it or not?'

'I must believe it,' I answered.

'Must believe it only because you've got to pass the exams. Must! So you don't yet believe.'

'My teacher, Miss Magda Peters . . .'

'Magda Peters again,' cut in Sarah.

'She is my teacher. According to her: everything comes from being taught,' I answered, 'and from practice. Even beliefs. You two would not ever have come to believe in Jesus Christ without being taught and then practising to believe.'

'Yes, yes, perhaps your teacher is right,' Sarah was confused.

Miriam, on the other hand, watched me as if she was looking at her lover's portrait. 'This year we've begun hearing a new word: 'modern'. Do you know what it means?' the aggressive Miriam began again, forgetting all about the question of thunder.

'I know. But only from Miss Magda Peters.'

'It seems you don't have any other teachers,' interrupted Sarah.

'What's to be done? It's she that can answer your question.'

'Then what does this fantastic teacher of yours mean by "modern"?' Miriam cut in.

'It isn't in the dictionary. But according to this fantastic teacher of mine it is the name for a spirit, an attitude, a way of looking at things that emphasises the qualities of scholarship, aesthetics and efficiency. I don't know any other explanation. She is a member of the schismatic group in the Catholic Church that's been expelled by the Pope. Perhaps there's another explanation?' I asked finally.

Sarah and Miriam exchanged stares. I couldn't see their faces clearly. Twilight had arrived, though it had seemed ages in coming. And now they just sat silently, exchanging stares, and they began to busily eliminate mosquitoes getting over-friendly with their skin.

'These mosquitoes,' Sarah frowned. 'They think I'm a restaurant.'

Now it was I who burst into laughter.

'Ah, we've forgotten our drinks,' said Sarah, 'Please!'

And the tension began to subside. I began to breathe freely again. And I remembered the servant dressed in white who had put the glasses and cakes on the garden table a while ago. For the first time I smiled to myself. Not only because the tension was subsiding, but because I knew that they knew no more than me.

'Do you know who Dr Snouck Hurgronje is?' once again Miriam attacked.

If the Assistant Resident turned up now, I would be saved from this torment. Where are you, my saviour? Why don't you appear? And these children of yours are no less fierce than the twilight mosquitoes. Or did you deliberately invite me here so that your daughters, my seniors, could do me in? These thoughts suddenly made me understand: the Assistant Resident was deliberately confronting me with his two daughters as a test. He probably had some specific purpose in mind.

'How about if I have a turn at asking a question now?'

Sarah and Miriam burst into laughter again.

'Just a minute,' forbade Miriam. 'Answer first. Your beloved teacher is indeed extraordinary. You, her student, are no less extraordinary. It's only natural you're so fond of her. Perhaps I also would be as fond of her as you are. Now, about my last question, perhaps your beloved teacher has spoken about him too,'

'A pity, but no,' I answered briefly, 'Tell me.'

It appeared she had long awaited this opportunity to come forward as a teacher. Skilfully, she told this story:

Dr Snouck Hurgronje was a jewel of a scholar: daring to think, daring to act, daring to risk himself for the advancement of knowledge, and was an important adviser in ensuring a Dutch victory in the Aceh war. It's a pity he was now involved in an argument with General Van Heutz. An argument about Aceh. What's the meaning of this argument? There isn't

105

any, said Miriam. The important thing is that he has undertaken a valuable experiment with three Native youths. The purpose: to find out if Natives were able to truly understand and bring to life within themselves European learning and science. The three students are going to a European school. He interviews them every week to try to find out if there is any change in their inner character and whether they are able to absorb it all, whether their scientific knowledge and learning from school was only a thin, dry, easily shattered coating on the surface, or something that had really taken root. This scholar had not yet come to a decision.

Now it was I who laughed again. These two misses were aping the scholar. And I was the guinea pig caught by them along the side of the road. Oho! Incredible! But they might be doing it on their father's orders which were probably not ill-intended, so I restrained my desire to launch a counterattack. I continued listening to Miriam's story. Not as a junior, nor as a student – but as an observer.

All was still and calm. Sarah did not speak. Then:

'Have you heard about the Association Theory?'

'Miss Miriam, you are now my teacher,' I answered quickly, avoiding the question.

'No, not a teacher,' she said with a sudden humility. 'These days it's only normal that there should be an exchange of views between educated people. Yes, isn't that right? So you've never heard about it?'

'Not yet.'

'Very well. This theory comes from that scholar. A new theory. His idea is that if the experiment succeeds, the Netherlands Indies government could put his theory into practice. That's right, isn't it, Sarah.'

'Tell it yourself,' said Sarah avoiding the question.

'Association means direct co-operation, based on European ways, between European officials and educated Natives. Those of you who have advanced would be invited to join together with us in governing the Indies. So the responsibility would no longer be the burden of the white race alone. So there no longer would be a need for the position of the Controller liaising between Native and White administrations. The *bupatis* could co-operate directly with the white government. Do you understand?'

'Keep going,' I said.

'What's your opinion?'

'Very simple,' I answered. 'We Natives have read what you have not read: Our chronicle *Babad Tanah Jawi*. Reading and writing Javanese has long been something our familes have studied. Look, in ELS and HBS we are taught to admire the Indies army's brilliance in subjugating us, the Natives.'

'The Indies army is indeed outstanding. That's a fact,' Miriam defended her nation.

106

'Yes, indeed, it's a fact. Do you know that the Chronicles written by the Natives tell of how we withstood your attacks for centuries?'

'But were always defeated?' charged Miriam.

'Yes, indeed, always defeated.' Suddenly the courage to continue my words disappeared. Instead I came out with a question:

'Why didn't you come up with this theory three centuries ago? When no Native would have had any objection to Europeans sharing responsibility with them?'

'I don't quite understand what you mean?' interrupted Sarah.

'I mean, this fantastic scholar, Doctor . . . what's his name again? . . . he's three hundred years behind the Natives of that time,' I answered proudly.

And with that I excused myself, leaving those two annoying seniors sitting there . . .

8

Father and Mother were very proud that I had received an invitation from Assistant Resident Herbert de la Croix.

Invitations from local Native notables continued to arrive at our house.

It was better that my parents didn't know how their son, of whom they were so proud, was made to look a fool.

With all my might I resisted their demands that I tell them what had happened. Instead, I announced that I would be quickly returning to Surabaya.

I was busy replying to all the invitations.

My father was no longer angry with me. The invitation from the Assistant Resident absolved me of all my sins.

I had telegrammed Wonokromo, giving them the day and time of my return to Surabaya, and asking that I be met at the station by a carriage.

Father and Mother weren't able, and perhaps also didn't feel it proper, to hold back my departure. There were no further accusations relating to the issue of Nyai Ontosoroh. Someone who had received an invitation from the Assistant Resident was immediately thereupon immune; it was impossible for him to have done wrong, on the contrary it was as if a sign had appeared over the gateway to his future proclaiming the certainty of his attainment of a high and important position. But they did insist I take leave of and say goodbye to the European official.

I didn't want to go but left for his house anyway. Once again I had to meet with Sarah and Miriam de la Croix. It turned out that when with their father they were not aggressive, but instead orderly and polite.

'Your school Director used to be my schoolfriend,' said the official. 'When you get back to school, pass on my greetings and respects.'

Then he explained: his children wanted to go home to the Netherlands. They had been without a mother for the last ten years. If they go, he would be very lonely. Because of that:

'Write to me often about how you're getting on. I will be very happy to read them. And correspond with Sarah and Miriam too,' he requested. 'These days people should exchange views, shouldn't they? Who knows, perhaps such discussions could turn out to be the foundation for a better life later on? Especially if you all become important people!'

I promised I would write.

'Minke, if you maintain your present attitude, I mean your European attitude, not a slavish attitude like most Javanese, perhaps one day you will be an important person. You can become a leader, a pioneer, an example to your race. You, as an educated person, surely understand that your people have fallen very low, humiliatingly low. Europeans can no longer do anything to help. The Natives themselves must begin to do something.'

His words hurt. Yes, every time the essence of Java was insulted, offended by outsiders, my feelings were also hurt. I felt so totally Javanese. But when the ignorance and stupidity of Java was mentioned, I felt European. So these messages, which had brought me so many thoughts, I took with me in my heart, I took with me in the express train, which took me back to Surabaya.

If Mr de la Croix had been a Javanese, it would have been easy to guess his intention: he wanted me as a son-in-law. But he was a European: so that was impossible. Especially as both Sarah and Miriam were several years older than me. The colonial official hoped I would become a leader, a pioneer, an example to my people. Like in a fairy tale! Nothing like this was ever mentioned in the tales of my ancestors. Is it possible that there could be a European who truly desired such a thing? In the history of the Indies no such thing had ever occured. The Dutch army had never rested its rifles and cannons for a single moment during their three hundred years in the Indies. Suddenly there was a European who wanted me to become a leader, a pioneer, and an example to my people. An uninteresting fairy story. An unfunny joke. It appeared he wanted to make me a guinea pig in an experiment to test the 'Association Theory' of Dr Snouck Hurgronje. To the devil with it all! Nothing to do with me. It's lucky I liked to make notes, so that I had a treasury that at every moment could supply me with guidelines and warnings.

I groped in my suitcase to find and read those letters that I had still not yet read. It was true, they told of the plan for a reception for the investiture of Father, and ordered and requested that I come home quickly. With my brother's letter there was even a note to my school director requesting leave. Uh! everything had passed by with victory to me.

He, he! why was Fatso, that fat man, with the rather slanted eyes, watching only me? His clothes were from brown drill, both his shirt and his trousers. His shoes were brown too – shoes that were normal for first-class carriages. His hat, from felt, with a silk hat-band, never left his head, but was sometimes lowered to cover his forehead in order to give him the freedom to look around the carriage as he liked. His baggage consisted of a small leather case that was located on the rack over his head. And he sat on the bench over there, on the other side. When the conductor was checking the tickets, he handed over his white ticket, but his eyes glanced across at me.

Between B— and Surabaya there were only a few places where the express train stopped. And Fatso didn't get off, nor were there any signs he was getting ready to do so. He was obviously heading for the last station. 'Stop!' I'm not going to take any notice of him. I want to enjoy this trip, as if it were a holiday. I wanted to sleep deeply. I needed my own strength and health.

The train hissed on rapidly towards Surabaya. By five in the evening Surabaya rattled under the wheels of the train. The train shot past the cemetery and stopped at the station. The platform looked deserted. Just a few people were standing or sitting, waiting or walking back and forth.

'Ann! Annelies!' I called from my window. She was there to meet me.

The maiden ran to my carriage, stopped below it and put out her hand: 'Everything's all right, Mas?' she asked.

Fatso passed me carrying his little case. He alighted first, looked briefly at Annelies, then slowly walked towards the station exit. I followed him with my eyes. He didn't go out, but stopped, and glanced back at us.

'Come on, get out. What else are you waiting for?' coaxed Annelies.

I alighted. The coolie followed, carrying my baggage.

'Come on, Darsam has been waiting for a long time.'

Fatso still hadn't gone out through the platform gate, so we ended up passing by him. His skin was a clear *langsat* colour, his face reddish. Every few moments he wiped his neck with a blue handkerchief. Just as he did in the carriage. As soon as we passed him, he moved as if he wanted to follow us.

'Greetings, Young Master!' called Darsam from beside the *andong*. (Mama had told him he was not to call me Sinyo.)

Fatso watched us as we climbed up into the carriage. Now I really began to be suspicious. Who was he? Why hadn't he gone yet, why was he still watching us? And as soon as we boarded, he hurriedly rented a *dokar*. As soon as our *andong* moved, his *dokar* set off following us. It was obvious he was following us.

When I glanced back at his *dokar*, he was wiping his neck. He was not paying any attention to us. The second time I looked, he was looking at us.

'Heh! Darsam! Why aren't you turning right?' I protested.

'Why to the left, Darsam?' asked Annelies in Madurese.

'I've got a little business,' he answered briefly.

The carriage turned left away from the station square, then to the right passing the green field in front of the residency building. And where was Darsam off to? And he looked so serious.

'Why aren't you turning right again?' protested Annelies. 'It's already evening.'

'Patient, Non, it's not dark yet. A lantern has been prepared. Don't worry.'

And it was turning out that Fatso's *dokar* was indeed following our *andong*. When, for the umpteenth time, I glanced back he bent down, sheltering his face behind the driver's back.

'Slow down a little, Darsam,' I ordered.

The *andong* entered into a third-class street, travelling slowly. The *dokar* behind us also slowed down. It had to, the street was too narrow. The *dokar* could have rung its bell if it wanted us to move over. But it didn't. Nor did it try to overtake us.

All of a sudden our *andong* stopped.

'Why here?' protested Annelies.

'Just a moment, Non. I have a little business,' answered Darsam jumping down and guiding the horse to the side of the road, tying the reins to a fence post.

Fatso's *dokar* hesitated to pass, but in the end it had no choice. The passenger himself turned the other way while blowing his nose with his blue handkerchief. He didn't look Chinese, or like a Mixed-Blood Chinese, nor like a merchant. Anyway, if he was a Mixed-Blood Chinese, he was probably an educated one, perhaps an employee at the office of the *Majoor der Chineezen* – the Dutch-installed leader of the local Chinese community? Or perhaps a Mixed-Blood European-Chinese returning from holidays to his workplace in Surabaya? He was clearly not a merchant. They weren't the clothes of a trader. Or perhaps he was a cashier at one of the 'Big Five' Dutch trading companies – Borsumij or Geowehrij? Or perhaps he was the Majoor der Chineezen himself? But the *majoor* were always arrogant, considering themselves equals with Europeans and so wouldn't take any notice of me, or any other Native for that matter. Or perhaps he was interested in Annelies? No. This had been going on since I left B—.

'Non, wait here a moment. Darsam has a little business in this food-stall,' said Darsam. With his eyes directed at me, he continued, 'Young Master, could you come down for a moment?'

I climbed down. Vigilantly, of course. We entered the café, a bamboo shack with a tiled roof.

'What's going on there?' asked Annelies suspiciously, from the top of the *andong*.

Darsam glanced back, answering:

'Since when hasn't Noni trusted Darsam?'

I was also becoming suspicious. Fatso and his *dokar* had stopped some way down the road. Now it was Darsam who was up to something.

'Stay there, Ann,' I said to calm her. Yet I felt my eyes following the hands and machete of the Madurese fighter.

There was only one customer drinking coffee in the stall. He didn't look up when we entered. It looked as if he was day-dreaming. Or pretending not to notice? Or an ally too of Fatso, like Darsam?

In the manner of giving an order he invited me to take a seat on the long bench across from the other customer. He sat so close to me that I could hear his breathing and smell his sweat.

'Take some tea and cake to the carriage outside,' Darsam instructed the stall woman. His eyes scrutinised her sharply until she took the food out on a wooden tray.

His eyes shone wildly as he brought his curly moustache up close to me, and whispered in heavy and awkward Javanese:

'Young Master, something has happened at the house. Only I know. Noni and Nyai don't. Young Master mustn't be startled. For the moment Young Master mustn't stay at Wonokromo. It's dangerous.'

'What's the matter, Darsam?'

Now his voice was calmer:

'Darsam is loyal only to Nyai, Young Master. Whoever is loved by Nyai, is loved by Darsam. Whatever she orders, Darsam carries out. I don't care what sort of order it is. Nyai has ordered me to look after Young Master. I will do it, Young Master. Young Master's safety is now my work. You don't need to believe everything I say, Young Master, but at least take my advice.'

'I understand your task. Thank you for being so conscientious. But what has happened?'

'Nyai is my employer. Noni is my employer too, but only number two. Now Noni is in love with Young Master. Darsam must also make sure that nothing happens to you. So I pass on this advice. Not because Darsam's machete can't guarantee your safety. No, Young Master. There is still something not yet clear to Darsam.'

'I understand. But what has happened?'

'In short Darsam will take Young Master back to his room at Kranggan, not to Wonokromo.'

'I must know why.'

He was silent and closely observed the stall woman as she went by.

'Finished yet, Darsam?' came Annelies's voice.

'Be patient, Non,' he answered without looking outside. Seeing that the stall woman had gone, he resumed his whispering. 'It is Sinyo Robert, Young Master. Making many promises, he has ordered me, Darsam, to kill Young Master.'

I wasn't at all surprised. I had already noted the signs of that youth's ill-intent. Only:

'How have I wronged him?'

'Only jealousy, I think. Nyai is fonder of Young Master. He feels unhappy with another man in the house.'

'He can tell me to my face. Why is he going to you?'

'He thinks too little, Young Master. That's what makes him so dangerous. Now Young Master knows, understands my advice. Don't tell this to Nyai or Noni. Don't ever. Nah, let's go.' He paid for what we'd eaten, not asking my opinion about any of this.

Fatso's buggy had disappeared.

Our carriage set off. And in Wonokromo – if Darsam was right – someone wanted to take my life, the only one I had. Fatso had been spying on me since B—. Perhaps my father's anger with me was justified after all. And my mother's warning that I must be ready to accept all the consequences of my own deeds was not to be wasted either.

Yes, yes, Robert Mellema had the right to look upon me as an intruder into his kingdom. At the very least I was another thing for him to worry about. He was fully entitled to think that way about me.

Annelies didn't want to let go of my hand, as if I was a slippery fish that might jump out of the carriage at any moment. She didn't speak. Her eyes showed her thoughts were far away.

'Ann, I found your money in my case,' I said.

'Yes, I put it there. You might have needed it. You were on an unknown journey and you had to return to me quickly.'

'Thank you, Ann. I didn't use it.'

She laughed for the first time. But her laughter didn't interest me. The carriage lantern didn't throw its rays back into the carriage. Darkness. Annelies's beauty was swallowed up by the blackness. Even if that hadn't been so, I'd still not have been interested. My mind was preoccupied with more forbidding matters, thieving all that could be said to be enjoyable. My earth, this earth of mankind, had lost all its certainty. All the science and learning that had made me what I am evaporated into nothingness. Nothing could be trusted. Robert? Yes, I understood him. Fatso? I would recognise his shape, even, I think, in the dark. But it could be someone I didn't know, someone I'd never predict, who was going to carry out this evil against me. Surabaya was famous for its paid killers – who charged only a half to two *rupiahs*. Every week there were corpses found sprawled on the beach, in the forests, on the roadside, in the markets; and their bodies always exhibited knife wounds.

The carriage headed for Kranggan.

'Why are we going this way?' Annelies protested again.

What could I say to Annelies? Before I'd a chance to think up an explanation, we stopped in front of the Telinga's house. Without speaking Darsam off-loaded my things.

'Why are they being off-loaded here?' protested Annelies again.

'Ann,' I said gently, 'I have to prepare for my lessons this week. So for the time being, I can't accompany you home. I'm really sorry. Thank you for meeting me, Ann. Say sorry to Mama for me, yes? I really can't go on to Wonokromo yet. I must stay here where I am closer to my teachers. My regards and thanks to Mama. Once I'm free again I'll definitely come back to Wonokromo.'

'Mas hasn't been able to study while he's been at Wonokromo? No one bothered you. Forgive me if I've been a bother to you,' she was on the verge of crying.

'No, Ann, of course not.'

'Tell me if I've been a bother, so I know what I've done wrong,' her voice trembled as she came closer to crying.

'No, Ann; truly, no.'

There was no way it could have been avoided. She cried. Cried like a little child.

'Why are you crying? It's only for a week, Ann, only a week. After that I'll be there again for sure. Isn't that so, Darsam?'

'Yes, Non. Don't cry like this, at somebody else's house.'

At that moment my sense of being a Javanese knight disappeared; a knight beyond compare, but only in my own imagination. Now I was just a coward – scared because of a report, just a report, that my life was in danger.

'Don't get down, Ann, just sit here in the carriage,' and I kissed her on her cheek in the darkness of the vehicle. I felt wetness on her face.

'Mas must come home quickly to Wonokromo,' she entreated, crying, surrendering to her feelings.

'So you understand, yes?' She nodded. 'When everything is over, I will come back quickly. For the moment I hope that you will listen to me and understand my situation.'

'Yes, Mas, I'm not disagreeing,' she answered faintly.

'Until we meet again, my goddess.'

'Mas.'

I got down. Darsam was still waiting in front of the door.

It was already night and lamps were shimmering everywhere. It was only my thoughts that weren't clear.

'Why don't you tell Mama?' I whispered to Darsam.

'No. Nyai already has enough troubles because of her children and her Tuan. Darsam must take care of this matter himself. Young Master must be patient.'

Mr and Mrs Telinga sat on the settee waiting for me to come out of my room and tell them what had happened. Such a good and happy couple! I don't know how they felt about me. I didn't go out, but locked the door from inside, changed clothes and got into bed without eating dinner. Before I put out the lamp I still needed to look up at the portrait of Queen Wilhelmina. This earth of mankind! She was secure in her palace, free of all problems, except perhaps within her own heart and mind. And me? Her subject, promised by the astrologer's stars the same fate, yet I may glimpse at any moment, springing from out of the corners of this room, a death arranged by Robert Mellema.

114

The room was enveloped in darkness. The conversation in the middle room came indistinctly to my ears. No meaning. Uh, as young as this, and already there was somebody desiring to take my life. The promise of the modern age, glorious and exciting as told by my teachers, showed not a single sign or indication of its whereabouts. Robert, why are you as mad as this? Murder because of jealous love still occurs the world over – a remnant of bestiality among men. Something unique to man. Murder out of greed was also another remnant from man's bestial life. Yes? It's true, isn't it? But you, you're more complex still. You hate your mother, your origins, and obtain no love from them. You beg love from your father, who pays you no heed either. You're jealous, Robert, because you mother's love now flows to me. Because you're afraid that your inheritance will flow to me also – somebody who has no right to it just as depicted in European fiction. Probably in your eyes I'm no better than a criminal.

I've been honest to myself, haven't I? And to the world? Look: I want no more than to enjoy what I've created by my own hard strivings. I need nothing else. A happy life, in my view, does not come from that which is given to one, but from one's own struggles. My separation from my own family had taught me that. Uh, a problem more complicated than all my school lessons put together.

And you too, Darsam! Let's hope your mouth cannot be believed. Let's hope Robert is not as evil as that. But you too are hiding some other purpose, and an evil one.

And you, Fatso, with clear, *langsat* skin and slight slanted eyes – great balls of fire! – what is your business with me? Someone as neatly dressed as you, is it possible you're just a paid killer? Because you want the Mellema girl and the Mellema wealth?

And Sarah, and Miriam de la Croix, and Assistant Resident B— . . . and Association . . .

My heart shrivelled up. Why was I such a coward?

9

So that this story of mine runs in order, let me first of all relate what happened to Robert after I left Wonokromo for B— in the company of that police agent.

I've put together the story below based on what Annelies, Nyai, Darsam and others told me; and this is how it has ended up:

When the buggy I was travelling in disappeared, swallowed up by the morning darkness, Annelies cried, embracing Mama. (I don't know why she was such a cry-baby and was so spoiled, just like a little child.)

'Quiet, Ann, he'll be safe,' said Nyai.

'Why did Mama let him be taken away?' protested Annelies.

'That slave of the law, Ann; there's no way we can fight him.'

'Let's follow him, Ma.'

'No point. It's still too early. And it's clear he's being taken to B—.'

'Mama, ah Mama.'

'You really love him?'

'Don't torment me like this, Ma.'

'So what should I do? Nothing, Ann. We must wait. We can't just do whatever we feel like.'

'Do something, Ma. Do something.'

'You think Minke is just your doll, Ann. He's not a doll. Do something, do something! Of course, I'm going to do something. Be patient. It's still too early in the morning.'

'You're going to leave me like this, Ma? Do you want to kill me?'

Nyai became confused. She had never heard that sort of lamentation from her daughter who usually never complained about anything. She knew and understood that Annelies was going through a crisis. Annelies: her trusted work companion. She knew she must do everything that Annelies wanted, that Annelies considered her right. She took her daughter inside to let her rest in her room.

And Annelies refused. She wanted to wait for Minke until he returned.

'It's not possible, Ann. Not possible. Maybe it'll be the day after tomorrow or the next day before he's back.'

And Annelies began to withdraw into silence.

Mama became even more confused. She knew: ever since Annelies was little she had never asked for anything. And now over the last few weeks she had been asking – not just asking, but urging, demanding – all concerning Minke. She had always been obedient, behaved sweetly, had been a sweetheart. Now she was beginning to be rebellious.

Annelies demanded her doll back. And the only person she could go to was her mother.

Nyai worried that her daughter might fall ill. She began to see more and more signs of all not being well with her daughter. Could it be that this obedient child was unable to deal with personal traumas, just like her father?

And the sun slowly began to rise.

Darsam arrived to open the doors and windows. He was startled to see the behaviour of his Noni. He was powerless to solve a problem requiring neither machete nor muscles.

'Yes, this is government business,' said Mama softly, in a rustling voice. 'Affairs that can neither be felt nor seen, affairs of the spirit world.'

For a second, Mama remembered her eldest child. In the next moment, she suspected him of sending an anonymous letter to the police. She suspected him! In the next moment: she would investigate.

'Call Robert here,' Mama ordered Darsam.

And Robert came, rubbing his eyes. He stood silently. If it wasn't for Darsam, he wouldn't have come. Everyone knew that. And he stood without speaking a word. His eyes shone with lack of interest.

'How many times and to whom have you sent your poison pen letters?'

He didn't answer. Darsam went up closer to him.

'Answer, Nyo,' the fighter urged.

Annelies was clinging to Nyai, holding herself up.

'I've got nothing to do with any anonymous letters,' he answered viciously, his face towards Darsam. 'Do I look like a poison pen letter writer?'

'Answer to Nyai, not to me,' hissed Darsam.

'I've never written any, let alone sent any,' now he faced Mama.

'Good. I always try to believe what you say. Why do you hate Minke? Because he's better and more educated than you?'

'I've got no business with Minke. He's only a Native.'

'And its because he's a Native that you hate him.'

'So, what's the point of having European blood?' he challenged her.

'Good. You hate Minke because he is a Native and you have European blood. Good. It's obvious I'm not capable of educating and teaching you. Only a European could do that for you. Good, Rob. Now I, your mother, this Native, know that people with European blood are, of course, wiser, more educated than Natives. You know what I mean. Now, I ask the Native blood in you – not the European in you – to go to the Surabaya Police Station. Find out what's happened to Minke. Darsam can't do that. I can't either. The work here won't allow it. You speak Dutch well and you can read and write. Darsam can't. I want to see what you're capable of doing. Go by horse, and be quick.'

Robert didn't reply.

'Go, Nyo!' ordered Darsam.

Without answering, Robert Mellema turned around and walked off, dragging his sandals, went into his room and didn't come out again.

'Warn him, Darsam!' ordered Mama.

Darsam went after Robert into his room.

The world outside was beginning to clear. Robert left his room escorted by the Madurese fighter. He went out the back, to the horse stables. He had put on jodhpurs, riding boots and in his hand was a leather whip.

'You just sleep, Ann,' consoled Nyai.

'No.'

Nyai checked Annelies's temperature and it was rising. The girl was falling ill. Her mother was very anxious.

'Put the sofa in the office, Darsam. So I can be with her while I work. Don't forget the blanket. Then fetch Dr Martinet.' She sat her child on the chair. 'Be patient, Ann, patient. Do you really love him?'

'Mama, my Mama!' whispered Annelies.

'Falling sick like this, Ann! No, Mama won't forbid you loving him. No, darling. You can marry him, any time you like, if he agrees. But now, be patient.'

'Mama,' called Annelies with her eyes closed. 'Where's your cheek, Ma; here, Ma, so I can kiss it,' and she kissed her mother's cheek.

'But don't fall ill. Who will help me? Could you bear to watch your Mama work like a horse?'

'Mama, I'll always help you.'

'So you mustn't get sick like this, darling.'

'I don't want to be sick, Ma.'

'Your temperature is rising, Ann. You must learn wisdom, child; people can only do their best, and be patient in awaiting the outcome.'

Darsam moved the sofa into the office. Annelies refused to be moved until she'd seen Robert leave on his horse. And her brother still wasn't to be seen.

'Chase Robert, Darsam!' exclaimed Mama.

Darsam ran to the back. Ten minutes later that tall, handsome youth raced off on his horse, without looking back, straight down onto the main road. And a quarter of an hour later Darsam drove off in the buggy to fetch Dr Martinet.

Only then was Annelies willing to be led into the office. And Nyai padded her daughter's forehead with a brown onion and vinegar compress.

118

'Forgive me, Ann, I'm not strong enough to carry you. Sleep now. The doctor will be here in a little while, and Robert will be back with news.'

Nyai went to the corner of the office, turned on the tap, and washed her face and combed her hair.

From under the blanket, Annelies asked in a whisper:

'Do you like him, Ma?'

'Of course, Ann, a good boy,' answered Nyai, still combing her hair. 'How could Mama not like him, when you do? Any parent would be proud to have a son like him. And what woman wouldn't be proud to be his wife one day? His legal wife? Mama too would be proud to have him as a son-in-law.'

'Mama, my own Mama!'

'So you shouldn't worry about a thing.'

'Does he like me, Ma?'

'What boy wouldn't be mad about you, Ann? Pure-Blood, Indo, Native. All of them. Mama knows, Ann. There's no girl as beautiful as you, Ann. Don't worry about a thing. Close your eyes.'

The girl had already closed her eyes for some time. She asked:

'If his parents forbid it, Ma, then what?'

'I told you not to worry about anything. Mama will arrange everything. Sleep. Stay quiet there. Let me get some milk. Remember, you must be healthy. What would Minke say if you became unattractive and gloomy. Even the prettiest girl looks unattractive if she's sick.'

Nyai cried out from the office calling after someone from the kitchen. Not longer after, someone brought some hot milk.

'Nah, have a drink. Mama will bathe first. Then try to sleep, Ann.'

Nyai went to bathe. On her return she brought warm water and a towel and took care of her daughter.

Annelies didn't say a single word.

Dr Martinet came, examined her for a moment, and then gave her some medicine. He was fortyish, polite, quiet and friendly. He was dressed all in white except for his grey felt hat. His right eye used a monocle that was attached by a gold chain to the top button hole.

Darsam hurried around preparing some breakfast for the doctor to eat in the office. And the guest breakfasted with Nyai.

'I'll come back this afternoon, Nyai. Give her some breakfast before she sleeps, but no solids. Keep her away from any din. Make sure everything is quiet. Sleep is her best medicine. Move her into her own room. Don't leave her in the office like this. Or move the sofa into the middle room. Keep the windows and the doors closed.'

And what about Robert Mellema?

According to the people at Boerderij, eyewitnesses and the accused at a trial later on, the events unfolded as I've put together below:

After leaving the stables, Robert raced the horse along the road. Then he turned right, towards Surabaya. When he got onto the main road he pulled up his horse, looked left and right, and slowed down to enjoy the morning view. He probably felt resentful. Just to protect an adventurer like Minke he had to wake as early as this! and go to a police station too. And what for? Let Minke disappear forever. The world won't be any poorer, won't have to undergo any extra suffering without him; a speck of dust brought in by the wind from who knows where, and wanting to dwell in his house for who knows how long.

The horse walked on unhappily because, of course, it hadn't eaten that morning, hadn't had its sweet drink yet. Robert hadn't breakfasted yet either, and already he had to be off working.

The morning was more than just cool. The buffalo carts carrying the oil drums from Wonokromo hadn't appeared yet in their usual long, seemingly unbroken, convoy. Only the traders from the villages were out walking in a line, carrying on their backs produce for the markets of Surabaya.

And the horse had covered about fifty metres at a slow walk. Robert's thoughts were wandering everywhere. From behind the hedge on the right a voice could be heard calling out a greeting.

'Regards, Sinyo Lobert.'

He pulled up his horse, and had a look over the top of the hedge. He could see a Chinese man in striped pyjamas smiling sweetly at him. The man had very little hair so that even his pig-tail was very thin. When he smiled, his cheeks pulled upwards and his eyes became even more narrow and slanted. Even his moustache was thin, long, dropping impotently at the ends of his mouth. His beard was also very thin, and out of a birthmark, a part of his beard formed a tassel and was darker.

'Gleetings, Nyo,' he repeated, when he saw Robert was unsure whether to answer.

'Greetings, Babah Ah Tjong!' Robert answered politely, nodding and smiling.

'Regards, regards, Nyo. How are things with Nyai?'

'Well, Babah. This is the first time I've seen Babah. Where have you been all this time?'

'As usual, Nyo, much business. And how are things with Tuan?'

'Well, Babah.'

'I haven't seen him alound for a long time.'

'As usual, Bah, a lot of business. The door to Babah's house is open today. The windows too. What's going on today, Bah? something special perhaps?'

'A good day, Nyo. A day for pleasure. Come on, Nyo, dlop in,' Ah Tjong's smile mollified Robert's resentment and also his hatred of every-

120

thing Chinese. He'd never had any desire to meet a Chinese. On any other occasion, he wouldn't even have responded to a greeting from one, let alone enter his yard or house; but now there was something he really wanted to find out.

'Good, Bah, I'll drop in for a moment,' and Robert turned his horse into his neighbour's yard.

He had never met Babah Ah Tjong, so he was only guessing that this was who he was speaking to. Babah ran down to greet Robert. Robert saw the pigtailed man clap his hands. A *sinkeh*, a full-blooded, immigrant Chinese, a gardener, came running; and he took the horse from Robert's hands, then led the horse around the back of the house.

Robert and Ah Tjong walked together, slowly, along the rocky path towards that building whose doors and windows were usually never open. They entered. And now the front stairs vanished behind a curtain of coconut-husk cords. And the veranda-less front area was very large, furnished with a number of carved teak settees. In one corner there was a brown-spotted bamboo settee. The walls were decorated with different-sized mirrors with red Chinese calligraphy on them. A carved wooden partition closed off the mouth of the corridor in the middle of the building. Several big empty porcelain vases decorated the room; they stood on legs with a dragon curled around them. There was no floor decorations. Neither was there a picture of Queen Wilhelmina. There were no flowers anywhere in the front room either.

Ah Tjong took him to the bamboo settee, which consisted of three chairs and a long bench and which faced the front courtyard. The host sat there and Robert opposite him.

'Ah, Nyo, we've been neighbours so long and you've never come to visit.'

'How could I when the doors and windows are always closed?'

'Ah, Nyo, come on. How could this house be kept shut all the time?'

'This is the first time I've seen it open.'

'If it's opened up like this, Nyo Lobert, it means, of course, that I'm home.'

'So where do you go when its closed up.'

'Where do I go?' he laughed happily. 'What will you dlink, Nyo? What's your usual? Whisky, Blandy, Cognac, Bolsh, *chiu* or *alak*? *Sausing* perhaps? White, yellow, warm, cold. Or Malaga wine? Or dly?'

'Ah, Babah, as early as this.'

'What's wlong with that? with flied peanuts, heh?'

'I agree, Bah, agree very much.'

'Good, Nyo. It's pleasing to leceive a guest like Sinyo: handsome, dashing, not shy, young . . . Sinyo has evelything. Wealthy . . . *wah*,' he clapped hands haughtily, without moving his head, without turning, just like a sultan.

From behind the partition emerged a Chinese girl in a long, sleeveless gown. The side of her gown was split high up exposing her thigh. Her hair was braided into two pig-tails.

Robert stared open-eyed at the alabaster-skinned girl. His eyes couldn't move from the split in her gown until the girl came up close so as to put the whisky bottle, glasses and fried peanuts on the table.

Ah Tjong spoke quickly to the girl in Chinese, who then stood up straight in front of Robert.

'Nah, Nyo, look over this girl yourself.'

And Robert was acutely embarrassed. He couldn't speak. His eyes and face shifted away as if tugged by a demon.

'This is Miss Min Hwa. Sinyo doesn't like her?' he ahemmed. 'Just out flom Hong Kong.'

Min Hwa bowed, put the tray on the table and sat on the chair near Robert.

'It's a gleat pity, Nyo. Min Hwa can't speak Malay, or Dutch, or Javanese. Only Chinese. What can one do. Why is Sinyo silent? Why? She's next to you now. Ai-ai don't pletend Sinyo has never done this before! Come on, Nyo, eh, you don't need to be shy with Babah?'

Min Hwa pushed the whisky glass onto Robert's lips who received it hesitantly.

And Ah Tjong smiled sweetly, deliberately encouraging him on. Min Hwa laughed shrilly and friskily, throwing her head back, her face muscles pulled tight, her mouth open and her pearl teeth, except for one which was gold, on display inside. Then the girl spoke quickly and loudly without commas, without full-stops. And Robert didn't understand, instead he became even more unsure of himself as the girl moved her chair closer.

Seeing Robert go pale and the glass in his hand almost fall, Min Hwa pushed the glass up to the tall youth's lips again. And Robert swallowed it down without hesitating. Suddenly he started coughing – he had never drunk liquor before. Whisky sprayed all over Ah Tjong and Min Hwa. They weren't angry, but laughed happily.

'Another glass, Nyo,' the host suggested.

Min Hwa poured more whisky into the glass and once more ordered the young guest to drink. He refused and wiped his mouth with a handkerchief. He was even more embarrassed.

'Come on, Sinyo, you aren't going to pletend you've never dlank whisky before?' and he teased, 'You don't like whisky, you don't like Min Hwa?' he waved his hand and the girl left, disappearing behind the carved partition. He clapped again.

Now another Chinese girl appeared, wearing a silk shirt and brightly coloured slacks. She wiggled as she walked up to the bamboo settee carrying a bamboo tray on which were various delicacies. She put it on the table, on top of the tray left by Min Hwa.

She bowed to Robert and smiled enticingly. Like the first girl, she wore lipstick. Before the delicacies were all laid out Min Hwa entered again bringing a glass of clear water on a glass tray. She put it before Robert. Then sat down again on the same seat as before.

'Wah, Nyo, there are two now. Which is the more intelesting? Come on, don't be shy. This one is Sie-sie.'

Several carriages began arriving at the front of the house. The guests all came straight inside. Some wore Chinese clothes, others pyjamas. All were men and had pig-tails. Without worrying whether the host was there or not they sat down straight away and began busily chatting, laughing and gambling.

'It looks like there's none you like, Nyo,' breathed Ah Tjong and he moved his hand to order them to leave to serve the other guests. 'Sinyo doesn't like Sie-Sie either . . . ,' he stood and called Sie-sie over.

As soon as the woman had come back, Ah Tjong sat her down next to Robert.

'Who knows perhaps Sinyo plefers this one.'

And Robert still appeared very embarrassed, confused; wanting to, but afraid. Babah broke into laughter again, enjoying seeing the youth in his confusion. And the other guests took no notice of the three of them sitting in the corner.

Now Sie-sie started noisily chatting with a loud, fast voice, then she began to seduce him, putting his shirt and belt in place, pinching the crease on his shirt. Babah kept observing it all and laughing too. Robert shrank up still more. Then the two Chinese spoke noisily to each other. And Robert still couldn't understand a word.

'Vely well, Nyo; Nyo doesn't like either of them.'

Sie-sie rose and disappeared behind the partition and Ah Tjong clapped four times.

Robert, perhaps, greatly regretted her going. He bowed his head. From behind the partition there now appeared a Japanese woman in a kimono with pictures of big flowers on it. Her face was reddish. She took short, quick steps. Her face was round and her lips were lipsticked and always smiling. Her hair was in a bun. She sat straight down beside the host. When she laughed, one gold tooth was visible.

'Look here; Nyo; here is another one.'

Perhaps because he didn't want to have still more regrets Robert got up the courage to look at the Japanese woman.

'Nah, Nyo, this is Maiko. Just two months out flom Japan.'

Before he stopped talking, Maiko spoke in a high voice in rapid Japanese. Robert didn't understand this either. Yet he still got up the courage to gaze at her.

Ah Tjong put his hand across the woman's mouth and said:

123

'This is my own one. Sinyo can have her if you like. Sit here, near her.'

Like a dog scared of his master's stick, Robert stood, and slowly moved over to sit on the divan, so Maiko was squeezed between them.

'So Sinyo likes this one? Maiko? good,' he laughed, understanding. 'In that case I'll go. I'll leave it up to Sinyo.'

The guest followed his host with his eyes.

And Ah Tjong mixed with his many guests, playing cards, *carambol* or *mahjong*. He walked around slowly, checking each table. Then he went back to the bamboo settee and stood in front of the couple, neither of whom could say a meaningful word to the other.

'Yes, it's difficult, Nyo. Maiko doesn't understand Malay. Let alone Dutch. How come Sinyo has nevel mixed with Japanese ladies? You've nevel been to the Japanese Galdens pelhaps?'

'I've never even seen one before now, Bah,' Robert at last got up the courage to speak.

'A loss, Nyo, a loss for a youth with money. In neally evely Chinese pleasure house like this, there is a Japanese miss. A loss, Nyo, a loss. You've never been into places in the led light distlict down town? In the Japanese Galdens? In Batavia? Indeed you've leally missed out on something, Nyo Lobert . . . Japanese Misses evelywhere . . . A pity. Come on . . .' he summonsed Robert with an emperor's flourish.

The three of them left the room. Babah out front, Robert behind him. And Maiko at the rear. Ah Tjong's pig-tail swayed a little at each step because it was so thin and it swept across the back of his pyjama shirt. They passed the carved partition. Maiko continued to talk in her enticing voice and to walk in those short, quick steps. The smell of perfume filled the air.

They entered a corridor that was hemmed in on left and right by rooms, and had no furniture except wall decorations. Here and there a few young Chinese girls were standing talking to each other. They were all dressed up and neatly made up and greeted Ah Tjong with great respect, then also Robert, but not Maiko.

Robert paid attention to every person. Short, tall, thin, fat, well-built and weak-looking; they all wore lipstick, smiled or laughed.

'Such pletty gills are life's pleasure, Nyo. It's a pity you don't like the Chinese ones,' he laughed piercingly. 'Nah, all the looms face each othel. Sinyo can take whichever he likes, as long as the door is left unlocked.'

He opened a door so Robert could see inside. Its furniture was as good as that in his own room, and it was just as clean, only it wasn't as big, and the bed was more beautiful.

'For Sinyo here is a king's loom, a loom of honour, if Sinyo likes it,' he walked along again and opened another door. 'Nah, only Tuan Majoor may use this loom. It happens he's in Hong Kong at the moment.'

124

All the furniture inside was new and in a style Robert didn't recognise – had never come across. Babah asked his guest's opinion. And Robert had no opinion except to agree that it was beautiful.

Ah Tjong entered, Robert and Maiko followed.

'The best furniture, Nyo. Just finished, Flench style in teak. Made by famous Flench claftsmen. Indeed Tuan Majoor likes evelything Flench. Most expensive furnishings in the building, Nyo. In the corner is a little cupboard, on top of that little table there's whisky and sake, whatever Sinyo likes. Settee, sofa and divan,' he said pointing out each in turn. 'Such a beautifully carved wooden bed makes for lestful and pleasant sleeping. Yes, Maiko?'

And Maiko answered with a bow and with a soft, fast, frisky voice, like a magpie.

'Nah, Nyo, enjoy yourself!'

Robert's eyes followed Ah Tjong as he walked outside, watching his pigtail until he disappeared behind the door.

10

Also because I consider the time sequence to be important I've prepared this section out of material I obtained from the court testimony later. Most of it is based on Maiko's – given through a sworn translator and written down in my own words.

I went to Hong Kong from Nagoya, Japan, where I was born. I went as a prostitute. My boss was a Japanese who then sold me to a Chinese boss in Hong Kong. I can no longer remember the name of my second boss. Just a few weeks in his hands were not enough for me to be able to remember his name, so hard to pronounce. He sold me to another boss, also a Chinese, and so I was brought out by ship to Singapore. I knew this third boss only by the name of Ming. I knew no more than that. He was very satisfied and pleased with me because of the profit my body and the service I gave earned for him.

My fourth boss was a Singapore Japanese. He had a great passion to own me. The bargaining went on for quite a while. Finally I was bought for seventy-five Singapore dollars, the highest price ever paid for a Japanese public-woman in Singapore. I was indeed proud that my body was more highly valued than those of the Sundanese public-women, who occupied the highest position and were the most expensive in South-east Asia's pleasure world.

But my pride in this didn't last long. Only five months. My boss, the Japanese one, came to hate me greatly. He beat me often. He even tortured me once with live cigarette butts. Because my customers were declining in numbers. Such was indeed the fate that could befall even the most famous prostitute: syphilis. And what I had caught was no ordinary syphilis. In this cursed world of prostitution the disease was called: 'Burmese' syphilis. I don't know why it is called that.

It was famous for being incurable, and the men were ruined and destroyed more quickly and more painfully. Women could go without feeling anything for a long time.

So I was sold for twenty-five dollars to a Chinese boss, my fifth boss. He took me to Betawi. Before the sale took place, my old boss took me into a room. He beat me on my chest and back until I fainted. After I regained consciousness I was stripped naked and parts of me underwent acupuncture so as to kill all physical sexual desire. His name was Nakagawa. I was handed over to my new boss the next day.

On the first day with my new boss, he wanted to try me. I refused. If he found out I had that accursed disease, I'd suffer still more torture. Perhaps I'd be killed. It was nothing unusual for a prostitute to be killed by her boss and the corpse destroyed or hidden who knows where. A prostitute is a weak being without a protector. Especially too as I knew that symptoms of my declining sexual desire were beginning to show. I asked my boss to hire an acupuncturist. Three times I received treatment and my sexual desire began to revive. Yet I still refused to be tried out by my boss. He was lucky he didn't try to force me.

It was only three months later that my boss found out I had a disease. He was angry. I could tell only from his face and the tone of his voice because I understood no Chinese. My customers dwindled away. People avoided my body and he became annoyed and bad-tempered. Night and day I prayed that he wouldn't torment me. No. He could torment and torture me as long as he didn't steal my savings.

I hoped to return to Japan next year and marry Nakatani, who was waiting for me to bring home some capital.

My boss didn't torture me, and didn't steal my savings either. When I changed hands to become the property of Babah Ah Tjong at a price equivalent to ten Singapore dollars, he gave me half a *guilder* and said in broken Japanese:

'Actually I wanted to make you my concubine.'

It was such a disappointment to hear those words. A concubine's life was not so harsh as a prostitute's; you could live reasonably, and were freer than the wife of a Japanese youth who hoped for capital from his future woman. What could be done? This accursed disease had taken root within me.

Babah Ah Tjong lusted greatly after me. I tried to repulse him, afraid of some new disaster. If I was exposed again, the value of my body might have fallen as low as five dollars, and I'd have become street rubbish in someone else's country. So I asked he hire another acupuncturist. This one guaranteed I could be cured over a month with ten punctures each evening. Babah objected to the time it was going to take, and to the expense. He allowed only one treatemnt, as an experiment.

Before leaving for Surabaya, I ran out of excuses to refuse my boss. I was used by him alone until I was put in his pleasure-house at Wonokromo and I had the best room.

If he was there, he almost always stayed in my room, not in any of the other fourteen rooms.

Babah didn't seem to be infected by the disease. I no longer had to worry; I was happy. There were men who were immune from the diseases of the pleasure world. Or perhaps the acupuncture treatment had made me less contagious. Who knows? And my price might go up again. Yes, I thought, who knows? If Babah had taken me as a concubine I would have been grateful and would have served him as well as any concubine could. If not, eleven months would have been enough, and I could have gone home. At the very least I would have been able to afford to redeem myself from my last boss.

That month passed. Babah became infected with 'Burmese' syphilis too. He didn't know, he wasn't acquainted with that strange disease. He didn't accuse me straight away because there he had many other women. Neither of us could speak to each other either.

I knew he'd been affected by the disease when, one day, he lined up stark naked all fourteen of his prostitutes, all nationalities, and quizzed them one by one about their diseases. In his right hand he carried a leather whip and with his left hand he measured for suspicious temperatures in those poor women's vaginas.

As a Japanese, I was the only woman he did not suspect. In the pleasure world of this earth, Japanese prostitutes are considered the cleanest and the cleverest in looking after their health. Everyone assumes they are free of disease. So he didn't check on me.

Three of them were taken out from the line. Ah Tjong ordered the other women, except me, to tie those three up. They were gagged. Ah Tjong himself beat them with his leather whip, and there was no noise from their gagged mouths. They were my victims. And I remained silent.

It's hard being a prostitute. If you contract a disease you must quickly report it to your boss who will then oppress you. It's best to stay silent until he finds out for himself. But the torment and oppression will still come.

After the three women recovered from their maltreatment they were sold to a Singapore middleman to be taken to Medan. I still remained unaccused in Ah Tjong's pleasure-house. While I was servicing only him, I wasn't too tired. I was getting back my health and energy. Also my beauty.

Almost every wealthy Chinese had his own brothel, his own pleasure-house. In Hong Kong, Singapore, Batavia or Surabaya, they all had the same custom, namely, to take turns in visiting each other's places. So one day it was Babah Ah Tjong's turn to receive everyone.

Babah's clapping had already called me out in the early morning. I went out. There was supposed to be gambling that morning. The afternoon and evening would be for taking pleasure. Some guests had already arrived and were playing cards, mahjong or carambol in the front room.

I was already uneasy. It mustn't happen that Babah Ah Tjong surrender me to one of his guests. Who knew if they might like Japanese women very much? How many must I service if Babah allowed it?

It turned out that he did indeed order me to receive a guest: a tall, big-bodied youth, strong and handsome, healthy and attractive – of European descent. His name: Robert. My heart was moved and saddened to think of his future. I saw in a glance that he was a green one without much experience. Who wouldn't have felt compassion knowing as boy as young as that must contract such a disastrous disease if, in a little while, he desired my body. He'd carry it all his life, perhaps he'd be deformed by it or even die an early death?

I studied the look on Ah Tjong's face, was he kidding or serious? It seemed he had no worries about giving me to Robert. Then I understood: he knew that it was I who had infected him with the disease. Soon he would sell me to someone else, or he'd force me to redeem myself by paying who knows how much tens of dollars. I felt very, very sad that morning.

After Babah took Robert and me into the room and locked it from outside, I knew I had to work, and to work as well as possible. I had to throw off all my sadness and anxiousness.

Robert sat on the divan. I quickly knelt before him and took off his boots. So early in the morning! His socks were dirty and looked as if they had not been cared for properly. I took sandals from the wardrobe. None were the right size. His feet were very big. What could be done? It was only then I pulled his socks from those strong and firm legs of his. I just placed the sandals in front of him, I didn't put them on. Such sandals, made from rice-stalks, would be crushed under his feet.

He didn't put them on himself either. He seemed to be a person who thought a lot.

Robert said nothing, but only stared at me, and everything I did, with amazement.

I took off his shirt, which had two pockets. He was silent. I knew both pockets were empty. I invited him to stand up and I took off his riding trousers. I folded them and hung them up in the wardrobe, though I did so unwillingly as they were filthy and stank. His underclothes looked as if they hadn't been changed for a week. So dirty. He seemed rather embarrassed.

That was the youth Robert, he had nothing besides his youth and his health, his handsomeness and his own lust. I began to think again: why was Babah giving me to this boy who had nothing? Perhaps he wasn't going to sell me, or force me to redeem myself because of the accursed disease. Maybe he didn't know about my disease after all. These thoughts made me some-what happy and calm again.

From inside the wardrobe I took out one of the Majoor's kimonos. I took off Robert's underclothes and put the kimono on him. He sat silently. I gave him a goblet of special wine to strengthen him. I didn't want him to have any regrets in the future when he contracted the disease that would

129

nest in his body forever. Let him have beautiful memories from that which would one day cause him unlimited misery; a beauty and enjoyment that was his right.

He swallowed the wine, all the time watching me in amazement. I kept talking gently so as not to disturb his mood. That was one of the many aspects of my work as a prostitute.

Of course he didn't understand a single word. Even so I did not say a single nasty word. And what man didn't like to hear a Japanese woman talk and pronounce her words? And watch her way of moving and walking. And enjoy her services inside and outside the bedroom?

At eight-thirty in the morning we got into bed. Robert refused lunch. He was very strong. His body was bathed in sweat, which made it feel as if he was made from moulded copper. He didn't once let go of me. His movements were awkward, the movements of an inexperienced youth. If it wasn't for the special strengthening wine, he would have bled and not been able to erect by himself. Let it be. Not long and his tremendous body would be destroyed and broken. Everything he had would be destroyed: his youth, handsomeness, strength. Ah, ah, ah . . . blessings that not everybody receives. So I pricked him on parts of his body just as the acupuncturist had done to me. He didn't know what I was up to, yet he bore it like a retarded little child, and I did it all while in his powerful embrace.

At four o'clock in the afternoon he let me go and got down from the bed. I too got down and wiped his perspiration-covered body several times with wet towels and rosewater. Five towels! All his energy was gone. His strength and handsomeness disappeared, like old clothes piled on a chair. He asked for his clothes. I fetched them and piece by piece put them on him, including his filthy, smelly socks and his heavy leather boots. After that I scrubbed his hair and I massaged his head so his head would be free from aches. I combed his hair neatly, only then did I myself dress after scrubbing my body with a wet towel too.

He seemed very satisfied. He still availed himself of the chance to grab my arm and sit me on his lap and he spoke slowly and with a deep voice. I didn't understand what it meant but I liked listening to the deepness of his voice. And I struggled to free myself, afraid that his lust would be awakened again. I hadn't breakfasted or eaten lunch. I too would have been damaged if I'd serviced him again. Perhaps his stomach was empty too.

He was so pale, as if he'd just got over an illness. I couldn't bear to look at him. I fetched some more special wine for him so there'd be some blood in his face. Then I took him outside the room.

But he hesitated and stopped in the middle of the doorway. Suddenly he turned and came inside again, embraced me and kissed me lustfully. Respectfully and politely I pushed him outside and locked the door from inside. I was very tired . . .

130

Below is the evidence of Babah Ah Tjong at Court, spoken in Malay, and translated into Dutch by a sworn translator; and after I put it into order. It turned out as follows:

At the time, I was in the office of my pleasure-house. About four in the afternoon the bell from the emperor room rang, signalling a request to unlock the door from outside.

I myself went to look after it. Sinyo Lobert was indeed my very special guest. It's very strange that you ask why. He was the son of my neighbour, and it had long been our custom to be friendly with our neighbours. Especially as one day Sinyo Lobert would be my full neighbour, not just the son of my neighbour.

He came out. His face was pale. Everything attractive about him had dissolved away. He almost couldn't lift up his head. He didn't seem to know his limits. He was somebody who one day would surrender all his body and soul to lust. Even so, he looked satisfied. That was evident from his lips which bloomed with an unforced smile. Naturally I was happy to see this.

'Nyo,' I addressed him. 'We will be good neighbours beginning today and forever, yes?'

He suddenly looked at me with wide-open eyes and full of suspicion. He shrivelled up, frightened. Someone experienced like me could tell immediately: he realised he'd have to pay out a lot of money for the pleasure he had just taken.

'Let me sign the bill,' he said hesitantly.

'Ai, Nyo, we'll be good neighbours. Sinyo doesn't need to pay anything. Don't worry. Who knows one day we could become partners? In short you're welcome to leturn any time you like. You can use any room you like, as long as it's unlocked, without any time limits, night or day. You can choose anyone you like. If the flont doors and windows are locked Sinyo can come in thlough the back door. I'll tell the gardener and the watchman.'

His hesitation disappeared. Then he answered:

'Thank you very much, Babah. I never guessed Babah would be as good to me as this.'

'Sinyo should have come here a long time ago. Only now you come.'

'I'll come back, of course.'

'Of course!'

I was his neighbour, I could never have turned him away. Especially as he was a youth still in is prime. So I not only had to think of ways to give him the chance to vent his lust but in the end I had to surrender Maiko to him until he was fully satisfied and bored.

131

He took leave to return home.

'It's already evening,' he said.

And I didn't obstruct him in any way. I took him to my office first. His eyes went wild again when he saw the other women. He had changed; he was no longer the embarrassed youth of the morning. I pretended not to see – if I serviced him I'd be breaking all the rules. So I called a woman, a barber, and ordered her to cut his hair according to my instructions.

Sinyo didn't refuse. She cut his hair in the Spanish style, with the part in the middle. His hair was rubbed with special hair oil, the most expensive. Then I ordered him to drink some palm wine, from my private stock.

'So now Sinyo looks fresh again?' I said.

But that wasn't all. I gave him a dollar. A pure white dollar, like the sun, without fault. He accepted it shyly, nodded in thanks, silently; only:

'Babah is indeed the very best of neighbours.'

I escorted him out through all the guests. Several stopped as to ask for Maiko. Sinyo frowned and I refused them all. I accompanied him out to the yard. Only after his horse had reached the main road and turned left, did I go inside again to find Maiko.

After that I don't know what happened to Sinyo.

And below is the story I've put together from the words of Nyai and Annelies about Robert Mellema:

At two o'clock Annelies awoke from her sleep. Her temperature had subsided. She asked whether Robert had returned.

'Not yet, Ann. I don't know where he could have got to.'

Nyai was already very annoyed and angry with her son. She ordered Darsam not to leave his post. The delivery of the milk, cheese and butter to the town was handed over to other drivers. Even the supervision of work out the back was delegated to people not really ready to become foremen.

'Let me wait for him out front, Ma,' urged Annelies.

'No. Waiting inside and outside is the same. It's better in the front room with Mama.'

Nyai supported Annelies and they sat together on a chair.

And still Robert didn't come. The sound of the pendulum clock disturbed the expectant atmosphere. Every now and then Nyai checked the yard. Her eldest still hadn't appeared.

'How could this happen Ann, you falling so madly for him after just a few days. He should be the one falling madly in love with you.'

Annelies didn't answer. Mama's words seem to hurt her.

'I'll fetch some food, yes?'

'No need, Ma,' but Nyai went anyway and fetched two plates of rice, meat and vegetables, spoon and fork and drinks.

Nyai ate, spoon-feeding Annelies at the same time.

'If you don't want to chew, then just swallow,' she ordered.

And Annelies didn't chew anything, just swallowed. Still no sign of Robert.

Twice Nyai called Darsam to serve customers. And Annelies sat silently gazing into the far-off distance – very far off.

Two hours passed.

'Ah, the crazy child is back at last!' exclaimed Nyai.

Only then did Annelies focus her vision on the main road.

'Darsam!' called out Nyai from her place. When he came, she continued: 'Lock the office door. You stand here,' she pointed to the door which joined the office with the front room.

Robert rode in on his horse, calmly, unhurriedly. He stopped in front of the steps, let his horse go free without tying it up, and walked up the steps and stood before Nyai and Annelies.

Nyai raised her eyebrows when she saw her son's hair cut with the new part in the middle. She noted that he wasn't perspiring. There was no dust on him either. The horsewhip was gone. He wasn't wearing his hat. Who knows where they were.

'That part in the hair,' whispered Nyai. 'That paleness . . . she covered her mouth with her hand. 'See Ann, see what sort of brother you have. Your Papa was like this when he came home from his wanderings, just like this. That smell of perfume . . . the same. If he opens his mouth, perhaps there will be that same smell of palm-wine as five years ago . . .'

And Nyai didn't say a word to Robert.

Annelies gazed at her brother with dreamy eyes. Darsam stood silently. Seeing that no one else was beginning, the fighter from Madura ahemmed. And as if he'd received an order, Robert looked up at Darsam, then shifted his look to his mother.

'The police don't know where Minke was taken. They don't recognise that name at all.'

Nyai stood up, enraged. Her face was scarlet. Her finger pointed at her eldest son, she hissed:

'Liar!'

'I've been everywhere seeking an explanation.'

'All right, enough. You don't need to say anything. The smell on your mouth, your perfume, that hair-part . . . the same as your father five years ago and ever since. Look well, Ann, that was the beginning of your father losing all his sense of direction. Go, get out, you liar! I have no son, a cheat and liar.'

Darsam, standing before the office door, ahemmed again.

'Never forget this day, Ann. This was how your father arrived that time, and from then on I had to think of him as gone from my life. So today it is the same with your brother. He is following in the footsteps of Master." Annelies did not respond. 'So be it. So, because of this, Ann, you must be strong. You must be strong otherwise you will become a plaything, and will be played with by people like him. Stop crying. Do you want to follow your father and brother?'

'Mama, I want to be with you, Mama.'

'So don't indulge yourself. Strengthen your heart.'

Annelies was struck silent on seeing Nyai suffer her greatest disappointment.

The horse in front of the house neighed. Robert came out of his room in new clothes, neat and dashing. He walked out of the house quickly, paying no attention to his mother, sister and Darsam.

He made no attempt to tie up the horse either.

Since that day Nyai's eldest son hardly ever set foot in his family's house . . .

11

I woke up at nine o'clock in the morning with my head aching. There was something throbbing and pounding above my eyes. It was is if a *palakia* tree seed had, unbeknownst to me, penetrated through my skin, and was now growing roots in my brain in order to turn itself into a tree within my head.

And I remembered the newspaper reports hailing as the most powerful medicine discovered in the history of humanity, a medicine that would do away with headaches forever. They said the Germans had discovered it, and it was called *aspirin*. But so far it was no more than a report. It was not yet to be found in the Indies, or at least I didn't know of it. Uh, Indies, a country that can do nothing but wait upon the products of Europe!

Mrs Telinga had compressed my head several times with brown-onion vinegar. The whole room smelled of vinegar.

'Perhaps there's a letter for me, Ma'am?'

'Ha, only now Young Master asks about letters. Before, you were never interested in reading them. You've changed. Perhaps though there is one. The person was here a while ago. I said you were sleeping. I don't know his name. Perhaps he has gone. I said to him: Young Master Minke is now staying at Wonokromo, isn't he? He didn't seem to take any notice, but rather took leave to visit next door for a moment, to Marais's house.'

The boarding-house was still. The other boarders had all left for school.

And that good-hearted woman pulled the table over close to my bed, then put some hot chocolate and cakes on it. I mean by cakes: fried coconut patties.

'What would Young Master like to eat today?'

'Does Ma'am have shopping money?'

'If I run out, I can always ask Young Master for more, yes?'

'Perhaps a police agent has recently been here asking about me?'

'There was somebody. Not a police agent. A young man of Young Master's age. I thought he was a friend of yours, so I told him what had happened.'

'Indo? Pure European or Native?'

'Native.'

I didn't question her further. I reckoned he was none other than that same police agent.

'So what will Young Master eat tonight?'

'Macaroni soup, Ma'am.'

'Good. This is the first time you've wanted macaroni soup. So you know how much one packet costs? Five cents, Young Master. So . . .'

'Two packets will be enough no doubt.'

She laughed, relaxing when she received the shopping money of fifteen cents, then rushed hurriedly back to her kingdom: the kitchen.

That morning everything was still. Occasionally the bell of a passing buggy could be heard. It was only within my mind that there was great activity: murderers and future murderers formed long lines with all sorts of faces, all sorts of figures, even Magda Peters appeared with a threatening, unsheathed dagger. Magda Peters – my favourite teacher! It was as if I had gone mad, just because of what someone had said. Come on, I shouldn't be so afraid of something whose truth and real context are so uncertain? I, an educated person? Even if the report was true, is it proper that I surrender to this accursed fear?

You will have suffered twice, Minke, if this report turns out to be true. First of all, you're already afraid. Secondly, you'll be killed. It's enough to suffer once, Minke. Once is enough. Get up then. Why must you suffer twice? You're too stupid to be called educated.

These thoughts made me laugh at myself. So I got up from the bed, stood tottering for a second and started walking to the back of the house. Everything seemed to be moving. I grabbed for the back of a chair. I got my vision under control again and left the room. I didn't end up going out to the back but sat in the front room and began to try to read the newspapers.

My headache subsided somewhat but the smell of the onion vinegar continued to be a real annoyance.

A pampered body, I said to myself.

Finally I did go out the back and had a hot bath despite the protests of the garrulous Mrs Telinga. How fond she was of me, that sterile lady. She was an Indo who was more Native than European, without a single remaining trace of beauty, fat like a pillow. Even though her Dutch was terrible, it was still her day-to-day language; it was the language used by her family. She had never set foot in a school: illiterate. Her adopted child was a male mongrel dog. It was very clever at stealing fish from the market, which it would do two or three times a day. It brought the fish home to its adopted mother. She would grill it for the dog. After eating, the dog would go to sleep in the middle of the door only then to wake up and set off to steal again. This adopted child never barked at strangers, but would look them over with slowly blinking eyes as if waiting to be barked at first.

After getting dressed and combing my hair, I went to Jean Marais's house. The picture of May's mother fighting the soldier wasn't finished. He was putting an all-out effort into it. He wanted it to be his best work.

May sat on his lap enjoying being spoiled. She had missed me over the last few days. I usually brought her some sweets. This time there wasn't anything in my pockets.

'We're not going for a walk, Uncle?'

'I'm not feeling well, May.'

'You're pale, Minke,' Jean Marais admonished me.

'I didn't notice,' May said, using French too; then she got up from her father's lap and looked at me. 'Yes, Uncle, you're pale.'

'Not enough sleep,' I answered.

'Since you moved to Wonokromo all sorts of things have been happening to you, Minke,' Jean reprimanded. 'And you haven't been out looking for any new orders since then either.'

'If you knew what I've been through recently, Jean, you wouldn't be able to bring yourself to talk like that. Truly.'

'You're in trouble again,' he accused. 'Your eyes aren't calm as they usually are.'

'Come on, can you really know what's happened to somebody from their eyes?'

'May, buy some cigarettes for me, please.'

And the little girl went outside.

'Nah! Minke! tell me what troubles you now.'

Naturally I told him of my suspicions about Fatso. That I felt there was somebody waiting for the opportunity to kill me (and there is only one of me!). That I felt that everywhere there were people spying on me, ready to swing their machetes into action against my body.

'Just as I expected. This, of course, is the risk you face when you go to live in the house of a *nyai*. You once joined in condemning the *nyai*s and their morality. And what did I say? Don't sit in judgement over something about whose truth you are uncertain. I suggested you visit there two or three times, to observe things as an educated person.'

'I remember, Jean.'

'Nah, you have been there. But you didn't just visit, you stayed.'

'Yes.'

'You lived there not just to investigate how the common view of *nyai*s matches with reality; you decided to act out that common view yourself – dragged down to a low and unpraiseworthy level of moral behaviour. Then you receive threats, who knows from whom. No doubt from that quarter with the most at stake: and who you have now challenged. Now you fear someone is out to get you, Minke. But it is your own guilt that is pursuing you.'

'What else, Jean.'

'Am I wrong?'

'It's very possible you are right.'

'Why only possible?'

'That is, if it were true I had acted in the unpraiseworthy manner you imply.'

'So you haven't?'

'No, not at all.'

'At the very least I'm happy to hear that, Minke, my friend.'

'And it's also clear that Nyai is no ordinary woman. She is educated, Jean. I think she's the first educated Native woman I have met in my life. Wonderful, Jean. Some day I'll take you there to meet her. We'll take May. She'd like it very much there. Truly.'

'So why does someone want to kill you if you have done nothing wrong? You're educated, try to be true to your conscience. You are among the first of the educated Natives. Much is demanded of you. And if you can't deliver, the educated Natives after you will grow up more rotten than you yourself.'

'Quiet, Jean. Don't talk such nonsense. I'm in trouble.'

'It's only your imagination.'

May returned with a packet of corn-leaf cigarettes and Jean quickly started smoking.

'You smoke too much, Jean.'

He only laughed. On that day my French friend did not make me happy at all. He was wrong. And I was being reproached with unfounded allegations. Father too had made similar accusations at the beginning of our meeting. Now Jean Marais seemed not to believe the truth of what I was saying: he too, in the end, suffered the old prejudices. He thought I'd been defeated, dragged down to unpraiseworthy behaviour. It felt as if there was no use in continuing the conversation.

I took May's hand and we went home together. We sat on the long bench on the front porch.

'Why don't you go to school, May?'

'Papa likes me to wait on him while he paints.'

'So what else do you do?'

'Watch Papa paint, just watch.'

'He doesn't talk to you?'

'Of course he does. He said that under that clump of bamboo it should be cool because the wind whistled through all the time. But that poor person being stamped on by the soldier, Uncle!?'

She didn't know that the woman being trodden upon was her own mother.

'Come on, May, sing!' and the child straight away started into singing her favourite song. 'A French one, May. I already know all the Dutch songs.'

'French?' she tried to remember. Then: *'Ran, ran pata plan! Ran, plan, plan,'* from *Joli Tambour*. 'You're not listening, heh Uncle, come on!'

My eyes were observing a fat man wearing a *sarong* and sitting under a tamarind tree on the other side of the road, next to a chillied-fruit seller.

He wore a *peci*, but wasn't wearing sandals, let alone shoes. His shirt was from calico, and he wore loose, black trousers and a wide, leather belt. His shirt was unbuttoned. His figure and skin and his narrow, slanted eyes meant he could not fool me. Perhaps he was to be my future murderer. Fatso! Robert's man, now that he had failed in enlisting Darsam.

Every now and then, while eating his fruit, he glanced over at the two of us.

'Call Papa, May.'

The little girl ran off. And Jean appeared with his tall, thin body, walking lamely on his armpit crutch. He sat down beside me.

'I don't think I'm wrong, Jean, that's the one. He followed me from B—. Only his clothes are different now.'

'Ssst. It's just your own imagination, Minke,' he scolded me instead.

Just at that moment Mr Telinga arrived, who knows from where. In one hand he was carrying a basket – who knows what its contents were – and in the other hand he held a metre of steel pipe, obtained from who knows where.

'*Daag*, Jean, Minke, what's going on? You two sitting out here together so early in the morning?,' he greeted us in Malay.

'It's like this,' Jean Marais began the story about my fears. Then he pointed with his chin to the man I reckoned was Fatso.

The new arrival put his basket down on the ground: it proved to be full of young *kedondong* fruit. The steel pipe remained in his hand. His wild eyes were aimed across the road.

'Let me have a close-up look. Come on, Minke, you're the one who knows him. Perhaps it is him. Let me bash in his head if needs be.' I walked along behind him and Jean Marais followed us, limping.

It became clearer as we approached that it was Fatso. He was no doubt spying on me that very moment. And he was pretending not to notice us coming closer. He went on enjoying his fruit, thought I could see his eyes glance about vigilantly. That he was disguised only strengthened my suspicions.

'It's him all right,' I said without hesitation.

Telinga approached him threateningly. And with the steel pipe still in his hand. I myself no longer knew what I wanted to do. Jean Marais was still limping along behind us.

'Heh, Man,' Telinga snapped in Javanese, 'are you spying on my house?'

Fatso pretended not to hear and continued eating.

'So you're pretending not to hear, ya?' snapped the pensioned Indies army soldier, this time in Malay. He grabbed the plate of fruit and threw it on the ground.

It appeared that Fatso was not scared of Indos. He stood up, wiped his chilli-paste-covered hand on a piece of tamarind trunk bark, swallowed down the remains of his fruit, bent over and washed his hands in the fruit-salad seller's bucket of water and only then spoke, calmly, in High Javanese:

'I am not spying on anything or anyone,' he tried to glance across at me and smiled.

What did he think he was doing? The impudence! He smiled at me. My future murderer! He smiled.

'Go from here,' shouted Telinga.

The fruit seller, an old woman, frightened, moved away. Some distance away people began to congregate, no doubt curious to know why a Native dared confront an Indo European.

'I eat here almost every day, Ndoro Tuan.'

'I've never seen you. Go! If not . . .' he swung the steel pipe about.

And Fatso was still not frightened. He didn't lift up his head and just bowed, with eyes vigilant:

'There has never been any ban on eating here, Ndoro Tuan,' he retorted.

'You dare argue back? Don't you know I'm Dutch and was in the Indies army?'

Fatso was no doubt a fighter. He wasn't afraid of an Indies army Dutchman. Perhaps he was a *silat* fighter, or *kuntow* expert.

'Even so, there is no police ban. There has not been any public announcement of any ban, Ndoro Tuan. Allow me to just sit here and eat my fruit. I haven't paid yet, either,' and he was about to sit down again.

I became suspicious when I heard him talk about bans. He knew about regulations. Telinga must be more careful. But the former Indies army soldier, who only knew of violence, had already swung his arm, striking towards the side of Fatso's head. Fatso parried the blow, but did not return the attack.

'Enough, enough,' Jean Marais tried to intervene.

'Don't keep on, Ndoro Tuan,' appealed Fatso.

Telinga lost his temper: this person dared defy him! He no longer cared who Fatso was! His pride had been wounded. And his right hand swung a death blow down towards Fatso's head. And the rebel calmly moved out of its way. Telinga was thrown forward by his own blow as it missed its target. In fact Fatso could have easily punched Telinga in the ribs, but he didn't. Each time Fatso successfully avoided Telinga's blows, Telinga become angrier and he attacked again and again. Fatso retreated, then retreated a little more, and then ran off. Telinga chased after him. Fatso disappeared down a narrow alley, where there were heaps of rubbish piled up.

'Telinga's crazy!' frowned Jean Marais, 'he thinks he's still in the army.'

And the person Jean was frowing at went off hunting after Fatso, and disappeared down the same alley.

'What's all this in aid of? Come on, let's go home, Minke. You're the cause of all this,' he blamed me.

140

He wouldn't let me support him. May and Mrs Telinga rushed about asking us what was happening. No one would tell them. The two of us sat and waited for the hothead to return. Anxiously, of course.

Ten minutes later, Mr Telinga returned, bathed in sweat, red-faced and short of breath. He threw himself down into a canvas deck chair.

'Jan,' his wife complained, 'what's wrong with you? Have you forgotten that you're an invalid? Looking for enemies? Do you think you're still young?' she approached her husband, seized the pipe from his hand, and took it inside.

Mr Telinga didn't speak. It was as if there was a secret agreement between us. And no one regretted all that had happened more than myself. Within my heart I thanked God that no catastrophe had eventuated. And I felt it was fortunate that I hadn't told them Darsam's story. I would have really been blamed for everything then.

'Young Master is still ill,' called out Mrs Telinga from inside, 'don't sit outside in the breeze. It's better you get some sleep. Food will be ready in a little while.'

'Go home, May,' ordered Jean, and May went home.

The three of us sat silently until Telinga had got his breath back.

'Let's forget everything that has happened,' I proposed. Uh! What if the police became involved. Uh! I'd truly be the shameful cause of it all. 'My head is aching again, Jean. Excuse me Mr Telinga, Jean . . .'

Once in my room I became even more convinced: it had been Fatso and he had been spying on me. He was obviously one of Robert's men. Darsam's story could not be dismissed as nonsense. Be careful, Minke!

For the first time ever, I locked my door while it was daylight. Also the windows. I got ready a hard wooden stick, formerly a mop handle, ready in a corner. I could grab it at any moment. Even if only at a basic level, goat-class, we say in Malay, I too had studied self-defence when I was in T—.

Being an educated person, there was something I had to accept: someone wanted to take my life, but I could not report it to the police. It would be unwise to involve Nyai and Annelies or Father who had just been made a bupati or, most of all, Mother. I had to face all this silently, but with vigilance.

Four days passed and my headache still did not disappear. I certainly wasn't getting enough sleep. And every day milk arrived. But there was no news from Darsam . . .

I had been away from school too long. The doctor had given me a certificate to stay away three weeks. The palakia seed had grown into a full-grown tree inside my head, without permission from its one and only legitimate owner, me. You're right, palakia tree in my head, I have to forget Nyai and Annelies. I must cut all relations with them! There is no point in maintaining relations. Only trouble will come of them. My life would suffer no great loss. I would not catch leprosy by not knowing this strange and forbidding family. I must become well again. Go after orders as before. Write for the papers. Graduate from school as was hoped for by so many people. Whatever else, I still liked school. To mix openly with all my friends. To be free. Obtaining new, unlimited knowledge and learning. And: absorbing everything from this earth of mankind, from the past, the present and the future. At then end of next month, Magda Peters was going to hold discussions, lighting up this earth of mankind from every possible angle. And I was ill like this.

I had wasted these emergency holidays: A clot of time packed with tension. Sometimes I thought: should someone as young as I be with tension such as this? Sometimes I replied: no, not yet. Miss Magda once told us the story of Multatuli and his friend, the poet-journalist Roorda van Eysinga: they lived in tension because of their beliefs and their struggles to improve the fate of the people of the Indies. Against both all-European and all-Native oppression. For the sake of the peoples of the Indies, who knew nothing of the world, those two ended up in exile, without comrades who visited them, without a single hand stretched out in aid, Minke . . . Read Roorda van Eysinga's poem, written under the pseudonym Sentot, *The Last Days of the Hollanders in Java*. Every word was filled with the tension of somebody calling out in warning.

Multatuli and van Eysinga came under great pressure because of profound actions. And the pressure that I was under today? Nothing more than the result of the stumblings of a philogynist. I must let go of Annelies. I must and must be able to do it! But I still couldn't convince myself. A maiden as beautiful as that! And Nyai – such an inspiring and impressive character – a regal woman of great powers of bewitchment. Yes, yes: 'If attracted, no limits to one's praise; if hated, no limits to one's finding fault.'

Slowly but surely I began to understand: all this was the result of my reluctance to pay the price of entering the world of pleasure, the world where dreams become reality. Multatuli and van Eysinga paid the price but they wanted nothing for themselves. What do my writings mean compared to theirs? Everything I hope and lust after is for myself. The thought shamed me.

Yes, I must let go of Annelies. Adieu, ma belle! Happy separation, oh dream, which I'll never meet again, not at any time nor in any place. There are things more important than a maiden's beauty and a Nyai's charisma. There is no point to a meaningless death. And my life, and my body, are my basic capital and the only ones I have.

This decision chased away the headache. Though not all at once. That's how all illness develops: it comes on suddenly, but disappears lazily. The *palakia* tree stopped spreading its roots and seedlings. Then they too died but only because of the arrival of a letter: from Miriam de la Croix. Her writing was fine and small, neat.

142

She wrote:

My friend, You have no doubt arrived in Surabaya safely by now. I've waited for news from you but none has arrived. So it is I who give in.

Don't be surprised, but Papa is very interested in you. He's already asked twice whether there have been any letters. Papa wants very much to know how you're progressing. He was impressed by your attitudes. You, he said, were a different type of Javanese, made from different material, a pioneer and innovator at one and the same time.

I write this letter gladly. Indeed, I feel honoured that I am able to pass on Papa's opinions. Mir, Sarah, he said to us another time, that will be the face of Java in the future, a Java which has absorbed itself into our civilisation, no longer shrivelling up like a worm struck by the sun. Excuse him, Minke, if Papa uses such a coarse metaphor. He does not intend to insult. You're not angry are you? Don't be angry, my friend. Neither Papa nor the two of us have any evil thoughts towards Natives and especially not towards yourself.

Papa feels moved when he sees how the Javanese people have fallen so low. Listen to what Papa has also said, even though he still uses that earlier coarse metaphor: Do you know what is needed by this nation of worms? A leader who can give them dignity once again. Do you follow me, my friend? Don't get angry before you know what I mean.

Not all Europeans have been participants in, and causes of the fall of your people. Papa, for example, even though he is an assistant resident, is not one of them. Indeed, he is unable to do anything, just as Sarah and I are also unable to do anything, though we all desire so greatly to stretch out our hands to help. We can only guess now at what we must do. You yourself are fond of Multatuli, aren't you? Nah, that writer, so glorified by the radicals, had indeed been of great service to your people. Yes, Multatuli, as well as Domine Baron von Hoëvell and another person also, who your teacher perhaps forgot to tell you about, that is, Roorda van Eysinga. But all these people never spoke to the Javanese, only to their own people, the Dutch. They asked Europe to treat your people properly.

My friend,

But now, says Papa, at the close of the nineteenth century, nothing that they did is of use today. According to Papa, it is the Natives themselves who must now act. So when we talked about Dr Snouck Hurgronje that day, it was no coincidence. That particular scholar holds an honoured place in the thinking of our family. We praise Association, at which you laughed that day. So please understand, my friend, why Papa is so interested in you. Indeed, Papa, and the two of us too, had never met a Javanese like you. You, he said, were totally European. You showed no sign of the slave mentality that the Javanese developed during the era of their defeat, from the time the Europeans set foot on this, the land of your birth.

On those still nights in this big and empty building, if Papa is not tired, we like so much to sit and listen to his explanations about the fate of your people.

How they gave birth to hundreds and thousands of leaders and heroes in their struggle, against European oppression. One by one they fell, defeated, killed, surrendering, gone mad, dying in humiliation, forgotten in exile. Not one was every victorious in war. We listened and were moved, and became angry also to hear how your rulers sold concessions to the Company, benefiting no one but themselves. It was a sign that their character and souls were being corroded. Your heroes, according to Papa's stories, always emerged out of a background of selling concessions to the Company; and so it was over and over again, for centuries, and no one understood that it was all a repetition of what had gone before, and that as time went on the rebellions all became smaller and more and more stunted. And such is the fate of a people who have thrown all their body and soul and all their material wealth into saving a single abstract concept called honour.

According to Papa, the fate of humanity now and in the future is dependent on its mastery over science and learning. All humanity, both as individuals and as peoples, will come tumbling down without such mastery. To oppose those who have mastered science and learning is to surrender oneself to humiliation and death.

So Papa agrees with Association. That is the one and only road for Natives. He hopes, and so too do both of us, that one day in the future you will sit together, as an equal with Europeans, in advancing this people and this country. You have already begun this yourself. You understand what I mean. We love our father very much. He is not simply a father, but also a teacher who leads us in our efforts to see and understand the world. He is a friend, a mature man with great authority, an administrator who hopes for no profit from the woes and tribulations of those under him.

Let me tell you what he said after you left us following that first visit. You left feeling angry and irritated, didn't you? We could understand because we knew that you didn't understand our intentions. Papa left us alone on purpose, so you could speak freely with us. But a pity, you were so formal and tense. As soon as you left, Papa asked us our opinion of you. Sarah reported: Minke became angry in the end, Dr Snouck Hurgronje and his Association Theory were three hundred years behind the times; repeated just as you had said. Papa was surprised and had to ask me to explain further. Then Papa said: He is proud to be a Javanese, and that is good as long as he has self-respect as an individual as well as a child of his race. He mustn't become like the general run of his people; when among themselves they feel as if they are from a race which has no equal on the earth. But as soon as they are near a European, even just one, they shrivel up, lacking the courage even to lift up their eyes. I agree with this praise of you, my friend. May things go well for you.

Then from the wayang-orang building, gamelan music began to waft across to us. Papa had ordered us to study your people's music. You have studied gamelan for a long time now, he said to us, and perhaps you can already enjoy it. Listen to how all the tones wait upon the sound of the gong. That is how it is in Javanese music, but that is not how it is in real life, because this pathetic people has still not found their gong, a leader, a thinker, who can come forth with words of resolution.

My friend, I ask with all my heart that you try to understand these words which you will obtain nowhere else except from my father, not even from the great scholar Snouck Hurgronje. That is why we are so proud to have a father like him. Papa is sure that the reason you like gamelan better than European music is because you were born and brought up under the swaying sounds of your great gamelan.

Minke, my friend, when will Life's gong sound? Will you perhaps be the one? The great gong? May we pray for you?

Listen again to the gamelan, said Papa once more. It has been that way for centuries. And the gong in the life of the Javanese has still not arrived. The gamelan sings of a people's longing for a Messiah. Just longing after him, not seeking him out, not giving birth to him. The gamelan translates the life of the Javanese, a people who are unwilling to seek, to search, who just circle around, repeating, as in prayers and mantras, suppressing, killing thought, carrying people into a dispirited universe, which leads them astray, where there is no character. Those are the views of Europeans, my friend. No Javanese, not one, would think like that. Papa also says that if things remain like this for another twenty years this people will never find their Messiah.

Aduh! my friend, what will your so-saddening-a-people look like twenty years from now? One day, in the future, we will go home to the Netherlands. I will go into politics, Minke. It's a pity though that the Netherlands still doesn't allow a woman to sit in the Lower House. I have a dream, my friend, that one day, when it is no longer as it is now and I can become an Honourable Member of the Lower House, I will speak much about your country and your people. And when I return to Java I will, first of all, listen once again to your gamelan, a gamelan whose beautiful unity of sound has no equal on earth. If its theme is just the same, a longing without effort, it means no Messiah has yet arrived or has yet been born. It also means: you have not yet emerged as a gong, or indeed no Javanese ever will, and your people will drown forever in the overflow of repeated tones and vicious circles. If change has taken place, I will seek you out, and hold out my hand in respect.

Friend, twenty years! That is such a very long time in this pounding, racing era; and it is, of course, also a long time if looked at as part of somebody's life. Nah! my friend Minke, this is the first letter from your sincere and well-wishing friend: Miriam de la Croix.

As I folded up the letter I knew that tears had left blue smudges here and there, where the ink had run. Why had a letter from a girl who I had met only twice in my life made me cry? She was neither kith nor kin, not even of the same race. She had such hopes for me. While there I was totally confused because of my recent mistakes at Wonokromo. She wants me to be of value to my own people, not to her people. Is it possible there is now a new style of Multatuli and van Eysinga?

How should such a beautiful letter be answered? And I had begun to consider myself a writer and had been praised by Mr Maarten Nijman, Chief Editor of *S.N. v/d D.!* I felt too small to be able to equal Miriam's thoughts. Yet I still forced myself to answer. Thank you, and no more than thank you poured out in so very many words, perhaps just like the pouring out of Javanese musical tones that separately headed for and waited upon the gong. In the letter I stated my astonishment that Multatuli and Eysinga, who I had just been thinking about, should be mentioned in her letter. Perhaps, I wrote, because we live in the same liberal era, in the same era, and I ended my letter with:

My good friend Miriam, I am so lucky to have found a friend such as you. I do not know what is going to happen in the next twenty years. I myself have never felt that I would ever become a gong. Neither had I ever dreamed of being even a drum; I have never had such thoughts, perhaps would never have had such thoughts had your beautiful and moving letter not arrived. Especially as it has come from someone who is not of my people. Peace and well being be with you, my sincere Miriam. May you indeed one day become an Honourable Member of the Lower House.

I rested my face on the table. I tried to absorb up all of Miriam's letter, trying to ensure I would never forget it as long as I lived. Friendship is indeed beautiful. And my headache slipped away and slipped away, and then disappeared altogether, who knows to where. Miriam, you did not just send a letter. More than that: a charm to rid me of tension. If only you knew: suddenly I felt brave, and the world became brighter and clearer. Become a gong! to be heard booming out everywhere.

'Young Master!' I raised my head. On seeing the person in front of me the *palakia* in my head returned, spreading its roots and seedlings. But now more vigorously. Him: Darsam!

'Excuse me, Young Master. I must have surprised you, you're so pale.'

I tried to put on a smile, my eyes darting to his machete and his hands. He laughed in a friendly manner while stroking his moustache.

'Young Master suspects me,' he said, 'when Darsam is Young Master's friend.'

'So what's the matter?' I asked pretending not to know anything.

'A letter from Nyai, Noni is very ill.'

I started and my eyes opened wide. He stood across from me. I read the letter while every now and then glancing across at his machete and his hand. Yes, it was true, Annelies was very ill and was being looked after by Dr Martinet. Nyai had told him of the origins of her illness, and she requested very strongly that I come quickly as was also advised by the doctor. Dr Martinet said that without my presence Annelies had no hope of recovery, and her illness would probably get worse and there would be complications.

'Come, Young Master, to Wonokromo, now.'

My head throbbed as if it wanted to break open. I couldn't stand up straight, my body went flabby. I quickly grabbed for the corner of the table. With my shaky vision I gazed at the fighter. Darsam grabbed me by the shoulder.

'Don't be concerned. Sinyo Robert will not be able to worry you. Darsam still stands vigilant. Come.'

Miriam de la Croix vanished, evaporated into smoke, disappeared from circulation. The magical power of Wonokromo had regained control over everything. Aided by Darsam, these legs of mine carried me to the buggy waiting in front of the house.

'You're not going to take leave from the people here?'

My steps came to a halt. I called out to Mrs Telinga that I was excusing myself and was leaving. She stood at the door and did not at all seem happy.

'Don't be away long, Young Master,' she reminded me. 'Your health.'

'Young Master will recover quickly at Wonokromo,' answered Darsam.

Afraid of Darsam's frightening appearance, she didn't say anything more.

'Where are your things, Young Master?'

I didn't answer. And I never found out whether I fainted in the buggy or not. All I knew was that all this had occurred as a result of Robert Suurhof's invitation: and now so many people had become involved and this young life of mine had become so tense. And all the time I heard just one voice, one sentence emerging from out of the Madurese fighter's mouth: 'This *dokar* and this horse are henceforth Young Master's property.'

12

As soon as Darsam led me up the stairs, Nyai Ontosoroh came rushing out to greet me:

'You've gone too far, Nyo, we've been waiting and waiting so long for you. Annelies has fallen very ill longing for you!'

'Young Master was also ill, Nyai, I had to carry him here.'

'No matter. If the two of them get together again, everything will be all right. The sickness will disappear.'

Those words were so embarrassing, yet it already felt like they had started to work as an antitoxin dissolving away the *palakia* in my head. Nyai caught me by the shoulder, and whispered softly in my ear, smiling.

'Yes, your temperature is a bit high. No matter. Let's go upstairs, Child. Your little sister has had to wait too long. You didn't even send news.'

She spoke so gently, it went straight to my heart. It was as if she was my own mother, my beloved mother, and I no other than her little boy, under her guidance. Yet my eyes kept glancing about here and there. At any moment Robert could leap out of the darkness and thrust a knife into me with those mighty muscles of his.

'Where is Robert, Ma?' I asked, as we climbed the stairs.

'Sst. You don't need ask that. He's his father's son.'

Why did I become so malleable in the hands of this woman? Like a clot of clay that could be moulded just as she wished? Why was there no fight in me? Even the will to fight was missing. As if she understood and had mastery over my inner self, and could lead me in the direction I myself desired?

The upstairs was far more luxurious. Almost all the walls of the corridor were covered with carpet. It felt as if I was a cat, who could walk along without making a single sound. The open windows manipulated views that stretched far away out there into the distance. Paddy and fields and forest spread out everywhere, joined together one after the other. A small group of people were collecting the last of the harvest. The remaining paddy was still fallow, awaiting the beginning of the end of autumn.

The newspapers reported that there had been an abundant harvest that year. There was no need to import low-quality rice from Siam, even though the most fertile rice lands of east and central Java were, to all intents and purposes, producing only sugar. It was a sign, said one observer, that Queen Wilhelmina had been blessed by God as the youngest queen ever, at an age very young for a queen.

We stood in front of the bed. Nyai fixed the blanket that lay over Annelies. That maiden's breasts stood out underneath the blanket. And Nyai put her daughter's hand into mine.

'Annelies, darling.'

With great effort the girl opened her eyes. She didn't turn. She didn't look. Her eyes, and that effort-filled look, were swept up to the ceiling, then they closed again.

'Minke. Nyo, Child, take care of my sweetheart here,' whispered Nyai. 'If you too are sick, then get well now. Carry my child to recovery with you,' it sounded as if she was praying.

She looked at me with almost begging eyes.

'It's up to you, Child. As long as my daughter recovers . . . You're educated. You know what I mean,' she bowed down as if embarrassed to look at me. Her two hands held my arm. All of a sudden she turned and left the room.

I groped for Annelies's hands under the blanket. Cold. I neared my mouth to her ears and called and called her name, slowly. She smiled, but her eyes remained closed. Her temperature was not too high. And I knew then: the *palakia* inside my head had been flung out, plucked out with all its roots and seeds, crashing down to who knows where.

And she was so close to me. My heart began to pound rapidly, pumping hot blood all over my body and I began to perspire.

'Come on, haven't you been waiting for Minke to come?'

I didn't know whether it was just my imagination, or if it really happened, but I saw her nod weakly. Her eyes remained closed. Also her mouth.

'Do you miss him, Ann? Of course, you miss him. He misses you too. Truly. If you only knew how much he longs to be always near you, Ann, to make you the adornment of his life, all the world would then be his, because his happiness is you, you alone. Open your eyes, Ann, because Minke is here now, with you.'

I heard Annelies sigh. Her eyes remained closed. Also her lips.

Doesn't this girl recognise my voice anymore? So I caressed her face, her cheeks, her hair. She tilted her head and sighed once more. Was she going to die? A maiden as beautiful as this? I embraced her and I kissed her on her lips. The beat of the heart in her breast seemed too slow. Her fingers moved slowly, almost stilled.

'Ann, Annelies!' I finally cried into her ears. 'Wake up, Ann,' and I shook her shoulders.

She opened her eyes. Her eyes stared far into the distance, not seeing, and not reaching my face.

'Don't you know me any more, Ann? Me? Minke?'

She smiled. But she still stared right throught me.

'Ann, Ann, don't be like this. Aren't you happy now Minke is back? I've come. Or must I go again and leave you? Ann, Ann, my Annelies!'

She must not die here in my embrace. I stood before the bed and wiped sweat from my dripping forehead.

'Keep going, Nyo,' Nyai encouraged me from the door. 'Keep asking her to talk. That's exactly what Dr Martinet advised.'

I turned. Nyai was pulling the door shut from outside. Her encouragement calmed my anxiety. Annelies was not facing death. She just wasn't conscious.

I sat on the edge of the bed. Her eyes were open but she didn't see anything.

'You can't go on like this, Ann,' I said, trying to convince myself as well. I pulled back her blanket. I pulled her up by her two hands. I forced her to sit up. But her body was so weak it fell back upon the pillow as soon as I let go of her. I tried again. She still couldn't sit up.

What must I do now?

Once again I kissed her upon her lips. Her hands began to move almost imperceptibly, but a little more than they had done a minute ago. I shifted her neck across to my left arm. I began again to try to get her to talk:

'If you're sick like this, who'll help Mama? There is no one else. So you mustn't be ill. You must get better. So that you can work, and go walking with me. We can go riding, Ann, all around Surabaya.'

I looked into her eyes, which stared off into the distance and I could see myself in the depth of her eyes. But she still didn't see me. For a moment I thought my face was not even reflected in her eyes.

Nyai Ontosoroh came back, carrying two glasses of warm milk. One glass she put on the table. The other she brought over to me and she put it up to my lips so that I would drink it down quickly.

'Drink it all up, Nyo, Child, Minke,' I drank until it was finished and the glass was dry. 'You must be healthy and strong too. A weak and ill person is of no use to anybody.' Then to Annelies: 'Wake up, Ann, Minke is here with you now. Who else are you waiting for?'

Without waiting to see whether there was any reaction from Annelies, she left again.

There had been no change in the situation the next time Nyai returned, but this time she came with Dr Martinet. I put Annelies's head down on the pillow, in order to be able to greet him.

'This is Minke, Doctor, who has been looking after Annelies today,' and we shook hands. Nyai's eyes observed us for a moment, then she continued, 'Excuse me, I must go downstairs.'

'So you are Mr Minke, the HBS student? Excellent. Happy is any young man who obtains so deep a love from so beautiful a maiden,' he said in mumbled Dutch.

'I have only been here an hour, Doctor. This was how Annelies was when I arrived. I'm worried, Doctor . . .'

The forty-year-old man let go a laugh, shook his head and shook my shoulders.

'You like this girl? Answer frankly.'

'Yes, I do, Doctor.'

'You have no intention of playing foul with her, eh?' he fixed his gaze squarely upon me.

'Why would I do that?'

'Why? Because HBS students have always been the favourites of the girls. It has always been like that, ever since the schools were founded. In Batavia too, and Semarang also. I repeat, Mr Minke, you have only honourable intentions?' Seeing that I remained quiet, he went on: 'There is only one thing needed by this girl: you, Mr Minke. She has everything she needs, except you.'

I bowed my head. Confusion ran amok within my breast. I had no intention of manipulating Annelies. But neither had I ever intended becoming serious about any girl. Now Annelies wanted all of me, totally, for herself.. Truly: I was being tested by my own deeds. And it was my conscience that made me affirm things of which I was not yet really convinced.

'You want her to regain consciousness?'

'Of course, Doctor, I would like it very much, and would be very grateful if you make her better.'

'She will regain consciousness. I have been drugging her and waiting for you to arrive. So it is your fault that she has been drugged for so long. If I had left her conscious without you here, there is no telling what would have happened. If you hadn't come back and I was forced to keep her drugged, it would have damaged her heart. It all comes back to you – you are the cause of it all.'

'Forgive me.'

'She has chosen you to be the one to accept all the risks.'

I didn't respond. And he kept talking. Then:

'She will be conscious again soon. About another quarter of an hour. When she starts showing signs of waking, you must begin talking to her, just pleasant, happy things. Don't speak harshly or roughly. Everything depends on you. Don't disappoint her. Don't make her lose confidence or become afraid.'

'Very well, Doctor.'

'You passed this year's exams?'

'Yes, Doctor.'

'Congratulations. Wait on her until the drugs wear off. What is your family name, if I may ask?'

'I have none, Doctor.'

He ahemmed without swallowing. His eyes swept over my face. Just for a moment. Then he went over to the window, and looked out onto the fields and the garden beside the house.

'Come over here,' he invited without turning.

And I stood beside him by the window.

'Why do you hide your family name?'

'I don't have one.'

'What is your Christian name?'

'I don't have one, Doctor.'

'How is it possible that you're in the HBS and have neither family nor Christian name? You don't mean to tell me that you're a Native?'

'Yes, I'm a Native, Doctor.'

He glanced at me. He stood silently for quite a while. Perhaps trying to convince his own heart of something.

'One more question if I may. Do you feel you can remain friendly and sincere with Annelies?'

'Of course.'

'Forever.'

'Why, Doctor?'

'Pity on this child. She cannot face violence, or harshness. She dreams of someone who will love her, who will give her pure love. She feels like she is living alone, by herself, without knowing the world. She has put all her hopes for the future in you, Mr Minke.'

He was no doubt exaggerating. So:

'She has a mother who guides her, educates her, who loves her.'

'She doesn't fully believe that her mother's love will last. She waits in anticipation for that moment when her mother will explode and reject her.'

'Hmmm. Mama is a very wise woman, Doctor.'

'That cannot be denied. But Annelies cannot convince herself of that. Possibly, secretly, Annelies sees her mother as being more attached to the business than to her. This is just between the two of us. No one else need know of this conversation. You understand.'

He was silent again for quite a while. Suddenly:

'So you understand?'

'I think so.'

'There must not be any hard, harsh, disappointing words. She loves you. I speak to you like this, first of all, because Native men are not used to treating their women gently and politely, as friends and with sincerity. At least as far as I know, according to what I've heard and read. You have studied European civilisation, so you no doubt know the difference between the attitudes of European and Native men towards women. If you are the same as most other Natives, this child will not live long. Quite frankly she could fall into a living death. If it came about, if, I say, you married her, would you take a second woman at some later stage?'

'Marry her?'

'Yes, that is what she dreams of. That you will marry her, yes? You're in your last year at school, aren't you?'

'I've no desire to propose yet, Doctor.'

'If necessary I will propose on your behalf in order to save this girl.'

I couldn't say anything.

'So you will marry her and will not take a second woman,' he put out his hand to obtain the certainty of a promise from my lips.

I took his hand. I had never intended to take more than one wife. I always remembered the words of my grandmother: every man who takes more than one wife is a liar, and will certainly become a liar whether he wants to or not.

'Her heart is too soft, too gentle. She can't cope with hurt. You must always humour, caress, protect her. It seems her self has been taken from her.'

'Taken from her?'

'By someone very close to her.'

'Who, Doctor?'

'I don't know. You will find out for yourself. Something around here, for certain. There are many secret, suppressed problems within her young heart. She lives, in fact, as an orphan. She feels permanently dependent. Even here in her own private world, there is no-one she can rely on. She needs someone who will support her. Having grown up in the middle of wealth, she doesn't appreciate the security it gives. For her, wealth is nothing. That is what I can understand about this child. You're listening, yes?'

Dr Martinet took his monocle out of his top pocket and put it in his right eye. After looking at his watch, he stared at me.

'Thank you for listening so earnestly. Look at the calm and peaceful view from here. It is lucky that this girl lives in the middle of luxury and peace. I don't know what would happen otherwise.'

The *palakia* seed in my head was replaced by another type of seed: suspicion: what did the doctor really mean?

'Excuse me. I'm not a psychologist. I've spoken a lot with her mother – an amazing woman. She is a mature and civilised person. She has real strength of character, reinforced by the hardness of someone with revenge still in their heart. Just for her, as a woman, to be so educated, is extraordinary. Even in Europe it would be an astounding feat. I don't think she has developed in this way consciously. One or indeed many experiences have been the motor behind these changes. I don't know what they might have been. Her heart is very hard, her mind very sharp, but in all this: it is her own success in all her endeavours that has made her into such a strong individual, and so daring. But she has one big failure in a certain matter. It's understandable: every self-educated person has a failure that stands out.'

Dr Martinet didn't continue. He hoped that I would seek for myself the meaning of his words.

'She's beginning to regain consciousness, your Annelies,' he said all of a sudden. He looked over towards her, left me and approached his patient. He checked her pulse, then he waved to me. 'Yes, Mr Minke. In a few minutes she will return to being the Annelies you knew before. May she return to complete health now that you are here again. From this moment on, this girl is no longer my patient but yours. Everything I have told you is between us alone. Good afternoon.'

He left the room, closed the door behind him and disappeared from sight.

Now the moment had arrived when I could feel sorry for myself. Yes! One after the other over these last few days new experiences had fallen upon and rocked me. And now there was a new one that I had to face: Annelies!

Great artists, Minke, said Jean Marais once, whether they are painters, or something else, or leaders, or generals, become great because their life has been crammed with and based upon profound, intense experiences: emotional, spiritual or physical. He had said this after I had finished telling him the life story of the Dutch poets Vondel and Multatuli: Without such profound experiences, greatness is purely imaginary: their greatness is whistled up by the money-minded people of the world.

Jean Marais did not know that my own writings had begun to be published. If his words are true, I thought, maybe one day I could become a great writer. Like Hugo as Nyai hoped. Or a leader, or a teacher of a nation as hoped by the de la Croix family. Or perhaps I will end up as rotting flesh just as Robert Mellema (if Darsam's story was true) and Fatso planned.

Annelies sighed and moved her finger. She will be all right; I will not have to watch her die. I moved away and sat on a chair where I could watch her. Even ill she was gloriously beautiful: her skin was fine, her nose, eyebrows, lips, teeth, ears, hair . . . everything. And I began to doubt Dr Martinet's explanation of Annelies's psychology. Could such a beautiful body house such a disordered mind? And I – an outsider, just an acquaintance – must I also accept some responsibility for her just because of her beauty? Creole beauty. How involved my life was becoming! The result of my own actions as a philogynist.

'Mama!' uttered Annelies. Now her legs began to move.

'Ann!'

She opened her eyes. And her eyes still gazed off far away into the distance. From this moment on she was my patient; that's what Dr Martinet had said. I held back my laughter, understanding that I was now the doctor who must cure her.

154

I took the milk from the table. I raised her neck with my arm and I poured a little milk into her mouth. She began to sip it and smacked her lips a little. Yes, she was beginning to regain consciousness. I gave her some more to drink. She began to swallow.

'Ann, my Annelies, drink it all up,' I said and I gave her some more to drink.

She took one swallow after another.

Nyai entered carrying lunch for two people.

'Why are you doing it yourself, Ma?'

'It's not that. No one else is allowed to come up here. So the doctor was right – she is beginning to wake up now.'

'Almost, Ma.'

'Yes, Minke, the doctor said only you can look after her now. It's up to you,' and she went out again.

Annelies opened her eyes again and began to look at me.

'What's wrong with you, Ann?'

She didn't answer, but just gazed at me. I put her head down on the pillow again. The beautiful shape of her nose pulled my hand over to stroke it. The ends of her hair were a corn-yellow brown, and her eyebrows were lush as if they had been fertilised before she was born. And her eyelashes, so long and curly, made her eyes seem like a pair of daylight stars in a clear sky, her countenance itself the clearest sky of all.

Where else on this earth of mankind could one discover such perfect Creole beauty, such a beautifully harmonious form? God has created such a thing only once and only in this one body in front of me. I will never let go of you, Ann, whatever is going on inside you. I am ready to face whatever and whoever.

'Ann, today,' I said to her, 'the weather is beautiful. It is hotter than usual, but it's fresh, not too humid.'

The maiden still just looked at me. The focal point of her gaze was the top of my nose. She still hadn't spoken. Her eyes blinked so slowly. Yet her beauty was still profound, greater than all those things which have been made by man, richer than all the combined and individual meanings to be found in the treasuries of the languages. She was a gift from Allah, without equal, unique. And she was mine alone.

'Arise and awaken, of Flower of Surabaya! Do you not know? Alexander the Great, Napoleon, all would fall to their knees to gain your love? To touch your skin they would sacrifice their nation, their people? Awaken, My Flower, because the world is a lesser place without you,' and without knowing it I was kissing her on the lips, fully conscious of what I was doing.

The long breath she expelled blew over my face. Her lips smiled. Her eyes too. But she still could not speak. So I kept on with my chatter, like Solomon praising the virgins of Israel: chin, breasts, cheeks, legs, the look in her eyes, her eyes themselves, neck, hair – everything, all of her. I stopped only after I heard:

'Mas!'

'Ann, my Annelies!' I said cutting her off, 'you're better now. Come on, get up. Let's walk. Come on, my Goddess.'

She began to move. Her hand waved to me. And I responded to that hand.

'Let me carry you,' and I carried her. I carried her. Yes, I carried her. And I wasn't strong enough. What sort of body was this, incapable of even carrying a girl! I put her down. Her legs stepped forward, shaking; her body swayed. I supported her. To the devil with chairs, table and bed. I took her to the window where a minute ago I had stood with Dr Martinet and where he had appointed me her doctor. A vast panorama of fields opened up before us. And the sun had already begun to leave its midday position.

'Look over there, Ann, the forest is the limit of our view. And the mountains, and the sky, and the earth. You see, Ann? Do you really see it all?'

She nodded. The wind whistled as it launched a lusty attack from out of that great expanse of nature; and it felt as if it was being channelled into that one window. Annelies shuddered.

'Are you cold, Ann?'

'No.'

'You should get some more sleep.'

'I want to be close to you, like now, Mas. It was such a long time, and you still didn't come.'

'I'm here now, Ann.'

'Don't let go of me, Mas.'

'You're cold standing here.'

'I'm warm enough now. The forest seems different somehow. And the wind too. And the mountains. The birds also.'

'You're well now, Ann. You're beginning to be strong again.'

'I don't want to be ill. I'm not ill. I was only waiting for you to come.'

I no longer felt ill either, Ann, had you wanted to know. Something made me turn and through a small opening in the door, I saw Nyai and Dr Martinet. They didn't enter. Then the door closed again . . .

13

The school director excused my absence, which went over the period in my doctor's certificate. The greetings I passed on from Herbert de la Croix softened his attitude. For several days I worked hard to catch up on my studies. It was easy. My grandfather had planted within me a belief: you will be successful in all your studies and you must believe you will be successful, and then you will be successful; think of all study as easy, and all will be easy; be afraid of no kind of study, because such fear is the original ignorance that will make you ignorant of everything.

I followed his advice, I believed in the truth of his words of wisdom. I was never left behind in my studies, even though, yes, even though I did not study as hard as the others. But now I really studied hard, to catch up on what I had missed during the last few weeks.

A *dokar* and driver had been put aside by Mama especially for me. Night and day. And each time I left for school in my new vehicle I picked up May Marais to drop her off at her school in Simpang.

Everything had changed. Especially, and most of all, myself. I now felt like a man of real substance as I sat on top of my luxury buggy in the middle of Surabaya's traffic. It was easy to see too that my friends at school had also changed. Meaning: they seemed to be, and probably indeed were, distancing themselves from me. I interpreted all this as a sign of respect towards someone who has just scored a rise in his marks. It was possible I might have been wrong in this estimation of my position, so I looked upon it as provisional only. My teachers, now that I travelled by luxury *dokar*, seemed to treat me as someone they didn't know but who was of equal status. This too was a provisional guess.

I felt I was no longer the old Minke. My body was the same; but its contents and its perceptions were new. I no longer liked to joke. There was more to me now than that. I was more thoughtful, while my friends at school were still childish. I no longer wanted to simply float on the surface of problems. But in every conversation and discussion I wanted to dive straight down to the bottom of every problem.

See, even Robert Suurhof still didn't want to approach me. He always moved away if we passed near each other. And the girls at the school avoided me too, as if I were the source of some plague.

Several times the school Director summoned me to get assurances that I had not already married, because a student must leave the school once he is married. I think it was Suurhof who was doing the talking. It could be no one else. He alone knew what had happened. Eventually I found out for certain: my guess was not wrong. He'd spread rumours, inciting my friends against me. (So my estimation of myself was wrong after all!) So: the looks directed at me were from people I felt I no longer knew.

Everything had changed. Now, all around me at school, there was no enveloping aura of brightness, but only loneliness, a loneliness that called and summoned me to reflection.

The only teacher who did not change was Miss Magda Peters, the Dutch Language and Literature teacher. She still hadn't taken a husband. All over her exposed skin there were brown freckles. Her clear brown eyes were always sparkling. At first her appearance tended to make you laugh. She struck me as looking like a white, female monkey with an ever-surprised face. But then as people listened to her first lesson, we all became quiet. The impression of a white, female monkey disappeared. Her freckles vanished. A feeling of respect replaced all this. And here are her words, when, in her first class since travelling down from the Netherlands to the Indies, she said:

'Good afternoon, students of HBS Surabaya. My name is Magda Peters, your new teacher for Dutch Language and Literature. Please put up your hands if you don't like literature.'

Almost everyone put up their hands. There were even some who stood up to show their antipathy.

'Excellent. Thank you. Please sit down everybody. Even the people of the most primitive society – in the heart of Africa, for example – who have never sat in school, never seen a book in their life, who don't know how to read and write, are still able to love literature, even if only oral literature. Isn't it an outstanding achievement, that after at least ten years in school, HBS students still do not like literature and language? Yes, it's truly outstanding.'

No one laughed and there was nothing to laugh at. Total silence.

'You will all advance through school. Perhaps you will obtain a string of all sorts of degrees, but without a love of literature, you'll remain just a lot of clever animals. Most of you have never seen the Netherlands. I was born and brought up there. So I know that every Hollander loves and reads Dutch literature. People love and honour the paintings of van Gogh, Rembrandt – our own and the world's great painters. They who do not love and honour them and who do not learn to love and honour them are considered to be uncivilised. Painting is literature in colours. Literature is painting in language. Put up your hand if you don't understand.'

To make sure we weren't classified as uncivilised, from that moment on we all knew we would have to concentrate on the teacher's every word. She had us in the palm of her hand.

And Miss Magda Peters's attitude towards me never changed. She must surely have heard the rumours whispered by Robert Suurhof.

It was generally Magda Peters who opened the Saturday afternoon discussions. She did this not just happily but with great enthusiasm. Every student could put forward any topic – general, personal; local news or international developments – as the afternoon's subject. If no student had anything to put forward, only then would the teacher choose the subject. Students were not obliged to attend if they weren't interested. The most popular discussions were those led by Magda Peters. No one wanted to miss out, and so the discussion had to be held in the hall with the students sitting on the floor. Only the speaker would stand. The teachers also sat on the floor. The teacher leading the discussion would also stand. On those occasions, one could see that freckles covered all of Magda Peters's body.

In order to place my situation and my attitudes in context, so that you may judge the truth or otherwise of my views about myself and my surroundings, I think it is proper that I tell something about my experiences in those discussions:

Once I asked about the Association Theory of Dr Snouck Hurgronye. Magda Peters asked for comments from the other students. No one knew anything about it. She then looked politely at the teachers but none showed signs of wanting to respond. Then she herself spoke.

'I am not sure what it means, either. Perhaps it is something that has arisen in colonial political life. Do you know what colonial politics are?' No one answered. 'It is a system or power structure to consolidate hegemony over occupied countries and peoples. Someone who agrees with such a system is a colonialist, who not only agrees with it, but also legitimatises it, carries it out and defends it. The basic issue in all this is the one of earning a living. None of this need yet attract your attention, students. You're all still too young. If such matters were to become the subject of a literary work, it would be much more interesting, as in the case of Multatuli's works, which have been discussed with you in class several times. Try, Minke, to explain Dr Snouck Hurgronje's Association Theory.'

I explained what I'd heard from Miriam de la Croix and my own views on it.

'Stop!' said Magda Peters. 'Such subjects may not yet be discussed at HBS school. It's up to you if you want to discuss them outside school. Such matters are the affair of the Queen, the Netherlands Government, the Governor-General and the Netherlands Indies Government. If you have a desire to find out more, it's best you do so outside school. Because none of you have a topic for today's discussion, I will choose one myself.

'Just recently I came across an article about life in the Indies. Too few people write about this. Precisely because of that, it attracted my attention. Maybe the writer is Indo-European. Maybe, I say. Perhaps some of you may have already read it? It's called: *Uit het Schoone Leven van een Mooie Boerin* (The Beautiful Life of a Beautiful Peasant Girl). The writer's name is: Max Tollenaar.'

Several hands shot up. I kept a straight face. Max Tollenaar was my penname. The original title had been changed and the editor had made some alterations to the text, not all of which I agreed with.

Miss Magda Peters began to read it out, placing stresses and pauses in such a way that her voice sang and the essay sounded more beautiful than I had originally intended. Yes, you could say it sounded like a long poem, dense with emotion. Virtually no one even blinked while listening. And after the reading was over and people were freed from its hold over them, at last they were able to let go of their breath.

'It's a pity that this story was published in the Indies, about the Indies, about the people and society of the Indies. As a result no one has discussed it in class. All right, one of you come forward and give us your reactions and comments on this story, perhaps even a critique.'

Robert Suurhof immediately came forward. He stood there, legs apart, feet nailed to the floor, as if he was scared the wind would blow him over. All eyes were directed at him. Only I hesitated.

He looked around at his friends first. Perhaps he was looking for moral support.

'I've read four pieces by Max Tollenaar over recent weeks. They have all been about the same thing and have been coloured by the same emotions. The writer is in the power of some force outside himself. Yes, yes, the writer is suffering some drastic fever. The writings are the long deliriums of someone who has lost all control over himself, who has lost all touch with reality. I don't *know* who Max Tollenaar is. But I can make a good guess, because I am the only witness to the events that he writes about.

'Miss Magda Peters, I don't think we should be talking about such writings in a school discussion; it only makes us all dirty, Miss. If I'm not mistaken – and I'm certain I'm not – the writer of this doesn't even have a family name.'

He was quiet for a moment, glancing around at all the students within whom he was building up such tension. He raised his chin. His eyes shone victoriously. He was going to let go one more shot.

Miss Magda Peters looked taken aback. Her eyes were blinking rapidly.

I alone knew what Robert Suurhof was up to: to revenge himself upon me. So I began to understand better: it was he who wanted Annelies. There could be no reason other than jealousy for his hatred and his public insults to me. Yes, it was Robert who desired to possess Annelies. He took me with him that day to make himself look good, and as a witness. Why me? Because

I was a Native. Upper-class European ladies used to take a monkey with them everywhere so they would appear more beautiful in comparison. He took me. It was Suurhof's monkey that won Annelies' heart.

'The person in question, Miss,' Suurhof resumed, 'is not even an Indo. He is lower than an Indo, than someone whose father refused to acknowledge him. He is an *Inlander*, a Native who has smuggled himself in through the cracks of European civilisation.'

He bowed to pay respect to Magda Peters and then to the other teachers present, and then sat down anxiously on the floor.

'Students, Robert Suurhof has just given us his opinion on the author of this story; an author whose identity he alone knows. What I had hoped for was an opinion about the story itself. Very well. Who do you reckon is the author?'

All the students looked around at each other. Then all looks were directed towards their friends who were neither Pure, nor Mixed-Blood, towards the Natives, as if underlining Suurhof's words. The Natives all bowed down their heads. All those looks made us feel as if their gazes were piercing right into our stomachs.

I knew Suurhof's face was pointed towards me. The others followed his example. No, said my heart, no, don't be afraid. To the devil with all this; if need be, I can leave this school. If necessary, right now.

Suurhof stood up again. He said briefly:

'The author is among us now.'

It seemed his whisperings had spread throughout the school. Now every face was directed towards me. I looked straight at Suurhof. Rays of victory shone out of his eyes.

'Who is it, Suurhof?' asked Miss Magda Peters.

With Caesar's forefinger, he pointed at me:

'Minke!'

Magda Peters took a handkerchief from her bag and wiped her neck, then her two hands. She didn't know what to do. She turned for a moment towards the row of seated teachers, then at me, then at the students seated upon the floor. Then she walked over to the teachers and the Director who also happened to be present. She gave a little nod, returned to the middle of the meeting and made a path through the students, heading straight towards me.

Now I will be expelled and publicly humiliated.

She stood for a second before me. The freckles on her legs became clearly visible. And I heard her call:

'Minke!'

'Yes, Miss.' I stood up.

'Is it true you wrote this?' She held up the *S.N. v/d D.*, 'using the pen-name of Max Tollenaar?'

'Have I done something wrong, Miss?'

'Max Tollenaar!' she whispered and held out her hand. 'Come,' and she pulled me up and took me to the Director.

All eyes were directed my way. Standing there before all the teachers and the Director, I nodded respectfully. They hardly responded. Then I was taken across to stand before all the students.

Silence.

The woman teacher rested her hand on my shoulders. I was like someone at confession, who didn't really know what to confess.

'Students, teachers, Director, today I introduce to you all, especially to you students, an HBS pupil by the name of Minke, whom no doubt you all know. But I'm not introducing the Minke whom everybody knows, but rather a Minke of a different quality, a Minke whose use of Dutch to state his feelings and thoughts is brilliant, a Minke who has written a literary work. He has proven that he is capable of writing perfectly in a language that is not his mother tongue. He has brought to life a snippet of reality, which other people, even though they too have experienced that reality, could never explain. I'm proud to have a pupil like him.'

She shook hands with me. I still wasn't told to go. Her words of praise raised me up to the highest of heights. Now I waited for the final chop to fall.

'Minke! Is it true you do not have a family name?'

'Yes, Miss.'

'Students, having a family name is just a custom. Before Napoleon Bonaparte appeared on the stage of European history, not even our ancestors – not one of them – used family names'; and she began to tell how Napoleon's decision on this was made law in all the territories that he controlled. Those who could not find an appropriate name were given one at the whim of the local officials, and Jews were given the names of animals. 'Even so, the use of family names is not unique to Europe or to Napoleon, who got the idea from other peoples. Long before Europe was civilised, the Jews and Chinese were using clan names. It was through contact with other peoples that Europeans learnt the importance of family names.' She stopped.

I was still standing there for everybody to look at.

'Is it true you're not an Indo, Minke?' a formal question that I had to answer in the affirmative.

'*Inlander*, Miss: – Native.'

'Yes,' she said loudly, 'Europeans who feel themselves to be a hundred per cent pure do not really know how much Asian blood flows in their veins. From your study of history, you will all know that hundreds of years ago, many different Asian armies attacked Europe, and left descendants – Arabs, Turkish, Mongol – and this was after Rome had become Christian! And don't any of you forget that under the Roman Empire, the Asian blood, and perhaps even African, of those citizens of Rome from various Asian nations: Arabs, Jews, Syrians, Egyptians . . . now mingles with the blood of Europeans.'

Silence continued to reign supreme.

My heart was empty. Only my body seemed unsteady. My only desire was to sit down again.

'Much of Europe's science comes from Asia. Yes, even the numerals you use each day are Arab numerals. Including zero. Imagine, what would it be like to count and add up without Arab numerals and without zero? And zero in its turn was derived from Indian philosophy. Do you know what the meaning of philosophy is? Yes, another time we'll talk about this. Zero, a condition of emptiness. From emptiness comes the beginning, from the beginning there is a development until the climax, number 9, and then there is emptiness and we begin again with a higher value, tens, and so on, hundreds, thousands . . . there is no limit. Without zero the decimal system would vanish, and all of you would have to count using roman numerals. Most of your names are Asian, because Christianity was born in Asia.'

The students began to show their restlessness.

'If Natives do not have a family name that is because they don't, or don't yet, need one; and there is no humiliation in that. If the Netherlands doesn't have a Prambanan or a Borobudur temple, it means in that era Java was more advanced than the Netherlands. If the Netherlands still does not possess such things, yes, it is because they have never been needed . . .'

'Miss Magda Peters,' the Director intervened, 'it's best that this discussion be closed.'

The discussion closed; everybody dispersed. Except for Magda Peters everyone seemed to avoid me. No one called out as usual. No one laughed. No one raced ahead of each other as they usually did. They all walked off quietly, full of thought.

Jan Dapperste, a student whose appearance was more Native then European, stood at the fence following after me with his eyes. He always introduced himself as Indo. But to me alone he had admitted to being Native. Trusting in me as a friend, he had explained that he was the adopted child of a preacher named Dapperste. An adopted child! he himself was pure Native. He felt close to me. After I obtained the buggy, it was usual for him to ask to ride along with me. Now he too seemed to be keeping his distance.

This time it was Magda Peters who asked for a ride. She didn't say a word the whole way. Indeed, what's the use of speaking when your heart and mind are full of troubles? The traffic was invisible to me. I could see only one thing: the students' and the teachers' anger towards Magda Peters. Their Europeanness had been wounded.

Once or twice Magda Peters looked at me from beside me where she was sitting.

'What a pity,' she hissed into the wind.

I pretended not to hear.

The buggy stopped in front of her house. She said thank you. Then suddenly:

'Come in, Minke,' and that was the first time she invited me into her home.

I walked with her inside. So we sat facing each other on the settee in the main room.

'You're extraordinary, Minke. So you really wrote that.'

'It's so, Miss.'

'You are certainly my most successful student. I've taught Dutch language and literature for five years now. Almost four years in the Netherlands. None of my students could write as well as that – and to be published as well. You must be fond of me – are you?'

'There is no teacher of whom I'm more fond.'

'Is that true, Minke?'

'With all my heart, Miss.'

'I guessed so. You must have been following all my lessons very carefully, with all your mind and heart. Otherwise there is no way you could write as well as that. You're not angry with Suurhof, are you?'

'No, Miss.'

'Good. You're worth much more than he. You've proven what you can do.'

The flattery was so embarrassing. She told me to stand up.

'At the very least, Minke, my efforts, my strivings these five years have now achieved some results,' she pulled me near her.

Totally surprised I found myself in her embrace, and she kissed me until I was out of breath! Until out of breath!

Every day I had to visit Jean's house – to drop off or pick up May or to hand in some new order. Even if only for one or two minutes. I also had to drop in at my boarding-house.

Having my own buggy made everything easier: chasing after orders, writing advertising texts, writing other things as well. My time somehow seemed to last longer.

When I arrived home, I was usually exhausted and needed to sleep for a while. Usually Annelies woke me up, bringing a fresh towel, and ordering me to bathe. Afterwards we sat and talked, or read Indies newspapers, or Dutch magazines.

At night, I worked, studied or wrote, while waiting upon Annelies in her room. Her health was improving with every day. But she hadn't yet resumed working.

Mama was very busy in the office and out the back; she had no time for the two of us during the day.

That night, like the nights before, I sat at the table in Annelies's room.

She was reading Defoe's *Robinson Crusoe* in a Dutch translation, each page of which was divided into two columns. I'd prepared a list of books she had to read. All books for young people: Stevenson and Dumas. She had to finish them in one month. And beside her lay the old dictionary – that Mama used every day – and old dictionary that, over the last ten years, had become incapable of meeting the demands of new developments.

I sat across from Annelies reading letters from Miriam and Sarah before I started writing a story to be titled *A Father's Son*. I meant no other than Robert Mellema.

This time Miriam's letter was even more splendid:

Do you remember at all that 'other one'? I've received a letter from the Netherlands. From a friend, a close friend, who knows about 'the other Douwager' in South Africa, in the Transvaal. The writer of the letter returned home to the Netherlands after being wounded in a brief battle. He himself was once in the same unit as the 'other one'. The brigade was under the command of one Mellema, a young engineer who was hard, courageous, ambitious, he said.

Friend, I was so happy to receive his letter. As happy as I am to receive yours. In it, friend, there was something mentioned that might interest you. The 'other one' is a few years older than you perhaps. Answering the Dutch call to seize back and defend their independence from the British, and without thinking too much about it all, he left for Africa . . . and was greatly disappointed.

Though there are some reports on the war in the Indies press, there is a great deal that is not reported. The Dutch were immigrants there, my friend – I think your favourite teacher, Magda Peters, pays too little attention to wars – and they ruled over the native peoples. In their turn the Dutch immigrants were conquered by British power, also an immigrant power from Europe. So power was structured in layers, with the natives at the bottom.

Just think, isn't it the same in the Indies? Just as Papa explained? There are some small differences, but they don't alter the basic reality. Aren't the Natives here ruled by their own rulers? Kings, sultans, and bupatis? *In their turn this Brown Government is controlled by a White Government. The kings, sultans and* bupatis, *with all the facilities they have here, are the same as the immigrant Dutch power in South Africa.*

My friend, that 'other one' became so disappointed when he realised what the war between the British and the Boers – the Dutch immigrants – was really about: who would control the land, gold and natives. The young Dutchmen who were called to go there, from all over the world, came only to be wounded or to die for interests alien to Holland. While that 'other one', according to his letter, saw how the natives of South Africa were much worse off than the natives of the Indies, far worse off than the natives of Aceh. If he was honest to himself, he said, he felt no different from an Indies Army soldier in Aceh.

But he realised this all too late. And he only came to that realisation as a result of an unexpected meeting with a non-white inhabitant, though not a black, named Mard Wongs. This person, my friend, was only one of several wealthy farmers who could speak Javanese. He and all the others, even though they spoke Afrikaans, were Slameiers, of your own people. Mard Wongs was an Afrikaan version of his original name. I think it must have been: Mardi Wongso. And the Slameiers are none other than the descendants of Javanese and Bugis-Makassarese-Madurese Natives, who had been exiled to South Africa by the Company.

Interesting, yes?

Now, Mellema's platoon, so writes my friend from the Netherlands, entered Mard Wongs's house to shelter there for the night. The old man, who was white with age, refused them and angrily threw them out of his house. Mellema lost his temper and threatened the old man that he would be shot.

Mard Wongs became more enraged: What else do you Dutch want? In Java you robbed us of all that we rightfully owned, you robbed us of our freedom, and now here you beg for shelter under my roof. Have you never been taught the meaning of robbery and begging? Shoot me then! Here is the breast of Mard Wongs. I would not give you the shade from a single piece of roof nor shelter behind one board of my house. Go!

And do you know, my friend, that in this contest of wills, Mellema gave in. He and his platoon were forced to sleep out under the open sky.

It was that incident that made the 'other one' realise how Indies Natives hated the Dutch. He realised then that he and his platoon were not the upholders of noble ideals, but merely and no more than the tools of colonial power. He was ashamed. He was confused. He had dreamed of becoming a hero, of making some contribution to humanity. Now he was in the middle of tyranny's arena.

Pity on the 'other one'.

The next morning his platoon attacked a position held by the British South African Light Horse Brigade. People said that brigade was led by Lieutenant W.Ch. Early a Boer regiment had attacked in large numbers from another direction but was confronted, pushed back and almost totally surrounded and annihilated.

At the midst of all this, Mellema's company attacked the enemy. The British were surprised, fell into disarray, and dispersed under alternating attacks from two directions. The position fell to the Boers.

But, my friend, 'the other one' was shot and captured. My friend has written that perhaps he will be taken as a prisoner of war to England. During those last days he never tired of regretting his earlier stupidity.

The reason why I'm telling you all this, my friend, is simply to add another perspective about something that is not generally publicised in the Indies. Isn't it true you only read about the brutality of the British and the victories of the Dutch in the papers? On the other hand, says Papa, the British press reports are about the savagery and viciousness of the Dutch towards the natives. But there is no paper in either England, the Netherlands or the Indies that talks about the South African natives themselves. Let alone about the Slameiers people. Isn't the world strange?

I think the Javanese Natives are better off. There have been a few people who have spoken up on their behalf. Yes, even though their voices have been drowned in the sheer din of the bureaucracy. This is something we haven't talked abut and analysed yet. Let's try to discuss it another time. You agree, I hope?

Now Minke, my friend, don't let me wait so long for your next letter, Miriam de la Croix.

Sarah's letter was different again. She wrote:

I can understand it if Miss Magda Peters didn't know anything about the Association Theory. We didn't know anything more than we told you that day. No more than that.

I told Papa that you didn't know anything about it. He only laughed boisterously, and said: You also do not know any more than the little you told him.

After your letter arrived I told Papa that Magda Peters didn't seem to know anything about it either. Your other teachers couldn't offer an explanation either. Perhaps they were unwilling, deliberately stopping themselves from answering, or perhaps, indeed, they didn't know anything. So what did Papa say? Not everyone has an interest in colonial policy, just as not everyone is interested in the art of cooking. And don't forget too, that in this age in which we live all the Indies believes in the greatness, authority, wisdom, justice, and compassion of the government. There are no beggars dying of hunger in the streets. Neither are there sick people dying in the streets. They too are protected by the government's law. No foreigner is beaten to death, just because he is a foreigner; foreigners too are protected by the government's law.

There is something I feel you should know. Papa has been talking about you: a youth like that should continue his studies at a university in the Netherlands. Perhaps he should study law, Papa said of you. Even if he failed, he would still have learnt what Europe means by law.

What do you think? Is it possible that a Native could become a graduate in a European science? To be honest, Papa doubts it. Papa says – don't be angry like you were before – the Native psychology hasn't yet developed as far as that of the European: his wiser considerations are still too easily pushed aside by lustful passions. I don't know if this is true or not. It seems that it is true though, especially if you look at the upper echelons of your people. You too should think about this. What do you think?

There is another thing I should pass on to you: one of the youths being tried out by Dr Snouck Hurgronje is called Achmad, from Banten. I tell you this in case some day you meet, become acquainted and correspond . . .

'Why are you sighing?' Annelies suddenly asked.

'On fire.'

'What's on fire?'

'My head. My own head. All sorts of things keep coming up. There is already so much work and I'm still not allowed to go undisturbed for a single moment. Read!' and I pushed the letters over to her.

'They're not for me, Mas.'

'It's best you know too.'

Annelies read them slowly and carefully.

'It seems many people are fond of you. It's a pity I don't understand much of this.'

'There's no reason to say it's a pity, Ann. They all seem to want to be my teacher.'

'Isn't it good to have teachers?'

'You too, Ann! of course, it's good to find a teacher. No knowledge is useless. It's only that they all seem to have a passion to see me become an important person as a result of their own efforts. Aren't they capable of doing it themselves anyway? Boring teachers are a terrible torment, Ann,' I said.

'Then you don't need to answer.'

'That's not right either, Ann. I've read their letters. They wrote to get an answer.'

And Sarah had gone a bit too far. Unashamedly mentioning things like lust. Asking for a reply too. Does she want me to strip myself naked? Even in Europe this is not yet a matter for public discussion. It is a private, tightly closed matter. These de la Croix girls go too far!

Annelies resumed reading. I think it unsettled her that the letters came from two girls, sisters. She put the letters down on the table, folded them properly, and put them back into their envelopes. She didn't say anything else.

Neither of us spoke for some time.

'Ann,' I began, 'you seem to be getting better.'

'Thank you for your treatment, Mas Doctor.'

'From tomorrow you no longer need a friend to stay in your room with you.'

She looked at me suspiciously.

'You're not going back to Kranggan?'

'If you still want me to stay, then, of course, I won't go back.'

She frowned. For a moment, she glanced at the letters from Sarah and Miriam.

'Don't you want to stay with me anymore,' she said in a voice that sounded as if she was about to cry.

'Of course, Ann, while you're ill.'

'Must I become ill again?'

'Ann, what are you saying?' and at that moment I remembered Dr Martinet's warning. And I was sure I hadn't spoken roughly to her. I quickly added: 'You must recover fully, Mama needs you greatly!'

'Why don't you want to stay here with me just because I'm not sick any more?' she asked nervously.

'What will people say?'

'What will they say, Mas?'

'Look, Ann, let me explain it to you: you're better now. If you don't want me to go back to Kranggan, then I won't. Believe me. I'll stay here at Wonokromo as long as you want. But not, of course, in your room. So beginning tomorrow, Ann, I want to stay and work in my own room, near the garden. If you feel lonely, you can come and visit me. It's just the same, isn't it?'

'If it's just the same, let's just keep on like this forever. You stay here in my room.'

'But upstairs is out of bounds for everyone except Mama and you. We must respect the rules, mustn't we?' and there were still another twenty sentences that I uttered.

She didn't interrupt any more. But her stare reached farther and farther out into the distance. Annelies was jealous.

The next day I visited Jean Marais. Before I left home, I prepared a question about South Africa. He listened silently. Then:

'You know, Minke, as a European I'm already very ashamed that I have become involved in colonial affairs. Probably I'm very similar to the person you've just described, someone who neither of us has met. I fought in Aceh only because I assumed Natives would not be able to fight back, and so wouldn't fight back. But they fought back all right, really fought back, with all their might, ignoring all obstacles. And they were courageous and daring too. Just as in many of the great wars of Europe. It was something to be very ashamed of, Minke: Europe's latest weapons were pitted against the flesh of the Acehnese. Because you've asked me my opinion I'll answer, but never ask me about these things again – it tortures my conscience.'

Without us realising, Mr Telinga had begun to listen in from a distance; then he came closer, sat upon the table. It looked as if he was eager to join in the discussion.

'All the colonial wars for the last twenty-five years have been fought in the interests of capital; fought to ensure markets that would guarantee more profits for European capital. Capital has become very powerful, all-powerful. Capital decides the fate of humanity.'

'War has always been the clash of force and of strategies so as to emerge victor,' Telinga intervened.

'No, Mr Telinga,' Marais protested, 'there has never been a war conducted for its own sake. There are many peoples who go to war who have no desire to be victor. They go to war and die in their thousands, like the Acehnese now . . . because there is something they want to defend, something more important than death, life, or defeat and victory.'

'It's all the same in the end, Jean. A contest between force and strategies to emerge victor.'

'That's only how it ends up, Mr Telinga. But if that's your opinion, very good. Now if, for example, Aceh wins and Holland is defeated, will the Netherlands become an Acehnese possession?'

'There is no way Aceh can win.'

'Yes, that's precisely the point. The Acehnese themselves know they can't win. While the Dutch know too that victory will surely be theirs. Yet, Telinga, the Acehnese still descend to the battlefield. They don't fight to win. They're different from the Dutch. If the Dutch thought that Aceh was strong enough to defend itself, they would never dare attack, let alone start a war. The whole thing is a matter of calculating the profit and loss of capital. If the whole issue is just a matter of winning, why doesn't Holland attack Luxembourge or Belgium, since they're both closer and richer?'

'You're a Frenchman, Jean. You don't have any stake in the Indies.'

'Perhaps. At the very least I regret ever having taken part in the war here.'

'But you, like me, still accept the army pension!'

'Yes, just like you. But that pension is my right; due to me from those who sent me to war. Just like you. I lost my leg, you lost your health. That has been the only consequence of the war for both of us. We don't want to have an argument, do we, Telinga?'

'You never used to talk like that when you were in the platoon!' accused Telinga.

'Then I was your subordinate, now I'm not.'

'What's the point of this argument?' I intervened. 'I only asked about South Africa. Goodbye.'

Then I went away and visited Magda Peters. She shook her head: 'About South Africa? Do you want to become a politician?' she asked me in return.

'What is a politician really, Miss?'

Once again she shook her head and looked at me as if I was someone suffering some grief. All we could do was sit there in silence.

'Later, when you have graduated. Then we can talk about this calmly. There is no need to talk about it now. You must make sure you graduate. Your marks are, indeed, not bad. With better ones you're sure to pass. Don't think about other things. Eh, Minke, are the stories true – I don't know where they come from – that you're living with some *nyai* or whatever?'

'Yes, Miss.'

'You know what people think of them?'

'I know, Miss.'

'Why are you doing it then?'

'Because it is not important where you reside. Especially when someone we call a nyai on the outside, Miss, is actually no less than an educated person; indeed she is my teacher.'

'Teacher? What does she teach you?'

'How someone can, starting from nothing, become an outstanding, self-educated person.'

'Self-educated in what?'

'First of all in developing herself, then in developing a big business . . .'

'Don't defend yourself with lies.'

'I think I've never lied to you, Miss.'

'No, except this once,' she looked at me, her eyes blinking rapidly, a sign (according to my guess) that she was thinking hard, 'don't disappoint me, Minke. You're educated. It's not fitting that you should act as if you'd never been to school.'

'What I said just now was my answer, as an educated person.'

The worry in her eyes began to go away. She blinked rapidly again, only it didn't seem funny anymore.

'Explain to me how a *nyai* can become a self-educated person. Educated in a European way, is what you mean, isn't it?'

'At least as I understand it, Miss. Perhaps I'm wrong; but try to visit us when you're not busy – in the evening, for example. Miss will be escorted home. They don't usually receive guests, but Miss will be my guest.'

'Very well,' she said, accepting my challenge.

And I knew for certain that she would come.

'Would you like to visit now?'

'Very well. You should know Minke that I need to know what's really going on – to pass on to the Teachers' Council. Something could happen to you one day, Minke.'

So we departed. We arrived at five o'clock in the afternoon. I took her into the front parlour and asked her to sit down. I studied the look on her face.

'It's nothing like I expected,' she whispered. 'In the Netherlands and Europe, a house like this . . . so this is where you live?' I nodded. 'It's not easy to own a house like this. Or to live in one . . . oh, Minke, like the German houses of Central Europe.'

Her attention was caught by something. I followed her gaze.

Annelies, in her black, velvet gown, had entered the front room.

'Ann, this is my teacher, Miss Magda Peters.'

Annelies approached, bowed, smiled and held out her hand. And my teacher seemed bewitched. Her eyes had no chance to blink. She stood and shook hands, her mouth wide open.

'Annelies Mellema, Miss. Just recovering from an illness. Ann, would you like to call Mama?'

Annelies nodded as she took leave, and left without saying a word.

'Like a queen, Minke. Her face is so delicate. Like an Italian prima donna. Is she the *nyai*'s daughter?' I nodded. 'She seems well-educated, polite and grand. Is it because of her you're staying here, Minke?' and I didn't answer. She had to understand my silence. 'It looks as if she might be your character in *"Uit het Schoone Leven van een Mooie Boerin"*.'

'It's indeed her, Miss.'

'Prima donnas from Italy and Spain, ballerinas from Russia and France, none are as beautiful as her,' she said as if she was lamenting her own fate. Then, as if addressing herself, 'Yes, I can see why so many people talk so much about Creole beauty. It's a pity though, the gown should be worn in the evening.'

Mama arrived on the scene in her usual clothes: a white embroidered *kabaya* and a brown, red and green *kain*. She held out her hand to the guest.

'This is Mama, Miss, and this is my teacher, Mama. Miss Magda Peters, my Dutch Language and Literature teacher. Mama is not used to receiving guests, Miss,' I said excusing myself to both parties, and because I had brought my teacher here without Nyai's consent.

It appeared that Mama was not upset because of my audacity; rather, she began:

'Are Minke's studies going well, Miss?'

'He could do better if he wanted to,' she replied politely.

'We are not used to receiving guests, Miss,' said Mama in flawless Dutch. 'We're very happy that you have taken the trouble to visit.'

'Ma'am, my visit is actually related to school affairs. We want to find out for certain whether Minke can study properly here.'

'He leaves in the morning and returns in the afternoon. In the evening he reads, studies or writes. I'm sorry, Miss, I'm not used to be called "Ma'am" and indeed I'm not a Mrs. It's not an appropriate way to refer to me, not my right. Call me Nyai as other people do, because that's what I am, Miss.'

Magda Peters blinked rapidly. I could sense she had been shaken by this request from the woman standing before her.

'There's no harm in being called Ma'am? There's no insult involved, is there?'

'There's no harm. And there's no insult. It's only that it contradicts reality somewhat; it's also not in accord with the law. I've never had a husband. There has only ever been a master who owns me, my person,' in her voice I could hear the bitterness of her life; sharp, a protest directed at humanity.

'Owns?'

'That's what has happened, Miss. As a European woman you would no doubt shudder to hear about it.'

I began to feel uncomfortable listening to this conversation. Mama was

172

seeking compensation for her past wounds. An unhappy conversation, for the person listening and the person speaking.

'But slavery was abolished in the Indies almost thirty-five years ago, Nyai,' Magda Peters responded.

'Yes, Miss, as long as there are no reports about slavery. I have read somewhere that there is still slavery in many parts of the Indies.'

'From the *Missie* and *Zending* missionaries?'

'My situation is about the same.'

Magda Peters was silent for quite a while. She blinked rapidly. Then:

'Ma'am is not a slave, and is not like a slave either.'

'Nyai, Miss,' Mama corrected her. 'A slave can live in an emporer's palace, but still remain a slave.'

'Why does Nyai feel herself to be a slave?'

This personal problem, which had been buried so long, now, before this European woman, was seeking for a way out into the open, to protest, to complain, to condemn, to seek attention, to accuse, to charge, to judge – all at once. As I listened I became even more anxious. My thoughts were busy trying to find some excuse to slip quickly away. Meanwhile Nyai was opening the door to her past.

'A European, Pure European, bought me from my parents,' her voice was bitter and filled with a desire for revenge which would not be satisfied even with five palaces. 'I was bought to become the brood mother of his children.'

Magda Peters was silent. I hurriedly excused myself. Let them stand on their own consciences. I found Annelies upstairs by the window, reading a book.

'Why don't you come down, Ann?'

'I'm finishing this book.'

'Why are you in such a hurry to finish it?'

'Really, I prefer hearing your own stories, Mas. Mas still hasn't told me very many. You get me to read other people's stories – these books. You do want to tell me a story, don't you?'

'Of course.'

She resumed reading. All of a sudden she stopped, turned around towards me:

'Why have you come here? This is an out-of-bounds area, isn't it?'

'To call you down, Ann. Miss wants to talk with you.'

She didn't reply and kept on reading. I went up close to her. I stroked her hair. She didn't react. When I pulled the book away from her, her eyes didn't follow my action. Annelies wasn't reading. She was hiding her face.

'What's the matter with you, Ann? Angry?' there was no answer. 'It must be a good story you're reading.'

She bent over and I could feel her shoulders shuddering as she held back her sobs. I turned her around to face me. All of a sudden she hugged me and burst out crying.

'What's the matter with you, Ann? I haven't hurt you in any way, have I?'

And I don't know if it was tens or hundreds of sentences I threw about everywhere to humour her. And she still didn't speak. She hugged me tightly as if afraid I would come loose and fly up into the green heavens . . . Annelies was jealous.

Conversation between two people drifted in through the door, which wasn't properly shut. It became increasingly clear that it was originating from the upstairs corridor. Mama could be heard calling out. Annelies released her embrace by herself. I poked my head out to have a look. Miss Magda Peters and Nyai were waiting for me in front of one of the upstairs rooms.

'Miss wants to see our library, Minke. Come, I'm going to show her,' she opened the door to the room, a room I'd never entered.

The room was the library of Mr Herman Mellema. It was as big as Annelies's room. Three big cabinets full of heavily hound books stood side by side. There was also a glass cabinet in which was Herman Mellema's bamboo pipe collection. The furniture was all spotlessly clean. There was no carpet on the floor, exposing ordinary planks, neither parquetry nor polished wood. There was only one table with a chair and *fauteuil*. On the table there stood a white metal stand with fourteen candles. A book, which turned out to be a volume of magazines, lay open on the table.

'A very nice room, clean and quiet,' Magda Peters allowed her gaze to wander around the room until it fell upon the glass windows which exposed views of the country outside. 'So beautiful!' Then she went straight to the table and took up the volume of magazines. She asked without looking at any particular one, 'Who is reading the *Indische Gids*?'

'Bedside reading, Miss.'

'Bedside reading!' she stared wide-eyed at Nyai.

'The doctor advises that I read myself asleep.'

'Nyai doesn't sleep well?'

'True.'

'Nyai has had so many troubles for such a long time?'

'Five years now, Miss.'

'And Nyai hasn't fallen ill?'

Mama shook her head, smiling broadly.

'So what is Nyai looking for in these magazines?'

'Just something to make me sleep.'

'What is Nyai's other bedtime reading?' she asked like a prosecutor.

'Whatever I grab hold of, Miss. I don't really choose.'

Magda Peters blinked rapidly again.

'And what does Nyai prefer most?'

'What I can understand, Miss.'

'Does Nyai know anything about Snouck Hurgronje's Association Theory?'

'Excuse me,' Nyai took the magazine from my teacher's hands, looked for a specific place, then showed it to Magda Peters.

My teacher glanced over the page quickly, nodded, then looked at me, and:

'Why did you bring up the Association Theory at school? You should have just asked Nyai?'

'I only wanted to find out more about it,' I said, even though I never knew that this library existed or that there existed a magazine which published articles about such things.

Magda Peters then inspected the books in the cabinets. Most were beautifully bound volumes of magazines. It was as if she wanted to inspect the contents of Nyai's head. She didn't seem to find the collection very interesting: They were mostly about livestock, agriculture, commerce, forestry and timber. But there were also volumes of general and women's magazines from the Indies, Netherlands and Germany. Magda Peters swept quickly over most of the library with her eyes. Then she returned again to the row of colonial magazine volumes and stopped for quite a while in front of a row of books of world literature, all in Dutch translation.

'There is no Dutch literature here, Nyai.'

'My master wasn't very interested in Dutch literature, except for Flemish writings.'

'Then Nyai must have read some Flemish books also?'

'Yes, there are some.'

'May I ask why Mr Mellema did not like Dutch literature?'

'I don't really know, Miss. But he did use to say that it was dominated by trivialty, had no spirit, no fire.'

Magda Peters ahemmed and then swallowed. She didn't try to question Mama further. Then she shifted her attention again to the whole library, as if trying to give the impression that she had obtained a picture of the cultural level of Mama's family, a family much slandered at my school lately.

'May I speak with Annelies Mellema?'

'Ann, Annelies!' called out Mama.

I went to her room. I found her sitting by the window. Her gaze was occupied with the gread broad panorama in the distance, the mountain range and forests.

'Don't you want to come, Ann?'

She still frowned. Didn't answer.

'Very well. Stay in your room, Ann,' and I went and left her.

'Ann!' called Mama once more, softly.

'She's not feeling well. Forgive her, Miss, she's just recovered from an illness.'

The two women went downstairs to the garden verandah while busily chatting to each other. I don't know what about. One hour later I escorted my teacher home in the same buggy.

She invited me to come in and sit for a moment. But during the journey she did not speak at all.

'Firstly, Minke, after seeing what that family is like, Minke, I feel that I'd very much like to visit there often. Your Mama is indeed extraordinary. Her clothes, her appearance, her attitudes. But there are too many sides of her personality. And, except for the embroidery on her *kabaya* and her language, she is totally Native.

'That complicated personality of hers has come very close to taking on the progressive and bright aspects of Europe. And indeed she knows a great deal, too much for a Native to know, and a female Native at that. She is indeed fit to be your teacher. Only that growl of revenge in her voice and in the implications of her words . . . I couldn't bear to hear it. If that revengefulness was missing, ah, she'd be truly, brilliantly outstanding, Minke. This is the first time I've met someone, and a woman too, who didn't want to make peace with her own fate.' She let out a great long breath. 'And it's amazing, her consciousness of the law.'

I was silent. There were several things I did not understand at all. I will ask Jean when I get a chance.

'Just like something out of a legend from *A Thousand and One Nights*. Imagine, she feels it's more proper that she be called Nyai. I thought it was only a part of her revenge. But, indeed, Nyai is the proper term for the concubine of a non-Native. She doesn't like being treated in any special way. She continues to stand firm on her actual situation – with a grandness sown of revenge.'

I still didn't intervene. Mama was being analysed as if she was a character in a novel and Magda Peters was elucidating her personality in front of class.

'A person who is used to giving orders, running things, after giving everything proper consideration, Minke. She could run a much bigger business. I've never met a female entrepreneur like her. A degree from a Business Academy would not guarantee ability such as hers. You're right, Minke, she is a successful, self-educated person. And I've only talked about the business side. God!' she made noises with her mouth. 'That's what's called a historical jump, Minke, for a Native. God, God! She should be living in the next century. God!'

I still only listened.

'In literary matters she could still learn from you, but even there she is, all the same, amazing. But you know what I found most amazing about her? She dared state her opinions! Even though there was no guarantee they were correct. She was not afraid of being wrong. Determined, with the courage to study from her own mistakes. God!'

I followed what she was saying without comment.

'I'd like to write about this extraordinary thing. It's a great pity I can't write like you, Minke. It's true what she said: Without spirit, without fire. All I have is the desire, only the desire. Nothing more. You should be happy, Minke, being able to write. And that Association Theory, Minke, it lies collapsed and broken just because of that Native woman, your Mama, Minke. If there were just a thousand Natives like that in the Indies, Minke, these Netherlands Indies, Minke, these Netherlands Indies could just shut up shop. Perhaps I'm exaggerating, but it's only a first impression. Remember, first impressions, no matter how important, are not necessarily always correct.'

She was quiet for a while then let out a long breath again. Her eyes no longer blinked nervously.

'She could advance even further. It's a pity that such a person would not be able to live among her own people. She is like a meteor shooting off by itself, travelling through space, knowing no bounds, who knows where eventually to come to ground, on another planet or back on our earth again, or to disappear in the infinity of nature.'

'How much you praise her, Miss.'

'Because she's a Native, and a woman, and is indeed amazing . . .'

'Please come again, Miss.'

'Pity. It's not possible.'

'As my guest.'

'It's not possible, Minke.'

'Yes, Mama is always busy.'

'It's not that. It seems your prima donna doesn't like me, Minke. I'm sorry. Thank you for the invitation. She loves you very much, Minke, that prima donna of yours. You should be happy, Minke. Now I know what all the gossip has been about.'

14

I had come to feel at peace and safe at Wonokromo. Robert was never to be seen. Mama and Annelies never mentioned him. Even so it did not mean I could feel I'd taken his place. I put all my efforts into impressing people outside that I was not a bandit, and had no intention of acting like one. And that I was no more than a guest who could be told to leave at any time.

And one night after finishing some study I decided I would not do any writing. I would have a rest and then continue with some more schoolwork. I don't know why I had become so industrious all of a sudden. I wanted to get ahead at school. One thing was for sure: it was not because of pressure from my family or from Annelies.

And I received no particular encouragement from my mother's letters either. They always asked if I was being beset by difficulties. I answered her fourth letter to tell her that I was doing well financially and to suggest that my monthly allowance be used for my younger brothers and sisters.

Correspondence was the hardest work. And in every letter I still gave Telinga's address. I only used the Wonokromo address when writing to Sarah and Miriam. They had started this. And I never asked them where they obtained the address.

I'd finished three algebra exercises that evening. The clock's pendulum struck nine times. The moment the chime stopped there was a knock on my door. Before I could answer, Annelies had entered.

'According to our rules you should be in bed by nine o'clock!' I rebuked her.

'No!' she frowned sullenly. 'I don't want to sleep if Mas won't study in my room like before.'

'You're becoming more and more spoiled Ann,' and, puh! even Dr Martinet would not have been able to handle a patient as difficult as her. I knew for sure: she really wouldn't go to sleep until her wishes had been one hundred per cent fulfilled.

'Come on upstairs. Tell me a story until I fall asleep like you usually do.'

'I've run out of stories.'

'Don't make it impossible for me to sleep, Mas.'

'Mama knows a lot of stories, Ann.'

'Your stories are always better,' and she closed all my books and pulled me up from my chair.

This doctor, obedient to his patient, gave in to her tugging, left the verandah, went upstairs, past Mama's room and the library, and once again entered Annelies's room. Over the last few days I hadn't been putting her blankets on or pulling down the mosquito net. As soon as she seemed to be getting well, she had to do all that herself.

She climbed straight up into her bed, lay down, and said:

'Pull up my blanket, Mas.'

'You're not really going to keep on being as spoiled as this?' I protested.

"Who else will spoil me if you don't? Nah! now tell me a story. Don't just stand there. Sit here like you usually do.'

So I sat on the edge of the mattress, not knowing what I must do near this newly-recovered goddess of beauty.

'Come on, begin a beautiful story. One better than Stevenson's *Treasure Island* or *Kidnapped,* more beautiful than Dickens's *Our Mutual Friend.* Those stories don't speak, Mas.'

How I must always surrender for her health's sake!

'What kind of story, Ann? Javanese or European?'

'Whatever you like. I long for your voice, your words spoken close to my ears, so I can hear the sound of your breathing.'

'What language? Javanese or Dutch?'

'Don't be so argumentative, Mas. Start a story now.'

So I began to invent a story. I was unprepared. It couldn't just pop out of my head. And then I remembered the story of the love between Queen Susuhunan Amangkurat IV and Raden Sukra. It was a pity it was so frightening and wouldn't be good for her health. Dr Martinet had left me orders: You must tell her happy stories, that have nothing frightening in them. This child is amazing, he said further, even though her growth is normal, including her intelligence, her mentality is still that of a ten-year-old child. Be a good doctor, Minke. Only you can cure her. Strive so that she believes totally in you. She dreams of a beauty which does not exist in this world. Perhaps because she's been forced to take on too many responsibilities too quickly. Her hopes are for a freedom without responsibility. Minke, such beauty, such incomparable beauty, must not die. Try. If you can become a vessel into which her trust can flow, only then will you be able to build up her own self-confidence. Try hard.

So I began to make up a story as I went along. How it would end I didn't know myself. I'll plagiarise the characters at random. I thought. Let them complete their own tales.

'In a country, far, far away,' I began. 'You're not being annoyed by mosquitoes are you?'

'No. Why are there mosquitoes in that far-away country?' she laughed and her teeth were struck by light from the candles, and her voice chirped gaily.

'In that far, far-away country there were no mosquitoes as there are here. Neither were there lizards crawling on the walls ready to eat them. Clean. That country was very, very clean.'

As usual her gaze rested upon me. Her eyes shone dreamily as they did when she was ill.

' . . . This country was fertile and always green. Everything that was planted thrived. Neither were there any pests. There was no illness, there was no poverty. Everyone lived happily and enjoyed life. Everyone was clever and liked to sing and dance. Everyone had their own horse: white, red, black, brown, yellow, blue, pink, green. Not one was blemished with spots.'

'Kik-kik-kik,' Annelies restrained her giggling. 'There are blue and black horses!' she said to herself slowly.

'And in this country there lived a princess of incomparable beauty. Her skin was as smooth as ivory-white velvet. Her eyes were as brilliant as day-light stars. No one could bear to gaze upon her for too long a time. A pair of eyebrows, just like slopes of mountains, protected that pair of daylight stars. The form of her body was what every man dreamed of. So all the country loved her. Her voice was gentle, overcoming the heart of all who heard her. If she smiled, the resolve of every man was shaken. And when she smiled, her white, shining teeth gave hope to every admirer. And when she was angry, her gaze focussed and blood streamed to her face . . . amazing; she became more captivatingly beautiful still . . .'

'One day she was going around the garden, on a white horse . . .'

'What was her name Mas, this princess?'

I hadn't yet found a fitting name, because I didn't yet know whether this story was taking place in Europe, the Indies, China or Persia. So:

' . . . all the flowers bowed down, bending their stalks, shamed and defeated by her beauty. They paled, losing their splendour and their colour. Only after the princess passed by did the flowers stand straight again, look up at the sun and complain, "Oh, Great Sun God, why have we been shamed so? Did You not plant us on this earth as the most beautiful creatures in all of Your creation? and You gave us the task of bringing beauty to humanity's life? Why is there now someone more beautiful than us?!"

'The sun, too, was shamed because of these complaints and in his shame he hid behind a great, dense cloud. The wind blew, shaking the sad-hearted flowers. Then rain soon came and withered the leaves of all those multi-coloured flowers.

'The princess continued her ride, taking no notice of what had occurred behind her. The rain and wind could not find it in their hearts to disturb her. All along the road people stopped to admire . . .'

I saw that Annelies had closed her eyes. I took the mattress broom and shooed away the mosquitoes, then dropped down the mosquito net.

'Mas,' she called, opening her eyes, and holding onto my hand, forbidding me from carrying out my intention.

I sat down again. The story had broken off. I groped around trying to start it up again:

'Yes, the princess rode on upon her horse. Everyone who observed her dreamed of how happy they would be if the gods would just turn them into the horse she was riding. But the princess did not know how they felt. She felt no different from anyone else. She never felt herself to be beautiful, let alone beautiful without peer.'

'What was the name of the princess?'

'Yes?'

'Her name . . . her name . . .' she pressed. 'Wasn't her name Annelies?'

'Yes, yes, Annelies was her name,' and the story turned to tell about Annelies. 'She had all kinds of clothes. Her favourite was a black velvet evening dress, which she liked to wear at all times of the day.'

'Ah!'

'The princess longed for a beautiful love, more beautiful than had ever been glorified as having occurred among the gods and goddesses in the heavens. She longed for the arrival of a prince who was dashing, handsome, courageous and more grand than the gods themselves.

'And then one day it happened. The prince she longed for arrived. He was indeed handsome. Manly also. But he did not have a horse of his own. Indeed he couldn't even ride a horse.'

Annelies giggled again.

'He came on a rented buggy, a *karper*. There was no sword at his waist, because he had never gone to war. All he brought was a pencil, pen and paper.'

Annelies laughed again.

'Why are you laughing, Ann?'

'Was Minke the name of this Prince?'

'Yes, his name was Minke.'

Annelies closed her eyes. She still held my hand, afraid I would leave her.

'The prince entered the princess's palace as if he had just been victorious in battle. They chatted together. In no time at all the princess fell in love with him. There could have been no other outcome.'

'No,' protested Annelies, 'the prince kissed her first.'

'Yes, the prince almost forgot. He kissed the princess, and she went complaining to her mother. Not so her mother would be angry with the prince. But hoping her mother would approve of the prince's action. But her mother paid no attention.'

'This time your story is wrong, Mas. Her mother not only did pay attention. More than that. She was angry.'

'Is it true she was angry? What did she say?'

'She said: Why complain? You yourself hoped for and expected to be kissed.'

Now it was I who couldn't stop myself laughing. So as not to offend her, I hurriedly resumed the story again:

'How stupid was the prince. Twice now he has erred in his story. Indeed, the princess was hoping for and expecting his kiss.'

'Liar! She neither hoped for nor expected it. She had no idea at all about what was going to happen. The prince came. He couldn't ride a horse, was even afraid of horses. He came, and before she knew what was happening, he kissed her.

'And the princess had no objections. Yes, she even forgot her sandals . . .'

'Liar! Ah, you're lying, Mas,' and she pulled my arm hard, protesting against the untrue course of the story.

And so I fell into the softness of her embrace. My heart began to pound like the ocean whipped by the west wind. All my blood rushed to my head, dragging away my awareness and disrupting my work as a doctor. And I returned her embrace. And I heard her panting. And my own breathing too, or was it all my own, though I didn't realise it. The world, nature, dissolved into nothingness. There was only she and I who were raped by a force which turned us both into a pair of prehistoric animals.

And we lay there exhausted, beside each other; we had lost something. All of nature suddenly went silent, without meaning. The pounding of my heart had stopped. Black clots began to arise within my heart. What was all this?

And Annelies held my hand again. Mute. And silently there was enmity between us. Enmity?

'Regrets, Mas?' she asked as I let go of a long breath.

And I did have regrets: an educated person with a mandate as a doctor. The clots of blackness were spreading everywhere. And indeed there were other regrets emerging that were not of my own will.

Annelies demanded an answer. She sat and rocked my body, repeating her question. I never guessed she was so strong. My answer was only to let out another long breath, longer still than before. She brought her face up close to mine to convince herself. I knew she needed an answer.

'Speak, Mas!' she demanded.

Without looking at her, I asked:

'Is it true I'm not the first man, Ann?'

She struggled free of me. Collapsed on the bed. Turned towards the wall with her back to me. She sobbed slowly. And I didn't regret having been so cruel, asking her such a tormenting question.

She was still sobbing and I still didn't react.

'You regret it, Mas, you regret it,' she began to cry.

And I remembered my task.

'I'm sorry, Ann,' and I stroked her thick hair in the manner she stroked the mane of her horse. She became quiet.

'I knew,' she forced herself, 'that one day a man I loved would ask me that.' She became calmer and continued. 'I have concentrated all my courage to be able to answer that question. To face it. I'm afraid. Afraid you'll leave me. Will you leave me, Mas?' Her back was turned towards me.

'No, Annelies darling,' humoured the doctor.

'Will you marry me, Mas?'

'Yes.'

She cried again. So slowly. Her shoulders shook. I waited until it receded. Still with her back to me, she spoke slowly, word by word, almost whispering:

'Poor Mas, not the first man. But it was not my wish, Mas, a disaster I could not avoid.'

'Who was the first man?' I asked coldly.

She didn't answer for a long time.

'You'll seek revenge against him, Mas?'

'Who was he?'

'So shameful.' Her back was still towards me.

Slowly but surely I realised: I was jealous.

'That animal.' She pounded against the wall. 'Robert!'

'Robert!' I answered viciously. 'Suurhof. It's not possible!'

'Not Suurhof,' once again she pounded against the wall. 'Not him. Mellema.'

'Your brother?' I sat up shocked.

She cried again. I pulled her roughly, she fell down on the bed. She covered her face with her arm. Her face was soaked with tears.

'Liar!' I accused, as if it was now my right to treat her in such a way.

She shook her head. Her face was still covered by her arm. I pulled her arm, and she pulled herself free, resisting me.

'Don't cover your face if you're not lying.'

'I'm ashamed, Mas.'

'How many times have you done it?'

'Once. Truly. A horrible accident.'

'Liar.'

'Kill me if I'm lying,' she answered firmly. 'Then one day you'll find out what happened. What's the use of living if you don't believe me.'

'Who else beside Robert Mellema?'

'No one. You.'

I let her go. I began to think over her shattering explanation. Was this perhaps the moral level of the *nyai* families? I almost answered yes. But I heard Jean Marais's voice again: educated people must be just and fair, starting with how they think. I imagined Marais pointing and accusing: your morals are no better, Minke. And I became ashamed of myself. She, Annelies, was no worse than Minke.

We remained silent for a long time. Each busy with our own hearts. Then I heard:

'Mas, let me tell you about it,' her voice was calm now. She needed to defend herself. Her sobbing had been replaced by a determined heart. Only she covered her eyes again with her arm.

'I still remember the day, month, year and date. You can see it marked red on the wall calendar. Almost half a year ago. Mama ordered me to find Darsam. People said he had gone down to the villages. I went to find him on my favourite horse. I went into village after village calling out his name. They – the village people – ran about to help me. He couldn't be found anywhere.

'Then someone told me he was inspecting the peanut crop in the fields. I turned and headed for the peanut fields. He wasn't there either. Even though there were no high trees, he was not visible anywhere. His clothes, always black, made it easy for people to pick him out. And indeed, he wasn't there.

'A child I passed told me that he was on the other side of the swamp. Then I remembered: he was preparing a new field, one that was still dense with reeds. That field was to be planted with alfalfa and job's tears for the new cattle Mama was importing from Australia. You couldn't see the field because it was surrounded by tall reeds.

'Do you remember that one remaining clump of reeds that I refused to go and look at with you?'

'Yes,' and a picture of the bushes emerged; they were tall and bunched up together. She had refused. I could still remember how she shuddered.

'I turned my horse in that direction while shouting out for Darsam from across the swamp. There was no answer. I came across a narrow track, broken here and there by bunches of reeds. And it was Robert I found.

' "Ann," Robert greeted me with a funny gaze. He'd thrown down his rifle and the string of birds from his morning's hunting. "Darsam just passed here," he said, "He said he had to see Mama. He forgot he promised to see her at nine o'clock. He was two hours late."

'I relaxed when I heard the explanation. "And how many have you caught?" I asked. He fetched his string of birds and showed me. "This is nothing, Ann," he said again, "the usual. I caught a strange animal today, Ann. Come down."

'He walked a few metres and picked up the corpse of a big black-haired wild cat. I got down from my horse.

' "This is not just any cat," he said. "Maybe this is the wild cat they call a *blachan*."

'I patted the hair of the cat-victim which had been struck on the head.

' "No, I didn't shoot it. It was curled up asleep under a tree when I crept up and struck it dead."

184

'His dirty hand grabbed my shoulder and I spoke angrily to him. He attacked me like a mad buffalo, Mas. I lost my balance and fell into the reeds. Had there been one sharp reed trunk, I would have been speared and would have died for sure. He fell on top of me. He held me with his left arm, at the same time covering my mouth. I knew I was going to be killed. And I struggled to be free, scratching his face. I couldn't fight those mighty muscles of his. I called out for Mama and Darsam. My calls died under the palm of his hand. Then I remembered Mama's warning: "Don't go near your brother." Now I understood, but it was too late. For a long time Mama had been alluding to his greed for Papa's estate.

'Then I realised he was going to rape me before killing me. He tore open my clothes. He kept my mouth covered. And my horse neighed loudly. How I begged that she would help me now. I closed my legs together like a vice but he prised them open with his powerful knees. I could not avoid the disaster.

'An unavoidable disaster, Mas,' and she was silent for a long time again. I didn't say anything but transmuted her story into images.

'My horse neighed again, came forward and bit Robert on his bottom. My brother yelled out in pain, jumped up. The horse chased him for a moment. He ran out of the reed bush. I grabbed his rifle and ran out too. I shot at him. I don't know whether he was hit or not. In the distance I could see blood all over his pants, running down onto his trouser legs. The wound from the horse bite.

'I threw down the rifle. My body hurt all over. I tasted the salty taste of blood in my mouth. I couldn't climb up upon *Bawuk*, but when I neared the villagers I forced myself up on her so my dishevelled clothes were hidden . . .'

'Annelies!' I exclaimed and I embraced her. 'I believe you, Ann. I believe you.'

'Your trust is my life, Mas. I've known that from the beginning.'

Once again neither of us spoke for a while. It was then I had my doubts about the doctor's advice. She was adult enough. She knew how to defend herself, even if she hadn't been successful. She knew the meaning of death and trust.

'Didn't you say anything to Mama?'

'What good would that do? The situation would have got worse. If Mama found out, Robert would have been eliminated by Darsam, and then everyone would have been destroyed. Mama. Me. No one would come to our business any more. Our house would have become a house of Satan.'

She spoke these last words strongly. But suddenly her strength disappeared: she hugged me again and cried again . . . and cried again . . .

'Have I done wrong or not, Mas?'

I hugged her in return. And suddenly my heart pounded, whipped up by the east wind. And once again it happened; we formed a pair of prehistoric animals, until finally we rolled over on the bed again. This time there was no clot of blackness in my heart. And we lay in each other's embrace, like wooden dolls.

Annelies fell asleep.

Indistinctly, half-consciously, I thought I heard Mama come in, stop for a second in front of the bed, chase away the mosquitoes, and mumble:

'Hugging each other, like two crabs.'

Half-awake, half-dreaming, I felt that woman pull up our blankets, pull down the mosquito net, blow out the candles, and then leave, closing the door.

15

My schoolfriends still kept away from me. The only one who began to befriend me again was Jan Dapperste. All this time he was my admirer and
looked upon me as a *'Mei-kind'*, a 'child of May', a child of good fortune,
a child who would never suffer failure.

He studied industriously, yet his marks were always below mine. His
pocket-money also came from me. Perhaps because of that pocket-money
he looked upon me as his elder brother. We were in the same class.

Jan Dapperste always told me of any rumour about me. So I knew all the
ill-intentioned things Robert Suurhof planned against me. From Jan, I also
found out that Suurhof had reported me to the school Director. Who cares,
I thought. If they want to expel me, let them. I can't do anything in this
school anyway. Elsewhere? Free and able.

Once the School Director did call me in and ask why I had become
such a loner and didn't seem to be liked by the other students. I answered
that I liked them all, and that there was no way I could make them like
me. He then said that there must be some reason they don't like me. Of
course, Director. What's the reason? He asked again. I really don't know,
I answered, I only know that there have been rumours about me spread by
Robert Suurhof.

'Because you're not one of them any longer. Not a part of them, not the
same as them.'

I quickly understood: this was a sign I was to be expelled. Very well – I'd
prepared myself to face such an eventuality. No need to be afraid. I may
not continue my studies? No matter. In the final analysis school was no more
than just a way to fill in time anyway. If I could advance, good; if not, no
matter.

'We hope that you can improve your behaviour. You will be important
one day, an official. You're receiving a European education. You should
be continuing your studies in Europe. Don't you want to become a
bupati?'

'No.'

'No?' he stared at me more sharply. For a moment only. 'Ah yes, perhaps
you want to become a writer. Or a journalist. Even so, proper behaviour is

still required. Or do I need to write a letter to the *Bupati* of B— or Assistant Resident Herbert de la Croix?'

'If you feel that to write to them about me would be useful, of course there'd be no harm in doing so.'

'So you agree that I should write the letters?'

'It's no concern of mine. That's your affair, Director. It has nothing to do with me.'

'Nothing to do with you?' he gazed at me again, still more sharply. Then in amazement. Resuming hesitantly. 'So who am I talking to now? Minke or Max Tollenaar?'

'They're the same, Sir, the one individual with different names.'

He told me to go and didn't summon me again.

Miss Magda Peters also seemed to keep her distance, though she still seemed friendly, and I met her only during classes.

The school discussions were still suspended by the Director.

And amazingly, I felt that whatever was going to happen, I was dependent on nobody. I felt strong. My writings were being read by more and more people. More and more were being published – even though they hadn't brought in a single cent all this time. If the public knew I was a Native, I thought, maybe their interest would dissolve away; perhaps they would also feel deceived. Only a Native! I was prepared to face this also. Jan Dapperste had already warned me of Suurhof's plan to expose me to the public.

The interview with the school Director was not the only thing that occurred during that month however. Not long after Jan Dapperste's whispered warnings, the paper *S.N. v/d D.* summoned me to their office. The managing editor of the paper wanted to meet me.

Jan Dapperste did not refuse my invitation to accompany me.

Mr Maarten Nijman received us both and pushed across to me a reader's letter. Exactly as Jan had said: Max Tollenaar is only a Native. Jan and I recognised the writing. Jan nodded knowingly.

'Have you called me to obtain recompense because of this letter?' I asked.

'So what it says is true?'

'Yes.'

'Well indeed, we must make a claim upon you,' he smiled agreeably, 'we've prepared our claim. You no doubt know what we are going to demand?'

'No.'

'Mr Tollenaar, we demand that you work part-time for the paper, part-time but on a permanent basis.' He pushed across a receipt and I received an honorarium for my past writings, even though it wasn't all that much. 'From now on, as you're now a permanent helper, you'll receive more.'

'How can I help?'

'Write, write whatever you like; and may you have success, Sir.'

The buggy took us to a restaurant. Jan Dapperste congratulated me and ate with great spirit as if he had never eaten in all his life.

The third thing that occurred was a meeting with Dr Martinet. It happened straight after we left the restaurant. Jan Dapperste was still with me. The doctor was waiting for me on his verandah, and said he wanted to see only me.

'And, Doctor,' he addressed me, 'how is your patient?'

'Well, Doctor.'

'What do you mean?'

'She's healthier now, working as before, and reads a lot in her spare time. She rides her horse when visiting the fields or the villages. She adheres strictly to the reading schedule I've prepared. Sometimes the three of us sit together listening to music from the phonogram.'

'True. She seems well.'

And Jan Dapperste was left alone on the verandah.

'Seems? So she's not as well as you hoped for, Doctor?'

'It's like this, Mr Minke. I've already examined her five or six times over the last few weeks. I didn't notice at first. But after a third examination, I realised that she always shuddered and the hairs on her neck stood up whenever I touched her. Since then I have been suspicious. What is going on inside the body of this beautiful girl? I began to think there might be something amiss in her unconscious. I quickly started to study it. At first I thought she was revolted by me. Perhaps in her eyes I looked like an animal. Perhaps I was truly revolting. I examined myself in the mirror. I examined my face in great detail. No. I hadn't changed much over the last ten years except that I now wore a monocle in my right eye. Isn't my face normal and indeed, perhaps, even if only a little, handsome?'

'Not just a little, Doctor.'

'Ah! a little is enough, you're the one who is really handsome. That's why she's chosen you and not me.'

'Doctor!' I exclaimed protesting.

'Yes, Dr Minke,' he laughed. 'Only after I met you, did I realise that she didn't shudder because of my appearance. It seems she shuddered because of my skin. White skin.'

'Her father was also white-skinned. A Pure-Blood.'

'Ts, ts, this is only a guess. Her father was white-skinned. Pure-Blooded. Yes. Listen, I called you to help me solve this problem. Yes, her father was a Pure-Blood European. Precisely. How many children in this world feel revulsion towards their parents? Deeply or not? Permanently or only sometimes? There are indeed no statistics, but there are such children, and not a few. This revulsion can be caused by the parents' own behaviour, for example. If her parents had the same colour skin as her, she wouldn't be revolted by skin colour.'

'Annelies is also white.'

'Yes, but with a Native softness. I myself have dreamed of her becoming mine. Funny, isn't it, Dr Minke? It's a pity she's too young for me. Only a dream! Don't be angry. I'm not serious. The fact is that she's revolted by me. Yes, she does have white skin. I'll make the following guess: an outside influence, strong and beyond opposition, has given her a false image of herself. She feels herself a Native, a genuine, real Native. She has obtained a picture from her mother that all Europeans are disgusting, loathsome and act basely. My interviews with Nyai and Annelies encourage me to come to such conclusions. Nyai is indeed extraordinary. I think everybody acknowledges that. I've said before to you that she has unconsciously self-educated herself? And because of that she failed in another field? She doesn't understand how to bring up her children. She has placed them in the middle of her own personal conflicts. It's not just a deficiency – it's a failure, Mr Minke.'

It seemed that the conversation was going to go on for a long time. I excused myself for a moment and ordered the buggy driver take Jan Dapperste home.

'That child, who knows nothing, accepts everything that is crammed into her as part of her very self,' he continued.

'But Mama doesn't hate Europe. She does a lot of business with Europeans, and with professionals like yourself. She even reads European literature.'

'True. As long as it fits in with her interests. Just look at her relationship with Mr Mellema? She progressed because of her master, but her unconscious always had its reservations and distrusted him. Everyone among elite circles knows the tragic story of Mr Mellema and his concubine, except, perhaps, Annelies herself. Without being conscious of it, Nyai has moulded Annelies into her second personality. That child will never show any initiative if far from her mother. Initiative, in the form of commands that Annelies cannot refuse, will always be something that comes from her mother. Pity on that beautiful child. Her psyche is in confusion, Mr Minke. Her mind is inside her mother's head.'

I listened, staring, confused. It was an explanation that was involved, difficult, the first of its type that I'd ever heard, but clear and interesting. It was amazing how someone could peep into somebody's inside like peeping into the inside of a watch.

'The mother's personality is overwhelming, she knows so much: more than enough for her life's needs in this jungle of ignorance which is the Indies. People are afraid to face her, afraid that they will be unable to move once under her influence. I, too, often find myself at my wit's end to know what to do. If she was only an ordinary *nyai*, then with that sort of wealth, with that sort of beauty, with an uncertain man, there would have for sure already been many thrushes coming around showing off their beautiful whistling. But no. None at all. None have come. None are singing – as far as I know, Pure, Indo, let alone any Natives, who most clearly of all would never dare try. They all know they would be facing a tigress. With one growl from her, such a company of crickets would disappear tumbling head over heels in a daze.'

'Is all this true, Doctor?'

'You must help me think it out.'

'Is it proper for an HBS student to be involved in work like this?'

'Ts, ts, ts, you're the one who has something at stake here. And, Dr Minke, do you think I'm just making up a fairy tale? You're educated: try to prove me wrong. That's why I needed you here. You are closer to them. It is you who must investigate what is happening; it is you who must understand what's happening. I'm just trying to give you a starting-point. You are an adult. Furthermore, only you can be her doctor now. Not Martinet. She, that girl, loves you; and love comes from a source of power that has no equal. It can change people, destroy them or cause them to cease to exist, build them up or smash them down. It's her love for you that I put my hope in; my hope that she will be able to free herself from her mother, so she can develop a personality of her own. From my most recent observations, from her deliriums, from the look in her eyes, it is clear that she has surrendered her fate to you. This is no mere guess, not just some wild supposition.'

His analysis was becoming increasingly interesting – because it did indeed relate to my personal concerns.

'Once she begins to say no to her mother, it means that there is some movement towards change occurring inside her. Of course one result will be pain, just as with all births. Nyai herself has unconsciously prepared the way for such a birth within the psyche of her daughter: she hasn't opposed Annelies' relationship with you, and has rather suggested it and made positive proposals, and even enthusiastically encouraged it. But there is still something else that is troubling her.'

(There then followed, I think, a number of sentences which I couldn't quite understand because of my own limitations. I haven't noted those down here.)

'Annelies, your sweetheart, carries some burden that weighs heavily on that fragile heart of hers. All roads have been opened to you, cleared by her mother. It appears that it is you, Mr Minke, whom Nyai wishes as her son-in-law. And it looks as if you approve of Nyai's wish. Even so, whatever it is that is burdening the girl's heart should also be of concern to us. She has been able to capture your heart, if I'm not mistaken. She should have the right to feel happy. But no, Mr Minke. On the contrary, she is suffering very, very greatly: afraid of losing you, whom she loves with all her heart. Nah, this is piling up all sorts of sufferings on her. She could go mad, Mr

Minke, I'm not joking, a person could go insane, become totally unbalanced, lose their mind, go crazy . . .'

He stopped talking. He took out a handkerchief from his pocket and wiped his face and neck.

'Hot,' he said. Then he stood up and went over to the corner of the room where he wound up the spring of the fan. After it started up and began cooling down the room he came back and sat down. 'For me, if treated just as an intellectual problem this is all very absorbing; on the other hand, to see such youth and beauty dominated by uncertainties and fears is so saddening . . . do you understand what I mean?'

'Not yet, Doctor, these fears . . .'

'We'll come to them in a minute. Perhaps ever since Eve, beauty has excused the deficiencies and imperfections of people. Beauty lifts up a woman over her fellow women, higher, more honoured. But beauty, and indeed even life itself, is all in vain if it is dominated by fear. If you still don't understand, I'll tell you what the problem is: she must be liberated from her fears, all her fears.'

'Yes, Doctor.'

'Don't just give me yes, yes, yes. You are an educated person, not a yes-man. If you're not of the same opinion as me, then speak up. It's by no means certain that what I'm saying is correct, I'm not a psychologist by training. So if you have different opinions then say so frankly so that our work of curing her will be easier.'

'I have no opinion at all, Doctor.'

'Impossible. Come on, out with it.' I remained silent. 'It's not too hot now, is it? Look, Mr Minke, in science, the word "embarrassed" has no place. People should not be embarrassed of being in error or doing something incorrectly. Errors and mistakes like these will consolidate the truth and so also assist in our researches.'

'It's true, Doctor; I have no opinion on this.'

'I know you're trying to hide something. Educated people always have an opinion, even if a mistaken one. Come on, out with it.'

His transparent, marble-like eyes gazed at me. He placed his two hands on my back:

'Look into my eyes, speak frankly. Don't make things more difficult for me.'

I gazed at his eyes, and because of their transparency it was as if I could see through into his brain.

'With respect, tell me. Please don't make me fail in this work of mine.'

'Doctor,' I began to bray, 'truly, this is the first time I've ever heard an analysis of this kind. I'm still amazed by it all; how can I come to any conclusions? About Mama and Annelies, yes, I have often felt that there are some problems. Especially about Robert. My feelings about all this, my feeling mind you, not my opinion, or at least not yet my opinion, is that there isn't much wrong in what you've just said. On the contrary, I think it will help me to understand. Am I mistaken?'

'Good enough and not mistaken. In science, humility is sometimes needed. But only sometimes. But you don't need to be humble when answering my questions. But, yes, forgive me if it seems I'm acting like a prosecutor. I'm absolutely sure that all this is in your interests too.'

The spring in the fan had almost wound down so he went over to the corner and wound it up again.

'Good,' he said, without sitting down. 'Well now, please listen: what I'm about to say may be of some use to you in any deliberations at home. First of all, about her fear of losing you. This whole matter is in your hands. No one else can assist. As soon as she sees signs that you are going to leave her, she'll begin to become anxious. So you must not let her see any such signs, let alone actually leave her. To leave her would mean to break her.' He took a pencil from his desk. 'Like this,' and he snapped the pencil in two. 'This broken pencil can still be used. But not a broken psyche, Mr Minke. If such a person continued to live, she would be a burden upon all. If she dies it would be to everyone's regret. Haven't I already said you are her doctor? It could happen that, should you wound her love, you might end up killing her instead. Now, I've told you, as clearly as I could. Without embarrassment, without fear, without self-interest. It's up to you now whether you become her doctor or her killer. By telling you this my own responsibility diminishes.'

Now he sat down again. He put the broken pencil on the table. Then he gazed at me again, perhaps to convince me he wasn't just joking.

'Yes, Doctor.'

'On the other hand, Mr Minke, it is precisely because she has fallen in love with you that she is beginning to be born as a personality in her own right, because she is being confronted with a problem that is totally personal. This time no one else can give any commands. It is her birth as a personality in her own right that has made her fall ill.'

I didn't understand any of this. I gazed into his eyes calmly. I don't know why but all of a sudden I felt a surge of suspicion towards him, as a European. He seemed to know what I was feeling and hurriedly added:

'Once again, it is by no means certain that I am correct in what I'm saying, even half-correct, let alone wholly. But while you have no opinion of your own, it would be wise for you to accept what I've said as a guide. So you do not become confused. A temporary guide.'

He didn't resume his lecture for some time. I reckoned he was having doubts. The thought gave me great pleasure. At the very least I could breathe easily again. It was true, of course, that they were only words that he was

193

pouring out at me. But what a feeling! What a feeling! It felt as if I was the anvil upon which he was hammering out some new understanding.

'Yes, Doctor,' it was naturally I who began, but only as an indication that I was not an anvil without spirit.

'Yes,' he spoke as if it was a complaint. And a heavy exhalation escaped from his chest which was tight with problems. 'Yes, this is all just conjecture at the moment, conjecture based on a number of facts,' he resumed in defence of himself, asking for forgiveness at the same time. 'I won't say any more until you have your turn: now you must talk to me. In what room do you sleep?'

He knew I could not hide my embarrassment. Even at school such a question would be considered insolent, no one would ever question me like that.

'In science, embarrassment has no value, not even a tenth of a cent. Mr Minke, help me. Only the two of us together can rid her of those fears. So, where do you sleep?' I didn't answer. 'Very well. You are embarrassed – a feeling without value. But so my conjecture has been proved. So Nyai does desire the safety of her daughter. That is why you are embarrassed to tell me. You have already slept in the same room with her. I'm not mistaken?'

I could not look at his face any more.

'Don't misunderstand me,' he said hurriedly, 'I have no desire to interfere in your affairs. For me the only important thing is Annelies's well-being, her well-being as a patient – and therefore also, of course, your own and Nyai's well-being. All I hope from you is assistance. Aid in understanding. My guess needs to be verified. That is the only medicine for her. Your personal confidences and those of all my patients are safe and secure with me. I will always be a doctor, you are one only temporarily. Nah! Tell me about it.'

To give me a chance to put myself in order, he went out to the backroom for a minute. He returned carrying lemon drink and poured some into a glass for me.

'Why do you serve this yourself, Doctor?'

'There is no one else in this house. Only me.'

'No washer or houseboy?'

'No.'

'You do everything yourself?'

'A servant comes and works three hours a day, then goes.'

'Your food?'

'A restaurant looks after that. Nah, let's continue. Have a drink first. I know you need to get up some courage,' he smiled sweetly.

And I had no courage.

'When the need arises,' he began to advise me, 'you must dare to learn and learn to dare to look upon yourself as a third person. I don't mean a third person in the grammatical sense. Look: as a first person you think, plan, give orders. As a second person, you consider, you reject or on the other hand you could approve; accept what the first person suggests. And the third person – who is that? – that is you as somebody else, as a problem,' he tapped the table with his fingertips, 'as an actor, as somebody else that you see in the mirror. Nah!, tell me now about yourself as the third person, as seen in the mirror by yourself as first and second person.'

'What must I tell you?' I brayed once again.

'Anything at all about your relations with your patient.'

'How must I begin?'

'So you are willing. Let me lead the way into the problem. Actually it's not that you cannot begin, but rather it's because you, as second person, are not fully willing. Let us begin. You have begun to live in the same room as Annelies. Now, continue on yourself.'

'Yes, Doctor.'

'Excellent. Nyai has never forbidden you or become angry because of this?'

'You are not mistaken, Doctor.'

'It's not I that's not mistaken, but Nyai. She has done the better thing in looking after the well-being of her daughter. So she carried out that advice. Nah! let's go on further. You sleep separately or in the same bed?'

'Not separated.'

'When did this begin?'

'Two or three months ago.'

'Long enough to get to know Annelies's major fears. Nah! have you had intercourse with Annelies?'

I shook.

'Why are you shaking? Listen well: here the problem is the important thing. Who knows if a similar problem will confront us some day in the future? Do you need another drink?'

'Excuse me, Doctor, I need to visit the toilet.'

'Of course,' and he showed me the way.

I met no one inside or outside the house. Still and silent like a graveyard.

Once in the bathroom I washed my face. I wet my hair. I felt the refreshing coolness of the water and my heart was refreshed too. I wiped away the dripping water with my handkerchief. Then I used the comb and mirror that were there. Nah, that is the third Minke.

As soon as I had sat down before him, he resumed:

'The more you try to hide things, the more tense you will become.'

He was becoming increasingly able to peep into my psyche. I became nervous again. And there was nowhere I could hide my face.

'Nah, come on. Give me reason to be even more thankful to you. I don't need to ask questions anymore, do I? You can continue the story by yourself.'

I shook my head. I couldn't.

'Very well, if you still need a guide. You have slept in the same bed with her. You have had intercourse with her. Then you found out she was not a virgin. You had been preceded by some one else.'

'Doctor!' I exclaimed. Without my realising it, my nerves gave way and I began to sob uncontrollably.

'Yes, cry, Minke, cry like a baby; still innocent like at the time of your birth.'

Why was I crying like this? In front of another person? Neither my mother nor my father? What was it that was worrying me? Perhaps I did not want my secret, our secret together, to be found out by others?

'So my guess was right. *Truly* you do love this girl. Her loss is your loss. You have lost something, and you want to hide that loss from the world. She was no longer a virgin. Yes, keep on crying, but answer my question. It's not the last question. It's important to get a picture of Annelies's first sexual relations in order to understand its influence upon her. A person's first sexual relations are soldered into the emotions of human beings, and *can* indeed determine a person's sexual make-up. No, no, that's not quite right. I should have said: it can determine a person's sexual make-up in the future. Now the question is: Has Annelies ever said or even been willing to say who it was? That first one? Or more accurately the first of those before you?'

'I can't, Doctor,' I exclaimed in my pain.

'The third Minke must come forward. And it's not the last question yet. Who was he?'

I didn't answer.

'So you do know who he or they were?'

'Not them, Doctor, him.'

'Very well, *him*!' He closed his eyes as if absorbing something. Then that qustion of his, which I did not wish at all to hear, stuck like a thunderclap bringing me to consciousness: 'Yes, him. Of course, him. Who was he?'

'Ah, Doctor, Doctor!'

'Very well, you don't need mention his name. Do you consider this person to be a good person or not? I don't mean in relation to sexual passions but in his day-to-day behaviour.'

'I don't dare, Doctor, I haven't the right to judge.'

'It seems that you consider everything to be a personal secret or a family secret, or a secret of your future family at least. Yes, it's very moving – this loyalty of yours to all the members of your family or your family-to-be.' He looked the other way as if to give me some freedom to use my own face. 'At the very least I can make a guess at who the person was, especially now that I've seen your reaction. You are still young, very young, and it is you – even if only temporarily – who are Annelies's real doctor. So you must be strong. You are fond of her, even if you're unwilling to say you love her. I myself prefer to use the latter term. You have shown you are willing to accept the consequences of her deficiencies, to accept responsibility for her well-being. No matter what happens, you will not let go of her, because thousands of eagles will destroy her. Her beauty is indeed extraordinary, that Creole beauty which conquers people, no matter what country they come from. You will end up making her your wife, whichever way you look at it. Be a good doctor to her, now, tomorrow and forever. The older we become the more complex becomes this life which confronts us. So the more courageous we must be in facing it.'

The longer he spoke the clearer became the vision of Robert Mellema; scorning and insulting me, threatening me, glancing out of the corner of his eyes at me and waving his fists.

'Yes, it's your own reaction which have confirmed my guesses. If you're unprepared either to confirm or deny them, what can I do? . . .'

'Doctor, Doctor . . . her own brother, Robert Mellema.'

The glass of lemon cordial in my host's hand fell to the floor, broken. I jumped up from my chair and ran out to my buggy.

Dr Martinet visited us several more times. Usually he came in the late afternoon when Nyai Ontosoroh and Annelies had finished work. They all sat in the front yard chatting and listening to the music from the phonograph. I could see his buggy enter the compound and would come out to meet him after I had bathed.

After that earth-shaking interview, about which I never told anyone except my diary, my respect for him became deeper and more unqualified. I didn't just look upon him as a doctor of great skill, a scholar of great humanity, but also as somebody who was able to plant the seeds of new strength within me. How he strived to understand other people! Not only to understand – but to hold out a helping hand – as a doctor, as a human being, as a teacher. He was a friend of humanity – a title that Magda Peters was to use for him some time later. He could show his friendship in so many different ways. And no matter in what way he did it, people were moved to put their trust in him. Sometimes I felt ashamed that I had been suspicious of him, even though it was my right to feel that way.

After observing him for a long time, my estimation of his age changed. Not in his forties, but in his fifties. His face was always that fresh, reddish colour, and young. No lines of age disfigured his face. Every one of his statements was interesting and had content. He was a very clever story-teller and without them knowing, he noted down people's reactions to his stories as a way of becoming acquainted with and understanding his patients. That's my guess anyway. I could be wrong.

During a visit to the house of an important citizen to arrange an order for a family portrait, I found that person reading an English magazine. When he went inside to fetch something, the magazine was left lying open on the table. Indeed a coincidence. And even more a coincidence that I needed to take a peep into the magazine and found an article by Dr Martinet inside. It's title was: 'The Beginning of a New Age of Social Transformations as a Source of New Illnesses'. In a box there was a paragraph that announced that any therapy that did not take into account the patient's social background was still primitive.

The man returned and I put the magazine down again. Since that moment I knew that Dr Martinet was also a writer. Not a writer of stories like me, but a scientific writer.

And when he arrived that afternoon I tried to observe his behaviour more carefully. I no longer needed to fear him, scared that he would peep into my psyche.

As usual his story that time also contained a message, even though it was told jokingly. It was about twins who, ever since they were children, ate from the same plate and drank from the same bowl. As soon as they entered adulthood, though their faces were identical, they became different people. Each was moved by different desires and dreams. Their desires and dreams shared the same origins. They were born out of an unfulfilling reality: and also of differing images of themselves, of what they want to become.

At first I didn't understand what he was getting at. Mama and Annelies didn't say anything either. Perhaps they were bored except, he then added:

'Like Miss Annelies here. She has everything: money, a mother who loves her, incomparable beauty, many skills. But there is still something that she feels she does not or does not yet have. You must recognise that she has such a desire. If not it will become an illness. And unconscious desire can govern one's body with great viciousness, showing no pity. Both emotions and thoughts are controlled by it, governed by it. If such a desire is not recognised people can behave as if ill – as if disturbed. Nah, Miss, what is it that you want so much that you have fallen ill?'

'There isn't anything. Truly there's nothing.'

'And so why have you all of a sudden gone red? Isn't it true you want Mr Minke?'

Annelies glanced at me, then bowed down her head.

'Nah, Nyai, if I may make a suggestion, marry these two at the very first opportunity,' he looked straight at me. 'And Mr Minke, you have learnt to dare? learnt to be strong? as well as daring to learn . . .?'

He didn't continue. A rented *dokar* entered the compound. The *dokar* driver helped his passenger down: Jean Marais. May jumped down, then led her father along.

I introduced them to the others:

'Jean Marais, artist, designer of household furniture, French nationality, my friend doesn't speak Dutch.'

The atmosphere changed. The problem was that Dr Martinet didn't understand Malay. Mama and Annelies didn't understand French, even though Dr Martinet did. Only May and I knew all their languages. And May so quickly stuck to Annelies.

And Dr Martinet nodded his head seeing Annelies's joy in obtaining a younger sister while May obtained an elder sister. In a second he directed his eyes at Jean, and asked in French:

'How many children do you have?'

'There have been no opportunities for May to have brothers or sisters, Doctor,' and his answer and his eyes radiated his displeasure at having to answer that question.

But Martinet, with his practice of piercing through into another's psyche, paid no attention and continued in Dutch addressed to no one in particular:

'How beautiful it would be if it were possible for the two girls to get together. It should have been happening since long ago . . .'

Meanwhile Annelies had taken May inside the house. They didn't come out again. Their laughter and chatter could be heard in the distance, sometimes in Malay, sometimes in Dutch and Javanese. Jean Marais shook his head as he listened to his child's voice. His face shone. But the atmosphere still remained awkward. Dr Martinet felt uncomfortable. He excused himself, and climbed aboard the carriage that was waiting for him beside the house.

'Mr Martinet is a very clever Doctor,' I said in Malay. 'It was he who cured Annelies. We are very grateful. While this friend of mine here, Jean Marais, has come to ask permission to paint Mama, if Mama agrees and has time.'

'What's the use of being painted?'

'Madam,' Jan responded.

'Nyai, Sir, not Madam.'

'Minke greatly admires Madam . . .'

'Nyai, Sir.'

' . . . as an extraordinary Native woman. He is always singing Madam's praises.'

'Nyai, Sir.'

' . . . so we are in agreement that they should be made eternal in a picture. In the future, who knows if in one or forty years, people will still know who you are and be able to admire you.'

'I'm sorry, but I have no desire to be admired.'

'That can be understood. Only stupid people admire themselves. But it is not Madam herself that admires Madam, no – but rather the living witnesses of the age.'

'It's a pity, Sir – I'm not willing. Not even to have my photo taken.'

'If so, yes, it's indeed a great pity. If so – if so – may I then just look upon Madam so as to memorise you in my heart?' he asked politely and awkwardly. Nyai went red. 'So that I can do the painting at home.'

Nyai's gaze swept from me across to the house, then to the signboard in the distance. Finally it settled on the garden table. She looked disturbed, embarrassed, and her movements were awkward.

'No, no Sir,' she was embarrassed. 'And you, Minke, what have you been saying about me outside?'

'Nothing bad, Madam. Only praise.'

Seeing the confusion Nyai was in, I spoke up quickly: 'Mama doesn't want to be painted now. Perhaps at some other time.'

'Not at any time.'

'He's my friend, Mama.'

'Then he's my friend too.'

Jean Marais, who had always been sensitive, perhaps because of his deformity, looked nervous and as if he wanted to leave quickly. His eyes nervously sought out his daughter, but only her voice could be heard singing in the distance.

'She is inside, Sir,' said Nyai. 'Please come in.'

We entered. The gay singing of May and Annelies became clearer. And Nyai seemed to be very happy to hear it. I'd never heard Annelies singing while I'd been at Wonokromo. It seemed as if she was returning to her childhood – a period that was far too short, torn away from her by responsibilities and work.

Jean was lost in silent day-dreaming.

'Mr Marais,' said Mama after we had all been sitting silently in the front room. 'Your child, it seems, has brought a gush of fresh air to this house. What about if she comes here often, just as Dr Martinet suggested?'

'If the child wants to, I can see no reason why she shouldn't,' his voice was despondent, as if he was afraid of losing something.

'Minke, Nyo, invite Mr Marais to stay overnight.'

'What about it, Jean, would you like that?'

For the umpteenth time I saw how awkward this artist was, this creator of beauty. He couldn't even answer such a simple thing. He gazed at me, not knowing what to do.

'Yes, Jean, you should stay the night. Tomorrow, early in the morning, I'll take you back to the workshop so you don't have to open late.'

He nodded in agreement forgetting to say thankyou for such a friendly invitation.

That night as we lay in the same bed before going to sleep, trying out Dr Martinet's method of conversing, I asked:

'Jean, you seem dispirited lately. Are you still lamenting over your past? I'm sorry.'

'That is the question of a writer, Minke? You're truly a writer now, one hundred per cent.'

'It's not that Jean. I'm sorry. I'm far, far younger than you, Jean, with far less experience and knowledge. Will you answer, Jean?'

'It's a very personal thing. And moreover I'm going to close the matter with the completion of that painting I started a while ago. Are you going to write about me?'

'You are a very individual person, Jean. Yes, providing I can do it properly. What is it that you really desire, Jean?'

'Desire? Ah, you! You are an artist. I am an artist. Every artist desires – dreams about – reaching the peak of his success. Success! And he gathers together all his energy, Minke, only to defend that success, a success that always torments and oppresses him.'

'But your voice is so despondent, as if you no longer believe that such success will ever come.'

'Such a question! – you are truly already an artist. I hope that question was born from your own spiritual struggles, a fruit of your own recent work. It is truly not the question of somebody your age. A question that contains authority. Do you believe in your own questions?'

I stopped. I asked as confidently but casually as possible:

'What do you mean by authority?'

'In short: someone who truly understands his own questions.'

It was clear he wasn't sleepy. And it was clear too that my efforts to get him to open up had failed.

And on that night I submerged myself into so many problems. I felt I was saying goodbye to my youth, which had been so gloriously beautiful and full of victories. Yes, even though they mightn't mean anything to others. It was all these things that I had noted down that gave me the right to claim victories. And the greatest of these victories was Annelies' love. Even though, yes, even though she was no more than a fragile doll.

The evening silence was broken only by the sound of the pendulum clock.

Then I remembered a sentence once uttered by Dr Martinet:

'Nyai's dairy cattle, in the process of becoming dairy cows, fully developed cows, adult cows, need only thirteen or fourteen months. Months! Human beings need tens, even scores, of years before they grow into full adults, human beings at the peak of their abilities and their worth. There are indeed those who never grow into adults, who live off the handouts of other people and of society: the insane and criminals. The resilience and strength – or otherwise – of a person's abilities, and his worth, is directly related to the size and number of the trials he has undergone. Those who always run from tests and trials – the insane and the criminal – never reach adulthood. A cow is fully developed in only thirteen or fourteen months – and without undergoing any trials, any tests . . .'

Ya Allah, in truth, the trials and tests You have made me undergo have been too great for someone as young as me. My situation has forced me to grapple with questions that should not yet be my concern. Give me the strength to face every trial and test You confront me with, just as You have done with others before me . . . I am not insane. And neither am I a criminal. And never will be.

16

That morning the sky was overcast. It had been a fine, clear week. It was only my heart that was not clear. The grey clouds that suddenly appeared within my breast warned me that a storm was on the way. Yesterday when I was out riding (all of a sudden I could ride quite well!) with Annelies – a Saturday afternoon with no school discussion – I glimpsed Fatso for a moment. Since then I had begun to feel anxious again.

I saw him on a cheap horse riding out of one of the villages on company land. In the evening, when Darsam came to my room to study reading and arithmetic, I refused to teach him. I told him there was a fat man who was acting suspiciously, who had followed me from B—. (Yes, I had suddenly remembered: he had bought a ticket at the railway station at B— – immediately after I bought mine. And I remembered too that he had arrived earlier and had hung around the platform talking to somebody.)

'Is he slant-eyed, Young Master?' Darsam asked.

'A bit,' I affirmed.

'Yes, he's been seen several times now in the village.' Darsam continued, and he thought he was an ordinary pedlar.

'If he was a pedlar he'd have a pig-tail for sure. He didn't,' I said. 'Maybe he's on orders from Robert.'

Darsam didn't answer.

'Where is Robert now? He hasn't been seen since I returned from B—.'

'He wouldn't dare come home. Do you remember what I told you before, Young Master? He ordered me to kill Young Master? And I said to him: my employers are Nyai and Noni; their friends are my friends; if Sinyo wants Young Master dead, it's best that it is Sinyo himself that I cut down; you're not my employer; look out! I pulled out my machete, and he ran . . '

It was yesterday that our conversation took place. The appearance of Fatso cast a shadow over my soul. And the morning sun was not able to cast out the grey clouds inside me.

'So you've seen Fatso?' I had asked Darsam the night before. 'If you meet him again what will you do?'

'If it's true he's Robert's man, he'll feel the steel of my machete.'

'Hush! Don't be crazy,' I forbade. 'You mustn't do that. If you did, everyone would get into big trouble. You mustn't Darsam, you mustn't, understand?!?'

'I mustn't, all right, Young Master, I mustn't. But I'll beat him until all his bones are broken, so he won't be able to do anything again for the rest of his life.'

'No. We don't yet know what the situation really is. If the police become involved, who'll help Mama? I can't. I'm not able.'

And Darsam was silent. Then he spoke slowly and hesitantly: 'All right, I will listen to Young Master.'

'Yes,' I said, 'you must listen. I don't want to be the cause of some disaster befalling this family. And . . . we must ensure that no one else knows about Fatso.'

And that morning I saw Darsam walking hither and thither restlessly. He was deliberately making his presence known so that I could call him at any time if I needed him. I knew: he was guarding my life from Fatso.

The three of us – Mama, Annelies and I – were sitting on the front verandah listening to a recording of 'Stardust'. The music jumped about like a school of river prawns at flood time. My heart was still enveloped by those grey clouds. I had a premonition: something was going to happen.

I observed Mama and Annelies one after the other. And Mama was clearly suspicious of Darsam because of his unusual behaviour.

'You seem uneasy, Mama,' I said.

'It's always the same. If Darsam is running about like a kitchen mouse, I always become uneasy. Something always happens. I've been restless since last night. Darsam!'

And Darsam came and stood at attention.

'Why are you running about like that?' asked Mama in Madurese.

'These itchy feet of mine just don't seem to want to stay still; they keep moving about of their own accord, Nyai.'

'Why aren't your itchy feet itchy out the back?'

'What can I do, Nyai, these feet of mine keep taking me to the front.'

'All right. But your face is so frightening. Harsh. Your eyes are wide open and are thirsting for blood.'

Darsam forced himself to laugh exuberantly and left after raising his hand in respect. His moustache still waved up and down as if he was pronouncing some mantra. His eyes were indeed wide open today, as if his ears were capturing some mysterious voice from the heavens.

'Why are you so quiet, Ann?' I asked.

'It's nothing,' and she rose and went over to the phonograph and turned it off.

'Why did you turn it off?' Mama asked.

'I don't know, Ma, the music sounds like a real hubbub today.'

'Perhaps Minke still wants to listen to it?'

204

'It's all right, Ma. Ann, do you still remember the man who was riding the horse yesterday?'

'Wearing the brown-striped pyjamas?' I nodded. 'Who is he?'

'Who was riding a horse? Where?' Mama asked hurriedly.

'In the village, Ma,' Annelies explained.

'No one has ever visited the villages on horseback. Except for Mrs Karyo's son, the watchman at DPM.'

'It wasn't him, Ma. And he never wears pyjamas when he comes home to visit his parents. This man was fat, clear *langsat*-coloured skin, a bit slant-eyed.'

'Darsam!' Mama called.

'Ah, see Nyai, that's why I need to have itchy feet!'

And Mama didn't respond to his jest.

'Who was the fat man on the horse in the village yesterday?'

'Just a pedlar, Nyai.'

'Nonsense. Since when do pedlars ride horses? Your behaviour is strange today too. Even if he could rent one, he wouldn't know how to ride. Did he have a pig-tail?'

Darsam, very unusually, laughed boisterously for a second time, trying to hide something. Then:

'Since when has Nyai lost faith in Darsam?' he wiped his moustache with the back of his arm.

'Darsam! You're really strange today.'

And the Madurese fighter laughed again, saluted, and left without another word.

'He's hiding something!' Mama mumbled. 'I feel more and more uneasy. Let's go inside.'

Unable any more to read, she stood up and went inside.

'Darsam, and Mama too, Mas, they're behaving so strangely. Why?'

'How do I know? Let's go inside.'

Annelies went in. I stood there surveying the scene with my eyes, and then I saw Darsam running towards the main gate with his unsheathed machete in his right hand. And outside, for just a moment, I glimpsed Fatso walking along the road in the direction of Surabaya. He was wearing an ivory-yellow suit, white hat and white shoes, and was carrying a cane, like someone out on a picnic. My earlier suspicion, that he could be a *Majoor der Chineezen*, no longer held.

On seeing Darsam I called out straight away:

'No, Darsam! Noooooooo!' and I ran after him.

And Darsam didn't listen to me. He kept on after Fatso. I had no choice, I ran after Darsam to try to stop him. Nothing must happen. And Darsam kept on after Fatso. And I kept on running too, yelling out for him to stop – running with all my strength.

From behind me, I heard Annelies cry out:

'Mas! Mas!'

I glanced back for a moment. Annelies was running after me.

It seemed that Fatso knew he was being chased. He ran with all his might to save that abundance of flesh of his from the fighter's machete. Now and then he glanced back.

'Tso! Fatso! Stop!' Darsam shouted hoarsely.

Fatso bent down so he could run faster.

'Darsam! Come back! Don't go on!' I shouted.

'Mas, Mas, don't follow them!' exclaimed Annelies from behind me, shrilly and loudly.

I reached the main gate. Fatso was out ahead, heading straight for Surabaya. Darsam was getting closer.

'Anneliesss! Aaaaan! Anneliessssss! Come baaaack!' Nyai could be heard calling out.

When I looked back I saw Mama, holding her *kain* up high, chasing her daughter. Her hair had fallen free and loose. Fatso was running to save himself. Darsam chased after Fatso. I chased after Darsam. Annelies chased me. And Nyai chased her daughter.

'Darsam! Listen to me! Don't!'

And he took no notice. He ran and ran. In a moment he would catch up with Fatso who would then lose his head. No! It must not happen.

'Mas! Mas! Don't join in!' exclaimed Annelies.

'Ann, Anneliessss, come home!' exclaimed Mama.

And if Fatso had ran on in the direction of Surabaya, he would have died for sure. The road was quiet on a Sunday, with just paddy, paddy everywhere, Ah Tjong's pleasure house or brothel, and Nyai's paddy, paddy and fields, and more paddy, and only then forest. It seemed he knew the area. His only chance: to turn into Ah Tjong's yard. He did it. He disappeared from my view.

'Don't turn!' ordered Darsam to his candidate victim.

'Darsaaam! Alaaa! Darsam!' I exclaimed.

Then the fighter turned also and disappeared.

'Don't go in there!' came Nyai's indistinct shout.

'Don't go in there!' Annelies passed it on.

And now I too turned into Ah Tjong's compound. Fatso wasn't to be seen anywhere. There was only Darsam standing, confused, not knowing what to do next.

The front doors and windows were closed as usual. When I caught up with Darsam he was still panting. I too was out of breath.

'The rat has disappeared. I don't know where he's gone, Young Master.'

'All right, let's go home. Don't keep on.'

'No, he has to be taught a lesson.'

There was no stopping him. He walked past the row of windows along the side of the house.

'Mas! Don't go into that house!' called out Annelies from her neighbour's gate. 'Mama forbids it.' But she herself had entered, tottering, into the front of the yard.

Darsam looked left and right. I pulled at him to make him return. He ignored me. His naked machete remained outside its sheath. In the end, I too became wild-eyed.

It turned out that Babah Ah Tjong's building was much bigger than it appeared to be from the outside. There was still a long annex at the back. Almost all the surrounding grounds were garden with fruit trees and flowers. They were all very well looked after. Everywhere could be seen thick heavy-looking black-painted benches. A narrow path, covered with layers of river gravel, cut up the yard into little sections.

For just a moment I caught sight of a couple. They didn't see us. Such views were never visible from outside, closed off by high, thick, multi-rowed walls.

Darsam turned right, circling the main building. There didn't seem to be anybody around. A back door was standing wide open. Behind me, Annelies had passed the row of side windows. Nyai's shouts could be heard more clearly:

'No, don't go inside!!'

And without hesitating Darsam went inside. He stopped, looked left and right, with his machete still in his hand.

And I too entered.

A large room, a dining-room, opened up before us, complete with furniture: table and chairs, a buffet with all sorts of crockery inside. Mirrors painted with Chinese calligraphy hung on the walls. A few Japanese paper paintings of ocean prawns, bamboo and horses also hung on the walls.

Suddenly Darsam was startled, nailed to the floor. His two arms shot out and stopped me from going any further. I kept going on. What was there?

The body of a European lay in the corner of the dining-room. The body was long and big, fat, large-stomached. Its blonde hair was already threaded with grey and he was somewhat bald. His right hand was raised up on his head. His left hand lay on his chest. His throat and neck were covered in yellow vomit. The smell of liquor filled the room. His shirt and pants were filthy, as if they hadn't been washed for a month.

'Tuan!' whispered Darsam. 'Tuan Mellema!'

Hearing that name I shuddered, and shuddered again as I approached the person with that familiar body, fatter than I had seen before, sprawled in the corner like a meditating ascetic. He was possibly in an extraordinary state of drunkenness or had fallen asleep after vomiting.

Darsam approached, crouched, and felt and pushed the body with his left hand. In his right hand his unsheathed machete was alert. The body did not move. Darsam then shook it back and forward, then felt the man's breast.

I came up close. It was indeed Mellema.

'Dead!' hissed the fighter. Only then did he glance at me, and continue his hissed-out speech: 'Dead. Tuan Mellema is dead.' And the frightening look on his face disappeared at once.

Annelies appeared at the door, calling hoarsely, out of voice, panting.

'Mas, don't go into this house!'

I went outside, down the stairs, pulling her by the shoulder. Mama arrived, also gasping. Her face was red and her hair was dishevelled and all over the place, falling in a mess across her ears, face, neck and back. She was soaked in sweat.

'Come on, come home! Everyone! Don't go into that accursed house!' she whispered, gasping.

'Young Master!' called Darsam from inside.

'Don't enter!' I now forbade Annelies and Mama. And I entered.

Darsam was rocking Mellema's body. The machete was still in his right hand.

'He's dead all right,' he said, 'he's not breathing. The blood has stopped too.'

Annelies and Mama were suddenly behind me.

'Papa?' whispered Annelies.

'Yes, Ann, your Papa.'

'Tuan?' whispered Nyai.

'Dead, Nyai, Noni: Tuan Mellema is dead,' said Darsam.

The two women stepped closer, then stood still in a daze.

'That smell of liquor!' whispered Nyai.

'Ma?'

'Ann, take note of that smell,' whispered Nyai again, without stepping closer, 'do you remember it?'

'Like Robert that time, Mama?'

'Yes, when he began to go mad too,' continued Nyai, 'and like Tuan the first time. Tuan went that way too. Don't get close, Ann, don't.'

All of a sudden everyone looked up when they heard a woman's footsteps. And they saw a female in a yellow kimono patterned with big red and black flowers. Her skin was more white than yellow: a Japanese woman. Her quick, short steps brought her in our direction. Then she spoke to us in Japanese with a clear and attractive voice. We couldn't understand.

As an answer I pointed to the corpse strewn in the corner of the dining-room. She shook her head and shuddered, turned right, and ran off with those short steps, more quickly, and went into the inner section of the house through a corridor.

We followed her with our amazed looks. That was the first time I had seen a Japanese woman. The round face, slanted, narrow eyes, the cherry-red, parted lips, one gold tooth: I don't think I'll ever forget it.

Not long after, out of the same corridor, there emerged the body of a tall man, an Indo, thin, with sunken eyes.

'Mama,' whispered Annelies, 'Robert, Ma.'

Only then did I recognise that handsome youth who had changed so much. It was indeed Robert.

Hearing Robert's name spoken, Darsam jumped up forgetting Mellema's corpse.

'Nyo!' he shouted.

Robert stopped that moment. His eyes shot wide open. As soon as he recognised Darsam and saw the machete, he turned and ran. Darsam chased him.

Annelies, Nyai and I were nailed to the floor. Dazed. For a second I imagined Robert sprawled out covered in blood, with a gaping stab wound. But no! Darsam came back again. He wiped his moustache. His face was wild.

'He ran, Nyai. Went into a room, jumped out the window. I don't know where to.'

'Enough, Darsam, enough,' only then could Nyai talk. 'Don't keep on with this craziness. He's my son,' her voice vibrated. 'Look after your Tuan.'

'Very well, Nyai.'

Annelies held her mother's sleeve; she was shivering.

'See,' Nyai hissed, holding back her anger. 'Nothing goes right. You go home, Ann. What did I say? Don't come into this house of sin. Pick up and carry back your Tuan, Darsam.'

'Borrow a cart,' I instructed Darsam.

Only then did the fighter sheath his machete and go outside.

Now Nyai stiffened as she looked at her master's corpse, while Annelies buried her face in her mother's breasts.

'Didn't want to be looked after properly. Preferred to be looked after by a neighbour. Ah Tjong! Ah Tjong!' Nyai called out. 'Ah Tjong! Babah!' and the person being called did not appear.

Darsam entered again, frowning:

'The impudent caretaker won't lend us a carriage.'

'Where's Babah?'

'He's not here, he said.'

'Fetch our own carriage.'

'Let me go,' I said.

'You two stay here,' said Nyai. 'I'll go back. Come on, we'll go home, Ann!' and she pulled her child along.

The two women held hands, leading each other out of Mr Tjong's pleasure house through the back door. They took no notice of Mellema's gaping-mouthed corpse, sprawled out on the floor.

I saw then just how totally Nyai had broken with her master. She was not even prepared to touch him, even though he was the father of her children. She could never forgive him.

'Such a good beginning, such a hateful end, Young Master,' Darsam grumbled. 'What he hunted he lost, what he caught was cursed.'

Soon after, there was the sound of uproar from the rooms. Women could be heard running about.

'Babah Ah Tjong's whores,' hissed Darsam. 'Five years Tuan nested here, here too he died. Dying in a whore's nest. Uh! Tuan! Tuan Mellema! Five years Nyai maintained her wrath. Even on his death, she showed no concern . . . human trash!'

'And Robert was here too.'

'Under the same roof, with the same whores. Damned ones!'

'Mama had to pay for it all.'

'A bill came every month.'

'Don't move the corpse,' I forbade.

A carriage arrived. Not Annelies, not Mama. Four police agents and their commandant, an Indo. They made an examination. One took notes of everything said by his commandant.

'Has he been moved?' the commandant asked in Malay.

'A little. I shook him,' answered Darsam in Madurese.

'Where's the owner of the house?'

'Not here.'

'Who lives here?' he took out his pocket watch, looked at it for a moment, and then put it back.

Not one of the house's inhabitants appeared.

'Who saw the body first?'

Darsam coughed, as his answer.

'What's the explanation of why the whole of the *Boerderij* household turned up here?' he asked in Madurese.

My heart pounded fast. There was no way of stopping it from becoming a police affair now. And all will be involved in difficulties.

'I was chasing Fatso.'

'Who is this Fatso?'

'A suspicious character. He ran, I chased him and he disappeared into here,' Darsam explained.

'You entered someone else's house? Without permission?'

'There was no one here when we arrived. Anyone can enter here without permission. It's a pleasure house.'

'But you didn't come here for that.'

'I've already told you,' Darsam was offended, 'we came after Fatso. Perhaps a customer here.'

The commandant laughed insultingly. And the other agents lifted up the corpse. Not strong enough. Darsam helped, just to avoid more questions.

'Very well. What are your names?'

So Darsam and I were taken away in the government carriage. We were questioned more thoroughly at the station. And . . . ah! in the end Father would indeed read his son's name in the paper – the cleverest among his children, the one the whole family was proud of, involved in a police case, and a dirty one – in a pleasure house too – all just as Father predicted.

That day we found out: Mr Mellema died of poisoning. His vomit and the phlegm in his mouth and throat pointed to this fact. According to the investigations of Dr Martinet, who was asked to conduct the autopsy, the poison had been given in low dosages over a long period, so that the victim had become used to it. On the day of his death he had received a dosage two or three times greater than usual.

And in the end it did happen: reports began to appear in the daily press: the death of one of Surabaya's richest men, the owner of *Boerderij Buitenzorg*, Tuan Mellema, dead in Babah Ah Tjong's Wonokromo pleasure house; dying in poisoned alcoholic vomit! and our names were mentioned over and over again.

Reporters kept coming to our house: Native, Chinese, Indo and Pure European. Mama and Annelies refused to answer any questions. It was I who forbade them to open their mouths. And in the street outside, people collected to watch us. Yes, we were beginning to be regarded as freaks on show.

None of us was detained. I used the opportunity to write a report of what really happened and it was published by the *S.N. v/d D.* A long time later I found out that my reports had increased the paper's circulation. People in other towns also sought that Surabaya paper because it was considered a credible source. The unnatural death of a wealthy man always gives rise to many suspicions and rumours.

I used my week's leave from school to write: to repudiate all the false and tendentious reports. But then there appeared another report, allegedly from police sources, that the police were carrying out investigations and were hunting for Fatso and Robert Mellema, who was the eldest of the Mellema children, and both of whom were strongly suspected of conspiring to kill Robert's – his own – father.

Who was this Fatso? one Malay-Chinese daily declared. The article mentioned the possibility that he could be a recently-arrived Chinese illegal immigrant. Perhaps he was a member of that group calling itself the Chinese Young Generation and who wanted to overthrow the Empire. One of their special features: they wore no pig-tail! And, indeed, Fatso wore no pig-tail. Maybe he had come to Java because he was being pursued by the British police in Hong Kong or Singapore. Now he was making trouble in Surabaya.

211

Firm action needs to be taken against illegal immigrants, especially those without pig-tails, who obviously had criminal intentions.

This guess was based on no more than a sucking of one's thumb! I replied to that Malay-Chinese paper. He indeed was slant-eyed – but that is not a characteristic unique to Chinese. He had no pig-tail – but that too need not be interpreted as a sign he was a member of the Chinese Young Generation.

The result of my article was that the police questioned *S.N. v/d D.* about Fatso. Maarten Nijman refused on principle to give any explanation. Actually he didn't really know what it was all about anyway. For his refusal, he was detained for three days and nights.

Miriam and Sarah de la Croix expressed their sympathy to me, to us, and were sure that we were innocent of any wrongdoing. Greetings also came from Herbert de la Croix who hoped that we would be able to face all our trials with strength and patience and that we would get through them all safely.

Mother's letters, so moving, told of her sadness, as well as telling me of Father's fury, which had reached such a peak that he actually said he no longer acknowledged me as his son. He had even written a letter to the Director of my school withdrawing me from school!

In the next letter from Mother, also written in Javanese language and script, she said: it was not certain that I was in the wrong, and she hoped I would be the one who clears the matter up. And that Assistant Resident B— had visited Father to calm him down and to pass on to him the above words; and also to say that my living at *Boerderij Buitenzorg* did not necessarily have any connection with anything indecent; that such a matter can occur as a result of one's own actions, but also can occur as a completely unrelated accident; no one can guess when such an accident, such a disaster, would befall them. Father did not contradict him. But to his sons and daughters he said: to become involved with the police is to shame and humiliate me, and whoever does become mixed up in a police affair is unfit to be near me.

I replied to all the letters. Responding to Father's pronouncement I wrote: if that is what is desired by Father, so be it; so from now on I will devote myself only to a mother.

My elder brother wrote to me. Mother bathed in her own tears on reading your reply. She cried over your attitude, why did you approach your father, who was already so furious with you, with such lack of devotion, as if he was a father who had never wished anything good for you, his own son. You are his son, you are young; it is you who must surrender.

And I didn't reply to my brother's letter. Let my father be free with his only and his own attitude. Especially too as I didn't really know my father well. Since I was little I had lived with grandfather, so father was really no more than a title to me. Every time I met him, all he wanted was for his authority as a father to be acknowledged. It was up to him! I had no business with his anger and his attitude. If Father withdraws me from HBS that too is his right. And a Native only got into school if someone with position guaranteed him. Only it was not father that guaranteed me, but Grandfather. And it was not certain that the school Director would accept Father's request. If he did, so be it. I now felt that I had accumulated enough means to study by myself, to enter the world walking on my own two feet.

Four days after Mr Mellema's corpse was found he was buried at the European cemetery in Peneleh. We all attended. Most of those who attended were inhabitants of the business's villages. Seven reporters also witnessed the event. Also Dr Martinet. Also Jean Marais and Telinga. The burial was organised by the Verbrugge Burial Company.

Dr Martinet took the job of representing the Mellema family. During the burial ceremony he told of his great sympathy for the Mellema family, especially Nyai Ontosoroh and Annelies, all of whom had been put through such trials over the last five years. Only a person who was truly strong could bear them. And the person involved was a Native too, who was aided only by her clever and adroit daughter. And those trials weren't over yet, because the matter still had to come to court.

His pronouncements, expressed as they were as sympathy, were soon reproduced in the colonial press, both Malay and Dutch. Dr Martinet became a target for journalists who demanded an explanation of his speech. He, who understood that such an explanation would be turned into a sensational serialised story, remained unrelentingly silent. So the Dutch language press in their own way and style rejected Dr Martinet's sympathy which was directed at one who was only a Native woman, and a concubine too, who perhaps was not even clear of any wrongdoing in the case. There have been many proven cases of *nyai*s conspiring with outsiders to murder their masters. The motive: lust and wealth. In the nineteenth-century alone, there could be listed at least five *nyai*s who had gone to the gallows. Even Nyai Dasima could have carried out the same crime, had not her master Edward Williams been such a wise person. But even her story ended with a killing. Only it wasn't Edward Williams who was the victim – but Dasima herself. The paper closed its piece with the suggestion that Nyai Ontosoroh be investigated more thoroughly. Meanwhile a Batavia paper suggested that this person Minke was a character who should be more thoroughly investigated.

Dr Martinet and Maarten Nijman collected a great many newspapers from other towns and passed them on to us.

After reading all their comments and proposals, Mama stated:

'They can't stand seeing Natives not being trodden on under their feet. Natives must always be in the wrong, Europeans must be innocent, so therefore Natives must be wrong to start with. To be born a Native is in the wrong. We're facing a more difficult situation now, Minke! my son.' (That was the first time she called me 'my son', and tears came to my eyes when I heard it.) 'Will you run from us, Child?'

'No, Ma. We'll face it together. We too have friends. And, I ask Ma, don't think of this Minke here as a criminal.'

'They have all the means they need to make us scapegoats. But while none of us have been arrested – especially Darsam – it means the police haven't been influenced.'

Another article, obviously written by Robert Suurhof, accused me of being an unashamed sponger, sucking up other people's wealth and representing myself to the public as a 'church-bird-without-sin'; but I was actually someone without a family name, without anything. My only capital, it said, was my crocodile daring.

The paper wasn't, of course, the *S.N. v/d D.*, but a daily famous for its addiction to scandals and sensations in all fields, with staff who were sensation-maniacs. Or as Dr Martinet put it: sick people, like Titus in Roman times. Dr Martinet visited us to express his solidarity.

'*Boven water houden*, don't drown.'

No matter how one humoured oneself, no matter what salve one applied to one's heart, Suurhof's article struck hard. The pain was felt even in the hairs on my neck.

'I'll take him to court, Mama.'

'No!' forbade Nyai. 'You'll never win.'

'If Mama refuses to confirm what he says, I'll have already won.'

'Mama is on your side,' said the woman. 'But you'll never win if you take it before the law. You'd be facing a European, Nyo. The prosecutor and judge will do you in and you don't have any court experience. Not all attorneys and barristers can be trusted, especially where the case is one of a Native suing a European. Answer that article with another of your own. Challenge him with words.'

This person who says he knows me is perhaps my friend; a good friend or a bad friend, I answered in my article. Why doesn't he show his face in the open, why does he prefer to hide behind a mask when he launches his filth? Come out in the open, Sir, show your own face. Why are you ashamed of your own face, your own name, and your own deeds?

My article, which was first published by Maarten Nijman, was then circulated more widely through an auction paper that had been able to turn itself into a general daily as a result of the Herman Mellema affair. Though most of the paper was still advertisements. In all of Surabaya there were six auction companies. Each had their own auction paper. Only one was able to turn itself into a proper daily newspaper.

How much have I stolen from the late Herman Mellema? Tell us, Sir. Give it all in detail if you can. You can ask assistance from Herman Mellema's family. Hire an accountant if you like, I wrote.

Truly, I would never have guessed. The attacks on me came roaring in. Mama was right – and I hadn't even brought it to court. The controversy didn't focus on the truth or otherwise of the accusation that I was a sponger sucking on Herman Mellema's wealth. The burning issue shifted to colour difference: European versus Native. Papers in the other towns started meddling in the affair. So for one month I had not a single opportunity to look at school work. My daily business was to respond to people's ignorance. And Maarten Nijman gave me every report attacking us; and I had to reply.

Miss Magda Peters also came to express her sympathy:

'Yes, this is how it is in all colonies: Asia, Africa, America, Australia. Everything that is not European, and especially if it is not colonial, is trodden upon, laughed at, humiliated, for no other reason than to prove the supremacy of Europe and of colonial might in every matter – not excluding ignorance. Don't forget, Minke, those who first came to the Indies were mere adventurers, people Europe itself had exiled. Here they try to be even more European. Trash.'

We listened to her expressions of sympathy, and to the oaths, in silence.

We tried to ensure that Annelies was kept out of the affair. It seemed our efforts were fairly successful. In this way an alliance developed between Nyai and me as we confronted the world outside the house.

'If you agree to fight them at my side, Minke, Child, Nyo, you fight them to the end. If they later find themselves cornered – be careful – they will gang up on you. It's happened so often before. Do you dare?'

'We will never rest, Ma, in dealing with this problem. I think Minke is not a criminal. I reckon, Ma, he won't run.'

'Good. In that case you don't need to go back to school yet. This fight is more important than school. At school they will gang up on you and will hurt both your body and your feelings. By facing this situation now you will learn to defend yourself and to go on the attack in public, before all races. You will graduate with the diploma named fame.'

Unexpectedly, there appeared in a European-owned Malay paper an article defending me, written by someone calling himself Kommer.

If Minke, alias Max Tollenaar, has actually and quite plainly broken the law, he wrote, why have none of his accusers taken him to court? Do they consider that the law in the Netherlands Indies doesn't fulfil their needs? Or are they deliberately insulting the law and exposing the impotence of our honourable law officers? Or do these not-so-honourable gentlemen want to create a new law of their own?

As a consequence of this article several legal people began arguing among themselves, and attention was shifted away from me. And that diploma called fame, promised by Nyai, did not come my way.

Nyai Ontosoroh seemed nonplussed in facing all the possibilities. In all this extraordinary business Annelies became even more absorbed in her work. Relations with the outside world were surrendered to Mama and me. And all of a sudden I was acknowledged as the only man in the house. Though not formally, of course.

The court case couldn't be put off any longer. Robert Mellema and Fatso were still not to be found. So the court was to try Babah Ah Tjong as the accused. A White court, a European Court! not because Ah Tjong had *forum privilegiatum*, but because there was *connexiteit*, where the victim is European, though the accused is not, something I found out later. He was accused with the premeditated murder of Herman Mellema, murder carried out both gradually as well as in a final act.

Perhaps it was the biggest ever court case in Surabaya. Aroused by the reports and the arguments in the newspapers, the inhabitants of Surabaya, of all races, flocked to witness it. It was also reported that many people came from other towns. Nyai's brother from Tulangan also came.

People also said it was the most expensive court trial ever. No less than four sworn interpreters were used: for Javanese and Madurese, Chinese, Japanese, and Malay. All the interpreters were Pure-Blood Europeans.

Mr Telinga, Jean Marais and Kommer also came. Kommer said that for as long as he'd been a journalist this much-feared building had never experienced such a cheerful group of visitors.

An owner of an auction office and paper that I knew also attended.

The Surabaya HBS closed for the first time in its history: the teachers and students shifted their class to the court-building compound.

Dr Martinet was called as an expert medical witness.

Babah Ah Tjong hired a defence lawyer from Hong Kong who spoke in English. So they had to get another interpreter.

People said that this was also the first time a Chinese had been tried by a European court.

The trial passed quickly at first. Dutch was used. It was difficult to get from Ah Tjong a confession of the motive behind the murder, even though he did confess to the poisoning using a Chinese prescription unknown to the medical world. He wouldn't tell the formula. All he would admit was that it made the victim lose his sense of balance, as was proved at trials on ten murderers in Kalisosok gaol.

At first Ah Tjong denied that the mixture could do any damage. Its only use was as an aromatic for palm wine, he said. A Chinese physician was called as a witness. He repudiated Ah Tjong's explanation and the accused was pressed on this, the weakest aspect of his defence, which brought him to an eventual confession of murder.

What was his motive?

At first, Ah Tjong said he was fed up with his customer who, after five years, still didn't want to leave. But he couldn't answer the question: why was he fed up when all this time his customer returned him a profit? And why then was Robert Mellema taken in?

The questioning of Nyai Ontosoroh, who had become the star of the trial, made her go scarlet. She was not allowed to use Dutch and ordered to use Javanese. She refused, and used Malay. She explained that the late Herman Mellema's bill at Ah Tjong's was forty-five *guilders* a month. It was paid at her office to a messenger. Lately, she had received bills for Robert Mellema at sixty *guilders* a month.

Why did Robert have to pay so much?

Because, answered Ah Tjong, Sinyo Lobell only wanted Maiko, who was the most expensive girl; and he wanted her just for himself.

Was it true that Maiko only served Robert Mellema? Maiko said no. She served whoever Ah Tjong told her to serve, including Ah Tjong himself. Especially as Robert Mellema had recently begun to lose his strength and his sexual desires.

To satisfy those interested, Maiko was questioned as to whether she had ever contracted a venereal disease while she had been a prostitute. The expert witness, Dr Martinet, explained that it was true that Maiko had contracted syphilis.

Did not Maiko regret having spread such a sickness in another people's country? She answered that it was not her wish that she become ill. She did not make the sickness. Her task as a prostitute was only to serve the customers.

Still to satisfy those especially interested, another question was asked: Who gave the disease to you? With a clear and beautiful voice Maiko answered that she didn't know. If customers were infected because of me, it was not my fault.

Had Babah Ah Tjong ever expressed his dissatisfaction to Nyai? Nyai answered that she had never even met her neighbour. She had only ever met his bills. Their first meeting was in this courtroom.

Finally, the court ran into many issues that could not be cleared up and which therefore annoyed many people. The absence of Robert Mellema and Fatso was an obstacle that could not be overcome. But of all the questioning I thought out of order, the worst was that about my relationship with Annelies; it made people laugh and giggle; and both the prosecutor and judge, each in their turn, could not let pass the opportunity to ridicule our relationship in public. Also my relationship with Nyai was subjected to disgusting and uncivilised insinuating questions. I was amazed that Europeans, my teachers, my civilisers, could behave in such a way.

It was fortunate that the questioning did not become too involved, though I knew that the intention was to prove whether or not sexual relations had occurred between us, in order to use any such confession as the link to connect us with the murder.

Ah Tjong made things go lighter for us with his statement that Nyai, I and also Annelies had no connection with the murder. And that statement freed us from further involvement in the case.

The trial went on for two weeks. The motive for the murder still eluded the prosecutor. The judge decided to postpone his judgement. The prosecutor was ordered to find Robert Mellema, and for the latter to be detained and questioned. The court's decision seemed to disappoint many people. Many people, so it appeared, expected the judge to bring down a death sentence because an Oriental had carried out the premeditated murder of a European. The judge ordered that Ah Tjong be kept in temporary custody. His helpers received sentences between three and five years each. Maiko was ordered to be treated at a hospital under the care of a doctor, to be paid for by Ah Tjong, as he was her employer. Meanwhile everyone waited impatiently for Fatso and Robert to be caught.

17

The trial came to a temporary halt. I went back to school.

Everyone had collected in the school-yard by the time my buggy stopped in front of the main gate. They put off their other activities just to take a look and stare at me go past.

Even before I had gone into class I was given a message from the school Director. And so I reported to him. These were his words:

'Minke, both as an individual and as representative of all the school's teachers and students I would like to congratulate you on your victory in court. I would also like personally to congratulate you on your tenacity in defending yourself from public attack. I, and all of us, are proud to have a pupil as talented as you. The court trial was followed by all the students and teachers. You no doubt already know that. You have been the focus of much attention, because you are a pupil at this school. Now I'd like you to listen to the decision of the Teachers' Council that has come out of its meetings and its rather difficult discussions about you. Based on your answers in court – I mean those concerning your relations with Annelies Mellema – the Teachers' Council has decided that you are too adult to mix with your fellow students, and in particular that you are a danger to the female students. The Teachers' Council Meeting does not dare accept the responsibility of answering for the safety of the female pupils to their parents and guardians. Do you understand?'

'More than understand.'

'A great pity. A few more months and you would have graduated.'

'So be it. It's all up to you, Director, to decide.'

He put out his hand to me and said:

'Failure in school, Minke, but success in love and life.'

By the time I left the office, class had begun. I could see all the eyes directed at me through the window. I waved and they waved back. It was that response which suddenly made my heart sad at having to be parted from all these people who, it seemed, still did care about this Native, Minke.

The buggy and its driver were waiting outside. I climbed aboard quickly. As the buggy started to move, I ordered the driver to stop. Someone was running after me, calling out. Miss Magda Peters. And I climbed down.

'A pity, Minke. I was unable to successfully defend you. I fought as hard as I could. It was impudent of the court to ask you about such private matters in public.'

'Thank you, Miss.'

She went. I climbed aboard and, at my request, the buggy set off slowly.

Yes, the court was indeed impudent. The prosecutor deliberately wanted to turn our lives inside out in public – a desire that was a kind of extension of Robert Suurhof's feelings.

As if repeating Dr Martinet's question, the prosecutor asked in Dutch, which was then translated into Javanese: 'In which room do you sleep, Minke?' And indeed I refused to answer that malicious question. But with the speed of lightening the question was directed at Annelies and spoken directly in Dutch: 'With whom does Miss Annelies Mellema sleep?' And Annelies had no power to refuse to answer. So humiliating giggling and laughter was heard in the courtroom, quite demonstrative too.

The next question was flung at Nyai Ontosoroh: Nyai Ontosoroh, alias Sanikem, concubine of the late Mr Herman Mellema: 'How could Nyai allow such improper relations between Nyai's guest and Nyai's child?'

The surging laughter became more exuberant, more insulting, more demonstrative. The prosecutor, and the judge too, both smiled, pleased that they had been able to engage in the torment of the spirit of this Native woman, a woman envied by so many Pure and Indo of her own sex.

With a clear voice and in flawless Dutch – defying the judicial order that she use Javanese, and ignoring the pounding of the gavel – like the flood waters released from the grip of a hurricane, she began: 'Honourable Judge, Honourable Prosecutor, seeing that you have already begun to make public my family affairs . . . (hammer of the gavel; a reminder to answer questions directly), I, Nyai Ontosoroh alias Sanikem, concubine of the late Mr Herman Mellema, look upon the relations between my daughter and my guest in a different light. I, Sanikem, am only a concubine. Out of my concubinage my daughter Annelies was born. Nobody ever challenged my relationship with Herman Mellema. Why? For the simple reason he was a Pure-Blooded European. But now people are trying to make an issue of Mr Minke's relationship with Annelies. Why? Only because Mr Minke is a Native? Why then isn't something said about the parents of all Indos? Between Mr Mellema and I there were only the ties of slavery and they were never challenged by the law. Between Mr Minke and my daughter there is a mutual and pure love. Indeed there are no legal ties between them. But when my children were born without any such ties no one was heard objecting. Europeans are able to purchase Native women just as I was purchased. Are such purchases truer than pure love? If Europeans can act in these ways because of their superior wealth and power, why is it that a Native must become the target of scorn and insults because of pure love?'

220

There was turmoil in the courtroom. Nyai kept on speaking, paying no heed to the judge's gavel. She was forced to admit that Annelies was not a Native, but an Indo. And the prosecutor's voice thundered furiously: 'She is an Indo, an Indo, she's above you! Minke is a Native, though with *forum privilegiatum*, meaning he's above you Nyai, but his *forum* can be cancelled at a moment's notice. But Miss Annelies remains above Natives forever.'

'Annelies, my daughter, Sirs, is only an Indo, so is that why she may not do the things her father did? It was I who gave birth to her, who reared her, who educated her without a single cent of aid from you honourable gentlemen. Or perhaps it wasn't I who have been responsible for her all this time? You gentlemen have never worked for and worried after her. Why all the fuss now?'

Nyai no longer heeded the court's authority. A police agent was ordered to remove her from the courtroom. She was dragged from her place, unable to resist. But her tongue did not stop letting fly words, bullets of revenge:

'Who turned me into a concubine? Who turned us all into *nyais*? European gentlemen, made Masters. Why in these official forums are we laughed at? Humiliated? Or is it that you gentlemen want my daughter to become a concubine too?'

Her voice rang throughout the building. And all present were silenced. And the police agent dragging her away moved faster to finish the job. She, this Native woman, had now become the unofficial prosecutor, plaintiff against the European race – a race now ridiculing their own deeds.

She went on speaking all the time they were dragging her away . . .

And now the buggy travelled slowly along roads already showing signs of the early morning traffic. And at the school court too the gavel had struck: I was no longer the same as my fellow students, a danger to the girls, dismissed dishonourably from school. If, for example, the secrets of the teachers were to be exposed in public, cut open without mercy . . . Who can guarantee they wouldn't turn out to be more corrupt? Doesn't everyone have their personal secrets, which they carry with them until death? And that prosecutor and that judge, both of whom showed me no mercy, who knows, they themselves may be keeping concubines, openly or secretly? Perhaps if there was no public or legal controls, their behaviour might be even more rotten than that of Herman Mellema towards Sanikem?

Travelling along in the buggy I felt that every person I saw was pointing accusingly at me: that is Minke who sleeps in the same room as Annelies, a woman he hasn't yet married.

That is a Minke now different from all his friends, different from everybody else – his situation was exposed in court, wasn't it? While the others weren't? And the judge and prosecutor didn't expose themselves either?

What I was feeling then, such very depressed feelings, my ancestors called *nelangsa* – the feeling of a piece of coral still living among its fellows but no

221

longer the same; where the heat of the sun is borne by all, but the heat in one's heart is borne alone. The only way to obtain relief was communion with the hearts of those of a similar fate, similar values, similar ties, with the same burdens: Nyai Ontosoroh, Annelies, Jean Marais, Darsam.

So I went to Jean's house.

'You're dispirited Minke. Expelled from school? Chin up!'

And he whose chin was always buried deep could now say chin up! It felt as if all things joyous had been eliminated from my heart.

'Your school is too small for you now, Minke. If Minke has been broken like this, there's still Max Tollenaar, isn't there?'

He looked at me as if I had some secret store of spirit. He didn't realise that my humiliation meant it would now be more difficult to find orders. I told him. He was silent for a moment. Suddenly he burst out laughing. And I was somewhat hurt.

'Do you know, Minke, I see a joke in all this.'

'There's nothing funny,' I said, annoyed.

'There is. Do you know what? There is only one medicine that can cure you. Get married, Minke. You must marry Annelies. Show to the world that you're not afraid of confronting even the eye of Satan. You'll become like the others. They're not asking much, only that you return to their fold – stupid, uncultured people. Marry, Minke, just marry.'

'Magda Peters said she thought the court was unjust towards us, even insolent.'

'Yes, it was uncivilised. That's the most apt way of describing it. There are some Malay-Dutch papers that have said the same thing. Only not as strongly as that. Those sorts of questions should only be asked in closed court.'

'Yes. But there was one Dutch paper that called Mama insolent, said that she created turmoil in the court. But they didn't even print her words.'

'Read Kommer's article. His anger was like that of a wounded lion. He's on your side.'

'Tell me. I don't feel like reading.'

'He wrote that the actions of the judge and prosecutor were insults to all Indo-Europeans born out of concubinage, out of a relationship with a *nyai*. Their children, if acknowledged by the father, are not considered Natives. If the father doesn't acknowledge them, they become Natives. It means: Natives are the equivalent of children born of a concubine whose father won't acknowledge them. He also condemned the court's exposure of your private affairs. Kommer said that the prosecutor and judge did not have European morals; it was worse than the Native court set up by *Wiroguno* to try *Pronocitro* almost two hundred and fifty years ago. Who were they, Minke? I don't know.'

'I'll tell you another time,' I said leaving.

As soon as I arrived home, I went straight into the office, to report on the new disaster, and:

'Ma, what do you think about the idea of Annelies and I marrying?'

'Wait a while. What's the hurry?'

I told her about the troubles that had befallen my attempts to obtain orders. Troubles that might also befall Jean Marais.

'What can one do, Child? Regrets don't achieve anything. The days at court have brought considerable losses to the business, and my position could deteriorate to that of any ordinary *nyai*, to be humiliated in public, to be sneered at out of the corner of people's eyes. We have to make up those losses first, Child. Because without this company doing well, this family will lose its honour. I hope you can understand.'

I observed Nyai's lips as they spoke so calmly. She hoped so much for my understanding.

'Minke, I have reflected on the strangeness of life for a long time now. If I can't save this business, my position will fall to that of any ordinary *nyai* who can be humiliated and looked down upon out of the corner of people's eyes. Annelies would suffer greatly. I will have been a complete loss as a mother. She must be respected more than an ordinary Indo. She must become a Native honoured among her own people. Such honour and respect can only be obtained through this business. It's strange, Child, but that is what the world demands.'

Annelies herself was working out the back.

Sitting on the chair in the office, the question of Pures, Indos and Natives hovered before my mind's eye, clearing away that humiliating self-pity. Everything formed a network like that of a spider's web. And in the middle of the web were the concubines and *nyai*s. They don't catch all the victims that come to them. On the contrary, the net catches up all possible humiliations that they then must swallow. They aren't employers even though they live together in the same room with their masters. They are not included in the same class as the children they themselves have borne. They are not Pure, not Indo, and can even be said not to be Native. They are secret mountains.

And my hand moved fluently across the page. Kommer's ideas were the backbone of my article this time. And the sun set. And my article began to take form.

Ya Allah, even out of such humiliating self-pity can come greater understanding about Your people. It was You too who ordered humanity to form nations and multiply. You have blessed relationships between men and women of different social and economic levels. Why have You not blessed this relationship between people of the same social and economic level and formed of their own free will – only because it has not been carried out according to Your rules? And You have allowed all this to occur, so as to give birth to the Indos who have so much power over those born with Your blessing.

I turn to You now because those nearest to You will not answer me. You must answer now. I am writing only what I know and what I think I know. Does not all knowledge and learning originate, in the end, from You Yourself?

Ten days after Max Tollenaar's article about the issue of Pures, Indos and Natives was published, Magda Peters came to Mama's house during school hours. The school Director wanted to see me. And I refused to go on the basis that I no longer had any connection with the school.

Nyai also objected to me going.

Annelies ran away into her room.

'Something has happened,' said our guest, 'no matter how you feel, you must come. But first of all accept my congratulations. Your last article was a true call to humanity, a powerful incentive to people to think more wisely. And you're still so young . . .

So in the end I went.

All along the journey, Magda Peters twittered about how good it was to have a student of whom she could be so proud. After all my recent experiences I felt soothed by this.

The Director received me with a friendly smile. All the students were given the rest of the day off. All the teachers were called together. A kangaroo court? Why was all this being done just for one person? Why was I so important?

The Director opened the meeting, and:

'It has now become a European tradition to make judgements on people based only on their achievements. Even on this spot of land called Surabaya that tradition must be maintained. We are not going to ask: what is this man like? No, because that is a private affair. He is valued because of his achievements, because of what he has contributed to his fellow human beings.'

And this beginning soon brought him to my latest article.

'Moving. Touching upon our sense of sanity. More than that: true. It seems that the humanist conscience of Europe, for so long absent among the Indies Natives has begun to grow within Max Tollenaar, one of our own students . . . Minke.'

I didn't understand at all what was meant by European humanism.

'There have already been seven letters, two from graduates, which protested against our decision to expel Minke. One said: this person must be helped, not expelled, even if it means taking some kind of special measure. The Assistant Resident of B— even felt it necessary to come to Surabaya to see the Resident of Surabaya to discuss the matter. The Resident had no view on the matter, but the Assistant Resident offered to be Minke's guardian while he was at HBS. He was even going to seek a meeting with the Director of the Department of Teaching and Religion if his efforts in Surabaya were not successful.

'So, for the first time, one of our decisions is being tested and challenged. Though it is not because of those tests and challenges that we must review our decision, but because of what we call our European humanistic conscience, in the name of our ancestors, and European civilisation today.

'Now, here is Minke, Max Tollenaar, standing before this respected Council of Teachers. This council will review its earlier decision and decide on some new policy.'

Like a lioness who has lost her child, Magda Peters roared, clawed, attacked in the interest of her lost child. Her freckles stood out more sharply. Her eyes blinked more quickly. Finally, in a low voice, slow and halting, she closed with:

'Education and teaching are nothing if not works of humanity. If someone outside school has developed into an individual with a sense of humanity like Minke, we should be grateful and thank God, even though our part in the forming of this individual is so tiny. Such an outstanding individual can only be born out of extraordinary conditions and circumstances, as is the case with Minke. So I propose: let us accept him back in school so that he can be given a stronger foundation on which he may build his future.'

The council continued with myself as the mute accused who did not know why he was being obliged to witness it all and finally it was decided that I would be accepted back as a student. But with special conditions: I must sit at a special desk set apart from the others, and whether in class or out, I must not talk to fellow pupils, either to ask a question or to answer one.

'What is your opinion, Minke, now that you've heard all this?' asked the Director who appeared to want to wash his hands of any past sins.

'While ever there is the possibility, I will continue my schooling as I indeed originally desired. If the door is open to me, I will certainly enter! If it's closed to me, I have no objections either if I do not enter. Thank you for all your efforts.'

The meeting closed. With dark faces, except for Magda Peters, all the teachers shook hands to congratulate me. My Dutch Language and Literature teacher was so satisfied with herself and considered all that had occurred her own victory!

As a closing ceremony the school Director handed me unstamped letters from Miriam and Sarah de la Croix.

The school was still. The HBS building, compound, even the gravel all seemed foreign to me as if this was the first time I had seen the school. The teachers' looks could be felt tickling my back. I walked straight to the buggy without turning to look back again.

'Go slowly,' I ordered the driver, Marjuki, in Javanese. 'Straight to the newspaper office.'

Half-way there the driver said shyly:

'Master looks so pale and thin.'

'Yes.'

'Why don't you take a holiday, seek a cure, Master?'

'Yes, later, when I've graduated from school.'

'Three more months, Master?'

'Yes. Still three more months.'

'What's the use of school, Master, if you already have enough of everything?'

'Yes, what is the use? But if I don't succeed in school, Juki, I'll feel like I won't succeed in anything else later.'

'Master has already succeeded in everything.'

'Succeeded, how?'

'That's what people say, only what people say, Master. Noni . . . wealth, cleverness, you know important people, Dutchmen, not just anybody . . .'

'Is that what people say?'

'Yes, Master, and so young, handsome; and in a little while you'll become a *bupati*.'

'Ah, forget it, Juki, forget it . . .'

At the office of *S.N. v/d D.* Maarten Nijman offered me a full-time job with his paper if I was expelled from school. The work would be very interesting, he said, even if the wages somewhat low, only twelve and a half *guilders*. I told him all about the Teachers' Council meeting and the decision it had just taken.

'So Miss Magda Peters defended you with such great spirit? Ah yes, Magda Peters. Are you close to her?'

'The wisest of my teachers, Sir.'

'Hmm. I think it would be wise if you distanced yourself from her somewhat.'

'She is so kind.'

'Kind? Yes, that's her way of leading people astray, I think.'

'Leading people astray?'

'You must have heard at one time or other: people can be lead astray with kindness too.'

'Lead astray, how?' I asked, amazed.

'She is a fanatical radical. She's one of those busy with the "Indies for the Indies" movement. Have you heard of it?' I shook my head. 'They say the Indies should be equal with the Netherlands. She and her kind don't want to know about all the limitations that exist in the Indies. Only disaster will befall those who dare fight against, let alone defy, those limitations. And among all those limitations the most numerous are the

226

unwritten limitations. In the Netherlands, of course, there is total freedom. Here no such thing exists. There is nothing wrong with being a liberal as long as the limitations here are recognised and no one causes any commotions. That's something you should know. It's fortunate that no Natives have joined that movement. Imagine, if you had joined it! If a liberal is condemned by the government – no matter what he did wrong – if he's a Pure-Blood, exile from the Indies would be his most severe punishment. If he was an Indo, punishment would be more bitter: dismissal. If a Native: I think that he'd lose his freedom altogether, he'd be locked away without any trial – because there's no law dealing specifically with this sort of thing. Nah! Be careful you don't end up the one who gets in trouble. Your country is not the Netherlands, not Europe. If you get in trouble no one among the liberals will be able or willing to help you.'

'She's my teacher, Mr Nijman, my teacher.'

'Look, Mr Minke, the Netherlands Indies runs on rumours. And it's worth listening to those that come down from above. There have already been rumours about Miss Magda Peters. You've already experienced a lot of trouble lately. Don't add to it, Mr Minke.'

He spoke for a long time, but politely, about the activities of the liberals but in a tone that rejected and criticised them. At one stage, he accused them of wanting to overturn the situation in the Indies which, he said, was already consolidated, orderly, secure, tranquil and where its people were protected as each day they went about making a living.

'And, Mr Minke, under the Native kings, your people were never secure, never at peace; there was no legal protection, because indeed there was no law. What hasn't the Netherlands Indies Government done for the people? The liberals indeed have strange ideas about the Indies . . .'

'But they're Europeans too,' I said.

On the way home in the buggy, it kept occurring to me how all these conflicts made the situation so complicated. Now we had to add to all this: Pure against Pure. And there was still the position of the Orientals. While Maarten Nijman also wanted humanism, but rejected liberalism. It was turning out that the more one mixed with people the more often different types of issues emerged, ones that I had never dreamed existed: and they were popping up like mushrooms.

Nijman had warned me to be prepared for the present and the future. And, he said, it could be that in the near future Magda Peters may have to leave the Indies. It was not only possible but probable. The rumours were rife and that was taken as an omen. Before it actually took place it would be best if I distanced myself from Magda Peters, he said. 'Magda Peters may only be ordered to leave the Indies, but you could find yourself in a place that you would never be able to leave.'

Nijman didn't want to explain the limitations he talked about. Good. I will ask whoever is prepared to answer. Perhaps his words contained some truth, if there were such limitations, and they were real.

At the Telinga's house there was a letter from Mother and, as was usual, it was written in Javanese language and script.

Gus, everybody has felt both pain and sympathy as they followed your affairs in the papers. You are my manly son. That is all that supports me. As for your own affairs, you yourself must resolve them all. Don't forget what your Mother has said before: don't run! resolve your affairs well. You remember? If you ever run away from something, your schooling and your education will have been in vain, because my son would then only be a criminal. You are fond of the daughter of this Nyai Ontosoroh? That's up to you. I only say: don't run from your own problems. Because, to resolve them is your right, as a man. Seize the beautiful flowers, because they are there for him who is manly. And don't become a criminal in affairs of love either – one who conquers a woman with the jingle of coins, the sparkle of wealth and rank. Such a man is also a criminal, while the woman is a prostitute.

I hear too from those who read the Dutch papers that you've become a man of letters. Oh, Gus, why do you compose in a language that your mother cannot understand? Write the story of your love in the poetry of your ancestors so that your mother and the whole country may sing them.

Don't worry about your father, he has a poem of his own . . .

Ah, beloved Mother. How great a love from me do you deserve! You have never punished me, never passed judgement on this son of yours. Since I was little you have never even pinched me. Now you find no error in my relationship with Annelies. You seek of me that I write in Javanese, a language that you can pronounce with your own tongue. How I have disappointed you, Mother, not being able to write Javanese poems. The rhythm of my life writhes so wildly it could never be forced into the poetry of my ancestors.

My communion with Mother was destroyed by Mrs Telinga with her usual nagging:

'What about this, Young Master, there may be no shopping done to-morrow . . .' and that meant that I'd have to produce at least one *talen* from my pocket.

At Jean Marais' house I found May asleep on a bed, now equipped with a new mattress but still no sheets. Jean himself was day-dreaming. The workshop at the back of the house was rather quiet.

'Jean, tomorrow you can begin painting Mama. It's best if you paint while she's doing her correspondence in the office. I'm back at school beginning tomorrow. And May can stay at Wonokromo while you're painting, Jean.'

228

'I'll come, Minke,' his voice still sounded lonely. 'I don't really feel like painting now.'

'It was you that wanted to do it before.'

'She's so strong, Minke. Her personality is so strong. I admire her, no more so than during the court case. She's such a determined person, with such vision. I could drown before her.'

I looked at him calmly. What was he trying to say: that he had fallen in love with Mama? only that he had no way of communicating it?

The Frenchman didn't say anything more.

'Have you ever suffered because of love, Jean?'

He raised his head and smiled. He asked in return:

'Have you ever heard the life story of the great French painter Toulouse-Lautrec? His immortal paintings now hang on the walls of the Louvre?'

'Of course not.'

'He achieved everything in life.'

'Why, Jean?'

He smiled mysteriously and wouldn't say.

Still yawning, May climbed up into my lap.

'Have a bath, May. Let's go to Wonokromo. Tomorrow you can come with me on the way to school.'

'By buggy from Wonokromo?' she asked, her eyes gazing at her father.

Jean Marais nodded in confirmation.

'You too, Jean. No need to wait for tomorrow. Let's go now.'

The three of us departed. The buggy was very crammed.

And in the evening, with Jean Marais as a witness, it was decided: Annelies and I were to marry as soon as I passed the HBS exams.

The world and my heart greeted each other in peace.

18

The graduation party was also a party within a party.

For three months I studied and studied and that's all I did. I didn't do any work for Jean. Studied and studied. And in the meantime my life had been restored to something like it was earlier.

I would be allowed to socialise once again with the other students at the graduation ceremony. I would be a real part of the student body once again – even though only briefly. We would each soon be embarking on our separate journeys into that unlimited life before us.

The parents and guardians sat in rows. All of them: Pures, Indos, several Chinese, and not a single Native.

Mama refused to attend, so I came with Annelies. And it was the first time she had left the house to attend a party. She wore her favourite black velvet dress with a three-stringed pearl necklace and a brilliant bejewelled medallion. Also bracelets. And there could be no doubt: she now rivalled the Queen both in natural beauty and in her adorned appearance.

Like all the other students who were to receive their diploma, I wore white clothes like the civil servants, except without the yellow buttons with the letter *W* for Wilhelmina on them.

The two of us entered the hall where we were greeted by Magda Peters dressed in her formal clothes. She greeted Annelies with great enthusiasm, and:

'Prima donna! You are the queen of the party!'

With all eyes on her, Annelies did not refuse to be escorted to sit amongst the audience. Both girls and boys turned around to see my queen. Now they knew: the world had become my kingdom, and I had seized it without a duel. I sought out Robert Suurhof so he would have no chance to hide his face. Instead it was Jan Dapperste who came into view, waving his hand. I replied with a nod.

Sitting in the chair there, I remembered Mother. How glorious it would have been if she could have witnessed her son accepting his HBS diploma. That noble woman was not present. And I felt an emptiness in the merriment and the grandness of the occasion.

The hubbub turned to silence. 'Wilhelmus' boomed out as everyone joined in singing under the witness of the Tricolours: flags and ribbons. Then the Director spoke briefly. He congratulated those who had graduated, and wished them well as they set off on their brilliant careers and he prayed for the greatest success for everyone. To those who would continue their studies in the Netherlands at university, he wished them happy sailing, and prayed that they would become good scholars, of use to the Netherlands and the Indies and the World.

The European Inspector of Teaching did not speak.

Then the program moved on to calling up those who had passed the 1899 state exams. The teachers were standing in a row behind the Director.

Stillness and tension.

'At the close of this school year, approaching the close of the nineteenth century, of the forty-five pupils who sat for the state exams in the Indies, the one who came first was from HBS Batavia. Eleven failed and have been asked to repeat. The graduate with the second best score is from Surabaya, which means he was first in Surabaya.'

Everyone cheered loyally.

I guessed that every student's heart was palpitating as they imagined themselves as number two in all the Indies and number one in Surabaya. Even I had dreamt of it.

'Graduating second in all of the Indies, first in Surabaya, the student's name is . . . Min-ke.'

I shook. I had no idea. In fact no one ever imagined that a Native could beat Europeans. Such an idea was taboo in the Indies.

'Minke!' called the Director.

I still couldn't stand. My fellow students on each side of me forced themselves to help me get up.

'Minke!' called out Magda Peters, waving.

And so I stood up; my legs were still unsteady. Everyone would no doubt witness this pathetic condition I was in. There was no more applause supporting me. Only because the person called up was a Native. Even the teachers didn't applaud. Then came some weak clapping. It was easy to guess who: Miss Magda Peters. Perhaps even Annelies didn't clap. She had never participated in this type of gathering before. She was probably sitting there completely confounded – that child who'd never mixed socially – like the child of a mountain.

I went up on the stage and received the diploma and the congratulations. My hand shook visibly.

'Steady, Minke,' the Director whispered.

Slowly I walked back to my seat, accompanied by the weak clapping of the teachers, and then that of a few students, and then of some of the audience.

Number five after me was Robert Suurhof. Last was Jan Dapperste. When Jan returned to his seat, there appeared from amongst the audience, Preacher

Dapperste, a Pure, who greeted Jan with an intimate embrace. The preacher's wife too. If Annelies had understood what this was all about, she would have done likewise. She didn't.

The party began. First and second class were to put on a Bible play; it was entitled 'David and Bathsheba', and was produced by one of the teachers.

Audience and students sat together now. Annelies was beside me.

Before the play began, the Director came up to me and gave me a telegram from B—: congratulations on passing the state exam second in the Indies, from Miriam, Sarah and Herbert de la Croix. It seemed that they knew my results before me, the person it affected. The Director shook hands with Annelies and was very friendly. Even so I was tense and anxious, afraid that he still might let fly some insult, openly or not. But no, he didn't insult her. It seemed he greeted her sincerely.

'Would Sir accept our invitation to you, the other teachers, and the students, to attend our wedding party next Wednesday? At seven in the evening?'

'So fast?' once again he shook hands with us.

Annelies responded to his congratulations coldly. And if I recalled Dr Martinet's explanation, I could understand why.

He shook me vigorously by the hand and then clapped merrily so that people looked around at us.

'May I announce it in a moment?'

'Thank you, Sir, of course, as an official spoken invitation.'

'Why no printed invitations?'

'Well, Sir, after our past experiences . . .'

Magda Peters, who sat listening, also shook hands with us, without comment. I don't know what she was thinking. At the very least her eyes weren't blinking fast.

The Director went again. It was announced that scene one was about to begin. Slowly the curtain rose. Spread out before us was a stony landscape where later (perhaps) Bathsheba would bathe and where David would glimpse her body. But Bathsheba still didn't appear even though the curtain was fully raised. Nor the Prophet David. People began to stretch their necks forward, looking for the beautiful Bathsheba. Instead, out of the stony landscape there appeared the Director, smiling and taking off his bow-tie.

The whole gathering burst into hearty laughter. The Director couldn't help but burst into a big grin also. So this unrobed, unturbanned David (but one who did wear a bow-tie) apologised but he said there was something he had to do. It would diminish his announcement's significance if it was done after the performance. Then he announced our invitation.

'Invitees besides teachers, students and graduates? There aren't any.'

There was scattered laughter.

232

'On behalf of all those who may not be able to attend, perhaps because they'll be returning quickly to their own regions or because they already have plans, as Director of the Surabaya HBS I wish to congratulate the bride and groom-to-be and pray that they will live happily forever. Thank you.'

And he descended from the stage passing Bathsheba, who was sneaking a look from behind the curtain . . .

Our wedding party, which we had planned to be a simple affair, turned into something much grander as a result of the sudden invitation announced at the graduation. Nyai approved. She was very happy to hear Annelies's report of how it was announced.

'This party will also celebrate your victory in the examination, Child. Despite facing so many trials, you still passed brilliantly. You overcame all trials.'

A few days before the ceremony, Mother arrived. She was the only representative of my family. Nyai greeted her joyfully, as if they were old friends. Mother quickly came to love Annelies, her future daughter-in-law. It was as if she could not bear to be far from her future daughter-in-law and never grew tired of staring in admiration at her beauty.

'Ya, Sis,' she said to Nyai, the future mother-in-law of her son, 'a child so beautiful, like Nawangwulan. Perrhaps even more beautiful than Banowati. *Ya Allah*, Sis, I never guessed, I never thought that Sis would take my son as your son-in-law. Neither in this world or the next will I ever forget it, Sis . . .'

'Yes, Sis they love each other. Only I ask your forgiveness because my child has no race, stems from a . . .'

'Ah, Sis, if a girl is as beautiful as this, she already has everything.'

In the evening Mother whispered to me:

'Gus, you're truly fortunate to have obtained a wife so beautiful. In your ancestors time a woman as beautiful as that would spark a great war.'

'Does Mother think I did not go to war to win her?'

'Ah, yes, yes . . . you're right, Gus, and of course, your victory was glorious.'

We were married according to Islam. Darsam acted as witness and as guardian to Annelies as stipulated in Islamic Law. It took place at exactly nine o'clock in the morning. As was the custom, and with feelings of gratitude, we both knelt and paid obeisance to Mother and Mama.

Tears poured forth from both of them as they accepted our obeisance and they blessed us with halting words. And Annelies cried also. Perhaps she felt there was something missing because there was no father present to share in the happiness of the day. Perhaps.

Mother and Mama put their arms on each other's shoulder, gazed at each other with tear-filled eyes, and embraced. To be moved to tears that way is humanity's most pure emotion. Such emotion also means pain, hurt in one's psyche, because people come face to face with their own birth as humans, naked and bare of all pretension and civilisation.

A small feast followed. Then afterwards the real party.

For the inhabitants of all the company villages, our marriage meant a big feast. The paddy-drying area was turned into a big covered pavilion. Everyone was given a holiday with full pay. The herdsmen who couldn't leave their work received triple pay. Five young calves were slaughtered. Three hundred chickens met their end. Two thousand and twenty-five eggs. The whole of the day's milk production was surrendered to the kitchen. Every company carriage, whether being used or not, was decorated with multi-coloured paper.

Never had the inhabitants of Wonokromo witnessed so big a wedding party.

Annelies once told me: Mama will give me anything I ask for at this wedding party. And she said also: she wants to see as many people as possible around her child sharing in the joy. So she would never regret it all her life.

Neither Annelies nor Mama wanted any dowry. What more do we wish for? said Mama. Annelies had already got everything from her future husband. If there had to be a dowry, said Annelies, it is something I haven't yet got from him: his promise of faithfulness *while ever I live*. And I gave it to her during the marriage ceremony.

At five in the afternoon, there was a knock on my door. Jan Dapperste entered. He was well dressed in an old-fashioned style.

'Forgive me, Minke, if I've come too early. I've come early on purpose so I can help,' he then sat down as if he hadn't been acquainted with a single chair for the last fifteen years.

In a complaining tone, he continued. 'You're indeed a child of May, you've got everything you've ever wanted. You succeed in everything you do. A few more years and you will be a *bupati*.'

'You're talking like some ill-starred child lamenting his fate.'

'You're not wrong. I've run away from Papa and Mama. After the ship set sail for Europe, I jumped overboard and swam ashore. An adopted child who doesn't know how well off he is . . .'

'I've heard you curse yourself like that at least three times now.'

'I'm sorry, especially on this such a happy day for you. It's not proper. I'm sorry. Help me, Minke. I don't want to leave Java. I'm not Dutch, not Indo.'

'I've heard that often.'

'Ya. And there's more than that: I've never felt happy with the name Dapperste.'

The Preacher Dapperste's family had no children. They had taken care of Jan since he was small, baptised him and given him their family name, Dapperste. Since then he's been called Jan Dapperste. He didn't know what his name was before all that. The preacher had tried to adopt him through the courts. He never succeeded because Dutch law didn't recognise adoption. So his name was something recognised in the community, but not by the law.

'Since I was small I have always been a coward. You know that too. The name Dapperste – the courageous one – has always tormented me.'

Yes, all our fellow school students knew. Some even changed Dapperste to Lafste – Jan de Lafste – the coward. And if his story was true, then for no other reason than to free himself of that name he had changed into a brave person indeed: diving into the sea and running away from his parents. I still didn't really believe him.

'So who are you living with now?' I asked.

'Here and there . . . I want to get a job here in Surabaya with my HBS Diploma. The only problem, Minke, is that the name Dapperste is on that diploma too. Must I go through life carrying that name to the very end?'

'You can change your name.'

'Yes, I know. I've spent the last year seeking explanations of how to go about it.'

'And?'

'You put forward a letter to the Resident who sends it on to the Governor-General.'

'Why haven't you done it then?'

He gazed at me with stupid eyes, as if he wasn't an HBS graduate. He made a noise with his mouth and looked away.

'You can't write a letter? Come on, you can use other examples of official letters?'

'It's the duty-stamp, Minke; it's too expensive to get free of this name. Just the application alone costs one and a half *guilders*. For the Letter of Determination that I need there is another one and a half *guilder* stamp. I've thought and thought . . .'

'And why haven't you done it yet?'

'Come on, Minke, don't tell me you don't understand. Where would I get three *guilders*? And then there are still the postage stamps.'

'Why didn't you just say you didn't know where you could get the money? Wouldn't have that been easier?'

'I'm sorry. Forgive me, Minke, it's so embarrassing speaking to you like this on this day of happiness for you.'

'You don't regret my happiness.'

'No, of course not. I thank God too with all sincerity and honesty.'

'Then share too in my happiness.'

'That's why I have come.'

'Listen, Jan, Mama is going to expand the business. She's going to move into spices. You can try working there. You'd like that, yes? While waiting for the determination about your name to be issued?'

'Thank you, Minke. You've always been good and generous. It's a pity the Governor-General's letter has to be preceded by an application – I haven't even made it out yet.'

'The new company is being headed by an Indo, van Doornenbosch. I'll introduce you to him later. I'll look after everything myself.'

He took my hand. His head was bowed down. He didn't speak.

'Don't just be silent. Talk with me while there's still some time.'

'Thank you, Minke. That's not all. You yourself can guess my situation. My accommodation, Minke, and the cost of travelling around Surabaya?'

Mother entered my room to prepare my adornment. That noble woman had struggled hard to make sure she would get this job. No one else may adorn her child, of whom she was so proud, now that he was to be a groom. In her right hand she carried a paper bag and in her left, a basket of flowers, some untied and some in bunches.

On seeing Jan Dapperste, who looked at her in a demeaning way, she hesitated.

'This is my mother, Jan,' I said.

Only then did my friend force a smile and bow in respect.

'Mother doesn't speak Dutch,' I reminded him.

And Jan Dapperste began to speak in fluent High Javanese. I was quite dumbfounded to witness it. And I explained to Mother that he was a fellow graduate, the son of a preacher.

'The former picked-up son of a preacher,' he corrected me.

'Child, Mother wishes to adorn her son now. Excuse us.'

'Allow me to help, Mother.'

'A thousand thanks, Child. But no. This is the last job his mother will do for her child. I must do it myself. Do you think you could move to another place?'

Jan looked at me, his eyes shouting out for help. I knew he was tired. And more than that: hungry. I knew his behaviour off by heart. I took a piece of paper and wrote an order to Darsam to look after Jan.

'Find Darsam.' He took the letter and went.

I could now light the gas lamp in my room, a sign that it was exactly six o'clock. The mains, which Darsam himself looked after, and was located in a small stone house behind the main building, was now opened. The room lit up.

Mother scrubbed my face, neck, chest and arms with a liquid whose name I didn't know.

'In the bygone ages,' Mother began talking, just as she did when I was still small, 'countries would wage all-out wars to win a maiden like my daughter-in-law, *mbedah praja, mboyong putri,* was our ancestors proverb, *victory over kingdoms, possession of its princesses.* Today things are more secure. It's not like it was when I was little, let alone when your grandfather was little. Even though the Dutch are so very powerful they have never stolen people's wives or daughters like the kings who ruled our ancestors. Ah, Child, had you lived in those days you would have been constantly called to the battlefield to be able to keep possession of your wife, that angel. Maybe she's even more beautiful than that. Her cheeks, her lips, her forehead, her nose, even her ears – all are as if formed in wax, shaped according to all men's dreams. How proud I am to have her as my daughter-in-law, Gus. You have made me so happy.'

'She, Mother, this daughter-in-law of Mothers, there's not enough Java in her.'

'You are happy with her, aren't you? Be happy in the beginning, Gus, but then be ever vigilant – a child as beautiful as that . . . the gods will not be still.'

Mother kept on looking to my body, and kept on talking too, and talking.

'You are lucky you don't have to always be fighting like your ancestors.'

'Mother.'

'Ah, if only I could take her to B—, Gus, everyone would come out of their houses to greet her. What about it? Will you both later come to B— or not?'

'No, Mother.'

'Ya, ya, I understand, Gus. So your mother must be the one to come here to see you, and my daughter-in-law, and my grandchildren.'

'It would be Father who would object, Mother.'

'Sst. Silent, you. So you've forbidden your wife to have her teeth filed? Don't her sharp teeth disgust you?'

'Let my wife's teeth remain as they were given to her, Mother.'

'Like Dutch teeth, like the unfiled teeth of an ogre.'

'Why are you scrubbing me like this, as if I've never bathed?'

'Hush! On this your wedding day I want to see you look like the child of the gods. So neither you nor I will look back on this day with any disppointment.'

'What's the use of being the child of the gods?'

'Hush! It is not for yourself that you must be like the child of the gods. Today, all your ancestors will come to witness your wedding, and give their blessings. I would never miss an opportunity to see one of my descendants. Imagine how I'd feel to see my son ascend the wedding throne looking like anything but a Javanese knight? And what will I say when I'm dead and see my grandchildren fail to be Javanese only because their parents did not look to things properly?'

'Do the ancestors of the Dutch also attand the wedding of their descendants?'

'Hush! Why are you concerned with the Dutch? You're still not Javanese enough yet. You don't obey your own ancestors enough. People say you've become a man of letters, but where are your poems that I can sing at night when I miss you?'

'I cannot write in Javanese, Mother.'

'Ah, if you were Javanese, you would be able to write in Javanese. You write in Dutch, Gus, because you no longer want to be Javanese. You write for Dutch people. Why do you honour them so greatly? They drink and eat from the Javanese earth. You do not eat and drink from the Dutch earth. Why, why do you honour them so greatly?'

'Yes, Mother.'

'What are you *"yessing"*? Your ancestors, the kings of Java, all wrote in Javanese. Are you perhaps ashamed of being Javanese? Ashamed that you're not Dutch?'

It would have been stupid to answer Mother's words, spoken so gently but containing an unanswerable harshness. Yes, everybody makes demands on me. Now Mother too. Mother knew and I knew I would not answer. She was speaking more to her ancestors, pleading that they forgive me, her favourite child. The ancestors must not be furious at me. Ah, Mother, my beloved Mother, a mother who has never tried to force her will upon me, has never hurt me, not even with only a little pinch, no, not with words, nor with her fingers.

'Nah, put on this *batik kain*. Now. Mother made this *batik* for you herself, and for this occasion. Four years I have stored it in a special box; every week I sprinkled it with jasmine flowers, Gus. After I heard people's stories about the newspaper reports of the trial, I sacralised the *kain*, Gus. One of you, and one of my daughter-in-law. Inspect your Mother's *batik* work and smell the aroma of the years and years of jasmine.'

So I inspected it and I smelled it:

'Beautiful, Mother, wonderful. So sweet-smelling. And that delicious aroma has been absorbed right down into the threads.'

'Aah, what do you know about *batik*,' and deliberately she didn't look at me knowing that I'd be grimacing from the pain. 'I dyed it red and blue with my own hands, Gus. And the dyes, I made myself also. Smell its aroma again, the perfume of the dye is still there,' and the *kain* was pushed under my nose.

'Delicious, Mother.'

'Ah, you! I'm happy, Gus, to see you so clever at pretending, so as to please the heart of this old woman,' and once again she didn't look at me as I grimaced with the pain. 'I could tell my future daughter-in-law and her mother would not be able to make *batik*. So it had to be me who carried out this task. When I was a child, Gus, a woman who couldn't make *batik* was considered a poor woman indeed.'

'Mother's *batik* is so fine. It must have taken you at least a month to finish?'

'Two months, two *batiks*. Specially made to be worn on this day. If you both throw them out after today: that is up to you.'

'I will save them until I die, Mother.'

'How clever you've become in pleasing me. Those are the words of a devoted son . . . These chains of flowers have also been made by your mother. This *keris* was left to you by your grandfather. It is hundreds of years old; from before the time of Mataram, from before Pajang. From the time of Majapahit, Gus.'

'From where does Mother know this?'

'Hush! don't be silly, Gus. Don't you remember hearing the family tree explained in your Grandfather's house? You never listened to him. That is your fault. Maybe you only value what the Dutch say. This *keris* has been used by all your ancestors except your father. This *keris* was prepared for you, Gus. Ah, how must I speak to you? Truly, Mother no longer knows, Gus. Excuse this old woman who knows nothing, Gus.'

'Mother!'

'There is no Dutchman who can make a *keris*, Gus. None are or ever will be able to make one. Open it and you'll see the thumb-prints of the craftsman sage who made it.'

At that time I was putting on my *batik kain*, so I said:

'Sorry, Mother, could Mother pull the *keris* out for me so I can see it?'

'Hush! You're indeed no longer of Java. Do you equate this with a kitchen knife?'

When I saw tear drops on her face I quickly tied up my *kain* and knelt down before her:

'Forgive me, Mother, it was not my intent to hurt Mother. Forgive me, Mother, a thousand pardons, Mother.'

Mother turned away and wiped away the tears from her face.

'Don't go too far, Gus, don't go too far with your non-Javaneseness. Since when has a woman been allowed to pull out a *keris* from its scabbard? A *keris* is only for a man. That which is for a woman is not called a *keris*. Don't be so disrespectful. You too could not make the likes of this. Respect those who can do more than you. Later you can look in the mirror. When you have slipped the *keris* onto your waist, you will change. You will look more like your ancestors, you will be closer to your origins.'

And mother talked and talked. And finally my adornment was finished.

'Nah, sit down there on the floor. Bow down your head . . . ,' and I knew what would follow on such an occasion as this: the advice before the marriage ceremony. It could be no other way. Nah, the advice was beginning. 'You are a descendant of the knights of Java . . . the founders and destroyers of kingdoms . . . You yourself have the blood of a knight. You are a knight . . . What are the attributes of a knight of Java?'

'I don't know, Mother.'

'Hush! You who believe only in everything that is Dutch. The five attributes of the Javanese knight are: house, woman, horse, bird and *keris*. Can you remember that?'

'Of course I can, Mother.'

'Do you know the meanings of the words?'

'Yes, Mother.'

'And do you know what they symbolise?'

'No, Mother.'

'Child who doesn't know his own origins, you! Listen, and pass it on to your children one day . . .'

'Yes, Mother.'

'First a house, Gus. Without a house a person can never be a knight. He can only be a tramp. A house, Gus, is from where a knight departs, and the place to where he returns. A house is not just an address, Gus, it is a place trusted by he who lives there. Are you bored?'

'I'm listening.'

She pulled my ear:

'You have never listened to your parents . . .'

'I'm listening, Mother, truly.'

'Secondly, a woman, Gus, without a woman, a knight goes against his nature as a man. Woman is the symbol of life, and the bringer of life, of fertility, prosperity, of well-being. She is not just a wife to a husband. Woman is the centre around which circles and from which comes the giving of life, and life itself. This is how you should look upon this old mother of yours, and what should guide you in bringing up your daughters.'

'Yes, Mother.'

'The Dutch know none of this, Gus. But you must know, because you're Javanese.'

'Yes, Mother, they know none of this.'

'Third, Gus, a horse. The horse will carry you on your journeys: after learning, knowledge, ability, skills, expertise, and finally – advancement. Without a horse, your strides will not be long, your vision will be short.'

I nodded in agreement, understanding too that this was wisdom that had been born out of centuries of experience. Only I didn't really know for sure whose wisdom it was? The ancestors or Mother's own?

'The fourth, the bird, is a symbol of beauty, of distraction, of everything that has no connection with simple physical survival, of only the satisfaction of one's soul. Without this people are only a lump of soulless stone. And the fifth, the *keris*, Gus, The *keris* is the symbol of vigilance, of preparedness, of courage, the weapon with which to defend the other four. Without the *keris*, the others will vanish. They will be vulnerable to any attack . . . *Nah*, you, HBS graduate, your teachers have never taught you any of this? Those Dutchmen? Now you know all that a knight need know. Never be without even one of these things. Do not scoff at the knightly attributes. Each of them is a sign of yourself. You must listen to your ancestors. If you can't obey in the other things, then at least complete the attainment of these five. You hear, Gus?'

'Yes, Mother.'

'Now meditate. Ask for the blessings and forgiveness of your ancestors, that they may guard you from the oppression, slander, and malice of others.'

I remained seated on the floor, head bowed.

'Not like that. Sit properly, cross-legged. Your arms relaxed and placed on your lap. Be a good Javanese, even if only for a moment and just this once. Bow down your head more deeply, Gus.'

I had carried out all her orders and her wishes. And indeed I did seek forgiveness from those unknown ancestors of mine, ancestors whom I could not even imagine. Instead, just for a moment, Fatso flitted through my mind.

Mother knelt before me, placing a necklace of jasmine flowers around my neck. She was sobbing. Then she placed a small chain of flowers in each of my two hands. With her hands, and without speaking, she moved each of my fingers into gripping the chains. She kissed my forehead under the curved edge of my *blangkon*. And her sobbing became worse. I felt her tears drop onto my cheeks. And all of a sudden I too began to cry.

And those images of my ancestors, which had not yet had the chance to even take on faces, faded away, replaced by churning emotions inside my breast, squeezing the tears out in an even more abundantly-flowing stream.

'Bless this child, the child of your blood, my ancestors, your most-favoured child. Protect him from disasters, from oppression, slander and malice, because he is my beloved child. I gave birth to him in suffering, almost dying . . .'

'Mother!' I flung my body to the ground and embraced her knees.

'. . . I have lived until today only so that I may witness this event. This is the child of my own blood. Bring him closer to greatness and triumph.'

I felt Mother's hands on my back. And Mother ceased her sobbing. She corrected the way I was sitting, the position of the jasmine necklace and the chains of flowers gripped in my hands. With the corner of her *kebaya* she wiped away my tears. She put right the way I held up my chin, it being too high.

241

'Meditate, Gus, meditate by yourself, without my help.'

Guests started to arrive and fill up the front room, inside living-room and the pavilion set up outside. My own heart was still occupied with the deep impressions left by Mother and the ceremony she had carried out on the eve of my ascent to the wedding throne. I'd never seen a bridegroom undergo such a ceremony. It was probably Mother's own improvisation. Maybe it was a special ceremony for a child who was a renegade in the eyes of his family, but not in the eyes of his mother.

Kommer, who received a special invitation, arrived five minutes before seven o'clock. He stroke confidently up to me, put out his hand and shook mine warmly, then he greeted Annelies, returned to me and said:

'With this marriage, Mr Minke, the dirty mouths outside will be silenced. But not only that. You have finished what you started. And the future? We will continue working together, yes?'

'Of course, Mr Kommer, gladly. We can be good allies. And thank you for your congratulations.'

He was a very friendly Indo. Only the shape of his head and the pointedness of his nose manifested his European heritage. The rest was Native, perhaps also his psyche. He was much older than me, maybe ten or fifteen years older. His movements were agile. And from his face you could tell he was not used to staying inside his house.

Jean Marais and May, Telinga and his wife, arrived in a hired *andong*. Magda Peters and my other school friends, arrived in the same manner. Mr Maarten Nijman and his wife came in their own carriage.

The school Director and the other teachers did not come. They sent a letter of congratulations with Magda Peters.

One minute before seven o'clock a telegram arrived from Miriam, Sarah and Herbert de la Croix. And once again I was amazed: How did they know about the marriage?

As I predicted, Robert Suurhof was nowhere to be seen. His absence became the subject of lively conversations amongst my HBS friends.

And Jan Dapperste, always tired and still fed up with his name, was busy running around like a propeller, carrying out his duties as a volunteer waiter.

There were quite a few of my own friends. There was no other Native except for Jan Dapperste.

Mama's customers flocked in. The recent trial, where Mama emerged as the star of the court had, perhaps, turned out to be an attractive and effective advertisement for the business.

In his usual smooth manner Dr Martinet carried out the duties of master of ceremonies. At eight o'clock sharp he began very fluently to deliver his speech. He started off by telling of the love between Annelies and me and the great storm with which we had had to contend. Never had he heard of such a storm in any tale of love between two people – a tale well worth being made into a book. (And it was indeed because of that speech that I put together my experiences so that they became this document.)

'This tale is unique,' he continued his speech, 'It could never be repeated.'

One moment that fluent doctor had all his listeners mesmerised into silence, then the next moment he had them all laughing. He emphasised everything important with a movement of his hands. It was a pity he didn't speak Malay – many people couldn't understand Dutch.

Finished with the beautiful telling of the tale of our love, he turned to another and unexpected topic:

'Let us now all look at the portrait hanging above the throne upon which sit the happy newly-weds.'

With no less a beautiful movement of his hands, he guided the eyes of all those present to Mama's portrait up above the two of us.

That painting, he explained, is a portrait of a Native woman who indeed is extraordinary for her times. Nyai Ontosoroh, a very clever woman, mother of the bride and mother-in-law of Mr Minke. She is a brilliant individual. She is a ship's captain who will never allow her ship to be damaged, let alone sink. It is through her captaincy alone that this happy occasion is able to take place, the uniting of the gloriousness of a woman with the great skill and ability of a young author. Through this captaincy, two pairs of hands will now proceed forth into each other's clasp for the rest of their lives, as this couple begins what will surely be an equally glorious life in the future.

'And you all know who painted this wonderful portrait hanging here? A painter of great talent! Not just any painter. If we examine the painting carefully we can see that the painter truly understands his subject's spirit. He had brought out the greatness in her. I think that these words of mine are not mistaken. Is it not so, Mr Jean Marais? Yes, the painter hails from France, a country with a great artistic tradition. Mr Marais, please stand up . . .'

I saw Telinga help Jean Marais stand up, and everyone started cheering wildly. The Frenchman went red with embarrassment and quickly sat down again.

The doctor's short speech greatly soothed us. And it seemed as if he was launching a propaganda campaign for Mama, and Jean Marais as well.

From where I was sitting, I could also see Darsam, dressed all in black, standing away in the distance. His moustache was lush and shining, and curled up at the ends. His eyes were wandering about everywhere. I couldn't see any machete. But I was sure that there were daggers slipped down under his shirt.

Nyai Ontosoroh, my mother-in-law, sat behind the screen at the back of the wedding throne and never stopped crying. Mother stood beside her daughter-in-law and, without once stopping, kept Annelies cool with a peacock-feather fan.

Behind the screen also, Mrs Telinga was busy looking after the other women guests.

The pile of presents under our feet grew higher and higher. Who knew from where they all came? Wreaths of flowers were lined up in rows on either side of us. As time went on the rows grew longer.

At nine o'clock the start of the party for the village people could be heard as the East Javanese *gamelan* rang out: *tayub!* Every now and then cheering and shouting could be heard. Darsam's men had been ordered to keep watch to make sure no rioting or fighting broke out. And there was palm wine, and it flowed all night.

At nine-thirty people began to make their way home. Dr Martinet had to leave first because of a call from a patient. About six seconds later, a youth arrived, dressed all in black. His hair shone. A fancy handkerchief adorned his top pocket. A gold watch-chain indicated the presence of a gold watch in his pocket. He strode confidently, dashingly, among all the people preparing to leave. He made his way straight to where the two of us were seated. There could be no mistake: it was Robert Suurhof.

With great politeness, he held out his hand to me and offered his congratulations. Then to Annelies:

'Forgive me, for being somewhat late, Mrs Minke,' he bowed down even more politely.

'We're happy you were able to come, Rob,' I said.

'Forgive all the things that have happened in the past, Minke,' he said, without relaxing his politeness, as if he was a new acquaintance. 'Allow me to present a little something to your wife, in celebration of this occasion.'

Without waiting for an answer, he took out a gold ring with a very, very big diamond. He took my wife's hand and placed the ring on her finger. He twisted the ring around so the diamond was hidden in her palm. Then he bowed down to her hand, just like in the novels about the middle ages. As far as I was concerned he kissed her hand for far too long. Then he faced me.

'I will not go back on a promise, Minke; I admire and respect you greatly, much more than I have ever done before,' and he handed me a little box tied in pink ribbon: 'This is a little present from me on your wedding day. May you both live happily forever.'

'Thank you, Rob, for your kindness and concern.'

'I would also like to take this opportunity to take my leave of you. I'm sailing for Europe, to study law.'

'Safe sailing, happy studying, and success to you.'

He walked away in that confident, dashing manner of his and joined the others about to depart for home.

Magda Peters, glassy-eyed, came to excuse herself. She held my hands tightly:

'I would have liked very much to follow your development over the next three years. No matter. If you ever come to Europe – don't forget my address.' She walked quickly away from us.

Mr Telinga and wife, Jean Marais and child, did not go home. They stayed the night. Jan Dapperste also. Jan was busy carting the present to the newly-weds' room upstairs and making a list of the names and addresses of all those who gave something.

Amongst the pile of presents were some things from Miriam, Sarah and Herbert de la Croix. No one knew who had brought them. There was a little note slipped between them, in Miriam's writing, saying:

Were you embarrassed to invite us? Or perhaps we wouldn't have fitted in properly, my friend? We wanted to stand on either side of that angel so famed for her beauty. What can be done? All we can do now is offer our congratulations, and don't forget to keep up our correspondence. Best wishes, and our regards and all our compliments to your wife.

In Sarah's parcel there was a special letter:

I am leaving for Europe, Minke. I'm fortunate to be able to pass on my congratulations on your wedding day. Adieu! Until we meet again in Europe!

Miss Magda Peters' present included several books and a brochure without the name of the author or of the publisher, and without any year of publication either. Written inside the brochure were the following words:

For a newly-wed like you, Minke, the most appropriate thing to give are special books not everyone can own, and I have chosen those you will like best. By the time you read this note, I will have already arrived home, and will be too busy to reflect on the happiness of a favourite pupil. May you obtain happiness as you build yourselves a brilliant life together. If at some time you happen to remember your unworthy but sincere teacher, Minke, remember: there has been in this world someone proud to have had a student who has followed in the footsteps of the great humanist Multatuli. But now, Minke, some of the students' parents have succeeded in having me sacked from my teaching job. I have been advised to leave the Indies before I'm actually expelled. I'm leaving tomorrow on an English ship. Adieu!

'Read this yourself, Jan,' I said to Dapperste. 'Our teacher.'

'What is it, Mas?'

'The rumours have turned out to be true. The government is getting rid of Magda Peters, though in an indirect way. It moves me greatly, Ann. Even facing such great troubles, she still made time to come and see us!'

'Expelled from the Indies?' Jan whispered after reading the note.

'Yes, and you don't want to leave Java. Will you do something for us, Jan?'

'Of course, Mas, gladly.'

'Will you see Miss Magda Peters off at the harbour, on behalf of both of us, and Mama and you yourself? And for Mother too? Such a kind person should not be allowed to leave without anyone to see her off; it must not happen.'

One small, long parcel turned out to contain a beautiful pen with gold nib. There was a card on which someone had drawn their own picture. Then he had printed the following words:

Greetings and best wishes to the doves Minke and Annelies Mellema, with the hope that you will forgive and forget a person you do not know except by the name: Fatso.

The present fell to the floor.

'*Mas!*' exclaimed Annelies.

Jan Dapperste picked it up.

'This one is for you, Jan,' I said. I put the card into my pocket. I still had to decide whether I would destroy it or keep it for the trial that might resume later.

It was after one o'clock. Jan Dapperste had finished his work. After saying good night, the finale to his evening, he left the room.

I went up to Annelies.

'Now you are my wife, Ann.'

'And you are my husband, Mas.'

There was a knock on the door. I jumped up and opened it. Mama entered. Her eyes were swollen, having had her fill of shedding tears. She approached us and couldn't speak. We understood her intent: to pass on her final words of advice.

'Mama,' I got in first. 'the two of us would like to thank you for everything that you have bestowed upon us so freely, everything that you have done for us, felt for us and thought about for us. We will always remember and never forget all this.'

She nodded, and went out again.

Annelies came up near me under the gas lamp. She put out her two hands. She didn't want, however, either to be embraced or to embrace.

'This ring, take it off.'

I took off that suspicion-arousing ring with its even more suspicious manner of placement.

'You didn't like getting it?'

'I have never answered any of his letters.'

In one flash I at last understood how Robert had felt all this time. He too loved Annelies. I studied the ring carefully. It was twenty-two carat gold, with a diamond. It wasn't clear whether the diamond was real or only imitation. It was too big to be a diamond; it was impossible that Suurhof had enough money to give away a present like this. I knew that his pocket money had never been more than twenty-five cents a month. And I knew his parents too – they couldn't at all be classified as well off. Yes, even his mother had never been seen wearing a ring. And why didn't the ring come with it's own box?

So I put it into my pocket.

'Give it back, Mas.'

'Yes, I'll return it.'

Night marched on. Suurhof and Fatso kept on harassing my thoughts.

19

Science was giving birth to more and more miracles. The legends of my ancestors were being put to shame. No longer was it necessary to meditate in the mountains for years in order to be able to speak to somebody across the seas. The Germans had laid a cable reaching from England to India! And these cables were multiplying and spreading all over the face of the earth. The whole world could now observe the behaviour of any person. And people could now observe the behaviour of the whole world.

But mankind and its problems remained as they have always been. And no more so than in matters of love.

Take that box that I had in my pocket – a cardboard box lined with black linen. Only two people knew its contents: Robert Suurhof and myself. Neither riches nor money, not diamonds, and no magical charm either. Only a letter from one human being, unsuccessful in gaining a love, to another, who had won that love. What can be done! Even in the modern world, how to triumph in love could not be taught in schools.

'Minke, my friend,' he wrote in large handwriting, though one in which it was clear his pen shook as he wrote.

He asked forgiveness, expressed his great remorse that he had carried out injustices, had been dishonest, and even acted with malicious jealousy. It's strange, he wrote; the cause of all these acts was not evil but rather a pure and hopeful love for Miss Annelies Mellema. He told how he had seen Annelies five times but had never had the chance to speak to her, even the chance to say hello had almost eluded him. He admitted that he had fallen in love and could not then accept reality. He endured great pain on seeing one Minke so easily gain entrance to Annelies's home and heart. It was not that he had given up hope – he claimed that such surrender was alien to him. He still kept up his hopes. Using all kinds of methods, he sent her several letters. Not one had ever been answered. He was unable to forget her.

All is over for me now. For you it is just the beginning. I admit I still feel unwilling to give up those hopes. There is no other way to ensure I forget than to leave the Indies. Yes, Minke, I must learn to forget. Even though this is so, don't let the mistakes I have made in the past ruin our relations . . .

Twenty days after our marriage, a letter arrived from Colombo. Miss Magda Peters reported she had set sail on the same ship as Robert Suurhof. He was working as a sailor and seemed to be ashamed of the fact. Miss advised him that such shame was inappropriate: such a job was not a humiliation for an HBS student, especially as he had such strong intentions to continue his schooling.

At the same time a letter arrived from Sarah, telling of Singapore and all its wonders: its roadways, clean and wide; busy, yet without dust; and the ships in such great numbers it was as if the harbour did not have enough room. There was far more ships here, she wrote, than I have ever seen in Amsterdam. Even more, she wrote, than in Rotterdam.

On the other hand, a letter from Assistant Resident B— told how his request to the Netherlands Indies Government asking that the government help me continue my schooling in the Netherlands had been refused, even though my grades were quite high enough. The main thing required by the government was high moral character. And I didn't fulfil that, he wrote.

That too was a fruit of science's progress. Even my moral character had now been given a final unchallengeable brand. First of all by the school. Then by the reports on the course of the trial. I did not, of course, hope for much from other people, yet that brand – so final – still hurt me greatly. I had never done harm to anyone else. I had never harmed another's reputation. I had never done away with other people's goods. I had never dealt in contraband. How was I to defend myself from such arbitrary judgements? Perhaps only Jean Marais taught the truth on this matter: People must be just and fair, starting with what they thought. It turned out that the Europeans themselves, and not just any Europeans either, were the ones who were unjust.

And the modern world had also, perhaps, taken news of me to Europe via those German-made sea cables . . .

Three months passed. My daily work consisted only of writing in the office and keeping Mama company. Sometimes I also helped her.

Jan Dapperste had received his Letter of Determination from the Governor-General through the Resident of Surabaya. His name was now Panji Darman. He was then freed from that hated name of 'Dapperste'. Slowly, gradually, his character also changed – just as he had hoped. He was high-spirited, liked to work, and was generous and open. At first he helped Mama with the office work but then he was moved across to Mr Doornenbosch's office to help in running the spice business.

Another month passed. Mother visited us twice.

Five months passed. Sarah de la Croix sent letters to me twice. Miriam also reported that she was going to return to Europe following after her elder sister. Mr Herbert de la Croix would be staying on alone in that big, silent residency building and so she asked that I write to him more often.

Six months passed. And then happened what indeed inevitably had to happen: Annelies was summoned (along with Nyai) to appear before the (White) Court. Who wouldn't have been startled? The court again. Now it was Annelies who received the main summons.

They left together. I stayed to carry on Mama's work. I wasn't able to finish all that much. I wrote some replies to the military barracks and the harbour master's office as well as the ships' chandlers. I noted down some new orders and some changes of customers' addresses. But the most difficult task was getting rid of the ex-Indies Army soldiers who kept pestering me and who wanted to court Mama.

I once saw Mama turn away some of them four times. The soldiers back from Aceh seemed to have made Nyai a major topic of conversation among themselves, and then they would, like soldiers of fortune, set out to catch the rich Mellema widow.

One of these men, and Indo, claiming he was a former *Vaandrig* – a junior lieutenant – even approached me. He had been awarded the bronze medal, he said, and had received ten hectares of good agricultural land near Malang as a part of his pension, and he wanted to become acquainted with Mama. Who knows, he said, perhaps later the two of them could go into partnership. At the end of the meeting, this man who claimed to be a former *Vaandrig* asked my help: would I pass on all his words to Nyai? If I was successful, he said, he promised to give me whatever I asked for this was also a part of my work.

He went away – forgetting to tell me his name.

Otherwise I wrote for *S.N. v/d D.*

They had been gone for more than three hours. I became more and more anxious. I stopped writing. Each time a milk cart came in, I went outside to have a look.

Four hours passed. The carriage I had been waiting for arrived at last:

'Minke, quickly!'

I ran to meet her on the front steps. Mama got out of the carriage first. Her face was scarlet. She put out her hand to Annelies who was still inside. And then out came my wife, ghostly pale and her face bathed in tears, mute. As soon as she alighted she fell into my arms and embraced me.

'Take her in!' Mama ordered me, roughly.

She strode quickly inside and went into her office.

'Have you had a fight with Mama?' I asked Annelies.

She shook her head. But no sound came out of her mouth. I went to take her upstairs. Her body was cold.

'Why is Mama angry?' I asked.

She didn't answer. And she refused to be taken upstairs. She asked with her eyes to be put down on the front-parlour settee.

'Are you ill, Ann?' and she shook her head. 'What's the matter with you?' and I became anxious that something had seriously upset this fragile doll of mine. She seemed to be in a state of total confusion. 'I'll get you something to drink.'

I fetched a glass of water for her. She drank it, and it seemed that the tightness in her chest subsided.

'Darsam!' exclaimed Mama from the office.

I ran to fetch the Madurese fighter. I found him at home, in the middle of plucking out the unwanted hairs of his moustache.

'Quick, Darsam, Mama is angry.'

He jumped off his chair. The little mirror and the tweezers fell onto the mat. By the time I reached the office he was already inside. Annelies too.

'Why don't you go to sleep, Ann?' Nyai admonished her hurriedly. My wife shook her head. Mama's face was still scarlet.

'What's happened, Ma?'

Darsam saluted Nyai and departed from the office. There must have been a carriage ready, because it was only a second before the sound of wheels grinding the pebbles on the roadway in front of the office could be heard.

Mama paid no attention to my question, went over to the window, shouted outside:

'Hurry! Be careful!' she turned around and went across to Annelies, caressed her hair and generally tried to humour her. 'You don't need to think about it. Let us look after it, Ann, me and your husband.' Then to me, 'It's come at last, Child, Minke, Nyo, what I've worried about all this time. I don't know much about the law. But we must try to fight it with all our strength and all our wealth.'

'What's this all about, Ma?'

She pushed several documents into my hands, originals and copies, from the Amsterdam District Court, stamped by the Bureau of the Home Affairs Ministry, the Ministry for Colonies, the Ministry of Justice. On top of the pile was a letter from Engineer Maurits Mellema in South Africa to his mother, Amelia Mellema-Hammers, giving power of attorney to the latter party to make all arrangements in relation to rights of inheritance from the late Mr Herman Mellema, his father, who had been killed in Surabaya, as he had been informed in a letter from his mother. Then there was a copy of a letter from Maurits Mellema's mother, written on behalf of her son, to the Amsterdam Court, asking it to look after the rights of her son over the wealth and property of the late Mr Herman Mellema.

Furthermore: copies of the Surabaya Court and Prosecutor's Office's correspondence with the Amsterdam Court, concerning whether or not there was a marriage certificate for Herman Mellema with Sanikem, whether or not there was a will made up by Herman Mellema before he died, the decisions of the court in relation to the murder carried out by Ah Tjong, a determination relating to the disappearance of Robert Mellema, copies of the certificates of acknowledgement by Herman Mellema of his children, Annelies and Robert Mellema, both of whom were given birth to by Sanikem as registered in the civil registry office. Then again there was correspondence between Nyai's accountant and the Surabaya Court all relating to the accountant's refusal to make available any information relating to the assets of *Boerderij Buitenzorg* without permission from those with the proper authority. Copies of documents from the Tax Office regarding the amount of taxes paid by the company. Copies of documents from the Livestock and Agriculture Office regarding the number of cattle and their condition.

I read each of the letters one by one under the gaze of Mama and Annelies who seemed to be hoping for some opinion from me. I didn't know anything at all about any of the things mentioned in all those letters. And, indeed, I had never even dreamed that such letters existed in this world. And I never knew that there were people who were actually paid to write them.

Then there was the official document of the Amsterdam District Court. Its contents: an order that its decision on the case was to be executed by the Surabaya District Court. In brief it read:

Based upon the application to the Court by Maurits Mellema, son of the late Herman Mellema, made through his attorney Mr Hans Graeg, located in Amsterdam, the Amsterdam District Court, based upon official documents, provided by the Surabaya District Court, whose authenticity cannot be doubted, determines that the entire property and wealth of the late Herman Mellema, because of the absence of legal ties between Herman Mellema and Sanikem, be divided as follows: Maurits Mellema, as the legitimate child, to receive 4/6 of all property; Annelies and Robert Mellema, as legally recognised children, to receive 1/6 each. Because Robert Mellema's whereabouts has been officially declared unknown, both temporarily as well as permanently, his inheritance is to be managed by Mr Maurits Mellema.

The Amsterdam District Court also appointed Mr Maurits Mellema guardian over Miss Annelies Mellema, as the latter is still considered to be legally under age, and so therefore her inheritance will also be managed by Mr Maurits Mellema. Mr Maurits Mellema, as guardian of Annelies Mellema, through his attorney, Mr Graeg, authorised another advocate located in Surabaya to bring action against Sanikem alias Nyai Ontosoroh, and Annelies Mellema, in the Court in Surabaya, over the guardianship of Annelies Mellema and her future upbringing in the Netherlands.

I felt as if I was about to faint, as I read those official documents with their strange language. I could however, understand one aspect of their contents very well: they looked upon human beings as no more than items in an inventory.

'Mama didn't say anything to them?'

'Look, Minke, Child, Nyo, my attorney was waiting for us there when we arrived. He was the one who arranged to get all these letters. He too was the one who, before the judge, told us of the decision and explained it.'

As I listened, the words of Mother came back to me: 'the Dutch are very, very powerful but they have never stolen people's wives as did the kings of Java'. But now, Mother? It is no other than your own daughter-in-law they are theatening to steal, to steal a child from her mother, a wife from her husband; and they want, too, to steal the fruits of Mama's hard work and everything she has strived to achieve over the last twenty years without ever a holiday. And all this was based upon no more than beautiful documents written by expert scribes and clerks with their indelible black ink that soaked half-way through the thickness of the paper.

'It looks like we'll have to get help from a lawyer, Ma?'

'Mr Deradera will soon be here, I think.'

That strange name had already made itself familiar during my recent complex and multifarious problems.

'Mr Deradera Lelliobuttockx . . .'

For quite a long time I had tried to learn his name off by heart and to write it. I had never met the man himself. Mama often went to him for legal advice. My image of him was a big and fat man, like Herman Mellema, with thick blond hair all over his body. His name reminded me more of some kind of spirit. He must surely be a brilliant lawyer.

'Didn't Mama protest against the decision?'

'Protest? I did more than that – I completely rejected the decision. I know them, those Europeans, cold, hard like a wall. Their words are expensive. She is my child, I said. It is only I that have any rights over her. It was I that gave birth to her, who have brought her up. The judge only said: The documents show that Annelies Mellema is the acknowledged child of Herman Mellema. Who is her mother, who was it that gave birth to her? I asked. The documents state that her mother is the woman Sanikem alias Nyai Ontosoroh, but . . . I am Sanikem. Yes, he said, but Sanikem is not Mrs Mellema. I can bring witnesses, I said, to prove that I gave birth to her. He said: Annelies Mellema is under European Law, Nyai is not. Nyai is a Native. Had Miss Annelies Mellema not been legally acknowledged by Mr Mellema she too would be a Native and this Court would have had nothing to do with her. *Nah*, Minke, what could be more humiliating! So I said, I will fight this decision, using whatever attorney is able and willing. That's up to you, he said coldly. Annelies just cried and cried, so that I forgot about everything else.'

She took a deep breath.

'You should have come too, Minke. You could have at least defended your wife and your interests, even if the court wasn't actually in session. Yes, even the judge has a wife and children too.'

I am sure that everyone will know how I felt at that moment: angry, furious, annoyed, but not knowing what I had to do. In such matters I was still a snotty-nosed little boy.

'I said too: my child is already married. She is somebody's wife. He then just smiled, just a shadow of a smile, and answered: she is not yet married. She is under age. If there has been somebody who carried out a marriage of her to somebody or married her, the marriage is not legal. You hear, Minke? Not legal.'

'Mas?'

'They then threaten to charge me as an accessory to rape because I hadn't reported the marriage as illegal.'

The office was still, silent. There were no customers about.

The three of us were silenced. Once a brilliant and honest attorney would be able to successfully appeal against the decision of the Amsterdam District Court. Oh, Amsterdam Court! You had never even seen us. How can a court, and a European Court too, manned by very educated people, experienced in matters of justice, with the degree of Bachelor of Laws, carry out the law this way, so opposed to our sense of law? Our sense of justice?

'I didn't even get on to talking about the division of the property, which didn't even mention my rights. Yes, indeed, I don't have enough documentation to prove that this company is my property. All I tried to do was to defend Annelies. At the time, all I could think of was her. Actually our business is only with Annelies, the judge said. You are a *nyai*, a Native, you have no business with this court,' and Mama grimaced savagely.

'In the end,' she said later in a soft voice, 'the issue is always the same: European against Native, Minke, against me. Remember this well: it is Europe that swallows up Natives while torturing us sadistically . . . Eu-r-ope . . . only their skin is white,' she swore, 'their hearts are full of nothing but hate.'

'And the attorney, he's a European too, Ma?'

'Just a slave to money. The more money you give him, the more honest he is with you. That's Europe.'

I shuddered. Years and years of schooling were overturned with just the three short sentences of a *nyai*.

Annelies had fallen asleep, exhausted by all the emotional tension; she lay with her head on top of the table. I went up to her and woke her up:

'Let's go upstairs, Ann.'

She refused to move – and sat up straight again in her chair.

'Get some sleep, Ann. Let us look after you,' entreated Mama, and Annelies complied.

I took her upstairs, put her to bed, and began to humour her:

'Mama and I will work hard, Ann.'

She just nodded, and I knew with all my heart: I had lied to her – I knew nothing about all the ins and outs of the law, how then could I work hard at it?

'You stay here, yes, Ann?'

She nodded again. But I couldn't bring myself to leave her in this condition – like a fish that was already in the frying pan. How moving was the fate of this fragile doll, my wife. It looked as if she had lost the will to do anything at all.

'I'll call Dr Martinet, yes, Ann?'

She nodded.

I went downstairs and gave orders that someone fetch the family doctor. I saw Marjuki racing his buggy off towards Surabaya.

In the office, Mama was with a European man, who was small-bodied, like one's little finger, perhaps only up to my shoulder in height, thin and flat. His head was slippery bald, and his eyes just a little slanted. He wore horn-rimmed glasses. Mama was watching him reading the documents regarding Annelies from the Amsterdam District Court. So that was Mr Deradera Lelliobottockx. It was clear he was no spirit. And he had been Mama's lawyer all this time.

I was amazed Mama wanted to deal with him. Just a while ago, before the judge, he hadn't said or done anything, had he? I watched them both. Mama was no longer so red-faced. Her movements were calmer now.

'Minke, this is Mr Deradera . . .' and we shook hands. 'This is Minke, the husband of my daughter, my son-in-law.'

'Ah yes, I've heard a lot about you. Could I just finish studying these documents first?' and without waiting for an answer, he resumed his work.

A person no bigger than one's little finger, with a face full of craters from the explosions of so many pimples – just how far would he be able to go in confronting the arbitrariness and might and coldness of European law and justice? And as a European, on whose side would he ultimately stand?

And he studied the documents one by one, turning them over and reading them again.

Mama rushed about finishing her own work, then even served him drinks. And the lawyer kept on with his inspection of the documents as if nothing at all was going on around him.

Finally, one hour later, he piled the letters together and put a letter weight on top of them, a black stone. He meditated importantly, wiped his face with his handkerchief, ahemmed, and then gazed across at me, then at Mama, and he didn't say a word.

'So what about it, Mr Lelliobuttockx?' asked Mama, 'oh, I'm sorry, I'm still not sure how to pronounce your name properly.'

He smiled – just briefly – which turned out to be because of his missing teeth.

'Oh, that's all right, that's just my name for signatures, Nyai, I don't mind if people are unable to pronounce it, it doesn't even worry me if they don't even try.'

'You can still make jokes while we're suffering a situation such as this, Mr Lelliobuttockx! We're already half-crazy with all this!'

'That is the way it is, Nyai, when the matter is a legal one. There is no point in charging one's feelings or countenance. The result is just the same whether people laugh, jump up and down, or cry and wail. It is always she who determines things in the end: the law.'

'So we will be defeated in this matter?'

'It's better we don't talk about defeat, Nyai,' said the attorney and his hands began to finger the documents once again. 'We haven't begun trying yet. What I meant was that I hope Nyai will be as cold and calm as the law itself. Feelings have no influence over any of this. All anger and disappointment is in vain. Are you listening too, Sir?' suddenly he turned and faced me. 'You understand Dutch?'

'I'm listening, Sir.'

'This concerns the fate of your wife and your marriage. The other side is in the stronger position. We will try if you and Nyai still want to fight the decision; at the very least we will get its execution postponed.'

I understood at that moment, we would be defeated and that our only duty now was to fight back, to defend our rights, until we were unable to fight back any longer – like the Acehnese in their fight against the Dutch according to Jean Marais' story. Mama also bowed her head. She more than just understood. She was going to lose everything: her child, her business, all the fruits of her efforts and her personal property.

'Yes, Minke, Child, Nyo, we will fight back,' whispered Mama. And all of a sudden she looked old, and walked dispiritedly upstairs to check on her daughter.

Mr Deradera Lelliobuttockx LLB submerged himself once again in his study of the documents. My suspicion of this little-finger-sized lawyer suddenly swelled to become so great that I stayed and watched his hands closely to make sure he did not secrete away any of those documents.

Another hour passed. Mama came down again and entered the office. She sat beside me, across from the jurist.

'Do you still need to study them, Mr Deradera?' she asked in her old voice – one with character.

The man lifted up his head, held back a grin, and said:

'We can try, Nyai.'

'You do not believe we can win.'

'We can try,' he started his reading again.

Mama took the letters from him:

'Your fee will be sent to your office. Good afternoon.'

Mr Deradera Lelliobuttockx stood up, nodded to us both, and was then escorted home by Darsam.

'Minke, we will fight them. Do you have the courage, Child, Nyo?'

'We will fight, Ma, together.'

'Even if we don't have a lawyer, we will be the first Natives to oppose the European Court, Child, Nyo. Isn't that also an honour?'

I had no idea of how I was to fight back, what I had to fight, who and how. I did not know either what should be my tools or through what mechanism we should endeavour. But: We'll fight!

'Fight, Ma, fight. We will fight back.'

'If you could only get Annelies to get up and fight too, she wouldn't always be falling into illness and incapacity like this. She would become the best of all life companions for a husband such as you.'

While waiting upon Annelies, I let loose my thoughts and allowed myself to concentrate on everything that had happened and was happening.

Engineer Maurits Mellema, and his mother, did indeed have reason to seek revenge on Herman Mellema. But what was happening now? Their revenge did not make them spurn his inheritance; rather they wanted to make sure they got every cent. So: in fact they too had wanted Annelies's papa to die. In their hearts they too had participated in and approved of Ah Tjong's actions. But they would not be punished. The life of the soul and the psyche are not mentioned in official letters.

Yes, this was nothing more than a case of the white race swallowing up Natives, swallowing Mama, Annelies and me. Perhaps this was what was called a colonial case – if Magda Peters' explanation of things was right – a case of swallowing up a conquered Native people.

Suddenly I was reminded of the liberals who, according to my teacher, wanted to lessen the sufferings of the Natives. That, too, was what the SDAP – the Dutch Social Democratic Workers Party – wanted. Ah, my good teacher. I regret now that I didn't go to see you off. If you were still in Surabaya, you would, for sure, hold out your hand in assistance. At the very least you would offer us some guidance, to help us. And you would do so gladly.

And as I thought about Magda Peters, there arose suspicions that were perhaps too fantastic: she had been forced to leave the Indies to make the execution of the Amsterdam District Court's decision easier! Perhaps you weren't really exiled but just got out of the way for the coming case. My suspicions then took on an even clearer form: everything had been arranged beforehand by that satanic alliance between Maurits-Amelia and the Amsterdam District Court. If it was true that Magda Peters had been gotten out of the way, then it was the school Director and the other teachers who knew how close she and I were. If my suspicions were correct, this whole thing, everything, was no more than a prearranged drama whose purpose was the sadistic torment of human beings. So even my graduation as number two in all of the Indies (to be number one was out of the question) was also no more than a play, manufactured to keep the radicals or the SDAP happy.

Should I have such grandiose suspicions as this? Was my thinking, as an educated person, fair and just? Was I not both too young and too ignorant to have such suspicions? I thought it over and over again. I couldn't avoid always coming back to the same condition: being inclined the accept my suspicions. My dismissal from school, the withdrawal of my dismissal, the closing down of the school discussions, the expelling of Magda Peters, the intervention of the Assistant Resident of B—, the invitation that was announced by the school Director at the graduation party, and his own and the other teachers' absence at our wedding, and being only represented by the letter brought by Magda Peters . . . No, I was not too ignorant or too young to understand. Each event was linked and entwined together so as to give victory to Maurits Mellema over the Native woman Sanikem, her daughter and son-in-law, her wealth and property.

'You've got some ideas, Nyo?'

'Ma, this evening, if nothing goes wrong, my first writings on this affair will be published. If it is not greeted by common sense, Ma, we will be defeated, Ma. We need time.'

'Don't think about defeat, Deradera said, think first about the best way to fight back, the most honourable resistance. Deradera was right, it was only his motives that were wrong. He only wanted bigger fees. That shrunken-up crocodile.'

'We'll turn to the best of our European friends, Ma.'

'Don't make any mistakes.'

That afternoon I sent a cable to Herbert de la Croix, appealing to his conscience regarding our case. Also to Miriam. If no one wanted to listen, then I would know: all that glorified European science and learning was a load of nonsense, empty talk. Empty talk! In the end it would all be nothing more than a tool to rob us of all we loved, all we owned: honour, sweat, rights, even child and wife.

That night Mama and I waited upon Annelies who had to be drugged once again by Dr Martinet so that she could sleep. The doctor was moved and saddened by the situation of his patient, her mother and her husband, who were bound so tightly by man-made fate, a fate manufactured far away in the north.

'I am only a doctor, Nyai. I don't know about the law. I don't know about politics,' he said, expressing his disappointment in himself.

He was the second person who had mentioned the word 'politics'.

258

'It's only proper that I ask your forgiveness because I am unable to do anything to help lighten your sufferings. There are no important people among my close friends, because I have never joined any of the clubs.'

And in what a modest manner the doctor presented himself.

'My only friends are those who have needed my help. I don't have anything more than that. I'm sorry.'

'But you feel that the way we are being treated is unjust, yes?' asked Mama.

'Not just unjust. Barbaric!'

'That is enough, Doctor, if it has come from a sincere heart.'

'Forgive me, there is nothing I am able to do . . .'

He left us with such a pained face. At the door he spoke in a sighing voice:

'I used to think that the only real difficulty in the world was paying one's taxes. I never knew that under these heavens there could exist difficulties such as these.'

He disappeared into the darkness, escorted by Darsam.

Five hours had passed since I sent off the telegrams to the de la Croixs. Five hours! And still no answer had arrived. Were Herbert and Miriam de la Croix not at home? Or were they laughing at us Natives?

'Yes, Child, Nyo, we must fight back, we must resist. However good and kind any European has been to us, in the end they will be afraid to face up to the risks of resisting European law, their own law, especially if it's only to defend the interests of Natives. We need not be ashamed if we are defeated. We must know why. Look, Child, Nyo, we, all the Natives, are unable to hire attorneys. Even if we have money it doesn't mean we are able to do so. The main reason is that we don't have the courage. And more generally still, we haven't learnt anything. All their lives the Natives have suffered what we now are suffering. No one raises their voice – dumb like the river stones and mountains, even if cut up and made into no matter what. What a roar there would be if they all spoke out as we will now speak out. Perhaps even the sky itself would be shattered because of the din.'

Mama had begun to forget her own feelings. She was placing the matter in the context of a more basic problem, she had left behind her own heart and her family, she had now brought in the river stones, the mountains, the chalk and granite rocks that were strewn all over Java, throughout all the Indies; those with mouths but no voices, and yet with hearts within them.

'By fighting back we will not be wholly defeated,' and the tone of her voice was pregnant with the knowledge of coming defeat.

'They know no shame, Ma.'

'Shame is not a concern of European civilisation,' Mama stared wide-eyed at me as if she was angry with me. 'You who have mixed with them all this time, how can you talk like that? You, Child, Nyo, as a Native, should and must be ashamed to have such thoughts. Never again mention shame in relation to Europe. All they understand is getting their way. Never forget that, Child, Nyo.'

'Yes, Ma,' I answered acknowledging her superiority. The truth or otherwise of what she said was, of course, another matter.

'I've never been to school, Child, Nyo, I've never been taught to admire Europeans. You could study for years and years, and no matter what you studied, the spirit of you will be educated to do the same thing: to admire Europeans without limits or end, so that you no longer know who you are and where you are. Even so, those who have been to school are still more fortunate. At the very least you get to know other races who have their own ways of thieving the property of other peoples.'

My mother-in-law took a newspaper from the table. Inside, there was an article of mine, and comments on it by the editor.

'Your writings are so gentle, like the writings of a teenage girl waiting for a husband. Have you still not become hard with all your recent experiences, let alone this current one? Uncompromisingly hard? Minke, Child, Nyo.' she went on in a whisper, as if there was someone else there who was listening in on us. 'Now you must write in Malay, Child. The Malay papers are read by many more people.'

'It's a pity, Ma, I can't write in Malay.'

'If you're unable at the moment, let someone else translate for you.'

And straight away I thought of Kommer.

'Good, Mama,' I answered quickly.

'Your marriage is legitimate according to Islamic Law. To nullify it is to insult Islamic Law, to besmirch the laws honoured by the Islamic community . . . Ah, how I dreamed of a legitimate wedding for myself. Mellema always refused. Because he already had a wife. Now my child has married legitimately, more honourable than me. And it's not acknowledged.'

'I'll work on it now, Ma. Mama should get some sleep.'

And she went off to bed. Her strides were still strong and firm like those of a still-undefeated general.

It was ten minutes past three in the morning. My article was almost finished. Out of the pre-dawn silence came the pounding of a horse's hooves, coming closer and closer, and finally entering our grounds. Not long after Darsam was calling out from below my window.

'Young Master, wake up!'

Below, in the light of an oil-lamp held by Darsam, I saw Darsam with an Indo in the uniform of a postman. He saluted, and asked in Malay:

'Tuan Minke? There is a telegram from the Assistant Resident of B—.'

He left happily with a tip of five cents. The pounding of his horse's hooves disappeared in the distance to the accompaniment of the cock's crows.

'Young Master has already done a lot of work. It's already dawn. Get some sleep, Young Master. There will still be other days.'

He didn't know a thing about what was happening. But I could sense he was anxious at seeing all the activity that was going on. Ah, Darsam, a thousand such as you, even with two thousand machetes, would be unable to help us. This is not a problem of flesh and steel, Darsam. This was a matter of rights, law and justice – you cannot protect us with dagger and machete. Suddenly there was a reprimand: you must be fair and just, starting with how you think! Darsam the fighter with his machete, even the mute stones and rocks can help you – if you know and understand them. Never belittle the capabilities of a single person, let alone two!

'Very well, I'll get some sleep now, Darsam.'

'Yes, go to sleep, Young Master. A new day will bring new opportunities.'

How wise too was this black-clothed man. I went upstairs and read the telegram:

Minke, a well-known jurist will arrive from Semarang. The day after tomorrow. Trust him. Meet him at the station. Express train. Greetings to Nyai and Annelies. Miriam and Herbert.

Mother! Mother! at last my cries have been heard. And you yourself have not even heard what is happening. Sleep deeply, Mother. I will not awaken you. Not now either. And here, your beloved son will not run. He will stay and fight. He is no criminal, Mother. Your beloved daughter-in-law will not be stolen away. She will present to you the grandchildren you long for, so one day you will be able to attend their weddings as Javanese . . .

An article about the contravening of Islamic Law by European Law appeared in Dutch in *S.N. v/d D.* Malay versions appeared in the Malay-Dutch press. They all appeared on the same afternoon. Mr Maarten Nijman himself came around to our house to deliver the complimentary copy.

'You have helped us a lot all this time. Now it is our turn to help you as much as we can,' he said. 'But there is nothing else we can do to help lighten your own and your family's burdens. All of the editorial staff and the workers at the paper have high regard for your resistance, and express their true and sincere sympathy – so young, like a sparrow harassed by a storm, but yet still fighting back. Another person would have been broken even before the fight started, Mr Tollenaar.'

He borrowed a picture of Annelies to publish.

'If possible, also a picture of you and Nyai.'

Mama give him a big picture of my wife in full Javanese dress adorned with diamonds and pearls.

'It's only a pity that we won't be able to publish the picture soon. We'll have to wait almost two months,' Nijman explained. 'The Indies is still a wilderness. There is no factory here that can copy this picture onto tin: zyncography is still not yet known here. We'll get the negative made in Hong

Kong. If Hong Kong can't do it because of all the orders from South-east Asia, then we'll have to send it to Europe to get done. Longer still. If we succeed it will not only mean greater impact, but we will be the first in the Indies to publish from a tin negative.'

He talked a lot and asked to be introduced to and meet with Annelies herself. And we refused on the grounds that she was ill.

'Is Miss Annelies already with child?' asked Nijman. 'Forgive the question. It might seem improper, but it could change the situation. It could nullify Maurits Mellema's decision even if the Amsterdam Court's decision still stood.'

Annelies pregnant? I had never even thought about it. I couldn't answer. Neither could Mama, instead she looked questioningly at me.

After Nijman left, Kommer arrived, also bringing a complimentary copy of his paper.

'Nyai, Mr Minke,' he said, 'your writings will soon be in the villages. We've hired men to read them out to the people. People gather around and listen. Fifteen special copies with the relevant parts underlined in red have been sent off to the leading Islamic scholars. They must also speak out. I'm going to try to get their opinions tonight. You and Nyai will not stand alone. Look upon Kommer here as a friend of the family in its time of trouble.'

We set off to Surabaya together. He got off at Gunungsari. I went on to the station to meet the attorney whose name I still didn't know. Kommer, before I left him, shook my hand from outside the buggy. His eyes shone with his enthusiasm for the humanitarian task he was undertaking. Then he waved his hands, and my buggy started off again.

The attorney I met turned out to be middle aged. He had a calm demeanour and he smiled a lot, and liked to listen, not like Mr Deradera Lelliobuttockx. His name was Mr—. I'll not mention his name here. He was a famous jurist and a very wealthy man as a result of his practice as a brilliant attorney and advocate and his name was often mentioned in connection with many big cases.

He stayed at our house. He studied Annelies's file all night, and asked that two scribes be hired to make copies of every document. Panji Darmam, formerly Jan Dapperste, and I, acted as scribes. But I was sacked in the end because of my bad hand writing and because I made so many mistakes. So Darsam had to go out that night too and find a clerk from the DPM, who also brought the special ink used for official documents.

Mr— (whose name I don't dare mention; and who could tell if he might be unsuccessful in this case and his practice affected) studied it all until morning. The two scribes made two copies of each document. At six in the morning they had to leave for their real jobs so we had to hire two more people.

262

At seven o'clock in the morning Mr— began to write a long letter, which the new scribes made several copies of. Taking one set of the copies, he headed off to the European Court in Surabaya with Darsam. He arrived back again in the evening and went straight to sleep.

We didn't know what had happened at the court.

The afternoon news, as published by Kommer, reported that the Islamic scholars had gone to the European Court at Surabaya to protest the decision of the Amsterdam District Court and its execution by the Surabaya Court. They threatened to take the matter to the Islamic Religious Supreme Court in Betawi. And they were removed by the police especially brought in for that necessity.

The commentary, which seemed to have been written by Kommer himself, warned that it would be wise for those in power to act more tactfully in dealing with the Islamic scholars who were held in respect, honoured, exalted and listen to by the followers of Islam in this region. It is dangerous to play with the beliefs of the people, much more dangerous than to make fun of powerless subjects of the realm or rob them of their rightful property and their women and children.

For the second time Kommer emerged as a friend. He was so skilful at speaking for us, for our situation and for the general conditions of the Natives. His words were so simple and moving, yet confident and full of substance. And, not without risk.

S.N. v/d D. published an interview between Nijman and Nyai:

For more than twenty years now I have worked my bones, building, defending and keeping alive this business, both with and then without the late Herman Mellema. I've looked after this business better than I have my own children. Now it is all being stolen from me. The attitude, illness, and incapacity of the late Mr Mellema resulted in my losing my first child. Now another Mellema is going to steal my youngest also. Through the use of European law, he is having me torn from all that is mine by right, and all that I love. If that is indeed his deliberate intention towards us, all I can do is to ask: What is the point of having all these schools if they still don't teach what are people's rights and what are not, what is right and what is not?

And he wrote up his conversation with me as follows:

We married of our own accord, and our marriage was approved of by the girl's parents. Our persons are our own property; we are nobody else's property; slavery was abolished by law in 1860, at least so we have been taught in our history lessons. Now with the impending kidnapping of my wife, in accordance with the court's decision, I wish to ask the conscience of Europe: is that accursed slavery going to be brought back? How can human beings be looked upon purely from the point of view of official documents and without considering their essence as human beings?

Then there was an interview with Dr Martinet:

I have known this family quite some time now. So I understand the situation of Annelies Mellema's health, both before she married, and afterwards. With a heavy heart I have to say that this girl loves her husband, her mother and her surroundings very much. She is very, very attached to all three. If indeed the Amsterdam District Court's decision is executed, the life of this girl could be destroyed through the emotional turmoil that will result. Even now Annelies has to be sedated. She has lost all faith in the existence of security, certainty and legal guarantees. Her spirit has been crammed full of fears and uncertainties. Must I continue to drug her while outside there is the sun, laughter and joy? Why must this young angel become the plaything of decisions that have no real connection with her life and happiness? As a doctor I cannot accept the responsibility of what might happen if I have to continue drugging her.

The attorney from Semarang, Mr—, read through everything that was connected with our case. He made notes but never spoke to us. Nor did we bother him with any questions. In the evening he read the papers from other towns. Only after all this did he finally begin to speak about many things, and:

'We must be resolute, Nyai . . . Sir . . .' He asked Mama:

'Why, really, didn't Mr Mellema ever marry Nyai legally?'

Mama answered:

'I didn't understand why Mr Mellema didn't want to marry either, although I often pressed him to marry me. I only realised what the situation was after the sudden arrival here, at this house, of Maurits Mellema, his son, five years ago. Only then did I understand that Mr Mellema was still legally bound to the mother of that engineer.'

Mr— turned and looked at her in amazement.

'So they were never divorced? If that's so then it was impossible for Mr Mellema to legally acknowledge his children here, because such children are considered bastards and acknowledgement of them is not considered legal. But if that's so, then Nyai's position in this case is much stronger!'

Within Mama and me feelings of hope were awakened once again. Mama was angry: Why had not Mr Deradera Lelliobuttockx thought of that point. But some days later Mr— reported to us that such a defence would not help us either.

Mr— said: 'After sending off a telegram to Holland checking things out, it has been shown that Mrs Amelia Mellema-Hammers, after her husband had left her for five years without giving any address, did apply for a divorce in the Dutch courts on the grounds of desertion. After efforts to find Mr Mellema were unsuccessful, in 1879 the divorce was granted. So the marital ties between them were already nullified when your child, Robert, was born.' Then he asked: 'Did Mr Mellema know of this divorce?'

'I don't think so,' answered Mama. Mama thought for a moment then exploded: 'If this is all true then Maurits Mellema lied to his father when they met that time five years ago! He challenged his father to institute divorce proceedings against Mrs Mellema on the grounds that she had been unfaithful. He destroyed his father's spirit with that conversation.'

With fury in her eyes Mama sat silently not saying a single word but I saw her hands shaking because of the overflowing of her emotions. Our picture of Maurits Mellema was only getting worse. It seems he deliberately set out to destroy his father's spirit and so speed up his death. And all for money.

The next morning Mr— returned to Semarang.

We were left without the support of a jurist, without any direct means of fighting the court's decision.

'All right, Mama, only the pen is left,' and so I wrote, calling out, speechifying, complaining, roaring, swearing, crying out in a pain, agitating.

Kommer translated them all and gave them out to those who were prepared to publish them.

And it was not without results.

The Religious Supreme Court in Surabaya issued a statement: Our marriage was legitimate and could not be disturbed or nullified. On the other hand, some of the colonial papers started flinging insults, curses and slights to us. Nijman's and Kommer's papers were busy summarising all the various statements.

While Annelies, my wife, that fragile doll of mine, was lying like a corpse on her bed, Surabaya was in a fever over her, Nyai's and my troubles. Kommer kept on fighting too. His paper was being read, and also read out aloud in the villages, and big crowds of people stopped to listen everywhere. Without going via eyes, without going via ears and mouth, the news had spread and had become a matter of wide public controversy.

Finally Darsam also found out what was happening without ever having to ask us. He was busy reading the Malay papers with the help of his children . . .

Once again Annelies and Nyai received a summons from the court. It was impossible for Annelies to go. Only Mama and I went, unaccompanied by an attorney. Dr Martinet waited upon my wife.

The Judge immediately asked where Annelies Mellema was.

'Ill. In the care of Dr Martinet.'

'Have you brought a letter from the doctor?'

I was startled to hear Nyai answere coarsely:

'Has the court already decided that my mouth cannot be trusted?'

'Good,' answered the judge, red-faced. 'Nyai should be more polite.'

'Should someone about to lose everything show politeness in the face of her loss? Just tell us what you want.'

The judge deliberately avoided a clash with the Native woman. He gave in.

'Good. In my hand is the Surabaya Court's decision regarding Miss Annelies Mellema, the acknowledged child of the late Mr Herman Mellema. In accordance with this decision, Miss Annelies Mellema is to be transported from Surabaya by ship in five day's time.'

'She's ill,' retorted Mama.

'There are good doctors on board.'

'I refuse to let her go. I'm her husband.'

'We have no business with anyone who claims or who doesn't claim to be her husband. She is still unmarried, without a husband.'

There was no way to get this devil to be reasonable. He took out his pocket watch, rose from his chair and left us.

The two of us left the building in unexpected anger. I asked Mama to go on home first. I got in touch with Kommer and Nijman to tell them the news, and even helped in getting the report ready, right up to setting the capitals.

That afternoon the news was published.

I found Dr Martinet waiting upon Annelies and Mama. The two of them sat silently, heads bowed. Neither of them seemed to want to talk.

The next morning something amazing occurred.

The Surabaya Court's decision had angered and infuriated many people and groups. A crowd of Madurese, armed with machetes and large sickles, had surrounded our house, and were attacking any Europeans or state employees who tried to enter our compound.

The traffic felt it had to stop to watch what was happening.

A Madurese, wearing all-black clothes, walked back and forth with his shirt open, showing his chest, as if it was being deliberately readied to fight anyone and face any risk. The tip of his head-band with its long tail fell over his shoulder.

From Annelies' window they could be heard forever cursing and condemning the White Court's decision as the act of infidels, as sinful, damned in this world and the next. From early in the morning until eleven o'clock they controlled our compound.

All the activities of the business stopped. The workers dispersed in fear and went home to their villages.

Two companies of police arrived, escorted by government carriages. The ringing of their copper bells could be heard from afar. Not paying any heed to the Madurese, the carriages came straight into our grounds. We could see from our room some of the Madurese swinging their great sickles against the legs of the horses. Two carriages went out of control and into the garden, splashing into the swan pond. Out of the carriages that succeeded in entering the yard jumped uniformed men with carbines who tried to disperse the Madurese. Those under attack did not want to leave. A fight took place.

From where I was, I saw two agents felled, bathed in blood. The uniformed men finally didn't know what else to do and fired off their rifles into the air.

Here and there could be seen a Madurese laid out, also covered in blood.

The police commandant, a Pure-Blood, swore at his men for firing their rifles. A stone flew through the air and struck his temple. He swayed about, fell, and did not rise again. A black Dutchman, an Ambonese from the Moluccas, who seemed to take command, shouted out that the Madurese must be dealt with more harshly. His arm caught a machete and as quick as lightening his shirt turned brown. The wailing of the Madurese shouting out the greatness of God was unexpectedly frightening. But in the end they were chased away and ran in all possible directions.

On the grass, in the yard, bloodied bodies were strewn about.

A company of Marechaussee, fresh from training in Malang, were brought in to take over from the police, who were considered to have disobeyed orders by firing their rifles, even though only into the air. The police were sworn at and insulted by the Marechaussee and ordered to leave quickly and to pull out the two carriages that had gone into the pond.

A group made up of Madurese, as well as others, charged the compound. It seems they thought the police were still in charge of the operation. Realising that it was now the Marechaussee they were facing, they hesitated. Some even ran off before entering the compound. Indeed the whole of the Indies feared the Marechaussee, a special command made up of specially chosen troops of the Netherlands Indies Army! They only ever used rubber truncheons, no firearms or blade weapons. They were famous as a company of fighters.

From the window I saw their leaf-green bamboo hats with the shining copper lion symbol bob up and down amongst the new group of attackers. Their whistles sounded noisily again and again and their truncheons swung round and round, striking and poking, thrusting and thumping. The fight between truncheons and whistles and the other sharp and blunt instruments lasted about half an hour. Two Marechaussee died on the spot.

That time too the protesters were chased away. Darsam was arrested and taken away to who knows where.

After things had calmed down Sergeant Hammerstee banged on the door, wanting to enter. Mama opened it and blocked the way.

'Nyai Ontosoroh?' he asked in Malay.

'I have no business with the Marechaussee.'

'This complex is to be guarded by the Marechaussee.'

'It's nothing to do with me. No one steps inside my house without my permission.'

'I, Marechaussee Sergeant Hammerstee, have come to request permission.'

'I do not give permission.'

'In that case we will camp in the compound.'

Nyai slammed the door shut, locked it from inside, and stood behind it for some time. Looking at me, she said:

'Give in to them once and they'll end up doing as they please. Don't worry. Nothing will happen. They have no papers about this house. They only believe in papers. No matter how tremendous they are, it's all meaningless without papers. Paper determines more, is more powerful.' Her voice was bitter.

From the window too I saw Dr Martinet have his turn in being denied entry by Sergeant Hammerstee, after they argued at the main gate for a minute. Their voices couldn't be heard from where I was. But his motions indicated that Martinet wished to see his patient, but he was refused. He remained stubborn. But then the doctor climbed aboard his carriage and left.

Now we had to care for Annelies without a doctor.

In the afternoon, Annelies slowly began to awake from her sedation. She opened her big eyes, looked left and right, as if glimpsing the world for the first time ever, then closed them again, and after that opened them again.

'Ann, Annelies,' I called.

She looked at me. Her lips opened, pale and bloodless. No voice emerged. I took some chocolate milk and put the glass up to her lips. Silently she drank down almost half a glass, stopped and sat up in bed. Mama sat silently observing her. Suddenly Mama rose and left the room. At first I guessed she went out back to supervise the looking after of the cows.

And not long after I heard her voice, half-shouting, in Dutch:

'Everybody may go to the Netherlands, why can't I?'

I took a peep outside in the garden. Nyai was speaking to a Pure-Blood European who stood with hands on hips. His voice was too soft to me to catch his words. The man shook his head for a moment, sometimes shook his finger.

'What's it matter to you if I accompany my own child? I'll use my own money, nobody else's.'

The visitor shook his head again.

'Show me the rules where it is written down I can't accompany my own child?'

The visitor seemed to move his hands but not his body.

'Smallpox certificate? Health certificate? My child doesn't have one either. On the contrary, she is ill. Get inoculated on board? I can do that too.'

I left them both there in the garden. Annelies seemed to be trying to get down out of bed. I helped her to walk. I took her over to the window because that was her favourite place. And we stood there for a long time. But it was impossible to stay silent forever. I forced myself:

'You've never got as far as the mountains, Ann? From the top, you could see all of Wonokromo and Surabaya. We'll go there one day.'

You couldn't actually see the mountain. It was covered by clumps of clouds and overcast, like white coffee not properly stirred, made by some lazy person. Low-hanging clouds blocked off the usually black-green forest. Far off in the distance, I couldn't guess how far, lightning flashed, king of the heavens, for a moment. The clouds and greyness then disappeared again to who knows where. Nature was busy with its own affairs.

And beside me, my wife let out a long breath.

Mama entered again. She sat down on the chair, silently, without speaking, as if nothing had happened. When I looked her way, she waved her hand calling me over. I left Annelies by the window.

'Minke, you must tell her, Minke, her departure is in three days' time.'

I had to tell her, because I was her husband. It was indeed my responsibility – a responsibility I still hadn't carried out because of everything that had been keeping me so busy lately. Annelies had to know: we were defeated, crushed without ever being able to defend ourselves, let alone fight back.

In the distance, nature was still miserable and was becoming more so with every flash of lightning. Under the window our swan pond had been damaged but still hadn't been repaired. A company village, usually visible from the window, and full of playing children, was now still, without any signs of life.

I approached my wife. I put my hands on her shoulders. I placed my cheek up against her cold cheek. I gathered together all my courage.

'Ann!' She didn't look, neither was there any other response. 'Ann, my Annelies, my wife, will you listen to me?'

She ignored me. The fingers of her left hand slowly scratched her neck. That beautiful neck, covered by her crumpled hair, was more perfect than nature outside.

We had only three days left together. She would leave, my darling, my most beautiful doll in the world. What will happen to you later, Ann? And what about myself? Will you be like the lightning outside, flashing for a moment, reigning supreme over all around you, only then to disappear forever? Someone who does not know you at all has suddenly judged you and punished you this way. Someone else again, they too not knowing anything, will separate you from us, and from everything that you love. You were so thin and pale, Ann. Mama and I had become so scrawny ourselves.

How sad and moving you were, Ann, so beautiful, but never having the chance to enjoy your own beauty and youth.

'Don't you want to listen, Ann?' She still paid no heed. 'Do you like the mountains over there, Ann?'

There was a hint of a nod, affirming.

'We should have gone riding there, yes, Ann? And Mama will stay at home. We'll go by ourselves just the two of us, Ann.'

Once again she nodded imperceptibly.

'*Bawuk* neighs asking after you all the time, Ann.'

She bowed her head. Then, so slowly, she turned around and looked at me and her eyes were like a pair of dreaming daytime star eyes. Her mouth remained mute, and it smelled of medicine.

Mama couldn't hold back her feelings any more. I could hear her crying and she left the room. About ten minutes later she came in again with another European. He walked straight to where we were standing.

'Government doctor,' he said without giving his name, 'here to examine the health of Miss Annelies Mellema.'

'Mrs,' I retorted.

He paid no heed to me. He led my wife off and sat her down on the bed. He took out a stethoscope from his long coat and began the examination. With eyes popping out, he then checked her blood pressure, tilting his head towards the ceiling. He put the stethoscope back in his pocket. He then examined my wife's eyes. After that he smelt her breath coming from her nose and mouth. He shook his head.

Mama watched all this in silence. The government doctor odered his patient to lie down.

'Nyai!' he asked in the coarsest of Malay, 'Why have you allowed this child to be drugged so heavily?'

'Do you wish to leave this house immediately?' replied Nyai in a Malay whose tone was even coarser.

'*Verdomme*, don't you understand yet? I'm the government doctor.'

'So what do you want, heh?' snapped Mama.

'You can all be charged! Dr Martinet too! Watch out!'

'Make your charges in your own house, not here, there's no need for you to work your mouth so much here. The door can still swing on its hinges.'

The government doctor went scarlet. He turned to me.

'You listen too,' he said using, as with Mama, the coarsely familiar *kowe* for 'you', 'you can be a witness to this talk, eh?'

'Indeed the door hasn't been nailed shut yet,' I said.

Nyai and I went over to Annelies and raised her up so she could eat.

'She's weak, too weak. Let her sleep. Her heart. Don't disturb her,' ordered the government doctor.

We got her off the bed and sat her on the settee.

'I'll fetch some food, Ann. Pay no heed to anyone or anything.'

She nodded weakly.

The doctor approached me in a threatening manner, and indeed, threatened me:

'You're trying to oppose my orders, *hey*!'

'I know my wife better than any outsider,' I answered in Malay, without looking at him.

'Good,' he said and left the room, 'Watch out!'

270

'Why won't you speak, Ann?' She was still silent. 'Will you listen to me, Ann? That puffed-up doctor has gone. Don't be afraid.'

I followed her eyes that were directed out the window and let my eyes head for the mountains, which were still covered by clouds. Mama observed my actions without speaking.

Annelies chewed slowly, very slowly, each time hesitating at swallowing.

From behind me I heard Mama speak, more to herself:

'Maurits before dug up past blood sins. Now he demands the wages of those sins. Before I thought he was some holy prophet . . .'

'There's no use in remembering, Ma,' I said without turning to look at her.

'Yes, memories sometimes torture. Indeed there's no use in remembering. Have you told her, Child, Nyo?'

'Not yet, Ma.'

'Speak Ann. You've been silent so long.'

Annelies looked at me. She smiled. Smiled! Annelies smiled! Mama opened her eyes wide in amazement. You're getting better, Ann, I exclaimed in my heart.

Mama rose from her place, embraced her child, kissed her, mumbling:

'The sadness disappears because of your smile, Ann, for your husband too. It's been too much, you not speaking all this time.' And her tears streamed forth.

Annelies blinked slowly, so slowly, as if she didn't really want to open her eyes again.

Dr Martinet had once said: her difficulty was that she wanted to consolidate tightly what already was there. She didn't want to let go of what she already had seized hold of. But a crisis could one day occur which would force her to let go of everything and she would no longer care about anything that happened to her. Was this the stage my wife was at now? I didn't know. Dr Martinet was not allowed to see her. His last words had been: If Annelies could be convinced to surrender to the situation, she would be safe. And how were things now? I didn't know. Mama didn't know. How far away you were, Doctor!

While she was under Martinet's care she was, so he explained, still clinging tightly to things as they were. We'd all been defeated, he said, all our efforts had failed, while Annelies didn't want to understand any of this. She did not seem to rebel, but within her there was disarray as an uncertain war raged. Only being sedated could save her from psychological damage. If not, it might happen that nothing again would have value for her. Or, on the other hand: she could become worthless to anyone. Remember . . . Mr Mellema. So, if she becomes conscious, talk to her without pause, about things beautiful, good; things of hope and pleasant things.

And now it was my job as husband to tell her the bitter truth: three more days! and she wasn't drugged. Dr Martinet was not allowed to see her.

The doctor had also once said: Annelies has passed the crisis period. He said that just a little while before we married. Now a new crisis was upon her. This time also, he said, I'm not her doctor, but you, her husband, the person she loves. You must try to leave with her for the Netherlands. Nyai will be able to pay for the trip: one hundred and twenty *guilders*. That wouldn't be too expensive for her.

They had forbidden us to escort her.

Try, said Dr Martinet, by whatever means. Don't let the life of your wife be wasted. She will not be able to live without you. You now are the only thing to which she clings.

I felt that I had done everything within my power, and I had been defeated. The Amsterdam District Court could not be opposed. The Surabaya Court for Europeans had pronounced that Mama and I had no connection with my wife. Nyai herself cleverly ordered Pandji Darman, formerly Jan Dapperste, to set sail 'to look after the spice business' in the Netherlands and to befriend Annelies as my representative. Nyai had forbidden him to come to Wonokromo to avoid suspicion falling upon him. And a Netherlands Transport Company agent brilliantly placed him in a second-class cabin next door to Annelies' cabin. The agent was the one who also got his health certificate pre-dated.

The face of my wife was like chiselled marble, as if the nerves in her face had been severed from her brain. There was no movement, no expression whatsoever, and she still didn't speak. I had tried from every angle, used every approach to tell her of the day of her departure. It had all failed.

She ate no more than four spoonfuls, then did not want to open her mouth again. I don't know how many times Nyai nervously walked in and out of the room. Once when the room was empty I embraced my wife and I forced myself to have the courage to whisper in her ear:

'Ann, we're defeated, Ann; we were to go with you on the boat to the Netherlands, but they will not allow us. Ann, do you hear me, Ann?'

She still did not respond.

'I don't know what you're thinking. But you need to know, Ann: Jan Dapperste will be there in place of Mama and me. In three days he will escort you as you set sail for Europe. Don't be afraid, yes, Ann. Once you've arrived there, Mama and I will follow.'

And Annelies still paid no attention. Yet I had carried out my duty as her husband, a duty by no means fully accomplished: she still hadn't responded. How many times would I have to repeat the information? I kissed her. Still no response. Perhaps Dr Martinet was right: she had passed the crisis point and was now beginning to set everything free?

For the umpteenth time Mama entered. This time she handed over a telegram from Herbert de la Croix and a letter from Mother.

The Assistant Resident of B— passed on his regrets the attorney he had sent had failed. He shared our sadness and expressed his sympathy for us. In his rather long telegram he also stated that the Amsterdam Court's decision was unjust. He had telegrammed the Governor-General saying that he would resign from his position if the court's decision was carried out. He had also sent a telegram to protest to the Ministry of Justice, all to no avail – they didn't even bother to answer. So he was going to resign and return to Europe with Miriam.

And Annelies herself? She had still lost her interest in everything. And I talked and talked, told story after story. And she still wouldn't talk. Perhaps she wasn't even listening. I carried her back to bed and I laid her down, and myself lay down beside her. It was lucky I knew so many stories as well as the legends of my ancestors. And yet I had already told them all. The European story of Prince Genevieve at least four times, *Gulliver's Travels* twice, Baron von Munchhausen twice, and Little D— perhaps more than four times. And there was still the mouse-deer stories. My own voice was already hoarse. I still added to all these stories, others of my own experiences that were a bit funny.

Embracing my wife I told fairy-taile after fairy-tale, I brought my mouth close to her ears – something she liked.

When I awoke, the night had passed, the room was bright with the rays of the sun. Yet my tiredness hadn't been chased away by the sleep whose length I didn't know. And all of a sudden I realised: Annelies was embracing me, kissing me and caressing my hair. I sat up in a hurry.

'Ann, Annelies!' I shouted. I held her wrist and I felt how her pulse was not as slow as the day before.

'Mas!' she answered.

Was it true that my Annelies was beginning to speak? Or was I just dreaming? I rubbed my eyes. Heh, dream, don't bother me like this! But my eyes saw my wife smiling. Her face was pale, her teeth dirty. And her eyes did not share the smile.

'Ah, Annelies, my Annelies! You're well again, Ann!' I embraced her and kissed her. My efforts and labour all these last days hadn't been wasted.

'Food is ready, Mas, let's eat,' she said gently, exactly as she used to.

I looked at her. Was Dr Martinet right: had she been flung off balance, shocked, so her mind was no longer able to work properly? I looked closely at her eyes. And those eyes were sad. Her lips still smiled but her eyes did not; instead, it was as if she had gone cross-eyed.

'Mama!' I shouted. 'Annelies is well again.'

And Mama didn't appear.

And without having washed first, I sat in that room facing the dinner.

There was no spoon or fork or plate before me. Only before Annelies. Had she lost her mind or was I to eat alone?

She began to spoon up the food and feed it to me.

'I can eat myself, Ann. It's you who must eat, let me feed you.'

She didn't eat, but fed me again. And I had to chew and swallow. I must not offend her – I knew that with certainty – and so I ate until I was full.

'Why are you feeding me like this?'

'Once in my life let me feed my husband,' she went silent and did not want to speak again . . .

20

This day – the last day.

The business had come to a total standstill. The Marechaussee were stopping everybody from entering our front grounds. All we were allowed to do was milk the cows.

Mama's protests were ignored.

'It's not costing Nyai anything,' they retorted, 'it's the people of the Netherlands who are suffering the losses.'

Many letters arrived. There was no opportunity to reply. There was no time really to read them either. The papers sent by Nijman piled up untouched.

Mama, I, and especially Annelies, were not allowed to leave the house, except to wash and to go to the toilet. So we were under house arrest.

The Marechaussee soldiers only ever left their tents in the compound to chase off people who gathered on the edge of the road, who were expressing their sympathy for us perhaps, or were only there to have a look.

Annelies looked more like her usual self, although she was skinny, pale and her eyes were dead.

'Tell me about Holland according to Multatuli's stories,' she suddenly asked.

'There was a country on the edge of the North Sea . . .' I began as best I could, 'its land was low-lying, so it was called The Land of Low Country – Netherlands, or Holland.' When I reached that point I could find no way to continue. Those dreaming eyes of hers, still sad, looked at me so strangely, as if I was some new kind of blue-tailed lizard that she was seeing for the first time in her life. 'Because the land was so low-lying, people became bored of repairing their dikes, so it became their habit to leave their country, to wander, Ann, to admire those other countries with their mountains. Then to conquer them of course. In those high countries they made the people low, nobody was allowed to even approach the height of a Dutchman.'

'Tell me about the sea.'

A European woman in white clothes and hat entered without knocking. Nyai and I let her do so; during the last few days anyone and everyone had been coming in and out of our rooms. She would only annoy us anyway.

'In four more hours you will be sailing across the sea, and more sea, and more sea, darling,' the new arrival said, taking over my job. 'There are more fish than you would ever imagine. Waves, ripples, swell, spray and foam. Miss will be sailing on a big ship, beautiful, crossing the ocean, darling, entering the Suez canal, passing by other ships on the way. When they pass, darling, the ship's whistle will blow. The others will blow theirs as well. Have you seen Gibraltar? Ah, you will pass by that town of coral too. And after that, a few days later, you will set foot on the land of your ancestors. Its sands are a shining, golden yellow, flowers everywhere, all as Miss wishes. It makes people happy. Soon Autumn will arrive. Leaves will fall . . . How happy you will be, looked after by your own brother – a scholar, engineer, well-known, honoured and respected by people. How happy you will be . . . if you don't like it, *yah*, perhaps in one or two years you'll be able to decide your own life. Yes, Miss, just one or two years . . .'

'Mas, I like the waves, and foam, and swell more than ships and the Netherlands . . .'

'No, darling,' the newcomer cut in, 'in the Netherlands you will find everything. Everything that Miss wants she will be able to find there.'

'Mas, is there anything lacking here?'

'No, Ann. You have everything here. You are happy here.'

'If the Netherlands has everything,' Mama added angrily, 'why have Europeans come out here?'

'Don't make my work more difficult, Nyai. Get her clothes ready.'

'No, not just her clothes,' Mama began to become irritable, 'her jewellery, also her bank book, also the letter of acknowledgement of her father, and the prayers of her mother and husband.'

'Mama,' Annelies cut in, 'does Mama remember Mama's story before . . . ?'

'Yes, Ann, what story do you mean?'

'Mama left home forever . . .'

'Yes, Ann, why?'

'Mama took an old brown tin suitcase.'

'Yes, Ann.'

'Where is it now, Ma?'

'Stored in the attic, Ann.'

'I want to see it.'

Mama went to fetch it.

'It's nearly time, Miss,' the European woman cut in.

Neither Annelies nor I responded. And Mama brought a small, brown, rusted, dented suitcase. Annelies quickly greeted it.

'With this suitcase, I will go, Mama, my Mama.'

'It's too small and horrible. It's not fitting, Ann.'

'Mama, it was with this suitcase that Mama left that time resolving never to return. This suitcase weighs too heavily on Mama's memory. Let me take it, Mama, along with the burdensome memories it contains. I will take nothing but the *batik kains* of Minke's mother. Only this suitcase, Mama's memories and Mother's *batiks*, my wedding clothes, Ma. Put them in. My devoted obeisances to Mother B——. I will go Ma, don't remind yourself of all those things from the past. That which has passed, let it pass away, my Mama, my darling Mama.'

'What do you mean, Ann?'

'Like Mama before, Ma, I too will never return home.'

'Ann, Annelies, my darling child,' cried Mama and she embraced my wife. 'It's not that Mama didn't try, Ann, it's not that I didn't defend you, Child . . .'

Mama sank into remorseful sobbing. So did I.

'We both did all we could, Ann,' I added.

'Don't, don't cry, Ma, Mas; I still have a request, Ma, don't cry.'

'Tell us, Ann, tell us,' Mama began to wail.

'Ma, give me a little sister, Ma, a little sister, who will always be sweet to you . . .'

Mama wailed even more.

' . . . so sweet, Ma, not causing you trouble like this daughter of yours . . . until . . .'

'Until what, Ann?'

' . . . until Mama no longer misses Annelies.'

'Ann, Ann, my child, how can you talk so. Forgive us that we could not defend you, forgive us, forgive, forgive.'

'Mas, we were happy together?'

'Of course, Ann.'

'Remember only that happiness, Mas, nothing else.'

'Come on!' shouted out an Indo from the door. 'We're two minutes late already.'

'Come, darling, Miss,' the European woman guided Annelies.

Annelies at once submerged into muteness and disinterest. Her momentary dignity suddenly disappeared. She walked slowly out of the room and down the stairs, under the guidance of the European. Her body seemed so broken and exhausted.

Mama and I ran up to support her, to take over from the woman. But the Indo man and the European woman stopped us.

Marechaussee had congregated at the bottom of the stairs.

And we were kept away! So we were only able to watch our beloved Annelies led away like a cow, step by step.

Perhaps this was how Mama's mother felt when she was treated that way by Mama because she was unable to defend Mama from Mellema. But how did Annelies feel? Was it true she had let go of everything, her own feelings too?

I no longer knew anything. Suddenly I heard the sound of my own crying. Mother, your son had been defeated. Your beloved son did not run, Mother; he is no criminal, even though he's proven incapable of defending his own wife, your daughter-in-law. Is this how weak a Native is in the face of Europeans? Europe! you, my teacher, is this the manner of your deeds? So that even my wife, who knows so little about you, lost all belief in her little world – a world incapable of providing security for even her. Just one person.

I called after her. Annelies didn't answer, nor look back.

'I'll be following soon,' I shouted.

No answer, no look back.

'I too, Ann; have courage, Ann!' called out Mama, her voice hoarse, almost unable to escape from her throat.

Also no answer, no look back.

The gate was opened. A government carriage was waiting, hemmed in on either side by mounted Marechaussee. Mama and I weren't allowed past the door.

For a moment we could still see Annelies being helped into the carriage. She still didn't look this way, didn't make a sound.

The door was closed from outside.

The sound of the carriage wheels grinding over the gravel could be faintly heard fading away into the distance, finally disappearing. Annelies was setting sail for where Queen Wilhelmina sat on the throne. Behind the door, we bowed our heads.

'We've been defeated, Ma,' I whispered.

'We fought back, Child, Nyo, as well and honourably as possible.'

Buru.
Spoken, 1973
Written, 1975

Child of All Nations

1

Annelies had set sail. Her going was as a young branch wrenched away from the plant that nourished it. This parting was a turning point in my life. My youth was over, a youth beautifully full of hopes and dreams. It would never return to unfold again.

The sun was moving slowly, crawling like a snail, inch by inch across the heavens. Slowly, yes slowly – uncaring whether the distance it had traversed would ever be traversed again.

The clouds hung thinly across the sky, unwilling to release a single spray of drizzle. The atmosphere was grey, as though the world had lost its multitude of colours.

The old people teach us through their legends that there is a mighty god called *Batara Kala*. They say it is he who makes all things move further and further from their starting point, unable to resist, towards some unknown final destination. And I too, a human blind to the future, could do no more than hope to know. Uh! while we never really understand even what we have already lived through.

People say that before mankind stands only distance. And its limit is the horizon. Once the distance has been crossed, the horizon moves away again. There is no romance so strong that it could tame and hold them – the eternal distance and the horizon.

Batara Kala had pushed Annelies across many distances, and had pushed me across others. The further apart we were forced the clearer it became that no one could tell what the future held. The distance opening out before me made me understand she was not just a fragile doll. A woman who can love so deeply is not a doll. Perhaps, also, she was the only woman whose love for me was pure. And the further Batara Kala pulled us apart, the more I came to feel that truly, I loved her.

And love, like every other object and situation, has its shadow. And love's shadow is called pain. There is nothing without its shadow, except light itself . . .

Whether light or shadow, nothing can escape being pushed along by Batara Kala. No one can return to his starting point. Maybe this mighty god is the one whom the Dutch call 'the teeth of time' (*de tand des tijds*).

It makes the sharp blunt, and the blunt sharp; the small are made big and the big made small. All are pushed on towards that horizon, receding eternally beyond our reach. Pushed on towards annihilation. And it is that annihilation which in turn brings rebirth.

I don't really know whether this beginning to my notes is fitting or not. At the very least everything must have a beginning. And this is the beginning I have written.

Mama and I hadn't been allowed out of the house for three days, nor permitted to receive guests.

A District Police Head rode up on his horse. I didn't leave my room. It was Mama who met him, and hardly a moment passed before the shouting started in Malay. Mama called me out of my room. The two of them stood facing each other.

She pointed to a piece of paper on the table: 'Minke, Mr Police Chief here says we were never under arrest. Yet we haven't been able to leave the house for over a week now.'

'Yes,' the policeman explained, 'you now are being officially notified: the two inhabitants of this house are free to come and go.'

'Mr Police Chief here thinks that now with this written notice, our period of detention never existed.'

These last few days Mama's nerves had been so on edge that she was ready to fight with anyone at all, especially a servant of the state. I was reluctant to join in the fight. I could see that Mama, her face fiery red, was ready to erupt with rage.

The Police Chief jumped on his horse and made his escape.

'Why didn't you say something?' Mama rebuked me. 'Afraid?' Her voice subsided into a low rumble. 'They need us to be afraid, Child, no matter how badly we natives are treated.'

'Ah, everything is all over now anyway, Ma.'

'Indeed, all over. We were defeated, but still they have violated a principle. They have detained us illegally. Don't ever think that you can defend something, especially justice, if you don't care about principles, no matter how trifling the issue . . .'

So she began to lecture me about principles – a lesson I had never learned at school, had never read about in books, magazines or newspapers. My heart was not yet calm enough to receive such new teachings, no matter how beautiful and good. Yet still I listened.

'Look, no matter how rich you are,' she began, and I listened halfheartedly, 'you must resist anyone who takes what is yours. Even if it's only a clump of soil below the window. Not because that soil is so very valuable to you. A principle: taking someone's possession without permission is theft. It is not right; it must be opposed. And in the last few days, it is our very freedom they have robbed us of.'

'Yes, Ma,' I answered, hoping that she would end her lecture quickly.

But it wasn't so easy to stop her and, if I hadn't been there, she would probably have delivered it to whoever else was around.

'Those who are not faithful to principles become open to evil: to have evil done to them or to do evil themselves.'

Then she seemed to realise that her timing was wrong. 'Go out and get some fresh air, Child. You've been locked up too long. You look stale.'

I went back into my old room, which I had shared so briefly with Annelies. Yes I needed to go for a stroll, to get some fresh air. I opened the wardrobe to get out a change of clothes. All of a sudden I remembered Robert Suurhof. There was something of his in this wardrobe: a gold and diamond ring.

Mama had thought it was a very expensive gift for a friend to give as a wedding present. The diamond alone was about two carats. Only somebody who was rich, or who really loved you, would give such a present. Yes, Mama's guess was probably right – Robert Suurhof might indeed have given it as a sign of his love. Now that Annelies had gone, the time had come to return this thing to him, to his family. Now it seemed no mere coincidence that Mama had spoken of principles.

After I'd dressed I opened the wardrobe. I took out Annelies's metal jewellery box. Robert's ring wasn't there. I checked the drawer again. It was lying unwrapped in a corner. I picked it up and looked at it closely.

I had never taken much notice of women's jewellery. Yet I could still enjoy the stone's pure shining blueness, sparkling within itself, the rays multiplied by its polished walls. Uh, why must I admire this destructive object?

I put back the jewellery box, which I had just opened for the first time. Beside the box was a folder. Inside it was a Bank Escompto bank book, a pile of salary receipts from the business, and two letters from Robert Suurhof. They had never been opened! I fought my desire to open and read them. I had no right, I told myself. She had received those letters before she became my wife.

I rose to leave for my walk, then stood hesitantly at the door. There was something I hadn't done. Yes, of course: I usually read the newspapers before I went for a walk. Who knows how long it had been since I'd read one? I returned to the desk, sat down, groped through the pile of mail. The desire to read was gone.

Why was I feeling so listless? I forced myself to start on a newspaper. No. I couldn't. I separated the letters from the rest of the mail and went through them one by one: from Mother, from my elder brother, from . . . Robert Suurhof for Annelies. Anger burned in my heart, my jealousy was awakened. From Sarah de la Croix, from Magda Peters, from Robert Suurhof for . . . from Miriam de la Croix, from . . . again from Robert Suurhof for Annelies. My hands and eyes began to sort more quickly.

There were eleven letters from Suurhof. Scalding lava erupted into my heart. Madman! Damned one!

I took a letter, tore it open and read:

Miss Annelies Mellema, Goddess of My Dreams . . .

I didn't go on. I rushed outside and ordered Marjuki to prepare a buggy. The ring in my pocket weighed me down. I would go and hurl this thing to the ground before his parents.

'Quickly, Juki!'

The buggy flew off in the direction of Surabaya.

Neither my thoughts nor my vision would focus. All was blurred, without direction. Then, in the distance, I saw an old school friend, one who had never passed his exams. But even concern for my friends had faded away. Only after he had disappeared from sight did I feel ashamed for having treated a school friend so dishonourably. Perhaps he was one who had been sympathetic to us in our troubles.

Near Kranggan I saw Victor Roomers strolling happily along, kicking the roadside pebbles. This Pure European fellow graduate didn't seem to have anything to do that afternoon. He was wearing white shorts, white shirt, white shoes; as usual, he looked quite fresh. After three years of studying with him, I had grown to like him. He was a lover of athletics; he had a sportsmanlike attitude towards the world and never turned a sour face to it. And most important of all, he held no racial prejudices.

'Hi, Vic!' I ordered Marjuki to pull the buggy over to the side of the road. I jumped down and shook hands. Victor invited me into a roadside drinks stall.

He began quickly: 'Forgive me, Minke, for not being able to help you in your difficulties. I came once to see you at Wonokromo, but the Field Police broke up any groups that collected around or near your fence. Some of our other friends also tried to visit you, but in vain. No one could help, Minke, especially not someone like me. I asked Papa about it all once. It had never happened before, he said, a Native daring to oppose a decision of the White Court. All our friends regretted not being able to ease your suffering. We truly share your sorrow in all this, Minke.'

'Thank you, Vic.'

'Where are you off to? You look so pale.'

'Would you like to come along?'

'Very much, but I can't just now. Where are you going?'

'I've got a bit of business to fix up, Vic, at Robert Suurhof's house.'

'A waste of time. What do you want to go there for?'

'There is something . . .'

'Robert's vanished. Who knows where he's gone,' Vic said casually, as if nothing of note had happened.

'Vanished?' Somehow it didn't feel right to use that word about a fellow graduate.

'Yes. So you haven't been reading the newspapers. Robert's name wasn't mentioned. It was Ezekiel's name that was printed.'

'You're right, I haven't been reading the papers. You mean the Ezekiel who owns the jewellery shop?'

'Who else? Surely there is only one Ezekiel left in this world, eh?'

The diamond ring jumped in my pocket, piercing my thighs and demanding to be taken to Ezekiel's shop. So Suurhof had stolen it.

'That's the kind of person our friend Robert Suurhof is,' Vic said with disappointment. 'He had big ambitions. He wanted to master the world in a week. In the end . . .'

'Oh, so now it's *in the end*, Vic. So Robert stole from Ezekiel's.'

'If I were you, Minke, perhaps I wouldn't be reading newspapers either. You've been through too much lately.'

'Forget it, Vic. Tell me about Robert.'

The diamond ring started jabbing and stabbing me in the thigh again. Imagine what would happen if a policeman stopped and frisked me; it would mean another trial.

'It's just like any other crime story. It always starts with someone's great ambition to overwhelm the world in a week. Pity the Suurhofs, Mr and Mrs Suurhof. Both are already so gaunt, perhaps now they're even worse. Two of their children give up school altogether just so Robert can graduate from H.B.S. Straight after graduating, he turns into a bandit, and a cheap bandit at that.'

'What did he take from Ezekiel's?'

'Not even that! If he'd robbed Ezekiel's shop, at least he'd have had some style. At least he would have had to fight the *hermandad* or speak with a golden tongue and outwit them. All he did was rob a Chinese grave, shaming his school friends, his school and his teachers. It's lucky he's disappeared and escaped arrest. Who knows where he is now?'

'I know where he is. But keep on with the story.'

'The story's quite simple. Remember how he used to carry on about becoming a lawyer? His parents would never have been able to pay for it, especially as he'd have to finish another five years of H.B.S. in Holland. His parents could never pay his fare, let alone his school fees. They're both ill; they've used up all their money for medicines. Ah! that Robert! He wanted to be rich, to have a wife of unrivalled beauty, to be number one man, a lawyer – and all in a week. Straight after graduating he goes and knocks down the cemetery watchman, at the Chinese cemetery, hitting him from behind and stealing from one of the graves.'

So that's the story, I thought. Oh damned and bejewelled ring, that's how you've come to be in my pocket! If something went wrong and the police knew where to find you now ... I became a bit nervous. I asked: 'How was the crime discovered?'

'You're going pale, Minke. Are you ill?'

I shook my head.

'He sold the booty to Ezekiel. It was discovered by the dead man's family. They checked all the jewellery shops and found one of their things at Ezekiel's; then they reported it.'

Vic then told the rest of the story; it was easy to guess. The crime was exposed; the police searched Suurhof's house. Robert had vanished. Nothing was found. No one knew where Robert had gone, not even his parents.

'You say you know where he is, Minke?'

'Well, at least where he's been sending his letters from.'

'Letters? To you?' he asked, amazed. His eyes questioned mine. Then, abruptly, he turned the conversation: 'There's no point, Minke. There's no point complaining to his parents about those letters. You'll only cause more sorrow.'

I became suspicious. How embarrassing if he knew about Suurhof's letters to my wife! How humiliated I would be as a husband! The ring itched in my pocket. Damned ring! Perhaps this accursed thing was the cause of all our misfortune. Oh-oh, trouble!

Victor could tell I was trying to hide something, to avoid answering. 'No, Minke, don't go there. That scoundrel Robert is capable of anything.'

I turned the conversation: 'What are you doing these days, Vic?'

'Just as you see me now: in and out of the villages. You know what I am? Don't laugh. An agent for a shipping company, taking pilgrims to Mecca. Being a *Sinyo* like this, it's hard to get my customers' trust. I intend to get some other kind of work, but ... ah well. Hey, Minke, do you know how many pilgrims will go on the *haj* from South Africa this year? Five hundred! From an English colony! If I could just get five hundred people here in Surabaya ...'

He too wanted to avoid talk about Robert's letters. He must have known they were addressed to my wife. So it was no secret. How did people know?

'Hey, Minke, would you like to swap jobs with me?'

'Thanks, Vic. But I must get on now.'

I left Victor Roomers in the stall. I left with an angry heart – hot, jealous, furious.

The buggy raced off towards Peneleh. From others I met along the way I got the same story and the same advice: stay away from the Suurhofs. One even said, straight out: 'Don't take any notice if you get letters from him. He's crazy.'

So all my school friends knew about the letters to Annelies. I was the only one who didn't. How blind I had been. Oh, Minke!

Willem Vos, who was working in a timber yard, even went so far as to say: 'He made it clear, that he was out to get you, Minke. Be careful. He made threats at the graduation party that day. But people like him would never dare say such things openly.'

I deliberately avoided the girls from school. Now that they had graduated they were no longer school friends but maidens awaiting proposals from one official or another – Pure European if possible. I would only disturb their waiting.

Late in the day, another friend pointed out: 'Ezekiel has been kept under detention, yet Suurhofs' name has never even been mentioned. Why? Because he has European Status. Ezekiel is a Jew from Baghdad, with only Oriental status.'

At five-thirty in the afternoon, my buggy entered the Suurhofs' front compound. My eyes went straight for the mango tree, where the family liked to sit and enjoy the afternoon air. Yes, there they were, all sitting on the wooden benches around the tree trunk, talking amongst themselves.

I had not been to this house since the incident between Robert and me, when I first met Annelies at Wonokromo. When they saw my fine buggy enter the yard they all stood up and stared in amazement. I recognised Mr and Mrs Suurhof straight away. Both were thin and wasted from consumption. Of their twelve children, only Robert, the eldest, was missing.

As soon as I alighted, Mrs Suurhof called out in her Indo accent, 'Ai-ai, Nyo, it looks like you're a big *tuan* now!'

'Good afternoon, Mr Suurhof, Mrs Suurhof, children,' I greeted them, thinking at that moment that my friends were right: I shouldn't have come.

The whole family looked thin and sickly. What was the use of showing them this cursed ring? And what was the use in protesting about Robert's letters? Pent-up anger, fury, a hot and jealous heart – all were slowly pushed aside by pity.

The children stood up and moved aside to make a place for me. They sat surrounding me in a horse-shoe shape.

'Wah! the newspapers were full indeed of reports about you, Sinyo,' Mr Suurhof began.

'Yes, but things have eased now. It's all over.'

'It's a great pity that it ended so unhappily, Nyo,' Mrs Suurhof added.

'What can be done,' and the conversation ended.

But our quiet reflections were interrupted. One of the children attacked with the news: 'Brother Robert has gone. He's not here any more. Didn't he say good-bye to you?' On seeing me shake my head he went on, 'He's gone to the Netherlands.'

'Who said he's gone to the Netherlands?' Mr Suurhof quickly took over the conversation. 'He went away just before Sinyo got married. You must know, as a child he was never at ease with himself. A young person, an H.B.S. graduate, restless, forgetful, never wanting to stay at home. Sinyo knows what he was like.' Old Suurhof threw a hard look toward his children. It seemed he meant to forbid them talking about their elder brother.

But one of the younger children didn't understand the signals. He came up to me and passed on some proud news: 'Yes, *Bang*, in the afternoon Bang Robert would work and in the morning go to H.B.S.'

'That's very fine. He was a very advanced pupil. What kind of work did he do?' I asked.

'He never used to say, Bang.'

'He might be restless,' Mrs Suurhof took over from her children, 'but we never believed there was evil in his heart. Yes, sometimes he was naughty, uncontrolled, Nyo – you know what he's like from school, yes? – but a wicked boy? No.'

The smaller child wasn't going to be ignored. He went on with his report with great enthusiasm: 'He sent us some money once, Bang! Fifteen guilders!'

'What are you talking about, Wim?' his mother reprimanded.

'Yes, it's true, Bang,' another little brother affirmed. 'Mama used the money for clothes for us children.'

'It's true, Bang, they're being made up now,' Wim added.

'Uh! children!' Mr Suurhof cut in. He wanted to say something else, but his coughing stopped him.

'It's true, Bang, it's true,' some of the other children supported their brothers.

'Hussy! That wasn't from Robert. You heard wrong. The money is from your father's pension,' Mrs Suurhof scolded.

'Back pay for a wage increase due five months ago, Nyo,' Mr Suurhof explained, then tried to divert the conversation: 'So Sinyo works for *Nyai* now?'

'Yes, just helping around the place, Sir, that's all.'

'How does it pay?'

'Well enough, Sir.'

'Yes, it's a big company; the salary would be big too.'

'Bang, Bang,' Wim charged in head first again, 'Bang Robert has been adopted by a wealthy merchant. He's living in a three-storied building, in Heerengracht.'

'Where's Heerengracht?' I asked.

'Ah, fancy listening to children's talk. Don't take any notice, Nyo.'

The eldest child – who hadn't been able to continue his schooling – observed the conversation with big suspicious eyes. He listened to each of his parents' words, and to what I said, but paid no heed to his younger brothers and sisters.

'Robert said' – another child came forward – 'after he becomes a lawyer, he's going to open an office in Surabaya.'

'So he's living in Heerengracht now?' I repeated my question.

'It's not true, Nyo. Even my husband and I don't know where he is now,' Mrs Suurhof contradicted her children.

Husband and wife were trying to avoid each other's eyes, while doing their utmost to silence their children.

The eldest, the one who hadn't even graduated from E.L.S., didn't relax his attention for a moment.

'Go on, over there, fix some drinks for Nyo Minke.'

The eldest moved slowly away from the mango tree, his head bowed.

'*Ayoh*! all out the back! Check that all the dishes have been washed. You too!' she ordered the smallest. They all obeyed.

'I don't know where those children learnt to fantasise about their brother,' said Mr Suurhof, frowning at his wife.

'Yes, that's children for you, Nyo,' Mrs Suurhof added. 'If Sinyo has many children later on, you'll find out. They eat out your heart. Don't pay them any attention now, Nyo.'

It was pathetic to see how these two parents tried to defend their family's good name by refusing to admit anything to the world, and by painting for their other children a flawless picture of their eldest son.

And what of the ring in my pocket? What must I do with this object, this bringer of misfortune? Must it smoulder forever in my pocket and my thoughts? These people will be even more tormented if I return it and tell them it came from Robert. Look: both of them are waiting to see what will come out of my mouth next, like the accused awaiting the judge's sentence.

Seeing I was hesitating, Mr Suurhof began: 'You must know yourself, Nyo, what Robert was like. I myself don't know what he wants, Nyo. He has never given any thought to the troubles he causes his parents.'

'Tuan, where is Robert now?'

'No one knows, Nyo.'

'I know he set sail for Europe on board an English ship,' I said.

Both husband and wife looked at me with hopeless eyes. The approach of one of their younger children, crying, from the direction of the house, saved them from their desperation. The child complained: 'Someone's stamped on my foot, Ma . . .'

'Nah! Nyo, this is how it is. Fighting every day. If God permits, you'll end up thin and dried up! Even when they're grown up, there's no guarantee they'll be of any use to you,' Mrs Suurhof advised me once more. She spoke to the child and led him back.

Now, left with four eyes only, I at last felt more at ease. Yet still there was not enough resolve in my heart to act on my intentions. The ring began to burn again in my pocket. The gaunt man before me was still trying to guess the reason for my visit.

'So how is your wife, Sinyo?'

His question gave me an opening: 'I am here precisely on my wife's behalf, Tuan.'

'Ha? She had no business with us.'

Pity returned to erode my resolve. No, you must not be weak! Do what you must, I encouraged myself.

Tuan Suurhof searched my face with guesses and anticipations.

'Yes, Tuan,' and I reached down into my trouser pocket. But once again I became unsure and couldn't do it 'My wife, yes, Tuan, my wife . . .'

'We've never had anything to do with Sinyo's wife.' Old Suurhof was beginning to feel boxed in.

'. . . is returning something that she received from Tuan's family, the Suurhof family.'

'Returning something? We've never lent anything to your wife.' He was becoming more and more guarded.

Before I lost my nerve again I reached into my pocket and drew out the handkerchief in which the ring was wrapped. I put it on the table, explaining, 'Yes, Tuan, only a small object. On the day we were married, my wife received this gift from Robert. We felt it was too valuable. We wanted to return it.'

'Nah-nah! we never agreed with Robert about any present.'

I opened the handkerchief. The diamond glistened in the bright twilight, lying there like an eyeball gouged from its socket.

Tuan Suurhof was abruptly seized by a coughing fit, turning his face away and bending over. His right cheek quivered uncontrollably. He waved the object away: 'Wrap it up again, Nyo. I know for certain that Robert had gone before Sinyo was married. Robert, and even we ourselves, have never owned anything like that.'

'It is indeed a very expensive ring, Tuan, perhaps worth more than four hundred guilder, but it did come from Robert.'

'No, Sinyo is mistaken. It couldn't have been from him. He had long gone.'

'Yes, he was indeed gone, Tuan, but not before our marriage. Even now he is sending letters.'

'How is that possible, Nyo? He doesn't even write to us. They must be fake.'

'No, Tuan, I know his handwriting well. So what about the ring?'

'No, Nyo, Robert never owned a ring like that. Put it back in your pocket, before anyone sees it,' he said nervously.

'Robert himself put this ring on my wife's finger. I thought that if we gave it back to you, you could use it for something.'

'No, Nyo, I am happy enough as I am, a clerk in the Post Office.'

'But we don't want it,' I persisted.

'Neither do we, Nyo. Indeed we don't have any right to it.'

The haggard man's eyes darted everywhere, even behind himself, steadfastly refusing to look at the ring.

'If that is the case, let me take my leave of you.' I stood up.

He too stood up. I walked away but he jumped up and blocked my path. He pleaded: 'Take the thing back, Nyo. Don't be angry with me. Don't make things even more difficult for us.' He held my hand, pleading.

'It's up to you, Tuan; you can throw it away. You can burn it.'

'Don't, Nyo. I daren't even touch it.'

I kept walking away. He tugged at me to stop me from going.

'Why are you afraid? It's Robert's. If you don't like it, then keep it and give it back to him when he returns.'

'Don't, Nyo, don't cause us more trouble, Nyo. Sinyo knows how many children we have.' His tugs grew stronger.

I stopped, unsure. Indeed I had no right to make trouble for him and his family. They had already suffered enough because of Robert. Victor Roomers was right after all. I shouldn't be adding to their troubles. Mama's teachings about principles were being tested. But it wouldn't be just to go on with this.

I allowed myself to be pulled back, and sat again under the mango tree. I listened to his pleas: 'Take it back, Nyo,' he said, pointing with his chin to the ring, which still lay on the handkerchief.

I wrapped up that accursed ring and put it back in my pocket. For the second time, I took my leave. He seemed relieved. All of a sudden, he asked: 'Where to now, Nyo?'

'To hand this ring over to the District Police Officer, Tuan.'

'God, Nyo, is there no other way?'

'No, Tuan,' I answered firmly.

'If that's what Sinyo wants.' He paused momentarily, then didn't go on. He escorted me back to the buggy. Before climbing aboard, I felt I had to ask his pardon: 'I'm sorry, Tuan. There is nothing else I can do.'

The buggy took me to the District Police Chief's office. Along the way I couldn't but help but marvel at the presence of the police in this world. In troubles such as these, they appear as a kind of godfather – able to solve almost any problem. The civilised world could not continue without them. People say they began as groups of private individuals in Spain, hired to protect the wealthy and powerful from criminals and from the poor. Later they were taken over by governments. As in other places, the police had not been around long in the Indies, only for the last few decades. Imagine if criminal cases had still been in the hands of the *Baleo*. There would be even more trouble before I could get rid of this ring.

The District Police Officer received me politely, listened to my story, took the ring and examined it. He seemed to know what he was doing. It was not fake, he said, and was about two carats, but he called someone else in to examine it more closely.

He handed me a receipt to sign which gave details of the ring's diamond carat value, its gold carat value and weight.

'Can you get witnesses that this was indeed a gift from Robert Suurhof?'

He took down the names I gave.

'Do you know where Suurhof is now?'

'I do know, Tuan, from his letters.'

'Can we borrow those letters?' he asked politely. 'No? Very well. If you have no objections, could you give us the address?'

'His actual address isn't written there, Tuan. But the stamps on the envelope were marked Amsterdam Post Office.'

'Good. Then let us borrow the envelopes. The more the better.'

'Just the envelopes?'

'If you have no objections, Tuan. Otherwise, please just write out a declaration giving the details.'

I wrote out the declaration he asked for.

On the way home I felt freed from the disturbances caused by that accursed object, as though freed from some thorn stuck in my throat.

'Only rich people like going to the police, Young Master,' Marjuki suddenly said. 'Little people like me are afraid. If I weren't your driver, I swear I'd never have entered that yard, Young Master.'

'Yes, Juki,' I answered. Indeed they had no need of the police. They had little interest in the security of their wealth, selves and name; in fact, they owned nothing. These thoughts, emerging so suddenly, aroused feelings of sympathy for them – those who had nothing, who had no need of the services of the police. To them a ring, especially a two-carat one, was like a legend from the heavens, not something of this earth. What need did they have of the police?

On arriving home, I went straight into my room. Once inside, I began to relax. The wardrobe no longer housed any accursed object. The police would do their job and search out Robert in the Netherlands. The Suurhofs would have to understand; their son would have to accept the consequences of his actions.

If I had not acted, perhaps those old people and their children would still go on living in a fantasy world forever. It would only hurt them all in the end. And me? I had been able to resolve quite a difficult problem, to balance pity and justice – and still ensure the triumph of principle.

And more that that: I had overcome my own weakness of heart, overcome out-of-place sentimentalism. I saw all this as a personal victory.

2

It was none other than Mama who said: A name can change a hundred times a day, but the object itself stays the same. The bureaucrats and aristocrats of Java, my people, liked to give themselves wonderful names as adornments, to impress everything and everyone around them, including themselves, with the beauty of these names. Shakespeare, that English dramatist, never knew the powerful men of Java who liked to wax lyrical with names, to ensconce their positions and offices in the security of names. A clerk likes to use the name *Sastra*, meaning 'of letters'; so *Sastradiwirya* will mean a clerk who is good and firm of will. A bureaucrat *priyayi* in charge of irrigation will strengthen his standing with the name *Tirta*, meaning water, so *Tirtanta* will mean an official who administers irrigation.

What's in a name? People called me Minke. Perhaps it was indeed a mispronunciation of the word 'monkey'. But it is a name, and it will still make me respond if I hear it called out.

Is it true that a name cannot change the substance of a thing? Was Shakespeare right? For the time being we'll have to reject the proposition. Take, for example, Robert Jan Dapperste, the Native child who was adopted by the preacher Dapperste. His body was thin and weak. He always needed protection and support. Every day he was the object of insults; he was called *de Lafste*. The more people he came to know the more he became the object of insults and laughter. Because of a name, just a name, he developed into a shy, introverted person, full of resentment and cunning.

Yet he was loyal to people who helped him and protected him, who didn't insult or torment him. He ran away from his adopted parents because of that name too. Now he had obtained a Determination of the Governor-General of the Netherlands Indies. He had a new name: Panji Darman. And he himself had indeed changed. Imagine: only three weeks after obtaining his new name, he had already become gay, free of the name Dapperste, free of any burden, with his good characteristics unchanged. And he turned out to be a very courageous person.

While still so young, two years younger than me, he was ready to carry out Mama's order to escort Annelies to the Netherlands or wherever else she might be taken.

I will not say much about him. It will be enough if I show you his letters. They are in the order in which they were written.

I write this letter on board a ship heading for Betawi, on the Java Sea, this calm and windless day. Mama and my good Minke, this is the first time I have sailed on a ship. Even so I have had no chance to dwell on my own feelings.

Before boarding the ship, my carriage waited at the edge of the road, waiting for the carriage that was bringing Madame Annelies. I saw several other people sitting along the side of the road also waiting to see Annelies pass. It seems that newspaper reports about Madame Annelies being taken away from Mama and Minke and being sent back to the Netherlands had spread by word of mouth, and had reached right down into the villages. There were many people who felt they must come and express their sympathy, by standing for hours along the side of the street.

Then there appeared a military carriage escorted by a troop of Marechausee in other carriages. That particular carriage was closed. In there was Madame Annelies. She must have been there. I ordered Marjuki to follow them after the troop escort had passed by. I couldn't help but watch the faces of those who were standing along the road. They were all disappointed that they couldn't see inside the carriage. Many of the older women, Natives, were wiping away their precious tears with a handkerchief or the corner of their selendang.

The closer we came to Tanjung Perak harbour, the bigger were the crowds along the road. In some places people threw stones at the Marechausee. Even some little children showed their sympathy with catapults and small slings. I could not but be moved by all this. They were enveloped in a sense of justice – a sense of justice that had been offended. It was as if Madame Annelies had become one of them, a member of their own families.

I had never seen so many people come together to express their sympathy and solidarity for another person.

The Marechausee rode on, ignoring the flying stones. But some soldiers were actually hit and were bleeding. They rode on as if nothing had happened. How resolved were their hearts in carrying out their evil orders! I worried, worried very much: it musn't happen that any of these stones hit Madame Annelies's carriage. But no, neither her carriage nor its driver became targets.

The closer we came to Perak, the greater the number of people waiting along the road. And now they weren't just throwing stones, they were shouting out too: 'Infidel! Infidel! Thieves!'

About five hundred metres from the harbour, across a road hemmed in on either side by mangrove trees, a string of Madurese buffalo carts were lined up, blocking the way. The carriages of Marechausee stopped, as did Madame Annelies's. My heart pounded anxiously as I watched the incident from a distance. Would there be another fight?

'Oh no! It's terrible, Young Master,' said Marjuki, 'Miss Annelies, Nyai and Young Master Minke are all in that carriage.'

It was indeed a tense moment, and neither of us could do anything. The Marechausee were all jumping down from their carriages, blowing on their whistles. They all charged the Madurese buffalo cart drivers. The fight was over quickly. The Marechausee were quickly in control of the situation. The now-driverless buffalo carts were pushed aside; many tumbled over into deep channels along the side of the road. Injured cattle and damaged carts now filled the channels.

I'm not really sure whether all this is the proper subject of my letters to you. Marjuki must have told it all to you already. My intention is to let you know just how many people came to express their sympathy in their own way, perhaps in a way that is unknown in Europe. But maybe it too is a European way, if we remember how people expressed their anger against Lodewijk the Sixteenth.

Madame Annelies's carriage now went straight on to the harbour without stopping at Customs. We arrived not long after. When I went into Customs, I suddenly realised: Mama and Minke were not accompanying Madame Annelies. They must have been forbidden from doing so, I thought. And because of that thought, a great, deep anger arose within me: Mama and Minke weren't even allowed to come with her to the ship. And these Dutchmen confessed themselves the servants of Christ in the Indies. My feelings were outraged by this. Christ would never have become involved in an abomination such as this. Mama, Minke, let alone Madame Annelies had never slapped anybody's cheek, but now you were being forced to put forward your right cheek, I thought. Those Dutchmen were not following the Christianity I was taught, yet your own behaviour had been Christian enough.

Perhaps it is also because of that great anger that I am able to write such a long letter as this. Forgive me, Minke, if this letter is not well put together, because, of course, I cannot write as you can. I write this because of my responsibility to report to you everything that you should know.

I waited on the wharf as the skiff took Madame Annelies out to the ship. My turn to be taken hadn't yet arrived. Forgive me for not being able to keep close to Madame Annelies. But I could see from a distance that she was being watched over by a European woman dressed in white, perhaps a nurse.

Even as I boarded the ship, I heard someone discussing the decision of the White Court, saying that it was not very wise or just and was too harsh, as if Mama's family were criminals. I pretended I knew nothing about it so I could get to hear more. But, a pity, the talk went no further than that.

I saw several Marechausee disembark from the ship. And with that I judged that the incident was over.

Two hours later, the ship blew its steam whistle, and departed.

Through the efforts of the shipping agent, I had been given the cabin next to Madame Annelies's. But, from the beginning, she has never used it. It appears that she was in a special room under the care of the ship's doctor. I have tried to get close to her: she might feel I am a friend, or at least an acquaintance. But she is never to be seen. I don't know exactly where she is being kept. And I don't yet dare ask about her, being afraid that such enquiries may give away my true purpose. Forgive my stupidity and clumsiness.

But I am still trying to find out which is her room. Don't be disappointed, Mama and Minke, if this is all I am able to tell you now. I will write again soon, and please pray that my efforts might bear fruit, just as we all hope.

My unbounded respects, Panji Darman

Several days later, eight days to be exact, his second letter arrived. This time it was post-marked Medan.

It was only when the ship entered Singapore harbour that I got to see Madame Annelies. She was in a white gown and was escorted by the nurse. She was brought up on deck so she could have a look at Singapore. But it was clear she wasn't really taking any notice of anything at all. I guessed from the first that it was actually the nurse who wanted to get a look at Singapore, not Madame Annelies. It was as if she had lost interest in everything.

I quickly moved closer to her, pretending not to know her. She was not looking at Singapore at all. Her head was bowed down as if to watch the waves playing against the side of the ship. But it was clear she wasn't paying attention to anything really. Her hair was neatly combed, and from where I stood I could smell perfume.

Her face was very pale. The nurse never let go of Madame's waist, a sign that she was in a very weak state.

A few score passengers went ashore to have a look around Singapore. Before disembarking they all had to stop and take a look at Madame Annelies. Those who intended to get their view of Singapore from the ship's deck felt, just like me, that they must seek a place close to her. Their feeling of pity and compassion showed on their faces, but no one spoke. Except here and there, somebody might whisper.

Madame Annelies's paleness was most evident in her lips, and she took no notice of anybody's stares.

I tried to get as close as possible without arousing suspicion. I was going to try to let her know that she wasn't alone on her journey to the Netherlands. But it seemed she paid no heed to either sound or voice. I spoke out my name as loudly as possible to an old Chinaman who, in fact, did not at all wish for my company: Robert Jan Dapperste alias Panji Darman.

The old Chinaman was quite surprised at my attentions but Annelies still didn't seem to care about anything going on around her. She didn't even glance around. She just kept on with her observation of the sea below. It was her nurse who turned around. I couldn't look her in the eye because of a feeling that I was doing something wrong. And the nurse seemed to understand: I had deliberately spoken my name aloud.

She pulled Madame along, leading her off by the hand away from that spot. I didn't dare follow close behind. But then just for a moment, no more than a moment, Madame looked at me; I think she recognised me. But she stayed silent, not showing any special interest.

I followed them from a distance. I watched Annelies led up and down other stairs with great difficulty and effort until, at last, they went into a cabin that was clearly not a passenger cabin. Perhaps that was her room, perhaps not. There was no name on the door, just a number.

After I discovered this cabin, I began to hang about there. But there was still no sign of Annelies. Perhaps tomorrow or the day after. But her nurse did from time to time come out of the cabin. Perhaps it was the ship's clinic? But I soon rejected that idea, because the clinic clearly isn't there; I know that for sure.

My good Mama and Minke, this is as much as I can report at the moment. Perhaps at our next port of call there will be some further progress which I can report . . .

Then there was Panji Darman's letter stamped Colombo.

It appears that the nurse did notice me. One day I was summoned by the Captain. His letter was addressed to Panji Darman alias Robert Jan Dapperste. I went to the cabin mentioned in the letter and, indeed, I found the Captain there.

'You are going to the Netherlands, yes?' I nodded. 'You came on board at Surabaya, yes?' I nodded again. 'You will continue your schooling there?'

'No, I am going on business,' I answered.

'Business. As young as you?'

'Yes. I think the younger one starts the better.'

'Very good. What will you be trading in?'

'Spices, cinnamon from East Java mainly.'

'Yes, Europe has a craze for cinnamon at the moment. What is the name of your company? Oh, yes, Speceraria, isn't it?'

The Captain just watched me, completely at ease, then asked as if totally disinterested: 'You no doubt have heard the name "Mellema"?'

'Everybody in Surabaya has.'

'What about Annelies Mellema?'

'I saw her with her husband once at the H.B.S. graduation ceremony.'

'Does she know you?'

'Perhaps. Her husband did introduce me to her once.'

'Don't keep using that word husband. She has no husband yet.'

'I know her husband. We graduated together.'

'Forget all that, Tuan. Are you then willing to help us, that is, if you do know Miss Mellema? Her condition is very pathetic, very sad. Every day she must be forced to eat porridge and half-cooked egg. She must even be forced to take a drink. She no longer wants to care for herself. She has handed herself over to others to do as they wish with her. She has lost all her will. It is her beauty that moves the heart of all who see her.'

Even though I tried my best to hide my feelings, I still feel my words were too enthusiastic.

'What can I do to help?'

'She doesn't want to speak at all. If she was willing to talk to someone, her condition might improve. Will you help us? Though I must remind you again that she is not Mrs but Miss.'

'Of course I am willing to help, Captain.'

'As long as you remember, she is not Mrs,' he repeated.

Mama and Minke,

Now I will try to tell you in as much detail as possible of my meeting with Madame Annelies. But forgive these inadequate writings of mine. As I said in my earlier letter, I write not because I am good at writing, but in order to carry out my responsibilities.

The Captain took me to the cabin where I had earlier seen the nurse take Madame Annelies. He knocked and then entered. I followed behind. Madame Annelies was sitting propped up in bed. Her eyes were closed. The nurse inside greeted the Captain with a 'Good morning' and reported on the patient's health.

'Has the Doctor been in yet?'

'Yes, Captain.'

'This is Mr Dapperste.'

'Oh, yes, Mr Dapperste, can you help us? Keep Miss Mellema company? She won't speak to us. We will leave you here with Miss Mellema. Perhaps because she knows you, she will want to talk. We thank you beforehand, Mr Dapperste,' and she left with the Captain.

Madame Annelies just sat there propped up in the bed. Under the bed there was a chamber pot and bottles of water. Everything was tidy, lacking in nothing. The port-hole seemed to be kept always half-closed. The wash basin and cupboard were both clean. There were no cockroaches to be seen anywhere.

I came up close to Annelies and whispered into her ear: Mevrouw, Mevrouw *Annelies!'*

She showed no reaction. I pulled a chair over and, sitting down, I watched her. She looked so thin and weak. I took hold of her arm and I felt how loose and thin her flesh was. I tried to think what I must do. I tried to recall everything I had ever heard about her and about how she was looked after when she was ill the other time. After observing her for quite some time, I sat on the edge of the bed. I repeated my earlier whisperings. Still no reaction.

I whispered again: 'Mevrouw, Mevrouw, Minke!'

She opened her eyes but still had no desire to look at me. Then I remembered what Mama said once, as she herself had been told by Dr Martinet: Annelies didn't like white people. I held out my arm under her eyes and called her again. She lifted up her eyes and looked at me.

Mama, Minke, how startled I was to see those eyes without any sparkle in them. How different she was on that day of the graduation party! How different she was on her wedding day when I was so busily tidying up all the wedding presents in the wedding room! How great was the torment she had suffered that it could cause the light in her eyes to be put out!

I know Annelies well; and Mama and Minke too. How much she has suffered, Mama and Minke. I know you all as people of noble heart. No, Mama, Minke, I have no regrets at shedding tears for people who are so generous, helpful, noble; and all these are things praised highly in Christianity. Why now are you all suffering this torment, which none of you deserve?

I repeated my whispering: 'Robert Jan Dapperste alias Panji Darman is here. Mevrouw is not alone.'

Her eyes blinked quickly. How grateful I was to have my efforts and strivings answered! She was going to talk. But no. She didn't blink again, her awareness died away, and I heard a long drawn-out breath blown out from her chest. She held my hand. She was going to speak: Madame Annelies moved her lips. But no sound came from her mouth. She nodded weakly.

I also knew that Dr Martinet had drugged her the other time. As if I were a doctor, I took a sniff of her breath. There was no smell of medicine. She was obviously not being drugged. But her condition was no different to that of someone under sedation: she was half awake, half asleep.

All right, it doesn't matter if there is no response to my whispers. Who knows, she still might be awake. So I explained to her that I had been sent by Mama and Minke to guard her and befriend her on her journey. On hearing the name Minke, her eyes blinked out a flash of light again. But it too lasted only for a moment, then it died away once more.

I had heard about the advice Dr Martinet had once given to Minke, so I began to carry out that advice. As if I were Minke himself, I began to tell her beautiful and wonderful stories. I didn't know whether she was listening or not. I whispered close into her ears. Ah, even if she wasn't conscious, at least my whisperings would find their way into her dreams. Sometimes I came so near to her as I whispered that I felt ashamed because I was so intimately close to the wife of a true friend. I shook myself free of those feelings. Forgive me, Minke.

For about an hour I talked and talked; then I realised that she had fallen asleep, really asleep, propped up against the wall. I laid her down on the bed and covered her with a blanket.

To be honest, my dear Mama and Minke, I have not been successful. She is still shutting herself off from the outside world.

Mama and Minke, I promise I will keep on trying. Whatever the results. It is God who decides in the end.

The next letter from Panji Darman was post-marked Port Said and it spoke as follows.

Since leaving Colombo and right up until entering the Red Sea, the weather has been exceedingly hot during the day. I can hardly stand staying in the cabin. And on top of all that, there were the great waves and ocean swell before the entrance to the Bab-el-Mandeb Straits; it has been almost unbearable. The ship's clinic is always full of people. But despite these conditions, Madame Annelies hasn't been affected at all. It is as if she has become immune to the effects of changes in weather, or has already lost her sensitivity to such things.

She was never taken to the clinic. The nurse says that the doctor always visits her cabin. But I never meet him, even though I care for Annelies and keep her company every single day. Perhaps he visits her before I come to the cabin.

Mama, Minke, I am caring for and befriending her in name only. The reality is not what I hoped for. I still haven't been able to get her to speak. It is like there is some dense mist that is blanketed over her mind. I don't know whether that mist is the result of medicines or something that has grown from within herself. I don't know. Because I have never met the doctor, I have never been able to get an explanation.

The nurse too has never been willing to give an explanation.

Forgive my stupidity.

In that hot weather and during those high seas, Madame Annelies has never left her bed. Her health is worsening. Several times I have seen the food spoon-fed into her mouth by the nurse only to stop there, unchewed. I began to worry that the nurse would become cranky with all this. So I have taken over her task. Let her go up on deck to get some fresh air, or do whatever she likes.

Mama, Minke, forgive me, because I don't know what Madame Annelies's religion actually is, even though I know she was married according to Islam. I need to ask your forgiveness because every time I leave her cabin I need to

300

pray at her bedside. I pray for her safety, health and happiness, then I say good night and return to my own cabin.

I am not in error to do that, am I? I only know Christian teachings and I only know how to pray in the Christian way. I could never bring myself to surrender her at night to that nurse without leaving her with a little prayer.

Every night before I sleep I pray also for Mama and Minke, that you both stay strong and wise.

I am never able to sleep before eleven o'clock. My thoughts do not seem able to get away from Madame Annelies and her withdrawal from the world. Ya, God, Allah, allow me a day when I can meet Annelies again in good health, smiling and talking happily as I have so often seen her in Wonokromo. So far it is only her muteness that I meet.

Even so, I have not lost hope. God will always give me the strength to guard and befriend Madame.

The letter post-marked Amsterdam was the longest.

As time goes on I become more anxious and saddened. Mama, Minke: Madame Annelies's health is deteriorating rapidly. This started happening after we left the Mediterranean Sea and the Straits of Gibraltar. Somewhere near the Bay of Biscay the ship was attacked by a storm. Great waves rolled over, washing froth all over the ship's deck. All the ship's port-holes were closed up tight. For the first time, Madame Annelies groaned. Only I was there to befriend her. The floor of the cabin swayed beneath my feet and it felt like it was going to turn over. The engine's voice trembled as if giving up all hope. I didn't stop vomiting.

In this situation I knelt down beside Madame Annelies's bed, gripping it with one hand, and I prayed that the ship would not sink, and that Madame would quickly recover once we had made land and that she would be recovered forever and that she be given the strength to endure the period of her guardianship, only one or two years.

Only twice she groaned; then she gave voice no more.

This storm receded about four hours later. It was then that Madame Annelies started to soil her bed. The nurse only rarely attended her now. Forgive me, Minke, that I had to care for your wife in such a situation. Christ was leading me in this work. May His love lighten her suffering.

And that was the situation as we entered the Channel, I prayed even more, because that was all I could do, pray and pray. If the hearts and minds of men can accomplish no more, is it not to God that we then call out?

I had such high hopes when the ship entered the 't Ij Canal. I whispered to her:

'Mevrouw, we have arrived in the Netherlands, the land of your own ances-

tors. Awaken now, Mevrouw. We will not be tormented by the sea any longer. You can laugh and smile now! Face these new things with courage and in health.'

She still didn't speak, just lay there, rolled over on the bed.

'Mevrouw, we've arrived in the Netherlands.'

Ya Allah! Mama, Minke, she opened her eyes. Her hand moved; she seemed to be looking for my hand.

'Jan Dapperste is here, Mevrouw,' I said to her.

'Jan,' she called out weakly for the first time.

'Mevrouw, Jan is here.'

Without looking at me, she said weakly: 'Be a friend to my husband.'

'Of course, Mevrouw. He is following on the next ship. You must get well quickly, Mevrouw.'

She didn't speak again.

Then the Captain came into the cabin with the nurse. He thanked me and requested me to leave Madame Annelies. I hesitated but I had no choice; it was an order.

All the passengers were ordered to assemble so that their identity papers could be examined, as well as, for those who weren't Netherlands Indies subjects, their health cards and passports. Because I had been in the cabin all this time, I didn't know where these officials had boarded. There were also Marechausee among them.

After the inspection I hurriedly found my suitcase and then took up a position where I could keep an eye on the cabin. Two dock workers stood outside. Without my realising it, the ship had already docked. A policeman then passed me accompanied by an old woman dressed all in black. They too were headed towards Madame's cabin.

Perhaps that was Mrs Amelia Mellema-Hammers?

Then I heard them talking as they walked past me, frowning seriously: 'Why has no one from the Mellema family come to meet her?'

'It's enough that I am here with that letter of authority I showed you,' answered the old woman who, it now turned out, was not Madame Annelies's guardian.

'She is seriously ill. You will not be able to take her. She must go straight into a hospital.'

'A contagious disease?'

'No!'

'I will take care of it all in the proper manner.'

They headed for the cabin where I had spent so much time lately. They ordered the dockers to enter the cabin too. Not long afterwards, Annelies was carried out on a stretcher, accompanied by the nurse, Marechausee, policeman and the old woman in her black clothes. I trailed behind them as they disembarked.

It was drizzling rain and the cold made its way into my bones.

Seeing me, the nurse said: 'You don't have to follow us.'

'I only want to know which hospital she's being taken to. I would like to visit her.'

'This lady,' she spoke again and pointed politely to the old woman, 'will take her straight to Huizen.'

'If that's the case, then let me help her.'

'I won't be able to pay you anything,' said the old woman.

'I hope for no payment, Mevrouw,' I answered.

'I have no money to pay for your train fare,' she said.

'I will pay for it myself. You don't need worry.'

'I have no money for food for you either,' she said.

'I will buy my own food.'

'You can buy your food from me.'

'Good.'

'Very well. Then let's go.'

We left for the station in a horse carriage. The old woman got down and went to buy the train tickets. Madame Annelies was left in my care. We all climbed aboard the train. We laid Annelies down on a seat with her head on my lap. By coincidence there weren't many passengers that day, that is, if my reckoning is accurate.

The woman sat across from me. She didn't speak. I forced myself to speak to her. Her name was Annie Ronkel, a widow.

'I already regret taking on this work,' she then said. 'If I had known it was going to be like this . . .'

'I don't, Mevrouw.'

'Who is paying you?'

'God Almighty, Mevrouw.'

Madame Annelies didn't move at all, at least not of her own will. Sometimes the swaying of the train would heave up her body a little. She no longer even opened her eyes. She wasn't interested in seeing the Netherlands.

The nurse hadn't stayed with us. The train moved off slowly, as if it hated leaving its stable.

'Where are we taking this sick one?' I asked.

'According to the agreement, to my own house,' answered the old crow, who still showed no interest in either my name or where I hailed from.

'Agreement with whom, Mevrouw?'

'With those who have hired me.'

'Mrs Amelia Mellema-Hammers?'

'How did you know that?'

'Let's take her to a hospital,' I proposed.

She wouldn't agree. It would mean disobeying her orders and she might lose her job.

It seemed a very long time. My legs had gone to sleep. Madame Annelies showed she was alive only by her breathing. The train stopped at Huizen. We transferred her to a hired horse cart. Only then did I realise that all Annelies had with her was an old suitcase. It was very light, as if it had nothing in it. Were there other things left on board ship? Ah, what meaning did they have, I thought almost in the same second. So I looked upon that lone suitcase as all that came with her from the Indies.

The horse cart left Huizen and made its way straight to a village, B., a peasant hamlet. The road was rough and rocky and in bad repair.

We carried Annelies upstairs. It was a small room, smelling of new hay. The house itself was a farmer's cottage made from earth and stones and with a hay roof, just like in all the pictures. Its occupants were the old woman herself, her daughter and son-in-law and their two children, both still very small.

After all this was finished, Mama and Minke, and Annelies lay in an old iron bed, maybe two centuries old, covered in a thick blanket, I fed her some hot milk. She finished half a glass.

After many different approaches, I was finally able to obtain the address of Mrs Amelia Mellema-Hammers. I returned to Huizen and sent off a telegram telling her of Madame Annelies's severe illness. After that I looked for some accommodation. The innkeeper only wanted to take me in if I paid more than the normal tariff – because I wasn't European. Perhaps they equated me with a demon or devil. It was there, in that inn, that I started to think about what I must do next in order to help Madame Annelies. If there was no word from Mellema-Hammers within two days, I would go and see her.

My dear Minke, that event which shook all of Surabaya did not reach the attention of a single person here. There is no concern over Madame Annelies anywhere. Everyone seems busy with their own affairs. So I thought again of Miss Magda Peters, our teacher who was expelled from the Indies. Didn't she once tell us that progress in this age was pioneered by the radicals? I will find Magda Peters and get her help. Sooner or later I will find out her address.

I write this letter in the inn in Huizen. Forgive me, for I have left Madame Annelies now for almost twenty-four hours. As soon as I finish this letter, I will be off to the hamlet of B. again.

May God continue to give strength to Mama and Minke.

Another letter stamped Huizen read like this.

I don't know what I must write under these anxious and worrying circumstances, ya, Mama and Minke. But even so I must write and tell you. I must not make Mama and Minke wait too long. Perhaps you, dear friends, may be even more worried and anxious than myself.

I have already been to Amsterdam and protested to Mrs Amelia Mellema-

Hammers. Engineer Mellema wasn't to be found at home that day. That woman only hunched her shoulders and then said: 'There is no need for you to involve yourself. There is already somebody taking care of the matter.'

At that moment I came to understand why one human being could murder another. But Christ still guided me. Nothing happened.

I explained to her that I had been looking after Madame Annelies ever since she set sail from Java.

'Are you demanding to be paid?' she asked.

'If it was only a matter of being paid, Madame Annelies's husband and mother would be far more able to look after that than you,' I answered, infuriated. 'Are you not her guardian? At least you could visit her while she is so ill.'

She answered with words of expulsion. I threatened that I would take the whole affair to the liberal press. She became even more fierce. She slammed the door shut in my face. I had no formal rights in any of this; I knew that, so I could do nothing else but go away.

Amelia Mellema-Hammers never did come to Huizen, let alone B., that three-house hamlet. She owned a dairy business, but it wasn't as big as Boerderig Buitenzorg *in Wonokromo.*

I returned to Huizen without being able to get in contact with Speceraria. *I was lucky that the old woman looking after Annelies still allowed me to come and visit each day. I made up a flower arrangement and placed it on the bedside table, near Annelies's head.*

Madame Annelies herself is no longer conscious of anything. Only God knows what her condition really is at this moment.

Just a few hours after this last letter a telegram arrived.

MY DEEPEST AND SAD CONDOLENCES ON THE PASSING AWAY OF MADAME ANNELIES. PANJI DARMAN.

And so the tension of all this time, which could have utterly destroyed a person's nerves, reached the moment of explosion.

And Mama looked calm, though of course I knew that inside she would be feeling the same as me. She had lost her daughter, and was soon to lose her business. I had lost my wife.

After reading the telegram she covered her face with both her hands. Her cries were stifled by her palms. She groaned and moaned, and then ran upstairs. My head collapsed upon the table, as if a sword had cut through my neck. How cheap was life. We will never while away the time talking as we used to. You will never again listen to my stories. Between us there is only a cluster of beautiful memories, and they were all beautiful.

Her smile, the light from her eyes; her voice, her sometimes so childlike words; all were now lost forever, to me, Mama and the world. Mother, your daughter-in-law is no longer with us. You will have no grandchildren from your *Banowati*. You will never attend their wedding.

I don't know how long my head lay on the table. Rapid footsteps from behind startled me. Mama was standing there, still a little overcome: 'It's as I predicted, Child, they set out to destroy her and for no other reason than to obtain this company. They have murdered her in the manner available and permitted to them.'

'Ma . . .'

'The same as Ah Tjong, but more vile, more cruel, more barbaric.'

'Ma,' and I could say no more than that.

'And there is nowhere we can turn.'

'Ma.'

'A satanic alliance more evil that Satan himself. Everything has come to pass.'

'That a human being could be treated that way, Ma.'

Mama stroked my hair, as if I were her own small child, and as if I were the only person in the world in mourning at that moment.

'Ya, Child, this is what they have been doing all along, only now it is our turn to experience it.' She spoke again but as if it had nothing to do with her own grief. 'Three years ago we did not know one another existed; we had never met. In just a little while we have become friends. Now this grief we shall bear together forever.'

'Ma.'

'My two children have gone, and this business too will soon go. I do not want to lose my son-in-law too – you, Child.'

Even in my grief I could sense that Mama would now become isolated from everything outside. She would return to being the maiden-girl who was thrown out by her family, sold to the house of *Meneer* Mellema.

'Child, if I ask you to remain my son . . .?'

Ah, what is the use of writing about this dark time in our lives. Let me just say that from the arrival of that telegram Mama felt closer to me. And I to her.

Panji Darman's letter that followed the telegram said his task was over so now he would come home to the Indies. Mama answered in a telegram that it was best he rested for a while in the Netherlands. If he wanted to continue his studies, she would pay for it.

Panji Darman answered with another telegram. He was a thousand times grateful, but he was not willing to be a burden on someone who was threatened by disaster. Indeed, it was he that should be helping Mama. Anyway, the Netherlands had given him only bad things to remember it by. He would come home quickly.

His letters kept coming.

The newspapers presented all sorts of reports from all over the world. But I saw only Annelies.

'For nine months I bore her, then I gave birth to her in pain. I brought her up. I educated her to be a good administrator. I married her to you ... She should be now growing into her full beauty ... Murdered, dying in the grip of somebody who did not even ever know her, who had never done a single good thing for her, and who only ever abused her,' Mama moaned during those days.

Finally I marshalled the courage to answer her: 'All we can do is pray, Ma, pray,' I repeated Panji Darman's words.

'No, Child, these are the deeds of human beings. Planned by the brains of humans, and by the warped hearts of humans. It is to people we must speak our words. God has never sided with the defeated.'

'Ma.'

'It is to people we must speak.'

I knew that revenge was raging inside her heart. She needed nobody's pity.

And so it was that I too began to learn to feel the fire of revenge.

3

Life went on without Annelies.

I returned to my old activities: reading the papers and certain magazines, books and letters; writing notes and articles; and helping Mama in the office as well as with the outside work.

All this reading taught me a great deal, about myself, about my place in my environment, in the world at large, and in the unrelenting march of time. Looking at myself this way, I felt I was being carried along by the wind, with no place on earth where I could stand secure.

This is the story, put together in my own way:

1899 – the closing year of the nineteenth century.

Japan has become increasingly interesting. These people, who arouse such admiration, are achieving more and more amazing things. I read from my notes: the Netherlands and Japan signed a treaty of friendship about half a century ago. One by one the European nations have come to look upon Japan as an Asian people different from the others, exceptional. And about five years ago I read in an article: Japan has entered the arena not wanting to be left behind by the white nations in dividing up the world. Japan has been taking its share too. She attacked Manchuria, the territory of China. And the Netherlands, and the Netherlands Indies itself, announced official neutrality in that war. Neutral! Neutral towards an ally that is on the attack. I could see in my imagination: a small child, clever and strong, thieving the possessions of an old giant riddled with disease – an old giant, laid out on a stretcher, powerless.

Elsewhere, a war had broken out between Greece and Turkey: the whole civilised world, they said, was watching the Bosporus Straits. Meanwhile, Japan continued to overrun the possessions of the decrepit giant China. The Spanish-American war broke out in the Philippines at the edge of the Indies. Two Dutch frigates sailed back and forth around the waters of Menado Sangir-Talaud on the one hand, and in the waters between Geelvinkbaai and the Mapia Islands on the other: both, no doubt, ready to defend the neutrality of the Indies. So the civilised world then turned its eyes to the Philippines. And Japan was still overrunning the possessions of the decrepit giant China. Victory after victory. Her power swelled; she became more resolute, more self-confident. Oi! amazing Japan!

Three years ago, one history book said, a treaty was signed between the Netherlands Indies and Japan. Japan again! In it the Netherlands Indies claimed the right to look upon Japanese residents of the Indies as having the status of Orientals. That was three years ago. One year after that agreement the Indies government hurriedly prepared a new law which gave the same legal status to Japanese residents as to Europeans.

Now, at the time of my writing, Japanese residents in the Indies have the same status as Europeans.

How proud must the Japanese be. How proud must Maiko be. And why not? They were the only people in all of Asia that had the same status as the white-skinned peoples! I could only sit, mouth agape, in wonderment. What had transformed these people? As a single grain of sand of the great sand-mountains of Asian peoples, I secretly felt some pride too, even though, yes, even though as a Javanese youth I felt far below them. I was a child of a conquered race. The European teaching that I had received had not equipped me to understand Japan, let alone the greatness of Europe.

What I was feeling then was that Europe had obtained its glory from swallowing up the world, and Japan from overrunning China. How strange it was if every glory was obtained only at the cost of the suffering of others. How confused I was surrounded by the reality of this world. I was overcome by directionless ideas and feelings. Perhaps I was still too young to expect to reach any clear conclusions. Yet it was precisely conclusions that I needed. Conclusions – the mother of a clear and firm stance.

The conferring of equal status on the Japanese in these Dutch-conquered islands startled all who heard of it. Japan had left the Arabs, the Chinese and the Turks behind – flying by themselves up into the heavens to join the ranks of the Europeans, and not just on paper, but in the treatment they received.

People said that, on the plantations and in the workshops, the business-men and foreman no longer called them *Koh* or *Engkoh*, but tuan. But Maiko certainly marred Japan's good image. It was even being said that the Japanese had the right to be paid the same wage as Pure Europeans for the same work. I didn't know if it was true. The Japanese, it happens, don't like working for employers who aren't Japanese themselves.

Perhaps, in all of the Indies, I am the one and only Native who keeps notes like these. Who else is interested in other peoples? Notes like these bring no respect, let alone any material benefit.

Mama, like the others, was not interested. It is true that she once said there was no point in hiring Europeans if Natives could do the work. Even so, because she had never paid attention to the matter, she was surprised to find several auction papers urging 'Sack all the Japanese coolies! Their labour is too expensive!' In the midst of all these proposals and demands the papers also got an opportunity to advertise the goods they had for auction. Indeed, several of our own workers told how three Japanese had been sacked from a *delman* workshop and a bakery. Both businesses were owned by Europeans.

Then the news was announced: The Country of the Setting Sun, of the Meiji Emperor, was appealing to all its overseas people, advising them: Learn to stand on your own feet! Don't just sell your labour to whomever is willing to hire you. Change your status from a coolie to an entrepreneur, no matter how small. You have no capital? Join together, form capital! Learn together! Be diligent in your work.

I felt that appeal was addressed to me too, like a voice from the heavens. Just like in the *wayang* when a god calls out from above the heavenly ether.

The reality however, was that the colonial newspapers and magazines were savagely and angrily opposed to the new legal reality. They did not want the position of the Japanese equalised with that of the Europeans.

And Jean Marais said that those accustomed to enjoying the suffering of the Asian peoples will, of course, never be ready to lose even a small part of the respect that they consider their right, as well as a gift to them from God.

Then there were others who wrote rudely – in auction and advertisement papers naturally. Japan, they said, the biggest exporter of prostitutes and cooks in the world, with its new status, will be able to ruin the world with its pleasures and its delicious food, bankrupting good families, bringing the disaster of moral collapse, creating chaos in Indies European society. The cities will fill up with red-light areas, with slant-eyed, kimono-wearing misses; their behaviour will offend the hearts of civilised European ladies. Will granting equal status to Japanese mean the acceptance of prostitution? Before it is too late and things have gone too far, would it not be better for this Indies State Decision No. 202 to be reconsidered?

Just imagine, growled my old landlord Telinga, what would become of the world if Europeans had to accept equality with coloured peoples, peoples who in no way can properly be considered equals? All sit on the same level? Perhaps it could happen. Stand at the same level?: no-o-o-o! All this while our heads have been bowed in obedience to the knives and scissors of Japanese barbers, our stomachs have been caressed by their restaurants, and perhaps even our fertility and potency has been thieved by their prostitutes . . . as if there aren't enough Indos in the Indies already!

Another fellow graduate angrily gave his ideas on the whole matter. He was well known as a regular patron of the 'Japanese Gardens'. 'If things keep on like this, one day that slant-eyed dwarf, with legs shortened by too much sitting cross-legged, will be found everywhere – sitting in our offices, where we ourselves should be sitting. How shameful! Would we have to bow first? Sadly, I feel this will happen. But I will refuse to look at even a Chinese officer! Even if they have hundreds of sacks of money!'

Another friend, the son of a former consul to Japan, had something different again to say. It was, perhaps, a rather imperfect repetition of something his father or mother once said: 'Japan? But they have been of great service to us, the Dutch. In the battles and wars to conquer the Indies, didn't a great many die for the V.O.C.? When we had to defend Batavia from the attacks of Mataram? Puh! Even so, it doesn't seem quite right.'

And Maarten Nijman: 'Indeed the concern, unease and disagreement with this decision to give equal status to Japanese has succeeded in casting a shadow over the hearts of all you colonial Indo gentlemen. There are grounds for your fear, but there is also something strange about it. The great Roman Empire never entertained such feelings, not even towards those peoples it had defeated and then colonised. And in this matter, the Netherlands never defeated and colonised the Japanese. Relations between Japan and the Netherlands have always been without blemish since the beginning of the seventeenth century. Yes, there was a fight in 1863-4, but that was only with one particular lord of the central government of the Dai Nippon Empire. And in the end that gave birth to the Shimoneski Convention of 1864 which improved Dutch-Japanese relations even further. So it is indeed strange that you Indo-colonial gentlemen feel so worried and unhappy over this!

'You gentlemen have defeated the peoples of the Indies, so you have the right to expect their respect. You have the right to demand anything whatsoever from them: a right that the law of history, where victory in war determines all, has conferred upon you. But in the case of the Japanese, it makes sense to acknowledge them as equals.'

And Telinga again: 'It's a pity I don't know anything about the Romans, though it must be true if it's written in the histories. But there is a difference with the Japanese. It's not possible to acknowledge them to be equally tall in all climes. That would be directly violating the laws of nature.'

And Jean Marais: 'Why can't those who disagree with the decision restrain their need to hurl insults? Amongst ourselves – if all we want to do is hurl insults – it has to be acknowledged that we all don't stand equally tall, stupid insults will only strike back at ourselves. It's true, isn't it, that you could get together a number of colonial gentlemen who are dwarfs, either because their growth was stunted, or because they were naturally small.'

Another voice again: 'Japan has been given equal status with Europe. And that is only possible because of our own generosity and sense of charity. Now it is law. And this is the question: if China achieves some little

311

progress like Japan, will China also be given equal status? There's nothing wrong with daring to put such a question. We must dare also to answer it. If it turns out that we must answer yes, what then will become of these Indies? What will our position be then?'

'The Japanese and Chinese people are famous for their wandering, a wandering caused by their poverty. The latest news is that the Japanese are flooding into Hawaii, and have already begun arriving in America – both north and south. The Chinese have come into South-east Asia in wave after wave. Those who know say it started before Christ. In the Indies itself, the number of Chinese is several times greater than the grand total of all the Pure and Mixed-Blood Europeans. Ai! can we forget the Chinese War of 1741-3 when the Chinese Imperial Fleet swept the Dutch East Indies Company from all its footholds on the north coast of Java? And then the fall of the Court of Katasura? It is hoped that our great colonial leaders, whom we all honour and respect, will spare some moments to contemplate these things.

'Look at our colonial investments: how much money and how many lives have we already flushed down the drain to put down every resistance of the Natives – from the moment we set foot here up to this very second? How many thousands of our soldiers have died in Java and Sumatra because of war and malaria? We have waged continuous war in order to retain power. Every barracks-child can tell you! Even now in the very centre of the Indies there are enclaves of power that have not bowed down before Her Majesty the Queen. Now there is a yellow-skinned people who have been made our equals: a nation of imitators. With our European technology, they have tried to sow the seeds of pride in their breasts by attacking and conquering Manchuria. The scholars say Japan wants to strengthen itself with the iron and steel of Manchuria.

'With iron and steel, and the science and learning of Europe, we dare not imagine what will happen to the fruits of all our strivings and efforts in the future. Ask any soldier who has had to go into battle time and time again! Ask the men who have served in the Field Police. Just count up how many have died or been disabled for life for the glory of the Greater Netherlands! Be careful!'

I myself, as a result of all this, was forced to imagine Japan as very very close to the Indies, ready at any moment to replace the power and authority of the Netherlands.

The Malay-Chinese papers, which mostly printed advertisements, remained silent; they gave no opinion. Even the turmoil in China itself was hardly ever reported.

If I may present my own conclusions on this matter. There was fear among the colonial classes in the Indies. It was as if they had lost faith in their own strength. And how can such a tall-statured people be so afraid

312

of another race – a race it despises, upon which it is always heaping insults? I did not understand. But I could sense that something was making the Europeans and their Mixed-Blood relatives very anxious.

Mama had not been reading the newspapers over the last several days. She was still busy, and not paying much attention to her make-up and dress. Dark rings shadowed her eyes. She rarely spoke, rarely greeted me. Whenever she wasn't working, I usually found her lost in thought. I didn't bother her with my questions.

If I forced myself to understand what was going on – even with my current limited capabilities – I came to the conclusion that the colonials were frightened of their own imaginings – imaginings of things far away on the distant horizon. For me Japan still represented something abstract. My admiration of her was admiration of an abstraction. In my mind I could not yet feel Japan in its concreteness. It was different with the Chinese, who could be seen and met almost anywhere in the Indies: their bare feet tramp the highways and village lanes, their backs loaded with pedlar's merchandise; their clear, clean skin. And they never complained! No one ever got to know them well because of their different language, their different habits and beliefs. But for me there was always something special about them. Without ever swinging a hoe or machete, without ever turning the soil or planting seeds, they were able to eat and live better than most Natives. Nobody wanted to see this special achievement, only to stare pop-eyed at their foreignness. But if the Chinese had this extra ability, surely the Japanese would be even further advanced.

Then an image of Maiko came to me – the one and only Japanese I'd ever seen and whom I met during the court trials. She was just one among so many Japanese prostitutes who had left the land of their birth, determined to accumulate some capital – so that they could return and set up a business with their husbands! And how much capital had already been gathered by all these prostitutes throughout the world? How much had been taken back to Japan by people other than prostitutes? How many businesses had been set up in Japan by now? I could not even imagine – except for how busy that nation must be with every kind of business and enterprise.

Even though I was a great admirer of Japan I had never dreamed that this people, who had never been conquered by Europe, could become so highly respected among the international community of advanced nations. Their warships patrolled all the world's waterways. The mouths of their cannons gaped out at both sky and sea. How proud any Asian would be to be so respected, never having to crawl and kowtow to some foreign power.

And then one day, quite unexpectedly, Maarten Nijman started a new controversy: 'The Yellow Peril From the North'. In contrast to his earlier

313

article, he gave the following warning: 'Only one step away from Japan is China'. A sense of restlessness has lately been in the air among all the peoples of the European colonies of South-east Asia, from Cochin China to the Indies. The target of this restlessness has been colonial authority. And there's another restlessness which is not so well known but deeper and more hidden – the restlessness of conquered peoples who have had enough, who are tired of satisfying the wants of those who have made themselves masters – all those who must be called 'Sir'. This is the restlessness of the religious leaders of the people in the conquered areas. It has been there for a very, very long time. But an even more important source of restlessness, which hasn't been recognised as such is the 'yellow peril from the north'. The reform movement, the renaissance in China, however small and meaningless it may seem, will, as time goes on, grow larger and larger.

I didn't really understand what he meant by 'restlessness', so I made sure I remembered that word. Restless! restless!

And it was none other than Herbert de la Croix who, through a letter from Miriam, completely dumbfounded me.

My good Minke, please don't become bored with us because we're always nagging you with our opinions about your people and your country. Papa says that right up to today, Minke, the nations of the north have come to your country to tread upon you. Yes, even in our times, Minke. You yourself have experienced this. The north has always been sacred to your people, even in their dreams. Isn't a dream of sailing northwards considered an omen of approaching death? And haven't your people, since the forgotten ages, buried their corpses pointing to the north? And your ideal home, isn't that one which faces north? According to Papa, this is because it is from the north that the marching feet of conquering peoples have come, ensuring your backwardness, then deserting you, and leaving you only the waste of their civilisation, their diseases and only a little of their learning.

I write this with a heavy heart, my dear Minke, not to hurt your feelings, but only to pass on a message: the north contains no magic. But it is true that you must keep your eyes to the north always in vigilance.

While Jean Marais said: 'I think, Minke, that your country is too isolated – it can't hear the life-beat of other countries. They can come out here into warm and gentle lands, relax, live like kings. Even a small nation like the Dutch. And your people can do nothing about it. Three hundred years, Minke. Not an insignificant time.'

Shameful. And there was more. I felt furious in my impotence.

This tumult of ideas and opinions from so many people made me more and more confused. School was simpler; you just had to listen and have faith in a few teachers. The best marks went to the student who could turn himself into what the teachers wanted.

Maarten Nijman wrote: 'The Chinese Young Generation, so well schooled, are jealous of Japan's achievements. The same Japan that is robbing China of parts of its own territory. They are jealous! And furious and angry because they are aware but powerless.'

Just like me.

'Pity on the Chinese Young Generation,' said Nijman. 'They are forty years behind the Japanese, the cousins they're so jealous of. Imagine, just to rid themselves of their *thau-cang* – pigtails – and to free the feet of their women from that tormenting, deforming custom, will need at least fifteen more years. Even then there is no guarantee of success. Ah yes, because "custom" will oppose the Chinese Young Generation with the force of arms. If they do succeed in ridding the byways of the world of pigtails and the tiny deformed feet of their women, they will still not have freed themselves from that habit of coughing up phlegm – a revolting habit that makes one's hair stand on end – a habit that has caused the Chinese to lose the sympathy of the whole world! To get rid of that habit the Young Generation would have to work for another twenty-five years at least. So it will still be about seventy-five years before the world won't feel disgusted when standing near a Chinese.'

Still Nijman's opinion: 'Japan is now looked upon as equal with Europe; China not yet. What people say is true: there is only one step between China and Japan. But it cannot be measured in miles or kilometers. It is a step in civilisation. It can be measured only in terms of the Chinese people's own capacities.'

Nijman's writings were interesting. One day I would ask his opinion of my own people. Are my people as pathetic as the de la Croix family says? Perhaps he has some kind of abacus he can use to calculate how many dozens of years it will take the Javanese to reach the same level as the Japanese.

And still with Nijman: 'That distance in civilization, however many steps it may be, is not important. In the end the strong always swallow the weak, even if the strong are only small in number. Just try to imagine: the Chinese nation is a big nation; what if it were strong as well? The Yellow Peril, sirs, the Yellow Peril. Be careful, very careful. Japan is already a reality; China too can likewise become a reality, whether we like it or not. Perhaps we won't ever see it ourselves. But be very careful, because time keeps moving on, whether we like it or not.'

———◆———

Then one day a letter from Nijman landed on my desk – for me. He hoped that I could come to the editorial offices, to write up an English-language interview with a Chinese youth.

An interview in English, not Dutch! If there is anyone who cannot see that this is a great advance, I don't know what to say to them. Mama had no objections. Like my own mother, she never forbade me anything. Also like Mother, she supported everything I did, as long as I was prepared to bear the risk, and as long as it did not harm anyone else.

So it seemed that it was only Jean Marais who objected. He began the argument a week ago. 'Minke, I've wanted to talk to you for some time, but I've always held back,' he said, 'even though I feel it my duty.'

'What is it, Jean?'

'It's like this, Minke. You have become famous and respected because of your writings. No one can deny that. But my opinion is different. Perhaps this opinion of mine comes originally from you. Look, Minke, I feel the respect you have obtained doesn't come from your writing. It is respect for your character. You present and show things differently. It is all uniquely Minke. Your writing is only an emanation, no, not even that, just a reflection of your character. You are a very interesting individual. Fortunately you have mastered Dutch, so you write in Dutch.'

From the very beginning my suspicions were aroused. Perhaps his opinions were only second-hand too – he didn't read Dutch. And he didn't normally speak for so long at once. I didn't like being lectured like this. If all he wanted to do was to free himself of his dependence on me, I didn't see why he had to start off with a speech. It was his right to stand on his own feet. It was good if he felt he could stand alone now. I too would join in thanking God.

But the way he delivered his little speech made me feel he was letting out some suppressed emotion, ready to explode.

'Yes, Jean?'

'There is something I feel is a great pity. Something which thousands of other people feel is a great pity too: why do you only write in Dutch? Why do you only speak to the Dutch and the others who understand their language? You owe nothing to them, just as your mother once told you. What do you expect from them that makes you want to speak only to them?'

My prejudice made me feel his words were jumping out at me, ignoring all humility: arrogant, piercingly lecturing, even reprimanding me. My anger welled up and overflowed. I sensed he was preparing to entrap me. He wanted me to write in Malay, so that he himself could read my writings directly, while destroying my fame and achievement and prestige. I gazed at him with bulging, angry eyes.

'Are you angry, Minke?' he asked in that arrogant tone of voice.

I restrained my fury. Whatever else, he was my friend, not an enemy.

He must not become a former friend. Perhaps he simply didn't want to face reality: my character, my individuality, could not be separated from the Dutch language. To separate these things would only make this person named Minke nothing but roadside rubbish.

'So you want me to write in Malay,' I asked, 'so that no one will read what I write? In a language that you can understand?'

'You've got it wrong, Minke. I personally am not a factor in this matter. I'm only speaking like this for your own benefit. Malay is used more than any other language in the Indies: much more than Dutch.'

I rejected his proposition. 'Why don't you accept reality? Only those with little or no education read Malay.'

Jean Marais seemed to be offended, because he himself couldn't speak Dutch. And indeed I wanted him to be offended, to be hurt. His heart must suffer the hurt that mine was now feeling.

However he then whispered harshly: 'You're an educated Native! While Native people are not educated, it is you who must ensure they become educated. You must, must, must speak to them in a language they understand.'

'Malay readers are, at the most, only uneducated European Mixed-Bloods who work in the plantations and factories.'

'Don't belittle,' he said more harshly. 'Do you consider Kommer uneducated? He writes Malay. He translates your writings into Malay. Do you think it was Dutchmen who defended you in your difficulties? How many of those uneducated ones were prepared to go to gaol to defend you? And for how long? They defended your marriage because of Kommer's translations, because of Kommer's writings, not because of your Dutch articles.'

'You're lying!' I pointed at his face.

'That's what Kommer said.'

'You're a liar!' I roared.

'He understands Natives better than you!' he hissed in accusation. 'You don't know your own people.'

'You're going too far now!'

'Through the Malay readers, even the illiterate among the people eventually found out. Their feelings were moved, their sense of justice was offended . . .'

I left his house, no longer able to control my fury. I went straight to the buggy, jumped aboard, and ordered Marjuki to get going.

'Just had an argument, Young Master?' Marjuki asked.

I didn't answer.

The buggy started off. From behind I could hear the sharp-pitched cries of little Maysoroh Marais: 'Uncle! Uncle!'

Damn! Keep going, Juki! Maysoroh be damned as well! It's no loss to me if I no longer know you. Then suddenly the words of Marais from two years ago echoed in my mind: 'You are educated! You must be fair and just – beginning with your thoughts.'

Have I been just? I turned around. The little girl was still chasing after the buggy, crying out and calling me to come back. Is it right for me to treat her this way, this child who had done me no wrong? Was my treatment of her father proper? Was I right that he only wanted me to write in a language that he knew? What has this girl done to you, Minke?

'Go back!' I ordered Marjuki.

'Go back where, Young Master?'

'To where we've just come from. Stop by that little girl.'

By the time we reached May, she was panting desperately. I jumped down. Her face was wet with tears and her hand was still waving futilely in the air. I picked her up and carried her.

'What's the matter, May?'

Between her sobs she said in French: 'Don't be angry with Papa. Uncle is Papa's only friend.'

That truly cut my heart. I hurriedly whispered in her ear: 'No, May, I'm not angry with your papa. Truly, I'm not. Let's go home.'

'Uncle shouted so loudly at Papa,' she protested.

'I won't shout at your papa again, May,' I promised.

'I prepared a drink for you,' she spoke again, 'and you wanted to leave, just like that. Doesn't Uncle love May any more?'

Wiping away her tears with a handkerchief, I carried her back inside the house on my shoulder. Jean Marais was still sitting thinking. He didn't lift his eyes to look at me, as if he no longer wanted to know me. Maysoroh ran out to the back and returned with drinks. Then she rushed to her father's side. Her clearly spoken words were interspersed with sobs: 'Papa, Uncle is not angry with you any more.'

Jean Marais was silent.

I regretted everything that had happened, as did he. I swallowed the drink May had brought. I caressed her hair, then excused myself.

'No!' protested May. She began to cry again. 'You still haven't spoken to Papa.' She collided into me, her red eyes moist, protesting in her own way. I too was now shedding tears. I ran to Jean Marais; I embraced him; I kissed him on his thickly whiskered cheeks: 'Forgive me, Jean, forgive me.' I cried and Jean cried.

All this happened a week ago.

Now, with Nijman's letter in my hand, I went to Jean's place again. Eight-thirty in the morning. May was at school. Jean was painting. My anger would now avenge itself; Not only does Minke not need to write in Malay, but has taken another step upwards: he is going to do an interview in English.

He didn't seem bothered by my arrival. I went up to him and began:

'Jean, once more forgive me my unworthy behaviour of the other day.'

Without turning, and while still sweeping the canvas with his brush, he answered: 'I understand your difficulties, Minke. You've suffered a lot of sadness lately. You're still in mourning. I was also in the wrong; I wasn't very clever in choosing the time. Forget it, Minke. And more than that, it's not right for me to interfere in how you dedicate your life. I didn't mean anything bad by what I said.'

His pronouncement sounded long and formal – a warning bell.

'Of course, nothing bad would come from you.'

Now the moment had arrived for me to avenge his earlier arrogance. I would show him the letter from Nijman, so that he would know: Minke was always advancing. He would be startled. He must be startled. He had to understand just who this person Minke was.

'Jean, Nijman has written to me. He wants to see me at his office, but not to write in Dutch. You don't agree, do you, with me writing in Dutch?'

He put down his brush and stared at me in great surprise.

'It's not that I don't agree,' he answered, but didn't continue.

'Nijman has asked me to write. Do you know in what, Jean? English!'

As if he understood that this was my revenge, his hand nervously sought his brush; he knocked it and it fell to the floor. He didn't retrieve it. He brushed his hands on his trouser legs and then held one out to me. He said coldly: 'Congratulations, Minke. You are indeed progressing.'

Now feel what it's like! I shouted silently, thrilled, in my heart. Filled with my victory, I examined his paintings.

Following Dr Martinet's sales talk on my wedding night, Jean had received many orders for portraits that didn't come through me. He'd already finished more than ten paintings. The one of Dr Martinet was the only one I recognised. Quite accurate, with the dusky sky as background. His eyes gazed at me without blinking. The point of his nose shone in its sharpness. I could recognise in the painting both Dr Martinet and his kindness.

'Those pictures are all finished, Minke. They just need to be collected.' Suddenly he turned the conversation, 'You're still an admirer of Japan, Minke, aren't you?'

'That's right, Jean.'

He didn't go on, but began to identify each of the portraits for me: this administrator, that official or police officer . . . as if showing off his triumphs, showing that he could succeed without me, and even succeed better.

'You're doing very well too, Jean,' I praised him.

'No, Minke. None of this is the proper work of an artist. Just the work of a day-labourer, a coolie.'

'But these pictures are all of important people – all of them.'

'That's got nothing to do with the art of painting. It's only to make a living, not for making life fulfilling. There is nothing that I want to say, to speak about, that I can put in those portraits. Except perhaps for the one of Dr Martinet.'

'I understand your words, Jean, but not what they mean.' I glanced at him out of the corner of my eye, and my impression was that he wasn't jealous of my success – he really was dissatisfied with his work.

'Do you remember Maiko, the Japanese prostitute?'

'Of course, Jean. That small, frail-bodied woman?'

'Servicing people for no other reason than to make a living. I'm no different to Maiko. It makes me ashamed.'

'The comparison is too extreme,' I said.

'Just think: I get paid for pleasing other people who have no spiritual or emotional relationship with me. In art, that's called prostitution. You're lucky to be able to pour out what you feel in your writings. I can't.'

He limped across to the window on his crutches. With his back to me, he said: 'So you're still an admirer of Japan?'

'Why, Jean?'

'If all the Japanese didn't want to write in their own language . . .'

Straight away I knew he was launching a counter-attack. I returned to my earlier vigilance.

But he changed direction: 'Do you remember what I once said about Jepara carving? I got more satisfaction out of working Jepara-type motifs into my furniture. At least it meant I was doing something to ensure that one of the beautiful creations of your people would be permanently preserved for others to see. I often hear from Kommer that the Javanese have many beautiful writings. I think that if I knew about Java, I'd be more happy translating and bringing them to the French people than working like Maiko with all this.'

Now I was at an even greater loss to understand. Yet I had the feeling that with this puzzle too he was still on the attack.

'You're confused, Jean.'

'Yes, I'm confused.'

We both went silent. I began to think over his words. Then all of a sudden the hidden meaning came to me, emerging as the meaning of one sentence linked up with another: an admirer of Japan . . . if all Japanese didn't want to speak in their own language . . . preserve forever some of the beautiful creations of Java . . . translate and bring them to the French people rather than work like Maiko . . . Yes. He was still on the attack. And I could sense that the purpose behind his attack was the same as before: to get me to change from writing in Dutch to writing in Malay or Javanese. It was clear he didn't think much of my getting the English interview after all.

320

I steered his attention in another direction: 'How's the picture of my wife going, Jean?'

'Annelies is so beautiful and alluring. She doesn't need any adornments. Her last experiences gave a special substance to her character. Only the brush stoke of a painter who truly knew her, Minke, can realise her potential as a subject for a portrait.'

I didn't understand about art. So: 'Naturally, Jean.'

'Moreover, I don't need to lie to you or Nyai.' It seemed he was reading my thoughts. He stressed the word *lie* as if inviting me to recall our argument of a week ago.

'It's not right to lie to a friend,' he said.

So he was still pushing me to write in Malay or Javanese. 'If you're in a hurry, Jean, I'll meet May later,' I said, ending that unpleasant conversation.

'You're always so kind, Minke.'

And I left him there with his thoughts.

I arrived too early. There was a Chinese youth sitting in the waiting room. His pigtail, his thau-cang, looked too long for his thin body. Its light brown colour also didn't seem right for his ivory-yellow, clear skin. It was as though you could see the whole system of blood vessels through his transparent skin. Uh! that too-long pigtail trailing right down to the waist! Strange! Long and not very thick. Not in balance with the round, fat and healthy red face. Just his face though, his body was gaunt. I looked at the thau-cang's hairs again: coarse and very thick.

I don't know why the pigtailed youth nodded to me, smiling so that his narrow eyes almost disappeared. His teeth became visible: one row, few and far between and very sharp. His clothes of Shantung silk were ivory-yellow, clean but old. His reddish face reminded me of a guava fruit.

After nodding and smiling, he just sat silently and didn't try to start a conversation.

I made a guess: this is the Chinese youth Nijman wants interviewed. I was disappointed at the idea that this might be him – just a youth dressed in Shantung pyjamas, without any shoes, with pointed and few-and-far-between teeth – just a *Sinkeh*. There's no way some Sinkeh boy would have any business with a Dutch newspaper! And if this was the one, why didn't he appear to be educated? Coming into a European's office wearing pyjamas, even if they were from Shantung silk. He looked more like a pedlar from the villages. He wasn't even wearing sandals – chicken-clawed.

A Pure-Blood sinyo requested that I go upstairs, to the editorial office. Nijman was sitting down, writing at his desk. He put his quill back into the ink bottle, stood up and shook hands with me. His words were merry, friendly, yet very polite and gentle.

'I trust that you have now got over your troubles, Tuan. That is why I took the decision to write to you.'

'Thank you, Tuan Nijman.'

'We all greatly admire the resolve and patience of you and Nyai. How is your wife's health, Tuan?'

'Fine, Tuan, fine.'

'I'm glad to hear it. Do you remember your last article? You compared something with a sparrow in a storm? It's my own opinion the comparison is not quite right. In my view, and it's not just my own, it is you, Tuan, that is the storm, and that which you considered was a storm was really the sparrow.'

'This time you are truly exaggerating,' I answered, and I remembered Mother's warning always to be wary of flatterers.

'No,' – he took out his pocket-watch and looked at it for a moment – 'I doubt if one in a thousand people could get through what you have got through safely. The reality is that you yourself progress further and further because of these difficulties. That is why I decided to write to you: begin with English! Defeated in one field of battle, but victorious in another. What's the difference? Isn't that so, Tuan Minke? If you succeed, your voice will be able to reach the international audience without going via the translations of others, yes?'

'You exaggerate.'

'Not at all,' he said firmly. 'Since the Japanese have been given equal status, all sorts of strange things have been happening in South-east Asia.'

'I've studied all your articles but, excuse me, I haven't read about anything strange happening.'

He laughed and invited me to sit on the settee: 'Not everything is reported in the papers, Tuan. Look, you've read my writings about the Chinese young people who are restless and jealous of Japan?' His eyes pierced mine with the question.

'Yes, and I read a lot more after I received your letter.'

'Excellent. It looks like these young Chinese have a real passion to catch up with Japan. Once you have begun to write in English, you'll be able to establish direct contact with publishers in Singapore and Hong Kong. That will bring you closer to the British Empire, to the international audience. To write about these strange goings-on will be very interesting to the international community, Tuan. Who knows, you might be a big success in this too?'

'Ah, you are exaggerating very much, Tuan.'

'Not at all. We'll try. To start with, you will note down an interview between myself and a young Chinaman, about your age.'

I had not been wrong. It was indeed the young Sinkeh with the guava-ball face that was going to be interviewed.

'And besides that,' Nijman went on, 'you will be able to see close up just how these strange goings-on are taking form. It will be very interesting. These young Chinese are nothing but clowns making unfunny and danger-ous jokes. Not at all funny, even saddening. And everyone knows you are far more educated than all of them. The Dutch education system is rated among the best in the world. Just look upon this experiment as an enjoyable game.'

The Pure sinyo who was outside a while ago opened the door. My guess was right: it was Guava Face whose words I was going to note down. He stood in the doorway, bowing his head deeply. When he stood up straight again he seemed even skinnier than before.

'Please come in,' Nijman said in English, without moving from his chair. I followed his example.

The Chinaman's bare feet nimbly and quickly made their way across the room and brought him up to us. He stopped in front of Nijman's desk, where he bowed once again and expressed his greetings in an English with which I wasn't familiar.

I got in first by holding out my hand. Then I sensed my own nervous-ness: I mustn't fail in this test. I will suffer great embarrassment if I am unable to catch what he says.

Nijman still sat in his chair. His English was clear.

'Please sit down, sir,' he said. 'Nah! Mr Minke, this is Mr Khouw Ah Soe. Mr Khouw Ah Soe, you must have come across Mr Minke's name in the newspapers.'

Guava Face bowed even while seated. He bowed so often I began to wonder whether it really was Chinese custom, real Chinese custom, in its pure form.

'Ya-ya-ya, Mr Minke . . .'

I sharpened my listening to accustom myself to his accent.

'The waves of events involving yourself and your family – we followed them closely . . . We all have sympathy for you and your family. May you remain strong. And what is the news of your wife now?'

'Very good, thank you, Mr Khouw.'

His narrow eyes penetrated mine. I observed them for a second. Standing there with nothing on his feet, wearing only pyjamas, he didn't seem to suffer any sense of inferiority at all. He moved and spoke as if he weren't arraigned before Europeans, but among his own best friends. This approach might not be very pleasing for Nijman, who would be used to being fawned upon by Natives. And that's what made Khouw's behaviour so interesting to me. He didn't try to pretend to be anything more than he really was. His face reddened as he talked. His few pointed teeth appeared and disappeared from behind his lips.

'I'd like to talk to you one day if you have the time,' he said to me. 'In any case, sir, we are very grateful to you, that, no matter what the means and route was, you played a role in the destruction of the corrupt Old Generation group that Ah Tjong symbolised.'

Word by word I followed what he was saying. Damn it, I didn't know what he meant. All I could do was grimace. It seemed he had already become used to speaking English in his own way. I tuned my ear so as to hear better.

'Your contribution was really greater than ours. May I know where you live? Are you still with that business?' he asked.

'Still, Mr Khouw.' I was amazed he knew all that.

'May I, perhaps, visit there one day?'

'Of course. And just wait there for me, if I haven't arrived home yet.'

Nijman intervened: 'Let's begin our interview, gentlemen.'

I readied myself with pencil and paper. The Pure sinyo appeared at the door again, but Nijman waved him away.

'Nah! Mr Khouw,' Nijman began, 'would you like to tell us where you come from and what education you have?'

'Of course. I am from Tientsin, the son of a merchant . . .'

'What kind of merchant, Mr Khouw?'

'Everything that can be sold, sir. I'm a graduate from the English-language secondary school at Shanghai . . .'

'But it's not close to Shanghai – Tientsin – is it?'

'Not at all close.'

'Are you a graduate from a Protestant or Catholic mission school?'

I wrote and wrote. Not sentences – just words.

'What kind of school it was and who owned it aren't important. In the beginning I wanted to continue my schooling in Japan. But knowing that there were very few places put aside for foreign students, I didn't try. Especially as I knew that several of my fellow countrymen there returned before finishing their studies.'

He was silent a moment. It seemed he was giving me time to take down what he was saying.

'Was their action a protest or the result of discrimination against them?' asked Nijman.

'Neither. They had taken an oath to become good workers for the Chinese Young Generation movement.'

'So then you joined them?'

'Exactly. There is no point in becoming a clever expert, as clever as a May tree . . .'

'What is a May tree?'

'Just the name of a tree that turns the mountains yellow whenever it flowers.'

'And it is really tall, this tree?'

'No, not really . . . anyway, any education would be wasted if one had to take orders from the corrupt and ignorant Older Generation which holds power, or if you had to become ignorant and corrupt yourself in order to be able to maintain that power. All a waste, sir. Even the cleverest of experts who became part of an ignorant power would become ignorant also.'

'So you object to the nature of the power of the Chinese Empire at the moment?' asked Nijman.

'Exactly!'

'But that is rebellion against the Emperor.'

'Is there any other way?'

'Japan still has an Emperor.'

'We are not Japan. Japan is experiencing her awakening. China is in the process of collapse. We want to speed up that collapse so as to rise again, free of oppression.'

'But the Chinese Older Generation is famed for its wisdom, the great heritage it has left China, books and cultural artifacts, a high civilisation . . .'

'True, but that was the Older Generation when it was the Young Generation. This is the modern age. Any nation and people that cannot absorb the power of Europe, and then arise and utilise it, will be swallowed up by Europe. We have to make our China equal with Europe without becoming Europe, as Japan is doing.'

'Do you really believe in what you are saying?'

'That belief is, indeed, precisely the power that mobilises us. We have never been conquered by another race, and we are not willing to undergo that experience. On the other hand, we have no dreams of conquering other races. That is our belief. Our people have a saying: "In the sky there is heaven, on earth there is Hanchou," and we young people have added: "In the heart is faith." '

'You speak like a member of the English parliament,' Nijman flattered him. 'You desire and are struggling for a new form of authority . . .' there was insult in Nijman's voice. 'You want China to become a republic?'

'Yes.'

'You want to rival the United States and France?' Nijman smiled arrogantly.

'Is there any other road that new nations can take in this modern age?'

'While most of the countries of Europe are not yet republics!'

'That's nothing to do with us.'

'Yet you yourself still wear the thau-cang.'

Khouw Ah Soe smiled politely, bowing. Nijman seemed unable to restrain his amusement and laughed also. I, on the other hand, was offended. Nijman's words went too far. It was Khouw Ah Soe's right to wear a pigtail.

'Do you know the meaning of the pigtail?' Khouw Ah Soe suddenly asked in reply.

'No. It must be very important.' There was a smile on Nijman's face. 'Tell us about it.'

'It's an unusual story, the story of the pigtail. There was once a time when Europe so admired our civilisation that the French took to wearing pigtails. Then, sir, the Dutch took on the practice also. So too did the Americans wear thau-cangs.'

Nijman was white. He murmured agreement.

'But that was when Europe had not known us long. Of course it is not like that now. Even so, it is still quite amazing: Europeans wearing pigtails! Even the Americans, during their revolution! During France's period of triumph and glory, they not only copied the pigtail but also the habit of eating frogs, which the rest of humanity looked upon as degrading. And what was, in truth, the thau-cang, sir? Nothing more than a symbol of slavery and obedience, originating during the period when China was ruled by the people from the north. Nah! sir, the pigtail in China was a symbol of humiliation. In Europe it was the other way around; it was a symbol of triumph, at one time, during one era. In China people used to eat frogs because of their poverty; in Europe it was a part of its grandeur. So topsy-turvy is history. The mighty race that forced us to wear pigtails is now being subjugated by the Japanese, who seek iron and steel and coal, to make themselves strong. That is if I'm not mistaken.'

'A very interesting interview,' Nijman gave his assessment, 'almost a lecture.'

'Forgive me, Mr Editor, it was not my intention to give a lecture. This is a very important moment for me. It is the first time, perhaps, that a member of the Chinese Young Generation has been interviewed like this.'

'This Young Generation – it has no publications of its own?'

'In this modern era, there is no movement that does not have its own publications, sir. And vice versa, sir, isn't it so? Every publication must present some specific interest or power group, even your own publication. I'm not wrong am I?'

'And when will you cut off your humiliating pigtail?'

'There will be a time for that, sir.'

'What was your purpose in coming to the Indies?'

'To see the world.'

'Oh-ya. You are the son of a merchant who sells anything that can be sold, yes?'

326

Khouw Ah Soe nodded in affirmation.

'You came by yourself. But you are a member of the Young Generation. How is it possible you have no friends, and have just come here to see the world?'

'Perhaps we have a different idea of what the word "friend" means. Our members are just workers, carrying out history. That is what I am as well. We are only ants who want to erect a new castle of history.'

'Mr Khouw Ah Soe, it seems to me that you are not just a high-school graduate. It appears that you have studied at university. The way you bow is not Chinese but Japanese. It seems you are trying to hide the fact that you have lived in Japan – for at least two or three years. You are, at the very least, a very intelligent university student.'

'Truly a compliment to be valued highly, sir.'

'And you haven't come to the Indies by yourself?'

'I wish that were true; I would not be so lonely.'

'It is not the Chinese way to wander around by oneself.'

'Oh yes? It appears you have a great knowledge of the Chinese. Well, if you are right, let me ask you: may not a Chinese with some European education be somewhat different from his own group and people?'

'Mr Khouw Ah Soe, what is your opinion of an elephant that leaves its herd? Isn't he a very dangerous elephant? Can't you too be compared to such an elephant? You are a member of the Chinese Young Generation, a member that has left its group. It is certain you are not here just to wander around and look at the sights.'

'Wonderful. Then you must be right.'

'Why is that?'

'Because according to our ancestors, the host must always be honoured.'

'You have a very clever tongue. May I now put to you the last question? Did you enter the Indies legally or did you sneak in?'

'A very good question, one that history will also put to the peoples of Europe: oh you peoples of Europe – and not just individuals – did you enter the Indies legally or did you sneak in? It is you yourself who must answer that question, not me. Good afternoon.'

Khouw Ah Soe rose from his chair. Smiling, he shook hands with me, then with Nijman, bowed and left the office.

For several moments Nijman sat numbed, his gaze riveted on the door now closed behind his guest. Then, realising his condition, he turned to me, saying: 'Yes, Mr Minke, write up the interview in English. It looks like he is hiding quite a lot. He says he's from north China, but he has a southerner's name. Says he has never been to Japan but is unable to rid himself of Japanese customs like that bowing of his . . .' He didn't go on with his grumblings.

I began to write it up. Less than an hour later I left the office. I still had time to pick up May. I dropped into a shop: I had to buy something for the little girl. I found a doll that was exactly like Annelies.

May's school hadn't finished for the day. I had to wait a few minutes. As soon as school was over, May caught sight of my buggy, ran to us, climbed aboard and called out to some of her friends to join her. So we had no choice but to transport this gang of little chatterboxes to their homes. May's house was the last one.

As she was about to climb down from the buggy, I opened up the box and handed her the doll. She jumped up and down in excitement. She kissed me over and over again. She kissed the plump, pretty doll too.

'Climb down, May. I have to go straight on.'

'No, I don't want to climb down!' she rebelled.

'Ah, you're being naughty. I've still got a lot of work to do.'

'Everyone's got a lot of work to do. Me too. Come on, come in.'

'No, May.'

She went silent. Her eyes moistened, then she bleated in French: 'Here's your doll. I'm giving it back. Uncle doesn't like Papa any more.'

'You're getting more and more spoilt, May,' I said, but the words kneaded my heart. How great was this child's love for her father; she didn't want to see her father lose a friend. 'All right then, I'll take you inside.'

I climbed down ahead of her, carrying her schoolbag. She carried the doll herself. She ran inside. 'Papa!' she shouted. 'May was given a present of a doll by Uncle Minke. Isn't Uncle Minke kind, Papa?'

I came in and saw the child cuddle up to her father. I heard Jean Marais answer, 'Very kind, May.'

I avoided looking at the paintings. My heart was troubled by the girl's behaviour, which had thrown my feelings into confusion. In a flurry she brought in some drinks. After putting the glasses on the table she gave me a long look, then those big eyes of hers gazed at her father.

'Why doesn't Papa talk to Uncle Minke?' she demanded.

'That painting is finished now, Minke.'

The child observed her father, then me.

'Are there other things that you want to paint, Jean?'

'Yes, there are many more.'

'Why isn't Uncle laughing, or smiling and grinning as you usually do?' May demanded.

So I laughed and laughed until I felt my jaw would drop off. Seeing all this, Jean Marais also laughed boisterously. May was the only one who didn't laugh. All of a sudden she embraced her father, and wouldn't let go.

Jean Marais and I went silent on seeing the child's strange behaviour.

'What is it, May?' She let go of her papa and ran into her room. We heard her howling; it seemed she would never stop.

328

I ran into her room. She was hiding her face under her pillow and her arms were hugging the edges of the mattress of the small wooden divan.

'May, May, what's the matter?'

I took the pillow from her face and caressed her head. Slowly the crying faded. I sat her up; she didn't resist.

'Don't cry, May. Don't make Papa and Uncle Minke sad.' She didn't want to look at me. Jean Marais came in, limping, and sat on the divan.

'The two of us don't understand, May. What is it?' I asked. Still she wouldn't look at either of us.

'Do you love your papa?' I asked.

She nodded.

'Do you love Uncle Minke?'

She nodded again.

'We both love you very, very much. Don't cry!'

But she started howling again. Between her sobs she protested: 'You're lying to me. You've become enemies . . .'

Later in the evening, having convinced May that the two of us hadn't become enemies, I was able to go home.

Soerabaiaasch Nieuws van den Dag hadn't yet published the interview with Khouw.

The next afternoon the much awaited report finally appeared. It wasn't a headline, but it was placed in a prominent corner with an attention-getting title: 'A Meeting with a member of the Chinese Young Generation'. I was tremendously pleased that my first work in English was good enough to be used by Nijman. I would enjoy it after dinner.

After dinner I sat with Mama in the front room. Seeing her so busy with all kinds of calculations, I quickly asked: 'It's late, Ma; give them here; let me do them.'

'No, this is very personal. That wolf wants fifteen percent. I'm only prepared to let him have five.'

I knew the wolf was Mijnheer Dalmeyer, an accountant. There was no need for me to interfere. Heh, why bargain over percentages? But my curiosity aroused; I asked about it.

'Just read your newspaper.'

I began to read. Now and then I caught a glimpse of the figures on the sheets of paper. Figures and totals with six digits. I made a quick guess: the value of the whole business. She didn't take much longer to finish her work; then she told me: 'Tomorrow I'm going to withdraw Annelies's money from the bank, Minke. I want to know how you feel: do you feel I'm violating your rights by doing that?'

'Mama! What are you saying? I don't have any such rights!'

'No, Minke. No matter what, you are my own son, the same age as Robert. And you know that this business is going to be taken over by somebody that the Law says has a greater right to it. I want to start another business. I need Annelies's money. Her savings from the last six years aren't all that much. She saved all of it – less than three thousand. I can invest that money in your name.'

'No, Mama, thank you very much. But no.'

I began to read. But heh! What was this? From the very first line, there was no similarity with the interview that had taken place. It read like this:

At eleven o'clock last Monday morning there fronted up to the editorial office of this paper a member of the Chinese Young Generation. This person wanted to sell us information about his movement. He gave his name as Khouw Ah Soe, his place of birth as Tientsin, and said he was a graduate of the English-language High School in Shanghai, and was aged about twenty years. His entry into the Indies was no doubt illegal! And we would not be wrong in assuming that he arrived as a member of a large group with orders from their organisation's headquarters in Japan.

As we all know, there have been many disturbances in the Indies since the arrival of members of this Young Generation. They openly seek the rapid abolition of the pigtail. The violation of this time-honoured custom of China must be resisted.

From the very moment they arrived, they have been opposed by the Chinese Sinkeh and Mixed-Blood subjects of the Indies. These latter love and respect their ancestors, and feel that to lose one's pigtail is to lose one's Chineseness. They condemn the idea and any effort to abolish the pigtail.

Khouw Ah Soe came to Surabaya about two months ago. He doesn't speak Malay, but speaks good English, Mandarin and Hokkien, and there are reports he has mastered two other southern dialects as well. Within a week of his arrival in Surabaya it appears he was able to influence several people. Together with these he organised a public meeting in the Kong Koan building. There he explained his lie, that the thau-cang was a symbol of humiliation that had its origins during the period of Mongol domination. And that it was a sign of the Chinese people's slavery under the northerners. The pigtail is no symbol of honour for the Chinese, he said.

The Kong Koan building burst into uproar. The fury of the crowd couldn't be restrained. The whole debate was conducted in Hokkien. They all demanded: cut his pigtail so he will be cursed by his ancestors!

According to our reporter, Khouw Ah Soe alone remained calm. He was not unnerved by the threats. He shifted his pigtail from his back across to his chest. Smiling he spoke: 'Don't worry! I myself have already begun.'

He lifted up his hair, and the pigtail was false. His hair was cut short; he was almost bald.

The crowd charged the speaker and the meeting's organisers. Fighting broke out and there were many cries and shouts. Kuntow *and* silat *left many people sprawled on the floor, some with broken bones. Khouw Ah Soe himself, with his false thau-cang, was taken to the hospital where he was to undergo treatment for fifteen days.*

He has escaped from the hospital and it looks like he has run out of both energy and money. The Chinese community of Surabaya has rejected him. He has not received any support, especially not funds. His attempt to sell us information is a sign of his failure. He is in very, very difficult straits . . .

What I had written was nowhere to be found; there wasn't even the slightest similarity. One thing was clear however: Khouw Ah Soe would be in great difficulty as a result of this article.

'Why are you gasping for breath like that?' asked Mama.

I told her what had happened. She also read the report.

'How could they lie in an article like this? Something that should be respected because it's going to be read by thousands of people?' I exclaimed.

Mama looked at me with pity in her eyes.

'Don't be sentimental. You've been educated to respect and even deify Europe, to trust in it unreservedly. Then, every time you discover reality – that there are Europeans without honour – you become sentimental. Europe is no more honourable than you, Child! Europe is only superior in the fields of science, learning and self-restraint. No more than that. Look at me, an example that is near to you – me, a villager, but I can hire Europeans and their skills. You can too. If they can be hired by anyone who can pay them, why can't the devil hire them too?'

Why can't the devil hire them? I lifted my eyes to look at her. Nyai was standing before me. She looked so tall, like a giant, like a mountain of coral. What kind of person was she? The whole world admired Europe because of its glorious history, because of its extraordinary achievements, its literary works, because of Europeans' abilities, for their forever-new creations, and their newest creation of all: the modern age. My thoughts flew quickly to that anonymous tract that Magda Peters had given me. Among other things, it had said: the Natives of the Indies, and especially the Javanese, who have been defeated again and again in battle for hundreds of years now, have not only been forced to acknowledge the superiority of Europe, but have also been forced to feel inferior. And the Europeans, wherever they saw Natives not contracting the disease of inferiority, viewed them as a fortress of resistance that must be subjugated.

The tract went on to say: Is the European colonial view appropriate? It is not only inappropriate, it is not right. But colonial Europe doesn't stop there. After the Natives have fallen into this humiliation and are no

331

longer able to defend themselves, they are ridiculed with the most humiliating abuse. Europeans make fun of the Native rulers of Java who use superstition to control their own people, and who are thereby spared the expense of hiring police forces to defend their interests. *Nyai Royo Kidul* is a glorious creation of Java whose purpose is to help preserve the authority of the native kings of Java. But Europe too maintains superstitions – the superstition of the magnificence of science and learning. This superstition prevents the conquered peoples from seeing the true face of Europe, the true nature of the Europe that uses that science and learning. The European colonial rulers and the Native rulers are equally corrupt.

'So why are you still so easily surprised?' asked Nyai, as if she had just finished reading that anonymous tract which, in fact, she had never seen. 'Not only newspapers, Child, but also the courts, and the law itself, can and may be used by criminals to carry out their purposes. Minke, Child, don't be so easily swayed by names. Wasn't it you yourself who told me that our ancestors used great and splendid names in order to impress the world with their magnificence – an empty magnificence? Europe's show of magnificence isn't based on names; Europeans strut around with their science and learning. But the cheat remains a cheat, the liar remains a liar, even with his science and his learning.'

Her voice was pregnant with anger. I could understand why: her already destroyed family was soon to lose all its property. It was about to be confiscated by the person the law said was the only heir; Engineer Maurits Mellema. I mustn't rub salt into her wounds.

'If they can, and indeed do, do such things to us, why shouldn't they treat the Chinese boy in the same way?' she said.

'That anyone would lie in a newspaper report, Ma . . .'

'In everything that they can get their hands on, Child. The predicament of that Chinese boy is the same as ours. He can't defend himself either. There was a time when mankind was oppressed by kings, Child; now he is oppressed by Europe.'

'It looks like Khouw Ah Soe is in real trouble,' I turned the conversation, 'not only with his own people, who don't want to see the end of the pigtail, but also with the police, because of the accusation that he entered the Indies illegally.'

'So now you know *your* newspaper, Child.'

'It is not *my* newspaper, Ma.'

'I'm glad to hear that. But you must have the courage to bear the risks, Child.'

'What risks, Ma?'

'What risks? At the very least that Chinese boy will suspect you of being involved in this shameless lie.'

'Maybe he will come here.'

'If he suspects you of being a liar and accomplice in all this, he won't come here.'

'I hope he won't think that, Ma.'

'If he doesn't, and he comes here, he is to receive our protection. He can stay in Darsam's house.' She sat down again. 'He mustn't stay in this building. He mustn't be seen. Give him a good welcome, Child. No doubt his customs and manners will be different. But you will still be able to learn from him, from other ideas that aren't European.'

Learn from ideas that aren't European! What is alive in the mind of my mother-in-law?

'Why are you gaping like that? Did I say something wrong? Something not in accord with what your teachers have taught you? You're looking at me as if you've just met me for the first time!'

'Yes, Ma, each day you amaze me more and more.'

'So what have you learnt from your Mama?'

'You're truly my teacher, Ma, a teacher who isn't European. I will try to make your teachings not just something I possess, but something I practise as well.'

'That's not what I meant.'

'Mama!'

'Child, you are all I have left in the world now. I am alone in the world now. Why should I go on working like this? I could easily see out my days without doing any more work. But this business must not die of neglect. It is my own child, my first child. It must remain my beloved child, even if it does fall into the hands of others. It may not be hurt or damaged like the others. It may not be treated just like some dairy cow.

Her thoughts were on the predicament of her business; but she still thought of the interests of others.

'It is my first child. Soon none of it will be left. Just you, Child, my son-in-law, indeed my son. You are more to me than my own children. Sometimes my empty heart is tormented, wondering why Robert didn't turn out like you.' She paused a moment. Then: '. . . I often say to myself: an imperfect seedling will die before it bears fruit. Indeed it hurts, Child, to have to accept that reality. And it is more painful still when my conscience accuses me of being unable to educate my own children. That is why I talk so much, lecture you so much.'

She picked up the *Soerabaiaasch Nieuws* again and fanned herself with it. Only after a lengthy silence did her words come out, slowly and with conviction: 'That Chinese boy knows how to learn from Europe, knows how to reject its sickness. He is no doubt a wise young man. He can be trusted much more than this newspaper,' and she threw the paper onto the table.

4

The atmosphere in that big house at Wonokromo became more oppressive every day. I didn't even want to write. The office work was equally uninteresting. Working near Mama, I felt like a dwarf at the back of a giant, a pebble at the foot of a mountain. I was insignificant; my individuality drowned in the immensity of her thinking.

If I allowed things to go on like this, I would surely end up overpowered by her shadow. I had already made up my mind to leave this place – Wonokromo and Surabaya – forever. But whenever my eyes fell upon this extraordinary woman, who, like me, had lost so much, I could not bring myself to carry out my decision. How lonely she would be without me. There would be no one to talk to, no one she could confront with her toughness of mind. She would be like a rock of coral in the middle of the ocean.

I must go; I must become an individual in my own right, my growth not stunted because of someone else's sun-obstructing shadow.

Then one day in her office I told her of my intentions: 'When Panji Darman returns, Ma, I will be leaving.'

I had not reckoned on how much I would regret saying that. She looked so sad and pained. She groped for something in one of the desk drawers to try to hide her face.

'I have no right to hold you back, Child. But you must know that your place here can not be filled by anyone else, not even Panji Darman.'

She could not make herself accept my going.

Suddenly she asked, as if she had just finished making a judgement on the way she had treated me all this time: 'What is it you really want?'

'I just want to get away from Surabaya, Ma, to Betawi perhaps. I think I will do some more study, some real study, so that one day maybe I can become like Dr Martinet.'

'If you leave now, Child, with your heart still wounded and in turmoil as it is . . . no, don't. You will never be able to study. You'll end up just wandering about like a hobo. You won't find what you're looking for. You'll be even more depressed. Stay here until you feel better. You'll be better able to decide what to do.' Then she was silent.

There was an agreement between the two of us not to think back on what had happened to Annelies, or at least not to talk about her. Even Dr Marti-net, who started to visit us again after the charges against him were dropped, never mentioned the subject of my late wife. It was even more the case with Darsam.

During a week-long trial, Darsam, who was charged with resisting the police and the Marechausee, managed to escape conviction. Now he went on with his daily work as if a person called Annelies, who had been so much a part of his life, had never existed.

Once every three days Darsam would come to me for lessons. He could not only read and write a little, but began to read the Malay-language news-papers, and he was also learning arithmetic. Sometimes he would even force himself to study how to handle the office work.

On certain days he would go to Kalisosok gaol to visit those who were imprisoned as a result of that earlier rioting. Mama always examined the parcels that were going to them, and told Darsam to pass on her greetings. Once she even wanted to go herself, but Darsam forbade her.

About eighteen people had been caught in the fighting against the police. The sentences ranged from two to five years of hard labour, in chains. Their great sympathy and support for us was something we could never fully repay; all we could offer was our equally great gratitude and the monthly assistance Mama provided for their families. Yes, it was true: the river stones, pebbles and rocks could also make their feelings known. Never belittle or scorn a single person, let alone two, because every individual contains unlimited possibilities.

That morning too I sensed a loneliness in Mama's heart. To alter the mood, I summed up the courage to begin: 'Ma, there was Annelies's hope, Ma, that Mama would give me a little sister, Ma. Shouldn't we respect that hope?'

'Come here!' she said. She stood up and moved away from the desk. 'Nah! here is the key to the drawer. Open it and examine the letters inside.'

I didn't understand what she was getting at. I opened the drawer. Inside there were only letters. Some were tied together with thread.

'Yes, read some from that bundle.'

I pulled one out. The envelope hadn't been opened. From somebody with a European name, a cashier in a bank.

'Read it,' she said.

'The envelope hasn't been opened, Ma.'

'Open it, and read it. No need to read it out to me, just read it for your-self.'

It proved to be a letter proposing marriage to Mama.

'You can read them all; they're all the same. I've only read three of them. Count how many there are, Minke.'

I counted them one by one. Among the names I came across were: Doctor Frans Martinet, Controller H. Sneedijck, Lieutenant ter Zee Jakob de Haene . . . and also Kommer! My heart fluttered; maybe even Jean Marais's name would be among them. Letter by letter I counted, but his name wasn't there. Before I could total them up, Mama's voice came to me: 'Enough, Child, put them back. What do you think?'

'Mama is still young.'

'When I see those letters, yes, I do feel young. How old is your mother?'

'A little over forty I think,' I answered.

'Then I would be her youngest sister.'

'Mama, I'm glad Mama intends one day to carry out that hope.'

'Yes, Minke, but my intentions are based on hard calculations. Life like this is so lonely. But who knows how long a human being will live? So it is you, who are with me now, whom I value most of all. It is you who I hope has learnt from these last experiences. Don't worship Europe in its totality. There is good as well as evil everywhere. There are angels and devils everywhere. There are devils with the faces of angels, and angels with the faces of devils everywhere. And there is one thing that stays the same, Child, that is eternal: the colonialist is always a devil.

'You live in a colonial world, you can't get away from that. But it doesn't matter, as long as you understand: he is a devil until the end of the world. He is Satan.'

I sensed the bitterness in her words. I recognised that she was confronting an enemy who could neither be opposed nor threatened, a devil immune to insults, blows, tears or pain.

'If you understand and know the satanic nature of colonialism, then any action you take against it will be justified, except collaboration with it.' She blew out a great breath.

'Mama.'

'Yes?'

'What do you mean by colonial?'

'It's something that must be not only explained but also experienced. You will never understand by reading alone. I've already tried to find it in the dictionaries, Child, three dictionaries. All in vain.'

'It should be able to be explained, Ma.'

'I can't. It is you who should be able to explain it.'

'What if we define it as "that which has the character of conquest"?'

Mama laughed. I was happy to see her laugh but my heart was not really happy, she was laughing at me. She went on ignoring my suggestion: 'Everybody in authority praises that which is colonial. That which is not colonial is considered not to have the right to life, including Mama here. Millions upon millions of people suffer silently, like the river stones. You, Child, must at least be able to shout. Do you know why I love you above all others? Because you write. Your voice will not be silenced and

336

swallowed up by the wind; it will be eternal, reaching far, far into the future. As to defining what is colonial: isn't it just the conditions insisted upon by a victorious nation over the defeated nation so that the latter may give the victor sustenance – conditions that are made possible by the sharpness and might of weapons?'

How confusing were this morning's experiences. Everything was indistinct and without a central focus. Every issue and problem was travelling about, crossing back and forth over previous paths, without direction.

'Your hopes for me are too great, Mama.'

'No. You have only one deficiency. You don't really know what that word "colonial" means. You must learn to understand. Your new Chinese acquaintance – what's his name again?'

'Khouw Ah Soe, Mama.'

'A very difficult name. From what I can tell from your story about him, he has come to understand that which you don't yet understand.'

'But China has never been conquered, Ma.'

'Every nation that is backward is conquered and colonised by every nation that has progressed.'

That morning's conversation, cluttered with criss-crossing traffic heading in no particular direction, was followed by a mutual silence.

Then one evening Khouw Ah Soe arrived. It was obvious he was in trouble. He was still wearing the same Shantung silk pyjamas, but they were not as clean as before. They were dirty and torn.

We sat in the small garden next to my room, on the concrete bench. Mama observed his round face intently (it was no longer reddish, but already going brown), as well as his thin reddish pigtail, his narrow eyes. I heard her mumble in Dutch: 'So young, leaving country and family, to come so far – what for?'

Khouw Ah Soe bent to catch her words, then said he was sorry, he didn't understand. I put it into English.

'Thank you very much for such kind words. Thank you.'

Unasked, I became the interpreter.

'My child here is confused, Mr Khouw, after reading the report published about you. It was the opposite of what he wrote.'

'Only to be expected.'

'Not that. I worried that you would be angry with my son.'

'No. That's the way it had to be. Their own actions will educate the people to hate them and oppose them – that has also been the case with the concessions in China . . .'

'My child had already sent a letter of protest . . . tell him yourself, Child.'

Khouw Ah Soe laughed happily on hearing my story, as if he wasn't at that moment being harried by his own troubles. Then he added: 'That is how they are – those that hold power in the conquered nations. It is even more sickening to witness the behaviour of those whites who live in countries they consider to be their colonies. To hope for anything else from them is a big mistake.'

'Nah!' attacked Mama, 'my guess is proved correct, Child. But don't translate that for him. This person is very clever. You can learn much from him.'

Khouw Ah Soe looked at me, waiting for the translation.

'Mama says,' I said, 'that you are now in trouble because of the *Soerabaiasch Nieuws*. Mama guesses you would find it difficult to find anywhere to stay.'

Khouw Ah Soe offered neither a denial nor an affirmation. He dropped his gaze to the floor. At once we understood that things were as we imagined. Someone strong like him would not get into some minor, trifling trouble. His problem would be that he had run out of friends.

'Let me arrange a place for him in Darsam's house,' Mama said. Then she excused herself.

Khouw Ah Soe continued his talk. I listened carefully to his every word. 'How happy I am to have met your mother-in-law – a very advanced woman.' He tapped on the table as a way of channelling his nervousness.

'You will stay here, in Darsam's place. He is a fighter.'

'The Darsam that was arrested by the Marechausee? He's free?'

Perhaps Darsam too had been mentioned in the newspapers of foreign lands to the north.

'No doubt he is a fighter,' he suddenly affirmed. It seemed he didn't know what else to say. He was nervous.

Not long after arriving in Surabaya he received news: a comrade who had been sent to Fiji had been murdered. Another who had been sent to South America was found murdered not far from the salt-petre mines of Chile.

Finally I summoned the courage to ask: 'What is it that you actually do?'

'Call out, no more than that. Call out to my fellow countrymen who have wandered overseas, that the times have changed, that China is no longer the centre of the world; that China has made great contributions to human civilisation, but that it is not the only civilised nation in the world, as so many Chinese believe.'

So they were like my own people, I thought, the Javanese, who looked upon themselves as the most polite, most civilised, and most noble of all people. A smile appeared on my face.

'My fellow countrymen must come to realise: it is not that the white people are simply superior; they are the ones who control the world, it is their countries that are the centre of the world. Without that awareness they will never be shaken free from their wrong views and false dreams. Arise,' suddenly his voice became louder, 'because the eastern peoples too can triumph in this new age. Look at Japan,' and his voice became softer, 'but my fellow countrymen look upon the Japanese as a people of no consequence, a young people, a small nation, and always only pupils and imitators of China.'

On another occasion he condemned the backwardness of his fellow countrymen, especially those working overseas. They were not like the overseas Japanese, who always returned with some new learning, who humbly set out to learn all they could from the countries where they sought their livelihood, and who took home what they learnt as a contribution to the development of their own nation and people.

'I'm sorry, Minke, perhaps I'm too sentimental in the way I talk about Japan, and too enthusiastic when I talk about my own work.'

'What's wrong with sentimentality and enthusiasm, if they're expressed at the right time and place?'

'You will be safe here,' I said again.

He had ran out of words, realising that there was someone going out of his way to help him. He looked embarrassed, and was silent.

Nyai invited him to eat, alone because we had already eaten. Afterwards I took him across to Darsam's house. The Madurese man greeted him by running about showing him where everything was: where the toilet was, which was the best way out of the complex if there was danger. I translated.

He thanked us over and over again with an elegant bow, not the Japanese bending that he used with Nijman. He thanked Darsam too for his help in overthrowing Ah Tjong's empire. But I didn't translate that.

Sitting in Darsam's front room, it seemed Khouw Ah Soe was able to wrest back his character, his confidence. Darsam didn't sit with us. Khouw Ah Soe spoke a great deal, for about two hours.

On my return to the main building I found Mama had not gone to bed. She wanted to hear what Khouw Ah Soe had said, and I told her.

'To come to another country without knowing the language,' she commented, 'just because he wants to help his people advance! Meeting danger after danger. Child, that's what a young person should be like. The Europeans came here as gangs of robbers and pirates. You must note the difference!'

Three days and nights he stayed with us.

From his other stories, I was able to gather that Nijman's guesses were not wrong. Almost everything Nijman had said was right.

He had left China with thirty or so others, who headed east, west, southwest or south. He himself, a university student from Waseda, and four others, set off for the Indies. He entered through Bagan Siapi-api in Sumatra by fishing boat from Singapore. Two of his friends headed for Pontianak in Netherlands Borneo. One stayed in Bagan Siapi-api. He and one of his friends went to Betawi. His friend was left to work there. He himself made his way to Surabaya, an area known to be difficult to handle. Surabaya was the centre for the Chinese gang, *Thong*, which, through its use of terror, controlled the lives of all the Chinese subjects of the Indies. The Thong gangs throughout the Indies were controlled from Surabaya.

'Yes, the Japanese have even sent people overseas to learn to play and to make pianos – to Europe and to the United States.' He went on to tell how his people who went overseas weren't like that. They broke their backs all over the world for no other purpose than to accumulate wealth. Then they came home hoping only to be admired, and to rebuild the graves of their ancestors. And only to fall into the power of bandits, who squeezed money from them every month and every year. For all time, forever, would they be the milk-cows of those bandit-ancestors as well as of the Thong bandits. If the bandit-ancestors weren't satisfied, their families at home would become the playthings of torment and torture.

In the end they once again left home, spreading out through the whole world, sucking up more of the world's wealth in order to please their bandit-ancestors. Not in order to build something grand, to convince the bandits that what China really needs is knowledge and learning, awareness of the need for change and for a new man with a new spirit, ready to work for his people and his country

So the children of the overseas Chinese must be prepared to receive a modern education. A great, a very great, amount of money must be gathered. The tribute paid to the ancestral and Thong bandits must be stopped. Modern schools must be founded, both for now and for the future. If not, the country of our ancestors will be swallowed up by Japan, just as Africa has been swallowed whole by the English.

Even though is words sounded like an advertisement, they were interesting and impressive.

'Every country in Asia which begins to arise and awaken is not just awakening itself, but is helping to awaken every other nation that has been left behind, including China.'

'But science and learning is not the one and only key,' I said.

'You are right,' he answered. 'They are only the conditions. Equipped with modern science and learning, a wild beast will only become wilder and more bestial, and a vicious human will only become more vicious and cruel. But don't forget, with science and learning even the most wild and bestial of all animals can be made to submit. You know whom I mean: Europe.'

The hair on the back of my neck stood up on hearng his last words. Mama would be quick to express her agreement with this young unsandalled and pyjamaed Sinkeh.

'So don't hold out any hopes that a modern education will ever be given to the conquered countries, such as this country of yours. Only the conquered people themselves know what their country and people need. The colonising nation will only suck up the honey of your land and the labour of your people. In the end it is the educated among the conquered people who need to recognise their responsibilities.' Suddenly he stopped, changing the subject: 'You no doubt know what happened in the Philippines.'.

His words came at me like an accusation. The Philippines was for me no more than a place on a map, a geographical location. The Philippines could not even be said to be far from my own country but I knew almost nothing about it.

'A pity, but no,' I answered.

He laughed and his narrow eyes disappeared completely from his face. His sparse pointed teeth emerged to represent his absent eyes.

'They studied well from the Spanish, from Europe, even before the Japanese. Even before the Chinese. It is a pity they were a colonised people, unlike Japan. The Filipinos could not develop because they were colonised. The Japanese have developed – developed too well. The Filipinos were good pupils of the Spanish. And the Spanish were bad teachers, rotten and corrupting. But the Filipinos didn't just accept their teachings uncritically. The Filipinos are also great teachers for the other conquered peoples of Asia. They were the founders of the first Asian republic. And it collapsed. A great historical experiment.'

I watched his lips closely, and their movements, which seemed somehow not quite rapid enough. His pointed teeth rose and sunk behind those lips.

'So you don't know anything about the Philippines?'

'Unfortunately, no. I only know there was a war between the Spanish and the Americans there.'

He ahemmed, then laughed.

'What's the matter?'

'The Spaniards and Americans – their war – it was all an act. There was no conflict between them; it was all to do with letting the Spaniards sell the Filipino people to the United States without having to lose face before the eyes of the world.'

'How do you know all this?'

'How? Wasn't all this reported in the newspapers?'

'I've never come across any such reports.'

He nodded. 'Do not university students here have their own newspapers? Oh, I'm sorry, there are no universities in the Indies yet, are there?'

'So students have their own papers?'

'Of course, newspapers that are devoted to ideals, not yet side-tracked by personal and vested interests.'

I couldn't say a thing. The way he linked one thing neatly with another made it seem they were indeed all entwined. His explanations rose before me as a great construction. I couldn't see through it. Yes, some great construction where every part contributed to strengthening every other part. All the peculiar things about him disappeared at that moment: his round and now brown face, his reddish pigtail . . . suddenly I was discovering something else about him, that emanated from his presence. And that something was: life! Life itself. You could hear the groans, the cries and complaints, and the pounding of his heart; the glow and lightning brightness of his thoughts. None of the things he had spoken about had ever come under my scrutiny. Now I could move on to wonder and imagine about many new things.

I told Mama all about it. She meditated for a moment. Her eyes glassed over in emotion, and finally tears made the journey across her cheeks.

'He has shown us how Europe and America are no more than evil adventurers, Child. If they had no cannons, would anyone honour them?'

Before the guava-faced youth left our house, I felt I had to ask one more question: Was Nijman's report true, that he had been beaten up in the Kong Koan building? He confirmed it.

'Dangerous work,' I commented.

'There may be worse yet to come.'

'You are not afraid?'

'The Philippines cannot be forgotten, can they? Even if they were deceived by Spain and America? It is inevitable that other conquered peoples will follow in their footsteps. Yes, even in the Indies. If not now, then later, when people know how to handle their teachers . . .'

He left one dark night, refusing the use of a vehicle. He walked off to who knows where. He said he might return at any time to seek protection. Only Nyai and I knew of the help we had given him. He had needed friends and help.

I think I can say it was from Khouw Ah Soe that Mama and I heard for the first time about the awakening of a whole people, rising up, advancing and respected, building a modern culture and civilisation.

I still remember those words of his, so beautiful, as if they came from some legend:

'In the past peoples could live at peace in the middle of deserts and forests. Now they cannot. Science and modern learning will pursue everyone everywhere. Human beings, both as individuals and social beings, can no longer feel secure. Mankind is forever being pursued because modern science and learning constantly provide the inspiration and desire to control Nature and man together. There is no power that can bring to a halt this passion to control, except greater science and learning, in the hands of more virtuous people . . .'

———◆———

The Surabaya newspapers reported that the police were busy with the hunt for illegal immigrants from China.

A Malay-Chinese newspaper published a report quoted from a Chinese newspaper:

It is true that Khouw Ah Soe entered the Indies illegally. It is now also known that he entered the Indies with several others. There were reports that one of these was a girl, a graduate from the Catholic High School in Shanghai. They have all been using false names since they left the Chinese mainland. In Hong Kong, Khouw Ah Soe was known as Tjok Kiem Eng and was wanted by the Hong Kong police. He was the troublemaker responsible for the cutting off of pigtails along the pleasure waterways of Hong Kong. From Hong Kong, he ran to Hainan.

The paper also published some background. It was estimated that during the previous year 240 Chinese had entered the Indies illegally, and they were mainly concentrated in Bagan Siapi-api and Pontianak. None of them spoke any Native language.

Not long after that there appeared another report:

Differing from most of the immigrants who came to the Indies, this small group of illegal immigrants did not become involved in the smuggling trade. Their intention was to create trouble in the Netherlands Indies by inciting the young people to defy their ancestors and their own parents.

They are anarchists, nihilists, good-for-nothing agitators . . .

And I myself?

After the appearance of Nijman's article about Khouw Ah Soe, I did not visit the editorial office again. Several times he wrote me letters in an attempt to humour my disappointment, saying forget it, forget it; if you come and see me, I will explain the whole matter to you. I did not go. Instead it was he who came to see me. Nyai did not come out to meet him.

He seemed much younger than usual. His clothes, even his shoes, were all brown. He took out a parcel from his briefcase and handed it to me.

'You will find this book very interesting,' he said.

It was about America, a continent that was totally unknown to educated Natives, except for the names of a few people and places, some geography and a little information about its produce. He didn't say anything more about the book.

'I understand. You are very disappointed, perhaps even angry because of the interview affair. There was nothing else we could do. Look, this is your country, Mr Minke. If you read this book, you will come to understand why America is thirsty for more inhabitants. It has vast areas of land, it is rich and empty. Different from Java, Mr Minke. Fifteen years ago this country of yours had maybe only fourteen million people; now it is closer to thirty million. The land is shrinking because of the number of people. Some action must be taken against these illegal immigrants. It is in the interests of the Javanese themselves. If not, in just a few decades, this island could become just another little China. I'm sure that is not what you want?'

Another cause for anxiety! I'd never thought of it like that. On some other occasion I would discuss it with Khouw Ah Soe.

'Look, Mr Minke, although the Dutch are the rulers, you can see for yourself that there is no great stream of Dutch families coming out here. It has never been the intention of the Dutch to pour out here to set up a colony. Wasn't it right to publish that article, if it can help stop the flow of all these Chinese coming out to our country? The Netherlands Indies has spent great amounts of money for this purpose, working in your own interests Mr Minke!'

So far I had not found any ground upon which to stand to analyse this problem. All I could do was listen.

'The recognition of Japan as an equal has produced a number of problems,' he went on. 'The Chinese of Singapore have already become restless. We don't need that sort of thing in the Indies, especially not in Java. Be frank, Mr Minke, do you agree with the ideas of Khouw Ah Soe?'

'In some things he is right.'

'Very true. But the truth does not necessarily bring any advantage.' He quickly set up defences. 'I think you would prefer to support your country than a truth that brought disadvantage to your country.'

Another point that wasn't without grounds! I had never thought about any of this. I just had to listen.

He left after he was convinced that he had influenced me. I had to promise to bring some new articles to the paper.

Mama laughed when she heard the story. 'You've forgotten already, Child; everything colonial is from the devil. There has never been any colonialist that has cared anything about our people. They are afraid of China itself. They're jealous.'

I forced myself to think how all these things came together: the progress Japan was making, the restlessness among the Chinese Young Generation, the rebellion of the Filipino natives against Spain and then the United States, the jealousy of the colonial Netherlands Indies towards China, the colonial hatred of Japan. And why wasn't the Filipino rebellion reported in all the newspapers?

And to the north, Siam was crying out because its silk, so popular in the Indies, was being pushed out of the market by Japan's cheaper and shinier silk. In the land of my own livelihood, Japanese handicrafts were

344

surreptitiously entering the market. The Javanese makers of blouses, combs and brushes were losing their share of the market, because the Japanese goods were cheaper and shinier. But the Javanese were silent. They did not cry out. They did not understand why their livelihood was drying up.

And the women of South-east Asia could not live without combs, brushes, and tweezers to catch head-lice – also all made in Japan.

With my inner eye I scattered my vision over my own surroundings. There was no movement at all. All Java was fast asleep, dreaming. And I was confused, angry, aware but impotent.

5

Something completely unexpected happened: a letter arrived from Robert Mellema.

I was working in the office at the time. Mama called me from her desk and pushed the letters across for me to read. From Robert, from Panji Darman, from Miriam de la Croix.

There was no address on the envelope. There was a picture of the sea and coconut palms on the stamp. The printing on the stamp said Hawaii. The post mark was illegible.

My far away Mama, it started.

I didn't know why that phrase filled my heart with emotion and my eyes with tears. The cry of a regretful child.

'What's the matter, Child?' asked Mama.

'This letter is not for me, Ma. It is written for Mama and Mama alone.'

'Read it,' she encouraged me.

'I'll read it slowly, ya Ma?' and I began to read aloud:

I know, Ma, that you will probably never forgive me. That's up to you. Even so, Ma, your son Rob, so far away now, begs your forgiveness, both in this world and the next. Ma, my Mama. Sun, moon and stars have all been witnesses to my sins against you.

And what meaning does my life have now? As low as your work might ever be, you will always be far more honourable than this child of yours, who has fought against you and caused you much sorrow.

I have heard the village people say: the greatest forgiveness is that which a child asks of his mother; the greatest of all sins is that of a child against his mother. I am the most sinful of children, Ma, your son Robert needs your most profound forgiveness, Ma, my Mama . . .

I glanced from the corners of my eyes at Mama. The look on her face hadn't changed. She kept on with her work, calmly, as if she weren't listening.

I know my Mama so well, so I know you won't want to read these writings of mine. No matter. That is a risk I must take. What is important is that at least there has arisen the intent to ask forgiveness of the person who gave birth to me, who has shed blood for me, who has groaned with pain for my life's sake, and that intent has now been put into words. So if you do not answer this letter or even if you don't read it, if I remain alive, I will know you have forgiven me, even though you may never say it. If I die in the near future, that will be a sign that you did not forgive me.

Once, on a ship, someone said to me: you can ask forgiveness of God at any time at all, if you sin against Him. Sins against your fellow man are different again; it is much more difficult to get him to forgive you. God is all-compassionate; mankind is uncompassionate.

I am not telling you where I am. What would be the point? It would only cause problems. I am on a ship. And I don't need to give its name, nationality or the flag it is flying under.

After what happened in Ah Tjong's house, I ran. By chance a horse cart was passing by. I jumped aboard and headed for Tanjung Perak. I was able to get aboard a junk heading for Manila. I did whatever work I was given: even that of cleaning the toilets – everyone's toilet, not just the one I used myself.

Completely humiliated – that is the condition that befell me as soon as I was away from you, my Mama. I could do nothing to resist what befell me. I had to stay alive. And what kind of life is it, Ma, crawling around people's toilets like this?

I was only a few days in Manila. Attacks by bandits threw the whole harbour into confusion. Many sailors disappeared without a trace. From Manila I travelled on board a small ship to Hong Kong. In that small, crowded city I got a job as a gardener in the house of an English officer. Soon after, he found out that I had caught a certain disease and he threw me out.

Yes, Ma, I am ill. The easiest thing for me to do was to visit a sinshe. He said I had caught a 'dirty disease' and that it was getting worse. I handed myself over to him. He treated me with potions and acupuncture until I looked fresh and healthy again. In the meantime I had become a vagabond, owning nothing at all. All I had was the clothes on my body. This is all a punishment from Mama, so I must accept it.

Because I could no longer pay the sinshe, I had to find another job on a ship. I was amazed that I was still allowed to live. I sailed all over the world, going from ship to ship. No one recognised or knew me, because I always used different names. People didn't care whether I was human, animal or devil.

But then the symptoms returned. I did everything I could to avoid destruction. As soon as I was in Hong Kong again I looked up the sinshe who had treated me before. Treat me until I am cured, I begged. But he told me something new: the disease can only be controlled; there is no real cure. I knew I would be tied to him forever. It's not that I didn't try the doctors. None of them were able to help me, not even to ease the suffering a bit. My heart shriv-

*elled up – all I could see hovering before me was death. Mama, it was you,
Mama, that I then remembered. Nothing can help me, except your forgiveness.*

*My illness meant I had to stay close to my sinshe in Hong Kong. I had
to have more money. He said I would have to visit him at least once a month.
My livelihood was not so generous as to bring me to Hong Kong every month.
And to work in Hong Kong itself was not easy for me, because I didn't want
to be known by anybody, as the child of anybody, the citizen of any country.
I had no address and did not want to have an address.*

Mama, I know my disease is a death sentence for me.

*I talked to another sinshe and his words frightened me: there is no cure, he
said; there is no one strong enough to survive for more than two years. How
frightening, Ma, two years for someone as young as me. Mama, my Mama . . .*

Nyai Ontosoroh stood up and left. Before leaving the room, she turned
to me and said:

'There are some other letters. For you.'

I didn't go on reading Rob's letter. I picked up the other letters from
Mama's desk. From Betawi, from the Stovia Medical School: I had been
accepted as a student beginning the next academic year; details were to follow.

Was it Robert's letter or the one from the Stovia that made Mama so
unhappy that she had to leave the room? I didn't know.

There was a letter from Robert to Annelies. Suddenly I realised that he
knew nothing of what had happened to the family. The letter carried the
same stamp as the first one. There was no date, nor mention of place.

*Ann, Annelies, my little sister. I have now travelled around the world as I
once dreamed of doing. More than twice, Ann. I have set my feet down in
all the great ports of the world. And I have met with too many people. Not
one has ever invited me to visit their house. They all look upon me as being
not of the same species, from a people too far away and too strange, perhaps
like a race of animals.*

*I had wanted to be a sailor. Now I am a sailor. But I am not happy. Even
in the most meaningless of jobs, I am still considered incapable. My thoughts
are always going back and forth between Mama and you. You know the
reasons. Until now you have refused to talk to me. Yes, Ann, I understand,
understand only too well. And I know too why people never invite me to their
houses. Your brother is indeed not worthy of being spoken to by you. He is
only an animal, lower still than the horses you ride.*

*The incident in the reed-marshes continues to haunt me. Forgive me, Ann,
forgive me . . .*

At that moment I had to stop reading a moment and reflect again on Annelies's story. So it was true. I read on.

I pray always that you may be happy, Ann. Perhaps indeed Minke is the right man for you, despite Suurhof's making fun of him. I think Robert Suurhof will turn out to be no better than me.

I have seen all kinds of people now, Ann: Indians, Chinese, Europeans, Japanese, Arabs, Hawaiians, Malays, Africans . . . and Ann, there is none among their women, young or old, as beautiful as you, as glorious as you. You are a pearl among women. Your husband will be such a happy man . . .

I shoved the letter quickly into my pocket. No, I must not think about Annelies any more.

When Mama came back in, she did not ask anything. She sat down and continued her work. I went on reading Robert's letter to her.

My contract with life is for two years, Ma. Who knows whether the sinshe's prediction will turn out to be right. When I left my sinshe, I swore that once I boarded a ship, I would never set foot on land again. I will stay on board until I receive your forgiveness.

The letter ended.

'Where should I put the letter, Ma?'

'Burn it. What's the use of saving such a letter?' she said without lifting her eyes, without diverting her attention from the papers before her.

So I put it in my pocket as well. There was indeed an extraordinary amount of mail that day. There was a letter from Panji Darman addressed to me:

Minke, my good friend,

There is something I must tell you; I think you should know about it. But first, forgive me, as I don't know whether this is the right time to tell you or not.

I was walking one day in the Java Kade *at Amsterdam harbour. I saw a young, strong worker, and he clearly wasn't a Pure-Blood Dutchman. He was pushing a cart. Do you know who he was? Robert Suurhof! He stopped, startled at seeing me. He pulled down his hat to hide his eyes. He was ashamed of his work. Then he went back to pushing the cartload of goods. I called out to him. He kept on going.*

I followed him from behind and I called out again: 'Rob! Rob Suurhof! Don't tell me you've forgotten me already?'

He stopped, turned, greeted me: 'You? When did you arrive? It's a pity I'm working just now. Come to my place later. After seven in the evening, all right?'

He gave me an address. And I have never found that address, let alone the person. I went again to the wharves. I asked several people whether they knew a harbour worker, a young Indisch I knew Suurhof was registered as a Dutch citizen, but his citizenship could be of no use for identification here. They didn't know what I meant by Indisch or Indies Native. A labourer, a youth and dark, I said. They mentioned several names but none of them was Robert Suurhof. There is no one by the name of Robert Suurhof known here, they said. There was one worker from the Indies, someone said, dark, not called Suurhof, but he was arrested about three days ago by the police. He was working in the Java Kade at the time.

I went to the Harbour District Police Station. It was true; Suurhof had been arrested and was being returned to the Indies. They said he was suspected of assault and robbery in Surabaya.

He may already be back in Surabaya by the time you receive this letter, Minke.

I have also met Miss Magda Peters. I will tell you about it another time. I will write to Mama about things to do with her new company, Speceraria.

My greetings and respect to her and to you too.

The letter from Miriam de la Croix was from the Netherlands. There was also a letter from Herbert de la Croix with it. Here is what it said:

My dear Mr Minke,

With this letter, both Miriam and I, even if somewhat belatedly, take our leave of you. We have left the Indies and are now in the Netherlands. We are truly sorrowed by all that has befallen yourself and your family. We ourselves are very much to blame for what happened to you and your family, though our intentions were good and honourable ...

I stopped reading and thought over again each incident. There were no grounds for Herbert de la Croix and his daughter to feel they shared any blame. Why, they had gone as far as sending us a famous jurist, even though he had failed. And why was their letter so excessively polite? They had defended me when I was dismissed from school, they had helped me to obtain a place in the Civil Service Academy or Stovia. They had kept up correspondence with me all this time. Mr de la Croix himself had even put his position on the line over my case. They had no reason to feel guilty.

Mr Minke, the Governor-General very quickly issued my discharge papers; we then left for Europe. The three of us are together as one again. Whatever has happened, my dear Mr Minke, whatever I have experienced, it is nothing and indeed means nothing compared to what you have suffered, or what was suffered by your beloved teachers, Multatuli and Roorda van Eysinga.

All these events have come and gone so quickly. There has been almost no opportunity to follow them properly or reflect upon them.

Before we finish this letter we need to let you know that the request for a place for you at Stovia has been approved. You may start there next academic year. If you don't wish to do so, because you are still upset by the events of recent times, you only need to write to the school and cancel your enrolment.

Greetings and respects from Sarah, Miriam and myself. May you triumph in life. Adieu . . .

There was a letter from Mother but I pocketed it too. I would read it later.

Miriam's letter was different again:

Minke, I don't feel right writing to you about serious issues while you're still in mourning. But at a meeting of housewives in my neighbourhood, someone read out one of Raden Adjeng Kartini's letters to Miss Zeehandelaar. People were dumbfounded to hear her reports of life among the Javanese. Relations between men and women seemed so strange and tense. In the discussion which followed, I concluded: Javanese women were living in darkness. Kartini's version did differ from what I knew of the life of Javanese village women, though, of course, I never witnessed it myself. Our servants used to tell how the women would sing while planting or harvesting, and how their men would carry off the harvested paddy. And how the little children would play under the full moon singing praises to the rice goddess . . . Perhaps Kartini knew nothing of all this.

But I didn't say anything that would change the women's response to Kartini's letters. The gloom of the letters might make it easier for them to sympathise with the plight of Javanese women, and with Kartini herself.

Actually I had planned to bring up your case for discussion at the meeting. Father also agreed, as did Sarah too. Yours was the only such case during the whole of the nineteenth century. They would be interested. The story of the love between an educated Native and a Mixed-Blood European girl, which proved to involve many issues, which could have just as easily taken place in Europe itself.

I was determined to call out to their Christian and European consciences. I was convinced I would succeed. I must admit: it wasn't the time or place to divert people's attention from Kartini and her problems.

The ladies were completely amazed to hear of a Native Javanese woman writing in their language. They had always thought of Native woman as still living in the stone age.

And you, my friend, how are you? Someone like you – young, strong, edu-

cated – will surely be able to face all things with great resolve. We all have faith in you. And we all believe we will meet with you again one day in circumstances much, much happier than those of today. We believe this, Minke. In the end, all was created by God for us to share. And there is no happiness without testing.

And for Kartini too, I pray that she will pass all her tests, because beyond those tests lies the garden of happiness.

You're not bored with my letter yet, are you? And can you sense how the length of this letter is a symptom of how I miss the Indies, how I miss Java? You can, can't you? You surely must be able to sense it.

If I may make a suggestion, Minke, you should correspond with that extraordinary girl Kartini. It would not be difficult to find out her address, because she is the daughter of the Bupati of Jepara. I am also going to try to write to her.

Our new life in the Netherlands, just as in Java, has its ups and downs, as is the case with people's lives everywhere. Do you know, Minke, the Germans and English and French are racing to make all kinds of machines that will help make life more comfortable for people? There are people racing to make a machine that will replace the horse carriage, not so huge as a train, and it will be able to travel on ordinary roads.

It seems that the fever to discover new things, new tools, will not allow people to be satisfied with how things are. People are entranced and possessed by everything that is new; new etiquette, new behaviour. Women are beginning to lose their shyness and are riding bicycles in the evenings. New, new, new, new! People forget that life basically stays the same, the same as yesterday. New, new, new, anything which is not new is looked upon as a remnant of the Middle Ages. People have become so childish, like little school children, thinking that with these new things life will be better than yesterday. This is the modern age! Anything which is not new is looked upon as being out-of-date, suitable only for peasants and villagers. People have been so easily lulled to the fact that behind all these shouts, these urgings, this madness for what is new, there stands a supernatural power whose appetite for victims is never satisfied. This magical power is the columns of protozoa, of figures, which is called capital.

In the Indies, Minke, it is different than in Europe. In the Indies people stand helpless before the might of authority. In Europe people collapse before these rows of protozoa called capital. Under the banner of furthering science and service to humanity, there are people racing to discover how to make a machine, which, together with its passengers, will be able to traverse the heavens, physically overcoming all distance. There is a report from another country that there are others who have caught a fever to make a vessel that can take people to the floor of the oceans. There are even predictions that it *will not be long before mankind not only has control over new sources of power but will have mastered vibrations to reach a certain destination.*

You were right, Minke, the nature and countenance of mankind stays the same, no better than what it was before. The sermons in the churches continually remind us of that. Man remains a being that does not really know what it wants. The busier people become with their searching and their discoveries, the clearer it becomes that they are in fact being pursued by the anxiousness of their own hearts.

You still blame Europe. Naturally I could not bring myself to fault you for this after your recent experiences. If you lived in Europe for one or two years, though, perhaps your views might change. The percentage of those who are evil is probably the same as among your own people. Only the conditions of life are different. When I listen to Papa's stories from the Babad Tanah Jawi, *it is not rare for me to shiver in horror at the viciousness, barbarism, and cruelty: all a luxury, Minke, and all only to achieve control of that small island called Java. I am of the same opinion as Papa: there was indeed a time and an era when Europe was no different to what is described in the Babad. Only I hope you don't forget one thing, Minke. At the time the Babad was being compiled, your people were still worshipping individual all-powerful rulers, while the European nations were gradually forming world empires. The world for your people is Java. Take a look at the names of the kings of Java, even of those who still live today. Inscribed in them is always a sense of them constituting the whole universe.*

What I am getting at, Minke, is that the Javanese view of things, from the very first time foreigners set foot in your country, had already been left far behind in Europe. It is not true that Java and the Indies were taken over by Europe purely because of Europe's greed. The problem in the first place was the warped attitude of the people of Java and the Indies towards the world. I, of course, worry that all this stems from Papa's opinions, because he is more accomplished in reading classical Javanese literature, but I agree with what he says.

If, for example, the Javanese and the Indies peoples had been more advanced than Europe and had sailed to Europe and conquered it, do you think Europe would have been a happy place? I really believe, Minke, no one could doubt that any occupation of Europe by the Javanese would have been far more brutal than what you are experiencing now. The European nations have studied the character and capabilities of the Indies Natives. While on the other hand the Natives hardly know anything about Europe. Come to the Netherlands, Minke, you will be astounded to see the collection of material we have about the thinking of your ancestors, beginning with what was chiselled onto stone up until what was inscribed onto palm leaves. And none of it, not one thing, was saved by its heirs, your people, but by Europeans, Minke, Europeans.

353

I don't know whether these notes of mine are representative of European thinking or not. Even so, allow me to consider them a European girl's ideas about the Indies Natives. So, Minke, let us work together to do whatever is good for Java, the Indies, Europe and the world. We will fight European, Javanese, Indies and the world's evil together. Let us provide Europe, Java, the Indies, and the world with a healthier understanding as was struggled for by the great humanists, and particularly Multatuli who suffered so much in life.

I am now throwing myself into social and political activities. Sarah has gone on to Teachers' College. In other letters we will discuss new issues. Like Papa, I call out to you! be triumphant in your life. From Miriam far away near the North Pole . . .

How adroit was this girl. I didn't really know what her situation was like, but I was sure life in the Netherlands would not be as easy as it was here. The three of them would have to force their bones to stay above water. Yet she still possessed her adroitness as well as her faith in the gloriousness of the future. She accepts all of life's difficulties and tries to overcome them. Maybe, in that way, all troubles become a sport to exercise brain and muscles. Difficulties make her stronger, not weaker. Her resilience aroused me from my depression. She was truly clever to be able to sweep the cloud from my mind. Very well, I will accept that you represent Europe, Mir, represent Europe's view of the reality of the Indies today. You represent the good side of Europe, Mir. Perhaps – and this is closer to the truth – you represent your own idealisation of Europe. I will answer your letter, Mir.

I don't know how long I had been sitting thinking. Mama spoke: 'What are you thinking about now, Child?'

'Ma?'

'I've been watching you lately. You've lost your liveliness. I know things have been difficult lately. Even so, I don't think you need become a day-dreamer. I've got an idea, Child: have you ever thought about getting married again?'

A shameful question. I knew what she intended, of course: she was trying to stop me leaving Surabaya and Wonokromo. I was her son-in-law, but the question still struck my ears as going too far, not right or proper, as if I were someone who'd never set foot in a European school. And before I could reassert my dignity, her voice came across again: 'I can't look at those eyes of yours – so depressed. You must try much harder, much, much harder to forget the past.'

This humouring of each other was beginning to seem like a game of handball.

'Does it still look like I haven't begun to forget, Ma?'

'You don't read seriously any more, you don't write, you're not your old spirited self. Sometimes you pick up a newspaper, but then only read a little bit here and there. Your thoughts are all over the place, Child.'

'Mama doesn't seem as fresh as before,' I said, hoping to end the ball game.

'Of course. Not without reason. I was born earlier. But I have decided what to do.'

'When Panji Darman returns . . .'

'No need to await Panji Darman's return. I have a suggestion, Child. Will you accompany me on a trip out of town? Perhaps our mood will change as a result.'

'Of course, Ma, I'd like that very much. In the meantime perhaps Panji Darman will return.'

'And then will you go to Betawi?'

'I think so, Ma.'

'You're the wrong kind of person to be a doctor. You know Dr Martinet. What was he able to do when we were in trouble? You were able to do much more than him to defend us, even though we were defeated in the end. I value the work you do much more than the work of a doctor.'

'Let it be, Ma. At least I can study, and have a livelihood at the same time.'

'You don't really believe your own words. Panji Darman will not be returning quickly. According to his latest telegram he has had to postpone his departure again.'

'Yes, Ma, maybe it would be good if we took a holiday. Mama has never taken time off from work. But who will look after things while we're away?'

'Darsam.'

'Darsam? What can he do?'

'Don't be insulting. He has a lot of experience now, except in the office. I want to try him, so he begins to know what a headache it is to have to manage everything.'

'Do you dare do it?'

'He must begin sooner or later. Someone as loyal as him must be encouraged, be given an opportunity. He has a sharp sense of who is a good foreman and who isn't.'

'But office work?'

'He must be given a chance to do that too. The correspondence can afford to stop for a few days.'

'You really dare do it?'

For the first time a big smile appeared on Mama's face. Her teeth gleamed. She had decided a long time ago to take a holiday. Now she wanted to carry out that decision. Do it without hesitation or doubt.

'Forget those letters. Forget them all,' she said. 'What's life for anyway? Not for taking aboard a whole lot of unnecessary worries.'

6

I went to Jean Marais's place to see how far he had got with his painting of Annelies. He had refused to copy from a photograph. 'With Annelies, Minke,' he said one time, 'I am going to paint her exactly as you and I knew her – not just as we saw her, but as we really knew her, when she was at her peak.' And so he painted from memory alone. A month had passed and the picture was still not ready. He was working on it when I arrived.

Out of a gloomy Rembrandt-like background there emerged the face of my angel like the moon coming out from behind clouds. Yes, it was only that overcast that had threatened her life – so young, pure, beautiful, without equal. I saw once again that hair of hers which I had so many times caressed, the smoothness of her clear skin, the almost imperceptible furrows on her forehead. She was my wife, my Annelies, always so spoiled with my embraces.

'When it's finished,' said Jean, 'you mustn't put the picture up for everybody to see, Minke.'

'I've got to just store it away?'

'Put it in the most beautiful cover you can find. You don't need to look at it again. You could go mad.'

Jean Marais wasn't talking nonsense. Every time I looked at that unfinished picture my heart started to gallop and my thoughts began to wander.

'Put it in a cover of beautiful grape-red velvet, Minke. I will make one for you.'

'Will it be ready, do you think, when I leave Surabaya?'

'So it's true you're going to Betawi?'

'I have the right to grow and develop too, don't I?'

'You are right, Minke; while you are too close to Nyai you will not develop.' He smiled broadly, but I didn't know what he was smiling at. 'You haven't the same charisma. You need to be in another place, another region, breathing other air, with other opportunities, other possibilities.'

He wouldn't let go when I excused myself. 'Don't rush off. There is something else.'

'How is May doing at school?'

'She seems a bit behind.'

'Perhaps she's too busy at home, Jean.'

'Perhaps. What's the point of being clever if you're not happy at home? Learning to work is also important – learning to build a life. School is no more than something to finish things off, isn't it?'

'When I have a child, perhaps I will think the same way.'

'There's no need to copy me. My outlook is based upon this deformity of mine. Without her near me I feel so alone. What do you think of this picture, Minke?'

'You're brilliant, Jean.'

'I have never painted so well. It should be hanging on the walls of the Louvre. You must see Paris, Minke: the palaces, gardens, statues, the most beautiful works of art in the history of mankind – the most beautiful and most grand, the biggest churches. There is nothing which rivals them . . . I'm sorry, I shouldn't boast about the achievements of my own ancestors.'

'Keep going, Jean. France is indeed greatly admired, by my teachers at school too. I am only their student and haven't ever been to France.'

'A guest will be arriving soon,' Jean Marais turned the line of conversation. 'Kommer. Maybe another ten minutes. You should meet him.'

'So he comes here often?'

'We have a little business together. He's asked me to design a trap to catch a black panther,' he said, continuing with his painting.

There was a sound of footsteps, and Kommer walked in carrying a leather briefcase. He shook hands with me. When he offered his hand to Jean, he didn't take it, just nodded.

'You're angry with me?' asked Kommer.

'It's not a good idea to shake hands with a painter at work, Kommer,' he smiled.

Kommer laughed: 'You believe in that superstition?'

'It's not that. The paint has poison in it. Let me wash my hands first.'

'And how are you, Mr Minke?' asked Kommer. 'You haven't written anything for a long time.'

Jean hobbled back and straight away butted in: 'Mr Kommer, Minke was once very angry with me for doing no more than suggesting he write in Malay. You try to talk to him.'

Now I was being incited to explode again, after my disappointment with Nijman. I attacked: 'What can you say in Malay? An impoverished language like that? Riddled with borrowed words from every country in the world? And even to say "I am not an animal", you need all these borrowed words.'

'Very true.' Kommer smiled broadly. From out of his bag he took several newspapers and put them on the table. 'Look, Mr Minke. This is the *Pelapor Betawi*. This is the *Bintang Surabaya* from Surabaya. Of course you must know it, or at least have heard its name. This is the *Taman Sari*. This new newspaper, the *Penghantar*, is from far-away Ambon. In Javanese? You can see for yourself, here – *Retno Doemilah, Djawi Kondo*. This one is in Malay, from East Sumatra, *Percikan Barat*. Nah, here is a pile of auction and advertisement papers. All published in Surabaya. You know them all. Study them page by page. All of them owned by Dutchmen, Eurasians and one of them, *Percikan Barat*, by a Chinaman.'

I couldn't see where his chattering was leading.

'Yes, Minke, it is not Natives who feel it is important to report the news in Malay or Javanese. Fantastic, isn't it, Mr Minke. Not Natives. And it isn't Natives either who feel it is important to encourage Malay and Javanese to develop and grow as languages. An impoverished language? Certainly. Everything is born into this world with no more than a body and a spirit. You too are no exception to that rule.'

My heart no longer felt incited to explode. The reality of it all was making me gasp for breath.

'I myself have just started with the *Primbon Soerabaya*. Just forget my own involvement in it for a moment. Take a look for yourself at all these newspapers which are escorting the Natives to a wider world, to the world of humanity. Looked at in that way, can't you agree that their contribution to the advancement of Natives is indeed outstanding? Even though the Natives don't recognise that contribution or feel they're being helped? Especially when none is able to afford a subscription so that they have to join together to be able to read them?'

It seemed Kommer's speech was going to go on and on. It was boring, even though it was helping me to understand the situation of the Malay press.

'Nah! Minke, it's not me that's talking now. It's Mr Kommer.' Once again Jean began to interfere. 'If you still want to be angry, be angry with him.'

But I wasn't angry, just bored. Kommer's way of presenting things was different and didn't anger me: he was actually inviting me to understand the issues. Then the Eurasian Mixed-Blood journalist arranged all the papers in such a way that they just called out to be read. My hands grasped out at one page, another page, and another page. I examined their appearance and typography, the columns, bent and untidily joined together, the wave-like interlinea, the uneven print.

'The typography!' I protested.

'Yes. Still not very good. The Dutch papers aren't perfect yet either. The point is the things that can be passed on to the Malay reader – issues that touch significantly the interests of the readers themselves. Not just things affecting Europeans.'

I understood all that he was saying. But my heart still wouldn't accept it.

'You could begin to learn to write in Malay, Minke,' Jean Marais began again.

'Yes, you can see for yourself' – now Kommer got his bit in – 'Malay is understood and read in every town, big and small, throughout the Indies. Dutch is not.'

I was still examining the Malay-language newspapers. There were too many advertisements and the serialised stories took too prominent a place on the front page. They all carried serials, most of them foreign.

'It won't be long, Mr Minke. Once you begin writing in Malay, you'll soon discover the key to it. That you have mastered Dutch so well is, of course, deserving of great admiration. But to write in Malay, your own people's language, is a sign of your love for your country and people.'

All of a sudden he stopped. He was probably preparing a whole new set of demands. So it was not only Mother, but also Jean Marais, also Kommer, who were making demands of me. And now Kommer – a person whose origins I knew nothing about at all – who knew if he was from heaven or earth – had appeared before me like a prosecutor with a shortage of victims. And I was not angered. And if I accepted these demands now, there could be no doubt that tomorrow or the day after other new demands would follow.

'Are you making demands of me, Mr Kommer?'

'Yes, I think, indeed, that is the case.'

'And do I not have the right to reject them?'

'Of course, Mr Minke. Look, he who emerges at the top of his society will always face demands from that society – it is his society which has allowed him to rise. You must know the Dutch proverb "The tall tree catches much wind." If you don't want to catch so much wind, don't grow so tall.'

'Where is there a tall tree that can turn away the wind?' Jean Marais backed Kommer up.

'The important thing, Mr Minke, is loyalty to one's own country and people.'

This Eurasian Mixed-Blood was getting more and more out of hand in his rudeness. Mother had argued the same point without pressuring or pushing. Kommer was not just asking, hoping, demanding. He was pushing me into a corner. And still he didn't seem satisfied. He added: 'Who gives a damn if Europeans want to read Malay or not? Just think about it: who will urge Natives to speak out if their own writers, such as yourself, won't do it?'

'Why do you write in Malay, Kommer?' It was my turn to interrogate. 'You are not a Native. You're more European than Native.'

He laughed. He didn't answer quickly. The whole of my attention was focussed on him. The skin of his face, burnt by the sun, shone with sweat. He groped in his pocket for a handkerchief, but he didn't wipe his face.

He rubbed his lips and the tips of his teeth. With a smile that was both a little upset and a little amused, he said, 'Look, Mr Minke, lineage is not important. Loyalty to this country and people, Sir. This is my country and my people: not Europe. Only my name is Dutch. It is not impossible for a non-Native to love this country and people. Look around you, Native society is so still, so quiet, so alone - they never speak with anyone outside themselves. Day and night their lives revolve around just one pivot, in the same space, in the same circle. Busy with their own dreams. Just the same thing over and over again. I'm sorry.'

His words were becoming more twisted and winding. And I was more and more caught up by them: 'An unbearable life, Mr Minke. Anyone who is aware of this condition must surely try to speak to them. To speak face to face with such a huge number of people is, of course, impossible. That is why I write, one person speaking to many.'

Whether he knew it or not, he was lighting my way, my life as a writer. I saw him anew, as a teacher without a name, a great man without origins. I respected him, even loved him, as if he were a part of my own body and brain. He had no hesitation in stating ideas he felt were true. He was a little prophet.

'Minke,' Jean Marais interrupted again, 'I can't express myself well. Mr Kommer speaks for me also. I too have hopes for you - my heart still can't bring itself to demand - you must speak to your own people. You are needed by your own people much more than you are needed by any other people anywhere. Europe and Holland will not miss your absence.' He was silent a moment as he looked at me, waiting for my anger to sweep down upon his head. 'See, you aren't angry with Mr Kommer, are you?' He was silent again, awaiting my reaction.

I didn't react at all. Kommer's words were as a great surging wave, moving, alive, shifting me away from earlier opinions.

'If I were a writer, I would write in my own language. Because I am a painter, my language is colour, a language between people, not between peoples.'

'So there is no need to study other peoples' languages, especially those of Europe?' I asked.

'Nobody has said that. Without studying the languages of other peoples, especially European languages, we wouldn't understand foreign peoples. And, equally, if you don't study your own language you can never understand your own people.' Kommer answered quickly, as if he had readied such a reply.

My question seemed childish, like foam frothed on the surging wave that was Kommer.

'And without knowing other peoples,' he continued without letting me regain my composure, 'we will never come to know our own society properly either.'

I felt like Romulus and Remus, the twins who founded Rome, being suckled by a wolf.

'Why aren't you saying anything, Minke?' Jean Marais returned with his own small wave. 'We are talking to your conscience, not just playing at moving our lips. Have you still an excuse for not writing in your own tongue?'

The great wave came again: 'People of whatever race who do not write in their own language are usually seeking their own self-satisfaction. They do not care about the needs of the people who give them life. Most of them do not know their own people.'

Do not know their own people! The accusation went too far; it was like a blow from a blunt adze. And it hurt even more that it came from people who weren't Natives: from an Indo and a Frenchman. In their eyes I didn't know my own people. Me!

'You still haven't spoken,' Jean pressed.

'He needs time to think things over, Mr Marais. Remember Multatuli, Mr Minke. "If the Dutch won't read or print my writings", he said, "I will translate them into Native languages – Malay, Javanese and Sudanese." He was your own teacher, and indeed he did go on to write in Malay.'

'You think I don't know my own people.'

'The truth is often painful. But that is it, more or less. From your articles, it seems that you know more about Dutchmen and Indos.'

'That's not true. I speak excellent Javanese.'

'That doesn't mean you know the Javanese people. Have you ever known the villages and hamlets of Java, where most of our people live? You've only passed through them. Do you know what the farmers of Java eat, your own country's farmers? Most Javanese are farmers. The Javanese peasant farmers are your people.'

'And what do you mean by "know"?' I grabbed at whatever straw I could to save myself from the surging wave around me.

Perhaps because he saw that my blood pressure was rising, Kommer headed off in another direction: 'I have another appointment. Mr Marais, where is the design for that panther trap?'

Marais pulled out the desk drawer and extracted a sheet of paper. 'This is the best possible, Mr Kommer. You will get that black one, if the animal does indeed exist.'

'Nah! Mr Minke, this is a trap to catch a panther. Please drop in to my home from time to time. I keep a number of different animals: tigers, crocodiles, snakes, monkeys, all kinds of birds . . . I like to watch their antics.'

'We will finish our discussion?'

'Another time, all right? Perhaps this isn't the right time. Yes, Mr Marais?'

'You catch these animals yourself?'

Kommer nodded.

'The panther is to be an addition to the collection?' I asked, relieved to be free of the wave's pounding.

'No, the German Consul has ordered one for the Berlin zoo. The wild black panther is the most dangerous of them all. It lives on the ground, amongst the brush, the tall grass and the trees. They can only be caught while asleep or if they are still cubs.'

'Where will you trap it?'

'In the forests around Sidoarjo. The panther is famous because of its black fur which is bluish, like hardened steel. With this design, I will get the carpenters of Sidoarjo to make a trap. Mr Marais, aren't these wheels too small?'

'No, the thing is that the trap musn't be too far off the ground. The measurements of these wheels are such that they will still be able to cope with uneven ground and channels or low embankments.'

'Right!' Kommer agreed. 'Nah, Minke, I would be honoured if you would join me in trapping this animal. You will have an opportunity to mix with your own people. Believe me, sir, I know these people better than you do. You will realise that there is too much that you don't know about them.' His words were confident and challenging, almost insolent.

Perhaps he was right; but his words weren't friendly. They offended, yet I was unable to refute them. I would test the truth of his boast. I would ask him whether he read Javanese writing or not. If he answered yes, I would ask which books he had read. If he answered no, I would have him cornered. But I hesitated, and he spoke first: 'Once you have come to know your people, sir, you will discover a source of material for your writings that will never dry up, an eternal source of material. Didn't Kartini, in one of her letters to her friend, once say that to write is a work for eternity. If the source is eternal, maybe then the writing will be eternal also.'

'You know a great deal about Kartini.'

'What can one do, sir – someone as important as her, her letters are being read everywhere.'

'When do you leave for Sidoarjo?'

'You are accepting my invitation?'

'When do you leave?'

'Tomorrow.'

'Good. Tomorrow we too are going to Sidoarjo.'

Kommer frowned on hearing the word *we*. Then his eyes twinkled: 'A coincidence,' he said.

'If possible I will join you, Mr Kommer. If possible. And you, Jean?'

'I must finish this painting. Who knows, perhaps one day it will end up in the Louvre? What do you think I should call it, Minke?'

' "The Flower that Closed the Century", Jean.'

Jean Marais went silent. Then his eyes shone with life: 'That gives me a new idea. The background, and the sparkle in her eyes must be adjusted. Also her lips, Minke; they must be able to talk about the century that has passed, and speak about the hope of the future.'

I didn't understand what he was talking about. 'You're the painter. It's up to you.'

'A painting has a language of its own, too, Minke.'

'Indeed your wife was too beautiful, Mr Minke, like the beauty we dream about,' Kommer said spiritedly.

'That is its form, Mr Kommer,' interjected Jean. 'Appreciation of a painting must not stop with the form. It must include the story contained in the brush strokes, the mood, the character, and the life created through the integration of the colours.'

Kommer gazed, head forward in incomprehension, like me, before this copy of Annelies. Jean Marais's eyes came alight as we listened to him. Though his Malay was limited, he was able to explain with the help of his eyes and the movements of his hands.

The longer he went on, the more I came to understand: the art of painting is a branch of learning all of its own, whose language cannot be understood by everyone. Better just to be quiet and listen. For the umpteenth time now, I thought: to graduate from H.B.S. only made you realise your own ignorance. You must learn to be humble, Minke! you, graduate from H.B.S! Your schooling doesn't amount to much after all . . .

Before setting off for the station, Darsam reminded me: 'Be careful, Young Master, guard Nyai well. This time I am not escorting her. Her safety is your responsibility now.'

'I will look after her, Darsam.'

Marjuki wanted to get the carriage moving. Mama stopped him and called Darsam. From on top of the carriage, she reminded him, 'You're in charge now, Darsam; be careful.'

Darsam smiled proudly, his moustache spreading: 'All under control, Nyai!'

'You're always saying "all under control, all under control". You haven't even got your moustache under control.'

It was true too. That great moustache of his wasn't symmetrical: one corner was drooping. Darsam's hand immediately went to his mouth, brushing back the moustache.

'Now tell me, all is under control.'

'Yes, Nyai, I forgot to tidy it up this morning, everything was done in such a hurry.'

' "Yes – yes – yes" is all you ever come out with when spoken to. Must

I be the one who has to check things every day? If even your moustache isn't looked after properly . . . look, what am I always telling you?'

'Yes, Nyai . . . If you feel spritely, then . . .'

'So you haven't forgotten. Perhaps because you weren't in such a big hurry. Marjuki, get going!'

The carriage left the front grounds. As we moved onto the main road, my mood changed. You don't know your own people! You don't know your own country! I felt shame and knew that it was deserved. I would redeem myself from these accusations which I could not deny. How many *kati* do you reckon that man with the scruffy black pants over there is carrying on his back? I don't know. He was carting a tall basket of peanuts. To whom will he sell it? I don't know. Where? I don't know. What is it worth? I don't know. Will it bring in enough money to provide food for, say, a week? I don't know. Don't know! Don't know! Is he strong and healthy enough to carry such a load? I don't know that either. Has he been forced to cart it? My ignorance showed its depths. What was the harvest from each hundred square metres? Crazy! These questions tormented my mind. Yes, and they all stemmed from observing just one man carting peanuts – you, you arrogant-hearted ignoramus! If your ignorance is so great that you can't answer any of these questions about this man, then all you must see is his body and his movements. It would be so embarrassing if you tried to write about him, hei! you big-headed writer!

Kommer was waiting at the station. I knew he had proposed to Mama. And would never get a reply. She hadn't even bothered to read his letter. He already had a wife and children. I had heard that his wife was also a Mixed-Blood. How he had got up the courage to propose, was something I could hardly understand. Wasn't he younger than Mama?

He ran about making sure he bought first-class tickets, as if he were richer than Mama. He stood with his back to me at the ticket window. I shifted my gaze from it – uh! that back which accused me of not knowing my own people and country! The platform was quiet, as usual. Several people sat on benches. Mama went into the first-class waiting room. I walked slowly along the platform. From one of the benches a woman could be heard reminding her husband that he should hide his white *haji* cap; it would attract attention. There was a railway regulation: Europeans, Chinese and haji were forbidden to travel third class. They had to travel first or second class. The man put his haji cap into a basket of souvenirs. His wife went off to buy their tickets. Her husband watched from his seat.

Was this the way to come to know your people? I laughed in my heart. I reckoned there must be more to it than this.

Once Kommer obtained the tickets, we quickly boarded our carriage. I sat next to Mama; Kommer sought a place opposite us.

'It's been more than twenty years since I've seen the villages,' Mama began. 'Perhaps nothing has changed in all this time.'

'Nothing has changed, Nyai; it is just the same,' Kommer responded, and then asked: 'People say Nyai comes from Sidoarjo. Is it true, Nyai?'

And so Nyai and Kommer became engrossed in conversation. You could tell the journalist was trying hard to find things to talk about, wanting to chat forever while the creaking train rocked on. He was trying to impress Mama with his education, with his interest in commerce, reading and agriculture, hunting, folk legend, and especially colonial politics.

I woke up because I heard my name mentioned; I didn't know in connection with what.

'I have suggested to Mr Minke that he write in Malay or Javanese. It seems he still has his doubts,' said Kommer.

'His own mother longs for him to write in the Javanese rhythm,' Mama explained.

'Nah, Mr Minke,' Kommer attacked as soon as he saw my eyes were open, – 'your own mother! None other than your own mother!'

His voice seemed to condemn my sleepiness. I wasn't even given a chance to yawn.

'Perhaps he's right, Child,' Mama joined in. 'When I read the works of Francis or Wiggers – senior and junior – and also those of Mr Kommer himself and Johannies, I feel Malay has a deliciousness of its own. You should try, I think.'

'There's no point in ending up being *forced* to write in Malay; why not start of one's own accord?' Kommer was getting carried away again.

'Why *forced*, Mr Kommer?' asked Mama.

'Forced, Nyai. Sooner or later, Native people will be greatly disillusioned by the Dutch colonial press, and they will be forced to write in their own language. The Dutch papers never discuss matters of concern to Natives, as though the only people in the Indies were Europeans. I reckon every honest writer will, in the end, be disappointed by them, Nyai.'

I watched them and watched them. They didn't talk about me any more. I think I fell asleep – giving Kommer a chance to show off his cock's plumage. He wouldn't ask about the fate of his proposal, I thought. And when I awoke again, he was asleep, propped up against the wall in the corner. Mama was looking out at the view. I'm embarrassed to admit it, but this was really the first time I ever took a proper look at my mother-in-law. In her own right, not in relation to Annelies. Her grace and beauty now revealed itself in its full naturalness. Nobody could say she looked old. Her cheeks were still full; There were no crow's feet at the corners of her eyes. She always dressed up as a businesswoman should. Her hair was always shining and the creases in her *kain* were never untidy. From the side she looked exactly like Annelies, only not quite as white and her nose wasn't as pointed. Her eyebrows were dense, which gave her eyes a sinister look.

Kommer was sleeping with his mouth open. One gold tooth sparkled at the corner of his lips. My heart beat anxiously: I hoped this manly and courageous newspaperman would not let saliva drip from behind his gold teeth. If Mama saw that, he might never get a reply to his proposal.

The train was very slow and stopped every other minute. First class and second class shared one carriage. All the passengers wore shoes or slipper-sandals. The second-class compartment carried passengers wearing slippers or sandals, no shoes. The third-class carriages were all 'chicken-clawed'. Pedlars going either to or from the markets walked up and down the carriage, accompanied by every kind of market smell; also flies. In first class there were only the three of us. In second class there were maybe ten Chinese and a haji who hadn't taken off his white haji cap.

There was so much dust and soot, it was guaranteed that passengers from all classes would leave the train with dirty clothes. In a number of places, when the train travelled slowly, I would see a gang of labourers repairing the railway tracks and a Eurasian seated on a horse, with a sword, keeping watch over them. The gangs were mobilised by the Native Civil Service and Village Heads, and the Village Heads also mobilised the farmers who worked on government-owned lands. Nobody was paid for this corvee work. They never received food, or money for transport. They even had to provide their own water for tea.

Had I been born a landless farmer, perhaps I too would have been among those being supervised by the Mixed-Blood on his horse. And perhaps his knowledge wasn't any better than that of a village child who looked after the buffalos. Perhaps too I would have been spat upon by one of the overseer's assistants, a village official in his black shirt, his batik kain, with his *destar* on his head and his *keris* at his back. But I was not a tenant farmer working government land. The comparison made me feel fortunate, and that I had the responsibility to be compassionate towards them. Responsible: because these feelings of mine arose not from the heart, but from the mind. You are right, Kommer; as soon as I start paying them attention, all kinds of ideas and thoughts, and not just material for later moulding, arise impressively before me. It is likely that among that corvee gang there are people with skills that neither the overseer nor his assistants have. Perhaps there are *gamelan* makers or experts in making wayang puppets, perhaps experts in Javanese literature. At the very least, they are all master farmers. Their miserable fate is caused only by the fact that they have no land of their own.

I knew for certain that besides being liable for corvee, they would also be conscripted to take part in night patrols and guarding the village, and in emergency collective labour if something had to be done in the public interest. They would have to pay tribute to their chiefs. Their chickens and eggs could be confiscated whenever some chief they had never seen before came visiting their village.

I had known all this since I was small. But only now, travelling along in the train, did they abruptly become real inhabitants of my thoughts. From Multatuli's novel *Saidja and Adinda*, I knew about the suffering of these peasants; but that knowledge had never lived in my mind as it did now. People also said that the peasants had to pay eggs and chickens and coconuts and fruit and herbs, which the Village Head would take with him each time he sought audience with the Ndoro Wedono, the Native District Chief. Sometimes the chiefs would voice the need, and the village officials would collect special tribute from the peasants to buy a cow or goat on his behalf. It all came from the peasantry, who owned nothing except their hoes and their labour.

The anonymous tract Magda Peters had given me spoke about them as the cork upon which the kingdom of the Netherlands floats. And what kind of cork-float? The pamphlet said it was a cork that will be forced to sink one day when its buoyancy has been soaked up. The whole of the kingdom's and the colony's life floated upon that cork. Any and every foot could step upon its head and shoulders, just as the Governor-General Daendels had literally done long ago, and they, the peasants, would accept every burden without protest. They would not complain, it went on to say, because for centuries they had known only one kind of fate: the fate of a peasant.

As soon as we entered the area around Sidoarjo, sugar cane enveloped the train, nothing but sugar cane, rippling in waves like a green sea upon purple-green sands. All of it would be cut and carried off to the sugar mills. This, it seemed, was the land where Nyai Ontosoroh was born. Everything centred on sugar. Even so, not everything tasted sweet. Mama's own experiences had already proved that. Perhaps I shall be able to discover other things . . .

Our destination was the family of Sastro Kassier, Mama's elder brother. I did not know much about him. From what I knew I wrote up these notes:

The plague had attacked the village of Tulangan. Every day people fell down sprawled out, dead, including Dr Van Niel, who was brought in from Surabaya. The Tulangan clinic, just a three-by-four-metre room, could do nothing. After burying their neighbours each morning, people would roll over and join their friends in death.

Sastrotomo, Sanikem's father, died; his children too, except for Paiman, Sanikem's elder brother. He ran away from the house to escape the epidemic that was sweeping down all around him. He knew his father and brothers and sisters had not been buried yet. He ran. Ran.

He didn't realise it then, but the plague bacteria had already began to multiply within him.

He wandered aimlessly. In the evening he collapsed in the darkness far outside the sugar factory complex. He knew he must keep walking but his strength was gone. He rolled his body under a tamarind tree. He remembered that the tree stood at an intersection. The narrow road to the right led to the graveyard. He did not want to end up there. He must live. He did not want to die just yet.

His body was burning with fever. Pain tormented his extremities. The night was dense with darkness; there was no wind. Those eyes, ah, why are those eyes always pulled towards the graveyard? How many of his aquaintances had been planted there like mandarin seedlings? and mangos and guavas? – seedlings that would never grow or sprout, vanishing, sucked up by the earth. Twenty people? Twenty-five? He could not count. His head was aflame.

In the darkness and stillness of the night, he could see from time to time tongues of fire leaping up from the graveyard, as if blown up into the sky to pierce the darkness of the windless night. They reached their peak, then fell back in a long curve, so long – as if they were flying away to vanish into nowhere. He saw too other fiery flames pointing back down towards the villages, including Tulangan.

He was afraid. And his body could not carry out its longing to be away from this frightening place. There was only one thing that proved he was still alive: the never-subsiding shout in his heart – live, live, I must live, live, live!

The morning dew woke him. In some obscure way, he felt that the dew had subdued his fever. As the sun began its ascent, he found himself approached by an old man. He heard the old man's voice, full of compassion, whisper: 'So young as this! It's not the right time for you to die yet, Child. You probably have never even been out of our village before now.'

The man wore a white beard and moustache. Paiman wanted very much to ask for help, but even his tongue would not work for him.

He dimly saw the old grandfather take down his woven rattan shoulder bag. From inside it he took a bottle. He poured something into Paiman's mouth, then went away. Almost four hours later, he returned and poured liquid from the bottle into Paiman's mouth once more. Like some god who had descended from heaven, the old man looked healthy and fresh amid the squalor of the epidemic. There was no fear in his face.

The bottle was empty. He put it back in his bag.

Paiman was saved because of that liquid. He didn't know what the old man had made him drink the second time; it tasted like kerosene. Several more times the old man returned to minister to him.

That was Paiman, who was now called Sastro Kassier, and he was more successful than Sastrotomo, his father, the father of Sanikem alias Nyai Ontosoroh.

Sastrotomo never succeeded in becoming paymaster. He was never thought worthy of consideration. Because he knew that the new manager would not adhere to the agreement made between Sastrotomo and Herman Mellema, Mellema went to Tulangan to ask that Sastrotomo's son be taken on as an apprentice clerk. He was to be trained so that later he could become a cashier. Mellema did not tell Mama about this act of conscience of his.

The new manager of the sugar factory had come to Wonokromo a few times. Herman Mellema used such opportunities to pass on 'aid' to his 'brother-in-law'. It was through such visits that Mama eventually found out: her elder brother had quickly advanced from being a clerk, to an apprentice cashier, and then had become full cashier.

Silently, Mama felt proud to have a brother who had achieved such a high position – the only Native paymaster in a sugar factory in all of Java.

On the day of his promotion, the factory put on a small *slametan*. Paiman, who had changed his name when he married Sastrowongso – meaning Descendant or With the Blood of a Scribe – announced a new name change: Sastro Kassier with two *s*'s. His new name was published in the newspapers as a Determination of the Governor-General.

He had eight children.

Several times Paiman alias Sastrowongso alias Sastro Kassier came to Wonokromo. Mama always received him happily. But as time went on, his visits became less and less frequent. His own position was becoming stronger. After Herman Mellema's death, he was never seen again at Wonokromo.

He did come with his whole family when Annelies and I were married. That time too, Mama received him very affably. His youngest child, a girl, was two or three years younger than Annelies. Twice I saw her from a distance. I guessed that was how Sanikem looked when she was a maiden. Her body, as well as her face, eyes, lips, and nose, were all exactly the same.

From the moment we boarded the train I suspected: perhaps Mama isn't going to Sidoarjo for a holiday but to ask for Sastro Kassier's permission for his youngest daughter, Surati, and me to marry. No, Ma, it would be impossible for Minke to marry and to live with a woman who was still pure Javanese. Impossible, Ma. I don't mean to insult my Mother or any woman who is still fully Javanese in their thoughts and customs. But I must make my own choice. You too, Ma, would never be able to take a husband who was still fully a Native. European ideas, whether a little or a lot, have

changed the way we look at things, have provided us with new require-
ments that must be met. And the matter of husband and wife wasn't just
one of man and woman. You know that too, Ma. If the purpose of this
visit is indeed to propose on my behalf – however beautiful and honourable
are your intentions – you must forgive me: I cannot marry her. I just
couldn't do it!

These suspicions and presentiments made me anxious, vigilant. On the
other hand Mama seemed quite merry, like a young girl. Like a butterfly
emerging from its cocoon, she lost that gloomy fearsomeness which had
dominated her all this time. She was becoming gayer, she laughed, smiled
and chattered. She was no longer engrossed in her business which was soon
to be stolen away by Maurits Mellema.

There was no one from Sastro Kassier's family to meet us at the station.
Mama had not told them of our visit. Kommer hailed a *dokar* and offered
to escort us to Tulangan. Mama laughed and refused: 'Tulangan is still
a long way from here, Mr Kommer.'

'I know Tulangan, Nyai.'

'Yes?'

'It is no more than ten kilometres,' he said.

'You can come and visit if you like. But not now, please.' And our dokar
trotted off towards Tulangan.

Sugar cane, sugar cane, sugar cane for almost the whole length of our
journey. The unshirted farmers stopped along the road to take a look at
who was riding in the dokar. Small, stark naked children, wet-nosed, filthy,
were playing along the edge of the road, looking after livestock. I would
be among them, had I been born into a farmer's family.

'This is what my country is like, Child. Only cane. It is true what you
said; everything revolves around sugar, whether evil or dreams. There are
more than ten sugar mills in my country, Nyo. When the factory starts to
mill, there's a big festival, nothing but festivals and parties. Everyone
stakes their wealth and their reputations as fighters. Everywhere people lay
sprawled in the streets, drunk. And on the gambling mats, children, wives,
younger brothers and sisters, all change hands as the wages of bets. You
need to have a look at one sometime. It's a pity the milling season isn't
about to start.'

The dokar driver tried to turn around, to catch the words he couldn't
understand. He asked 'Yes, *Ndoro?*'

'No, Man, I wasn't speaking to you.'

I was amazed that Mama followed Dutch practice and called the driver
Man. The word did indeed mean 'man' or 'person', yet I sensed that it still
contained an derogatory element: it was used only when talking to lower-
class men. The problem was that there was no neutral way to speak to such
people in Javanese and Malay. Perhaps this is an aspect of the poverty of

my mother tongue, a poverty that forces people to accustom their hearts to the constant degrading of others? Uh! why does my mind go crazy like this? why won't it stop looking for work?

'Tomorrow or the day after, Child, you can take a look at the villages. Didn't you say yesterday that Kommer had accused you of not knowing your own people? Actually I feel he was accusing me too. He is not totally mistaken. Perhaps he was a bit extreme, but I understand what he meant. He loves all that is Native so much, except their deficiencies and ignorance. He loves all that was ever possessed, created or known by his mother's ancestors. On the train, he spoke with tremendous enthusiasm about the *candi* temples. He said that he once invited Jean Marais to go on a trip with him to see some. Jean laughed. He didn't understand what a candi was. Kommer tried to explain. Jean only laughed more. Kommer became cranky, and took his revenge by belittling the monuments of France that the rest of world so glorifies.'

Not an interesting subject. Suddenly Mama asked 'Have you ever seen a candi? Neither have I. They were built to last forever; there must be something about them that their builders wanted to immortalise.'

The conversation was becoming even less interesting.

'Have you ever read anything about Paris? about France?'

'Nothing specifically, no, Ma.'

'I don't know why, but sometimes that country interests me very much. I can't imagine what it is like, but I'm still interested.'

Perhaps it was Jean Marais that Mama was really interested in. But I didn't say anything.

'And Kommer?'

'What about Kommer?'

'What do you think of him?' I asked, fishing.

'He has a lot of enthusiasm. That's all. A little while, five or ten years maybe, and you will far outshine him.'

'Ma, I don't mean that.'

'Sst! You'd be pleased if I accepted his proposal?'

'What is it that Ma wants?' Mama's face went red like that of an inexperienced maiden. How happy she was at that moment.

It seemed that Sastro Kassier was very well known in Sidoarjo. The dokar driver knew exactly where his house was. It was a stone house, a respectable house. It was located on the Tulangan sugar-mill complex. Sastro Kassier was the only Native to have a house inside the complex.

The front door was closed, but the windows were open. Beyond the curtains could be seen a reception area that wasn't at all small, and furniture one usually finds in the houses of Europeans. The differences were few: no books were in evidence, whereas in a European house they usually took pride of place among the furniture.

'Yu! Yu Djumilah!' Nyai called out several times. She was calling for her sister-in-law, the wife of Sastro Kassier. I had never seen her, though she had come to my wedding, but I knew her husband.

A woman, looking much older than Mama, opened the door. She stood there not understanding what was happening.

'Yu Milah, have your forgotten me? Sanikem?'

'Ai!ai! Sis Ikem, is this Sis Ikem? ai! ai! come in. Come in. Still so young too?' She ran hither and thither welcoming us, and invited us to sit on the settee of which they were so proud.

'Yes, this is how we live. Please don't compare it to your building, Sis Ikem.'

The dokar driver took down all our things and carried them inside the house. Djumilah herself prepared a room. She came back into the parlour and began again: 'Yes, just a simple room, please don't be disappointed,' she always spoke in Javanese, the only language she knew. 'You must be very tired. Let me get you something to drink,' and she disappeared to the back.

Not long after that a pock-marked girl came out, bending and bowing as she brought out a tray of drinks. She went down on her knees as she approached us.

From the back came Djumilah's voice: 'Have a drink, Sis. There just happens to be water boiling.'

The pock-marked girl put the drinks out on the table, shifting them to their right places.

Nyai got up from her chair and had a look around. Above one of the doors were two pictures of Her Majesty Wilhelmina, a sign that here lived two graduates from the Factory School. No doubt two of Sastro Kassier's children, and it was unusual for children – boys or girls – from small towns like Tulangan to go to school.

After having a good look around, Nyai went to the other room. I could hear Djumilah's voice, loud and harsh, but friendly: 'Yes, Sis, this shirt was woven in Gedangan. There are no weavers in Tulangan. There is no cotton grown here. Very nice?' Laughter. 'If you'd like, I'll order one for you later . . . yes-yes, I'm amazed too, Sis, why the factories over there don't want to make shirts like this. They'd be much better too of course.'

They came out together. Then Djumilah took Mama's suitcase and my suitcase into a room. I looked at Mama for a second. I heard her hiss: 'Stupid woman!'

The basket of souvenirs had been carted into the kitchen by the dokar driver.

As soon as Djumilah re-emerged from the room, she said: 'Ah, you've stayed home, Sis Iken. Sir, please feel free to change your clothes and rest up.'

'I want to see out the back first.' Nyai stood up again and Djumilah took her to the back part of the house.

I was left alone there with my heart in turmoil – I was thought to be Mama's new man! Perhaps worse than that: the kept man of a Nyai. Why didn't Mama put things right straight away when only one room was prepared? Why did she merely hiss 'stupid woman'? At least it would be good material for a story. I laughed, seeing the funny side of it.

They came in again and sat down, still chattering away and laughing about I don't know what. I was silent, meditating on what I heard. Usually the male guest is received by the man of the house in the front parlour and the female guests by his wife in the back parlour or kitchen. The host wasn't here, so I was now included among the female guests. Another funny side to this awful situation.

The pock-marked girl came in again, bowing and bending as before. Now she put out some of the sponge cake we had brought from Wonokromo. At that moment Mama put the following question to Djumilah: 'Lha! *Yu*, where is Surati? I didn't see her out the back there just now.'

'Surati? Alaa, *Nduk*,' she shouted out shrilly, 'Even your auntie doesn't recognise you any more!'

The pock-marked girl, curling her lip, bowed down: 'It is I, Surati,' she whispered. 'Yes, Aunt, pocked like this is how I am now.'

I too was startled. This was Surati, that pretty girl I had seen twice before. Marked with big broad pocks, some deep and blackish.

'Alah-alah! Nduk,' Nyai stood up and pulled the girl up too. 'How could this happen to you?'

'It is my fate, Aunt.'

'It was her father's doing, Sis Ikem's own brother, a man with no backbone. He wanted to follow in Sastrotomo's footsteps, and sell his own daughter to the *Tuan Besar Kuasa* Factory Manager!' Djumilah burst out.

'What? Paiman?' Nyai was suddenly in a fury. 'Paiman could do that to his daughter? Didn't he know what I had to suffer? Sit here, Nduk!'

Surati sat down, bowing her head as custom required a young girl to do before her elders, especially before a man she had never met before.

Djumilah began to screech out curses on her husband, like a stream of river water which had found a free path in the steepest part of the gully. Every now and then her words would be punctuated by a shrill shout from Nyai: 'A child as pretty as her, as sweet as her, look how she is now!'

Silently I followed the three women's conversation. Their questions and answers provided the structure of a story. Mama was overcome by the fire of her emotions. Back here in the environment from which she originally came, she seemed for a moment no more educated than Djumilah, thrown about by waves of excessive emotion. While Surati told her the story as if it were the story of someone else's life; as though she had never felt sorrow or regrets at the loss of her handsomeness.

They kept on talking. Mama groaned, accused, attacked; she laughed and smiled no more. The experiences of this once-beautiful blossom of Tulangan, the story of how she came to be pock-marked like this, unattractive to anyone, even to Mama and me, formed the basis of a great short story. It truly moved me and I wanted to write it. I promised myself that I would immortalise her suffering, even if the story was similar to Mama's own.

They talked and talked for more than an hour. They forgot I was there with them. Then the factory whistle reminded us all that it was already five o'clock. The cane workers in the fields now knew the working day was over.

'Ah, Tuan hasn't been able to rest yet?' Djumilah said in a tone that asked forgiveness. 'Sis, Ikem, please show Sir into the room . . .'

'I see there is another room, he can use that one,' said Nyai.

'Why must you be separated?' protested Djumilah.

'Don't be stupid! This is Annelies's husband!'

'Oh, ah, oh, Annelies's husband! ya-ya, and how is Annelies – people say she was taken to Holland?'

'She's fine, Yu.'

'No news yet?'

'Oh, yes.'

'Well, I had better prepare another room.'

Then I realised: her own sister looked upon Nyai as a woman of low morals. I ahemmed. So that unspoken matter was now resolved. I got a room of my own, perhaps Surati's.

As I settled into that room, with its tidy bed and clean linen, I began to muse upon how disappointed Mama must be. Pity on her, that woman who wanted to tie me down. She would not try to marry me to Surati now. Her failure was an omen: I would soon be able to escape from Surabaya and Wonokromo.

Twilight arrived. The lights came on and I suddenly realised: electricity! For several minutes I stood gazing in admiration at the globe that gave off light but burnt no oil, no gas, no wick. I thought of Edison and I bowed my head in his honour. I had now actually enjoyed two of his discoveries, the phonograph and the electric light bulb. And I was actually seeing an electric light bulb itself, not just a picture in a newspaper or magazine.

After I bathed, instead of taking the usual afternoon stroll, I began to note down the story of Surati's life. But I wasn't able to do it in peace. All of a sudden I heard Mama, running amok with words – and a man's low voice occasionally responding. Sastro Kassier had arrived home and was feeling Mama's wrath.

There was silence at the dinner table that evening and an atmosphere of enmity. I withdrew from the table before the battle began again.

It was Djumilah's voice that first broke the silence in my room: 'You were always a man without a backbone. Like a wayang puppet that's lost its stick. It's lucky there's not a war on. How would you behave if you had to go to war, heh?'

'Nothing but the descendant of a slave!' Mama re-entered the fray.

'You keep out of this, Sanikem. You've done all right as a nyai,' Paiman alias Sastrowongso alias Kassier answered.

'No! You're the one who benefited from my sale as a nyai. You were made a clerk!'

'But you're doing all right too!'

'I'm doing all right now because I've worked and fought hard, not because I was made into a nyai! Idiot!'

I closed the door, and my ears too, and went on writing my notes . . .

7

These are the notes I made about what happened to Surati, rearranged and rounded out with further material.

The citizens of Tulangan were busy preparing for a party to farewell the Tuan Manager, Tuan Besar Kuasa. His contract had expired. As soon as his replacement arrived, he would set off for Surabaya, among much festivity. He wanted to leave the people with something nice to remember. To the employees whom he was leaving, he would keep saying: 'May my replacement be better than I. Please help him!'

All the employees, workers and other ordinary citizens held the same hope. The Manager of the sugar mill was a powerful man in Tulangan; more powerful than the *Bupati*, Assistant Resident or even the Resident. He was a little king. People said his wage was bigger than that of the Governor-General. Though people didn't bow down and abase themselves before him, as they had to before a bupati, *patih* or *wedana*, his word was law. The old people of the village could still tell the story of the first Tuan Kuasa, the one whom Herman Mellema replaced, and how he ordered the execution of seven farmers who rebelled and refused to surrender their land. Five others had died of fright after carrying out orders to remove stones from the temples to be used as the foundation of giant constructions for the factory.

The laugh of a Manager is something that puts people at ease; his threat is something else: the plantation supervisors, foremen, office employees, even the coolies, will obey him without question. At the crook of his finger, people will come; with just an ahem, people can be knocked to the ground.

The Manager of the sugar mill, Tuan Besar Kuasa: a man with a tongue of fire.

So it was the time for preparations for the arrival of the new Manager. The hand-over ceremony was attended by the Controller and Ndoro Bupati of Sidoarjo. Two hours after the ceremony, the new and the old Managers came out from the office and went among the festive throng. The gong sounded, and the party began. At the same time, carriages were readied to escort the old Manager as he left Tulangan.

The party itself was kept going with hired *joged* dancers, with palm wine and with dice and brawling.

The new Tuan Manager was called Frits Homerus Vlekkenbaaij. He accompanied his predecessor as far as Sidoarjo railway station. As soon as he returned he strode into the partying crowd. Through an interpreter he rebuked: 'What kind of infidel's party is this? Such noise – barbaric! Everyone leave! Go! Quickly!'

Everyone realised at once that gloomy clouds hovered before them.

Mijnheer Frits Homerus Vlekkenbaaij was not at all tall, not even compared to Natives. His body was like a ball, with a bloated stomach – the stomach of someone who always sat and did no physical work. His eyes were deep, and peered from out under his eyelids, a greenish yellow, but clear, like marbles. He was the first European to appear there in public wearing short-sleeved shirts and short trousers, so that his dense, long, blond body hair was visible. He was bald; his cheeks were round and loose. His heavily lidded eyes gave the impression that he never slept at the right time. He kept to himself, avoiding speech except to spray abuse at people (though his lips weren't thick and heavy enough to be frightening).

Not only the coolies and villagers, but especially the office employees and foremen were frightened of his power. It was the Mixed-Blood employees who whispered to the villagers and coolies: the new Tuan was '*Plikemboh*' – 'Ugly Penis'. The name stuck. The women would look away or giggle, covering their mouths, whenever they heard that name.

From the time of the party a tense atmosphere oppressed all of Tulangan – villagers, employees and labourers. Plikemboh seemed capable of doing anything, to anyone – Native, Pure or Mixed-Blood. The workers and office employees, as usual, reacted in their normal way: they would accept any treatment as long as they weren't dismissed.

Plikemboh understood that people were afraid of him. He was pleased. Now he was really someone. He was feared; he was master. He didn't have to work. Fear was his trusted foreman. He was rarely seen at his desk. His only order during the whole first month was: tighten the supervision over the manufacture of spirits and hard drink.

Plikemboh was a drinker and a drunkard. Yet he never drank what he had manufactured himself. So one or two sample bottles of drink from his own factory were brought to him, and he would sniff them to assess their alcoholic content.

In the second month he started to wander around outside the complex. He would visit the cane plantations and the factory's electricity plant. He liked to stand watching the plant's steam generator, proud that it was the very first in the Surabaya area. He would walk around carrying an air rifle with which he hunted birds. He didn't ride horses – unusual for a sugar-mill manager.

In the late afternoons he could be seen sitting in front of his house, perhaps half-drunk, with the air rifle on his table. He would take aim and shoot at any Native child who passed by on the street. Soon all the children were afraid of him. They would run away as soon as he appeared in the distance, carrying his rifle. So began the practice that mothers would use his name to frighten disobedient children.

Whenever he spent time outdoors, his face went very red, like that of a hen about to lay an egg. His head hardly ever turned, as if it were just a piece of twisted fire-wood.

Everyone knew he was a bad shot. He never took home a single bird. Whenever he went hunting a black leather bag hung from his shoulder. People guessed the bag had never held a bird, only a bottle of brandy.

After realising that the birds would always elude his black leather bag, Plikemboh became bored with his rifle. Now he discovered a new kind of hunting: entering the homes of the Natives who lived near the factory complex, opening the doors to their rooms, their cupboards, even their cooking pots and rice-steamers. His reasoning was that Natives could not be trusted; they were all thieves, or half-thieves, smugglers of contraband, manufacturers of illegal whisky. He never found what he was looking for. Then he began to worry the women. People began to lock their doors and wouldn't open them even if he pounded on the door.

Both men and women felt disgust whenever near Tuan Plikemboh. Not just because of his appearance; more so because of his character. Wherever he was present, people felt the air to be polluted. His body hair, his bloatedness, his transparent eyes, his glistening baldness . . .

One day Djumilah cried out startled. Plikemboh had entered the house, perhaps through a window. Djumilah ran to the back part of the house, into the kitchen. All the boys were at school. The girls were in the kitchen. Plikemboh came into the kitchen too. The girls, in a daze, scattered in every direction, running faster even than their mother.

Djumilah ran out into the back yard. She shivered; she was unable to speak. She saw Surati pulling up water from the well, ready to do the family washing. Her mother signalled her to run. The girl didn't understand. Plikemboh had rushed out and reached the well. Now he stood before Surati, who was shaking with fear, unable to stand up any longer.

In the distance she could hear Djumilah calling for help. People came running. Seeing Tuan Besar Kuasa up to one of his tricks again, they all disappeared, guarding their own fates.

Fear and revulsion made Surati shiver and collapse into a squat. Seeing this, Plikemboh didn't know what to do. He slunk away behind the other houses and disappeared from view.

Only then did the neighbours return to Surati. They picked her up and carried her to the kitchen sitting-bench and changed her wet, stinking *kain*. Her face was white and she still couldn't speak.

The Tuan Manager, carrying his shoulder-bag, descended again to the main road and returned to his office. From his books he found out that house number fifteen was occupied by the Sastro Kassier family. He summoned the Paymaster. Before coming to the Indies he had prepared himself by learning a little Malay from a retired Controller. The conversation took place in Malay:

'You are Sastro Kassier?'

'Yes, Tuan Besar Kuasa.'

'You are the Paymaster here?'

'Yes, Tuan Besar.'

'You have worked here a long time?'

'More than fourteen years, Tuan Besar Kuasa.'

'How many wives do you have?'

'Only one, Tuan Besar Kuasa.'

'Liar. No Javanese like you has only one wife.'

'On my life, Tuan Besar Kuasa, only one.'

'How many children?'

'Eight, Tuan Besar.'

'Good. Do you have a virgin daughter?'

Sastro Kassier sat up, startled. The father in him warned him to be careful. The beginning of some catastrophe hovered before his soul's eye. But there was no way to avoid answering. All his children were listed in the company books. He would lose his position straight away if he was discovered to be lying. He admitted he did have one. Plikemboh asked about her age, her schooling, everything about Surati except her name.

'Good. You can go now.'

Sastro Kassier returned to his work. He was anxious. He thought of sending his daughter away to Wonokromo. Impossible. From the Eurasian-owned Malay-language press, he knew that Sanikem herself was in trouble. His youngest niece, Annelies, was under the threat of being taken off to the Netherlands under guardianship. He knew too what a big affair that had become. He had wanted to go to Wonokromo to ask about it and at least to show his sympathy. He had hesitated, and ended up not leaving. Now it was impossible to take Surati there.

In the afternoon, after work, he was summoned again by Tuan Manager. He was received in Plikemboh's house. He was served cakes and alcohol. He couldn't refuse any of the things offered to him, afraid of exciting Plikemboh's wrath. All that he drank and ate there he felt was poisoning him, destroying his whole world.

Not a single person knows what they said to each other. Neither Sastro Kassier nor Plikemboh have ever spoken about it to anyone else.

It was evening when he returned home. His wife greeted him roughly – the first time he had ever been treated that way by her: 'Look out, you, if you try anything crazy with that Plikemboh!' she threatened.

He realised that the whole of Tulangan knew what was happening. That night he didn't eat, but went straight to his room. He couldn't sleep either. His eyes blinked open and shut like those of an old doll.

No paymaster was ever popular. It was the same with Sastro Kassier. The labourers suspected that he and the foremen conspired to take a ten per cent cut from their wages. None of the coolies could read or write. They could only frown, distrust, hate, make threats behind the backs of those concerned. Sastro Kassier indeed needed the money – for gambling, and to pay for his mistresses, an honoured custom among Native employees.

But one's position – that was everything to a Native who was neither farmer nor tradesman. His wealth might be destroyed, his family shattered, his name dishonoured, but his position must be saved. It was not just his livelihood; with it also went honour, and self-respect. People would fight, pray, fast, libel, lie, force their bones to the limit, bring disaster down on others, all for Position. People were prepared to give up anything for Position, because, with it, all might be redeemed. The closer Position took a person to the Europeans, the more he was respected. Even if all he owned was his one *blangkon* hat. Europeans were the symbol of unlimited power, and power brings money. They had defeated the kings, the sultans and the princes of Java, and the *ulamas* and the *jawara*. Man and things they subjugated without the slightest quiver of fear.

The next morning Paiman alias Sastro Kassier was called before Plikemboh again. Once again their conversation remained a secret to themselves. That night Sastro Kassier did not come home. He walked and walked through the villages to the north of Tulangan, like a burglar without a job. He thought and he didn't think. He prayed and then forgot what he prayed for. He did not make the rounds of his mistresses. He did not pick up the cards. He had resolved to cleanse himself of all such pollution. He neither drank nor ate. He walked and walked. He did not sleep; just walked.

He went back to his office after bathing in the river and meditating on top of a rock. He would work through the day without visiting home. As soon as he unlocked the door to his office, a messenger arrived: 'An order from Tuan Besar Kuasa: as soon as Ndoro Paymaster arrives he must report immediately.'

His meditation and ascetic exercises of the night before had not been blessed. Already Plikemboh was calling for him. His heart was still in turmoil. Now people would find out what the two of them talked about. A young coolie was scrubbing the office floor with carbolic acid.

'Eh, Sastro Kassier have you come up with an idea yet?'

'Not yet, Tuan Besar Kuasa,' he answered.

'Why not?' he mispronounced his Malay.

'I haven't dared discuss it with my wife, Tuan Besar.'

'Don't you know yet who Vlekkenbaaij is?'

'I know, Tuan Besar, I know very well.'

'How come then you haven't spoken with your wife yet?' he said in even worse Malay.

'Afraid, Tuan Besar.'

'And not afraid of me?'

Sastro Kassier was afraid of them both. He didn't answer.

'So then bring this wife of yours to see me. Why are you still here? Ayoh! bring her here to me! Ayoh! Get going!'

'She's *tetirah* to another village, Tuan Besar Kuasa.'

'What's this tetirah?'

'Gone, Tuan Besar, gone to rest at her mother-in-law's.'

Vlekkenbaaij's eyes popped out. His forefinger wagged up and down as it pointed threateningly: 'Watch out if you're lying. You'll regret it later. Get to work!'

Sastro Kassier went to his work. His anxiety did not prevent him from preparing his accounts. Tomorrow, Saturday, was payday. After finishing this, he recklessly reported sick and went home early.

His wife was not at all surprised to see her husband not sleeping at home. That indeed was the way of a man with position. She would never ask where he'd been. It was not the custom of a wife to challenge a husband who had position. Indeed even without her ever challenging him, she could be kicked out without *talaq*, a formal divorce. In some matters, the wife of a man with position might dare ask something, but never concerning her husband's 'leisure'. She was silent, silent in every way, feeling indeed inadequate in her inability to serve her husband as he desired.

Now Djumilah prepared something to eat, even though the day was still young. But Sastro Kassier did not eat. He pulled his wife over and ordered her to sit on the chair beside him.

'Don't think you can trick me,' she erected battlements around her daughter.

'He wants to see you.'

'No.' Djumilah knew she would be powerless once faced with Plikemboh himself.

'It's true; he wants to see you.'

'I cannot. Rather than my child be sold ... Shameful. Times have changed. That kind of thing shouldn't happen any more.'

Sastro Kassier knew his wife's answer was a challenge to divorce her. 'Then you should go away.'

'No. I will defend my daughter.'

'Surati!' called Sastro Kassier. The girl came out and squatted, bowing before her father. 'You know what's happened. What do you say?'

'Pay no attention to your father!' Djumilah incited her daughter. 'You mustn't be like Sanikem, your aunt. May God forgive her.'

'Sanikem is now richer than the Queen of Solo,' Sastro Kassier contradicted. 'Surati could be rich like that too. Well, Rati?'

'The mouth of Satan! Don't answer, Child, don't!'

'Yes, she doesn't have to answer. But both of you have a duty to understand how things are.'

'Don't listen.'

'Tuan Besar Kuasa,' Sastro Kassier went on, not heeding the protests of his wife, ' has ordered that I hand you, Surati, over to him. He wants to take you as his mistress. That's enough. That's all you need to know from your father. It's up to you whether you want to reject him or accept. If you don't want to answer, that's all right too. Nah! go!'

Surati left.

'Satan!' cursed Djumilah. 'Do you think I gave birth to her so she could become someone's concubine? You were always a man without backbone!'

'Don't make me angry. I'm still meditating, trying to find an answer to this.' Now it was Sastro Kassier who shouted.

'Meditation! No need to meditate to know the answer: *No*! and the whole thing is over.'

'It's not as simple as that.'

'Are you afraid of becoming a farmer? A trader at the market? Ashamed? If I were the man, that would be my answer: no!'

'What does a woman know? Your world is no more than the tamarind seed. A wrong step and all of this could fall apart.'

The whole day Sastro Kassier did not eat or drink. He left the house and walked and walked as he had the day before, across the dikes around the infertile paddy land which the village people still owned. The most fertile lands, all of them, had been taken over, rented by the mill, every cane season for eighteen months. Peasant farmers who rebelled courted disaster; the factory also controlled the Civil Service right down to the village officials.

The time of the full moon had passed. The night was shimmering with the half-light of its yellowish glow. The wind blew strongly. Sastro Kassier took no notice of the wind, of the moon, of himself. A sugar-mill official was one of the elect, one of the beloved of God. If that were not so, then could not any Native become a paymaster? Now he longed for an answer, one that didn't come from a human mouth, but from the realm of the supernatural, through some non-human being as an intermediary. Perhaps tonight some supernatural being was roaming the dark like him on this half-lit night. Perhaps this being might whisper the answer to him. And, indeed, if at that moment a goat had stood up on its two hind legs, or squatted, or rolled over, or sat legs tucked under as if at prayer, and spoke, and said: hai! Sastro Kassier, carry out the orders of Tuan Plikemboh; he would carry them out no matter what the consequences. As long as Sastro Kassier himself could not be held responsible for his own deeds, did not have to use his own brain. So long as the sign did not come from a human mouth, such as his own.

And if that goat said No!, he would never do what Plikemboh wanted, no matter what the cost.

For people like Sastro Kassier, Europeans were only one level below supernatural beings. And they could be found about the place almost any time you wanted one. But he would never dare contradict a European. Like the others, he preferred to hope for a supernatural being. They had to be obeyed as well, but they were much more difficult to find when you needed their advice.

Sastro Kassier had complete faith that he would not collapse or faint for lack of food and drink. Fasting too was a much honoured practice. But he came across nothing supernatural. As if nothing had happened, he turned up for work as usual the next morning. His duties at the office must be carried out as efficiently as possible.

He took out the key to his office. He started: the door wasn't locked! He searched his mind: had he forgotten to lock the door when leaving yesterday? He didn't go into his office. His eyes examined the steel latticed walls. It was impossible for anyone to get their hands through and undo the lock from inside. He could see the whole office inside. Everything was lying peacefully in its place. Who had opened the door?

He didn't feel he'd been negligent. He had locked the door when he went home yesterday. He could still remember the click as he had turned the key in the lock and said to the attendant that he was going because he had a headache. Wasn't it the attendant himself who had reminded him: don't forget the key, Ndoro?

Sastro Kassier was absolutely certain he hadn't forgotten. Locking up was one of his many responsibilities; he could not possibly have forgotten. He turned around and found yesterday's attendant on duty today as well – he was sitting on a bench in the corner. Sastro Kassier asked uncertainly: 'Who opened this door?'

'There hasn't been anyone, Ndoro.'

'Nah! Look, the door's already open. The key's still in my hand.'

· The attendant went pale, and didn't say anything.

'Go and get the night attendant.' He was sure now: someone had entered his office without permission. Only two people held a key: himself and Tuan Besar Kuasa. It was possible Plikemboh had come in and forgotten to lock up again. But if it were someone else using a copied key, and with evil intentions?

Half an hour later the night attendant arrived.

'You were on guard last night?'

'Yes, Ndoro.'

'Who entered my office?'

'Tuan Besar Kuasa, Ndoro.'

'You saw him yourself?'

'Yes, Ndoro.'

'Watch out if you're lying! What did he do inside?'

'I don't know, Ndoro. I came outside to keep watch on the other doors and windows.'

Sastro Kassier felt a bit calmer; yet his suspicions could not be put at rest. He went uncertainly into the office. From his desk drawer he took out his accounting books, anxious. He knew with great certainty: people might do anything for the sake of Position.

He opened his cash box. Yesterday he had sorted the money into piles for today's wages. All he had to do now was set it out on the table. He jumped back in shock. The cash box was empty, its lock undone, a gaping emptiness. He took another step back, his eyes wide open. He bumped into the next table.

'Attendant!' he shouted.

'Yes, Ndoro,' replied the attendant from behind the latticed wall.

'Look!' he shouted again. 'You are a witness! The cash box is empty. Someone has been in here and opened the cash box. You are a witness! The night attendant said Tuan Besar Kuasa came here last night. You're a witness! a witness!'

'Ndoro!' The attendant was shaking.

'You're the one who guards my office. Go and report to Tuan Besar Kuasa.' The attendant tottered off to find Plikemboh. 'Today there will be no wages, no pay!' Sastro Kassier cried hysterically.

People gathered around outside the latticed wall gasping at the sight of the open, empty cash box.

'No wages! The cash box has been emptied! Emptied! There will be no wages today, no pay for anyone!' Sastro Kassier shouted more and more hysterically as the crowd watched.

The office work stopped altogether. All came to have a look: European – both Pure and Mixed-Blood – and Natives. Not a single person dared enter the paymaster's office. Only two people had that right: Paymaster and Manager.

Sastro Kassier was still screaming hysterically when Frits Homerus Vlekkenbaaij arrived and growled: 'Shut your snout!' Immediately Sastro Kassier was silent.

384

Plikemboh entered through the crowd, which was parted by the aura of his power. Sastro huddled in a corner, his eyes unable to move from the gaping cash box.

'What's all this about, you, monkey Sastro Kassier?'

The Paymaster, no longer able to feel the sharpness of such an insult, reported nervously: 'Someone has broken into the office, broken into the cash-box.'

'You're the only one here.'

'Night attendant! Here!' shouted Sastro.

The night attendant pushed his face up against the iron lattice. 'Yes, Ndoro.'

'Ayoh! tell us: who was here last night?'

The attendant stared at Plikemboh for quite some time, and the Manager stared back at him with those marble-like eyes.

'No one, Ndoro. No one was here.'

'But what did you just tell me? You said Tuan Besar Kuasa was here last night. Now you're going back on what you said. The day attendant heard you. Day attendant!'

Now the day attendant pushed his face up against the partition. His eyes followed the look of the night attendant, to Plikemboh, to the Paymaster, then to the floor.

'You witnessed what the night attendant said to me.'

'Yes, Master, Ndoro.'

'Tell us what he said: that Tuan Besar Kuasa came in last night.'

'The night attendant said that no one entered here.'

'Liar! Both of them are liars!'

'You are the liar!' Plikemboh pointed to Sastro Kassier. 'What time did you go home yesterday? Eleven! Who inspected your things before you left? Attendant! Did you examine his things when he left, day attendant?'

'No, Tuan Besar.'

'Who can witness that you didn't take the factory's money? Who's your witness?'

'Who can witness that I *did* take the money?' Sastro Kassier protested weakly.

'Answer first: who can witness that you *didn't* take it?'

'There is no witness,' answered Sastro.

'So it was you who took it. Report this to the Marechausee!'

'Not yet, Tuan Besar Kuasa. Not yet! We must investigate who has been here first. Only Tuan Besar and I have keys. There are no signs that either the door or the cash-box lock have been forced. They must have been opened by the right key.'

'You dare accuse me? The Manager?'

'Who knows?' Sastro Kassier began to fight back. 'If it wasn't Tuan, it could only have been me. There is no one else who could have opened this cash box except us two.'

'Very well, let me just call in the Marechausee. We'll see you admit it all under their riding whips.' He started to move away, stopped, and called out, 'Karl, Karl!' When the person he had called arrived he gave the order in Dutch: 'Draw up a letter of accusation to give to the authorities, for the Marechausee too. Do it now. I'll take it to them myself.' And then speaking in Malay: 'Ayoh! everyone back to work! You too, monkey!'

The crowd dispersed. The Paymaster was left facing Plikemboh. The closest people to them were the day and night attendants. Both were pale. They were facing away from the Paymaster's office but their ears were alert, straining to hear.

'In short,' said Plikemboh, 'who took the factory's money is not the important thing now. What is important is that all wages due to the foremen and coolies must be paid today. Must be!'

'If there is no money, it's impossible.'

'That's your affair, Paymaster. Your name is Kassier isn't it, eh? The factory put its trust in you. It is your responsibility. How much was lost altogether?'

Without opening his books, the Paymaster replied: 'Forty-five thousand guilders and five cents.'

'Quite a lot. No one has ever had that much money. How much are the coolies' wages this week?'

'Nine thousand and forty-four guilders.'

'Good. Pay up that nine thousand and forty-four guilders. Don't fall down on your job.'

'I don't have even one guilder.'

'Where did you go from here yesterday?'

'Home.'

'And didn't go out again? People saw you leaving your house. Who did you go to see? Why are you silent? You must have been going somewhere.'

Now Sastro Kassier understood: he had fallen into a trap, prepared especially for him. He also understood that in a case like this where two people are accused, one a Pure-Blood Manager, perhaps also a shareholder, and the other a Native, the Native is in the wrong and the Pure is in the right. Since he had been Paymaster, the money in his care had never been short one cent. That was before; it was different now. Where were you last night? Who is your witness? The night attendant would stand fast with his lies. It was enough to keep saying that no one had come in, for there was no reason for anyone to visit the office at night. And a Manager who was perhaps even a shareholder would never rob money from his own factory.

'Come on, tell me. Where did you go? You still won't confess? Whom

386

did you meet? Why are you silent? Fine – you don't want to answer. In short, you still have to pay today's wages and salaries. No delay – that is a factory regulation, part of our agreement with the Government. Do you hear? The Government!'

Before leaving, he still needed to turn around and add: 'Do you want to try to fool the Government? The troops of the *Kompeni*? The Marechausee? The police? You can try if you like.' Then he left.

Everyone stared across at the Paymaster's office, now like an iron cage. Each thanked God not to be the one singled out for this disaster.

The Paymaster stood gazing at the yawning cash box. He did not know what he must do. He was no longer concerned with the disappearance of the money, but with his responsibility to ensure that the wages and salaries were paid. He sensed his fingers going cold because he wasn't counting out the money. In a moment, the foremen would start arriving to collect their pay. A gang of coolies would be waiting upon each of them. He knew the danger that threatened if the money wasn't paid over as it should be. He also knew with certainty that the agreement between the factory and the Government did exist.

Slowly he closed the cash box, and locked it. Without looking at anyone, he left his office, locked the door and headed for Plikemboh's office, walking with his head bowed.

'Ha, you've come, heh. What do you have to say?'

He wanted to gouge out those marble-like eyes, from that European face.

'Tuan Besar Kuasa Manager, I don't have the money to pay the wages. It is up to Tuan Besar Kuasa to decide what is best.'

'Sit!' ordered Plikemboh.

For the first time in his fourteen years at the factory he sat on the chair opposite the Manager.

'What do you want now?'

'The coolies and foremen must be paid today. There is no time to borrow money from the bank. Tuan must lend me the money.'

'Lend you money?' Plikemboh hissed. 'That's an insolent request indeed. Nine thousand and forty-four guilders – the same price as four new stone houses with land and furniture. You're crazy!'

'Only Tuan Besar Kuasa can help me.'

'You shall be dismissed, punished, everything you own will be taken from you. You'll be a pauper, a vagabond, a beggar. And it will happen today, if you can't pay those wages . . .'

'Whatever may happen, then let it happen. But Tuan too will be in trouble if the wages can't be paid. The factory will be closed – for breaking the agreement with the Government. What can one do?'

Frits Homerus Vlekkenbaaij laughed to hide his surprise. Then: 'You're clever heh; you've a lot of cunning in you. You want to drag me into it, eh?' Now his tone was more friendly. 'Yes, I must help you to pay out those wages. Here, sign this agreement first. Put your signature and your thumb-print on it. You'd better do it.'

It became clearer still to Sastro Kassier. It was Plikemboh who had arranged all this. Plikemboh had already prepared the letter of agreement: it demanded the handing over of Sastro's grown-up daughter within three days of signing the letter. On handing her over, his debt to Plikemboh and all the remaining missing money would be taken care of by the Manager himself.

Sastro Kassier forced himself to believe that this was indeed the genuine fruit of his meditation and fasting over the last two nights. He had not yet eaten or taken any drink. But today, anyway, the foremen and coolies would receive their money. He knew he could not avoid his responsibilities as Paymaster. With a prayer that God lay a curse upon it, he signed the agreement, then added his thumb-print.

He received the money. Plikemboh observed it all, smiling.

The days now passed tensely for Surati. She knew the story of Auntie Sanikem well. She was unwilling to go freely to become someone's concubine, isolated from the world, looked upon by everyone as something strange, a public spectacle to be gaped at.

Her mother kept pressuring her not to agree to anything her father suggested. She was afraid of her father, but sad for her mother. From childhood she had been taught to fear and obey her parents, with words, with beatings, with pinchings. Fear of her parents was a part of her personality. But she was still more afraid of the Europeans and their weapons.

The happiness in her life vanished. Her mother's rebellion against her father turned everything topsy-turvy. She could not stand to see her father so abused by her mother; neither could she stand to see her mother belittled and ignored by her father. If the gods and goddesses in the heavens fought each other as viciously as her parents now fought, the earth would tremble and be forced to find a place to anchor itself.

'Don't make your mother and your sisters carry a burden of shame. Become a concubine? Be a nyai? May God protect us, may it never happen. It's not proper, not right. No one can say it's right.'

Surati understood. She must carry out her mother's wishes and not shame her sisters. The whole neighbourhood agreed with her mother. She understood too, better than they that it was her father who held power over her, more power than anyone else. If her father wanted her to do it, there was no power that could stop him. Not the police, not the Kompeni, and certainly not just the Village Head. And she would not dare oppose him.

She lost all desires during those tense days. Must she just surrender herself to whatever was to happen? And so save her parent's marriage? Bring them together again in an atmosphere of perpetual enmity? Or must she rebel, so that when her mother sides with her, a divorce would follow? What would be the fate then of her little sisters? She couldn't decide. She herself had come face to face with Plikemboh. She would never willingly be taken by him! She shivered.

That evening, after the factory whistle had finished its repetitive screaming, she was lying despairingly on her bed. In the front parlour, her mother was venting all her fury on Sastro Kassier: 'Miserable descendant of the seller of children! As long as you're all right yourself! A man with no backbone! A worm could still crawl on and try!' Her voice was harsh and furious but her muscles were powerless.

'Surati!' called her father.

Surati came out of her room and stood with head bowed and hands clasped before her as was proper. At that moment, she knew: her voice had volume but no power.

'So, Rati,' Sastro Kassier opened his speech, 'three more days and I will take you to him, to Tuan Besar Kuasa Manager. In all things it is Allah that hands out fate and good fortune. It is He who decides all things in accord with His wishes.'

Surati understood that she must now answer, with an answer from a fearing and obedient child. She knew too that such obedience and fear meant her own destruction. All of a sudden she remembered the smallpox epidemic that was spreading wildly in the south. In a little while everyone would be lashed by the disease. Tulangan too. What was the difference between the destruction looming before her now and the viciousness of smallpox? As a good daughter, she would not disappoint her father.

'I just obey, Father.'

'You will do what I say, Child, my Child? What do you mean?'

'In whatever way it is Father's wish.'

'Yes, Child, it is only you that can save your father, that can stop your father from being dismissed, from being put in gaol.'

'Let him be dismissed. Let him be accused, Rati, so that he knows what it means to be a man.'

'No, Mother. We would all be ashamed as a result.'

'Ah, you, Rati, Surati, to accept being the concubine of an infidel, a cursed devil.'

'We all eat from him,' Sastro reminded everyone.

'Let it be, Mother; my sisters are still many. What does it mean to lose just one egg? I will go there myself. No need to be escorted like Sanikem.'

'Thanks be to God, Rati, praise be to God. You are a child who truly understand the difficulties of her parents. A child so devoted to her parents will be honoured both in this world and the next.'

'Mouth of a liar!' Djumilah agitated. 'Not honour. He doesn't know the difference between honour and humiliation.'

'But,' Surati went on, 'allow me to go out tonight to meditate. Don't look for me. When the time has come, I will go myself to the house of Tuan Besar Kuasa Manager.'

'What kind of meditation, Child? Late at night like this?' Djumilah could not hold back her tears. All her anger melted away in pity for her daughter. 'With so much illness about now?'

'Yes, Mother. If its parents can no longer do anything for an egg, then the egg must roll away itself to find its own way in life.'

Djumilah could no longer hold back her heart's emotions. She embraced her daughter.

'Where are you going? All this is your own father's . . .'

'Let it be, Mother. Now let me leave.'

'Where are you going? I will come with you.'

'Let it be, Ma. What need is there? This daughter of yours is an egg that must be sacrificed. Stay and live in happiness with Father.'

And so it was. With a small bag containing clothes, matches, kerosene and dried foods, the girl left to make her way into the thick blackness of the night. Her feet took her southwards. After travelling quite a long way, she sat down in a daze beside the road. What must she do? All she knew was that she must leave that house. The roof that had always sheltered her from rain and heat now housed a nest of quarrels, had lost its power to shelter and protect, its peacefulness; and all because of her. But where must she go now? She knew her mother and sisters would try to follow her. She stood up and walked a bit further. Quickly, faster and faster. She slipped behind a hedge, disappearing from the view of anyone following her.

She pressed on, her strides quicker. She did not want blame to arise in her heart.

She must resolve the problem herself, because it was she herself who would undergo it all. None of this would be happening if there were no Plikemboh. Plikemboh – Surati shivered. She was supposed to accept that disgusting person as her man. For a moment the vision of Plikemboh disappeared, and was replaced with one of her mother, her father, her little sisters, Aunt Sanikem. Then for a moment she saw Annelies's marriage again – Annelies sitting beside her husband, looking so happy. Surati knew such happiness as that was not now for her, nor would it ever be. A tear dropped. She too wished for such happiness. But it seemed her fate was to be different. And she was afraid of her parents.

'Why is Father like Grandfather Sastrotomo?' she whispered angrily to herself. 'How could he do it to his own daughter, just to keep himself safe? What was the use of having me? Why can't I be like other girls?'

Like lightning, memories flashed by of other friends who had suffered this same fate. All beautiful and handsome girls, stolen from their houses, through all kinds of means, by Europeans. Now it was her turn, because now she had reached the age for theft. Like them, she could do nothing. She knew she would have surrendered like the others, had not Plikemboh been so hideous.

The air was cold and the wind whistled and whistled. Her legs walked as if they had a will of their own. To the south, to one particular spot: a village that was at that moment being destroyed by smallpox.

'No one will protect me,' she whispered to the night as it covered her in darkness. 'If my own parents can't do anything, what is to be done, as long as they never come to curse me.'

Without her realising it, a plan had formed, the plan of a winged ant that wanted to fly into the flames of a fire.

During those tense days, she had tried to gather together the courage to decide. And she could not decide. A maiden dwells in silent loneliness, alone in life. Her only friend is the hope of happiness. Without the hope of happiness, she has lost everything. There is no one that she can talk with. If she makes what seems like a decision, it is in reality only a surrender to what is going to happen. At the moment Sastro Kassier had decided, such a surrender became an unshakeable resolve. One thing that had made its way into her mind at the time was the smallpox epidemic. What must happen now? The coming together of herself and the smallpox epidemic. She would do it.

From behind her came the howls of a pack of wolves, that had recently roamed about seeking victims. The curfew had allowed the wolf packs to become kings of the night. Several times already, villagers' stock had been attacked and destroyed. She was not afraid; the oppression in her spirit had overcome fear. She walked on. Only if she heard the lonely cry of a bird did she stop and look. Perhaps the bird was calling after the moon, or crying out its longing for a lover who would never arrive.

She had covered almost fifteen kilometres. Sweat soaked her body. The moon was starting to peek out from behind the horizon of silhouetted trees. She stopped under one tree, checking whether she could see anything in the distance. She did not want to be seen by anybody, or meet anybody. She checked behind her, and to her left and right. There was nothing suspicious. But she remained alert at the places shrouded in thicker darkness. Still and quiet, as if she were the only person on this earth. And the cries of the night birds made the night seem even stiller.

Many times during the last two weeks the army had ordered a curfew. People obeyed. Only the army and police were allowed out, but she did not see even a single soldier.

She travelled on for about another ten kilometres. In the distance she could see a blinking glow in the night sky, like a lamp that had almost run out of oil: campfires among clusters of bamboo. That was the village where she was headed. The campfires were army posts. The soldiers weren't visible. She kept on walking. She knew the army had issued orders that no one was to approach closer than two kilometres. The people in the village weren't allowed out. Those outside weren't allowed in. Those in the village were pitilessly given up to die, without compassion – sacrifice to Lord Smallpox.

If I die there with them, then I will be dead, her heart whisperd to the night wind. It would not be long, and all would be over. Surati was going to kill herself. She had accepted what was to nappen. And she felt as though she could still decide, not like Aunt Sanikem. She herself must bring an end to herself.

And if I do not die, it must truly be my destiny to become the woman of that hateful and hideous man. What is to be done, Father, Mother . . .

The closer she came to the village, the further she moved away from the roads, plunging into the paddy and through the broken-down, neglected fields. The scratches on her feet and body from the leaves about her went unfelt. She did not even lift up her kain.

She was startled when she disturbed some ducks sleeping peacefully under a bush. The animals scattered, screeching their frightened protests. The ducks had no one looking after them, she thought; perhaps their owners had been killed by the smallpox.

Now she plunged through fields wrecked by wild pigs and deer. Her clothes were covered with grass blossoms. Her *sanggul* had fallen loose and her hair was tangled. She didn't care. Her hairpin had fallen who knows where.

The moon shone brighter and brighter. The tongues of fire in the distance seemed to grow larger. Some Kompeni soldiers could now be seen running back and forth. The wind began to blow strongly. She knew the village perimeter was patrolled continuously. The nearer she came, the lower she crouched. Finally she began to crawl, like a forest pig.

The fires that lit the soldiers' camp receded into the distance as she moved away. She kept crawling, making no sound, like a cat. Her hands and feet were covered in blood, cut by the thorns and sharp brush along the way. She sought a rift in the bamboo that fenced off the village. In vain. It was not easy: the clusters of bamboo weren't *ampel* bamboo, but thickets of the thorny variety.

She had forgotten her own problems, her own troubles. Her whole being was concentrated on the effort to enter that village, to break through the bamboo fence. Every hole, every gateway, was guarded by Kompeni men and tongues of fire. Without any sharp instrument, with only her bare hands – the hands of a young girl who had never done any real physical work – she was unable to break through. She had to climb over. So she began her attempts to climb over the bamboo – the first such experience in her whole life.

In the distance she could hear soldiers greeting each other:

'*Hordah!*'

'*Preng!*'

In silence, she listened alertly. The voices went away.

I must climb down, she whispered to a stalk of bamboo. But still she didn't climb down. She cast her eyes across the village on the other side of the bamboo fence. Here and there stood huts with grass roofs, like giant animals trying to hide themselves. A lone, gaunt cow dawdled silently along. She could vaguely hear the hungry lowing of other cattle. The moon shone brighter, reluctantly throwing its light upon all that lived on the earth. She no longer wanted to look up at the moon, where in the past she had so often gazed while singing with her friends. This time she had to force herself to look; perhaps it would be the last time.

She climbed down into the village, carefully, freeing herself from the view of the Kompeni men and from the jabs of the bamboo's thorns. The ground below the cluster of bamboo was blanketed in fallen leaves. They rustled under the tread of her feet. She stood silently, listening for sounds. Between the whistling shrieks of the harsh wind as it charged into the bamboo clusters, she heard again the lowing of starving cattle. Perhaps they were still tethered in their corrals. No human sound could be heard. Now she was a member of this village. Like the others, she was surrendered unconditionally to the smallpox. She walked on, looking for the cattle that were lowing so weakly. The moon lit her way to a house, with a corral at the back. She lit a match and looked for the cross-bar. There was no human inside, just a pregnant cow. She undid the rope that tied the cow. The animal walked slowly, heading towards a spot from where the grass sent out its delicious aroma. She gazed at the animal, which had no intention of saying thank you, then walked on again. Under a jamblang bush, she saw a she-goat and its kids, sprawled out dead from hunger and thirst. The she-goat was still tethered. It seemed it had just given birth, unwitnessed by anyone.

The moon was shrouded in cloud. Once again Surati forced herself to look up, as if she wished to memorise forever its face before the smallpox entered her body and escorted her to the universe of souls.

Those that live, let them live, she whispered; the dead, lie still in your muteness; don't disturb me.

Then, confidently, without hesitation, she stepped into a hut. She heard a weak voice coming from inside.

'Is there someone there?'

There was no answer. She opened another door. Darkness gaped out at her from the doorway. Yes, she had heard a voice, a very weak one. She lit a match, and saw a bloated, wheezing baby lying beside its dead mother. A gaunt baby, fleshless, covered in filth. Both lay on a tattered bamboo mat. The match burnt out. She lit another and then the kerosene lamp that hung from a nail on a wall.

The Kompeni would never dare come here, she thought.

Behind the door, she found another corpse – a man, bare chested, sprawled on the ground, dead. His right hand reached out. Perhaps he was trying to reach his baby, his loved one.

The man looked very young, less than twenty years old. Surati herself was younger.

The still living baby she took and cuddled. It had the smell of rotten fish about it and its body was hot. She took a bottle of drinking water from her bag and gave some to the baby, but the child was no longer able to swallow. The end for it too was near.

Far away she could hear the trumpets of the Kompeni. She didn't know what they signalled. She didn't care. She held the dry, shrivelled child, dirty and rotten-smelling, as though holding one of her little sisters at home. She hugged the small weightless body to her breast. She kissed it as if saying goodbye, goodbye forever, then to be together again, also forever.

Under the rays of light from the kerosene lamp, the baby finally reached death's door. Surati began to sing a lullaby so that this very young soul would be able to sleep in eternity caressed by the love of another human being – a human being it had never known. She cleaned the child's face with the corner of her *kebaya*.

The child convulsed for a moment, quickly expelling its final breaths. Surati did not know the child's name. She had never seen a human being on its deathbed. She was not afraid in this encirclement of death. She felt so close, such a friend to them all; soon she too would be a part of it all. Death? What lies beyond death? At least, for sure, she would not be meeting Plikemboh. Why are people afraid of death? And why am I not afraid? When the smallpox has entered my body, and death arrives . . . no, she was not afraid. The curse of one's parents was more terrible than death. Enter, you smallpox, come into me.

She put the baby down beside its mother. She pulled its father over with great difficulty. The corpse was already stiff. At least, now, the baby was sleeping together with its Mama and Papa. For a moment she looked at the two parents at peace in death, together again forever. She felt happy that she had done this, as if she had done some deed of unrivalled goodness, that had never been done by anyone else ever, except by Surati.

She found nothing in the hut except some torn cloths, piled up on an overturned bench. With these she covered them as with a blanket. She put out the lamp, went outside and closed the door.

She had heard rumours that the Kompeni was going to spray the village with kerosene and set it on fire. Not now; that was still five days away. The Village Heads in the district had protested against the Kompeni's plans: it wasn't right to burn people alive. It was not certain that everyone would be killed by the smallpox. But the Kompeni doctor, Lieutenant Doctor H. H. Mortsinger, had calculated that everyone would die within two more days. Even if some hadn't died, they might spread the epidemic; so they should be wiped out as well. The Village Heads' protests resulted in the decision to postpone the burning for a few days, to give everyone a chance to die naturally. The burning was still to go ahead.

To die by fire, there was nothing wrong with that either, thought Surati.

She found more corpses outside the house. Some parts of the bodies had been bitten by animals. They had all began to ooze blood, corrupting the air with their smell. She became aware of the stench of carcasses coming at her from all directions. The dense rottenness was like the rising scent of incense sticks, bearing her to a far-away universe, a place she had never realised existed until now.

Surati lived thus for three days and two nights in that village. She began to feel the hair on her body creep whenever the wind blew. I have caught the disease, she told herself. Very early in the morning she found a well and bathed. She took out the best clothes in her bag. She began to adorn herself. She put on all the jewellery and other adornments that she owned. She knew the fever was starting to attack. In the darkness of the night, she climbed once more over the bamboo. She moved quickly, as if she knew by instinct exactly how far she must travel. It was as if she were racing against the fever that was dancing within her. A few more days and I will be dead. And I will take you with me, Plikemboh! Everybody then will be free from your torments; children, women and your workers! Perhaps the world will be a little more beautiful without you.

The fever in her seemed to weaken, subjugated by her will, unable to suck up her strength and her determination. I must get safely to your house, Plikemboh, looking fresh, young and pretty.

A girl who was not from a peasant family would never have been taught to walk quickly; indeed they would be forbidden from doing so. But Surati's legs took stride after stride, penetrating the darkness and the night mist, half-running over the paddy-field dikes, now overgrown with weeds. Now she held her kain by its corners so it would not be soiled by the weeds' blossoms.

Ten kilometres she had covered. Yet there was still no sweat on her. She walked another five kilometres, and five more again. Then she stopped under some trees, and descended into a big ditch. She washed herself again. At the peak of the moon's mist-covered brightness, she put on her make-up once more. For a long time she sat under the tree, not thinking of anything.

395

During those last few days, she had stopped thinking, surrendering herself to the flow of events as they happened, as though she were part of nature itself, like the wind, like the water, like the earth. She began to see people out walking on that dark morning. She too stood up, walking slowly so as not to ruin her make-up and her adornments, just like a woman of the aristocracy. Slowly enough even to control her sway.

As the sun rose, Tulangan became vaguely visible behind the mist. She saw several dokar carrying goods and heading for the markets of Sidoarjo.

On entering Tulangan she stopped and whispered to herself. Here I am, coming to you, Tuan Besar Kuasa Manager, greet me: Surati!

The factory office was open when she arrived. The roads around the factory were busy with coolies pushing loaded carts. She didn't know what they carried, nor did she have any desire to know. Her legs took her straight to Plikemboh's house.

She announced herself formally: '*Kulo-nuwun*'. In her imagination she could see Aunt Sanikem, a score or more years ago, standing before this same house, there to become the concubine of Tuan Mellema. The door was open, but no one answered her. She sat on the steps with her back to the house. Her dried food was finished. She felt hungry. The fever was still obedient to her plan.

She heard slippered footsteps behind her. She stood facing the door, bowed and once again said: 'Kulo-nuwun'.

Plikemboh emerged still wearing his pyjamas. He stood gazing at her, and at once recognised who she was.

'Sastro Kassier's daughter?' he asked joyfully, and sped down the stairs to fetch her.

'It is I, your servant, the daughter of Sastro Kassier, Tuan Besar Kuasa.'

She ascended the steps, escorted by Plikemboh, and surrendered herself to be taken into his room – the place which forever would be the boundary that marked the end of her life as a virgin and the beginning of her condition as a kept mistress.

Take me! Take all you can get from me, she thought, and may you soon be destroyed.

As soon as she entered the room, the smallpox ran amok within her. Her strength was broken. From the moment she lay prostrate on Plikemboh's bed, she was unable to rise again. And very quickly Plikemboh too became infected. During those last few days, they both lay sprawled out on the bed, awaiting death.

Tulangan was pronounced an epidemic area. All work stopped. The traffic was stilled. Those who managed to speak through the Kompeni's encirclement ran for their life, forgetting position and income. The sugarcane fields were left unattended. The steam-generated electric plant was mute. The factory whistle went dumb. Tulangan was in darkness. The chimneys lost their grandness, craning forward, looking down on Tulangan as if wanting to know what was happening, nodding sadly, but no eyes cared to look up at them.

The village across the fields, which Surati had left behind, was burnt out by the Kompeni – destroyed together with all its trees that the villagers had looked after for many years. Tulangan itself was not set on fire. Doctors were brought in from all over Java to end the epidemic. A big sugar mill must not be destroyed just because of smallpox. Capital must be kept alive to grow; and people may die.

Lieutenant Doctor Mortsinger was also called to Tulangan with all the medic troops from the Anti-Epidemic Service in Bandung. Inoculation was carried out in Tulangan and all the surrounding areas. But the Kompeni encirclement of Tulangan was kept unmercifully tight. People could neither leave nor enter. People were even forbidden from leaving their houses. Food was brought in and shared out. Every day people buried the victims.

The first to die was Tuan Besar Kuasa Manager, Frits Homerus Vlikkenbaaij, alias Plikemboh.

Surati was still prostrate on the bed when that heavy corpse was taken from beside her to be buried. Only then did people find out that the maiden had already begun her life as a nyai. And hadn't died.

Even while facing the threat of death by smallpox, all the people of Tulangan, regardless of race, Pure or Mixed-Blood, stopped to thank God for the death of Tuan Besar Kuasa Manager. To them his corpse was a talisman that would protect Tulangan from disaster. But no one ever found out who it was that had really killed him.

The young mistress was carried home by her mother, whose insults and abuse of Sastro Kassier never stopped.

Sastro Kassier himself did not stay silent. The death of his boss gave him the chance to make his accusations. Witnessed by local officials, a search was made of his late employer's things. There, in a cupboard, they found the missing money, still intact. Sastro Kassier remained triumphant as the honest Paymaster, but his honour as a husband and father was gone, and would never return.

So, too, was Surati's beauty gone forever.

And the sugar mill of Tulangan remained grand in its command over all of Tulangan: man, animals and growing things.

8

For three days we had been resting in Tulangan. The new manager who replaced Plikemboh sent a letter to Mama, inviting her to come and have a look around the factory. Mama turned down the invitation. He then came to Sastro Kassier's house to invite her in person. He was very young, perhaps about thirty years old. Mama refused the invitation again.

I don't know why the master of that sugar mill felt he had to invite Mama. Mama herself had never mentioned having any special business with him.

Kommer also sent us a letter: he would not be able to visit us. He couldn't leave the carpenters while they were making his trap. It was proving to be quite difficult to make.

Every day Mama and I went for a walk through the paddy fields, plantations and villages. She was really changed; the dark, eerie aura about her had vanished. She was truly enjoying her holidays. She didn't look at all like a widow, nor like someone out walking with her son-in-law, himself a widower, She looked like a young maiden, not yet married.

Her walk was confident and free like that of a European woman. She always wore the kebaya that for a century had been the fashion for Indos, nyais and now for Chinese women to wear. Very few Native women wore them, at most a few from the elite classes, and perhaps their children. Most just wore *kembans*, or even went totally bare-breasted.

Nyai Ontosoroh's beautiful and delicately embroidered kebaya became the focus of everybody's attention. Such a kebaya was still rare in the villages, and its whiteness and the brightness of its embroidery shone out in the middle of all this greenness, drawing all eyes to it.

On the fourth day she wouldn't go for a walk and sent me out by myself.

So on that day, in European clothes (people called them Christian clothes), carrying a bag containing pen and paper, a bottle of water and a little dried food, I set off alone in a southerly direction. My plan was to visit the village that the Kompeni had burnt down, the one that Surati had visited.

In the middle of the ocean of sugar cane I saw something odd: the tiled roof of a house. Whose? Somebody's home, or a place for toilers to take shade? The trees behind it showed that cane did not grow around it. Probably somebody's house-garden.

It wasn't out of mere curiosity that I set off in the direction of the house, but because I wanted to accustom myself to taking an interest in everything that was related to the lives of the Natives, my people.

The track, hemmed in on either side by the cane, was still and quiet. Not a single person passed me. But from the direction of the tiled house came the sound of muffled shouts, roughly spoken.

The sun radiated shafts of heat. Sweat soaked my back. The air was fresh and invigorating. My body felt unconstrained by the etiquette required when escorting Mama. I walked along, enjoying it all to the full, savouring how healthy I was. I felt fortunate to be alone in the middle of this greenness, free like a bird. I had never in all my life gone for a hike alone and so far. Perhaps I had already travelled more than five kilometres.

This was the same road that Surati had once travelled, not in the midday heat like this, but in night's pitch darkness, before the moon had risen.

The cane to my right and left would ripen in a few months' time. It would become sugar, helping to make Java the second biggest producer of sugar in the world. The sugar would be dispersed over the earth to many countries and give enjoyment and health to millions of people. And the name 'Tulangan'? No one would ever hear of it.

There were those shouts again.

The track I was following branched out. A lane lead to the suspicion - arousing house.

A farmer with a hoe at his waist passed me. He raised his bamboo hat, bowed without looking at me – only because I was wearing European clothes, Christian clothes. He was heading towards the main road. Perhaps he was a cane cutter.

'What's all the shouting about?' I asked in Javanese.

'The usual, Ndoro. Old Truno is not like everyone else.'

'Who is this Truno?'

'The one who lives there, Ndoro.'

'In that house?'

'Yes, Ndoro.'

'Why are they shouting at him like that?'

'He won't move out of his house.'

'Why must he move?'

These barrage of questions made the peasant afraid. He shrank back, bowed, raised his bamboo hat again, excused himself. Perhaps he had been among those shouting just now.

The shouts came again. Now it was clear what they were saying, in crude Javanese: 'When are you getting out of there?'

Other shouts followed from several mouths at once, but I was unable to pick up what they were saying. Then there were more disputatious exchanges and cries for Truno to get out. What was happening in the middle of this ocean of cane?

Because of the accusation of not knowing my own people, yes, and because of curiosity, my legs took me closer to the location of the quarrel. Perhaps I could learn to understand their problems. Without my realising, my feet were now carrying me more quickly. I no longer took any notice of the foliage above me as the branches and twigs squeaked against each other whenever the wind blew.

In this very lane the tiled house stood. It was made out of thick *betung* bamboo. The walls were from *anyam* bamboo. In front of the house stood a moustached man with a thick beard, bare-chested, wearing black trousers down to just below his knee. In his hand was a machete with that just-honed shine about it. His eyes were wild. On seeing me, his eyes popped out in challenge.

'Oi, *Pak*!' I shouted, in friendly Javanese. 'Who was making all the noise just now?'

He still stared at me wild-eyed as if I were his enemy. I stopped in front of the bamboo gate.

'What?' he hissed in low Javanese. 'You too?' I was offended. I could feel the blood rise into my face. A Javanese had never spoken so roughly towards me, let alone used the familiarity *kowe* for 'you'. No doubt he was that kind of insolent Javanese, hadn't been properly educated, I thought. Then quick as lightning came the voice of Jean Marais, accusing me: you are not just, Minke; what right do you have to abuse him? What have you done for him? Just because you are the grandson and the son of a bupati? You say you understand the great call of the French Revolution? What's the use of having graduated from H.B.S.?

A smile of awareness crept onto my lips. I must remain friendly.

'Don't be angry with me, Pak. I'm not your enemy.'

'Every single day . . .' the man frowned, yet my friendliness did relax him a little.

'What is it, Pak?'

'. . . like a pack of barking dogs!' It poured out in sharp tones.

'Who, Pak,' I asked affably, 'is like a pack of barking dogs?'

He observed me with suspicion. It was unusual for a Javanese peasant farmer to be suspicious of his superiors. Peasants had no right to be suspicious. It was clear that this one peasant had *mrojol selaning garu*, had 'escaped the prongs of the rake' and turned his back on the proper way of behaving. Like an elephant that had left its herd, as Nijmann had said about Khouw Ah Soe, a Javanese peasant who refused to fit himself to the old mould was also dangerous. Machete in hand, loud voice, not listening to orders: all this was evidence.

400

'Don't get me wrong, Pak, I've only just arrived.'

He wouldn't give up his suspicions. His smallish eyes stood out as if they were not interested in ever having to blink again. Indeed they seemed ready to hurl themselves out of their sockets at any minute. I must try to win his trust. Must! Must! There's no way of getting close to somebody without first making contact with his heart.

Daring myself to go on, I took a step forward, passing through the gate, not without having to suppress my fear.

'What's really going on here?' I asked affably.

'Is Ndoro a *priyayi* from the mill?' he suddenly asked in high Javanese, a question which also struck me as insolent.

'No. I have just arrived from Surabaya. I am not an official from the mill. I'm still at school, Pak. I write for newspapers, that's my work, Pak.'

With savage eyes – not normal for a Javanese peasant either – he looked me over from the top of my head to the tips of my shoes.

'This machete is not just good for cutting down banana trees,' he growled threateningly in low Javanese. 'One more time, and someone will cop it.'

'What is it? What is it?' I asked, in the politest of ways.

'I don't care who he is, Javanese, Madurese, Kompeni, one more howl from them . . .'

His anger passed its climax with these growls and threats.

'Is Ndoro one of them or not?' he turned abruptly, interrogating me. More insolence.

'Who do you mean by *them*?'

Once more he challenged my eyes, and looked at my bag. '*They*,' he said savagely, 'are those factory dogs. This is my own land. What business is it of theirs what I do with it.' He wiped sweat from his back.

Unease squatted in my heart; he had gone back to speaking in *ngoko*, in low Javanese. He had forgotten what class he belonged to. So why should I treat him so well? But you have resolved to become more familiar with your own people! You must understand their troubles. He is one of those fellow countrymen of yours about whom you know nothing, one of your own people, a people you say you want to write about, once you have begun to understand them.

'Of course this is your own land,' I encouraged him, and myself too.

'Five *bahu*, inherited from my parents.'

'You're right,' I said, 'I saw it noted down in the Land Office.'

'Nah, it's registered in the Land Office.' He spoke to himself. The tension began to recede. Slowly he was returning to being a humble Javanese peasant.

'Can I visit you, Pak?' I said in an even more friendly way. His grip on the machete began to relax. I took another step forward.

'If Bapak isn't angry with me, I'd liked to know what this is all about. Who knows, perhaps I can help?' I took another step.

He didn't answer, but turned around and headed for the house. I followed. He threw his machete down inside the house. He fetched a straw broom and swept clean the bamboo bench at the entrance.

'Please, Ndoro, this is the best I can offer.'

So I sat on the bamboo bench, adorned with a *pandan* bamboo mat. He stood with hands clasped before me. He was beginning to trust me, I hoped. 'All right, tell me why you are so angry,' I asked.

'Yes, Ndoro, I have already been very patient. My inheritance was five bahu, three paddy fields, two dry fields and this house garden. Three bahu are being used by the mill. I didn't happily rent them out but was brutally forced to do so, by the mill priyayi, the Village Head, all kinds of officials and God knows how many others! The land was contracted for eighteen months. Eighteen months! But now it has been two years! You have to wait until the cane stumps have all been dug out. Except if you want to put your thumb-print to another contract for the next harvest season. What's the contract money worth anyway? You can count it up as much as you like, they never pay in full anyway. Those dogs, Ndoro . . . now even my dry-fields – they want those too. The trees will be torn down to make way for the cane!'

'How much do you get for one bahu?' I asked, as I took my writing implements from my bag, knowing that all of Java's peasants respected a pen. I was ready to take notes.

'Twenty-two, Ndoro,' he answered fluently. Amazing.

'Twenty-two *perak*, for every bahu, for use for over eighteen months!' I exclaimed.

'Yes, Ndoro.'

'How much did you receive?'

'Fifteen perak.'

'Where did the other seven go?'

'How would I know, Ndoro? Put your thumb-print down, they said. No more than fifteen perak a bahu. Eighteen months, they said. In reality, two years, until the cane stump and roots were dug out.'

'They dig out the roots themselves?'

'Of course, Ndoro. They don't want to see the stumps grow and ripen again, become new cane fields again. They don't want the farmers around here to get any leftover cane without paying, without working.'

I wrote and wrote; and I saw that he was beginning to respect me. But I didn't know what he really thought of me.

'Nah, now you must listen, let me read out to you everything that you have just told me. Eh, what's Bapak's name?'

'Trunodongso, Ndoro.'

I stopped a moment on hearing that name. My grandfather had once warned me against peasants who use the name 'Truno'. Such people, he said, are usually quick-tempered, especially when young. And sometimes they are even quicker-tempered in their old age. People choose that name hoping they will be able to maintain the spirit of their youth, to keep their strength and health right to the end. And, said my grandfather, such people usually study the martial arts before they marry. I didn't know whether he was right or not.

'So Trunodongso is your name. Good, let me read this to you.'

I read out in Javanese what I had written and he nodded at the end of each sentence.

'This will be printed in the newspapers. All the clever and important people up there will read it. Perhaps Tuan Besar Governor-General, Bupatis, Residents, Controllers, all of them. They will investigate all this. They will then know that there is a farmer named Trunodongso who is being forced from his land and his paddy, and is recovering only fifteen perak for each bahu that is rented by the mill.'

'Wah, Ndoro.' He freed his hand from its polite clasp, ready to protest. 'It's not like that,' he began.

'You're taking back what you've told me?'

'No, Ndoro, it's all true. But I am not the only one who has received only fifteen perak. That's all any of the farmers around here have received, Ndoro.'

'Everyone?'

'Everyone, except the village officials.'

'How much did they get?'

'No one knows, Ndoro. But we do know that none of them are complaining. Never!'

'But people have the right not to rent their land if that's what they want.'

'Yes. That is my situation, Ndoro, I don't want to rent out my land but every day I'm threatened, taunted, insulted. Now they threaten that the lane to my house will be closed off. If you want to get to your house and land, they say, you'll have to fly. They have already closed the channels bringing water to my paddy fields. I couldn't farm the paddy, so I had to rent it out.'

This kind of thing was something I had never come across before. I wrote everything down. Trunodongso went on and on. All that he had been unable to say for so long was now poured out to me. I was no longer noting down just words, but the fate of who knows how many thousands, how many tens of thousands peasant farmers like him. Perhaps this was the fate of all the sugar region's farmers. And he was not facing just Europeans, but Natives too: village officials, civil officials, the factory officials, including Sastro Kassier no doubt. My note-taking became even more enthusastic. And Trunodongso became even more open with me.

A girl appeared, carrying a bamboo basket, walking towards a well beside that bamboo house. She pulled up the water using a bamboo scoop and started washing some clothes in an earthenware dish.

'Is that your daughter?' I asked.

He nodded.

'How many children do you have altogether?'

'Five, Ndoro. Two boys – they're out hoeing in the field now. The others are girls.'

'Five. May I come in and have a look around Bapak's house?' I asked politely.

'Please come in, but it's very dirty.'

I went inside the house. There were no windows. There was no cow or buffalo inside, but a tethering post standing in the corner indicated that a large animal had lived with the family at some other time or other.

'Where's the cow, Pak?'

'What's the use of a cow if you have no paddy, Ndoro? I've sold it.'

There was no furniture except for a big bamboo bench and a kerosene lamp hanging from a bamboo pole. In the corner lay a hoe with lumps of fresh dirt clinging to it.

I thanked God that this quick-tempered farmer had been restored to the original Trunodongso, friendly, generous with his smiles, polite and humble, no longer hiding evil feelings.

'Where's your wife, Pak?'

'Just left for the market, Ndoro.'

'Nduk, Nduk!' I called to the little girl doing the washing. She ran to her father. Her eyes were tired, as though she had never had her proper fill of dreams – or perhaps because she had ringworm.

'What are you cooking today, Nduk?'

'Depends what Ma brings home, Ndoro, from the market,' she answered, looking into her father's eyes.

'Nah, look, Nduk, I want to eat here tonight, yes; would you like to cook for me?'

Once more she quizzed her father with her sleepy eyes. Her father answered with a little bow of the head. Her voice was very, very polite: 'Of course, Ndoro, si Piah would be very happy to cook for Ndoro, but it's sure to taste terrible. A village child, remember, that's what I am.'

'So we'll eat together tonight. How many altogether? Seven?'

'Then I must get some firewood,' Trunodongso excused himself. 'But Ndoro won't be ashamed to eat here?'

How happy was my heart to feel this family was beginning to lose its suspicion of me. I added quickly: 'Is the market far from here?'

'No, Ndoro, it's quite close,' answered little Piah. I knew in fact that the market was near Tulangan.

'Here is some money. Go and buy something. It's up to you what you cook,' and I handed her two coins.

Once more the child looked up at her father. Trunodongso glanced around, pretending not to see. I put my bag down on the bench, and went outside the house.

I felt a happiness blooming in my breast. I drew the free air deep into my lungs and threw out my two arms like a *garuda* about to fly into the sky. What Kommer had said indeed seemed true: if you're willing to pay a little attention, a whole new continent arises, with mountains and rivers, islands and waterways. I will stay upon this new continent for a while longer. Columbus was not the only person to discover a new continent. So too have I.

I strolled around outside the house. At the back, clothes were drying – clean rags, really. And he was a farmer with five bahu of his own land, including three bahu of first-class paddy fields! If he'd been able to refuse surrendering his dry fields, why hadn't he been able to refuse handing over his paddy? His remaining dry fields were the last bastion of his livelihood. He has to defend it to the end. If he didn't, his whole family could be turned into vagabonds.

The air streaming through the thickets of trees was truly refreshing. The freshness of the air was present, but also the staleness of life – a continent with great mountain peaks, deep chasms.

A drain carrying the dirty water from the well wound aimlessly about; ducks were scratching in the mud looking for worms. Under a *laos* bush, three chicks fought over who was the eldest. A pregnant cat – yellow-coloured – slept in the sun on a pile of old leaves. A row of banana trees, not one of which had an upright trunk, leaned sleepily to one side. In the distance, Trunodongso was cutting down a tree with his machete. He chopped it up and piled the wood together in the middle of the thicket.

As I moved further away from the house, I could see more closely the nature of the tidily farmed corn and sweet-potato fields. The border between the back-yard garden and the fields proper was marked by a row of coffee trees, thick with fruit, and protected by the umbrella of closely planted coconut palms. It seemed that this family could live off their own fields – except for clothes and sugar.

Trunodongso had disappeared into the house carrying a hand of bananas. No smoke came from the kitchen yet. At the edge of the field, where it met the mill's cane, I found two of Trunodongso's sons hoeing the ground. They stopped working as soon as they saw me and laid down their hoes. They showed me great respect, yet were also obviously surprised and afraid. More than that: suspicious.

'Pak Truno's sons?'

'Yes, Ndoro.' They took off their bamboo hats and threw them on the ground. They were aged sixteen and fourteen. There were no pictures of Queen Wilhelmina back in their house – neither had finished primary school.

'This is the border with the factory's cane?'

'Yes, Ndora.'

'Aren't they suspicious of you two if any cane goes missing?'

The two of them consulted with their eyes. I saw suspicion in those consultations, and fear.

'No, I'm not from the factory,' I said. Still they didn't seem to believe, and were afraid. 'I'm staying at your house at the moment. Later on we'll eat together.' They glanced back and forth at each other again; then without answering dropped their gaze to their feet.

'You've never been accused of stealing cane?' I asked again.

They shot a look at me from the corners of their eyes, then their eyes consulted once more.

'Don't really know, Ndoro,' the eldest answered.

They were still suspicious and afraid; that's how all farmers felt towards non-farmers. The anonymous pamphlet that my exiled teacher Magda Peters gave me had said: The peasant farmers of Java were afraid of all outsiders, because their experiences over the centuries had shown them that outsiders – individuals or groups – would thieve everything they owned. These two young boys, with hoe in hand, sickle at their feet, were afraid of me for no other reason than because I was not one of them. Because my clothes were not the kind they wore.

What that pamphlet said was exactly right. A European had written it. He knew about the Javanese peasants. And I was just now discovering this continent. I was now witnessing that bottom point in their lives: being under the sway of fear and suspicion.

If one day they should cross the limits of their fear and suspicion – so that brochure said – this group of people living under God's sun, who aren't used to thinking rationally, will rise up in an explosion of blind fury; they will run amok. They could explode individually or in a group. And their targets would be anyone who was not one of them, who wasn't a peasant farmer. Such indeed was the condition of these pitiable beings who had never known the learning of the world: in no time at all their fury would be suppressed by the Army, and they would be broken forever. For three hundred years! So that anyone from whatever group who can humour and capture their hearts they will follow – in religion, to the battlefield or to annihilation.

I remembered the pamphlet's words well, and so as not to arouse any more fear in these boys' hearts, I moved away. I walked back towards the house, thinking to myself along the way: perhaps if I had not come and shown my sympathy to Trunodongso, he might have wielded his machete, cutting down whomever he could. The pamphlet had also said: they would run amok not really in self-defence, nor to attack or to take revenge, but only because they no longer knew what else to do once their last opportunity of life had been stolen.

That pamphlet's author, Anonymous, I had to admit, was very knowledgeable. It was clear that the peasants themselves did not understand their own condition. But in that other corner of the world, in the Netherlands, people did know; they knew exactly what the situation was. They even understood the psychology of the peasantry as a class. And all this was in a pamphlet written by a Dutchman living in the Netherlands. It was true what Jean Marais had said: you study the languages of Europe to understand Europe. Through Europe you can learn to understand your own people. To study the languages of Europe does not mean you cannot speak to your own people, and that you should speak only to Europeans.

I went on towards the bamboo house. It was not only from Europe that so much could be learned! This modern age had provided many breasts to suckle me – from among the Natives themselves, from Japan, China, America, India, Arabia, from all the peoples on the face of this earth. They were the mother wolves that gave me life to become a builder of Rome! Is it true you will build a Rome? Yes, I answered myself. How? I don't know. In humility, I admitted: I was a child of all nations, of all ages, past and present. Place and time of birth, parents, all were coincidence: such things were not sacred.

Back in the house I went on with my writing. But the first sentence was not what I had been thinking as I walked back: 'And evil too came from all nations, from all ages.'

I wrote and wrote until all that I wished to write was finished. I flopped my body down upon the bamboo sleeping bench and fell asleep, forgetting all that had been happening around me.

Who knows how long I slept. Indeed I hadn't had enough sleep the night before. I had been overcome by my passion to finish the notes about Surati. Shouting startled my eyes open, but I still lay there on the divan-bench.

'Nduk! I only got five *beggol* for the chicken, Nduk. Not enough to buy any clothes for you, just some pants for your father.'

Realising that the voice was that of an adult woman, I quickly got up. No doubt it was Trunodongso's wife, home from the market. Her smallest daughters followed behind. On seeing me Truno's wife stopped in front of the house, bowed down again and again, then walked off around the side of the house to the back.

It appeared that Piah had begun cooking in the kitchen. I could smell the aroma of frying chicken. All of a sudden my stomach was calling out for food.

Now I could hear Piah speaking in low Javanese to her mama: 'When will I get some clothes, Ma?'

I couldn't hear the answer; perhaps, she anwered slowly: when the other chicks grow large. I took out the gold pocket watch my mother had given me for a wedding present. It was four o'clock, and my stomach was making wild demands.

Trunodongso came outside to the bench and invited me in to eat. He apologised for not daring to awaken me earlier. Inside there was a woven bamboo mat with the edibles laid out on it. There was only one plate. The curry was in an earthenware bowl and the rice in a bamboo basket. Ground chilli and dried fish lay crushed in the earthen bowl. The stone pestle stood in the bowl on top of the chillied fish.

'Please, Ndoro.'

'Let us eat together, Pak, with all the children and Ma Trunodongso.'

'It's all right like this, Ndoro; there's only one plate.'

'Then we can all eat from banana leaves.'

An argument started. Finally Trunodongso gave in. Everybody was mobilised to eat together off banana leaves. More food was brought out from the kitchen. I did not regret doing this, even though I knew it was torture for them to eat with me. They were so afraid of taking any of the chicken, especially the fried chicken. It turned out to be as hard as wood. So then I knew: this family had never cooked chicken before, not even the ones they owned themselves.

Seeing that they were hesitating to start, I finished my meal quickly and went for a stroll outside, to get some fresh air.

After dinner the following conversation took place.

'If Bapak worked that land yourself, would you be much better off?'

For the first time Trunodongso laughed. 'When my parents were still alive, heaps of paddy surrounded this house. There were many chickens and ducks. A few years before they died, the factory starting pressuring them to give over the land. My father refused. Then the Village Chief came, then the Ndoro *Satan*. My father still refused. Then the paddy-field water canals were blocked further up, on factory land. There was no more water. My father . . .'

'Weren't the canals built by the farmers themselves? Not the factory?'

'Sure, Ndoro. I myself helped build them. A week it took, I remember it well. At the end of clearing my section of land there was a great pile of fallen leaves. There were many snakes. No less than seven there were.'

'No one was bitten?'

'Ah, just little lizards really, Ndoro.'

'How much were you paid?'

'Paid? No one paid us.'

He liked to watch me write down his answers. And I was certainly not going to disappoint him. I would pour it all out in the newspapers. I could already guess that there would be a great commotion. Perhaps this man before me now would become the main figure in some great story about the farmers of the sugar-cane regions. He was becoming more and more interesting. The more marks I made on the paper, the more he trusted me, and the easier it became to enter his psyche.

I recalled again my grandfather's warning about people with the name Truno. (Perhaps we were still afraid then of Trunajaya.) Such people, my grandfather told me, would fight the Government, or become rebel bandits. Uh! the names of Javanese! As a writer of newspaper advertisements, it was my view that if grandfather's words were true, the names that Javanese took were no different than advertisements, whose messages were by no means truthful.

Very carefully I asked him: did he like to fight?

'No,' he said, 'but indeed I did study martial arts when I was young.' So he was a fighter; my grandfather's words were right. 'Bapak has been involved in fights?'

His eyes narrowed, as if defending themselves from an attack. Realising that the question had aroused his suspicion again, I quickly added that my grandfather had made me study silat too. I studied for three years, before graduating. But, I said, I had never been in a real fight.

He listened to my story with eyes full of life – the narrowness disappeared. He was indeed a fighter. No wonder the factory people didn't dare any reckless attempt to throw him out.

I quickly turned the conversation away from fighting and silat. He must not become suspicious again. Issue after issue emerged. I wrote and wrote. This person was interesting: unlike other peasant farmers, he dared state his opinion, even though his approach was roundabout and he never went directly to the issue. I reckoned he was indeed a peasant with character. And the more questions I asked him, the happier he was giving his answers. I thought he might have been a labourer in a town once. But I didn't ask.

'Might I stay here tonight?' I asked.

He was surprised at my request. I wanted to stay overnight so I could study a little about how he lived. As expected, out came excuse after excuse. But I was unyielding. With great reluctance he finally gave his agreement. His youngest child was sent off with a letter to Mama in Tulangan.

So it was that I stayed the night.

That night the fireplace was lit, as was the custom if you kept livestock. Smoke filled the windowless space. My lungs were hot and tight. As the evening wore on, the silence was broken by the croaking of the tree frogs.

I was given a place on the edge of the big sleeping bench. The other children, boys and girls, slept on my left. Their breathings seemed to speak to each other; they took turns in coughing. The fire finally went out. Then the mosquitoes attacked from above, the bed bugs from below. Ya Allah, how peaceful they all were in their sleep, and I could not even keep my eyes closed in my torment.

For how many hundreds, thousands, of years, generation after generation, have they slept like this? Human beings with great resilience, great strength. Every other moment, my hand moved to get rid of a mosquito or bedbug. My eyes still wouldn't close. Slowly my irritation increased. I sat up in the dark. But the mosquitoes and bedbugs took no notice of my irritation; they were just as blood-thirsty as ever, as if they alone were the only beings who had to live. How high was the price I had to pay so that no one might ever accuse me again of not knowing my own people! Perhaps if I had not given them shopping money, I would not have eaten at all that night. What did they really eat each day? I still didn't know.

I had just rested my head back on the sheath of dried paddy stalks, when I heard singing outside the hut. Who would be singing on this insect-ridden night? The voice seemed to hesitate. Before even one verse was finished, I heard the scrape of a door being opened carefully. I attuned my hearing. I could make out the shuffle of a long sarong on the floor. Obviously Ma Trunodongso. Then another scrape of an opening door. So husband and wife were up, and going outside.

They wouldn't be going out to relieve themselves. It was the midnight village song that called them. This was interesting material for my story.

Before I knew it, I was groping my way through the darkness to the door. I must add to my knowledge about them. Not long after, there was another sound of a door scraping open, but this time it was my hand that did the opening. I was now outside the house, with the mosquitoes, but without the bedbugs. A black starless sky. My eyes tried to locate any human movement. Nothing but blackness. Where had the husband and wife gone? I tried to remember from what direction the singing had come. My arms and legs groped in that direction. I reckoned I had reached the jackfruit trees. The singing had long since died away.

'Impossible,' I heard a warning spoken emphatically.

There were several people under the jackfruit tree – at least three. The voice dropped to a soft whisper. Of course I was drawn in that direction.

'The priyayi staying with you is a factory spy for sure!' I heard. 'And you haven't the courage to kill him.'

'No, in the name of Allah, he is not a spy.'

'He's Sastro Kassier's family!'

'Even so, he is not like the factory people, he's not arrogant like them.

410

From Surabaya, writes for a newspaper, he says. He's going to write for the papers about how we've been cheated all this time.'

'Rubbish. As if you didn't know what they're like. Kill him and get it over with.'

'No blood shall be spilt in my house,' came the voice of Trunodongso's wife. 'Factory spies aren't like that.'

'Very well, I will tell all this to the *Kyai*. Perhaps tomorrow I'll be back again.'

I rushed back to the house while they were still talking. My hands and feet began to grope around again. Now it felt as if the house was far away, another kilometre or perhaps two. They must not find me outside.

Suddenly my feet slipped into a drain. I must be on the wrong path. The foul-smelling drain mud became my second layer of clothes. I must be near the well. I had indeed come the wrong way. The humiliation of it! For the first time in my life I had to bathe at night. And for the first time in my life I had to wash my own clothes, in the darkness in the cold.

With my teeth rattling, I finally reached my sleeping-bench. I had no dry clothes. I lay down but now pulled the bedbug-ridden mat over me as a blanket.

Even so I did not feel any more tormented than before. Rather I felt thankful to God: Trunodongso and his wife's trust in me was a far greater blessing, overcoming the cold and torment.

In the morning, wearing only my underclothes, I washed my pants and shirt again and dried them. Then I wrote and wrote. It was clear they were involved in some kind of conspiracy. My guess was that they were banding together to fight against the factory. Perhaps I was mistaken. I must stay here perhaps another day.

Once again I strolled out the back to get to know my new field of action better.

That night I again heard the singing. I awoke and waited for the Mr and Mrs to leave. The sky wasn't as dark as the night before. The stars lit up the earth. The two figures before me made their way quickly to the jackfruit thicket. This time I didn't dare go so close. From behind the *laos* bushes I could make out the silhouettes of several people. They didn't stay long, but left for who knows where.

I returned to the house. For a long time I tried to light the kerosene lamp. When I succeeded, I discovered that Trunodongso's two sons had also gone. So too had their machete and sickle, which usually leaned against the wall. Only their hoes were left, lying side by side near one of the roof supports.

That morning only the smaller children were at home. Little Piah quickly brought water into the kitchen, aided by her younger sisters. I befriended her while she cooked, and she became restless as a result. I fetched a hoe from its place and went out the back. In bare feet, chafed by the cold, dirty ground, I began to hoe where the boys had finished yesterday. After only five minutes I had to stop. I was panting. I was ashamed of myself. Those boys were far younger than me, and they could hoe the ground for four hours without stopping.

There were no witnesses to my condition. How embarrassed and ashamed I would be if someone saw me out of breath like this. I began to hoe the ground again, but this time more slowly. Then little Piah arrived.

'Ndoro, don't work like that, you'll get dirty, you'll fall ill. There's coffee ready back at the house. Let me carry the hoe.'

I was lucky the offer of a drink arrived, otherwise I would have been obliged to continue that voluntary but murderous work.

'Don't keep on hoeing, Ndoro,' forbade Piah politely. 'If you blister your hand, you won't be able to write.'

I didn't even have a blister yet, but already I was unable to write; my hands shook uncontrollably. Still I had now, at least once in my life, hoed the ground. Clearly I would never be a farmer like them.

That afternoon I asked permission to go home. I considered that I had enough notes. But the main thing was that I could not live any longer in these conditions. I now understood that these people were far stronger than me. They had the strength of iron; they were tempered by suffering. It was strange. Why should such a class of people made so strong by their suffering, just keep on suffering?

Trunodongso stood bowing with hands folded before him and said how he regretted not being able to show the kind of hospitality that was proper. His eyes were red from lack of sleep.

'If Bapak is ever in Wonokromo, come to our house. Make sure you visit us,' I told him.

The whole family escorted me. I groped in my pocket. There was still one rupiah and fifteen cents, and I gave it to little Piah.

'Don't forget to visit us at Wonokromo. Look for the house of Nyai Ontosoroh. Remember it, Pak: *Nyai On-to-so-roh*.'

His wife's and sons' eyes were also red.

Now only Trunodongso was left to escort me. He carried my bag respectfully, as if he were my servant. In the middle of the cane I stopped, and said to him: 'Pak Truno, by Allah, I am not a spy.' He glanced at me for a moment, then bowed his head. He must have guessed that I had heard the conversation on that dark night.

'I respect Pak Truno and all those suffering the same fate. Through my writings I will try to lighten you burden. More than that is beyond me. Let's hope my help may produce some results. Troubles such as these can't always be overcome with machete and anger. It's all right, Pak, go home, get some sleep, you're exhausted. Here, let me carry my bags.'

He handed them over. I walked along without looking back. Yet somehow I could tell he was still standing there. All of a sudden he shouted out and ran up to me: 'Forgive me, Ndoro; may I ask what is Ndoro's name?'

9

On our tenth day in Tulangan, Kommer arrived with a cut of venison. He looked happy and his face was tanned.

Mama went out to meet him. I still had to finish off a few lines more about Trunodongso. I paid no heed to the chattering of the newspaperman, but the sound of his voice was loud, joyful, full of hope.

After finishing my writing, I went out to meet him.

'How's your panther, Mr Kommer?'

'Haven't caught it yet. I'm going to have to go home first. They'll pull up the traps themselves,' he answered. 'What can one do? The paper is also important.'

'You look very well,' I spoke again.

'Nyai also looks very well,' he answered, 'but you seem a little pale yourself.'

'He has spent too much time inside, Mr Kommer,' said Nyai.

'What a pity,' said Kommer. 'If all you do is write, Mr Minke, life will be short. You must engage in some outdoor activities as well. It's a pity you didn't want to come hunting with me. Perhaps you have never seen how a deer runs along, jumping and constantly turning to look back to glimpse its hunter. Its beautiful many-branched antlers can't save its skin and its life. How beautiful they are, those antlers, especially if the deer is running with its head thrust towards the sky. A futile beauty: those antlers prevent it from hiding in the brush and running through the jungle. Because of the antlers, Mr Minke, only because of its antlers that animal is cursed with the fate of having to live always in the open, on the plains, and is therefore open also to the hunter's bullets. Just because of its beautiful antlers!'

'Perhaps you are engaging in some satire.'

'If you want to take it that way, you may. Look, the beauty of your life is your writing. So you seclude yourself in your room, and that indeed is a suicidal kind of activity.'

I laughed belittlingly.

'I'm totally serious, Mr Minke. At the moment you are still very, very young. You are healthy; you've never been ill. If you keep on staying indoors like this, you will lose much of life's richness.'

'Well, as far as that goes . . .'

'Five years indoors like this, stuck in your room, will use up the health and strength of ten years. What a pity if all of a sudden you feel dried up and worn out.'

I told him how I'd finished two articles, one of them being the best thing I'd ever written.

'I'm glad to hear that, Mr Minke; may I read that one?'

'You can read it in printed form later. But you are welcome to read the other one if you like.'

I handed him the manuscript 'Nyai Surati' and watched his face. Mama went out the back.

'You can comment on it now too, but don't mention any of the names I've used,' I warned him.

The manuscript was quite long. Kommer had not finished it by the time Mama came back with food. He was submerged in the story. Letting out a great breath, he placed it down on the table carefully, as if it would break, stared at me with shining eyes, and commented: 'It's becoming clearer from your writing.'

I was afraid he might mention Surati's name; but he mentioned no name.

'What do you think?' I asked coolly.

'Your unique characteristics are becoming more and more evident. It's true what people say, that you're going further and further in the direction of humanism, expanding its scope. If people like us say 'expanding its scope' then you must look for the aspect that isn't mentioned.' He didn't explain what that unmentioned aspect was. 'Your writings cry out to people's sense of humanity, rejecting barbarism, cheating, libel and weakness. You dream of human beings who are strong and whose humanity is strong also. Indeed, sir, only when all people are strong like that will we have true fraternity. You are truly a child of the French Revolution. As long as you retain these personal characteristics of yours . . .'

Mama listened with great seriousness, not involving herself. I saw Kommer sweep his gaze across to Mama, inviting her opinion. His request wasn't answered, but, as though he'd received some encouragement, the journalist continued: 'It seems you have studied many of the French writers.'

'No, sir.'

'No? Nah, that's why your outlook on life is so heavy, so serious, just like Multatuli. You have no sense of humour. If you started reading the French writers, you might be able to change.'

'So the piece isn't any good?'

'Good, very good indeed. There's no grounds for doubting how good it is. I'm talking about this outlook of yours. No humour, no sense of fun, heavy like a one-tonne weight. You face life and mankind too seriously; you are tense, as though you'd never taken any pleasure, never played.'

'Is it wrong to be serious?'

'No, not at all. But you don't mix with enough different kinds of people, from different classes. This constant tension and seriousness could kill you. Have you never had any interest in the lighter side of life?'

'Yes, Minke, you're always gloomy and serious, Child,' Mama intervened.

'Yes, Nyai, gloomy. That's exactly the right word,' Kommer flashed.

'I haven't seen any happy side to life yet,' I defended myself. Now the newspaper man listened with his full attention.

'The situation is still not very happy for many people, Mr Kommer, and that story is about maltreatment, oppression. Where is the light side of it? If I agreed with that kind of treatment of other people, perhaps I could see something funny in the grimaces of others' suffering,' I went on. 'I'm not among those who oppress others, Mr Kommer.'

'True, it's all true. You've brought it all to life within you as it has brought you to life. You have become one with your material. That is a matter of intellect and emotion. You are right on every point; isn't that so, Nyai?'

'Ah, I don't understand this sort of thing.' Mama was washing her hands of the whole thing.

'Life is a matter of balance, Mr Minke. A person who concerns himself only with the light side of things is a madman; but someone who is interested only in suffering is sick.'

'So you count me among the sick?'

'If you keep on this way – yes. You will lose your resilience, your adroitness will be suffocated by all the suffering you concern yourself with. It would be best if you learnt to change, if I may make a suggestion.'

Kommer seemed so sure of his words, as if there were no other possibility.

'He only needs a change of atmosphere, Mr Kommer,' Mama interrupted. 'I think you exaggerate a bit.'

The journalist was silenced by her reprimand. He turned to face Mama, and listened intently.

'He is still in mourning. If he sees suffering about him, then it's only proper and natural that it colours his writing. He sees all those who suffer as his friends, and all injustice as his enemy. People don't have to see merriment and suffering as being in some kind of balance. Isn't reality itself more real than anybody's opinion about reality?'

A debate then ensued. All in Dutch. Mama proved to know a lot about life. As a child, a latecomer to life, I listened more than I took part. Abruptly the debate stopped. Kommer's question came at me like the point of a cutlass: 'You write quite well. I think everyone would agree with me. This last article of yours is your best piece so far. If you continue like this, you won't be able to write stories. You will be making speeches, and you will stop being a writer. Do you want to be a writer or a speechmaker?'

That question hurt me greatly, partly because I couldn't understand his argument properly.

'Why does he have to choose between these two things?' Mama protested. 'He has the right to grow and develop. He has the right not to choose between those two things. He is still young; at the very least he still has twenty years in which to develop. Have you been more successful in your career than Minke?'

'Don't get me wrong, Nyai.' Kommer began to soften his line. 'Minke is the hope of his people. What other Native is there like him? If Minke doesn't accept this challenge, it will be difficult later for him to possess the resilience, the toughness he'll need. He'll be quickly discouraged and won't finish the work he began. Look, Nyai, even in this piece I have just read, already he has begun, although in a disguised manner, to speak out on behalf of his people . . .'

'Now *you're* making a speech,' Mama said.

'What do the Natives hope for from me? Nothing. But much is expected of Minke, with all his talents - too much. I have already urged him to acquaint himself with his people and their lives, a source of material that will never dry up. With this latest piece, he has started on that road. Isn't that so, Minke?'

'Yes,' I answered.

'Nyai, if Mr Minke here is unable to see the happier side of life, how is he going to be able to show his people what happier future they might build? Suffering is a narrow window through which to look on life, Nyai. And there are many ways to overcome it. Without some joy, some merriment, even in the defeat of suffering people will only go round and round in circles inside that suffering.'

Mama was silent. She seemed to be groping, not knowing what to say.

'Twenty years, Nyai. We have both experienced it ourselves - twenty years is not all that long. Twenty years can pass by and see a person no cleverer than he was before. There are many who become more and more unable to learn from their experiences. These are indeed harsh words, these words I direct at Mr Minke, and also to myself. But they are better than the flattery so generously handed out by Maarten Nijman. Minke here has been flattered too often. But the seeds which will grow within him, Nyai, where will he get them if not from those of his friends who are honest with him?'

'In twenty years, Tuan, he will have had much greater success, I am sure, than you, Mr Kommer.'

I turned the other way, embarrassed to hear my mother-in-law defend me and boast about me like that. She would rather see me victorious than see the truth.

'Nah, that is exactly what I hope will happen. Let me explain. Recently there has been a lot of talk in elite circles about those letters of Kartini, which have been read again for the umpteenth time before the conference of the League Against Moral Corruption in the Netherlands. She talks about the coming of the modern era in Europe, which she only knows second-hand. But in these Indies there is only the darkness of night. The modern era? Ha! Not a single spot of light is yet to be found. The Natives live in pitch darkness. In their ignorance, they make themselves the laughing stock of everyone, for their stupidity. One of the lines of her letters – as I understand it from what others have reported – goes: how happy people would be if they could sleep for who knows how long and then wake up to find that the modern era had already arrived. Nah, Nyai, many people have interpreted this sentence as a sign that she has given up, lost all hope. And in my opinion, she has indeed given up.'

'Nah, now it's you, Mr Kommer, who have become the speechmaker.'

'Indeed I am a giver of speeches. I speak a lot, Nyai, in many places.'

'But you too write like Minke.'

'True, Nyai.'

'Nah, well then, what is wrong with doing both things?'

'It would be a dangerous thing if Mr Minke made speeches in his writings instead of confining it to his conversations. Mr Minke doesn't seem to be as clever in, nor as inclined to talking as me. And a speech-dominated story is the very worst kind of writing.'

'What's all this got to do with Kartini?'

'What's it got to do with Kartini, Nyai? Kartini has given up hope. She no longer knows what to do for her people. So she feels tired, because she always sees suffering and suffering alone. She longs to sleep, and then to wake up and enjoy the bright modern era. The modern era is not being built in people's sleep, by their dreams. Mr Minke, I, and many others – and indeed your own people themselves – do not hope that it will be like that.'

'You deliver a clever speech,' Nyai praised him.

'I will do anything, Nyai, if it will be of use. And whatever else might be said about this Kartini, she is the only Native girl to speak out like this, in her letters and articles.'

'Nah, Child,' Nyai said finally, 'you have to decide what is best for yourself.'

'Mr Kommer,' I began, 'I don't really understand what you're getting at. What exactly is it you object to in my writings?'

'The piece is very good; I said so just now. But there are signs that you are turning your story into a speech. And that tendency will become more prominent in your writings if you are not warned. In these Indies there has been what we might call 'criticism'. Criticism can be rejected, but it has to be listened to first, reflected upon. If it isn't necessary to reject it, then it can be taken as a suggestion. No one need be angry just because they have been criticised.'

That was the first time that I had come across what Kommer called 'criticism'.

Lunch brought a halt to the conversation. Afterwards listlessness conquered us all. Kommer's enthusiasm for speech-making dwindled away. He sat sleepily in his chair, but didn't want to go home either; he enjoyed displaying his knowledge, and the opportunity to sit near Mama. As the day wore on our heads became heavier from the heat and humidity.

In a voice that had lost its spirit and enthusiasm, Kommer began again: 'A good author, Mr Minke, should be able to provide his readers with some joy, not a false joy, but some faith that life is beautiful. While suffering is man-made, and not some natural disaster, then it can surely be resisted by men. Give hope to your readers, to your fellow countrymen. Haven't I already advised you to learn to write in Malay or Javanese? Give your people the best that you are capable of.'

'I will not forget, Mr Kommer.'

'Between my two suggestions there are reciprocal connections.'

'I still need time to understand all of what you've said.'

'Of course, and you are still young, with plenty of time for that.'

'That's why I have brought him here, Mr Kommer,' said Mama, 'so he can get some fresh air. A new atmosphere, a new environment, new ideas, a new vigour. It's clear he has found much new material.'

'Exactly, Nyai, new material. But the way he approaches the material is exactly as before. Pessimistic. Suffering and gloom are his horizon. But the horizon itself is the base of the sky, where the sun sinks and then rises again, the place where boats and ships disappear from sight, and also the place where they emerge into view as they approach the shore.'

Only then did I realise that Kommer wasn't smoking. Because I too didn't smoke, I didn't say anything. Mama also took no notice.

'Mama, what Mr Kommer says is beginning to make sense to me. But, yes, I need to think about it calmly.'

'Yes, Mr Minke, you are an admirer of the French Revolution; you want to see human dignity given its proper place. If you look at people from one point of view, that of suffering alone, you will lose the many other aspects of humanity. Reflection upon suffering alone will only give rise to revenge, revenge and nothing else . . .'

'We're on holidays,' Mama suggested, 'Why don't we talk about something else, something happier?'

'Nothing happy has happened to me just lately, Nyai. I didn't catch the panther I wanted. Tomorrow I've got to go back to Surabaya. When are you going home, Nyai?'

'I think it will be after you go back.'

The conversation stagnated. Kommer began to lose his sharpness. He had already yawned three times. I myself had just yawned for the second time. Perhaps also it was because he was such a sleeper that he hadn't caught that panther, and hadn't caught Mama's heart either. He could fall asleep in front of Mama on the train, precisely at the time he was hoping she would say 'Yes' to his proposal. Maybe he could even fall asleep in the middle of giving a speech.

'If you're already sleepy,' Mama prodded him, 'you . . .'

'It's better I go home straight away, Nyai, Mr Minke.'

We went with him out to his horse. Then he rode slowly out of Tulangan.

'He was just showing off what he thinks he knows,' Mama growled, 'like a little child showing off her doll.'

'Perhaps there is some truth in his words, Ma.'

'Of course. But it was the way he put them across, Child, his excessive enthusiasm, his pride . . . that wasn't his heart's voice. He wanted to put his knowledge on display. Perhaps he doesn't really believe what he says.'

'He is a good man, Ma,' I said.

'Yes, he is a good man. That help he gave us was without any self-interest; at least I hope that's the case. But that speech of his just now, there was self-interest there . . .'

'What self-interest, Ma?' I asked like a whining child.

'Are you bored with staying here?'

'Perhaps Panji Darman has arrived back in Surabaya.'

'So you do really intend to leave me?'

'Whatever else happens, Ma, I hope that you will give me a little sister-in-law.'

'*Husy,*' and Nyai quickly walked back into the house.

Sastro Kassier's house was usually busy with the sounds of children. It was three o'clock in the afternoon and this time no sounds could be heard. Sitting in the front parlour by myself, gazing at the two portraits of Her Majesty Wilhelmina, I thought over all Kommer had said. He always ordered and insisted, suppressing me and robbing me of my freedom. I knew his intentions were good, not everything he wished from me was wrong. Perhaps indeed he was right about everything. But why did he have to push his ideas so aggressively? Why was he more interested in bragging about his own greatness and in flooding those around him with his enthusiasm? So he can control them? *Must* and *Don't* are his banners, no matter what the particular idea – as if there were no other point of view. Earlier, when I had only known him a little, and superficially at that, I had been attracted to him. I saw him as a man of decision, and without rival. But the more I got to know him, the more my feelings changed. They were no longer sympathetic, indeed the opposite. Even Mama didn't want to continue the debate with him.

How different he was from Sarah and Miriam de la Croix. Even Magda Peters had not gone around *ordering, insisting*. Jean Marais, who was such a gentle and shy man, was not like that, except for the one time he pressed me about using Malay. And that was probably a result of Kommer's influence.

My father and elder brother were exactly the same as Kommer, full of *musts* and *don'ts*. I smiled: perhaps that was how they were, those backward people who had never been touched by the spirit of the French Revolution? Men who had become comfortable with ordering around their wives and children and their neighbours and their relatives who had no power? My smile developed into a laugh. I was pleased with this idea of mine – an idea that was by no means certain to be true.

Yes, perhaps Kommer was right this time. Very likely so. But with so many *musts* and *don'ts* he should entertain no hopes of getting close to Mama's heart.

Why was Jean Marais so easily influenced by him, trying to coerce me to learn Malay? Such a polite and shy person? I tried to recollect what he had said that had hurt me so much. All I recalled was that old reminder of his: be just and fair, starting with your thoughts. I have always tried to think and act justly, my heart assured me. Have a go now at weighing things up again, as if Marais were testing your true inner thoughts. You still spend more time weighing up the good and bad of other people: what about yourself? Have you really considered all this fairly?

Is it true that you write for Dutch readers when you have not the slightest debt to them? Just as your beloved Mother says?

I am about to start to learn Malay, I answered. That cannot be achieved in just a day.

Are you absolutely sure that you have never forced and pressured people into doing things, nor gone around forbidding them to do things just because you liked it, as some kind of luxury or enjoyment? Like Kommer?

No, never. Really, never.

If it is true you are an admirer of the French Revolution, why were you so offended when a farmer, like Trunodongso, spoke in low Javanese to you?

I was ashamed in my heart and unable to answer. And I admitted it: The spirit and ideals of the French Revolution still had not cleared away my old attitudes as I lived my day-to-day life. It was still just something I'd read about, no more than an ornament to my thoughts.

Good, you have admitted that. Now, if a Native starts to talk to you in high Javanese will you advise him to switch to low Javanese? Ha, you can't answer. You are still not able to give up the comforts and pleasures that are yours as an inheritance from your ancestors – rulers over your own Native fellow countrymen. You're a cheat! The ideals of Freedom, Equality and Fraternity of the French Revolution? – you have betrayed them, for the benefits of that inheritance. It is only the ideal of Freedom that lives within you, and then it is only freedom for yourself, no more. Don't you feel ashamed that you dare call yourself an admirer of the French Revolution?

I shrivelled up in shame. Yes, I had to admit it: I was still unable to give up the benefits of my heritage. When someone spoke to me in low Javanese, I felt my rights had been stolen away. On the other hand, if people spoke to me in high Javanese, I felt I was among those chosen few, placed on some higher plane, a god in a human's body, and these pleasures from my heritage caressed me.

You are not being honest as an educated person should be, Minke.

Those peasants addressed me that way of their own free will.

They do not do it of their own free will. They behave that way because of their experiences over the ages, as the slaves of both great and little kings. They would be flattened flush to the ground if they themselves did not flatten their bodies napkin-like before their kings – indeed they had been forced to prostrate themselves that way. If that is how they act towards you, a fellow Native, they will behave the same way before other peoples too. Then why should you be offended when Natives abase themselves before the Europeans? You have not learnt and practised justice; it is not yet part of your character.

One can't throw away all those benefits and pleasures in just one go, I rebutted.

You are learning to know more about your people. You now have a little knowledge about them: how through the Javanese language you yourself actually help to enslave your own people. And then you pretend you want to defend Trunodongso through your writings in the newspapers.

I will defend him.

Do you really want to defend him?

Yes. Truly, I do, by Allah.

Mama says: God is always on the side of those who win.

And so people must struggle to be victors, and thus God will bless their efforts. When Mama speaks like that, she is speaking in the name of her own experiences. She did not accept defeat. But in the final confrontation with Europe she was defeated; God has not yet blessed her struggles.

So now you want to defend them from oppression, using Dutch, your language? Ha, you can't answer. Then they are right: you must begin to write in Malay, Minke; Malay does not hold within it any oppressive character. It is in accord with the aims of the French Revolution.

'Are you daydreaming, Tuan?'

I was startled. Djumilah moved my manuscript away to make room for banana-coconut custard and some thick black coffee. I answered with a laugh and nodded my thanks. I put the manuscript away.

'Perhaps you're thinking of someone, heh?' she jibed me. 'Is there someone you've met here in Tulangan?'

'I've met so many people, many indeed,' I answered.

'Thanks be to God,' and she went out to the back again. I watched Djumilah as she left, a lioness without strength, except to roar. Truly different from the wife of Trunodongso – without needing to roar she goes side by side with her husband, as a friend in life, and as an ally as well. Different too from Mother, who knows only devotion and doing good. Different again from educated Kartini, who longs for the arrival of the modern age. Different also from Mama, an independent human being – the essence of the ideal of Liberty from the French Revolution – who sees the modern era as containing no blessings beyond the advances in tools and technique.

From among all those women it is Mama who most closely resembles the ideal of the French Revolution.

And you yourself? You too are a free human being, like Nyai, but you are not trying to live up to the ideals of Equality and Fraternity. Wasn't the Revolution over more than a hundred years ago? What do you say now? More than one hundred years have passed!

Yes, there is very little of these ideals within me. Jean Marais works towards his ideal of filling his life with his paintings, not just obtaining his livelihood from them. Why do I want to write just to be famous? Just to feel satisfied with myself? You are being unjust again, Minke. Does your search for your own satisfaction give you the right to fame? Unjust! Others work until they sweat blood, to the edge of death – and there is no fame for them. They may not even be sure of eating two meals a day.

And you are no different from others. You are no taller, no more to be honoured than Trunodongso. That is, if you truly understand what the French Revolution was all about. What do you think now, Minke?

And I remembered Khouw Ah Soe. He was fulfilling his life.

And the Filipino Natives who had tried to oust the Spanish, they too had given substance to their lives. And they had fought back against the Americans as well.

Writing is obviously not just a means towards self-satisfaction. Writing must be a way of giving substance to your life, as Jean said. And I was happy: my story about Trunodongso would do that. I would publish it. No need to take notice of Kommer's opinions . . .

10

On stepping down onto Surabaya station I asked Mama's permission to go straight to Nijman's office. In my bag were two manuscripts. One I thought was very good, the other perfect. Both contained eternal values, both were dedicated to eternity. I was proud most of all of the second article: a defence of all those suffering the same fate as Trunodongso. The world must be told how Java's farmers are being thrown off their rice lands – the most fertile lands with the best irrigation – by the sugar factories, and with the aid of the Native civil servants in colonial employ and of the village officials. If Multatuli had been here in Surabaya, I would have come to him and said: Teacher, today I begin to follow where you have trod before.

Today I am important.

All who have fallen from on high, I began my story about Trunodongso, *have been saved and then restored by the farmers: kings, ministers, soldiers. And all the treading feet of men: they too have been borne on the backs of the farmers* . . .

There had never been any fiction written about farmers. Mine was the first. People said I did not understand my own people. Just let them wait! Soon they would know.

At Nijman's offices, the Pure-Blood boy invited me to go straight upstairs. Nijman stood, and held out his hand: 'It's been so long since you have been here. The readers have been waiting for another article from you.'

I took out the article about Trunodongso. Proudly I handed it over to him: 'Mr Nijman, here are the results of my silence all this while.'

He took it, politely, and asked would I allow him to read it now. I nodded. He would be amazed by the advances I had made.

'Poetic!' he nodded very politely and went on reading.

He had never used that word before. Just one word, and I felt it was a measure of the article's worth.

I observed his face. He hadn't finished one page; the smile had disappeared. On the second page, his forehead wrinkled. Before he went on to the third page he raised his eyes and looked at me.

It could be no other way, Mr Nijman; this is the first time you would have read such a story as this!

He went on again. His face was turning red. On the fifth page, he put the manuscript down. He took up his pipe and began to suck on it. He blew out the smoke slowly into the air. Then: 'Do you remember the person who sat on the same chair as you now sit?'

'Of course: Khouw Ah Soe.'

'Yes.'

He didn't go on. He seemed to be groping for the right words. Why bring up Khouw Ah Soe? I became vigilant.

'Yes, Mr Minke. All of a sudden I'm reminded of him. It seems you became friends with him after that meeting.'

'I never met him again after that.'

'True? As I read this, I get the feeling that you must have talked with him again.'

His words came at me like accusations. What was the connection between Trunodongso and Khouw Ah Soe? My pride in the story was overshadowed by a new fear.

'The spirit of this story – your spirit, your enthusiasm – has influenced the story too much.'

'Influenced it? How?' I asked anxiously.

He didn't answer, but asked instead: 'What were you thinking of when you wrote this?'

'What was I thinking of? The person about whom I was writing.'

'A true character or just someone out of your imagination?'

'A real person.'

'So you would dare to claim that all this here is more than just imagination? That it is factual?'

'Of course it is.'

'You would dare guarantee that?'

'Yes, I would,' I answered, once again the hero, my pride returned.

He said nothing more. He read the story again, starting from the beginning. I was still nervous about being connected that way to Khouw Ah Soe. That wouldn't happen, would it?

Nijman stopped reading and fell into thought.

Yes, he would be impressed by this – my best writing, perfect – a protest about the injustices suffered by who knows how many thousands of Trunodongsos. I would reveal to the world the conspiracy of blood-sucking vampires who were cheating those illiterate farmers of their rents. Who could tell how many tens of years this deception had been going on?

Before reaching the end of the second page, Nijman raised his eyes again, looked at me very sharply, and asked: 'You are the son-in-law of the late Mr Mellema, yes? And what would your father-in-law think if he were still alive and saw what you have written here?'

My expectation that he would be impressed disappeared abruptly. On his face were signs of restrained fury.

'What's the connection with the late Mr Mellema?'

'You yourself know, don't you, that he was the Administrator of a sugar factory? You yourself have written: "And who knows for how many tens of years this deception has been going on?" If it has only been twenty-five years, it means you have accused the late Mr Mellema of carrying out such deceptions for at least four years.'

My eyes almost popped out. Such a thing had never crossed my mind. Nijman's lips were still moving; his voice continued: 'You have accused your father-in-law of being involved in a conspiracy to defraud people of their rents. And you must know the implications of such a deception: Boederij Buitenzorg was set up with money obtained from such conspiracies. Yes? Or wasn't that what you meant? Why are you silent? Do you still wish to say that all you have written is true? Not just fantasy?'

I was speechless. My mind worked faster and faster, but whatever I thought of, it was Mama's face that I saw.

'Good; what you have written here is not just fantasy,' Nijman went on. His voice was soft but its lashes still hurt. 'Could you prove these embezzlements if the appropriate officials demanded evidence from you?' He stared at me as though he would never blink again. 'Or indeed is it your intention to publish a libel?'

'No! But these peasants – they have no place to air their grievances.'

'Nowhere to take their grievances? There are police everywhere. That's what police are for. They can ask for protection from the police.'

'The police are closer to the factory officials than the peasants, Mr Nijman. You must know that yourself.'

'So now you're accusing the police of being in on the conspiracy too?' He awaited my answer. 'Are you out to multiply your accusations? Look, Mr Minke, if another person were here with us now, and he later made accusations against you, as a witness I would naturally have to recount everything that had been said. You are lucky there is no other witness here. And you're luckier still that I am not a police official. If I were, and if I made a case of this, you would be involved in a case of libel, and you yourself, I think, would find many difficulties in obtaining both evidence and witnesses.'

Now I began to realise how dangerous it was to be a writer. But why had there been silence about this issue for so long? And why now that I was writing about peasants did Nijman no longer like my writings?

'Don't worry,' he finally humoured me. 'In my opinion, this story is totally untrue, its just *smaadschrift*. This character of yours, if he does in fact exist, is just a liar. You have been taken in by his lies. He's nothing but a liar.'

My honour was offended. His words implied the accusation: you too are lying through that character of yours, Minke!

'But you know, sir; Minke is not a liar.'

'Of course you are not a liar. But a wrong original conception can give birth to many errors,' he answered. 'There are no peasant farmers who have become poor as a result of renting their land to the sugar mills. They receive a fair rent. They are happy to work as plantation labourers, on their own land that they have rented out.'

He was silent and I was silent. The atmosphere of enmity pressed down upon my heart.

'Do you know what the wage of a sugar-mill worker is?' Seeing that I could not answer, he went on, 'At least one *talen* a day. By working for a factory just one week, he receives the equivalent of the rent he receives himself for one bahu of his land.'

At that moment, I was envious of Kommer's skill in debate. Someone like him would easily be able to parry the attacks of this other experienced newspaper man. I was not able to do so yet. At that moment I could do nothing. I had to admit that there was still much that I had not yet learnt from Trunodongso.

'You are still silent. I'm not going to do anything, sir. We are friends, yes? Your only lack is that you have not yet mastered all the material about sugar. You need to study the sugar mill's Annual Report. The Tulangan one, in particular. Or for all of Sidoarjo, or even all of Java. Or you can study the Memorial Edition of the *Factorij*. If you are indeed interested in these things, I will be very happy to help you.'

I could not dam back Nijman's words with talk about justice and truth. He looked at the issue from a completely different angle. It was clear he sided with the factories, that he did not want to know who this Trunodongso was.

'And a good wage for a sugar-cane labourer, Mr Minke: how much is that? Three talens. Someone working as a coolie, after just five days' work, if he is a good worker, can earn the equivalent of twice the rent he receives for one bahu of land. Who says people prefer to work their own land rather than become sugar-mill coolies? What's the price of a day's labour hoeing? Three beggol, no more than that.'

His words kept on sliding out, unstoppable, unparried. All kinds of emotions wrestled within my breast. All kinds of information about sugar came forth from his mouth: the cost of the foreman's labour, of the employees, the cost of the hulling machinery, the cost of the sack material and of having them sewn up, the expertise of the sugar-mill engineers, whose education was not available in every town or country.

My pride in this, my best manuscript, the most perfect of all, dissolved in disarray. My faith in myself melted. I saw myself as the most stupid of people, thoughtless, not knowing how to weigh things up, ignorant. But still I felt I was on the side of truth.

'You are a good writer, but not a good journalist. In this you have lost the beauty of writing. You are making a speech . . .' – exactly what Kommer said.

He didn't read the fifth page.

'It's a pity we have such different opinions,' I said. My hand was ready to take the manuscript from his desk.

'We don't have different opinions, Mr Minke. Don't be mistaken. When you are writing about reality, you must make sure that you provide enough documentation. There are specific ways of doing that.'

'I am sure my writings do not contain errors.'

'People can believe in many things that are not right. History is indeed the story of liberation from wrong beliefs, of struggle against stupidity, against ignorance.'

He looked the other way, as if to give me the chance to regain possession of myself.

'It's best that you keep clear of things that might end up getting you in trouble. One or two untrue explanations in the hands of an educated person could develop into some kind of general disturbance. It will be Natives who suffer in the end. Do you still remember Khouw Ah Soe? Hmm, an educated young man, with wrong thoughts stemming from a wrong explanation of things. He left his own country, and came to make trouble here in the Indies. It was lucky the Chinese of Surabaya weren't able to be stirred up by him. So in the end he had to suffer the consequences of his own errors. You've heard what happened?'

'What do you mean?'

'He was killed.'

'Khouw Ah Soe?'

'That's who I'm talking about.'

'Where, Mr Nijman?'

'You seem very keen to know. I can tell from that, and from your writings, that you did indeed become friends with him.' He put his pipe down on the table; it had gone out. 'If you ended up as Khouw Ah Soe did, I too would feel a loss, as would many others, Mr Minke.'

'If you yourself experienced what Khouw Ah Soe experienced, Meneer Nijman, I would be just as keen to know what happened, even though you and I have never really been close friends.'

No doubt he knew what my answer meant: I no longer looked upon him as a teacher. I saw him now as a competitor who wanted to box me into a corner. I took my manuscript, put it in my briefcase. And, just as Khouw Ah Soe had done that day, I left his office without excusing myself.

I hired a carriage and headed straight for Jean Marais's house. Along the journey I thought over and over again about those threat-filled words of Nijman's. Perhaps he could do some evil against me, and my story about Trunodongso could be used as evidence. He was happy, even joyful, about Khouw Ah Soe's death. He could be equally as pleased by my own.

Quickly I took out the manuscript. Ah, my most beautiful of all works, perfect! I held it in both hands. I tore it once, twice, three times. The paper was now tiny shreds, becoming even smaller, scattered along the road.

Trunodongso, forgive me. I am not yet able!

I found Maysoroh bringing water into the kitchen. She was so happy to see me. Jean was engrossed in watching his workmen. I took him into his own work room.

'You look upset, Minke,' he greeted me.

'You're not wrong, Jean.'

'What trouble are you in now?'

'No, it's this . . . for the first time ever, I have torn up my own writing. I scattered it over the road.' I told him everything that had happened. And I ended with: 'I will never have anything to do with *Soerabaiaasch Nieuws* again. Nor with Nijman. This is the second time he's done wrong by me.'

I waited to hear Jean's opinion. He sat silently in his chair. He didn't even look at me, as if my anger, my worries, my fury were of no interest to him. All he did was call May and tell her to be quicker getting dinner ready.

'Don't you have any opinion on this, Jean?' I pressed him. 'You're siding with him because he's European?'

He blinked, startled, and turned to stare at me. He spoke slowly: 'That is just prejudice,' he said in French, then went on in Malay: 'I have often tried to explain to you what prejudice is. What you just said is a kind of prejudice, colour prejudice, cultural prejudice. You are educated, aren't you?'

'Nijman is no less educated than me. He is more prejudiced. He is siding with the factories rather than with justice and what is right.'

'Just a minute, Minke. You haven't seen how things are. Perhaps you're right, but are unable yet to prove that you are right. I am absolutely sure you are right about the factories. Your only weakness is that you don't have any proof. As far as the law goes, you are in the wrong. Charges could indeed be brought against you. You would be found guilty. You could not

430

produce evidence. On the other hand, the Court would definitely be able to prove you were making unsubstantiated allegations.'

'I could get the testimony of Trunodongso and others like him.'

'He has put his thumb-print to every receipt he has received. And the amounts he would have received would be exactly as written on the receipt, not a cent less.'

'But that's where the deception lies!' my fury exploded again.

'And that is what you must prove. You must take on a new task besides that of writer; you must become a detective. If you succed in obtaining evidence that embezzlement and deception are occurring, your writing will be of much greater value. No one will be able to reject it. That indeed is the method used by the great social writers of Europe. Behind each of their works, there is full documentation. They are not afraid of any court. It is rather the courts that are sometimes afraid of them.'

I had to listen. This kind of thing had never been taught by Magda Peters.

'They too are like you, writing to achieve a victory for humanity and justice; but your position before the law is much weaker. I hope you will be stronger. You are not in the wrong, you are in the right. It is just that your position is not yet strong enough. Ah, Minke, you must never think that I am not on your side. I know you. And it is not just the Indies, but the whole world, that needs writers like you, writers who take positions on what they write about.'

'You know all this; why don't you write it yourself?'

'If I could write, why would I become a painter?'

'Thank you, Jean. I understand. You are my friend.'

'Don't be discouraged, Minke. There was no need to tear up that story. We could have studied it together. I am always happy to help you.'

'I'm furious, worried, bitter, Jean.'

'I understand. But your writings pose no danger while they remain unpublished. That's the trouble with looking on Nijman as a god. The time had to come when you would be disappointed. He does not make the rules. He is just one man among millions upon this earth, and every one of those millions has the right to his own opinion. Why then are you angry? Why does the fact that Nijman has a different opinion to you offend you, upset you? He too has the right to his own opinion.'

'He was so rude, Jean. He has never been like that before.'

'You must see Kommer. He predicted this: that you would be disappointed.'

'Yes, I remember.'

'He was let down earlier than you.'

'Thank you, Jean. I understand.'

Maysoroh came out looking for me. Seeing we were engaged in serious

431

conversation, she didn't join us but sat at a distance looking at me with questioning eyes.

'Kommer was here yesterday,' Jean said. 'He was upset that his trap didn't work. He was more upset still that you seemed disappointed with his opinions.'

'Yes.'

'Where's Uncle Minke's drink, May?' May left and returned carrying a tray with drinks – hot, steaming tea. Then she moved away again.

'Perhaps he is a bit rough, a bit rude even. But that doesn't mean he is necessarily wrong, Minke. He was disappointed too that you still wanted to write for the *Soerabaiaasch Nieuws*.'

'May, let's go to Wonokromo,' I said to her.

'I've got a friend coming over this afternoon, Uncle. A pity.'

After drinking what May had brought in, I excused myself. Jean Marais felt he had to limp out with me to the carriage. 'Where's your buggy?'

'I'm using a hired one, Jean.'

'Don't be discouraged; don't let this break you. It would be a loss to me too.'

The carriage took me back towards Wonokromo. About a hundred metres from Jean's house, I saw Kommer. Perhaps he was going to Jean's place. He didn't see me, and I didn't really want to be seen by him.

Darsam greeted me with his arm in a sling and his hand bandaged.

'Cursed bad luck, Young Master,' he complained.

'Fall off a carriage?'

He shook his head and stroked his moustache with his left hand.

'Just bad luck, Young Master, stupid luck!'

'Fall from a horse? But you don't ride.'

'It's all taken care of now, Young Master. It's all in the hands of the police.'

'Police? What's happened?'

'Fatso, Young Master, he came back. I'll tell you later tonight, so Nyai can hear at the same time.'

On entering the house, I found Mama sitting reading the *Soerabaiaasch Nieuws*. She stopped reading and motioned me to sit down. Then: 'Your friend, Child . . . read this.' She pushed the paper across to me.

In a big headline the news was reported: THE DEATH OF A RABBLE-ROUSER. I read the report. The person named as a rabble-rouser was none other than Khouw Ah Soe.

This report followed. One morning a wig was found nailed to the wooden pylons of the Merah Bridge. The wig had a long pigtail and was covered in blood. It had obviously been nailed there deliberately; the nail

432

was not at all rusted. The police who examined it ordered a Chinaman to translate the writing inside. It read: 'If this wig is found forcibly freed from my head, it means they have got me. They – the Thong Terror Society.'

Three hours later, a fisherman had to climb down out of his *sampan*, twelve metres from the bridge. His net had snagged on something. He hurriedly climbed aboard again, and headed for shore, shouting: 'A body! A body! Dead! In the water!'

Once again the police arrived on the scene. All the fishermen nearby were ordered to haul in the net. The victim was a young Chinaman with short hair and sharp but few teeth. His feet were bound together and tied to a bundle of rocks. On his body they found thirty wounds from sharp instruments.

In a short time the police discovered who the man was: he had gone by the name of Khouw Ah Soe, a rabble-rouser on the run from Shanghai, chased out of Hong Kong, who finally met his end in the Mas River, Surabaya.

No one had come to claim his body.

'Don't try to do anything about the body, Child. He has finished his work. Dying in someone else's country, without friend or family.'

'I heard from Nijman, Ma. He seemed happy about Khouw's death.'

Nyai Ontosoroh paid no heed to my words. She gazed into the far distance.

'He knew the danger, Ma,' I said to humour her.

'It seems anybody who has an opinion must be expelled or annihilated here in the Indies,' she said, half to herself.

Mama then bowed her head, and so did I. We paid our respects to a young foreigner, a few years older than me, a lone wanderer. Here in the Indies to call out to his people to rise and awaken; that the danger of Japan had already touched upon China, that Japan would swallow up their country if they remained stagnant in this modern era. Any nation would be proud to have a son such as him.

Khouw Ah Soe appeared in my mind's eye as a giant. I felt very, very small: a youth hanging onto a nyai, whose own country had been swallowed up by the Dutch for three hundred years.

Mama was the first to raise her head. It seemed she was still half thinking to herself: 'Any mother would be happy to have such a son as him, even though her heart would be in turmoil.

'He was an orphan, Ma.'

'Happy then will his parents be to have him back with them.'

The two of us sat silently, recalling all we could of that young Chinaman.

'There was once another orphan like him, like your friend. Even today he is loved by the people in the village, perhaps in all the villages of Java, Child, even though hundreds of years have passed. He too was killed in the end like your friend. Except that he died on the battlefield. He too was brave, intelligent, clever. You know his name: Surapati – Untung Surapati.' She pronounced his name syllable by syllable, as if savouring its sound, and its memory.

My thoughts moved to Untung Surapati. Mama admired him and loved him. And I felt ashamed, because all this time I had never thought of him as more than a character in a story.

'There is not a single Javanese who does not know of Untung Surapati. Every one of them loves him.'

The atmosphere of mourning was abruptly ended by the arrival of a hired carriage. Kommer jumped down and then helped Jean Marais out. The two of them came up to the house.

'Excuse us, Nyai, we've come after hearing of Mr Minke's recent unhappy experience.'

'You mean the report in the paper?'

'Newspaper report?' Kommer asked. 'No, his bitter experience with Maarten Nijman.'

I quickly told Mama what had happened.

'It wasn't the manuscript I read?' Kommer asked.

'No.'

'That one you considered was your best article ever?'

'I think,' Mama intervened, 'it must have been his best. There was something he wanted to achieve with it.'

'I think so too,' Kommer agreed. 'But Jean Marais's comments are right; Mr Minke's legal position is weak. But Trunodongso's position is weaker still. He will never be able to prove the truth of his statements, even though he is telling the truth. But I want to give you some more information about Nijman's paper. You should have been told this long ago. Nyai, Mr Minke, it is only natural that Nijman takes the side of sugar, because he himself lives from sugar. His paper is owned by sugar interests, funded by the sugar companies, to protect the interests of the sugar lobby.'

Mama and I removed Khouw Ah Soe, and Untung Surapati, and Darsam from our thoughts. We also put aside Jean Marais, who was always being caught dreamily admiring Mama.

I was impressed by Kommer's explanation. When he was still a teenager, having just graduated from E.L.S., he went to work for the weekly paper *De Evenaar*. It was a small and insignificant paper. Its printery was owned by a sugar mill. Then he found out that the paper itself was also owned by Lord Sugar.

'I knew Mr Mellema already twenty-five years ago,' he went on. 'He arrived one day with a text he wanted printed in the paper. It attacked the attitude of the Patih of Sidoarjo, who was putting obstacles in the way of the sugar mill's attempts to expand the area of land it controlled. It rejected the Patih's opinion that sugar was impoverishing the region of Sidoarjo; it claimed that sugar was making the region prosperous. The Patih was later moved to Bondowoso. Two years later a Sub-District Head, a *camat*, argued with Mr Mellema. The camat himself owned fifty hectares of first-class paddy fields, but he was still greedy to obtain more. A competition arose between the factory and the camat, each trying to expand their land holdings. Mr Mellema came to the paper again, and ordered me to spy on the camat. Officially I was to go there as a reporter.'

'You did it?' Nyai Ontosoroh asked.

'I was just a low-level employee then, Nyai. I did what I was told.'

'What else were you ordered to do?'

'Just to report back on his habits and so on. I reported everything to Mr Mellema.'

'That's all?'

'That's all. I returned to Surabaya and continued with my work at the paper. Then I received news: the camat had been replaced. It's not clear where the old camat was moved to. All his land went to an executor and from there across to the sugar mill.'

'Did the camat die?' Nyai asked, upset.

'No one knows, Nyai.'

'You're not being honest with me,' Mama pressed.

'After the camat disappeared, I felt I had been part of something evil too. I was disappointed in my paper. I left it and went to work for the *Surabaya Star*. The paper I left behind grew, coming out twice a week. Once it became a daily it changed its name to *D.D.*, just for a week. It was accused from Batavia of violating a trade name. *D.D. Surabaya* changed its name to *Soerabaiaasch Nieuws*. But it was the same paper it is today: a creature of the sugar lobby. It must defend the interests of sugar. Anything can happen, so long as sugar remains safe! Your writings delivered you into a trap, Mr Minke. A sugar trap!'

'Just a minute, Mr Kommer,' Mama intervened, 'I once heard of a body that was found in the paddy fields. Gored by a buffalo, the rumours said. The camat of Sidoarjo . . .?'

'I don't know about that, Nyai; the papers never reported it . . .'

Mama was silent. Perhaps she was asking herself what other things there were that she didn't know about Herman Mellema. Her face showed the signs of an unsettled heart.

'It wasn't my intention to remind you of the late Mr Mellema,' said Kommer, asking forgiveness.

'I understand, Mr Kommer; excuse me,' she answered, arose, then withdrew.

We all watched Mama as she went out.

'Was she angry, do you think Mr Minke?' asked Kommer.

'There have been too many shocks just lately, Mr Kommer,' I answered. 'So many deaths, so many injustices, and now you bring up another matter. Too shocking – to find out that Herman Mellema did such things. I am shocked myself. It's understandable.'

'That wasn't my intention, Mr Minke, truly.'

'You have only told us what you know. We should be thankful for your frankness.'

'It disappoints me too, Minke; it saddens me, not that there is such a good explanation for Nijman's actions, but that it should bring so much hurt and sourness with it,' Jean Marais added.

'There is nothing to regret, Jean. We would have been even more disappointed if nobody had told us. Eh, Mr Kommer? We are truly grateful you have been prepared to tell us all this. It must have taken a lot of courage to tell us. And it was all brought about by my writings. Indeed that story of mine, the one I considered the best of all, I tore up and scattered along the road even before you had a chance to read it. But this other one, Mr Kommer' – I opened my bag and took out the story 'Nyai Surati' – 'would you accept this manuscript as a souvenir of this dark day?'

'Why, Minke?' asked Jean Marais. 'Do you mean for it to be put into Malay and published by Mr Kommer?'

'No, Jean. It's for Mr Kommer himself. Who knows, perhaps one day Mr Kommer will have time to go through it and change it, rewrite it, as a remembrance of our friendship, and of this day too.'

Kommer was unsure, but accepted it.

'You often go to Sidoarjo,' I added. 'You can do some more research, and won't be in a hurry, as I was. You did say you thought the story had merit, even if written like a speech?'

'Why don't you perfect it yourself?'

'Beginning this day, Mr Kommer, I close one book. I accept your suggestion. I will learn to see the brighter side of life. The way I am now, all my strength is being sucked away.'

'Close one book, Minke? What do you mean? You mean you're not going to write again?'

'Yes, Jean. I must stop writing, at least for a while.'

'You're tired, Minke,' said Marais gently, 'not your body, your soul. You need a new environment, a new atmosphere.'

'Yes. I must go.'

'Go where, Minke? You'll leave Nyai alone, by herself?'

I couldn't answer. What Jean had said made me realise just how tired and dispirited I was.

'Good, you must get some rest,' Kommer proposed. 'You have the right to a rest. We only came to let you know about Maarten Nijman and his paper, a sugar paper. You musn't be discouraged. Come, Mr Marais; we'll go now. Pass on our goodbyes to Nyai.'

They left. I escorted them to the front steps. My eyes accompanied their carriage as it left our property. Further and further away they moved, finally disappearing from sight.

However unrefined Kommer might be, he's proved to be a good and reliable friend. And Jean Marais too. What would happen to me if I had no friends? They have felt all that I have felt over the last months. I will write a letter to Mother, and tell her of the beauty of friendship – something she always advised me about but which I never thought about seriously until now.

Back inside the house, I remembered Mama. The news Kommer brought had shaken her greatly. She had lost something which she had always been able to hold on to. I should be with her now.

Slowly I made my way up the stairs. I didn't knock. The door wasn't locked; indeed it was open a little. Coming from inside the room were sounds of crying, almost inaudible. That a heart as hard as hers could shed tears! How much she had suffered already. Still, Kommer's information about *De Evenaar* and *Soerabaiaasch Nieuws* and their connection with Herman Mellema had deeply shocked her.

11

But the book wasn't completely closed. Unpleasant matters still pursued us.

That night I sat beside Nyai in the front parlour. Her eyes were still swollen, though she seemed more lively. The look in her eyes showed that she was still meditating on things; then they would change and you could see she was becoming anxious again.

'Yes, Minke, Child, you should look for a new environment. How I too would like to leave here, leave for some distant place and rid myself of all this. Kommer is right. We could petrify like rocks if we keep getting knocked around like this.'

'Where does Mama want to go, so far away?'

'I'm bored with Wonokromo. Perhaps I'm bored too with this kind of life. Wherever we go, it is always bandits that we find.'

'To Europe? Or Siam maybe?'

'Perhaps one day I will leave the Indies. This country becomes more and more foreign to me with every day.'

'Europe or Siam would be even more foreign, Ma.'

She didn't answer. All I could hear was a sigh of complaint. And that was the first time I had ever heard her complain. She was much disturbed by Kommer's news, I knew what was troubling her. Nijman had snidely hinted to me that Herman Mellema was also involved in the conspiracy to cheat people of their rents. While I had not passed on Nijman's remarks to anyone, especially not to Nyai, a woman so clever could easily work out her late master's involvement in the crimes.

'If I had known before that his capital was obtained by deception, black-mail . . . murder,' Mama spoke.

'We only know now, Ma.'

'It's lucky you wrote about Trunodongso. If you hadn't, I'd still feel . . . feel clean. Even after his death that damned man still deceived me. Devil! Barbarian!' she began to burn with fury, exploding into insults and curses. 'Acting like a man of honour – in reality just a deceiver of powerless peasants!'

In my mind's eye I saw the young administrator of the mill at Tulangan who had twice invited Mama to his house. He would be no different from Plikemboh and Mellema, my father-in-law.

All of a sudden Mama lost control and began to cry.

'Let me take you upstairs, Ma.'

'Let it be, Minke, let my heart speak now. Listen to me. Listen. If you will not, then who will listen to me?'

Her wave of weeping reached a peak, words held back by sobbing, the crying of a strong-hearted woman, courageous, experienced, educated and intelligent – the weeping of someone who realises she has built her life on top of mud.

I could do nothing but bow my head. This woman who was used to standing straight and firm needed no crutch.

As the weeping ebbed her words came, one by one, the sentence broken by sobs: 'I have never felt such regret as I feel now, that I was soiled by the touch of his body. That I gave birth to his children. Bastard, bandit, scum! That I ever served him: cheater of peasants, creator of poverty, oppressor, blackmailer . . .'

'Ya, Ma, forgive me for writing that story.'

'Murdered. That camat was murdered on his orders. They said he was gored to death by a buffalo, but it was Mellema who killed him. Mellema!'

'Ma.'

'Surati did the right thing, killing that man. She killed him. That's what I should have done, not with smallpox, but with my own hands. Dog! Crocodile!'

'If I hadn't written about Trunodongso . . .'

'You have done nothing wrong at all, Child. Mellema is lucky he is dead.'

'Ma.'

'Otherwise, I could do the worst and have Darsam kill him, so that he would die before my very eyes!'

Nyai Ontosoroh covered her face with both hands.

I could see Darsam out at the back, walking about with his arm in a sling, wanting to come inside and report. I signalled to him to go. He turned off to the right and disappeared from sight.

'What is my situation now? For twenty years I have developed our capital, evilly gained capital, won by cheating those without power.'

'It's not all from deception, Ma.'

'Who knows? I don't dare have such hopes. How dare he! How dare he! Barbarian! Animal! Damned! Cursed!' Once again she burned with fury and disillusionment.

'I'll get something to drink.' Without waiting I went off to the kitchen.

I found Darsam sitting at the table. A cook was making coffee for him.

'Cold water, please, cook, one glass.'

'Good, Young Master, let me take it to her.'

'I'll take it myself, cook.'

Darsam stood up, paid his respects, and asked: 'Is there still something important being discussed, Young Master?'

'Perhaps you won't be able to make your report tonight, Darsam.'

'Perhaps or definitely not?'

'Perhaps.'

'Let me take the drink in, Young Master.'

'No.'

I took the water in myself, leaving the two in the kitchen staring at each other in amazement.

Mama took the glass and drank it all down at once. She seemed to have calmed down.

'Life seems so empty, futile, knowing where all our money has come from.'

I could understand her feelings: she had devoted herself to the business, always doing things the honest way; now it turned out that the business itself was born of *haram* capital.

'Have you ever heard or read about anyone having to go through what I have? Accursed experiences like these?'

'No, Ma.'

'Don't write about this last thing. Now talk to me. Ah, how lonely it will be if you're not here, Minke.'

'Ma, even if there had been more capital, if Mama hadn't worked, this business would never have grown.'

She looked at me for a moment. Her lips were taut as she held back another explosion of anger. Then slowly the tension disappeared, and she was calm again.

'What do you really mean, Minke?' she asked, somehow seeming unsure of herself.

I told her what I had been taught about Robinson Crusoe.

'Yes, I've read that book,' she cut in. 'He was marooned on an island by himself.'

'True, Ma. It wasn't his money that enabled him to live, but his labour. Gold and coins were of no use to him on an uninhabited island. A mountain of gold and three mountains of coins would have been of no use to that Robinson, Ma. Without the labour of humans, nothing has value. Under the ground, under our feet, Ma, there are many things to be found: gold, silver, copper, iron, coal, salt and gas – wealth that is beyond our imagination. But it is all useless, valueless, without the labour of human beings, while people do not dig it out from the womb of the earth, to use it.'

'You mean you value what I have done, Child, rather than that accursed capital?' she asked, somewhat comforted, a little child-like.

'I value all that Mama has done rather than the things you have accumulated as your property.'

She let out a long breath. She was confused as to how she should look upon all her successes.

'Not everything that you have come to own,' I said, daring to offer her advice, 'are things which are not *halal*. Not all the capital came from conspiracy and deception.'

'That's where the problem lies, Child. We don't know how much of the money is halal and how much haram. If I knew, then it would be easy enough to separate them.'

'There's no need to know now, Ma.'

'It must be returned to them, to those peasants and farmers. And even that is not possible. We only know Trunodongso, and it would not be right to give it just to him. To share it out isn't really a possibility either. To hand it over to the Government would be folly. And how much each farmer has a right to – that isn't clear either.'

'You don't have to think about it now, Ma.'

'Yes, it doesn't have to be resolved now. But then again at any moment now, Engineer Maurits Mellema could turn up to take over the business. Everything must be arranged before he arrives.'

Then I remembered what a teacher had once said about the differences between rich Europeans and rich Natives. The Natives collected wives with the excuse that they were doing it to help out the women they married. Europeans gave a part of their wealth to help with projects in the public interest: schools, hospitals, publishing, meeting halls, research.

'You have an idea, Child.'

'Yes, Ma,' but I was unsure.

'If there were teachers . . .' began Mama.

'Yes, Ma,' I agreed, 'we could found some schools for the children of those who were cheated . . .'

That idea became a medicine that settled her spirits. Her anger began to subside, as did her regret and melancholy.

'Darsam!' she called out suddenly. She had recovered herself.

Darsam was already waiting between the back and front parlours. His unslung hand twiddled his moustache. I waved, signalling him to come closer. He saluted Nyai with his good arm.

'If Nyai isn't too tired, I want to make a report tonight,' he said.

'Fetch a chair!' Nyai ordered.

He pulled a chair across with his left hand. With his left hand too he apologised for sitting on a chair that made him higher than Nyai. He let out a long breath, releasing the tension within.

'What must you remember when reporting?' Mama asked in Madurese.

'Smoking is not allowed, Nyai.'

'Good. You may begin.'

'Not just yet, Nyai. There is one other thing.' He took a thick wad of paper from his pocket, a letter, and handed it over to his employer.

Mama read it for a moment, then pushed it over to me.

'I can't understand it. Read it,' she said.

The letter was in English, badly written in large, round letters. The address wasn't clear. But from the first lines it was clear that the writer was Khouw Ah Soe. I translated it into Dutch for Mama.

My beloved and honoured Mama, I began.

'He calls me Mama?' asked Nyai. 'Your translation isn't wrong?'

'Exactly as written, Ma. I'll read on . . .'

I cannot tell you how grateful I am for all the help you have given me. And that help means even more because it was given at a time when your own child was in such great difficulties. In the end, in all of Surabaya you were the only person to hold out your hand in aid, while my own people cursed me, abused me, derided me. They let themselves go on embracing the old beliefs that the Heavenly Kingdom cannot fall into the hands of foreigners. They forgot that Hong Kong, Kowloon, Macao have already long been in the hands of foreigners. Canton, and even Shanghai itself, the biggest city in China, in the world, has been cut up into concessions for the foreigners. More than ten foreign nations, Ma. And their rotten influence makes itself felt more and more as every moment passes. In those cities my people are abused and insulted in their own country. They blind themselves to reality. While you, my beloved and honoured Mama, a foreigner and stranger, not understanding my language, it was you who were able to understand what I wanted to do. In you I found a true mother.

My beloved and honoured Mama,

For the past few days I have been staying here. Darsam looked after me very well. He always left the door open for me whenever I came home around dusk. I lacked nothing, and I was able to lay my body down in its weariness and get rest without ever being disturbed. He looked after my safety, and took care of my every need. He did not understand at all what my secret was, nor did I understand him. We spoke to each other with nods and shakes of the head, but our hearts spoke much.

I shouldn't be really writing such a letter. But other considerations have forced me to do so, Mama. Over these past few days my room to manoeuvre has been getting smaller and smaller. Even smaller and narrower than the freedom allowed by the identity and residency regulations enforced among the Chinese of Surabaya. And it is only Mama's house that has provided me with protection and sustenance. It is because of the ever-narrowing room to move, that I write this letter.

442

Yes, the thanks I wish to pass on to you should not be in a letter but should be spoken to you, face to face, coming straight from a clear heart. But who knows, my beloved and honoured Mama, I may not have the chance to speak to you again.

Thank you, my Mama, a thousand thanks for all your sincere help and protection. From your son.

And beneath was his name written in Latin script.

There was another letter in the envelope, addressed to me. I translated it also for Mama:

My good friend Minke,

Perhaps this is the only way I can pass on my message to you. I very much need your help. My situation is desperate. Perhaps soon they, my own people, will succeed in having complete control over me . . . My mission in Surabaya was too difficult. I will never see you again and I ask you to pass on the other letter in the envelope to someone in Betawi, called [and he gave a name]. Forgive me, because you must obtain the address from someone else. His name is Dulrakim and he lives in Kedungkrem. I can no longer remember the address in Betawi, and I haven't been able to meet Dulrakim because he's a sailor and hasn't been in Surabya for a while.

Another thing, my friend – don't send this letter through the mail. You are going to Betawi soon, aren't you? This person lives there. Say that, right up until the end, I never forgot.

My profound thanks to a friend who I will never be able to repay for his kindness.

Then I saw the other letter, written in Chinese.

'It seems he knew it was coming, Child,' said Mama in Dutch. 'There's something I didn't understand though, Child. What is a concession?'

'I'll look it up in the dictionary later, Ma. I don't know either.'

Darsam's eyes went back and forth from Mama to me, as he tried to understand what was being said. Though his moustache be ten times bigger, he would never understand.

'Your guest, Darsam,' Mama said in Madurese, 'was forced to write this letter because he could not speak to you. He expressed his great thanks to you. You had been so good to him.'

Darsam's eyes shone and blinked slowly as he savoured Nyai's words.

'In this world and the next, he would never forget you.'

'That young Chinese, Nyai, he could say that?'

'Why wouldn't he be able to say something as simple as that, Darsam?'

'He wore a pigtail, Nyai, and would cough his phlegm up and spit it on the ground.'

'And what's the matter with a pigtail? Anyone with hair can grow one.

443

Cough up and spit out phlegm? Every one has phlegm. The only difference is that he spits it out making a noise and you swallow it secretly.'

'But he mentioned something about the next life,' Darsam protested.

'He was only saying he owed you a thousand thanks, Darsam, in this world and the next.'

'He was just a Chinese, Nyai.'

'Yes, like me, I'm just a Javanese. And a Dutchman is just a Dutchman.'

'He won't be coming back, Nyai?'

'He won't be coming back. And so he says his final thank you.'

'Returning to his country, no doubt.'

'To his ancestors.'

'By boat, naturally.'

'In every kind of boat, by every kind of vehicle that is available. Now Darsam, let us hear your report.'

12

Darsam's report turned out to be quite long. He told it all in Madurese, so I had to get Mama to help me put it down in written form, as it is given here:

The second day after Nyai Ontosoroh's departure for Tulangan, Mr Dalmeyer arrived.

As Nyai had ordered, I invited him to work in Nyai's office. The books and papers that Nyai had prepared I took from the cabinet and put before him on Nyai's desk. Food and drink were prepared for him and set in the office too.

He read everything, examined the papers page by page.

At four in the afternoon he asked to be shown the cattle pens. I took him out to the back. He counted all the dairy cows and noted the figures down. It shouldn't have taken long just to count how many cows, how many bulls, how many calves. But he ended up staying there for quite a while after meeting that other 'cow'.

Nyai must know who I mean.

So I left him with that frisky Minem girl. What can one do? They had met and got to chatting. Even as master of the house, I was no longer relevant. I left them at the cattle pens.

That girl Minem used to harass *Noni* Annelies, pressing Noni to make Minem a supervisor over the milking. As soon as Noni left, she began to try to win me over. And she is indeed clever at cajoling, that frisky one. If it hadn't been for her ever-enlarging stomach with that child inside it, and then not being able to work, and giving birth, she would have kept on harassing Noni forever.

Nyai herself knows what happened: she had her child several months before Noni Annelies went away. Working while she carried and suckled her baby meant that her output fell. There were no grounds to make her a supervisor. But even so without any hesitation, she began again to press and cajole Noni to make her a supervisor. Noni might even have given in and made her one if she had not gone away all of a sudden.

But that daughter of the devil really has a devil's tongue. When she saw

Nyai and Young Master go off to Sidoarjo, even before anyone had left for work, she came to my house. She paid no heed to my wife and my children, who hadn't yet been got off to school. She carried her baby with her.

'Look, look at him, *Cak* Darsam,' she said, pointing to what she was carrying. 'Is it right that this baby should be in such a condition when his grandmother is so rich?'

Impudent. Insolent. But even so, it was a startling statement.

'And I'm not even considered worthy to be a supervisor of the milking.'

'Why don't you hand the baby over to its rich grandmother then?' I asked, pretending not to understand what she was getting at.

'If her grandmother would acknowledge her, that would be easy. But if she won't?'

Minem had no husband. People said she was a widow. Others said her husband had left her or that she had left her husband. Nyai must still remember her, the one who flirted with the men all the time. The big problem was that she was pretty, her body was quite good, her skin wasn't too dark. She was very attractive. If she were a good *joged* dancer, she would be in demand for sure.

'So who is the child's father?' I asked her. She smiled coaxingly.

'That's what happens if you accept just any man,' I went on. 'Now the child is an excuse.'

'Not just any man,' she denied, still smiling invitingly. 'The father of this child is none other than the son of my employer. Now say it's just any man.'

'Don't try any blackmail here,' I warned her.

'Who would dare blackmail Cak Darsam? This is truly Sinyo Robert's child.'

Nah, Nyai, another problem. Actually I didn't want to tell you. But as I thought it over; I knew I must tell you. Yes, if she was lying, all right, but if she was telling the truth? Whatever else might be the case, if she wasn't lying, then perhaps indeed that child might have Nyai's blood. I had to tell you, Nyai.

'Give the child here!' I ordered, and I took the baby from her.

She didn't object. The baby was dirty with snot and spittle. Seeing how disgusted I was, she wiped the baby with her selendang. A boy, Nyai, healthy, plump, but not looked after properly. I somehow felt there was some of Nyai's blood in him. The face was like that of Noni Annelies. His nose was pointed but the skin was like that of Sinyo's.

The baby cried when I lifted him from Minem. His eyes were big, Dutch eyes. I became suspicious. Was it true that this was Sinyo's child or – forgive me, Nyai – Tuan Mellema's? I asked.

'Sinyo's!' she maintained.

'There are many sinyos and tuans in Wonokromo,' I said, though unsure of myself, because no sinyos and tuans came visiting the villages around here. And Minem spent her days working with the dairy cows. She'd be too tired to travel away from the village at night. She had never taken holidays. Whenever I visited the village, I never saw anything suspicious. The men who did the patrols never reported seeing any sinyo or tuan.

A few weeks before Nyai went away, though, the patrols did report seeing an outsider visit Minem's house several times. But they said there was nothing suspicious. Just a guest, not an outlaw or anything. Perhaps he wanted to marry her. We had no outlaw or anything. Perhaps he wanted to marry her. We had no right to stop him.

So I had never paid any attention to him, as he was not making trouble. But remembering those reports of her guest, I then asked Minem: 'Minem, you've never spoken about the child's father before. Why all of a sudden, after being visited regularly lately, do you begin to bring the subject up?'

'There's no connection with him,' she answered becoming even more cheeky. 'The thing is that I've been waiting for Sinyo to come back, but he never has. So what will become of the child? Sinyo Rober promised that when the child was born he would acknowledge him.'

'But he never has.'

'That's why I have come to Cak Darsam.'

'You want me to help you to convince Nyai to accept him?'

'Why not, if he is indeed her grandson? On my death, I'd swear anywhere, this is the child of Sinyo Rober.'

I sent my wife and children out; but they had already heard part of the story. I think Minem indeed planned that they hear, so the story would spread. Soon all of Wonokromo will hear, Nyai. That is one reason why I thought I had better report to you as soon as possible. Perhaps already she had begun to tell her story to her friends, with the intention of trying to squeeze something out of you later.

What I thought then, Nyai, was that a simple girl like Minem surely wouldn't know how to go about blackmailing someone. Then it occurred to me that she might have been encouraged by the man who has been visiting her lately. Perhaps he has been inciting her to try to make some profit out of the affair, squeeze something from Nyai. Was I wrong to think that, Nyai?

So I gave the baby back to her. He looked as though he would become a tall boy.

'Cak Darsam can see for yourself. His father isn't Javanese,' said Minem.

'Who is this man who has been visiting you lately?'

'*Babah* Kong,' she answered without shame.

'Perhaps this is Babah Kong's child,' I said.

'No. I've only known him for a little while.'

'Babah Kong wants to marry you?'

'No.'

'Take you as his concubine?'

'He only comes to chat.'

'Liar,' I said. 'As if I don't know what you are. Come on, say it again: he only comes to chat. Come on, say it.'

Minem didn't repeat her statement.

'Now if you have another child, you'll be accusing someone else of being the father.'

'No, Cak Darsam. This is Sinyo Rober's child.'

'What does your guest talk about?'

'This and that.'

'What does he say about this child?' I asked.

'He did once ask who the child's father was: Sinyo, Tuan, or Young Master. I answered: He's Sinyo's child.'

'How could he know there was a Sinyo, Tuan and Young Master. You're the one who has been running off at the mouth!'

'No, I didn't tell him anything about Nyai's family.'

'Good. So he knew before he met you. So it was he who told you to come to me now.'

Minem denied this ferociously, with all her being. But I don't know, Nyai, if she was telling the truth or not. She was always smiling, flirting, pinching me, and things.

'Why don't you claim that his father is the Tuan Resident, or the Governor-General?'

She didn't know what a resident or governor-general was. She answered like this: 'His father really is Sinyo Rober. I will always say so, Cak Darsam, because Sinyo made a promise to me. He said he would take me as his nyai and that we would live in a building and I wouldn't have to work but would be an employer instead.'

'But Babah Kong wants you as well. What are you up to?'

'I've already said no. I'm still waiting for Sinyo. And he still hasn't come home. Help this child, Cak Darsam. Talk to Nyai. Could you stand to see her grandson going without, like this?'

'Is it the child who needs help, or you?'

'What would be wrong with both of us receiving some help?' and she pinched my thigh so hard I let out a yell. I pushed her out of the house.

So I have told you the beginning of the story, Nyai. I mean about the matter of Minem's child. In Darsam's opinion, Nyai should examine both the child and her mother. I don't know what that girl, that Minem, really wants. She has the tongue of a devil. And even on the first day that Mr Dalmeyer arrived here, she was flirting with him – it was incredible. And Mr Dalmeyer responded to her flirtations. He worked here for four days, and every evening he disappeared into the barn. Everyone saw what was going on. Even though the two of them always talked in whispers, in the end they were overheard. I won't tell you what they said, Nyai; it wouldn't be proper.

Then one day, after Mr Dalmeyer's work here was finished, a watchman reported to me: Babah Kong had arrived to visit Minem. According to the schedule Minem shouldn't be at home yet. But she was. So I went after her, to her house. From a distance, I saw them go inside the house. I could see Babah Kong. Nyai, it was someone we all would recognise: Fatso!

But I only glimpsed him for a moment. I had to have another look. I went up closer to Minem's house. It seemed they knew I was coming. Minem came outside to greet me.

'Who is your guest?' I asked.

'I have no guest here,' she answered. She was carrying her baby.

I went inside. The only person there was her old mother. I checked under the sleeping benches. It was true, there was no guest. Minem went off again, back to the cattle pens to get on with her work. She paid no heed to me. But I had seen Babah Kong go into the house; I had seen him with my own eyes. He must have gone out the back door. I went out to the back of Minem's house. Yes, I was right; there he was, walking off quickly between the thickets of banana trees and taro bushes.

I was not mistaken, Nyai. There was nothing wrong with my sight. Babah Kong was none other than Fatso.

I pulled out my machete and set off after him. He knew I was chasing him. He began running too. He was fat all right, but there was still a lot of briskness in his stride. He ran fast, like a devil.

'Hey, stop, you, Fatso!' I shouted.

He paid no heed, so I kept chasing him. He tried to get out of the village and make his way into the fields. I kept after him. But he ran very well, that fat body of his bent over; he looked rounder, like a marble. Run! You will not escape me. You do not know these fields as I do.

I wanted to make sure he could not lose himself again in the compound of Ah Tjong's brothel. He must die unwitnessed at twilight in these fields. His sins against us have been too many. His reappearance was the omen of some new disaster. He must die.

It appeared he was indeed trying to get to Ah Tjong's brothel. I moved to cut off his path. He turned left. The distance between us seemed less and less. I saw his face was already scarlet when he turned to get a glimpse of me, and his chest was heaving and panting. Three people are not needed here – you will not escape Darsam, one man alone. Fatso! Ayoh, use up all your breath before this machete sweeps through the air to split your chest.

He finally reached an area that has never been planted because the ground is bad, too low and full of pot-holes and roots. Noni had once ordered it levelled and covered with peanut-shell waste. Some work had been carried out. The compost had begun to rot away and the pot-holes had re-emerged. We didn't put on enough in the first place really.

Fatso ran in that direction. Several times he fell, but he easily recovered himself. I also fell. I was having a hard time as well. Once I dropped my machete. It took quite a while to find it amongst all the dense bracken. Fatso ran on happily, even stopping to look while getting his breath back.

'Fatso!' I threatened him, 'don't enjoy the dusk air for too long. In a moment I will catch up with you again.'

Once I found my machete, I mobilised all my strength. The distance between us narrowed again. He began to run out of breath and strength. Now I've got you! 'Nah! you!' I shouted. Fatso was cornered in a dry canal. He had toppled into it and hidden himself there. His whole body was hidden from my view.

When I reached the dry canal I found him trying to free himself from an overgrown vine. His eyes showed no fear – this madman.

'Now you die!' I hissed.

'Don't kill me,' he said, panting softly, 'I'm not an enemy.'

'Shut your mouth!'

'Truly, I'm not an enemy.'

I raised my machete, to scare him into admitting who he was.

'I'm a friend,' he said, and he remained calm and unafraid.

I attacked with my machete, intending to cut off his head. He adroitly stepped aside. Although fat, he was tremendously fit, quick like a deer. That alone was enough to confuse me. I jumped into the canal to finish him off once and for all. I heard him still panting. I heard my own breathing too.

'No!' he shouted, seeing I was truly out to kill him. No matter. In a moment his neck would be sliced, as soon as he was no longer able to side-step the machete, which was already whistling in the air. He rolled over quickly. My machete missed again, hitting a clump of clove plants. I raised it once again.

All of a sudden there was an explosion. My hand holding the machete bent back. The machete snapped and the broken piece disappeared into the overgrowth.

I stopped in my place, Nyai. The machete did not cut through his neck. I glanced up at my weapon. All I could see was the top of a tree. All that was left of my machete was its stump. Fatso seemed to think I'd be worried by that. He smiled, that madman! He obviously didn't understand who Darsam was, Nyai.

Fatso leaned against the bank of the canal. My shortened machete was once again raised ready to smash down on his face. His fat lips and narrow eyes would disappear from his face. I no longer heeded the pistol in his hand.

'Don't go on,' he warned.

I paid no attention. The pistol exploded again. Now what was left on my machete fell to the ground amongst the weeds and ferns of the unused cana. Nyai, my hand felt hot. My fingers were unable to grip. He had shot me; I could do nothing.

'What did I say?' he said in Malay. 'I'm not an enemy. What could I do? You forced me to shoot.' He stood up straight. The pistol still pointed at me.

If he had shot once more, I wouldn't be here reporting today. I'd have preferred to be shot dead. But he didn't do it. The injury to my hand left me helpless. I wanted to attack with my left hand, but I realised in a moment that it would be useless. I stayed silent.

'Had enough?' he asked insolently. 'Not going to attack me again? Learnt your lesson?' I was silent, ashamed, fuming. 'If you're not going to attack again, I'll put this pistol away and help you. Well? Agreed?'

How insolent he was! I still said nothing; I was clenching my teeth. He only shook his head, smiling, perhaps in insult, perhaps in pleasure at my condition.

'What's the meaning of one person with one machete?' he said. 'Come on, out of the canal. I'll help you out. Out of there first.'

I performed that shameful act. I climbed up the bank of the canal. He heaved me up from below, pushing my buttocks. Insolent. Once I was up, he climbed up nimbly, that jungle cat.

'Let me stop the bleeding,' he said. 'If you lose too much blood, that'll be the end of you. Lift your wounded hand right up in the air. It hurts? Of course.'

He was so friendly; I don't know whether to make fun of me, or to rub in the shame, or whether it was sincere. I don't know. I raised high my wounded hand. He put away his pistol. He could have killed me; but he didn't. His attitude was not that of a troublemaker. I didn't know what to do. Carefully he put his hand into his pocket and took out a handkerchief. He twisted it around until it became like a piece of cord and he tied it tightly around my wrist. The blood stopped flowing.

'Let me take you home,' he said again.

It was true – he didn't want to kill me. His hands were well-muscled and strong. He wasn't just any fat man. I had underestimated him. It was lucky there were no villages about. When they heard the shooting, everyone had shut themselves in their houses, locked their doors. How ashamed I would have been, if they had seen me being escorted along by the man I was going to cut up! There was no patrol about either. The sun had set. Dark. No moon, Nyai. My own house was locked from the inside.

In front of the door, he said: 'Nah, tell your missus to take you to the hospital at the palm-oil factory at Wonokromo. Don't say you were shot. Don't go to the police. Say you've had an accident.'

And before disappearing into the darkness, he added again: 'I am not an enemy. Don't get things wrong. Behind all this, I'm your friend; only you don't know who I am. Go to the hospital straight away.'

After I shouted and banged on the door, my wife opened up. She took me to the hospital. Marjuki drove the buggy. I was lucky there were people still on duty. And, yes, they did ask what had happened.

'I fell, Tuan, was jabbed by some bamboo,' I answered.

The Dutch doctor treated me, washed and bandaged my hand himself and put it in this sling here. He didn't let me go home. The three of us were given coffee and told to wait a moment. We sat on a long bench.

Disaster, Nyai. It wasn't long before the police arrived. We were taken away to the police station. We were interrogated that night. They didn't believe my wound came from falling on bamboo. They said there were no signs of bamboo around the wound, but there were signs of a bullet passing through. I don't know how they could tell. But I still didn't admit anything. They threatened to detain all three of us until we confessed what had happened. I had to tell them, Nyai. If I didn't and they kept us, who would look after the business?

That night too a detail of policemen took us home. They took lamps to the canal and examined the place. They found not only the shell of a bullet but plenty of signs of a fight. They took away the spent shell and also the pieces of my broken machete.

That's what happened, Nyai. Once I started to tell them what happened, the whole story came out. Minem was interrogated that night too. She didn't know where Babah Kong lived. She admitted to sleeping with him a few times and said he had promised to make her his concubine. But Minem didn't believe him. Babah Kong wasn't very generous, according to Minem, so she wasn't sure about the idea.

It was all taken down. And you can see, Nyai, I wasn't arrested. Neither was Minem. Now it's Babah Kong who's being chased by the police. It seems, Nyai, maybe we'll end up in court again, if Babah Kong is caught.

I thought, at that point, that Darsam's report was over. Mama didn't ask him anything, though she must have realised there were a lot of issues to follow up: Minem's baby, Mr Dalmeyer's work, Dalmeyer's relationship with Minem, Fatso still being around the place, Darsam's new troubles, the upcoming trial . . .

This woman had so much to face.

But Darsam hadn't finished.

He put his bandaged hand on the table, having taken it out of the sling.

'Nyai,' he said, his voice taking on an even more serious tone, 'I have carried out Nyai's orders as well as I could. If I have made any mistakes, done anything incorrectly, I would like Nyai to say so.'

A tense silence followed. Nyai still said nothing.

'Have I done wrong, Nyai?'

Nyai Ontosoroh let out a big breath; both her cheeks sagged a little. She rubbed behind her ear with the finger of her left hand, then said slowly: 'You have made no mistakes, Darsam. You have not been in error in anything. Everything has been handled correctly.'

'In dealing with Fatso too, Nyai?' asked Darsam, childlike.

'You weren't entirely right there. The same as the other time, you wanted to go too far. If Babah Kong hadn't been armed with a pistol, would you have killed him?'

'No, Nyai, I just wanted to frighten him.'

'Don't lie! Fatso wouldn't have taken it so seriously if you hadn't been serious as well,' Nyai replied. 'How's your hand now?'

'Nyai,' he said sadly, 'my fingers no longer have the strength to carry a machete – to swing it, or to spin it – huh! I can't even hold it. I understand now, Nyai, how my livelihood has depended so much on these fingers of my right hand. With them I carried out all your orders, Nyai: remove trespassers, escort the milk wagons, take up my machete and fight, collect debts, take care of security, maintain authority over all the workers. Now these fingers are of no use. I have thought about this for a long time, Nyai, yes, these last few days; without these fingers Darsam is no longer of any use to Nyai. I'm no longer of use even to myself. I'm unable to work. I must admit it, Nyai: my service to you is at an end.' His voice slowed, serious and sad. 'Darsam will go home to his village, Nyai; home to Sampang.'

'And what will you do there? Make salt? It'll be no different. You won't be able to work there either, without those fingers.'

'That's the trouble indeed, Nyai.'

'Go and see Dr Martinet tomorrow. You can't be sure your fingers are damaged permanently.'

'And if they are, Nyai?'

'Get them checked first. Dr Martinet will do all he can.'

'And if they are damaged permanently, Nyai?' he repeated.

'Ah, see the doctor first.'

He didn't want to go. He remained motionless in his seat, waiting for his employer's decision.

'What are you waiting for now?'

'Will I be dismissed, Nyai?'

'Even if nothing can be done for your fingers, Darsam, you will stay here. Your children graduate from *Vervolg* this year, and must learn to

453

work. They can begin to learn Dutch. Who knows, Darsam; your children may not be as ignorant as you. And what does it matter that your right fingers are broken, if your heart is strong? Nah, go, get some sleep!'

'But Darsam will never hold a machete again.'

'Go to bed!' shouted Nyai.

Very hesitantly he rose, raised his left hand in salute to Nyai and me, put his chair back against the wall, then went. He walked erect, not looking back. He disappeared down the stairs.

'Do you know what has happened tonight?' Mama asked me.

'The police are out after Fatso, Ma, who is really Babah Kong.'

'That's not important.'

'There will be another trial, Ma, and more abuse and humiliation.'

'That's not important either. The case is over, although there are still loose ends. It's this, Child. Darsam, and others like him, only realise now: all this time life has depended on those right-hand fingers. Life comes from those fingers. All of a sudden those fingers cannot be used. He only realises it after his capital is damaged, the living capital of his fingers. Others pretend they work with their brains. For years and years, they study, they learn to think that they might live properly and as they wish to live. But a person's brain can be damaged too; remember Tuan Mellema. Years of learning and practice disappear in one moment – decades of learning disappear. Wandering at night like an animal, forgetting he is human . . .'

'Why, Ma?'

'And there are others who put their lives in the hands of money capital. For decades too, they make their capital grow, from a small seed to a banyan tree thick with foliage. Then, suddenly, they realise that the money was obtained immorally, the fruits of deception . . .'

'Ma!'

'So it seems we are all the same, Child: me, Tuan Mellema, and Darsam. What we thought to be solid, strong, trustworthy, something we could hold onto, turns out to be no more than a speck of sand. Perhaps this is what they call the tragedy of living. How fragile we are! And Khouw Ah Soe, young and intelligent, is now dead, killed by his own people – a people he was working to help. Perhaps his murderer knew who he was – a killer paid just one *rupiah* or perhaps two . . .'

'If they knew him well, they would never have killed him,' I objected. 'Maybe they would even have helped him.'

'That's what happens in the *wayang* stories, Minke. In real life, people are killed precisely by those who know and understand them. And the Acehnese, Minke – how many of them have been killed by Europeans, who have made it their business to know all there is to know about them? And your story about Trunodongso – who do we see there, impoverishing him

454

and forcing him off his land? Those who know more, more about farmers and farming. I'm sure Tuan Mellema was not involved only in deceiving those farmers, but in oppressing them and using force against them as well. A conspiracy to embezzle rent money means there must be cheap land to rent to start with.'

Mama wasn't really talking to me. She was testing her own thoughts. She was looking for something to grip hold of, some truth which had its very roots in truth. She was trying to face and not give in to the tragedy of life.

Slowly it was becoming clear that my own and the world's joyful greeting to the modern age was an act of folly. Only their tools and their methods were modern, Mama said. Man remained the same, never changing, on the sea, the land, at either pole, amongst the wealth and poverty that he himself makes.

'While listening to Darsam's report, I decided how much money I would return to the peasants, Child. An amount equivalent to all the capital we used to set up this business. I will build schools. I will employ one or two teachers. I will tell them to teach Dutch, and arithmetic.'

'That will be good, Ma.'

'If they knew Dutch, they wouldn't be so afraid when they had to deal with the Dutch. And if they knew some arithmetic, how to count, they wouldn't be tricked so easily. If you decided not to leave Wonokromo and Surabaya, you could visit there once a week. You could tell the children about the evil-doings of the colonialists.'

'They'd arrest me and put me on trial, Ma, and accuse me of agitation and incitement. They even expelled Magda Peters.'

'So who must begin, if not you? Do you too want to go to sleep, like in that story of Kommer's about Kartini, and wake up with the modern age already here?'

To be honest, I shook with fear as I heard that challenge.

'You're not saying anything, Minke, Child. Who must begin? Must I do everything myself?'

'Of course not, Ma.'

'Then who must do it? Yes, indeed, hundreds of people will carry out this work. But that is in the future. I don't know when. But who will begin?'

Indeed I was afraid of that idea – just an idea. I didn't have the courage to answer. I was ashamed to listen to my own voice. Cowed, that I might be exposed by that challenge for what I really was.

'Oh, yes,' Nyai Ontosoroh abruptly changed the subject. 'I forgot: you want to continue your schooling at the Medical School in Betawi . . .' Her voice held the hint of a sneer.

'Yes, Ma. I will leave as soon as Panji Darman arrives.'

'But still it must be you who begin, Child, wherever you are, whatever school you attend. You were the first to suffer all these things, you know how things really are, and the reasons, and how things are connected.'

'Ma –' I tried to defend myself.

'If you don't, you will be running away, Child. Do you remember that letter from your Mother you once told me about? To run away is to admit you are a criminal. All your education and experience will be in vain. I know you are not someone who runs away.'

13

But still we couldn't close the book. Events kept pursuing us one after another.

A newspaper story reported that a peasant rebellion had broken out in the region of Sidoarjo. The police were unable to handle it and had to call in the army. It took three days to quash the outbreak. Kyai Sukri, who was thought to be the mastermind, was arrested and brought in chains to the Tulangan sugar factory. The Tuan Besar Kuasa Manager was furious that the disturbances had held up production. He ordered that Kyai Sukri be punished with eighty lashes before being taken to stand trial.

The Kyai suffered his punishment witnessed by all the factory employees, foremen and coolies. He let out his last breath with the seventieth lash.

'If your article had been published that time . . .' Mama began.

'Yes, Ma; without wanting to, I've ended up betraying them.'

'Your article would have made Nijman smell that there was something going on. You have been in the position of a spy working for Nijman – and unpaid to boot – and you could still be in trouble yet.'

I felt so ashamed to hear her sum up my situation that way. I saw Trunodongso, and little Piah, and Mama Truno. I had told Trunodongso that not all problems can be solved with machete and anger. Did they tire of waiting to see my promise carried out? Yes, surely they must have hoped they had an ally in me.

'It is good that you destroyed your article. But you are still in danger, Minke. Nijman knows now who you are. Sastro Kassier and his family know you stayed overnight in Trunodongso's house. Jean Marais and Kommer know too, from the story you told them. I know too. Jean Marais probably wouldn't have said anything to anybody. But I don't know about Kommer and Sastro Kassier and his family. If Trunodongso is caught, and mentions your name . . .' She sighed deeply. 'If he is dead, then you should be all right, or at least things can't be too bad for you.'

I knew I had to get away from this house, from Wonokromo, from Surabaya; I had to disappear.

'And me too, Minke, Child, because you were always with me. We have been involved together in another case. And there is the incident now with Darsam. Our situation is getting worse and worse.'

Yet again we were bound together by an unhappy matter. I felt even closer to her.

'It's lucky you didn't take up the Tuan Manager's invitation while you were there, Ma.'

'Someone as young as that, well educated, just out from Europe, how could he be so heartless to order Kyai Sukri be whipped – and eighty times too. The Kyai was already old and bent, perhaps with arthritis . . .'

And with the words she spoke next, I felt orphaned: 'Yes, Minke, you must go. This house is not good for you. You are still young, you have the right to some joy as Kommer said. I can handle these troubles. No need for you to stay with me through all these difficulties. But I cannot help thinking now: Trunodongso will remember your promise.'

'I could never leave Mama at a time like this. Even though it has been only for a short while, Ma, I have been very happy as your son-in-law . . . and that happiness binds me to you . . . I could never leave you in a situation like this.'

'No, Minke; you must have some joy in your life. But remember Trunodongso. You owe him a promise.'

'I told him once, Ma, not everything can be solved with machete and anger.'

'He will always remember the help you promised him.'

The conversation was brought to a halt by the arrival of a carriage. We knew it would be Marjuki bringing back Panji Darman alias Robert Jan Dapperste from Tanjung Perak Harbour. We had told Marjuki to convey our sincere regrets that we were unable to meet him ourselves.

Exactly as the carriage pulled up noisily outside the front door, we heard someone announce himself with the formal *kulo-nuwun*. From behind the thick beard and moustache I recognised him: it was Trunodongso, about whom we had just been talking.

'Who is it, Child?' Mama asked, seeing me go pale.

'Trunodongso, Ma,' I whispered.

'Ha?' she rose from her chair, and ran to meet her guest.

We went outside to help him. He looked filthy. He had covered himself with a horribly dirty sarong, all torn; he looked like a beggar. Behind the beard and moustache his face was pallid.

Without talking, Mama led him inside and into her office.

His eyes still fixed on me, the one person here whom he knew, he said very slowly: 'Yes. Ndoro, I come to seek your protection.'

'You've got a fever, Truno,' Nyai Ontosoroh spoke to him.

'Ya, Ndoro, I am sick. Fever. Not harvest-time fever. I made myself come here even sick like this.'

458

Mama sat him down in a chair, unable to say anything more. Her eyes shot nervously about. Seeing her do that, I closed the office door. From the middle parlour came the sound of shoes heading our way. I jumped up and locked the door that led to the parlour.

'I have come, Master, Ndoro, to surrender my life into your hands, and that of my wife and my children.'

'Where are they?' asked Mama.

I hurried over to the window, to make sure no one was trying to peer inside.

'Still on the other side of the river, Ndoro.'

'Why are you covered in a sarong like this?'

He opened his sarong. He wore no shirt, and on the left side of his back was a fifteen-centimetre-long wound.

'From a Kompeni sword, Truno?' hissed Mama. Seeing the wound seemed to make her even more nervous. 'Pull up your sarong. We'll call a doctor soon.'

'I am afraid of doctors . . .'

From the window I saw Panji Darman walking towards the house. He waved, so pleased to be seeing everyone again. His face was bright, having lost some of its darkness while living in Europe. His cheeks were flushed, fresh, healthy.

'Hai, Minke.'

'Oi!' I answered. 'Welcome, Rob.' I was still reluctant to call him Panji Darman. 'We were too busy, we couldn't meet you.'

'Ah, doesn't matter. Where's Mama?' He came closer to the window.

'She is well, well.' He reached the window.

'We're busy right now, Rob; how about we get together tonight?'

He looked disappointed, nodded and moved away.

'So you left them all, Truno, paddy, dry fields, your house?' asked Mama. 'Minke, get someone to fetch Dr Martinet. Tell Darsam to prepare a place in the go-down.'

But Trunodongso didn't feel safe without me. His eyes called out to me. I explained: 'Wait here, Pak. Don't worry. You are safe here. As long as you don't speak. Understand?'

'Don't call a doctor for me.'

'Silence, you, Truno,' whispered Mama. 'It's all to help you.'

His head dropped in pain, and I went.

The grain go-down was almost empty. Mama had ordered that everything be sold. Grain was being sold every day. Usually she waited for buyers to come looking, but not now. She was selling everything she could.

As I walked off looking for Darsam I could still see Trunodongso covering his body with the sarong. As she lifted the sarong to cover his back, we could see his swollen feet. He was no longer the Trunodongso who dared stand and challenge everybody with his machete. He was more powerless than a wooden doll.

I found Marjuki unharnessing the horses from the carriage. Frowning, he protested at the new orders to go and fetch Dr Martinet. 'The horses are still tired, Young Master.'

'Take another horse.'

'They're all being used at the moment.'

'Then hitch up this horse again.'

'They're still tired,' he answered back.

So we had to argue. Darsam came along to help. Marjuki, with a very unwilling heart, harnessed his horses again. Darsam went off to carry out some other order.

When I got back to the office, I found Mama talking with Trunodongso. They were whispering to each other. As I came closer, I heard Mama say: 'You're ill; you can't go to get your family yourself.'

'They won't know how to get here,' he said.

'Minke will fetch them. Tell him where they are.'

'They won't trust him,' answered Trunodongso.

'Minke will be able to make them trust him. They have seen him and met him before.'

'They still won't believe he's there to help them.'

'You must go, Minke. Don't use one of our carriages: hire one. Truno, tell him where they're waiting.'

So I set off in a hired *andong* for the address he had given me: a ferry crossing along the Brantas River. I had never been to that area. The andong driver had to tell me where to start walking – for two kilometres to the south. I had to walk through villages. The andong had gone on one kilometre past the Brantas Bridge. The driver had agreed to wait for me.

While I walked I tried to think why Mama had ordered me to fetch Trunodongso's family. She could have sent anyone from the business. I was very tired and didn't know the Wonokromo area well at all.

The village lanes were dirt tracks, still and quiet, overgrown with grass, and looked as though they were never cleaned. There were no drains along the path's edges, which were lined with shady dadap trees, cactus and dead thorny branches. A number of people I passed moved to one side, hugging the edge of the path, because I wore European clothes and shoes, Christian clothes. Perhaps they thought I was some black Dutchman out looking for trouble.

As I got closer to the ferry crossing, it suddenly came to me: perhaps Mama was deliberately sending me away from the house – from Trunodongso. If he had been followed by spies, only Mama would be arrested. I would not be there. If this were not the case Mama must have had something else in mind. And it was all a result of my own actions.

460

Mama, ah, Mama, you have nothing to do with all this, but still you hold out your hand to help, involving yourself in new troubles.

The ferry crossing was quiet – no one about except the ferryman himself, poling his way across the Brantas. I had no choice but to wait for him to arrive at my side of the river. There were no signs of Trunodongso's family.

Seeing me waiting on the river bank, the ferryman stopped his work. Indeed, he started to pretend to have some trouble with his raft. You! I shouted in my heart, you're just pretending, you're afraid of this black Dutchman too!

'Hey! You! Quickly! Over here!' I ordered in Javanese.

His eyes darted about, startled. Fear was written all over his face. Yet he brought the raft over to the river bank and tied it to a wooden pole. He threw the rope over to the shore. He came up to me, bowing again and again, and stood, hands clasped in front of him: 'Ndoro Tuan, Master.'

'Where are the people who were here a while ago, the ones not waiting for the ferry?' I asked.

'There's been no one who hasn't been waiting for the raft.'

'A woman, two boys, a girl who had little sisters?'

'No, Ndoro Tuan, no one like that.'

'Look out! Tell me quickly, or . . .'

'Ah, oh, ah . . .'

'No need for "ah, oh, ah"; do you want me to take you to my office?'

'No, Ndoro Tuan. Truly, there is no one here.' He bowed his head and eyes; he didn't even dare look at my shoes.

'Is that true?' I asked threateningly.

He said nothing.

'Ayoh! to the Police Station.'

'Please, no, Ndoro Tuan. My children will be waiting for me at this time of day, Tuan.'

'Where is your wife?'

'I have none, Ndoro Tuan; I am a widower.'

'Who cares? Come along with me.'

'Mercy, Ndoro Tuan, I have done nothing.'

'No mercy for you. Come on.' I made a move to leave and he moved to follow.

From the great fear he showed, I guessed he was indeed hiding the people I was after.

'Where's your house?'

'I have never stolen anything, Ndoro Tuan. There's nothing in my house.'

'Walk in front of me. Show me your house.'

He walked along slowly before me, every now and then turning to see if I was still there. I began to feel badly about the way I had treated him, about coming here wearing European clothes and shoes – symbol of the bogeyman, enemy of the little people. They would all think I was here to steal their freedom or their possessions.

One behind the other we walked along a narrow path under thickets of riverside bamboo, passing fields of neglected banana trees.

'That's your house?' I saw a bamboo-thatched hut emerging from behind thicket. Smoke formed clouds as it passed through the roof, only to be dispersed by gusts of wind.

'My hut, Ndoro Tuan.'

'Who's doing the cooking?'

He kept walking, his head bowed, pretending not to hear. Seeing that, I quickened my pace, passed him and ran on alone to the hut.

The bamboo door was open. It was dark inside, full of smoke. I saw Piah boiling something in an earthen pot; she squatted facing the fire. Beside her squatted two smaller children.

'Piah!' I called.

She was startled when she saw me. Afraid. Her arms trembled. Her two younger sisters hugged close to her.

'You haven't forgotten me? Are you afraid of me?' She kept her eyes on my shoes as she stood up. She placed her shaking hands on her sisters' heads. 'Where's your mama?' I asked.

She still wouldn't answer. Her eyes wandered to the bamboo sleeping-bench. There *Mbok* Truno slept, beside her two boys.

'Tell Mbok Truno I've come to fetch you all. An andong is waiting at the main road.'

As I came out of the smoke-filled hut, the ferryman arrived. He kept his eyes to the ground, still afraid to look at me.

'Those little children are yours?'

'Yes, Ndoro Tuan.'

'You said you were a widower. Who's that woman in there?'

Trunodongso's wife came outside and up to me. Her eyes were still red. Obviously she hadn't had enough sleep. Her clothes were a mess; there were many new tears. Like Trunodongso, she had swollen feet. Then came her two sons. Their feet were swollen as well. They wore shorts that went down to their knees, and their torsos were wrapped in sarongs. They stood, hands clasped in front of them.

'Still tired, Mbok?'

'No, Ndoro. How did Ndoro know I was here?'

'From Pak Truno. He's at my house. He told me. Are you strong enough to walk another few hundred yards? There's an andong waiting.'

They all looked exhausted. Perhaps they hadn't eaten for a long time. Mbok Truno looked at the ferryman, seeking some kind of advice. The ferryman said nothing. He kept his head down, still afraid and suspicious.

'Good, have something to eat first. It's already afternoon.'

I waited outside the hut. The two boys came and waited with me, sitting on the ground. I sat on a felled banana-tree trunk. Neither said a word, neither looked me in the face. The ferryman went inside and didn't come out for a long while.

Five minutes later Piah came out carrying an earthenware dish containing three yellow sweet potatoes in one hand and a jug of water in the other. She put the dish down on the banana-tree trunk and the jug of water near my feet. She invited me to eat, ignoring her brothers.

I guessed this was the ferryman's daily meal – now it was being given to his guests. I pushed the dish across to the two boys.

'Eat. We will be leaving soon,' I said.

They didn't eat.

'Don't worry about me. I've already eaten. You still have to walk another three or four hundred metres.'

Unable to restrain their hunger any longer, they devoured the sweet potatoes, skin and all. Then they gulped down the water in the jug.

The ferryman had given them all he had, these guests on the run: a roof to shelter under, sweet potatoes, sleeping-bench, and even his own safety – he was ready to give them that too. In another place, Engineer Mellema, educated and quite well off, wanted to obtain other people's property. And it was none other than the late Herman Mellema who had turned families like Trunodongso's into vagabonds. And you too, Ah Tjong!

Trunodongso, this time I failed. But one day, you will still become one of my characters – you, who knew nothing of this modern age. No schooling, illiterate; merely the sight of someone in shoes makes you tremble! And you too, ferryman, you too will become a character in my stories. Perhaps you too are a farmer who has lost his land, and now hoes the waters of the Brantas.

I cannot do it now. Later, later when I have learnt more about my own people. The thing to do now is get them away from here. I myself may have to leave quickly, leave Wonokromo and Surabaya.

Still the ferryman didn't come out of the hut. Perhaps he was advising Trunodongso's wife not to trust me.

'Ayoh, we must leave now,' I said to the two eldest, the boys.

They went inside the hut. I waited a long time. They didn't come out, all apparently agreeing not to trust me. I went in. They all watched me, strange looks in their eyes.

'Ayoh, quickly. It's already late. Do you want to keep Pak Truno lying there in pain waiting for you?'

Surely it was the ferryman who was making things difficult for me; but I was not angry. I must respect him, no matter what. He himself didn't try to look at me, just kept his head bowed. Perhaps he avoided looking even at my dirty, dust-covered shoes.

'So Mbok Truno and you children don't want to come with me?' I asked. 'Then I will return by myself. Pak Truno can't come to fetch you until his wounds have healed.'

I went out, and walked away slowly, giving them more time to decide. I looked back, and still they hadn't come out. I began to quicken my pace. Only after fifty metres did I hear Piah shouting. I pretended not to hear, though I slowed my pace to let her catch up.

I could hear her footsteps as she got closer.

'Ndoro! Ndoro!' she called.

I stopped. Now I could hear her panting breath. I looked back. Extreme exhaustion was painted on her face – a face that looked so old and yet so childlike.

'Ndoro won't arrest us?'

'Your father is waiting for you and he is hurt. If you don't want me to take you to him, that's up to you, Piah. If you want to come, good, you can all catch up with me. I will walk slowly to the main road. It's still quite a way from here.'

Who wouldn't feel sorry for that most exhausted member of the group? Even in these circumstances, they still held important the ideal of freedom – just a tiny bit of freedom – without ever having heard of the French Revolution. But I could do no more than offer them my help.

She stood there, bewildered.

'If it's only you that is to come, then let's go.'

'I will go back first, Ndoro.'

'Yes, go back first. But I can't stop. I will keep on walking slowly.'

The child went back to get her mother. I kept walking, without looking back. It seemed a long distance I had to travel. The trust I had won from them in Tulangan was now lost. How many months ago was that? Two? Had things changed so much since then? I wore Christian clothes, I wore shoes, I was closer to Europeans than they were. And it was Europeans who wanted to catch Trunodongso, husband and father. They were people on the run, afraid, hungry and tired.

They will give in to me too, I decided in my heart. On the run, in other people's villages, without Trunodongso, they will have nothing. They will surrender to me.

When I arrived back at the main road, I found the andong driver sound asleep, snoring. I climbed aboard and sat beside him. His head was uncovered and his mouth open. His head-band had fallen to the floor; I could see his hair was greying.

For five minutes I sat there beside him. The andong swayed every now and then as the horses, worried by swarms of evening flies, kept shaking their bodies. The driver still didn't wake up. And Trunodongso's family still didn't appear.

My 'ahemm' awoke him. He blinked his eyes several times, startled, looking at me in great embarrassment. His hand groped about his head looking for the band of his destar. He became even more nervous when he realised his head was uncovered – very impolite according to Javanese custom. I picked up his fallen destar and gave it to him. He bowed again and again as he climbed down from the andong, all the while thanking me, feeling he had been too much honoured, that I had been too considerate in my actions.

'Forgive me, Ndoro.'

'It's all right, Pak.'

'Do we leave now, Ndoro?'

'We'll wait a bit longer.'

He didn't protest. The sun had almost sunk below the horizon. He asked nothing, said nothing. It was not yet an age where someone barefooted could start up a conversation with someone who wore shoes. In the stories of our ancestors only the priests and gods wore slippers and shoes. And these simple people equated shoes with the power of Europe, of the same essence as the Kompeni's rifles and cannons. They were more afraid of shoes than daggers and machetes, swords or *kris* or spears. You are right, Herbert, Sarah, and Miriam de la Croix: they have been made to abase themselves so low, by the Europeans, by their own Native leaders. They have become so full of fear: the wages of continuous defeat in the battlefield of confrontation with European civilisation.

Nah, Kommer, do I still not yet know my own people? Will people still think of me as incomplete, laugh behind my back, because I write only in Dutch? Now I can answer: even if only a little bit, I have begun to know my people, a peasant people.

Just watch: the Trunodongso family will be forced to overcome their fear and suspicion, called to the centre of their family who is called Trunodongso. That is the way of things in Java. They must come and will come. I know the Javanese way. I will wait. My efforts must succeed.

As twilight reached its climax they became visible in the distance, walking one behind the other. Slowly, hungrily. The two boys carried their little sisters on their backs. Little Piah walked in front.

I climbed down from the andong to greet them. They seemed unsure. The hope of seeing the centre of the family again shone a little in their faces. The ferryman followed behind, a little way in the distance.

'Ayoh, climb aboard, everyone.'

They climbed up silently, surrendering to whatever might befall them,

465

as long as they could see Trunodongso again – but not surrendering from hunger or exhaustion.

The ferryman stood watching us from a distance. I waved to him. He came closer, bowed his head.

'Thank you for looking after Trunodongso's family. When you go home, you'll be lonely?'

He just spat.

'Come here, closer.'

He took a step forward, but didn't dare come too close.

'For the hospitality you gave them, and for the sweet potatoes you need yourself, take this talen.'

He took it – silently.

'There's nothing else you want to say?'

'Can I come to see them soon?'

'They will come to see you, once things are all right.'

The andong began to move. I sat beside the driver. Looking over my shoulder, I examined them one by one. How many tens of kilometres had they travelled, circling to avoid the Kompeni men? I won't ask them here, on this andong. I saw how their gaze wandered everywhere without fixing on anything in particular, as though they had no interest in the difference between their one-hut village in the middle of the sugar cane and the town with all its factories and street lighting. Perhaps the town's activities were no more to them than the rustling and swaying of the cane leaves.

'Have you ever seen a train, Piah?'

'Yes, Ndoro,' she answered tiredly. But she wasn't really interested. Neither were the others. It was as if Stevenson, the inventor of trains, had never harnessed steam to move a locomotive engine which then carried the products of cane workers' sweat to Tanjung Perak harbour.

'Have your been on one?'

'No, Ndoro.'

'Wouldn't you like to?'

'No,' she answered slowly, paying more attention to the actual question than to the presence of a train in either her imagination or on this earth of mankind.

'Look at the train.' I pointed to a string of carriages with its engine puffing and hissing along from the south. 'Isn't it fantastic?'

They all shifted their gaze to the horseless iron carriage. Not one of them held it in particular admiration. It was not part of their world. Perhaps their own dreams were more beautiful.

The andong was being overtaken by the panting, breathless train, which puffed out clouds of smoke and ash like a dragon in the myths of bygone peoples. But my fellow passengers were still not interested. Perhaps they were exhausted by the uncertainty of their fate. Perhaps too Trunodongso, the centre of their lives, was the only grand thing in their thoughts.

'Do you know that Pak Truno's sick?'

No one answered. They knew; better not to speak out.

'You can work at Wonokromo,' I said to the two eldest children.

They didn't answer.

'You've never been to school?' I asked again.

'It's enough they know how to hoe the ground, Ndoro.' Now it was their mother who answered.

'Perhaps Pak Truno has already been seen by Tuan Doctor.'

In the glow of the street lights I could see them become anxious: a doctor had entered the life of Truno. Ah, how much everything European torments their peace of mind. I didn't feel able to keep the conversation going. I realised there was a centuries-wide gap between them and me. Centuries! Perhaps this was what my history teacher meant when he talked about the social gap, or maybe, better still, the historical gap. In one nation, where people eat and drink the same things, in one country, yes even in one andong, there can be such a gap, not yet or not at all bridged.

All of us in that andong sat silently, each with his own groping thoughts.

Our vehicle entered the Boerderij Buitenzorg long after the sun had set. Mama ordered that they all be taken straight into the go-down. Trunodongso was sitting on a bamboo mat, being examined by Dr Martinet. Seeing a European present, Mbok Truno and her children stopped, each gripping hold of the other.

'It's all right,' I said, encouraging them. 'Go on in.'

I set an example, and they moved forward, their feet dragging along the go-down floor, bowing again and again, keeping their gaze away from the white person in front of them.

Mama followed behind them.

'Ayoh, don't be afraid,' she too encouraged them, passing them and going up to the doctor.

'The wound is somewhat old,' said Dr Martinet in Dutch to Mama.

'A villager, doctor,' answered Mama.

'It's not a wound from being pierced by bamboo, Nyai,' he spoke again. 'A wound from a sharp weapon, perhaps a week ago. Has there been another fight here since the incident with Darsam?'

'No.'

'Remember, Nyai, what you say now I'll have to report if any investigation eventuates.'

'Of course, Mijnheer Doctor.'

'I know he didn't fall on any bamboo,' Dr Martinet pressed.

'What does it matter, Mijnheer Doctor? It's all the same. He is wounded and must be treated.'

'It might be a different matter before the law.'

'There's no need for a trial, Mijnheer Doctor,' answered Nyai Ontosoroh patiently.

'Very well. It was an accident with bamboo. Make him understand, Nyai. If he doesn't, he can get a lot of people in trouble.'

'Thank you, Doctor. You are always so good to us.'

Dr Martinet went home without joining us for dinner.

Only then did Trunodongso's wife and children sum up enough courage to approach. As quick as lightning Mama shifted her attention to her new guests: 'Nah, Mbok Truno, stay here with your man, you and all your children. Don't think about what's happened. Look after your man well. There are more mats over there. Roll them out on the floor when you want to sleep. The go-down is big. Don't talk to anyone. Don't tell anyone anything. Just one story to someone, and you could bring disaster upon us all. Do you understand, Mbok Truno?'

'They all understand, Ndoro,' Trunodongso answered from his place on the mat.

'Come on, Child,' Mama said.

As we walked away she put her hand on my shoulder and whispered slowly: 'After you left to fetch them I sent Panji Darman off to the shipping agent. There's a ship leaving for Betawi tomorrow. You must leave tomorrow, Child, Nyo. You must act as if nothing has happened. And don't speak to anyone.'

I took Mama's hand and clasped it. 'Your child will go, Mama. Mama has done so much for me. Thank you, Mama. Will I not be sinning to leave you here alone to face so many difficulties, Ma?'

'I've thought it all out, Minke.'

'Bless me, Ma, that my journey be a safe one, and that I will do well at medical school.'

'You will do well, Child, Minke. You have gone through so much with me. I understand the problems you face being so close to me. Go tomorrow, leave before dawn. Hire an andong. No one will go with you. Don't ever be afraid or discouraged.'

'I haven't been inoculated yet, Ma.'

'Panji Darman had his on board ship too. The shipping agent will arrange everything.'

I kissed the hand of this compassionate and loving woman, my mother-in-law. After tomorrow would I ever meet her again? She let me kiss her hand.

As we came closer to the house she whispered again: 'And don't forget the task your dead friend gave you.'

'Who, Ma?'

'Khouw Ah Soe. You haven't forgotten, have you?'

'I'll make sure his letter is delivered.'

'And so you must. A task given by someone who is dying, Minke, is sacred.'

'I've got a request too, Ma.'

She stopped. The night was black. The sky was thick with clouds. Not one star was to be seen. Darsam could be heard ahemming some distance away.

'What, Minke? I will help you in your difficulties. You have the right to ask that.'

'Not that, Ma. Trunodongso and his family.'

'Don't worry about him. He has a claim on this business. So too do all the other farmers who were cheated by Mellema.'

'And what about Mama herself?'

'Everything will be all right. And another thing – don't take your wife's portrait with you.'

'I miss her sometimes, Ma.'

'No. Your schooling – that picture will only hinder you. Forget her. Mix with other girls, Child, and be proper too. And when you are in Betawi don't forget about your Mother. You forget that wonderful woman too easily.'

Darsam ahemmed again. Mama called him over. 'Darsam, look after that man and his family well. When you're ready, give the two boys some work. Whatever you think is suitable. Put the woman to work in the main kitchen.'

'Who is he, Nyai?'

'Your faithful comrade in days to come.'

Mama went inside and I followed. She sat down in the front parlour where Panji Darman had been long awaiting her.

He had only been away a matter of months carrying out Mama's instructions yet Panji Darman now looked fully grown up. He stood up as we walked in and bowed to show his respect to Nyai Ontosoroh.

'Ya, Rob, you may begin.'

The youth nodded to me, sat down again, and began in Dutch: 'My Mama.' He stopped for a moment, watching for something in Mama's face. 'Please forgive my letters. I am not able to write any better than that.'

'Well enough,' answered Nyai.

'And not clever at talking either.'

'You're quite clever there too.'

'Minke, please forgive me. You look very tired. Please don't be angry if I say the wrong thing.'

Humbly, carefully, avoiding any chance of offending or hurting our feelings, he began to make his report. He first expressed his gratitude that

469

Mama should trust him enough to send him to Holland as Annelies's escort. He asked forgiveness for all his deficiencies. I don't know how many times he asked our forgiveness.

'You have carried out your task as well as you could, Rob. No one could have done better. You have represented Minke and me, perhaps even better than we could have ourselves. It is we who are grateful to you. There's no need to repeat what you have told us in your letters. About my late daughter, there's no need to mention her again. Your task is over, and so too is that whole affair.'

Panji Darman looked at Mama, amazed and bewildered. He asked quietly, 'Is Mama angry with me?'

'What about your reports on other matters, Rob?' I helped him.

Panji Darman understood. He went on: 'No, Mama, Minke, I must finish my report. I have not written to you everything that happened. It's not that I want to remind you of all that past sadness. My task isn't over until I have finished my report,' and ignoring what Mama and I had said, he went on.

Only Panji Darman escorted Annelies to her final resting place. A funeral parlour took care of all the arrangements. The preacher refused to carry out any service because he was unsure about my wife's religion. Panji Darman himself carried out a little Javanese ceremony.

'My Mama, forgive me if I did wrong.'

Mama's countenance didn't change. I bowed my head deeply as I listened. His words were clear and pure, from a heart that knew no self-interest.

'Even now I don't know what Mrs Ann's religion was. If it was Islam, please forgive me. I thought it was better to have some ceremony rather than none. I join in the deepest sadness with my Mama whom I love so deeply and with Minke, my truest friend. I know better than most just who Mama, Minke and Mrs Ann are. All people of character, to whom I owe so much.

The more he spoke the more formal it all sounded. And too much trivial detail. Mama cut in: 'Thank you for all your kindness, Rob. Minke also thanks you, isn't that so, Minke?'

'Yes, Rob.'

'Now, about the other things.'

Panji Darman, alias Robert Jan Dapperste, for the millionth time expressed his gratitude for Mama's offer of putting him through school in the Netherlands. Then there was another request for forgiveness because of his lateness in returning to the Indies.

'An unnecessary extra expense,' he went on. 'The thing was, while I was in Amsterdam I saw a report about preparations to publish a Malay journal. Its name was going to be the *Pewarta Wolanda*. The report said, Ma,

Minke, that this magazine was being published especially for people in the Indies, and that it would use good Malay. It was going to try to develop Malay into an appropriate administrative language and a language of polite social communication. But the most interesting thing was that they were looking for articles about life - real life - in the Indies. So I decided to visit the magazine's office. And who should I find there? None other than Miss Magda Peters.'

Panji Darman was sitting in the reception area. Magda Peters was arguing with some Indisch. With all the racket from the printing, he couldn't make out what they were disagreeing about. As she came outside she quickly recognised Panji Darman, but because he was then asked to see the editor, she only had time to give him her address.

The editor turned out to be a veteran of the Aceh War who knew a great deal about the Indies. He had been a lieutenant in the army. He was very happy to have Panji Darman visit him. He was assisted by a Sumatran, Abdul Rivai, a Java Doctor who was continuing his studies in Holland.

'Forgive me, because I can't remember that Dutchman's name now,' said Panji Darman. 'He asked me to write about my experiences in the Netherlands, in either Malay or Dutch. I was willing. And in a flash I was thinking about all that had happened in those last few weeks. I would tell the story of the unjust way Europeans had treated Mama's family. I said I'd be back in about two weeks. The only trouble was that he asked that I write it in proper Malay, not in the uneducated Malay of the marketplace. I wasn't able to say yes to that. I said I could only write in Dutch. He gave in.

'Before I left he showed me sample copies of coming editions. They were going to be very beautiful, Mama, Minke, full of attractive photos - just like European magazines. I went back to my lodgings and began to write. That's why I was late in returning home.'

Then one day Rob went to visit Miss Magda Peters. Our former teacher was renting a room in a very austere area. There was no carpet in her room. Her fireplace was an old iron stove. Her furniture comprised a bed, a wall cupboard and a table with two chairs. How different was her situation here compared to how she lived in the Indies - in a nicely furnished house, all to herself. But she didn't seem ashamed of her poverty.

I'd come to ask advice about my article. I'd changed the names of the people in the story. She said that an anti-colonial article like that could not be served up to the readers of a colonial magazine; that the magazine was to be published to help broaden the knowledge of those loyal to colonial power, so that the colonial masters would be able to converse occasionally with them.

'You are always so well-intentioned, Rob,' Mama cut in, 'but you needn't have done all that.'

'I felt it was my duty, Mama. I had to do all I could.'

'You've done so much for us, Rob,' I added.

'If I didn't finish my tasks properly, I thought, I will live in shame forever, Minke; I would never be able to finish another task ever.'

Mama watched Panji Darman with glassy eyes, moved by the loyalty of this simple young man.

'I didn't understand what Magda Peters meant,' he went on. 'I didn't get the chance to talk with her again. I excused myself and went to the editor's office. He read what I had written, not saying a word, and he gave me three guilders as payment.'

'I've never seen that magazine,' I said.

'Neither have I. I asked him to change the names in the article and use the real ones. He said there was no need. He didn't ask my address either.'

'They won't publish it, Rob,' said Mama.

'However that might be, at least I tried,' he answered.

'Is there anything else, Rob?' asked Mama, beginning to get impatient.

Panji Darman then reported on the use of the money he took with him, including the three guilders he earned from the article. Then: 'Now about the business side of things, Mama.'

The orders were for the cinnamon to be sent unpowdered by Mama's spice business, Speceraria.

'Good, Rob. As soon as you're ready to work, you can contact the cinnamon collectors. Now go and get some rest.' Mama stood up and went upstairs. She seemed very tired.

'Good night, sleep well, Mama.'

She didn't answer, but disappeared from sight.

'We'll meet again tomorrow, Rob. Rest now.' I didn't give him a chance to speak. As soon as he left, I locked the door. Then I went out to the back, and locked the back door from outside.

The clouds had disappeared from the heavens. The scattered stars sparkled peacefully. I went to the go-down to have one more look at Trunodongso.

The children and his wife were asleep. Truno himself was lying in a somewhat difficult position, not yet asleep. As the light from a wall lamp struck him, his eyes blinked open and shut. He didn't see me approaching. As soon as he saw the shadows, he became vigilant; then: 'Oh, Ndoro,' he said, and sat up with some difficulty.

'Feeling better?' I asked.

'My land, Ndoro,' he said anxiously. 'They will have taken it by now.'

'Husy, don't think about that. Get better first. Nyai will look after you all. You and your children will be able to work here until you want to go back to your village.'

'Ndoro promised you'd help me.'

'You were too impatient. I hadn't succeeded yet, and you were already up to all kinds of things. Didn't I warn you before?'

'I was bound by an oath, Ndoro.'

'My promise to you is still in force. But your oath, your promise to these other people, has only brought disaster. All right now, get some sleep. Don't worry about these things now. Nyai will take care of everything. Don't ever talk about Tulangan. Don't say that you've ever met me. Don't go anywhere without Darsam's permission. They will still be looking for you. Your moustache and beard – shave them off – everything.'

'Good, Ndoro.'

As I came out of the go-down I bumped into Darsam, who never seemed to sleep.

'Not asleep yet, Young Master?'

'And you, why aren't you asleep Darsam?'

'Young Master, I don't know, I'm always restless, ever since my hand's been like this.'

'Nyai has said you will stay here.'

'But what work can I do like this? I just end up wandering back and forth like a hungry mouse.'

'What do you want to do?'

'To work, Young Master, but I can't. Must I be just like a tree, doing no work but forever sucking strength from the earth?'

'You'll slowly adjust to your hand, Darsam. You'll be able to work again. Dr Martinet says not all your fingers will be useless. Some of them won't be able to move, but not all of them.'

I grabbed his shoulder and ushered him towards his house. We went inside. Everyone was asleep. He turned up the light.

'Darsam,' I called him softly.

He didn't hear me. He fetched a rag and cleaned the seat where I was to sit.

'Darsam,' I called again. 'No need to sit. I want to talk to you standing here like this. Darsam, I don't want ever to forget all the help you have given me during these difficult times. I don't really know whether I should consider you my brother or my uncle.'

'You're very strange tonight, Young Master,' he said, amazed.

I took out the gold pocket watch that Mother had given me. 'Look, Darsam, you can read and write now. You can read the time? Nah, here, what time is it?'

'Twelve o'clock less fifteen minutes, Young Master.'

'Very good.' I opened the back of the pocket watch and showed it to him. 'Can you read that writing?'

He tried and tried, but couldn't.

'No. You can't. It's Javanese writing. It says: "To my beloved son on his wedding day." Darsam, this was made by the best of the goldsmiths at Kota Gede, Yogya. From my mother. Try it on. It looks good, doesn't it?'

'No, Young Master, no.'

'Hush; don't wake anyone.' I put the watch into his shirt pocket. I hung the chain on the second button from the top of his shirt. 'Very good, Darsam; it suits you. This watch really suits you. Take it as a remembrance of a young man who can never forget the thanks he owes you.'

'Young Master,' he protested.

'Don't refuse. This is an order. Take that watch wherever you go.' I took his left hand and I shook it, trembling.

He became even more amazed. And in that condition, I left him.

The pendulum clock in the front parlour rang out twice. All my things were packed in my suitcase. My briefcase was full of writing paper. I had resolved not to sleep. I walked back and forth in the front rooms and the back, making sure I would remember all these things that I was about to leave behind for who knows how long, perhaps forever: the furniture, the phonograph which had not been used for so long, not even for recording, the ornaments on the walls, and the shiny, newly polished parquetry, all glowing in the light of the gloomy oil lamp.

For quite a while I gazed at the portrait painted by Jean Marais – the picture of Nyai Ontosoroh. In the dim light of the lamp it seemed more alive than even Mama herself. All her strength was there, as if she were a goddess immune from pain and death, remaining strong in all weather and situations. Yes, even the clouds in the background seemed to be running away to avoid her head. If she had lived ten or maybe thirty centuries ago, the painter would have had the right to paint her with a halo. In the future, if I am given a long life, long enough to become senile, this woman will still never leave my memory. Her face, her kindness, her wisdom, her patience and resolve, her strength, I will take them all with me to my death.

I went back into my room and took out from its wine-red velvet cover Jean Marais's painting and stood it near a lamp.

Ann, you are still smiling. It was you who first brought me into this room, and into the garden beside it. I am still here now, Ann, even though for the last time, and you left it before me to go who knows where. I know I will never see you again in this life. Nor will I ever meet a woman like you.

'Put the picture back!'

Mama was standing behind me. She was carrying a bamboo bag which she put on the table.

'Here is some bread and drink; you must breakfast before you board the ship.' From the basket she also took an envelope, and gave it to me. 'This is what you have saved while you have been working here. One hundred and fifty guilders. A carriage is waiting. Leave now. You must carry all your things yourself. No one must see you. Good luck, Child, Nyo. Good luck.'

She embraced me. She kissed my forehead. She helped me carry my things to the door. Before leaving the house I asked for her prayers for my safety and for her blessings. She gave them, then said once again: 'Good luck, Child. Live up to your ideals.'

She turned and went inside. I stood in a daze on the steps. It was here that I first met Annelies and came to know her, then became a member of this family. My breast felt heavy. What more could I hope for from this beautiful house? There is no longer anyone waiting for me to come home, waiting for my caresses. A tear dropped.

The cold wind struck my face. The basket and bag and suitcase I carried all together in my two hands. I had taken just a few steps.

'Let me help you Young Master!' My bag fell from my hands. It was Darsam.

'You won't talk to anyone!'

'Where is Young Master going?'

'You're the only one who knows. Keep quiet about it.'

We stealthily made our way to the road. Seeing us approach, the andong driver lit the carriage's lamps.

Silently Darsam lifted my things up onto the carriage.

'A safe journey, Young Master, wherever you are going.' From his waist he took a dagger in a leather sheath and handed it to me. 'Take this, Young Master.' He pushed the weapon into my belt.

'Come on, driver!'

Goodbye to you all: Wonokromo, memories both beautiful and sorrowful, Mama, Darsam, Trunodongso and your family. Goodbye; I will not return. Mama, the woman I admire most in my life, you, in whose hand I was no more than a lump of clay to shape however you wished, who could explain the great issues, who could dig deep into many things at once, who was intelligent and educated, who is ahead of your times, goodbye. All your hopes for me will be realised, Mama. All of them.

I sobbed in the darkness of the morning.

The carriage travelled slowly through the stillness, further and further away from Wonokromo. I ordered the driver to drive around Kranggan, past my old boarding house and Jean Marais's house. Maysoroh was no doubt still asleep under her blankets. Goodbye everybody, goodbye to you all. And to you too, Mr and Mrs Telinga! I had to use all my strength to resist the urge to see Maysoroh. That sweet child! How clever she had been in keeping her father's friendships alive! How deeply she loved him! All her father's hurt and pain became her hurt and pain. So young a little one! Goodbye May!

Goodbye to you all.

I instructed the driver to fill in a few hours travelling around, visiting the places I used to like, and also my old school, the H.B.S. The building was still blanketed in darkness – no light, either in the compound or along the street outside. Ah, you, my school, are you afraid to look me in the face? Because what you gave me has turned out to mean so little?

The carriage kept moving. Goodbye to you all. I will never return to see any of you again. I am on my way to become my own person, to become what I was meant to be.

Goodbye.

14

The ship *Oosthoek* set sail from Tanjung Perak.

The crowd that had come to say last farewells dwindled in the distance; the people now looked like ants swarming over the wharf. I knew not one among them. No, I was not afraid, not discouraged. Goodbye to everything, to men and their earth.

The sea took me further and further away from land. To become complete, not the shadow or image of someone else, no matter how much I respected and admired that someone else. I must not see this parting as a sad event. There was nothing more I could expect to gain or learn in Surabaya and Wonokromo – the places that had swallowed up my youth. As time passed the crowd on the wharf became a blur. In the end all I could see were the mountains to the south.

Though I hadn't slept at all the night before, I had no desire for sleep. This was the first time I had travelled by boat; my first view of the island of my birth from the ocean: a white line of beach pressed by heavy layers of green growth and mountains, looking like rows of grey-blue waves – Multatuli's 'Emerald Horizon'.

'Something wrong?' I heard someone greet me in Dutch.

Beside me stood a European – young, friendly-looking. His face was adorned by a smile. His lips were pale. His teeth were somewhat yellow from smoking. He was tall and slim. On his little finger he wore a gold ring with a small diamond, no more than five carats. His clothes were all of white cotton.

He held out his hand by way of introduction: 'My name is Ter Haar, Mr Minke, or is it Mr Max Tollenaar.'

'Oh, Mr Ter Haar – have we met?'

'I'm a former sub-editor at the *Soerabaiaasch Nieuws*, Mr Minke.'

'Why have I never seen you before?'

'Of course you have not. Mr Nijman does not wish others on the editorial staff to deal with Asians, especially not with Natives.'

'May I ask why not?'

'Especially in your case, Mr Minke. He did not want you to be influenced by anyone else.'

'Influenced? How?'

He laughed and slapped my shoulder. He took off his glasses and cleaned them with a handkerchief. After he had put them back on, he offered me a cigarette. I said I didn't smoke; he nodded: 'It's best you never take it up, Mr Minke. Once you try you'll never be able to give it up. But my smoking doesn't bother you?'

'Please, go ahead, sir.'

'It is good that you graduated from H.B.S. Too few Natives receive an education as good as that.'

How many times had I heard that? It was a signal: get ready to discuss a European-type matter. Like a mechanical voice-box I automatically produced from my mouth the usual ever-so-polite response: 'I will try to follow what you say as well as I can, Mr Ter Haar.'

He nodded, focusing his eyes on me. The lecture was about to begin.

'In these times we live in, Mr Minke, there are many different ideas floating about the place. Mr Nijman doesn't like people who don't think as he does.' He coughed several times and threw his cigarette into the sea. 'Ah, this is how it is for cigarette addicts. If you don't have a cigarette you must have one; once you get one your throat's hot and sore. You're lucky you don't smoke.'

Perhaps he threw his cigarette away not because his throat was sore, but because he needed time to make up his mind whether to tell me what Maarten Nijman was like.

'Mr Nijman doesn't like the radicals,' I said.

'Ah, you have sharp insight. You are right. And more than that, he is an Indo. He is a member of the *Indische Bond*.'

'You're a radical too?'

'A good guess, Mr Minke.'

I remembered Miriam de la Croix, who had joined a political party, so I asked: 'You're a member of the *Vrizinnige Democraat* party?'

'That's about right.'

'And you mean that Nijman doesn't approve of it?'

'Oh, he's a shareholder in T.V.K.' He scratched his neck. 'So people say, anyway. It seemed he didn't like my thinking. We often argued, even when it wasn't necessary. I had no involvement with the T.V.K. You know about the T.V.K.?'

'Of course. The Madurese call it *te-pe-ka*.'

'It'd be strange to find a Surabayan who didn't know of it.' He whistled, his cheeks collapsed, and his lips shook. 'We had so many fights, I gave in and left.'

'That's what you're doing here?'

'Yes.'

478

'Where are you heading?'

'Semarang, Mr Minke. I'm going to work for *De Locomotief*. Have you read that paper?'

'Not so far.'

'A pity. The oldest paper in the Indies. It has a long and brilliant history. It's read in the Netherlands too.'

'A strange name for a newspaper – *De Locomotief*.'

'To honour Mr Stevenson. The paper was founded at the time the very first locomotive was put to use on Java – thirty-six years ago.'

'How would you compare it to the *Soerabaiaasch Nieuws*?'

'There's no comparison, Mr Minke. The *Soerabaiaasch Nieuws* is no more than an extremist colonial paper.'

'So it is a sugar paper.'

'Yes. Many of its younger reporters have been let down, disappointed. They're sent off to do jobs that aren't really work for journalists at all.'

Ter Haar did not go on with his comments. Having heard about Kommer's experiences at Tulangan, it was easier for me to understand what he was saying.

'While nothing adverse is being said about sugar, it looks like any other neutral paper, but as soon as sugar interests are offended, it appears in its real colours. I heard you've had some bad experiences of your own with Mr Nijman.'

'No.'

'Even so, you should write for *De Locomotief* instead. It's more famous, has a bigger circulation. I'll try to get your writings published. The paper is not just read in Holland but in South Africa – the Transvaal and Oranje Vrijstaat – and wherever Dutch is understood: in Surinam, in Guiana, in the Antilles. It gives a realistic picture of the Indies to the world.'

He talked with great enthusiasm about the world of the press. I listened like a little boy being told a bedtime story like the *Pancatantra*.

There was virtually not a single neutral paper the world over, he said. In the Indies nearly all the papers were colonialist in the extreme. The plantation papers were even worse. Their job was to give indirect orders or make suggestions to government officials that suited the plantation owners. The news reports were merely a formality, so they could call themselves newspapers.

'Your pieces, for example, were published just to keep the readers entertained, humoured – to assure them that nothing was wrong in the Indies, that all was safe and secure – safe and secure for the sugar mills, so that the shareholders in the sugar companies would feel at ease, and the share prices back at the exchange in Amsterdam would remain stable.'

I felt he was accusing me: my writings were no more than a way of making the mill owners happy. But I had written those articles in full seriousness, mobilising all my abilities, all my emotions, and exhausting both in the process.

'And if I had talked about the sugar interests?'

'There would be no space in the paper for your work. On the other hand, everything must be done to keep the confidence of the shareholders: for example, if there were a sugar crisis because of a fall in prices.'

I didn't understand. How stupid and ignorant I was! A sugar crisis! Fall in prices! How much I did not know. And I was ashamed to ask – an H.B.S. graduate who doesn't know anything about sugar, who tried to make contact with a cane coolie and was laughed at by Nijman.

As time went on his lecturing became more and more overbearing. He became more enthusiastic – the enthusiasm of an unpaid teacher. It was killing the enthusiasm of the student, who had never paid his fees anyway. What I had heard and understood from Kommer's story about *Soerabaiaasch Nieuws* was no longer enough to help me. I couldn't understand. Couldn't understand! Who can fault someone who simply doesn't understand?

'So now you know why Nijman could get so upset about a peasant farmer.'

He became more and more carried away. Lustily were the wolf's teats pushed towards me. In anger and frustration my throat was seized and the nipples jammed into my mouth.

And that sugar-owned man, Nijman – his hands have never held cane, his trousers have never brushed with the earth of a cane plantation – why must he become so savage just because of one farmer? Doesn't the Government have enough soldiers and police?

Ter Haar nodded in his knowing-teacher fashion. He raised his head and lit a new cigarette. His sucking made the cloves in the cigarette crackle. The dirty white cigarette paper caught alight, curled and turned into ash. His threw his gaze towards the deck tower.

'Take this ship, Mr Minke. Listen to the engine. This is not owned by the Government. The Dutch company K.P.M. owns it. Yes, people say that most of the capital comes from the Queen. And that's why they can use the word Koninklijke – Royal – but it's not owned by the Government.'

His talk became even noisier, the milk from this wolf was becoming thicker and thicker, too sticky to swallow. His lips moved quickly, sometimes sucked in and almost disappearing, but his voice lashed out, overcoming the power of the wind that was crashing into my ears: 'Surprised? That there is a company owned by the Queen but not Government property? That's called a phenomenon, sir, a phenomenon of our age. Uh, don't ask me. I know what it is you want to protest. Ah no, you already know.'

I shook my head in a panic.

'No? Truly?' He gave a short, biting laugh. 'It is the Government that guards, that guarantees the security of the Queen's ships, the profit that comes from each trip. It is the same with all the sugar mills and plantations, all the private businesses.'

He went on to tell me all about all the giant businesses that were active in the Indies: figures, protozoa spread throughout my land, growing and multiplying, making the people of this land dance to the pull of the threads they held in their hands.

He flung his cigarette into the sea. It didn't sink, but bobbed with the waves as they broke against the ship's sides.

'Any kind of capital can enter the Indies. The Government has opened the door. The Government guarantees the security of that capital. A bitter thing to know, Mr Minke, where all that capital comes from. Mostly from the Netherlands, sir, but lately there has been more from the peasants of Java themselves. Have you read about this year's sensation?' He stared at me like a devil about to pluck out my eyes. 'No? Of course not: it hasn't been reported in the papers here. An incredible story, Mr Minke. Something uncovered in Holland and exposed to public view in the Parliament. N. P. van den Berg and Mr C. Th. van Deventer have made the accusation that the Royal Family has taken from the peasants of Java the amount of 951 million guilders. Have you ever seen a thousand guilders?'

The wolf's thick milk was gulped down in one clot.

'The Royal Family misappropriating the wealth of the Javanese peasants! Farmers, just farmers! That's what they have alleged – van den Berg and van Deventer.'

Ter Haar stared at me once again, as if he wanted to lift me up and fling me onto the deck. He was angry, frustrated: 'We here in the Indies have been waiting and waiting for something more to be done about the matter in Parliament. But no, that was all, Mr Minke, nothing more. I don't know how many mouths the palace gagged with wads of money, but all of a sudden the Members of Parliament went mute.'

I didn't understand, but I nodded. Even how one thing related to another I didn't understand.

'But the greatest outcry in Holland is over the debt the Indies accumulated – 100 million guilders in six years – to finance its lust to conquer Aceh.'

The image that appeared before me was of Jean Marais. And a question: Who was this man that I have called Ter Haar? As he watched me – perhaps I was standing open-mouthed in confusion – he laughed boisterously.

'What can one do? Your eyes must see these things clearly. Ignorance is shameful. Allowing someone to remain in ignorance is betrayal. Nah, I'm free from accusations of betrayal now.'

481

He slapped my shoulder. 'What a *De Locomotief* man says is different to what a *Soerabaiaasch Nieuws* man says.'

'Do you know Kommer?'

'Kommer? The reporter from the Malay paper? I've heard his name.'

'He's never spoken as you have.'

He didn't react. Instead he bent his tall body over so he could bring his lips close to my ears: 'And Governor-General Rooseboom, famed for his liberality and gentleness, no less a fraud – the deceit of a deer, Mr Minke.' Abruptly, he straightened his body. Leaning against a ship's ladder, his head thrown back, he broke into cascading laughter. And when he was free once more from laughter, he bent down again, his lips near my ears again: 'You read the newspapers.' And like Nijman: 'But not everything is printed in the papers. Have you heard about the decision to grant the Japanese equal status with Europeans?' I nodded. He ahemmed. 'Russia is furious with the Netherlands Indies.'

'Russia?'

'Yes, Mr Minke, the Czar. You know why?' I shook my head. 'Well, isn't Russia at odds at the moment in Manchuria with Japan?' Now it was I who ahemmed. 'Several weeks ago' – he tried to count it out on his figures but was unsuccessful – 'the Russian fleet turned up at Tanjung Perak harbour, Mr Minke, at Batavia itself. Old Governor-General Rooseboom, Mr Minke, he was rushing about everywhere looking for ways to make the Russians happy. Yes, Mr Minke, the Crown Prince was with the fleet. He was on his way to Port Arthur.' He let out a breath. 'Do you know where Port Arthur is? Nah, in the name of the neutrality of the Netherlands Indies, the Crown Prince was entertained with a hunting trip in the forests around Priok. And so there would be no complaints, Rooseboom ordered that some of the deer from the Governor's palace at Bogor be caught and let loose at Priok.' He broke out into that boisterous laughter again. 'Just imagine how happy the Crown Prince must have been to make those half-tame animals topple to kiss the earth. And the flattery from the Dutch officers, already prepared: what a great hunter is His Highness the noble Crown Prince of Russia. It was the first time in the history of the Indies a hunter could down three deer in one strike.'

Now his voice slowed down.

'That was during the day. At night the daughter of a Bupati was brought to him. God! In the name of the neutrality of the Indies! How old was that girl? Almost fourteen! God! In Europe, in the Indies, the lies are the same.'

I wasn't capable of following all his chatter and all his laughter, his bendings and straightenings. Now a new cigarette inhabited his mouth. The previous one had been elegant: this one was of corn-husk, tied with red thread.

'And that neutrality, Mr Minke, is all for the sake of big business in the Indies.'

It seemed he was relieving himself of some burden which had nothing to do with me. Now that he was released he was silent. I used the opportunity to question him about where he came from and where he received his education. He seemed so young. He laughed. He did not avoid my questions – but neither was he clear in his answers. From his sparse replies I gathered that at twelve he had become a cabin boy on a ship bound for the Indies. In Surabaya he had jumped ship. He then became a general run-about at a Factorij. Later he went into the interior of Borneo, and the land of the Torajas in the Celebes, and the Batak lands in North Sumatra – perhaps then too as general servant – with a research scholar. Since that time many researchers had sought after him as an assistant, especially people from the churches.

Humbly he acknowledged: 'It was from them I gleaned what knowledge I have of the world. But it was with my own eyes, my hearing, the soles of my feet, that I gathered a few clumps of knowledge about the Indies themselves.'

'What you've just been telling me – it's not about the jungles, is it?'

He laughed again, but not so boisterously this time. He was no longer smoking; his stock had been wiped out.

'What's the difference? All these great cities are just jungles, places to wield power over others, to get whatever life-essence can be sucked from people's bodies. Yes? Isn't that so?' His laughter was less and less convincing. Then, abruptly: 'Mr Minke, the Government is not as it used to be. Your people, Mr Minke, there's nothing left of them but the dregs after their bodies have been squeezed by forced cultivation. The great companies pay the fattest tribute to the Indies state now. So, if necessary, the Government will mobilise army and police, civil service and village officialdom to make sure their will is done.'

So we returned once again to that issue. I could find no way to escape the harangue.

He talked on and on, about a dozen things of which I had never heard before. The *Oosthoek* sailed calmly to the west. Everywhere there were sailboats of the fishermen, and of the Bugis and the Madurese.

'I don't know how long these Buginese and Madurese boats will be able to hold out against the ships of the K.P.M. There used to be many more; I myself have witnessed how the steamships – first the Arabs and then the Chinese – started to push them aside.'

'That's never been taught at school.'

'Sorry, Mr Minke, I've never been to school. And anyway, what would be the point of teaching things like that? Truly, this heart of mine is so happy to hear a Native say something like that. Uh, these times, Mr Minke: like a perforated rice-steamer, this age can never be filled up, no matter how many different questions are asked and answers given. Deceit is flourishing everywhere. Not the deceit of people who only want a dish of rice – that's no more than the cunning of a people already at the same level as the mud of their homeland – but deceit and falseness that ride the wind, Mr Minke, deceit as the legitimate child of excessive power. I'm sorry, Mr Minke, this person you speak to here is no more than the illegitimate child of one mother and who knows how many fathers . . .'

His confused talking, as if he were being hunted by some devil, ended abruptly. His hands groped in his pockets, left and right, but he couldn't find a single cigarette.

'Why would the Queen invest capital here?' A question flew from my mouth to mask my stupidity.

'What for? Ah, Mr Minke, what does it mean to be a queen in these mad times? Without capital she too would be the servant of capital. Even a king is best off being a king of capital.'

'But the teachers all say we are entering the age of modernity, not the age of capital.'

'They only half-know what's going on, Mr Minke. The journalists know more about what's actually happening. And to half-know something is not necessarily to know it at all. Look, Mr Tollenaar, didn't you use the pen name 'Max Tollenaar' to conjure up the image of Multatuli's 'Max Havelaar'? From that alone people will know you are the spiritual child of Multatuli. Your humanity is great; even so, Mr Minke, such humanity, without real knowledge of life in the Indies, could miss its mark altogether. What people call the modern age, Mr Tollenaar, is really the age of the triumph of capital. Everybody alive in this modern age is ordered about by big capital; even the education you receive in the H.B.S. is adjusted to its needs, not your own needs. So too the newspapers. Everything is arranged by it; including morality, law, truth and knowledge.'

As time went on Ter Haar's talk became more and more like a pamphlet. (I myself had some doubts about including all this here, especially as I wasn't really able to fathom it all. But not to include it would also not be right; Ter Haar took me on a journey to new continents which I had never encountered in my geography lessons. So if these notes read like a pamphlet – yes, that was the situation I found myself in. The ship, the past, Surabaya and Wonokromo back there – uh, they all became the pages of a pamphlet, splinters of an incomplete knowledge.)

And it was still difficult to accept the notion of the absolute sway of big capital over people's lives. In the villages people weave, spin, make batik, plant their fields, marry, reproduce, die and are born – and none of this is because of capital. And early in the morning people leave their beds, ritually wash themselves and face God – and is not that because of capital either?.

Now catching up with what Jean Marais had said about the power of capital in the Aceh war. But Ter Haar gave more than a glimpse: it was a flash of lightning. Marais had said that the Netherlands Indies was jealous of English capital which could fondle and control Andalas via Aceh, a buffer state. The independence of Aceh was violated by the Dutch, even though Holland always said that the Netherlands violated Aceh with the agreement of England.

'Yes' – now Ter Haar spoke again, 'but what people call capital is more than just money, Mr Minke. It is something invisible, abstract; it has a supernatural power over real objects: it causes everything that is scattered to collect together, that which is together to scatter, that which is liquid to solidify, and that which is solid to turn into liquid. Once in its grip, everything changes shape. The wet is made dry and the dry made wet. A new god has the world in its fist. Yes, it's a boring thing, but a fact. Production, trade, the sweat of the people, transport, communications, no one, not one person, is free from its power, influence and instructions. Also Mr Minke, the way people think, people's ideals, they too are approved or not approved, blessed or not blessed by it.'

The longer he spoke the more fantastic his story became, contradicting everything I had ever been taught at school. It burst from my lips – an attempt to restate a classic issue: 'Wouldn't it be as true to say that everything is ruled by science and its laws?'

He laughed amicably, 'Science and its laws are now no more than just an empty swelling, powerless . . .'

And Mama reckoned everything was ruled by authority, by power. Ter Haar broke into that uncontrollable laughter again. His tall body shivered. At that moment I reckoned he must have a nervous disorder. Neither he nor his rhetoric could be completely accepted.

'There is no power that does not stem from massed capital, Mr Minke, not these days. That other kind of power is to be found only among shepherd peoples wandering the grasslands, or other nomads in the deserts, jungles, and savannah. The cleverest of people, and even Stephenson, the hero of the century, would never have been able to give the locomotive to the world with no capital. It is only with capital that he was able to order the clouds of steam to make those carriages move tens of metres. Without capital people could not make light, bring to life the telegram, and telephone. Isn't it so? Without capital, those big men would be nothing more than leather wayang puppets with no backbone to keep them from flopping. Isn't it so?'

The wild wolf had spoken too much. It was too complicated to digest.

That afternoon I slept well. I used the evening to note down all his babblings and to think a little about the truth of his words. Everything my teachers had taught me was now threatened with being turned upside down, thanks to this Capital. What had Ter Haar said? Everything is subjugated by it: individuals, societies, and peoples. Those who don't wish to be subjugated remove themselves, run away. Kings, armies, the President of the United States, France, even the beggars by the roadside stalls or the churches, all, he said, are in its grip. Peoples who reject the power of capital will languish and die. Societies that run away from it will return to the Stone Age. All must accept it as a reality, like it or not.

I was on my way to Betawi to continue my schooling. After I graduated I would become a government doctor, curing the sick employees of the state. They must be able to carry on their work for the government. And the government, in its turn, would ensure the health of capital. Is that all that will become of me in the future? An insignificant expender of energy in the interests of capital?

I had not finished with my thoughts. The writing still stood on the paper, gaping open-mouthed. I had not closed it with a full stop when he came to my cabin. He invited me to eat with him.

On leaving the cabin I realised it was already night.

Dinner in the second-class dining room was all-European. My appetite died. Ter Haar, on the other hand, ate happily and lustily.

'You don't like European food very much,' he said. 'Yes, food is a matter of habit. I still to this day prefer pears to bananas.'

Back up on deck, however, it was I who began: 'Mr Ter Haar, why did Mr Nijman and his paper treat Khouw Ah Soe as an enemy?'

'You mean the Sinkeh Chinese murdered at the Red Bridge?'

He didn't know what had happened so I told him.

'Mr Minke,' he began, 'the situation is now safe, calm and orderly for big capital. People can get on with their work without any significant disturbances. Khouw Ah Soe and his Young Generation might have influenced the Chinese in the Indies, might have had some influence generally. If society is disturbed, then trade will most surely be disturbed as well, and prices too.'

'But there are always disturbances.' I told him about the troubles of the peasant farmers in Tulangan, which, it turned out, he knew about.

'Peasant rebellion is meaningless, Mr Minke.'

'But the situation is disturbed too.'

'Such small upsets are already calculated as part of general production costs.' Now he seemed to try very hard not to lecture. 'What kind of power do those capital-less peasants have? How much damage can they do? It won't cost the companies more than twenty sacks of sugar to put things back in order.' He laughed. 'What's twenty sacks compared to five thousand? The peasants will be put down. It takes a week at the most. Then they return to their original state. But, Mr Tollenaar, if the people themselves change . . . aduh! things will never be the same. The conditions of life will begin to change also, slowly moving further and further away from the original situation.'

'But it wouldn't be the farmers, but the Chinese that changed, that is, if Khouw Ah Soe had indeed succeeded in his efforts.'

'It's not as simple as that. All kinds of people influence one another – even into their kitchens. Perhaps you yourself are already a lover of *kecap*, bean curd, *taoco*, noodles, *bakso* and *hungkwee* without ever feeling you have been influenced by another race. And not just the Natives of the Indies, but the peoples of Europe too. People use spoons and forks, eat spaghetti and macaroni – all influences from China. Everything that gives pleasure to mankind, everything that does away with mankind's suffering and boredom, everything that lessens his fatigue, will, in these times, be copied by the whole world. That young Sinkeh too. He and his friends were only trying to copy the United States and France. In the end so too will the Natives of the Indies. And if the Natives started on that path, then soon there would be no more comfortable place for big capital in the Indies.

This last exposition of his was easier for me to follow and helped explain what had been said earlier. A spot of light appeared to expose the way ahead so I could travel it without the aid of others.

Before us, the island of Java was swallowed up by the darkness. Here and there were lights like yellow-reddish fireflies. There was life there, the greater family of my people. They are not allowed to copy America or France, either directly or via the influence of others; they have to stay in their present state for ever.

'They are the source of earnings for big capital,' Ter Haar went on. 'Everything must be turned into a source of profit. From every centimetre of thread that is sewn into a torn garment, from every stride that makes itself felt on the earth. And in the towns of Europe and America, from every mouthful of water. Maybe in the future they will take profits too from each cubic centimetre of air we breathe.'

Abruptly the tone of his voice changed. Stingingly: 'Do you know anything about the Indies' close neighbour, the Philippines?'

'A little. They rebelled against the Spanish colonisation, then against America.'

'Where did you hear that? It has never been reported here in the newspapers.'

'Ya, just a coincidence, Mr Ter Haar,' I answered. I could not say anything else not because of the subject itself, but because my source was Khouw Ah Soe. I still had his letter in my suitcase.

'News from the Philippines is very scarce. It seems the Government feels it has to restrict such reports.' Ter Haar's words came forth more and more quickly, more enthusiastically; he seemed now to be expounding his own

487

beliefs: 'The Government is afraid that if the Indies Natives find out a lot about what's happening, about how far the Filipino Natives have progressed under Spanish rule, they would be ashamed.'

'Many Filipinos are educated, really educated,' he went on. 'Already some are graduates. And the Indies Natives? Just a handful sit on the benches of universities in Holland. There is still not one graduate in all of the Indies. Public schools are not even three-quarters of a century old. In the Philippines they have been going for almost three hundred years. In the Indies ninety-nine per cent of Natives are illiterate. In the Philippines it is ten per cent less than that.'

Such progress. The Filipino natives were closer to European science and learning, to understand the power that rested with the European peoples, to know how to use that power; and so they rebelled. They had changed as human beings because of European education. They could never return to being the Natives of earlier times. And the Government of the Netherlands Indies was even more worried that the educated Natives of the Indies would find out that the Filipino rebellion against the Spanish was lead by educated Filipinos and was no mere peasant disturbance like that in Tulangan.

Before the rebellion itself took place, he went on, the port workers in the Philippines harbours refused to work. Coolies refusing to work! I thought, amazed. In a flash I remembered something like that being reported in the newspapers here, something they gave the name of 'work desertion' and in Holland 'striking'.

'The Filipinos have already carried out strikes,' said Ter Haar. 'But their rebellion is even more interesting; it rocked all of Europe, including Holland, Mr Minke.' He hurriedly lit another cigarette. 'They're all busy studying why it happened so they can make sure nothing similar occurs in their own colonies. A friend of mine knew one of the Native leaders there, someone called Dr Jose Rizal. My friend met him in Prague. Rizal was a poet, very brilliant, and a fiery lover also. The Spanish caught him in the end. A great pity – someone as outstanding as that. His faith wasn't strong enough. A pity.' He smacked his lips. 'Of course there can be no doubt now about his fate: the death sentence ended his life story. Someone as cultivated as that, writing poems in Spanish, just as you write in Dutch. A doctor, Mr Tollenaar, and you too intend to become a doctor. Perhaps that is no coincidence.'

'Somebody educated, a doctor, a poet . . . rebelling . . .'

'Maybe the Dutch are cleverer than the Spanish. There has never been any rebellion by educated Natives against the Dutch here. Here the educated Natives always follow the Dutch. The Indies is not the Philippines, Holland isn't Spain.'

'And he was sentenced to death?' I was reminded of Khouw Ah Soe.

'That's right. The Spanish military are famed for their viciousness.'

An educated person had rebelled against his own teachers . . . indeed there had never been anything like that in the Indies.

'And then even when isolated from his comrades, Jose Rizal did not stand alone. So many, so very many people loved him, because with all his knowledge and learning, he loved his own people so much. Many prominent people, clever people, in Europe pleaded with the Spanish Government to pardon that brilliant, educated Filipino.'

'What did he want to achieve with this rebellion?'

'You don't know? He wanted his people not to be ruled by the Spanish. He wanted them to rule themselves. A pity' – he made noises with his lips again – 'that inexperienced people in the end became the victims of an alliance between Spain and America.'

'I don't really understand, Mr Ter Haar. How could they rule themselves? You mean the educated Natives would replace the Spanish and the Americans to govern their own people?'

'Of course, that's what they wanted. National independence.'

I conjured up in my imagination the kings and bupatis of Java, mad with their lust for power, making people bow down and crawl before them, give obeisance to them, do their pleasure. And no guarantee that they would be better educated than those they ordered about. I shook my head. Even to imagine the Filipinos governing without white people was beyond me. And here, on my own earth to think of such a thing! Huh, to make any sense of it at all was impossible. Without the power of the whites the kings of Java would soon be mobilising every single inhabitant in the effort to annihilate each other, each trying to emerge the sole triumphant ruler. Wasn't that history for centuries?

'What's the matter?' Ter Haar reacted to my brief silence.

'And what would happen if the Native kings held power again? Imagine how the educated groups would suffer, Mr Ter Haar?'

'No. The Filipinos intended to govern along American and French lines: a republic – that is, if they had won. In such a great awakening as that there were of course many leaders whose thinking was European, and a modern organisation also. Not like the peasants of Tulangan. There was an organisation that was the engine of opposition. The one called *Katipunan* . . . or something like that.'

'A modern organisation?'

'So you are not familiar with the idea of a modern organisation?' Now it was he who shook his head.

I couldn't see his face clearly. The evening darkness provided him with a good disguise. Perhaps he was pitying me, a graduate of H.B.S. who didn't know about modern organisations! Probably Nyai Ontosoroh would have understood and been able to explain it clearly. But truly, I didn't understand. I stayed silent, no more questions; shame and embarrassment enveloped me now.

The drumming of the ship's motor shook everything inside my body, even my thoughts.

'In the end,' Ter Haar went on, 'the more European science and learning Natives obtain, whatever their race or nation, the more it is certain they will follow in the footsteps of the Filipino Natives, trying to free themselves from European rule. The Filipino Natives wanted to stand up themselves as a free nation, as Japan does now, acknowledged by all the civilised nations of the world.'

'And you include the Indies in this prediction?'

'Of course, though who knows when? And to prevent such a thing from occurring, or at least to postpone it, the Government here is especially miserly in handing out European education. Science and learning are sold at the highest price. But there can be do doubt that the Netherlands Indies will arrive at that point one day, as the numbers of educated grow. That day will arrive, perhaps as predicted by Sentot. You know that name?'

'You mean Multatuli's friend?'

'Yes, Let's walk. Standing here is not healthy, especially for a smoker like me.'

Perhaps he thought I wasn't following him; he moved onto another subject, but then turned back: 'One day, when you have read and studied more, you will understand better than you do now.'

'The Indies, Mr Ter Haar,' I said, because I didn't feel comfortable just listening and never contributing any words, 'has been confronted with the rifles and cannons of the Kompeni for three centuries and has always been defeated.' All of a sudden I remembered the story of Untung Surapati who had won. 'Only sometimes we have won, but that was only momentary.'

He laughed affably. 'Naturally, because those Natives were still back in the Middle Ages, or perhaps even earlier – maybe you could say the Stone Age. But if the Indies Natives – just one per cent – could master European science and learning – even less than one per cent, one-tenth of one per cent – those changed human beings could start changing their society – then their whole people would change. Especially if they had some capital as well. The rifles and cannons of the Kompeni army do not have the power to hold back change, Mr Tollenaar. Even if their numbers are small, if one class rises in rebellion, even the smallest nation will rise up along with them. You remember the Eighty Years' War, don't you? What was Holland compared with Spain at that time? But once Holland had risen, even Spain had to admit defeat. Do you know about Mexico?'

'No. A great pity.'

'The first conquered people to defeat their masters, the Spanish. What was the significance of the Mexican Natives compared to Spain then? But

490

once a group rises up, once a nation rises up, its power cannot be dammed back any longer. It cannot, Mr Minke.' And, as if to shout it out: 'It cannot!'

'You seem to believe the same thing will happen in the Indies too.'

'I'm not talking to you like this without reason.'

'Such a thing won't make the Dutch nation happy, including yourself,' I said.

'I believe in the French Revolution, Mr Tollenaar: Liberty, Equality, Fraternity – not just for ourselves, as is now the case on the European continent and in America, but for everyone, for all nations upon this earth. The true liberal point of view, Mr Minke.'

'But France herself has colonies in Africa and Asia, and America.'

'That is France's, and Europe's, wrongdoing. But the shout of the Revolution remains as grand as always. It was created from French blood, tears and pain, and French lives.'

'You amaze me, Mr Ter Haar.'

'I'm proud to be a liberal, Mr Minke, a liberal who sees things through. Yes, others call this sort of view "extreme liberal". Not just disliking being oppressed, but also disliking oppressing. And, indeed, more than that: disliking oppression anywhere.'

It was far into the evening when I returned to my cabin. I noted down only the main points Ter Haar had discussed, including those I didn't yet fully understand. Totally exhausted, I laid myself down on the upper bed. The others in my cabin had long been asleep. And I was absolutely sure that in a moment I too would be blessed with a health-giving sleep.

When I awoke it was light. The day was visible through the porthole. Two small fishing boats with small sails were attacking a wave. The howl of the ship's motor shook everything, including me. Washing my face in the basin, I went outside. And Ter Haar's words were still there, swooping down, attacking me, pursuing me. How could a Native become President? Would he not just fall back into the ways of the kings, which he would know from legends, and which he could see for himself in the bupatis? And then would not others emerge who wanted to be like him? Then wars would rage continuously, just as in the classic history of our rulers, *Babad Tanah Jawi*. War without end – each person pitted against the other, all against all? What would come of it?

We have had hundreds of years of experience of war, Mr Ter Haar. Defeat, always defeat. And according to Miriam – who knows whether it was her own opinion or just picked up in one of the alleys this world – it is Minke, and Minke's race that is perhaps the cleverest in the world at turning its back on reality, at drugging itself into sleep, at humouring itself with the fantasy that they have never been defeated.

That maiden had the hope, whether a just or an insane hope: don't be like your fellow countrymen, Minke. There must be one person who is aware, who can be their brain and their senses. Uh, another wolf, that Miriam.

And the Philippines – salute! Defeated? Defeated in its fight against America? At least this mighty people had defeated Spain. It's a pity, Mr Ter Haar, but we are not Filipinos. I could not imagine it: the Indies without the Dutch! We must draw as deeply as possible on the well of European knowledge and learning. Just as Japan is doing. There is no honour without European science and learning. Ah, Mr Ter Haar, you are truly a spirited coaxer, a harassing tantaliser, leading me astray.

With that last thought I went into the bathroom. But none of these things wanted to be shaken loose. They kept popping up, pursuing me and hopping up and down crazily everywhere. What torment such a little knowledge can wreak . . .

Private capital began to enter the Indies . . . yes, at the end of the Culture System. The Minister of Colonies, de Waal, legislated for the expropriation of land which was to be set aside for capital interests born of the corruption during the Culture System. And these interests wanted guarantees from the Governor-General of the Netherlands Indies, not against the possible depredations of Native rebels – they were considered insignificant – but against the incursions of the English, who were biding their time and quietly keeping their eyes on the situation from Singapore and Semenanjung. What was the meaning of the London Treaty of 1824? It was just a piece of paper. The English could use Aceh as a bridge into the Indies. Aceh had to be brought totally under Dutch control, to dispel the fears of big capital.

And Aceh proved to be unlike Java. The Dutch fell into a trap. The Acehnese war raged, the most costly during the whole of colonial history. Ninety per cent of the armed forces and seventy per cent of the budget were siphoned off to win that war. It went on for almost a quarter of a century! The commitment shown by the Netherlands Indies Government in subjugating Aceh acted as a guarantee for capital. More and more capital made its way to the Indies . . .

In the dining room Ter Haar was already waiting. He went on with the stories from yesterday. He tried to explain the power of big capital in our times, the modern era. He never mentioned the Acehnese War. All this talk he came out with now was almost a repetition of what was in that anonymous pamphlet that Magda Peters had given me.

I asked him whether he ever read an anonymous tract on this subject. He asked in turn, amazed: 'Do you mean *Onze Koloniale Modderpoel* ?'

'Exactly,' I said.

'So you have read it. Do you know that pamphlet is a banned publication?'

'I never knew there were banned publications in the Indies.'

'Be careful how you look after it, Mr Minke. There was an earlier banned book too, *Vrouwen naar Jacatra*, but it is nothing compared to that pamphlet. If you have already read it you should be a member of the Radical Group. I'll try to arrange it, if you agree. But keep away from the Indies Union.'

'What is this group?'

'Ya, just a discussion group. You agree?'

What was wrong with being honoured with membership? Ah, Ter Haar, you enticer! Discussions about the situation, you say. No doubt more interesting than school discussions. I agreed without thinking about it any further. Anyway, he knew more than I did.

He invited me to walk with him on deck. He was becoming more and more friendly and open. He went on with his story:

These days the big capital that came into the Indies was not only active in agriculture. Capitalists had their fingers in mining, transport, shipping, industry. The small Chinese tin miners on Bangka Island had been swept aside by big investors. The small sugar businesses of Java had been stamped out by the sugar factories. These small businessmen were now just coolies belonging to the new, powerful tuans.

'You know about de Waal's Agrarian Laws?' I shook my head. Another new continent.

'And you must know that it was former Minister of Colonies Van de Putte who was the brilliant mind behind them, and the cleverest of all the devils of heaven and earth. A sailor, Mr Minke, who came to the Indies and became a Tuan Besar Kuasa in charge of a sugar mill. It was he who drew up the sugar laws when he later became Minister for the Colonies. Now it has been revealed: all this time he was the owner of the biggest sugar-cane plantations in the Besuki-Bondowoso region. Him! While your people, Mr Minke, who lived all around those plantations, had nothing! That is the sort of thing you will find out by joining our discussions.'

What a huge range of things this one wolf knew! Perhaps there wasn't a grain of truth in any of it. But he did seem to know.

'Do you know the story of how the big farmers of Priangan were robbed of their most fertile lands?'

It had happened not long ago, he told me. The big farmers or rich villages had their own forests, rice lands, other fields and crops. They owned hundreds of buffalo, which roamed freely in the village or on private land. In order to seize those lands for the big capitalists the Government only had to issue land regulations. But in order to take the lands over without creating suspicion, Native agents were set to work. They put poison in the water holes where the buffalo drank. In one month ten thousand buffalo died. The villages stank of rotting carcasses. Disease was rampant. So it was announced: no cattle were allowed to roam freely in the forest lands or in the jungle. With Kompeni troops as their bully-men, and facing little resistance, the Government forced the villages and big farmers to give up their lands. Now it was all planted with tea. Not a single relic remained of the great cattle farms. Destroyed, totally annihilated.

'You would never find out such things without joining the Radical Group, Mr Minke. Please, don't look at me like that. Our group is only a vehicle to collect information about all the illegal, dark goings-on in the Indies. And then there is the gold rush around Pontainak. You surely wouldn't have heard about that. Isn't that right? Yes? And the secret societies of illegal immigrants from North Borneo.'

His words kept swooping down without a pause. I don't know when he had the opportunity to wet his throat and lips. Perhaps he had finished five or seven cigarettes. You could even smell the cigarette smoke on my clothes. He talked and talked:

Capital wanted to turn all the Natives into its coolies. The Natives' land would become its own land. So the capitalists resisted with all their might any moves for European education to be given to Natives. They were afraid the source of their power, cunning and evil, would be revealed. But capital needs more than just coolies; it also needs foremen who can at least read and write. So schools were set up to teach a few people to read and write. Then that too wasn't sufficient; they needed some who could count. And those schools needed teachers, so a Teachers' School was set up. Then they felt the need for a few people who could speak a little Dutch. The primary schools that were operating were divided into grades I and II; students in first grade received a little tutoring in Dutch. So, as things developed, capitalist interests in the Indies found they needed educated Natives for their own enterprises. And so on, and so on. More advanced schooling, at high-school level, in special subjects were instituted for Natives: Agriculture, Administration, Medicine, Law. It could not be avoided. It was necessary because of the growth and development of capitalism itself – including the medical school you yourself are about to enter. And you're given good money to stay with the Government, to make government service attractive.

And the most powerful of all capital was sugar capital. It was on behalf of sugar that the liberals in the Netherlands, calling their policy the Ethical Policy because they wanted to pay the Netherlands' debt to the Indies, accrued in the days of the Culture System, waved the banners of Education, Emigration and Irrigation for the Indies, and prosperity for the Natives. But in reality it was done in the interests of sugar. Education: to produce the literates and numerates and technicians needed for the sugar industry. Emigration: to move more Javanese off Java, providing much needed labour in Sumatra and opening up more land for canefields in Java. Irrigation: water for the cane plantations, for sugar.

'And that's not all, Mr Tollenaar,' Ter Haar went on.

'One need gave birth to another, because that is the law of life. Willing or unwilling, capital will bring Natives more and more into contact with western science and learning whether they want that to happen or not.

'And Mr Tollenaar, you yourself want to study to be a doctor. Yes, there must be doctors, so that the plantations and factories aren't disturbed with people falling ill.'

'If in the future I graduate as a doctor, it won't be my intention . . .'

'Willing or unwilling, you will become a part of the cane-crusher machine – like the sieve, or a cog, or steam kettle.'

'But a graduate of the medical school becomes a government doctor.'

'It's all the same, Mr Minke.'

He had succeeded in making me understand.

'The Government would not provide education and training if it wasn't in its own interests. Remember what happened in the Philippines. But they have no choice.'

I understand now why Jean Marais was so sickened by the Aceh War, something he experienced himself.

Another ship came into sight as it passed us from the west.

'Look at the ship, another K.P.M. ship. The Queen's capital is behind it – just like this one. Both made by clever engineers and tradesmen. The motors made by the best inventors. But it all belongs to capital. Those without capital are no more than coolies, no more than that, no matter whether they are more brilliant than all of the Roman and Greek gods together.'

Now I thought of Nyai. She too was able to employ Europeans to do her business. They came when she called. And Mr Deradera Lelliobuttockx was tossed out of the house in front of everyone because he was no longer of use. A Native throwing out a Pure! What a lot Nyai had learnt from Mr Mellema!

Ter Haar began again to discuss the Philippines, but this time choosing material he thought I would understand. Now he used a new term which was even more difficult: nationalism. He himself had great difficulty in explaining it.

Then he stopped. Like somebody who had just remembered something, he took out his pocket-watch: 'I have an appointment, Mr Tollenaar. You must be bored with this endless chatter of mine.'

'Not at all,' I said, though in fact I did feel more than just a little full.

'Then we'll take this all up again another time.'

'I have never met a European like you, Mr Ter Haar.'

'Not all Europeans are rotten.'

'You remind me of Miss Magda Peters.'

'Quite possibly. I only heard her name after she was expelled from the Indies.' He nodded, excusing himself, and walked off, disappearing down some stairs.

Back in my cabin, I opened the dictionary. But its explanation of nationalism was just as unenlightening as Ter Haar's. Nothing in the dictionary equated this nationalism with the greatness Ter Haar attributed to the rising up of the Filipinos against Spain and America.

I had not been long scribbling down the outline of Ter Haar's discourse when his servant arrived with two magazines: *Indische-Gids* and *Forschung und Prufung*. It seemed this was how he wanted to continue our discussions.

Only because I had never seen it before, I opened the German magazine first. There wasn't a single picture. My German was terrible, but there was an article about the Philippines. I felt I had no choice but to force myself to untangle its meaning. And it was more than just difficult. Knotted up and entangled by all my own recent experiences, my mind turned the article's complexity into complete confusion. On the other hand, it was those very experiences that enabled me to understand some things. Aided by those experiences, I came up with this picture of the situation.

The educated Natives of the Philippines put their hopes in the Spanish liberals back in Spain, just as I had put my hopes in the Pure Dutch liberals back in the Netherlands. Yes, in Europe, the land where the peak of human achievement and brilliance was stored as in a museum. And the Natives had beautiful dreams: one day the Spanish would, in their generosity, make them members of the Spanish parliament, and give them the full civil rights of subjects of Spain, and they would be able to feel they could do some good for their own people in their own land.

One thing I learnt, a basic piece of knowledge: that a small group with their dream tried to bring it to reality, inviting others to dream the same way. They set up a newspaper. A newspaper! Filipino Natives publishing their own newspaper! *La Solidaridad*! And the educated Native Dr Jose Rizal was one of its leading figures.

I had never seen a picture of him. But I imagined him as someone tall and slim, with big side-whiskers, moustache and heavy eyebrows. But that's not so important. What was important was that the authorities in Spain cursed him and took action against him. And I was forced to think about how things were in the Indies. There had never been anything like that Filipino group here. Never. And the indications were that there never would be. Poor Trunodongso; with machete and hoe he wanted to fight them, while even Rizal had been trampled so easily.

Still fortified with his hope in Spanish charity, he carried on with his attempts to make his dream a reality: he founded the Filipino League. But the Philippines colonial government continued their attacks upon him.

I know these notes won't be of much interest to anyone, but I have no choice but to include them. Why? Because these thoughts are so much a real part of my environment, the world I inhabited. Ah, knowledge: Trunodongso would never have heard that there is a nearby country called the Philippines. And knowledge, the result of my reading this article, made the Philippines a part of my own world. Even though only as an idea. The wonder of knowledge – without their eyes ever seeing the world, it makes people understand the breadth of the world: its richness, its depth, its height, and its womb, and all its pests and plagues as well.

And Rizal still dreamed of the honour and nobility of Europe, said that magazine. But European power was a monster that became hungrier and hungrier the more it gobbled up. I found myself thinking of *Buto Ijo*, the greedy ogre in the wayang stories of my ancestors.

But other groups of educated Filipino natives had long lost their faith in Spanish colonial power. They took up arms and rebelled. Poor Trunodongso and his friends: they knew no geography; they thought that if they could rid Tulangan of the sugar mills they would win an eternal victory. But Rizal was even more pathetic than Trunodongso. When his comrades took up arms, he was still dreaming of the generosity of the Spanish governors of the Philippines, even after he was arrested and exiled. And a few days before he was executed he was still urging his fellow Filipinos who had taken up arms to stop fighting. He was more pitiful than Trunodongso. Him – Rizal! Truno was defeated because of his lack of knowledge, Rizal because he did not believe in what he knew . . . in his intellectual conscience.

The Filipino Revolution broke out. The goal was to run the Spanish out of the Philippines. In my soul's eye I could see the educated Filipino Natives rising up, leading their fellow countrymen, uneducated like Trunodongso, in attacks against the Spanish garrisons – a war that could never be depicted on the wayang stage. Even in my fantasising I could not imagine it. They weren't led by individuals, but by a spirit of resistance, represented in the Katipunan. Represented too in its top leadership: Andres Bonifacio. Seven years ago. Poor Trunodongso – he knew nothing of such leadership. Poor Minke – I had only found out a few hours ago. Tens of thousands of Native Filipinos mobilised the whole people into resistance. And they did resist, they did fight back. The whole land seethed with rebellion, marching out of the houses to take part in the fighting, to live or to die. The Spanish in the Philippines were pressed hard and then pressed even harder. And the Filipino Natives chose their first president: Emilio Aguinaldo. In 1897! The first republic in Asia.

And they built their government on the French model! No wonder Khouw Ah Soe was so excited about the Philippines! He was still at the stage of crying out to his people like Rizal – at a time when his own country was suffering under the Americans, the English, the French, the Germans, and the Japanese, as well as parched by drought, the whole country, north to south, east to west. He too died, just as Rizal did. And this Javanese – he is still nothing. He is nobody.

The Filipino revolution was thrown into turmoil by traitors who loved money more than freedom for their country and their people (another piece of basic knowledge for me). The rebels, in their defeat, accepted the hand of friendship from America. The warships of America sailed to the Philippines and surrounded the Spanish armada. On land the Filipinos worked together with the American marines. No different than the wayang stories.

I have heard the explosion of a cannon, on Queen Wilhelmina's coronation day. But in my soul's eyes thousands of cannon explosions tore apart the garrisons and the earth of the Philippines. The sky was dark with cannon smoke. Death arrived to the sound of tumult. Not like the death that silently throttled the people to the south of Tulangan which Surati witnessed. How different is killing to the sounds of shouts and cries, from the strangulation of smallpox.

But the Filipinos, still inexperienced in these things, were finally deceived by the Americans. In the battle of 13 August 1898 – a show battle between Spain and America, like the show battle between Mataram and Surapati – Spain was defeated, America won. The Filipino patriots were the real losers; they were freed from the Spanish, but fell into the hands of the United States, which became their new master.

So far I had learnt one thing clearly: white power was equally greedy everywhere. Greed! Greed! No longer just a word, its meaning fused in my mind as the starting point for all understanding. Greed. But that was still better than war, killing, destruction. Especially a war where there is no hope of victory, as in Aceh, in the Philippines, like the one Truno wanted to wage. No, Ter Haar the Coaxer, I still need Europe as a teacher, including you yourself. Only through your own strength can we confront you, Europe.

Oosthoek's chains clashed and clanked as the anchor was lowered into the waters off Semarang. Night had fallen. Lamps flickered on land and sea. Stars twinkled in the sky, and the surface of the sea glimmered in shining yellow waves. Ter Haar was nowhere to be seen on deck, nor in the dining room either.

498

I went to his cabin. Not there either. His things were already tidily packed.

From the loudspeakers came an announcement: all passengers not leaving the boat at Semarang could make a four-hour visit beginning at eight o'clock the next morning. Passengers for Semarang were asked to disembark now.

I used the time to walk around watching the people disembark. I found Ter Haar speaking to another European near the gangway. It was he who spotted me first: 'Mr Max Tollenaar, may I introduce you to my friend from *De Locomotief*.'

'Pieters,' he told me his name.

Ter Haar explained who I was and about the *Soerabaiaasch Nieuws*.

'Oh, Mr Max Tollenaar is really quite young. I thought you'd be middle-aged at least. There is much wisdom in your writings.'

'We will be going ashore in a minute,' said Ter Haar.

'You will be visiting ashore tomorrow?' asked Pieters.

'Of course.'

'Good. Don't head off before we come to fetch you,' he said. 'You must come and visit our newspaper offices. Who knows?'

They boarded a small rowing boat and waved goodbye. Not long after, the few passengers for Semarang went ashore.

'Eh, Mr Minke.' Someone spoke to me. Beside me stood a Pure European – a police officer.

'I'm not mistaken, am I?' he asked. '*Tuan Raden Mas* Minke? Officer Van Duijnen. How was your journey? Enjoyable?'

'Very much so, sir – my first trip by ship.'

'Not seasick?'

'The weather has been beautiful and the sea calm.'

'Very good. You're not going ashore?'

'Tomorrow, sir, in accordance with the ship's announcement.'

My heart beat with suspicion. There had to be some reason for his approach. Perhaps Trunodongso had opened his mouth under interrogation. Truno, yes, that Truno. Who knows what stories he came with.

'I think it would be best if you went ashore now, sir,' he advised me. I became even more suspicious.

'A pity, sir, but I still need some rest.'

'You can rest in the hotel.'

'Thank you, but no.'

'I'm not joking, sir. Let's go ashore. Where are your things?'

Yes, Trunodongso had betrayed his promise. The policeman was obviously arresting me. I headed off to the cabin. He followed me. I packed all my things. He helped me.

499

'You got around to making notes even on this journey?'

'It seems you need me ashore?' I asked.

'Yes, sir.' He presented me with the order. 'There's no need to worry. You can see for yourself that it is an official order. I'm not here to kidnap you.'

'My destination is Betawi, not Semarang.'

'There's plenty of time to go to Betawi. Why didn't you go by train? The trip through the south is much more interesting.'

He was suspicious of me. I didn't answer, pretending not to hear. I picked up my suitcase and bag. I left the food basket behind.

'Let me help you,' he said. He carried my suitcase. 'You don't have anything stored in the hold?'

'Nothing, sir.'

We descended the steps under the gaze of many eyes. A young criminal had been arrested on board.

'What have I done wrong, sir?' I asked.

'I don't know. Don't be anxious. I don't think there is anything to worry about.'

'How can I be detained like this? I'm a Raden Mas. You know that.'

'Precisely. That is why a District Police Chief has been assigned to meet you.'

'Meet me?' My mind raced trying to make sense of it all. In the end I couldn't escape the thought of Trunodongso. New troubles hovered before me. More newspaper reports. More suffering for Mother. I still have given you nothing, Mother. It seems I can only fall into predicaments like this.

The last time I was met by a police agent, Father was made a bupati. Now it is a District Police Chief, but certainly Father has not been made Governor-General of the Netherlands Indies.

A special boat took us ashore. A government carriage was waiting to take us.

'. . . where to, sir?'

'No need to worry.'

The carriage took us to a hotel. 'The best in Semarang, sir,' he said.

Semarang was fast asleep in the light of the gas street lamps. He was not joking; it was indeed the biggest hotel in town. People looked after us very politely. I was given a big room, for two people, a bit too beautiful.

'Nah, Tuan Raden Mas Minke, just stay here and be good. Don't go out. Don't leave the hotel until someone comes to get you.'

'What's really happening? Why am I being detained like this?'

'Have you been treated improperly, Tuan?' – exactly as the police agent had behaved the last time.

Before leaving he repeated his warning. Once again I was a pawn in a chess game. Certainly, Father had not been made a Governor-General.

Perhaps he had been awarded the Lion Cross for his services to the state. Well then, it was Trunodongso I had to think about. Or Robert Suurhof?

Dinner was brought by a waiter. And the way he served me – how careful he was, as if he were afraid. All my questions went unanswered. Perhaps outside the door there was another policeman?

How I missed Ter Haar now – that tantaliser, that coaxer, that broadcaster of ideas. His whisperings still buzzed around me: they, those people, Mr Minke, build their power upon the ignorance and backwardness of the people of the Indies. Uh, that cajoler. Who are you, Ter Haar? A police spy? My suspicions were set in motion again. Maybe that's it. That school report of mine – that my moral character was wanting – that would be noted down in all the books of the offices that administer candidate civil servants for the bupatis. As an individual, I could do nothing to defend myself against those books, or the silence of the Police Chief.

For the rest of the night I lay with my eyes blinking open and shut, on that incredibly soft and comfortable mattress.

At four o'clock in the morning knocks on the door startled me awake. My heart beat like the mosque drums at *lebaran* time. A first-class police agent, a Mixed-Blood, was standing beside my bed. A short nod from his apparently wooden neck informed me it was time to get ready, to bathe, eat, and depart, though not a sound emerged from his mouth. Like a lamb who had lost its mother I did everything he ordered by those peremptory gestures.

Then District Police Chief Van Duijnen came to take me. Without much talking we left for the railway station. Five in the morning, and the train left for the south-east on my first journey into the hinterland of central Java. Dry and bare. Grey-coloured earth. Long bridges, wide river beds, yellow water, mountains.

The locomotive huffed and puffed wearily towards the central Javanese kingdom called *Vorstenlanden*, past indigo go-downs, coconut, sugar, tobacco, rice, cinammon – all property of the European landlords.

Locomotive! Locomotive! Locomotive! It announced itself constantly with its own incessant rhythm. Lo-co-mo-tive! Hissing crazily along the rails, spouting black smoke into the sky, screaming with its whistle, it woke the people from their dreams, declaring itself the mightiest being on earth.

Ter Haar had not repeated the clichés of others. 'It was this locomotive that inspired the *Semarangsch Nieuws – en Advertentieblad* to change its name to *De Locomotief*. Everybody remembers the year: 1862.' No, it was different with this person Ter Haar; he had had his own story:

'E-eh, Mr Minke, after Prince Dipanagara was defeated, the Culture System went on to great successes in the Vorstenlanden. Yes, isn't it so, Mr Minke; it is only in the Vorstenlanden that peasant farmers can be squeezed clean of everything and end up as dregs. It was to there that

Dutch capitalists migrated to steal the peasants' land and to become great landowners. Isn't it so? Yes? And when their go-downs could take no more indigo and sugar for export to Semarang, and the aristocrat's go-downs were full too, then the matter of transportation to Semarang became a problem. You couldn't ever have heard this story. I say couldn't, Mr Minke – why? because it involves another bigwig. Another Minister for Colonies: that lawyer Baud. He sent camels to Java. Real camels, truly, Mr Minke. Almost four dozen. And the thing was, Meneer, in the experiment of transporting the indigo, there was no trouble. From the Vorstenlanden to Semarang, those animals with their serious faces, like a caravan of philosophers, walked along in a line doing their duty.

'But then the forts at Ungaran and Semarang ran short of rice. Now the behaviour of the camels from Tanarifa was different. You know where Tanarifa is? Over on the west coast of Africa. Nah, after carrying the rice for a week, these immigrants from the Canary Islands lost their seriousness. They all began crying and howling; they couldn't stand the smell of the rice they carried. Every few moments they were turning around, scratching at the stones on the road, then knocking into each other and falling down. After two weeks of carrying rice there wasn't one that could stand. Some dropped beside the road; others died in their pens.'

'The kings of Java owned nothing but their grandeur and their harems. They had no horses, no cattle, no buffalo – nothing to use as beasts of burden. So Minister Baud sent donkeys to Java, ten times more than the now-dead camels. The battalion of donkeys put on a different act, Mr Tollenaar. During the first month they grouchily made their way along the Vorstenlanden – Semarang road with the sacks upon their backs. In the second month, their tongues hung out as they carried the sugar. Then, as they carted the indigo, they began to sneeze. In the end, they all died as well. And there was nobody fuller of spleen than the European landowners of the Vorstenlanden. Finally, in the end, Mr Minke, it was the iron horse that they decided upon – the locomotive. And more and more land was stolen.'

Now that first locomotive in Java, in the Indies, was hauling me in my carriage towards the Vorstenlanden, the warehouse of the indigo and the sugar and all the other commodities needed for the comfort of Europeans.

Van Duijnen didn't speak. He was reading a poetry book in Malay: *Pantoen Waktoe Kadatangan Prince Frederick Hendrik di Ambon* by Ang I Tong. The newspaper *Sinar Djawa* on his lap remained untouched, and he did not offer it to me. Now I saw for myself a Dutchman reading Malay books and newspapers. My thoughts didn't want to focus. I had no desire to read. My mind kept wandering, groping to discover what was about to happen to me.

That evening Van Duijnen was kind enough to pick me up at the hotel. He took me around in a luxurious carriage to see Surakarta. He spoke a lot about this centre of Javanese culture. He liked it here.

I think I know why he liked it so much. Ter Haar had also said 'Surakarta is the centre of your culture, and of 110 large European-owned plantations. Imagine! Imagine! Where could the peasant farmers possibly find land for their own needs? Just imagine! Do you know what that means? Heaven for the European planter, for every white person, like me.' His laugh boomed. 'Isn't it so? Yes? True, heh? And your people, Mr Minke, except for the aristocrats and a few successful traders, they got nothing. They had to crawl like worms to get a bowl of rice.'

It was as if Ter Haar's finger was pointing at my forehead: to whom should you speak now? Still to people like Van Duijnen, who can lounge on the cushions of your culture, your civilisation?

The streets were lantern-lit – *cempor* lamps at the mouth of every alley, peddlers' kerosene lamps along the road, everywhere, tiny, flickering, dim. Forgive this son of yours, Mother. I have not answered your letters. I have given you nothing you desired, even though your hope was simple: that I write in Javanese. Speak to the Javanese, said Jean Marais. Kommer too. But it is only the little lamps I see, Mother.

On the train to Surabaya, van Duijnen was silent again. His head lolled; then he jolted awake.

'You look pale. Ill? A chill?' he asked.

'No,' I shook my head. 'Perhaps it's just that I'm so tired.'

'Is that why you took the boat?'

'At least on a ship you can walk about, and bathe.'

'For a long journey it's true that ships are still superior.' He became more friendly.

But I had lost the desire to respond. I deliberately exhibited my tiredness and kept my eyes closed. I curled up in the corner.

At five o'clock in the evening we arrived at Surabaya station. A government carriage picked us up. Where were we heading? Wonokromo? I knew all the countryside; I didn't need to look.

All of a sudden there was a crowd of people on the road, blocking the traffic. The carriage had to stop. Van Duijnen stuck his head out, amazed to see this crowd cutting off the roadway. Our carriage bell rang out. The people wouldn't move out of the way. Van Duijnen rose to his feet, his face glowing.

'Look, Tuan Minke!'

Out of politeness I did what he wanted. In front of us were ... what were they? Ya Allah, the *velocipede*, the bicycle, the *kereta angin*! There were four Europeans spread across the road holding each other's shoulders. Each was slowly pedalling his own bicycle. I had seen these magical two-wheeled vehicles many times now. They looked so fragile, as if they could be taken apart, folded up and thrown anywhere you liked with one hand. They looked thin and tall and frail.

The onlookers were astounded that the riders did not go flying onto the ground.

The four Europeans seemed quite young. They raised their hands into the air – 'no hands! Nah!' Now while their feet pedalled they all began to sing. And they didn't fall! Once again Europe showed its magic.

Walking in front of the performing youths was a Mixed-Blood who shouted through a loudspeaker, in Malay: 'This is what they call the *kereta-angin*, sirs, the *velocipede*, the bicycle. Genuine German-made. Speedy, as fast as the wind. The Lord Wind gives his aid to the riders so they do not fall. You sit safely in the saddle. The feet start pedalling slowly . . . and rider and vehicle shoot off like an arrow! Anyone can buy! Cash or time payment with the Kolenberger Company, Tunjungan Street. And it is not expensive, sirs.

'Runs as fast as a horse. Needs no grass, needs no stable. Just takes quarter of an hour to learn how to ride, and you can travel anywhere. Far more comfortable than a horse. This vehicle never farts, never needs a drink, never dungs. Genuine German-made. You can take it straight inside the house; it never sweats.'

The government carriage we were travelling in moved to the side of the road, making way for the slowly advancing bicycle riders.

The pedestrian announced again: 'The Firm Kolenberger also gives lessons. Only one *tali* for as long as it takes to learn to ride. Don't miss this chance! The most faithful of all modern vehicles. The missus can ride at the back and a child at the front. Three people can set off together and pedal all around the town – no exhaustion, no cost.'

They passed us and our carriage returned into the traffic.

'Crazy!' whispered Van Duijnen. 'The world's gone mad!' Suddenly he laughed. 'Two wheels. Just think: two wheels! There's more and more of them nowadays too. Crazy! Just one bump and husband, wife and child would be over and injured. Who'd buy a thing like that? Like a mantis! It'll just end up messing up the traffic.' He laughed again. Perhaps he was imagining the victims of the bicycle falling in the middle of the road. 'And did you hear what he said?' he exclaimed. 'Better than a horse. Can that thing jump over a gully? Can it climb a mountain? Can it swim? Can it have children? Crazy! Yes, it's superior if all you worry about is that it doesn't drink or eat or dung.' He laughed again: 'It can't neigh either!'

I sat down again and rested my body against the seat. A number of Dutch magazines had begun criticising young women who rode bicycles. It wasn't polite, they said. If the wind blew, all eyes looked the girls' way, so not only was sin being encouraged, but accidents as well. The problem was that people had to stare goggled-eyed at every new thing. But once things got started, the world lined up behind. And these young women had begun riding around in public, just for the fun of it, without any real purpose! The Netherlands and Europe were being attacked by bicycle fever.

I remembered an article in another magazine: to oppose progress was no different from Don Quixote's attack on the windmill. If women now liked to ride the bicycle, why wasn't a special version made for them so that the wind couldn't be made the scapegoat? Did people think the world belonged only to men?

The bicycle of my imagination was in the Netherlands, and so my thoughts went to Annelies. She now lay in the earth. She never had the chance to see the two-wheelers proliferate in the land of her birth. Had her heart not been broken, this year she would have been free from her guardianship, able to return to Java, and we could have been together again.

Must I keep remembering her? And why do thoughts of the Netherlands always link me with her? She chose extinction without me. She made her own choice. And in the embrace of the earth of the Netherlands she would never witness the wave of women's emancipation that was roaring through the land: emancipation on bicycles.

Now my mind concentrated upon the wonder of this emancipation leaving Annelies alone in her grave. You will never hear the famous Dutch feminists, Ann. Humanity would collapse without womankind, they said. Why must women be just the substratum of life? Why do their own children, who happened to be born males, have such extraordinary objections to women appearing in public? Why does the Netherlands even today deny women the opportunity to become Ministers or Members of Parliament, even though twice consecutively it has been ruled by female monarchs?

Uh, this modern world! What blessings have you really brought us? The rotten heritages of the past have still not been flushed away: Natives are not allowed to be equal, let alone superior, to Europeans, and must always be defeated. Europeans are against each other too, liberals opposing non-liberals, liberals opposing liberals, and now there was the women's movement for emancipation: women fighting men. Is the modern age the age of the victory of capital? Machines and new discoveries cannot answer, cannot say anything. Humanity stays as it always was, complex and confused by those same old passions, just as in the wayang ages of yore.

I had fallen asleep in the government carriage. I awoke when it came to a stop. As soon as I climbed down the surroundings felt familiar. Yes, it was so: we had stopped in front of Nyai Ontosoroh's house in Wonokromo. What was the policeman doing? My heart beat strong and fast: Trunodongso! It was the Tulangan affair after all.

Nyai Ontosoroh came out, greeting me with a smile. No, that smile could not have anything to do with Trunodongso.

'Mevrouw,' said Van Duijnen, 'I have brought Tuan Minke back. I will leave now. Tuan Minke is not to leave this place, as ordered by the Prosecutor. My respects!' Having said this, he left in the carriage.

'Come in, Child. Let someone else look after your things. Don't be angry, don't be disappointed. You look so tired. I understand what you've been through. You want to forget your past as quickly as you can,' said Mama, 'and now it turns out things still have not finished. Even so this house and I are a part of your past. Ayoh, smile, sit down.'

'What is it this time, Ma? Trunodongso?'

'He's caused no problems.'

'Robert Suurhof?'

'No.'

'So what now, Ma?'

'Don't be so depressed, Child. You are not the only one who has experienced these new troubles. I too, and all those we love. I hope this will be the last incident. Forgive me, Child, a thousand pardons. We all want some happiness. If the other has come instead, forgive me. Have a bath first, then we can talk properly about all that has happened.'

Nothing had changed in the front parlour. The picture of Nyai still hung in the place of the picture of old Queen Emma.

'You've only been gone two or three days. Why do you look so foreign now? I'm sorry. A thousand pardons,' she said again.

She went into the office.

15

Something had happened in the household: Minem, that frisky girl, was now living in the main house. Minem, the milker of cows! She was sweeping the floor. Even from a distance I could see her eyes wandering.

As I passed I heard her soft greeting: 'Young Master has arrived,' like the whispering of seduction.

I pretended not to hear and kept walking to the bathroom.

Poor Mama. It seems you became so lonely after I left that you gave in to Minem's desires. Or is it that you want to be close to your grandson? At peace with your fate?

Close to dinner time when I was reading the paper, Mama came in carrying Minem's baby: 'This is Rono, Child.'

'Minem's son, Ma?' I put aside my newspaper.

'Robert's child; my grandson.' Her eyes shone. 'So my line will not be broken, Child. It was your child really that I hoped for.'

Seeing that I was still confounded by it all, she began to explain: 'It is Robert's child. See his eyes! The eyes of his grandfather. Rob himself has confirmed it.'

'Rob!' I cried.

'Yes, his last and concluding letter.'

'Last and concluding?'

'He is dead, Minke. Rob is dead. Venereal disease. In Los Angeles.'

'The United States?'

She nodded.

'So far away.'

'This child will never see his father.' She was speaking to herself rather than to me. Her voice was lonely, heavy.

I understood and bowed my head. Both her children had died in their youth, within months of each other. And before Robert, Annelies's beloved horse Bawuk had died too.

For a moment I remembered the horse's death. The stable hands had not been able to humour its heart. Every day Mama spent two or three minutes chatting to it, just as Annelies had. It ate its favourite sweets, but lazily. Slowly it became thinner and thinner. Finally the veterinarian announced there was no hope.

The animal could no longer stand; perhaps just like Annelies. It lay on the stable floor, without the desire even to raise its head.

Then, one day before we went to Sidoardjo, Mama and I were working in the office. Nyai asked the time. It was ten past nine. She covered her ears. Half a minute later there were two shots. Mama uncovered her ears and went on working. 'What was it?' I asked Mama. She answered: 'Bawuk, Bawuk has been put to sleep.'

Bawuk had made itself a member of the Mellema clan.

And now there was Rono.

'It's over with my children. I need Rono, this child.'

I looked at Nyai with questioning eyes. She started to tell the story, slowly like someone groping through the darkness of the night. It was not straightforward.

While the *Oosthoek* was carrying me to Semarang, a letter had arrived from Robert Mellema in Los Angeles. That afternoon Nyai took the letter to the Prosecutor's Office as evidence in the Ah Tjong case. She was received politely. The letter was copied by two clerks. Mama was asked to check that the two copies were the same as the original. She received a copy. The original was kept by the Prosecutor.

Then Mama had gone to the police to ask for help to contact Robert Mellema. Darsam had driven Mama there in the buggy. Then something had happened in the police station's courtyard. Like a plot devised by a playwright, Fatso, alias Babah Kong, had appeared in the yard.

'Fatso!' I stood up from my chair.

'It turns out he is a first class police agent.'

'What did Darsam do?'

'It was Fatso who quickly told Darsam not to say anything about the earlier shooting.'

'And Darsam, what about Darsam?' I asked impatiently.

'Darsam ran inside and reported everything to me. The police looking after me were surprised too, so they summoned him – not Babah Kong – but Jan Tantang.'

I couldn't picture how confused Mama must have been at the time, like a complicated melodrama unravelling on a stage.

'Jan Tantang was questioned in front of us,' Mama went on. And it turned out he wasn't a pedlar, but also a police agent, first class. A Menadonese-Dutch Mixed-Blood.'

'Did he admit everything, Ma?'

'From the very beginning, as soon as the questioning started.'

'Another trial, Ma?'

'Of course.'

Rono gurgled. Minem came and took him, leaving behind sharp glances.

'Yes, Child. A lot has happened. Yesterday the police came with a telegram from Los Angeles: they had found where Robert was living, but that's all they found; Robert himself had died four months earlier.'

'Ma.'

'Yes. So be it. That's what had to happen and indeed has happened.' She told me the month and day – exactly the same day Bawuk had been shot by the vet.

'I feel sorrow with you, Ma.'

'He has reached the destination he set off for. I think that's for the best. At least his dreams were fulfilled: to be a sailor, to sail the world.'

This extraordinary woman showed no signs of sadness; but I knew her heart was torn apart. It would not be long now before she had to lose the business as well – which had always been her first child, her honour, the crown of her life.

'Isn't it amazing, Child, all of a sudden, out of the blue, I have a grandson,' she turned the conversation.

So now I knew with more certainty: it wasn't because of Trunodongso that I had been brought back here. But because of the arrival of Robert's letter, and the discovery of the identity of Fatso alias Babah Kong alias Jan Tantang.

'You must read Rob's letter, Child; here's the copy.'

'It's not for me, Ma. I don't think it's necessary.'

'The trial will involve you, Minke. You must read it.'

After dinner Mama gave me the letter. I don't remember these days exactly what was in it as I only read it once, and there were so many errors of language. But I have written it up again to read like this:

Mama,

I know you have not forgiven me. Even so I ask again for the thousandth time: forgive me, Mama, forgive this son of yours, this Robert Mellema, whom you yourself brought into this world.

Ma, my Mama, as I write this letter I feel so close to you, as when I was a child who suckled at your breast. But it seems now that there is nothing for me in those breasts. The water of life, Ma, the water of forgiveness no longer flows. I know I will die young, Ma, without your forgiveness. With my head splitting with aching throbs, all my joints stiff and pained by any movement, I forced myself to write you this letter, Ma, news from a lost child. Fever attacks me again and again, my vision is almost gone, lost in the haze. I no longer know if I write in a straight line. But I must finish this letter. Perhaps it is my last. I will keep writing for the next week, until I can write no more.

The nurses here have been so good to me, giving me paper, and ink, and pen. They have promised to post it to you and even to pay for the stamps. They have promised to post it only after disinfecting the paper.

Now that I'm writing this last time, it is not to ask for your pity. I only ask forgiveness. I will face everything with resoluteness just as you have faced everything. So you must not feel at all sad if I talk about my illness. I only want to tell you what has happened, as a son to a mother. No more than that.

My illness spreads, each day becoming worse. My body is no longer of any use to me, let alone to anyone else. There is just a heap of rotting flesh and bruised bones. I have no pity for myself, Ma. I have more pity for you, who suffered so much pain and spent so much energy to give birth to someone whose fate is no better than this.

Mama, it is best that first of all I tell you from where I caught this disease.

I have a disease of pleasure. After thinking about it I am sure it was in Ah Tjong's place. May he and all his descendants be cursed. I was still very young and inexperienced. He invited me in and provided me with a Japanese woman. And it was because of that woman that I lied to Mama for the last time, the biggest lie I ever told.

There is no one here in the hospital who can treat this disease. They never talk about my illness, but I know what their silence means.

Because all this goes back to Ah Tjong, let me talk first about him. Cunningly, using a thousand tricks, he got me to sign a letter confessing to living in his house and that all my food, drink, accommodation, pleasures and everything I needed were provided by him. The next day he started a long conversation with me:

'If Tuan Mellema dies, Sinyo Robert will be the sole heir.'

'No, Bah, I have a younger sister.'

He nodded, then went on: 'You are discouraged just by a little sister?'

'And there is a step-brother from Papa's legal marriage.'

'A step-brother? What's his share in Sinyo's family in Wonokromo? He has no rights. I can help Sinyo get good lawyers to arrange everything. It'll all be fixed. Sinyo will be the sole heir.'

'It can't be, Bah.'

'Your only problem is your sister, and that can easily be fixed. Ah, she's only a sister anyway.'

'Maybe Papa's already made a will.'

'No,' he said, 'your Papa hasn't written anything.'

'How does Babah know that?'

Babah just laughed.

'How do you know that?' I repeated.

'Ah, don't worry, it'll all be fixed without you doing a thing. Sinyo will be sole heir.'

'Maybe my sister will soon marry this H.B.S. student. He might want to demand his wife's rights.'

510

He went silent. He asked who it was and where he lived. I told him that the person in question was staying at our house but that at the moment he was involved with the police. He asked me whether I liked my future brother-in-law. I said: 'He's just a disgusting Native. From the moment we first met I didn't like him.'

'Look, Nyo,' said Babah, 'if Sinyo becomes sole heir, Maiko can be Sinyo's concubine. And you won't have to do any work. Babah will look after the business. You will have no problems.'

'Mama wouldn't allow it.'

He nodded, then he spoke like this: 'Your sister is just a girl. Your mother is just a Native woman. What are they compared to Sinyo? Nothing. They're no more than banana-tree stumps, Nyo. Believe me. If I say Sinyo will be the sole heir, it means the two of them will be gone.'

'But they're not gone,' I rebutted him.

'Yes, now they are here. But who knows about tomorrow or the day after? But the business, it will all be Sinyo's alone. And no need to work. Just taking pleasure, while the profit rolls in by itself.'

'There's still Papa.'

'Sinyo's Papa is no longer a factor in anything. He's dead in life, alive in death. Neither his mouth nor his heart have any value. Everyone knows that. It's sad, but that's how it is.'

'Yes, I admitted.'

'How much pocket money do you get from Nyai?'

'Nothing now.'

He clapped his hands and smacked his lips reprovingly. But I know now why Mama never gave me any money. Mama wanted to teach me to earn money from my own efforts, and I didn't like working. How happy must Annelies be, wanting nothing and understanding what you wished to teach us. It was I who was in the wrong, Ma, and it's no use being sorry now. And, yes, you were right, Ma, it is only from their own efforts that people know happiness. At least, Ma, it is certain that you have obtained some happiness from your work. Ah, what's the use of talking about my own feelings, feelings that will have no value in your eyes, Ma?

But let me go on with this chat between the two of us, Ma.

It was clear he was proposing some possibility of inheritance for me. And how stupid I was; I was happy to hear those poisonous suggestions.

'About the possible brother-in-law, Nyo ... easy, especially if he's living there. Uh! what's the price of a brother-in-law?'

'Darsam will guard him,' I said.

'Darsam? he's just a hired fighter. How much does a hired machete earn? Three ringgits?'

'I don't know, Bah.'

511

'Just say it's three ringgits. At the most it'd be thirty guilders. If you give him fifty, he'll do what ever Sinyo wants.'

I said he was right. He told me how to approach Darsam. 'All hired machetes are the same,' he said. 'Pay them more and they'll betray their own employers. A hired machete from anywhere. Give him ten guilders as a deposit. Here's four ringgits. Sinyo doesn't like your sister or Nyai, do you?'

'I hate them both,' I answered.

'Easier still. But the candidate brother-in-law has to be taken care of first.'

Satan had entered into my heart. One evening I met with Darsam at his house. I invited him down to the go-down and he came with me but was suspicious. I lit a match and put down the four ringgits before him.

'Four ringgits, genuine, ten guilders altogether, new and shiny,' I began. He gave a short laugh.

'For you, Darsam.'

'You've become rich very quickly. Where's the money from, Nyo?'

'Ah, don't worry. Put it in your pocket. Next time I'll give you four times four ringgit more.'

'Forty guilders more?' he asked. 'Sinyo's not fooling around this time, hey?'

I put out the match so he wouldn't be embarrassed to take up the money. 'How much do you get each week from Mama, Darsam?'

'Ah, Sinyo's just pretending not to know.'

'Anyway, if you join with me, you'll be much better off.'

'Where did Sinyo get all this cash?'

'All taken care of, Darsam. Hey, Cak, people say you once killed a thief here.'

'Easy, Nyo, if only a thief and only one man.'

'Of course it'd be easy for you, Darsam. What isn't easy for Cak Darsam? Hey, Cak, if there was another thief, would you still dare fight him?'

'I'd have to check first who he was, Nyo. If the thief was Nyai's own son, it'd be best I didn't interfere.'

'You mean me, Darsam? I've never taken anything that didn't rightfully belong to my father, Papa, Cak.'

'Nah, that's why I'd have to see who the thief was first.'

That answer not only took away my confidence but scared me as well. Remembering Ah Tjong's assurances, I put aside those feelings and went on: 'There is a thief here again, Cak. He doesn't carry a rifle. Forty guilders more, Cak, if you take care of this other thief, and leave no trace.'

'What thief, Nyo?'

'Minke.'

I couldn't see his face in the dark, but I could tell he was furious. He growled like a leopard.

'Take back your money, Sinyo,' he shouted viciously. 'Darsam has never taken blood money. Don't go yet, before I say my piece: if you take another *step before I have spoken . . . I'll cut you down right here and now . . . un-witnessed by anyone. Listen: my employers are only Nyai and Noni. They liked Young Master. Look out! If anything happens to any one of the three of them, I'll know who did it. Look out! It'll be Sinyo I'll kill. Go, get! Don't trifle with Darsam!'*

Frightened by his threats, I ran all the way back to Ah Tjong's house. Babah shook his head but didn't say anything. I tried to forget that incident. I was afraid to meet Darsam. I had thought of him as a playboy and a hireling but he had frightened me into total collapse.

Babah ordered me to live secretly in his house. I lived in the midst of unlimited pleasure. Everything was made available to me. I didn't have to think about a thing.

Ah Tjong has some plan for our family, Ma. I feel so guilty now that I not only didn't resist letting him do whatever he wanted but – more than that – I actually agreed to all his plans. It's only proper that Mama is unwilling to forgive me.

Everything is catching up with me; I must look upon it all as a punishment which I must undergo to redeem myself. I don't want pity from anyone. Don't pity me, Ma. Don't remember and miss me, Ma. Forget me as if you had never given birth to me. As if the milk from your breasts had just spilt onto the ground. I'm too low to be your son; even the offspring of a dog knows how to be faithful and return kindnesses. I'm too low a person to be the child of anyone. Even so, once again, Ma, I say I need your forgiveness. And Annelies's and Minke's, even though I know they won't give it. At least I have done my duty and asked for it, petitioned for it.

Be careful, look out for Ah Tjong. Now I understand better: he wanted to gain control of Boerderij Buitenzorg and its land by means of murder and evil, cunning tricks.

Let's leave this horrible matter, Mama.

Does Mama remember a dairy herder called Minem? Annelies will know her. When Darsam, Mama and Annelies and Minke came to Ah Tjong's house, I had to run away. I knew how furious Mama felt towards Ah Tjong and towards me. I ran, Ma. It was then, Ma, that I left my seed in Minem. I mean: Minem is pregnant because of me, not because of anyone else. I don't know if she aborted the pregnancy or not. If she hasn't Mama, that is my child, your own grandchild.

Ma, my request to you is: look after that child, boy or girl. I hope she is a girl. Whatever else, she is your own blood, she has never sinned against you. Give the baby my name: Mellema. If she is a girl, call her Annelies Mellema, because she too will be wonderfully beautiful.

Don't let Minem keep on working in the dairy. Bring her into the house, because that is what I promised her. It's up to you, Ma, how you arrange it.

Mama, it's been a week now that I've been writing this letter. By tomorrow

I will not be able to write any more. Live your life in happiness, Ma . . . Good-bye, my great Mama. May you stay healthy and safe as long as you live. May you live long to see your grandchildren and great-grandchildren. May no one ever make trouble for you again. May there be some among your grandchildren that make you very proud. Best wishes too for Annelies and Minke . . .

Once again there was a trial. The Court wasn't packed this time. The public's interest in the case had waned. But one extraordinary thing did happen: for the first time the *Soerabaiaasch Nieuws* printed a photo on its front page: of Annelies wearing her diamond necklace. But it was a great pity the caption was so sensational: 'the beautiful victim of a struggle over an inheritance'.

What fantastic events and experiences lay behind that photograph. And how beautiful was all that had tied the two of us together for those months. So little was contained in that caption. And it hurt even more when Maarten Nijman came to our house to gloat over his success.

'Ah, we can't keep up with orders from other publishers, magazines and papers, from outside Surabaya as well. They all want to hire the negatives.' He didn't bother with our feelings; he was too involved with the photo's success. He went on: 'The royalties I'm charging are way too low; there are so many orders. Some would even pay three times as much.'

I no longer just hated but was now sickened by this man who once was a god to me. The more pictures of my wife appeared in the press, the more I was sickened by the behaviour of all the press. They were concerned only with trading on our feelings. Their profits and their success made them forget there was somebody who didn't like what they were doing. But there was nothing we could do.

Even with all the publicity, the trial did not attract much interest. But on the other hand, the pictures of my wife started to appear in people's houses, in the road-stalls and restaurants, even in the hotels. Anyway, that's what one Malay-language paper reported.

In this sickened mood we faced the trial.

The trial became convoluted and went on and on. The judge was Mijnheer Mr B. Jansen, the same one as before.

Ah Tjong looked thin, pale and bent. His pigtail had gone white. He wore silk clothes that were already far too big for him. His eyes were sunken and he hardly ever lifted his face.

Ah Tjong's platoon of prostitutes were paraded out again as witnesses, including Maiko. Fatso alias Babah Kong alias Jan Tantang was also a witness.

I'm not, of course, going to cover the whole course of the trial which went into the same trivial details as the earlier one. Just let it be said that the proceedings became so caught up with detail that the court had to adjourn several times. And it got even worse.

But the adjournments didn't spare me from the courtroom. For me there was another trial. I was a witness. A new case: that of Robert Suurhof.

He sat in the dock with the proprietor of Ezekiel's jewellery shop. Myself, Robert Jan Dapperste and a few other school friends were witnesses to his putting the stolen ring on Annelies's finger at our wedding. The family of the corpse whose grave was robbed were also witnesses. So too was the graveyard watchman who suffered Suurhof's thuggery.

The trial went smoothly, even though Suurhof gave the most indirect and complicated answers. But he couldn't escape from admitting his own deeds.

And behind me, Mrs Suurhof never stopped crying and sniffing. Her sadness was swept away by laughter in the courtroom, caused by the question and answer about the reason Robert Jan Dapperste changed his name to Panji Darman.

My friend frowned sullenly, his honour offended, sickened by the behaviour of the court. And the laughter and giggles were silenced by his challenging answer: 'It is my right to change my name to whatever I like. It did not cost you gentlemen one cent.'

I liked his answer.

The trial lasted only an hour and a half. Robert Suurhof was sentenced to eighteen months' gaol on top of the time he'd spent on remand. Ezekiel was sentenced to eight months for receiving stolen goods.

As soon as the trial ended everyone stood except Mrs Suurhof. My eyes met Robert's; his shone with revenge. He let me see his hate. He even bared his teeth at me. He showed the same hatred to Panji Darman.

Mrs Suurhof called out to him again and again. He pretended not to hear and walked off quickly with the police guards to Kalisosok gaol.

On the way home to Wonokromo Panji Darman began: 'He wants revenge, Minke.'

'I'm going to Betawi as soon as possible, Rob. And you'll be protected by Darsam.'

'Even so, Minke, he's still dangerous.'

'He's not the only one who is a man, Rob.'

The conversation ended but our hearts remained anxious.

'Yes, we must be more careful,' I said soon after. 'People like him can be nasty and tricky. Rob, I liked your answer in court. I felt offended too.'

'Yes. I had to take a stand against those honourable tuans.'

'Good for you, Rob. All the best to you.' I held out my hand. He took my hand, and without us realising it, we were embracing each other like little children taking an oath for life . . .

———◦◦———

In the trial sessions that followed in Ah Tjong's case, the proceedings concentrated on Jan Tantang, Minem and Darsam.

Jan Tantang explained that he had never met Ah Tjong. He had never even laid eyes on him. He was confronted with Ah Tjong's prostitutes but they all denied having met him or knowing him. Ah Tjong's gardener said he did see a fat man walking calmly through Ah Tjong's garden on the day of Herman Mellema's murder. The man did look like Jan Tantang, he said, except he only saw him from behind. He thought the man was just another customer out getting some fresh air. The man was wearing European clothes and had no pigtail. The gardener thought he must have been a Chinese Christian, perhaps the family of the 'Lieutenant of the Chinese'. Not only had he no desire to speak to the fat man, but he would not dare to do so, so he didn't pay the man any more attention.

The questioning then went to the matter of relations between Robert Mellema and Ah Tjong on the one hand and Mellema's relations with Jan Tantang on the other. Jan Tantang explained that he did not know Robert Mellema, though he had heard the name. He admitted he had been on Ah Tjong's property on the day of Herman Mellema's death, but claimed he had never set foot inside the house.

'I ran into Ah Tjong's yard to escape from the machete of a certain Madurese,' he said, 'a Madurese that people say has the name of Darsam.'

'Who told you that was his name?'

Jan Tantang thought for some time, trying to wriggle out of the question. The judge's persistence forced him to admit: 'Minem told me.'

The questioning about Minem caused some laughter.

Darsam admitted he wanted to teach the fat man a lesson because he thought he was a killer paid to murder Darsam himself.

'My duty is to guard the business and the family,' he said, 'and I have always tried to carry out that task to the best of my ability. I am paid to do my job.'

He was pressed on the question of whether he intended actually to kill Jan Tantang, because hadn't he already killed a man, and wasn't he also suspected of being involved in the fighting against the Marechausee and police on an earlier occasion? He answered: 'I only wanted to find out who was his boss; and if he was out to kill, then I would have done him in on the spot. That would be the fate of any hired killer.'

'And why were you suspicious of Jan Tantang?'

The convoluted questioning finally made its way to me. I told the story of being followed from Bojonegoro railway station to Wonokromo. My suspicions, I said, were passed on to others as well. Jan Tantang confirmed what had happened as a result, in front of the Telinga's house.

The trial had been going on a week already. Medical school would be starting in only six weeks' time. The questions and answers went on as if they would never end. I waited expectantly for Robert Mellema's letter to be read in court. It seemed I would have to wait even longer for that hoped-for event.

Days came and went. Still there was no sign that the trial was nearing an end. The whole issue of Herman Mellema's death was still not getting closer to any kind of resolution. Instead the court headed off once again in the direction of the internal affairs of Nyai Ontosoroh's family: How did she treat her children? Straight away Mama refused to answer all such questions and proclaimed that how she brought up her children was her own affair.

Then abruptly there came a question like a clap of thunder: 'Mr Minke, what are your feelings towards Nyai Ontosoroh alias Sanikem?'

My blood boiled. Mama went red as she watched my lips. But they did not succeed in making us the object of more laughter. The trial seemed to be trying to paint a certain picture: there was indeed no connection between Jan Tantang and either Robert Mellema or Ah Tjong. And so, precisely because of that, the questions were now being fired off in our direction. And Robert Mellema's letter still did not appear. The Prosecutor did all he could to discover what orders Nyai had given to Darsam.

Mama steadfastly refused to answer any questions that were intended to reflect upon her policies as manager and owner of the business. She restricted herself to answering that she had never given any orders to any-one to act against people, and she certainly had never ordered that trespassers into the villages on company land be killed.

A month had passed. Then a month and a week, two weeks, three weeks. I would not be able to start medical school that academic year . . .

Then I was asked: had I never received an order to take action against someone I was suspicious of while working for the business?

'What does the Prosecutor mean by "someone suspicious"?'

'Someone who was going to do harm to Nyai and you yourself?'

'So far I have never seen the person who has done harm against us,' I said.

'So there is such a person?'

'Yes, there is.'

'Where is he?'

'I don't know.'

'And what harm has he caused you?'

'The loss of my wife.'

It was becoming clearer. They were trying to prove that Nyai and I and Darsam were involved in a conspiracy against someone. Against whom, I didn't know. But I concluded definitely that the Court was out to get us.

At home I told Mama what I was thinking.

'Yes, they're pressuring us and deliberately wasting time. Your suspicions are right.'

'But why are they doing it?'

Mama began to explain. The day before I was brought back from Semarang, there had been a visit by three people: the Government Accountant, a Pure, and two assistants, Mixed-Bloods. They inspected the business's books, as well as the stables, rice lands and fields, and the dairy too. Mama showed them the S.E.&O. certificate from Mr Dalmeyer, but they ignored it.

'Is there something wrong with the examination made by Mr Dalmeyer?' Mama asked, and the Government Accountant just replied by giving a new S.E.&O. 'So, Child,' Mama went on, 'it seems the business will soon be taken over. Perhaps Engineer Mellema will be here shortly, or if not, at least the person he appoints to carry it out.'

'But what's that got to do with the trial, Ma?'

'If they can make us look bad in the public's eyes, then people will think the business has been run badly as well – run by bad people. So it will seem right that someone like me should be kicked out. Engineer Mellema will be able to take over much more easily. The public will be on his side. They will think it's right that we be got rid of.'

'Could somebody with education behave as deviously as that?'

'The more educated the person, the more educated the deviousness.'

Yes, I had to learn to think like that. Before it had been a kind of hidden knowledge I had. Now it seemed I was going to see the final proof.

'Yes, Minke, you've got to learn to think as daringly as that. They can even do worse things than that, Child.' Her words were pronounced slowly, as if nothing had happened at all. 'In the ins and outs of this life, Child, what you studied at school was just children's games. You are adult enough now to understand that the law of the wolf rules our lives, amongst them and amongst ourselves also. Soon you will see, Child, that what I am saying now is not missing the mark, nor will it.'

I was coming to understand better and better: for the thousandth time and for always we have to keep on fighting back. Just like the Filipinos, who did not know what the future held for them, yet still there was something that had to be done. And what was it that had to be done: yes, they had to fight back.

That night I went off to see Kommer and Maarten Nijman to show them Robert's letter to Mama – the copy made and approved by the Prosecutor's Office. I even helped Kommer with the task of putting into Malay the bit that concerned Robert's plotting with Ah Tjong. That night also the two men wrote commentaries and published them in special editions separate from their newspaper, which were distributed before dawn.

Kommer's comments were very courageous: that the Court should not keep pursuing and persecuting the witnesses, especially when it was clear that they were only witnesses and not the accused. That the Court should return to the crux of the matter, namely the role of Ah Tjong and Robert Mellema on the one hand, and Jan Tantang on the other.

At the next session of the trial Kommer and Nijman were called as witnesses. They were each asked where they got the quotes from Robert Mellema's letter. Both refused to give an explanation. Kommer was pressed harder: 'Was Robert Mellema's letter written in Malay?'

'Dutch.'

'If in Dutch, where did you get the right to translate it into Malay and publish it without using a sworn translator from the Court, because that letter is presently evidence in this trial.'

'As far as I am aware,' answered Kommer, 'that letter was not written for the Court but addressed to Nyai Ontosoroh. It is obvious then that it is not the sole prerogative of the Court to possess and control the letter, let alone translate it. As long as I have been a journalist I have never seen a law saying otherwise.'

'Do you not understand that the contents of your special edition could influence the course of the trial?'

'It is up to the Court whether or not it wishes to be influenced. Everyone is free to reject or accept such influence. And anyway, it is clear now that the letter does in fact exist.'

'Where is the original of the letter now?'

'With the Prosecutor.'

The Judge asked the Prosecutor whether he did have such a letter. The questions and answers now revolved around the letter.

Mama became involved and explained that she had earlier gone to the police to ask their help in contacting Robert Mellema in Los Angeles. It turned out that the sender of the letter had since died.

The bench felt the blow of the Judge's gavel again and again as Mama had to be reminded to restrict herself to answering the questions.

The proceedings became tense. So many issues came and went so fast. One witness after another was called. I was almost left behind by it all.

'Where is the letter? Why was the trial resumed if there were no new material such as the letter? And why was no more evidence brought forward in Jan Tantang's case?' So shouted Kommer from the pages of his newspaper.

Nijman's comments were almost the same. My dislike for him turned into vigilance. I viewed his involvement in all this as totally commercial. But as long as what he did helped us, there was no reason to hate him.

Both were trying with all their might and with great risk to themselves to ensure that the trial was not diverted from its true purpose. Who, after all, was the accused?

These comments aroused great interest among the more hot-blooded newspaper readers of Surabaya, and among all races. The courtroom became more and more crowded. On the day that the courtroom was at its fullest, the trial was adjourned for several days.

Medical school had started without me.

When the trial resumed again there was a new Judge, a tall, slim man, Mr D. Eisendraht. It wasn't clear why Mr Jansen was replaced. Perhaps he was sick.

The trial now proceeded smoothly, and on a straight course, as though rocketing along a railway line.

The new Chief Judge asked to see Robert Mellema's letter. Someone was appointed to read it out. Then the policeman who had contacted Los Angeles was summoned. He read out the telegram that was received from the Los Angeles police authorities, which confirmed that there had been a patient called Robert Mellema, a subject of the Netherland Indies, who had died four months and two days ago.

Based upon the letter, new questions were asked about the motive, but again the trial had to be adjourned because Ah Tjong was sick. And when he reappeared again, looking paler, thinner, and broken, he surrendered and confessed. He was sentenced to death by hanging. He died before the sentence could be implemented.

The Ah Tjong-Robert Mellema affair had been cleared up, with the aid of Kommer and Nijman.

And the Jan Tantang affair turned out to be a melodrama. This is the story.

Jan Tantang was a police agent, first class, from Bojonegoro. One day he was summoned before the Assistant Resident of Bojonegoro, Herbert de la Croix. Jan Tantang could give both the date and the time that the meeting took place. As an orderly servant of the state, he had indeed noted everything down.

As soon as he received the summons, he attended.

It was eight o'clock at night. The Assistant Resident was sitting in his rattan armchair in the *pendopo*. Tantang stood before him.

'You are the police agent, first class, that the District Chief has sent me?' asked Herbert de la Croix.

'Yes, Tuan Assistant Resident: agent first class, Jan Tantang.'

'From Menado?'

'Yes, Tuan Assistant Resident.'

'Can you speak Dutch?'

'A little, Tuan.'

The Assistant Resident seemed disappointed that he could speak only a little Dutch.

'Can you read and write?' He looked happy when he heard the answer Yes. 'Who can speak proper Dutch among the police agents?'

'As far as I know, Tuan, no one.'

'I need a clever man for a special assignment. Are you willing?'

He admitted to the Court he was hoping for a promotion. He had answered: 'Ready and willing, Tuan Assistant Resident.'

'Good. Tomorrow you leave for Surabaya. You must keep under surveillance the son of the new bupati. His name is Minke. Do you know him, what he looks like?'

'Not yet, Tuan Assistant Resident.'

'Wait for him before he leaves for the station. An H.B.S. student. You'll know him.'

De la Croix ordered him to report on all Minke's habits: his schooling, his diligence in study, how he mixed with other people, and with whom, outside school as well.

'Why did Assistant Resident Herbert de la Croix give you this task?'

Jan Tantang answered that he didn't know. He had explained what his job was. He sent back reports by letter and telegram.

'Why did you behave so suspiciously? Was that the only way you could carry out your orders from Tuan de la Croix?'

'I was given no guidelines on how to carry out my task.'

'Was acting suspiciously the only way you could have done it?'

'No.'

He went on to explain that he really wanted to become acquainted with Tuan Minke and so be able to converse and mix with him. But Tuan Minke was an H.B.S. student and Jan Tantang was embarrassed, felt awkward about approaching him. He felt inferior and so kept his distance.

There was almost a disaster when he was asked about my relations with Nyai Ontosoroh. He remained resolute with his answer: 'I don't know.' Several times the question was put to him in other ways, veiled; but he remained steadfast in his answer.

I reckoned he knew a lot about my relations with Mama. He was deliberately avoiding talking about our private affairs so as not to cause us harm. This moved me. Sometimes I thought he was indeed our friend, as he had told Darsam.

He sat calmly on the accused's chair, always polite, his two hands clasped in his lap. I didn't see his fatness so much any more, but rather his humanity. His answers were always polite, orderly and direct. He won my sympathy.

It was he who had been given the task of reporting on me for de la Croix's study of educated Natives. In his race to understand the Native psyche, Herbert de la Croix did not want, it seems, to be left behind by Snouck Hurgronje. He had become a victim of his studies, and had also got many people involved in all kinds of problems. He himself had lost his position, and perhaps had to live off uncertain earnings in Europe.

One of the witnesses was Minem. The frisky girl decided to sit next to me, so I was hemmed in by two women. Among the other witnesses was Darsam.

The questioning went on to the subject of Minem. The girl answered in Javanese.

One afternoon a fat man leading a horse passed in front of her house. 'That man smiled at me. He stopped and offered me some perfume. Without even asking me, he rubbed a little on my neck. It smelt so nice.' Minem spoke fluently, completely unembarrassed and unafraid. 'I asked him to come in.'

The Judge asked Jan Tantang: 'Why did you say your name was Babah Kong?'

'The one thing I knew I must not do was to give my own name.'

'You were no longer carrying out a task for an Assistant Resident.'

'I was still working for Tuan Herbert de la Croix, even though he was no longer an Assistant Resident.'

'And what were you doing still taking orders from him? You are an employee of the state.'

'I only used my own spare time.'

'You were paid for your services?'

'No,' he said without hesitating.

'Why were you willing then?'

'I slowly came to understand what de la Croix was concerned with doing, and I wanted to help him.'

'And how did you and Tuan de la Croix communicate after he was no longer an Assistant Resident?'

'Letters.'

'And what did he say in them?'

'They were addressed only to me, not to the Court or the public.'

It looked like Jan Tantang was a man with principles. He deserved to be honoured and respected.

Minem continued: 'Babah Kong kept asking about my child, where he was and who he was. I answered that his father had disappeared to parts unknown almost six months before. He asked if we were divorced. And I asked how could we be divorced if we hadn't even been married? Babah Kong took out a little bottle of perfume, poured out a little and rubbed it on my cheeks, pinching them too.'

The courtroom was filled with laughter. Jan Tantang bowed his head. Minem glowed happily at receiving so much attention. That young mother didn't hide anything. Her red, thin lips kept on talking without being stopped by either Judge or Prosecutor. It seemed they too enjoyed looking at this pretty village girl who spoke so frankly.

Without concealing anything, Minem announced that the child she was now suckling was the son of Robert Mellema, the son of her employer, and so was the grandchild of Nyai Ontosoroh.

Then: 'It seemed Babah Kong was jealous of the father of my baby Rono, Ndoro Judge. He kept on pressing me as to who was the baby's father.'

'Did Babah Kong alias Jan Tantang ever propose marriage to you?'

'Babah Kong did once ask me to become his woman.'

'And why were you unwilling?'

'My child had to be taken care of first.'

'Did not Nyai acknowledge him as her grandson?'

'She has now,' she stated with energy.

Nyai was frustrated, annoyed by Minem. Once again her private family affairs were being paraded in public view. The Prosecutor didn't allow such an opportunity to go unused; and it became even more obvious that the Prosecutor was out to confuse the course of the trial. Question after question was addressed to Nyai.

But the Chief Judge finally moved to bring a halt to the public's pleasure in these private affairs. The questioning shifted to Darsam: 'How many times in twenty-four hours would you meet Minem, Darsam?'

'I never counted,' answered Darsam, frowning sullenly.

'And you have never tried to seduce her?'

'A woman like her doesn't need to be seduced,' he answered furiously.

'And whom would you have preferred to seduce?' asked the Prosecutor, glancing at Mama.

Now it was I who was about to explode in fury.

The Chief Judge used his gavel again.

'This is important, to fill in the background, Your Honour Chief Judge,' objected the Prosecutor. 'Answer truthfully, Darsam. Why did you never try to seduce her?'

Darsam did not answer.

'You have never touched her?'

'No!' Darsam gnashed his teeth.

'Is he telling the truth, Minem?'

'Yes.'

'Did Tuan Minke ever visit your house?'

'No,' answered Minem.

'Have you ever spoken to him?'

'A few times, Ndoro Prosecutor.'

'And he never tried to seduce you?'

A tear of humiliation, of anger dropped from my eye.

'A pity, but no, Ndoro Prosecutor.'

'Why a pity? Did you have hopes in that direction?'

Minem giggled slowly. Mama shifted restlessly in her chair.

Back at home Mama didn't say anything to Minem. I gave her my opinion about what the Prosecutor was doing. She just smiled, explaining: 'He is trying to prove that Rono is not Robert's son, not my grandson.'

'But why, Ma?'

'If it is proved that he is Robert's son, then Rono will have rights to a part of his grandfather's property. It is clear now that the Prosecutor is definitely in league with Maurits Mellema. But there is nothing we can do. We have no proof.'

The next few days at Court were spent on the shooting incident. It could not be proved that there was any enmity between Darsam and Jan Tantang because of sexual jealousy over Minem. The police presented evidence of a fight.

Both Darsam and Jan Tantang admitted what happened. The motives were admitted by the Court: Darsam's suspicions. Darsam was labelled the aggressor; Jan Tantang, said the Court, was defending himself.

In the end Darsam was given a six months' suspended gaol sentence, two years suspended on condition he got into no more trouble. Jan Tantang was sentenced to eight months and was sacked from the police force.

With the end of the trial this whole convoluted affair was finally over.

16

One morning a man arrived on horseback, dressed in white shirt, trousers and white cap, but with no shoes. He was a chocolate-skinned Indo. Very, very politely, he handed me two letters. Mama wasn't in the office but out in the back doing Annelies's work.

One letter was from the Government Accountant confirming that the business's finances were in proper order and that nothing was amiss – reaffirming the S.E.&.O. The other letter was from Engineer Maurits Mellema. I didn't read that one, but left it on the table for Mama.

'Tuan,' said the messenger with the letters, 'allow me to meet with Minem.'

'Minem?'

'She lives here, doesn't she?'

'What do you want with her?'

'Allow me to tell her myself.'

I opened the door that led into the front parlour and called the girl over. She came, merry as ever, carrying her baby.

'Young Master called me?' she asked gaily. Her thin lips were all shiny; who knows what they had just eaten? She stood close and tilted her head.

'In here,' and she entered the office. She seemed a bit disappointed that there was another person there.

'This is Minem, if you're sure that's who you're after.'

'Minem?' the messenger asked in Malay.

'Yes, Tuan.'

'Can you leave today?'

'Leave for where?'

'Tuan Accountant de Visch.'

'Who is that? Tuan Accoun . . .'

'My employer. You said you'd live with him, didn't you?'

Minem thought for a moment, then laughed. 'Oh, that tuan? Just a minute, let me take leave from Nyai first. Can you wait?'

She left the office. I was astounded. How freely she behaved, no fear, no embarrassment, not like most Native women at all. Like a European girl from the H.B.S. This child was intelligent, I thought, but hadn't received a proper education. Quite a daring person, game to gamble with her fate. She saw her beautiful body and pretty face as the only capital she had and which she could use to obtain some of the pleasures of life. Perhaps with a proper education, she would have grown up to be an outstanding woman.

Not long after, Mama arrived with Darsam. With no greeting for the messenger, she sat down at her desk, took out some papers and gave them to Darsam.

'Our regards to them all. Try to meet Jan Tantang. Tell him not to worry because he's lost his job. As soon as he is free, we will employ him.'

Darsam saluted, then went again. I went to her and reported that there was a letter from Mr de Visch, and showed her the letter I had just finished reading.

She read it with shining eyes. A pleasant little smile played on her lips as she nodded.

I observed her face – still so young and fresh, as if she had never borne children. She was always dressed up and adorned, and her skin was always glowing. The events that had just taken place seemed erased from her soul and body. They had left no mark at all on the way her face glowed or on the way she moved.

Now Engineer Maurits Mellema's letter was in her hand. Her smile disappeared. She took her brass letter-opener, but hesitated to tear the envelope.

'The messenger awaits an answer, Ma.'

'You brought it?' she asked the messenger in Dutch.

'Yes, Nyai.'

'You work for Mr de Visch or Maurits Mellema?'

'The former, Nyai.'

'So this letter was with the other?'

'Yes.'

'Is Engineer Mellema at the Accountant's office? This letter has no stamp.'

'I don't know, Nyai.'

Mama knocked the edge of the envelope up and down on the desk. She tried to overcome her hesitation. She put the letter and the copper knife down.

'Read it to me, Child,' she said softly.

I opened the letter and read it in a whisper.

'Yes,' she then said. 'Write the reply, Child.'

After it was written she put it in an envelope and called the messenger over: 'You can take this back with you.' The messenger took the letter and then sat down again. 'That's all, you can go now, there's nothing else.'

'Yes, Nyai, there's still Minem.'

'Minem?'

'I'm taking her with me, Nyai.'

'Where did you meet her?'

'Just now, here.'

'Here?' Nyai glared, startled.

I quickly explained what had happened. She stood up, took out a handkerchief from a drawer and started to bite on it. Slowly she walked to the door, took a deep breath, then sat down on the settee with the messenger.

'When did Minem meet Tuan de Visch? No, let me call her.'

Before Mama reached the door, Minem entered without knocking, carrying Rono and a bamboo bag. She was dressed up and looked very attractive, slim but full-bodied. Unusually, she didn't drop her eyes before Mama, but spoke directly: 'Nyai, today Minem is taking leave to go to live with Tuan . . .'

'Sit down here, Minem, so we can talk calmly first. Minke, come over here, so you're a witness, and you too. What's your name?'

'Raymond de Bree, Nyai.'

So the four of us sat in a circle around the table; five of us actually – there was Rono too, asleep in his mother's arms.

'Minem,' Nyai began, 'you have been living in this house because that was what Robert wanted. You yourself have been living here of your own free will, and because I asked you if you wanted to. Isn't that right, Minem?'

'Yes, Nyai.'

'You haven't been here long, that's true, but no one so far has tried to get rid of you?'

'True, Nyai. No one.'

'Are you sure?'

'Yes, Nyai.'

'You are not pregnant now?'

'No, Nyai. I'm clean.'

'Good. Have you been treated well while you've been here?'

'I've been treated well, Nyai.'

'Good. So you won't say bad things about the place you're about to leave?'

'No, Nyai.'

'You're not going to regret later having gone with Tuan de Visch?'

'No, Nyai.'

'Think about it first. Because once you've left here, I will not take you back again. You understand that?'

'I understand, Nyai.'

'So you understand. You were taken in because of Robert's request. Now you're leaving of your own accord.'

'Yes, Nyai.'

'And what about Rono?'

'If Nyai wants to take him, I will leave him with Nyai.'

'Are you sure? You've thought it over properly?'

'What's the use of keeping a baby like this without a father, Nyai?'

'Good. Give me the child.' Rono changed embraces.

'You won't need the child again, will you? You won't be visiting him? Because that would disturb us and him.'

'No, Nyai, but give me some compensation.'

'You mean a payment?'

Without embarrassment, Minem nodded.

'I will look after this child well. And I will give you some going-away money, but I will not buy my own grandchild. You yourself are surrendering him freely. You yourself were the one who got so many people to press me to acknowledge him as my grandchild.'

The messenger looked restless. He kept shifting his position and moving his bag about. Mama humoured his impatience.

'This is about the fate of a human being, Tuan Raymond. We cannot be rash in what we do. Nah, Minem, so I will give you some going-away money. But I am not a buyer of people. Tuan Raymond de Bree is a witness. You will report all this to Mr de Visch, yes?'

'Let Minem report it herself, Nyai.'

'If you don't want to be a witness, all right. I have a witness: Mr Minke. But if anything happens in the future, I will still name you as a witness. The day, date and time you were here and took Minem, I will note down too. You can go.'

'But my orders to bring Minem?'

'Take her.'

'Come, Minem, let's go,' invited de Bree.

'The money, Nyai.'

'There must be a letter, Minem,' said Nyai, 'and you must put your thumb-print to it, if you agree to what it says. If you don't, you can leave without anything. If you want to wait, I'll draw it up now.'

The letter was short, explaining that Minem acknowledged that she surrendered her child to Nyai Ontosoroh on the day, date and time it occurred, with me and Raymond de Bree, the messenger of Accountant de Visch, as witnesses. And that the child was born on a certain date and was her own child with Robert Mellema born out of wedlock.

Nyai read it out and put it into Javanese. She put her signature to it, as did I. Minem put her thumb-print to it. But Raymond de Bree refused.

'It doesn't matter if you refuse,' said Nyai. 'Underneath your name it will explain that you heard the whole conversation but refused to sign the letter. Write that down, Minke, and that Minem was taken by Mr Raymond de Bree, who did not give clear information where he was taking her.'

I wrote all the additional explanation on the bottom of the letter. Nyai gave the messenger the letter for him to read.

Raymond de Bree still refused.

'Good, if you don't sign it, you'll be open one day to the accusation of kidnapping.'

The messenger looked frightened. He still hesitated, yet he had no choice but to sign.

They left. Minem left a kiss for her child. For a moment a tear formed, then she left with de Bree. Neither wore shoes. The toes of their feet pointed outwards.

'Minem,' called Mama, and the girl returned, leaving de Bree waiting under a tree.

'What about your mother? Are you going to leave her just like that?'

'I will come and get her another time, Nyai.'

'Who will feed her if you leave her now?'

She didn't answer and excused herself, walking quickly away from the office. Rono still slept in Nyai's arms.

'Wanton girl!' Mama whispered harshly. 'You are lucky, Rono, that you will never know who your mother is. Have you ever written about an itchy-passioned girl, Child? She is a good character for you to write about. You've known her from close up, too.'

That was the first time I heard that strange phrase: itchy-passioned girl!

'You can write something as a souvenir of this day.'

'It's her right, Ma. Perhaps she feels her future here is uncertain.'

Mama didn't want to listen.

'In this world there are not many women with that itch – women who seek a profit from their femininity while their breasts haven't dropped and their cheeks haven't drooped. In all places and amongst all classes there are such women, and they are always disgusting. If I could write like you, Child . . . Look at this baby; he meant nothing to her. A husband meant nothing to her; a home nothing, her parents nothing. Her youth is being dedicated to her wantonness. Nothing is important to her except if it will help satisfy her passions.'

Mama let her anger overflow. I didn't agree with what she said.

'No one knows what fate awaits this child. I hope it's good, yes Rono, much better than that of your mother and your father. Your nose is certainly that of Robert's; your skin is whiter than his when he was a baby, even whiter than your mother's.'

Suddenly she remembered something.

'At five o'clock this evening, Child, Engineer Maurits will be here.'

I pretended not to hear. He was undoubtedly coming to order Mama to leave.

'You look pale, Child. Don't worry. Who knows what he wants? Perhaps he wants to kick us all out, except for the wealth we've built.'

How ashamed I would be to be thrown out by somebody, kicked out from someone's house, shown no respect. How those people who hate us will cheer and shout. But I must stay with Mama through this final trouble.

'We will arrange a proper ceremony to greet him,' she spoke again.

'Greet him!'

'According to the law, he owns all this. He has profited because Robert and Annelies are gone.'

'Mama, and what about Mama?'

'You're worried about me? Thank you, Child. Are you afraid that I'll become a burden to you, that I'll want to go with you? No. But let's deal with this man first. You still have an account to settle with him. Indeed we can't fight the law or him, but we still have mouths to speak with. With our mouths we will confront him. And we still have friends.'

'What can they do?'

'Friends with you in times of trouble are friends in everything. Never belittle friendship. Its magnificence is greater than the fire of enmity. Do you agree with me that we call them over to help us make more merry the greeting we give Mr Maurits Mellema? Jean Marais and Kommer?'

I was silent as I thought over what use that would be. What could they do if the law wasn't behind them? One shy and limping, the other a speech-maker and hunter of wild animals.

'You don't agree, Child?'

'Very well, Ma. I'll fetch them.'

Rono jerked awake. Nyai rocked the unblanketed baby in her arms.

'Ah, he's wet himself, the baby. Yes, Child, call them over. That's the best thing to do now.'

And so I went out, putting behind me the memory of Minem who was taking her itch away with her, and of Rono and the futility of his birth. My mind was now filled with a new puzzle from my mother-in-law. She was about to confront the man who wanted to throw her out ...

17

So that the story runs in sequence, I have put together a selection of writings and opinions that I have heard at one time or another and which are connected with this story of my life. Some of the material I obtained several years after the events, but that is not important.

There had been a rumour: the Netherlands Indies was going to build a navy of its own which it would call the *Gouvernements Marine*. It would not be a part of the Royal Netherlands Navy. The rumour was not without foundation, and this is what it was all about:

Japan had been given equal status with the white races. Its international position was the same as that of the European countries. Japan had been taken off the Indies Government's Alien Orientals list and shifted to the European list. The colonials could shout, roar, and protest, but the decision of the state was more decisive.

The European Indies could hurl all the insults they liked: that the Japanese ships, for a maritime country, were old and decrepit, no better than chicken coops. Certain Japanese admitted that they were like a baby just beginning to crawl. In their hearts perhaps they were smiling to themselves – they were one people who had never bowed down and kowtowed to the Europeans, let alone slid along the floor before them – a people whose spirit could not be shaken by international criticism.

I once saw a small poster with a lithograph picture of a fleet of Japanese ships, all in tatters as they were battered by a storm. Their cannons shivered in the cold. A Japanese flag flew on every ship, almost as big as the ships themselves. And the picture's caption read: 'In the name of the geisha's kimono, forever forward!'

Whatever insults might have been hurled, the Netherlands Indies military experts felt they needed to organise a meeting, a seminar, to discuss defence matters, specifically in relation to the Indies, and precisely at the time of a visit to Indies waters by a Royal Netherlands Navy force under the leadership of Admiral —— (I won't give his name). What was the best defence for the Indies?

Japan was on everybody's lips; its name reverberated around the seminar again and again. They said that the Japanese Navy was many times bigger than the fleet of the V.O.C. - Dutch East Indies Company - when it conquered Java, Sumatra and the Moluccas. The distance between Japan and the Indies was much shorter than between the Netherlands and the Indies! The rise of Japan should not be met just with colonial insults. A country that has been able to stand up to western supremacy should not be belittled. Such a people would be able to achieve its ideals. Science and learning had become the property of the world, and were there to be used by all who were capable. In this new age, victory in war would not be determined by the colour of a people's skin, but by people rising with weapons in their hands. The flesh of no race was immune to cannon shot. Modern science and learning was not the sole property of Europeans.

People said that Japan was clever only at imitating. But, said another voice, the imitation of worthwhile things was a sign of advancement, not something base and undignified, as some colonial opinion had it. All peoples and races began by imitating before they could stand by themselves. People should indeed learn to get used to new realities. Reality doesn't go away because people don't like it, or just because they insult it. Even the European races, before they were as advanced as they were now, could only imitate. And they could imitate the bad things as well, like smoking and sucking on a pipe just as Indians do. Imitating was only a chapter in the life of all children. But then there comes a day when children are fully grown. People should prepare themselves to confront that day. Don't be startled, or shocked and overcome, if on that day reality rears up before you larger than you could ever imagine.

There was no preparation that could be carried out too early.

Yet it sounded like a fairy tale: that Japan could force its way onto the soil of the Indies. Japan would first have to face the French in Indo-China, then get past the English in that strongest of all South-east Asian forts called Singapore. Indeed the Indies were guarded by layers of European forts, which could never be penetrated. But don't forget, someone else added, that the distance between Europe and South-east Asia is very great indeed, and Europe's ships are spread throughout the waterways of its colonies: in America, Africa, Asia and Australia. The Japanese fleet is together, concentrated in one place, and its ground army even more so.

People should remember that all Japanese who have left their country - whether to become coolies in Hawaii's pineapple plantations, or cooks on the ships of other races, or a cook in a San Francisco mansion, or prostitutes in the big cities of the world - nevertheless remain like the heart and lungs of the Japanese race, inseparable from their country, their ancestors and their people. And more than that: even though they live from us, they still look upon us as a race of barbarians, and *come that day*, they will try to prove that they are right about us.

We mustn't laugh and think that it is all just the arrogance of an isolated people who have never had contact with the great nations of the world. Japan has opened its doors to western influence for tens of years now, and its citizens are busily extracting what is best from the achievements of all peoples, the world over. They are a thrifty people who know the purpose of their thrift: the greatness of the Japanese Empire. They had practised the principles of economy and thrift long before they learnt it from us.

Some of those attending the seminar, so people said, still refused to acknowledge Japan as significant, or to acknowledge the other speakers' opinions as worth consideration.

Views were put forward regarding the appropriate defence strategy for the Indies, given its peculiar geographical situation. In 1811, during Governor-General Jansen's time, the British Navy was easily able to take the Indies. That must not happen again. Up until now the Indies Army had stood as an autonomous force, a united force, the product of the power of the Netherlands Indies state. But at sea the Indies were still dependent on the Royal Netherlands Navy. Even the transport of supplies to Aceh and the Moluccas for the Army, especially before the forming of the K.P.M., depended on private merchant fleets: Arab and Chinese, Madurese and Buginese.

I had never thought about the sea before, but now it began to arouse my interest. My mind conjured up pictures of the centuries during which the ships of the V.O.C. had battled the ocean waves – those wooden ships – for months, even years, on end, seeking out spices. They found them. The profits were huge. And to defend and expand those profits they founded an empire. Mostly, and first of all, upon the earth of my homeland. They created an empire and they kept watch over it across the seas. It was the sea that took them to their greatness. And they knew that every forward-moving nation could use those same seas to build other empires. They were not going to let that happen. They had been cursed with the necessity of always defending what they had founded and what they owned.

The Netherlands Indies needed its own navy for its sea defences; we could never defend ourselves on the seas while the Royal armadas and squadrons were sailing around in the Atlantic. The Indies must have its own navy, and as quickly as possible. The defence of the Indies must adjust itself as quickly as possible to the natural circumstances of the Indies. It must have its own maritime defence strategy. There must be surveys to find suitable spots for naval bases. The bases must be built. The situation cannot remain as it is now: with the visiting Royal Navy ships harbouring wherever they like, as if they were on a honeymoon picnic.

The military people at the seminar were quite shaken by it all. And that Admiral – people said he represented the concern in the Netherlands – was also shaken.

That seminar left me with the impression that war was going to break out the next day, or perhaps the day after. The Netherlands Indies fighting – I'm not sure whom. How many conflicts there are in this world! Everyone against everyone: people against people, group against group, individuals against their group and vice versa; groups against their own broader class and the other way around too; women confronting men in Europe and men who didn't confront women; governments fighting their own citizens. And now empires in confrontation. All were just manifestations of one thing: conflicting interests!

And if the Netherlands found itself confronted with a defence problem – which had happened already a number of times – the Indies must be able to defend itself using its own strength. But to try to defend yourself in this modern age without a navy: unimaginable! People reminded each other that there were the Germans in East Papua, the English to the north, and to the south-east as well. The American Navy was now playing around in the Pacific; playing grave-making with the Filipino rebels and finally throwing out the Spanish . . .

Changes in 'the balance of power', people said, (and how tremendously did that idea loom in my thoughts) had placed the Indies in a new situation.

It was a pity I had never seen that grand epic of conflict, the *Bharatayuddha wayang* story. I had never met a puppet-master who dared to put it on. It was too complicated, and that complexity left an impression of the supernatural. So too it was with this 'balance of power'. In all these complications and this complexity, with all its supernaturalness, I had a vision of a child's playpen, inside of which was a jumbled pile of question marks. And my mind was tormented like this all as a result of thinking about other people's concerns, such as the fate of the Indies without a navy of its own.

In the history of the Netherlands Indies (I did not need to learn this from a book or a teacher) the Dutch were not just proud, but almost arrogant, about the strength of their army. But after seeing what happened in the Philippines people began to whisper: a strong land force is meaningless in an island country if there is no navy. The Spanish preferred to retreat from the Philippines rather than confront the American fleet. The Indies had to learn to look after itself, including its sea defences.

And the seminar itself produced a warning (and I will never be able to forget it): watch out, gentlemen! In a modern war, if the forts in the countries to the north are penetrated, and we do not have a strong navy, this country will fall in a matter of days . . .

Not long after the seminar the ship H.M.S. *Sumatra* was sent to the Indies to survey the best places to build a base for the Royal Netherlands Indies Navy of the future. On one of its trips it surveyed the waters around Jepara, on the southern coast of Java. (Later on I found out that three Native girls, one of them with a name famed through all Java, R. A. Kartini, along with their father, had boarded the ship to make an inspection. They were welcomed with full honours. The ship's crew knew them as Native girls who thought like Europeans and they called them the Princesses of Jepara.)

As I was writing these notes a question arose in my mind: did they know what the earlier tasks of H.M.S. *Sumatra* had been, even though they had been interested in the Boer War in South Africa?

Why South Africa? Because indeed there is a connection. After the H.M.S. *Sumatra* arrived, another ship followed from that northern corner of the world: the H.M.S. *Borneo*. One of its passengers was a war hero from South Africa: Engineer Maurits Mellema. That warship made its way to where I lived: Surabaya. He was commanding a team of marine engineers.

Now allow me to fantasise a bit about this particular character, and forgive me that I am unable to imagine what he looks like . . .

He was still commanding his troops in South Africa when he was summoned by the Royal Netherlands Navy. He had already gone through battle after battle under the command of General Christaan de Wet – victories and defeats. (Indeed there were more defeats than victories and the Dutch were becoming more and more pressed.) But in any case people need heroes to caress their souls. And if there aren't any, they'll scrape up anything. In short, Mellema was made a hero; he was honoured and praised by all. He had defended the honour of the House of Orange as well as the veins of gold running through the southern tip of the African continent.

Perhaps I have the right to picture him as an officer whose chest is covered with medals. I don't know how many Englishmen he had sent to the grave, how many square metres of land he had lost, how many of his men had been killed or taken prisoner or had disappeared or had gone mad or deserted. There were no other names along with his. And I don't think I'd be wrong in presenting the picture that from his mouth came a never-ending stream of curses, directed especially at the English General French.

Probably Holland was proud to have such a great son as Maurits Mellema. Probably he was famous throughout the land . . . and a pile of other probablys as well. My imagination can be squeezed no further.

The surveys to find a suitable place for the Royal Netherlands Indies Navy base was finally successful: the Surabaya peninsula. The docks were designed. Remembering Engineer Maurits Mellema's previous experience at Surabaya harbour when, seven years before, he had helped design new sugar and oil loading docks, the Royal Navy summoned him. He was chosen to build the new naval base at the tip of Surabaya harbour.

A telegram was sent to South Africa summoning him. He was seen off by his friends and the soldiers who served under him. He left Africa with glorious memories . . .

And if I keep on drawing upon my imagination, I can come up with some more ideas.

Every member of the ship's crew taking him home to Holland shared with him the happiness of his return. The journey was a refreshing outing for him, far from death and the spilling of blood, from groans and cries of *Aduh!* And if I let this imagination of mine get out of control altogether, this would be the next part of the story:

That morning at the *Sumatra Kade*, in Amsterdam harbour, a crowd of people had already gathered. There were many girls there and veterans of the Boer War too. A number of senior offices from the Royal Navy were there, and also a navy band. At exactly ten o'clock the ship from South Africa passed through the heads and entered the harbour.

I could see Minister Kuyper, who was so involved with the Boer War, also there to greet the ship.

A woman, dressed all in black, quickly attracted attention. She too was a welcomer, standing in the crowd: the widow Amelia Mellema-Hammers. In one hand she carried a black bag. In the other was an umbrella, also black. And she was ready to shed tears of welcome too.

The ship began to dock. The passengers stood along the deck rail. Slowly the navy band began to play.

The first person to disembark from the ship was none other than Engineer Mellema himself, accompanied by the ship's captain. People shouted and cheered to welcome their hero. The music blared, trying to make itself heard over the cheering. Things became merrier and merrier. Engineer Maurits Mellema smiled calmly. He waved his hand. As soon as he stepped ashore a crowd of people, who knows where from, charged forward and placed a garland of flowers around his neck. The officials and officers from the Royal Navy took turns in shaking his hand. The Royal Navy Music Corps kept up their playing. Kuyper was forgotten by everybody.

Not a single medal decorated Mellema's chest; yet through his veins ran the heroism of his ancestors who had defeated enemies from both land and sea. This great son of the nation was very friendly. He faced the world with a smile which reflected the great experiences now behind him. People said: whoever returned home from war as victor would see all the difficulties before him become as nothing.

His mother, having longed to see her son for so long now, ran forward to embrace and kiss him. And the hero Mellema loved his mother. There were kisses in return to her cheeks, left and right. This scene of a mother's love continued as she held her son's body. There must not be some irreplaceable part of the hero's body buried back in that unknown land. Amelia Mellema-Hammers suddenly burst into uncontrolled weeping – an expression of gratitude to her God. The body of the child she had given birth to was still whole; the English had not succeeded in breaking it.

The Royal Navy carriage took hero and mother to headquarters to the accompaniment of the crowd's shouts and cheers. In the background the ship and its crew stood along the deck watching this great event.

I don't think I could tell my imagination it was wrong if I said that the papers also reported this event. But there was nothing in the papers about the deaths of Herman Mellema, Annelies Mellema and Robert Mellema; nor was there any mention that the great hero was about to receive some free booty from Wonokromo, Surabaya.

There was no other news about the hero for a while. Then, later, a small report about a banquet held by Engineer Maurits Mellema and his mother – a banquet with speeches, ringing with *hosees*. Beneath that report was another: about the sacking of an English journalist in South Africa who wasn't doing his job properly but making up stories from his bedroom; while in that same room he was composing adventure stories about a white baby who grew up to be the king of the South African jungle . . .

I'm afraid I must end my fantasy here.

Dulrakim from Kedungrukem, whom I visited to get the address of Khouw Ah Soe's friend, well, he was the kind of person who liked to collect stories – I don't know if just for himself or to broadcast to others. He had a treasury of adventure stories that seemed unlimited. Because he doesn't have an important place at all in my story, I don't think I need say much about him. But he did have something to say about Engineer Maurits Mellema. Only a short tale, but he did have that one story. Of course it was just something he had picked up hanging around the harbour.

He reckoned the young marine engineer was quite a friendly person. He said he heard someone say once that heroes were usually like that; great experiences made such people more humble and sensitive to other people. Mellema liked music, and was a hero of the dance floor as well.

His favourite topic of conversation was the slowness with which the Netherlands Indies came to realise the need for its own navy. Didn't that great son of the Indies, Daendels, almost a century ago, realise the same thing? Hadn't he even recognised and indeed used Surabaya as a naval base? How quickly the Europeans in the Indies forgot! The lack of an international war for almost a century seemed to have turned them all senile.

According to another story, a Dutch seaman once asked the engineer: When the Surabaya project is finished where will Mijnheer Engineer go? His answer was simple and strong: to wherever the Netherlands call me.

Once he had to give a public talk. He talked about how the Dutch first entered South Africa. They had to face the resistance of the inhabitants, the black people who fought with spear and arrow. Do you all know how those black people fought? he asked. They crawled, wriggling along the ground, not standing, but like snakes, moving forward by using their

537

elbows. The Europeans stood straight, rifles ready. The blacks crept forward with spear and arrow – a symbol, and not one of our own making, that the black-skinned people will always crawl beneath our feet. In war and in peace, the white-skinned peoples will always be on top, superior, always standing tall above the crawling coloureds.

Dulrakim never told me if he himself attended that lecture. He couldn't tell me if the people there agreed with the engineer's opinions or not. What he did know was that Engineer Maurits Mellema had been entrusted with the job of building the base for the Netherlands Indies Navy on Perak peninsula, Surabaya, and had been given the honorary rank of Lieutenant-Colonel.

Yes, he is a capable man, Dulrakim commented. He had shown this while leading his men in South Africa, people were saying; and now as a marine engineer he was equally capable at managing the construction of the base. Hundreds of men – perhaps thousands, if you count those not directly involved with the project – obediently carried out his orders. All to bring into being the Netherlands Indies Navy base!

Almost a hundred years ago Daendels knew what had to be done, Mellema was always growling.

Whether all these stories are true or not, only Dulrakim knows. I was amazed at the number of stories he had stored away. He told all these stories as though they had nothing to do with him personally. Uh! you sailor, you untiring collector of stories . . .

It seemed the relationship between Maurits and Herman Mellema would not impose itself on people's awareness ever again. Except for me and Mama. And it was as though Mellema's way to us, both in my fantasy and in reality, had been swept clean and clear for him. Neither he himself nor his clothes need be dirtied or torn by walking some narrow pathway. He came as a god, the god of the Netherlands Indies Navy base project. It was the pet project of the Netherlands Indies Government. It was as though all the power and facilities of the colonial state were being mobilised to ensure the project's success. And Engineer Maurits Mellema was promoted from god of building to god of success.

In Wonokromo a woman would have to confront this double god, alone. This woman had been robbed, with the aid of the law, of her child and property, the products of her sweat, and weariness. She had no legal grounds to stand on. She had never travelled anywhere because the Netherlands had needed her. She had at her side only a youth named Minke and a man named Darsam who could no longer swing his machete. What other strength was still stored away in these three people which could help them confront Engineer Maurits Mellema, now so triumphant in all things?

538

This lone woman wished only for two more friends to be with her. Just two: one Jean Marais - painter, one-legged invalid, introvert; and one Kommer, a reporter from a Malay-Dutch newspaper whose writings had never been able to topple the mountainous combined power of the Indies and the Netherlands.

Mama had said Engineer Mellema was coming to kick her out. I thought the world 'kick' was too strong. That engineer would never have to raise his foot. He would not have to expand the slightest amount of energy. With just one puff, Mama would be exiled forever from her kingdom and her throne. But Mama still felt she had value and worth. Engineer Mellema would come. He would give a little puff, and all humankind living upon the land of the *boerderij* would be blown off, to flutter away like the feathers of a goose.

Jean Marais bowed his head when he heard Nyai Ontosoroh's request; he went pale, perhaps from fright.

'You don't think you can do it, Jean?' I asked.

He sucked on his corn-paper cigarette, then blew out rings of smoke: 'I'm only good with brush and palette, Minke.'

'All right, if you won't come, I'm going to Kommer's now, with the same request from Mama. I'll drop in here on the way back.' Jean could say nothing, but his eyes watched me closely. 'Perhaps you'll have changed your mind by then,' I added.

But his face had changed when he heard Kommer was needed by Mama too. He wiped his mouth and said, 'Go now. I'll wait for you. Perhaps I'll think differently then, Minke.'

I went.

I discovered that Kommer's place was quite large. There were cages everywhere, with their animal occupants: pythons, some mouse-deer, a bear, a leopard, forest roosters, orangutans. He himself was fast asleep in his own cage.

His wife - I don't know if a Mixed-Blood or a nyai, who hadn't given him any children - awakened him. I sat on a rattan settee. He stuck his head out from behind a door, his eyes still bleary: 'Have you been waiting long, Tuan Minke?' he asked in a sleepy voice, then disappeared.

He came out wearing batik pyjamas. His face was wet and his eyes were still red, but on hearing Nyai's request all sleepiness vanished.

'Good, let's go,' he said. 'Let me teach this Maurits Mellema a lesson. 'Give him a good going over, so he knows how it feels, hey?'

His wife followed the conversation from a distance. On hearing I had brought a request from Nyai Ontosoroh, I saw her face change. Her eyes shone with jealousy. She stood up and hurried away, disappearing behind an inner door.

Kommer stood up and went inside too. Not long after there were the sounds of an argument. I heard the noise of plates and cups being thrown about. A woman's scream followed, and crying. But in the end Kommer appeared in fresh and tidy clothes. His hair was parted on the right and shone from too much hair oil. He didn't wear the shoes he wore most days. In their place he put on a pair of patent leather ones from Europe, the latest fashion. On his coat, as an adornment to his watch pocket, hung a leopard's claw and a silver-bound wild boar's tusk, souvenirs of his proudest hunting successes. He looked handsome and dashing, not down and out, nor defeated.

'Can we confront him?' I asked, pretending not to have heard what had gone on inside.

'We'll see what happens.'

'You're optimistic,' I said as I climbed aboard the carriage.

'All great events should be witnessed first hand, Mr Minke; and not just so you can write about them properly for the newspapers. Apart from that . . .' he too climbed aboard.

'What, Tuan Kommer?'

'. . . it makes our own lives fuller.'

If I hadn't known he had proposed to Mama, perhaps I might have become a devoted admirer of the man. I admired what he had just said, but only a little.

The carriage set off nervously for Jean Marais's house.

'He's coming at five o'clock, hey? Just under two hours,' he said as he put his watch back in his pocket.

His eyes examined me. Perhaps he was surprised that I wasn't admiring his wild boar's tusk and his leopard's claw. Perhaps too he was surprised that I had no questions for him. Maybe he had forgotten he'd told me the stories of those souvenirs three times before.

Sitting beside me, he emanated an aroma of perfume that sent my head swimming. I sat silently, as if he were the normally attired Kommer. Who can forbid people from falling in or arousing love? Even the gods can not. The first few pages of the *Babad Tanah Jawi* tells of how the god *Batara Guru* falls madly in love with a woman of the earth. And even *Batara Kala*, the absolute ruler of Time, could not hold the other back, let alone break the power of their love.

The interesting thing was that the behaviour of a middle-aged man who had fallen in love was no different from that of a teenager. Both turned into heroic exhibitionists, out to get everyone's attention. No matter how clever a man is, said my grandmother's maid when I was still very young, if he's been smitten he becomes truly as stupid as the greatest idiot. Why should Kommer be an exception?

When we arrived at Jean Marais's house, we were met by Maysoroh in a new dress. As soon as I climbed down, she held out her hands, wanting to be spoiled.

'You're grown up now. It wouldn't be right to carry you,' I said. She cuddled up to me, so I had to take her by the hand. She looked clean and very pretty. 'You're very pretty today, May. Give me a kiss.' She kissed me on the hand.

We walked inside arm in arm. Kommer was behind us. He didn't seem interested in his surroundings. Perhaps he was busy readying himself for the big event, or preparing himself to look as dashing as possible for Nyai.

And who wouldn't have been surprised to see Jean Marais now? He rose from his chair with great difficulty. His smile was handsome. His moustache and beard had been combed.

'I combed Papa's beard,' said Maysoroh proudly. 'Isn't he handsome now?'

Jean Marais nodded his impatience to leave straight away. His trousers had been ironed. His vest boasted silver buttons. Fantastic! Had he fallen in love with Nyai Ontosoroh too?

'Afternoon, Mr Marais,' called Kommer.

'Afternoon, Mr Kommer. A pity you didn't catch that panther. A great pity that trap I designed didn't work.'

'That panther escaped, but now we're going after another, Mr Marais: Engineer Mellema,' he said in Malay.

'That's right!' answered Jean merrily.

'You're ready for it by the look of you, Tuan.'

'Hmmm. Let's go.'

So it was that we set off in the carriage. I sat next to the driver; Kommer, Marais and May sat in the back. I couldn't quite catch what they were talking about.

'Is Nyai having a party?' whispered the driver, Marjuki.

'A party, Juki, a big party.'

The carriage sped on.

18

That afternoon thick grey clouds hung umbrella-like over Surabaya. There was no wind, no thunder. The air was heavy with humidity. The trees around the house sleepily awaited the rain, and the clouds would not fulfil their promise.

Kommer and Jean Marais were in the front parlour. They sat close to each other, talking like two old bachelors planning illusory adventures.

In the back parlour I found Mama talking to Minem's old mother, who had been given the job of looking after Rono Mellema. Darsam was standing near the back door. Rono was nowhere to be seen.

'Ya, Nyai, I don't know what that Minem really wants. She's a crazy girl. A baby still feeding off the breast and she leaves him like he was just a pile of rags.'

'Darsam, check the gas tanks now. Quickly bathe and then go and turn on the lamps. Put on your very best clothes. And don't forget to tend to your moustache.'

I told Mama that our friends had arrived, all nattily dressed and dashing. Mama smiled happily.

'Is the office closed, Ma?'

'No, Jan Dapperste's there. Wash now, Child; dress in your best. We must be at our very best when we meet Engineer Mellema.'

She herself had changed her clothes and put on her make-up. She looked very attractive. For the first time, I noticed, she wore a necklace and a simple bracelet, along with her velvet slippers with silver embroidery and a black velvet kebaya. Dressed all in black like that she looked much younger, very pretty, with charisma about her. No one could guess what terrible strength she was going to throw against her enemy later. Those words of hers, which earlier had impressed me so much, now seemed ready to be fulfilled: 'Now all I'm left with is a mouth.'

After bathing and dressing, I prayed that she would not resort to violence. Her order to Darsam to dress in his best clothes meant that he was to meet the engineer too. Even that instruction to Darsam gave cause enough for worry.

I did not want to see our visitor die, cut down by Darsam's machete.

Nyai needed only to move her little finger or give Darsam the slightest nod, and the young engineer would die. No, ya Allah, no machete must cut apart his body, no blood bubble from his veins. Ya, Allah, protect us all from that horror. Give Nyai some sign, guide her in her confrontation with the enemy. Side now, Allah, with the weak!

Sitting in the back parlour, I observed her quietly thinking. Her face was clear and bright. I thanked God. She was holding Maysoroh's little hand, paying no attention to the girl's prattle.

May then came over and cuddled up to me. For the thousandth time she asked again: when will Annelies come home from Europe? She stopped her prattle when she heard Nyai call Minem's mother. The middle-aged woman entered obediently and bent to the floor.

'Bring Rono here, and his selendang too, so that I can carry him,' she ordered.

'Rono's still asleep, Nyai.'

'Bring him anyway.'

May now cuddled up to Mama. Seeing Minem's mother hand over a baby to Nyai, May asked straight away in a loud voice: 'Who's this, Nyai? He's beautiful! Whose child, Nyai? Is it Annelies's child?'

'Yes, he is a beautiful child, isn't he?'

'Very beautiful, Nyai. A boy?'

'Of course, May. He's your little brother. Rono, that's his name.'

'Rono, Nyai? What a wonderful name.'

'You wanted to have a little brother, May. He's your little brother now.'

Maysoroh jumped about the room excitedly. Then she took the baby's clean little feet and kissed them.

'Give him here, Nyai, so May can have a turn at holding him,' pleaded May. Her eyes shone with great hope.

'He's not a doll, May, a little brother.'

'Ayoh, come on, Nyai, let me hold him.'

And Nyai gave the baby to May to carry while still holding him herself. Then: 'That's enough, yes? Yes, that's enough. Tomorrow you will have another chance.' Maysoroh seemed satisfied. She jumped around merrily.

'Ma,' I called slowly, 'she wants a little brother or sister, Ma. She wants one very much.'

'You'd like a little brother, May?'

'Yes, Nyai, very much.'

'Does Mama remember that holy task, Ma? From her? She asked for a pretty little sister, Ma.'

Suddenly Mama's face went grey. She gazed at me silently. She embraced Maysoroh with one arm and kissed her forehead.

'Doesn't my little brother ever cry, Nyai?' asks May.

Only then did Mama and I realise that we'd never heard Rono cry.

543

Minem's mother brought in a new batik selendang and Mama used it to carry Rono.

'A bottle and a napkin, Mbok.'

As Minem's mother left, Darsam entered, wearing his best clothes, shining black, made from the best cloth. His machete was in his belt. The tips of his destar stood up in challenge like his symmetrical, thick, curling, pitch-black moustache. He saluted with his right hand, now healed.

'I didn't summon you, Darsam.'

'But there is something I have to report, Nyai,' he said.

'Oh yes. You've met with Jan Tantang.'

'That's right, Nyai. He expressed a thousand thanks and will make use of your offer. A pity, Nyai, such a good man.'

'And you were going to kill him. You were crazy!'

'It was his own fault. There are two other matters, Nyai. That Sinyo Robert . . . the sinyo who came here once and then I took him home . . .'

'Robert Suurhof, Ma,' I added.

'He was made chief gaol bully, Nyai, and beat up Jan Tantang, in the European block. Sinyo Robert was then beaten up in turn by some Madurese. He didn't die, Nyai – just some slight injuries.'

'And what about your friends, Darsam?' She ignored Robert Suurhof.

'That's the second thing, Nyai. They were sentenced to two months' solitary confinement – no visitors, of course.'

'Is that all?'

'That's all, Nyai.'

'Good. Wait with the other guests inside.'

He saluted once again, and left us. Minem's mother brought the bottle and napkin and Nyai tied them to the free end of the selendang. Carrying Rono, rocking him that way, Nyai didn't at all look like a grandmother with her grandson, but like a young mother with her first child.

'I forgot to tell you, Child: the Court acknowledged the child as Rono Mellema, as Robert's son, just after I received Robert's letter and the police message from Los Angeles.'

'That's good, Ma.'

I didn't have the chance to check any further whether Rono really had never cried all that time. All my attention was concentrated on Mama. I wanted to be ready to move if she ordered Darsam to kill Mellema. I hadn't heard her give any such order. But who could know for sure? In the meantime I could only hope and pray.

From the front parlour came the chimes of the pendulum clock; it was a quarter to five. Thunder began to growl in the distance, preceded each time by a flash of lightning. The day was turning gloomy.

'Come on, May, let's go out front.' Maysoroh ran out ahead of us.

'Remember, Child,' whispered Nyai as we walked, 'you will be facing your enemy, your own enemy. Don't be silent, as you usually are.'

'Ya, Ma, before him we only have our mouths. Nothing else.'

'So you need to understand now,' she observed my face, 'he will never read your writings, so he must listen to your voice.'

'How do you know, Ma?'

'People greedy for money and property, Child, never read stories; they are barbarians. They have no concern for the fate of other people, let alone people who exist only in a story. His revenge against his father has now turned into revenge against everything that was ever close to his father. It's a pity Dr Martinet is in Europe at the moment. If he were here . . .'

She nodded to her guests. Jean Marais strove with difficulty to stand as if honouring a great queen.

'Forgive me, gentlemen, that we're a little late,' she said in Malay. 'We thank you for your willingness to be with us as we meet Engineer Maurits Mellema.' She went on, in a somewhat official manner, 'We three believe that at the very least you have come freely to stand beside us in this matter, even if you should decide not to join us in what we do later.' She turned to me and asked 'Where's Darsam?'

Darsam wasn't there. I rushed out back again. I found him changing his destar for the blue-back of a *kain wulung*. And now he was wearing the pocket watch I had given him. Before leaving he took his machete from his belt and inspected it, then walked hurriedly along behind me.

'Do you need to bring the machete, Darsam?' I asked without turning. 'It'd be better if you left it at home.'

'And what is Darsam without his machete?' he asked in turn.

As I turned I saw him stroking his moustache. His eyes shone; he knew that there was some great work to be done.

'It looks like something important is going to happen today, Young Master?'

'Yes. But don't you do anything drastic this time.'

'This Darsam here, Young Master, he knows when he has to act. All is under control. Don't worry.'

My anxiety was aroused once again on hearing those confident words of his.

'Watch out. Don't cause any trouble. You have to realise, Darsam, this time Mama really needs your serious help. Her troubles are very great indeed. Don't you add to them with something new.'

'Don't worry, Young Master, I guarantee all will be well.'

The wind stilled; the world seemed to have stopped breathing. The layers of thick cloud began to sprinkle droplets of rain, hesitantly. The day became darker. The gas lamps were lit by Darsam. The front parlour and the back of the house were bathed in light; the house was magnificent in its grandness.

We each sat on our chairs, arranged in a row facing the front courtyard: Darsam, Jean Marais, Maysoroh Marais, Mama with Rono Mellema, Kommer and me. In front of us was a table and on the other side an armchair for the honoured guest.

It was all arranged so that the light from the lamps would shine down onto Engineer Maurits Mellema while his welcomers would be sheltered from it. Just like the preparations for a scene in a play, I thought – and that was exactly what it was.

No one spoke. Even Maysoroh, the little prattler, became submerged in the oppressive mute atmosphere, more oppressive than awaiting the decision of the Court.

Three times already Kommer had taken out his watch and told us the time. And again now: 'Two minutes past,' he said.

Darsam took out his gold watch, but said nothing.

The drizzle stopped. The atmosphere still oppressed us all.

At ten past five a navy carriage appeared at last in the front courtyard.

I rose and went to the edge of the steps. I had been given the task to greet this man who had murdered my wife. I still hadn't hit upon the right sentence: one evincing never-to-be-reconciled enmity or just the usual greeting to any guest?

The carriage stopped in front of the steps. A sailor jumped down from inside, saluted and opened the door. A young officer alighted, complete with epaulettes on his shoulders and a sword at his waist. He was dressed all in white from the top of his head down to his shoes and laces. He stood erect on the ground, then straightened his shirt. The sailor, also dressed in white, saluted.

'Good afternoon,' I extended my greetings in Dutch. 'Welcome, Mr Mellema.'

He merely nodded without looking at me. His attitude was offensive and hurtful. I felt I wanted to punch in his head, though my arm wouldn't have reached him because he was so tall. Yet I escorted my wife's murderer inside. So this, it appeared, was Engineer Maurits Mellema: tall, with the physique of a sportsman, broad and strong chested, a long pointed nose like those of Greek statues, handsome, dashing, no moustache, no beard, grey eyes. He strode up the stairs with confident steps.

On entering the parlour, he stopped, raised his hand, and said in Malay, 'Greetings!'

The people sitting in the chairs all stood up, as if on command. Jean Marais too, and Nyai carrying Rono Mellema, and Maysoroh too.

'Greetings!' they all answered together.

546

'Am I now meeting Nyai Ontosoroh alias Sanikem?' He continued in Malay, his gaze focused on Mama, ignoring the others.

'You are not wrong, Tuan Engineer Maurits Mellema. I am Sanikem,' answered Nyai. 'Please sit down.'

'No time to sit,' he answered arrogantly. 'This will only take a moment.'

'It does not feel right that it should be just for a moment. Look, the friends of your business have all come to greet you.'

He looked at them one by one, from Darsam at one end to me at the other.

'Let me introduce you to them. Over there, Tuan, is Darsam, our chief of security.'

Darsam ahemmed, and thrust forward his machete. Engineer Maurits Mellema was unsure what to do, and just nodded to the Madurese. The object of the nod showed his teeth.

'Then, there is Tuan Jean Marais, a painter, a French artist.'

The guest was even more unsure of himself now. His legs moved for a moment. Forcing himself, he moved forward, closer, and held out his hand. He asked in French: 'You are a Frenchman?'

'Yes, Mr Mellema.'

'A painter?' he asked, amazed.

'Not wrong, Mr Mellema. And this is my daughter – Maysoroh Marais. Greet Mr Mellema, May.'

The child held out her little hand, and the guest smiled as he took it. He pinched May's chin, saying in French, 'Good afternoon, pretty child.'

May quickly started prattling in French, admiring the embroidery and decorations on his shoulder and sleeves and asking if she could feel them. The guest bent down so she could feel his epaulettes, the gold embroidery on his back, the embellishments to his sleeves, even the decorative cords hanging from his sword.

The tension fell away. This arrogant man was a normal human being; he is fond of little children too, I thought.

And at that moment I felt Mama's sharp gaze piercing my back. I turned to her. Yes, her eyes were watching me to ensure that I was not taken in by this pretence.

'Enough, May. Say thank you,' said Nyai.

Engineer Mellema straightened again and Nyai Ontosoroh continued: 'And this is Tuan Kommer, a journalist, Tuan Mellema.'

The guest was startled again, nodding. Seeing that Kommer was an Indo he didn't offer his hand.

'And on the end there is Tuan Minke, my son-in-law, Annelies's husband.'

He seemed nervous. Standing erect before Nyai, he turned to look at me. I saw that he didn't know what he must do. With a reluctant heart and obviously forcing himself, he stepped towards me. Nyai went on, 'A graduate of H.B.S., a candidate doctor.'

He held out his hand to me, saying in Dutch: 'Yes Tuan, I am here above all else to express my sadness to you.' He turned to Mama and said the same thing to her in Malay.

'No need for that,' said Nyai in Malay when she saw Mellema coming across to her with hand extended. 'The loss of my daughter cannot be replaced by the handshake of her murderer.' Her voice trembled.

Despite the signs of his grandness – his uniform, his white skin – he shrivelled before us. I too shrivelled at those words. My breast tightened, knowing I did not have the courage of my mother-in-law.

'That is too harsh, Nyai,' Engineer Mellema defended himself. 'I understand how sad you and Tuan . . .' he turned to glance at me, 'but to accuse me of murder is going too far. It is not true.'

'Tuan has lost nothing, except respect, in my and our eyes. Yet you have gained everything from our loss,' Nyai went on. Her voice still quavered.

'I can't accept that. Everything has its rules,' the guest answered. He still stood, and all his welcomers still stood also.

'That's true,' said Nyai in Malay, 'there are rules to deprive us and to allow you to profit from everything.'

'I didn't make the rules.'

'But you have done your best to use those rules for your own profit.'

'Nyai can hire an advocate.'

'A thousand advocates cannot return my daughter to me.' Now it was not only her voice that trembled, but also her lips. 'There is not a single advocate who would take on the defence of a Native against a Pure. That is not possible here.'

'What can one do, if that is the will of God?'

'Yes, the will of Tuan has become the will of God.'

Engineer Maurits Mellema went silent, perhaps because his Malay was limited.

'You don't want to be responsible for any of this, so it is God that you order be held responsible. Very beautiful. Why won't you account for yourself to me? To her mother, who gave birth to her, raised her, educated her and looked after her financially?'

The tremble in her voice and her lips slowly disappeared. She turned to me. Now again I shrivelled up, having nothing of my own to fling at him.

'It has already happened,' the guest began again, 'that's why I have come here, to . . .'

'. . . to give up your guardianship over my wife and give it back to me?' I hacked at him, forcing myself, in Dutch.

'. . . to-to-to not to fight.'

548

'You don't need to fight with us. There are many other people you can use to do that, even to kill some of us,' parried Nyai. 'Tuan Kommer, what do you have to say?'

And with that fluency of his, he spoke in Malay: 'Tuan Engineer Maurits Mellema, as a journalist I promise you that everything you say here today will be made public. All of Surabaya will know what kind of man you are. Keep on talking, but maybe you had better sit down.'

Still the guest would not sit. He bit his lower lip.

'Tuan Marais,' asked my mother-in-law, 'this is Tuan Engineer Maurits Mellema about whom you have heard so much. Do you not feel that it is only proper you accept the honour of using this very valuable opportunity to speak with him?'

'*Monsieur Ingénieur* Mellema,' began Marais in French, 'Monsieur was born and educated in Europe, a scholar. So was I, though I did not graduate. But how great is the difference between us, Monsieur; you came here seeking wealth and power, I simply as a wanderer.'

'I came here for the Netherlands,' answered Mellema.

'You did not come to this house for the Netherlands. There is no Netherlands here, not even a picture of the Queen.'

The guest ahemmed; his eyes sought out a picture of the Queen but all he found was a painting of Nyai Ontosoroh, in all her grandness, hanging over the door which led into the back parlour.

'We are both pure-blood Europeans, Monsieur,' Jean Marais continued, 'and I can agree with some of what Nyai has said. You are to blame for Madame Annelies's death. Monsieur owes Nyai and Monsieur Minke a life.'

'There is someone who takes care of all that sort of thing, who is responsible,' answered Engineer Mellema.

'What you took care of, and what you are responsible for, is that death.'

'That's for the courts to say.'

'You are a liar! In your heart, in your conscience, do you feel guilt?'

'No.'

'An even greater lie!'

'We don't understand French,' protested Nyai in Malay. 'Now that you have killed my daughter, when do you want to throw us out?'

The guest was still standing, and went pale for a moment; then he went red with impotent anger. Seeing Mellema was still not ready to speak, Mama went on stabbing at him: 'Very beautiful.'

'So this is what the real Europe is like, the Europe without rival that has been stuffed into my head for so long,' I added in Dutch.

This educated man, this marine engineer turned to me. He answered softly: 'I understand your sorrow, Tuan, and I join with you in your sorrow. But what can be done; it is all over now.'

549

'Very easy. Do you think your life is more valuable than that of my wife?' I swore. 'You thought of my wife as a piece of portable property, that you could shift around at will, that could be treated as you wish. You don't recognise Native law, Moslem law; you did not honour our legal marriage.'

'I didn't come to discuss all that.'

'Yes, you didn't even bother to let us know that my wife had died. You wanted to surprise us with the news of her death. Yes?' I pressed.

Mama exploded in fury when she heard my accusation: 'Good. He doesn't want to talk about all this, the sins which weigh so heavily on his heart. Now just tell us: when do you want to throw us out so that your plan may be complete?'

'You are going to do that too?' asked Kommer.

'It's nothing to do with you,' riposted Mellema.

'Who said so?' Kommer contradicted. 'Everything that happens under the sun is the business of thinking people.'

Now this person, this officer who was used to having his every word listened to, was stuttering, unable to speak.

'If one's feelings of humanity are offended,' Kommer went on, 'everyone with feeling will also be offended, except for people who are mad and those with truly criminal mentalities, even though they may be university graduates.'

'As a European, and more especially as a Frenchman, I too feel offended. That is why I am here,' said Marais in French.

'That's it, Tuan Marais,' Kommer encouraged him, even though he didn't understand French.

'Dressed in your navy uniform like that, with your title of Engineer, you will surely be the subject of my next painting. And what will I call that painting? This: *L'Ingénieur Mellema, Le Vampire Hollandais.*'

Our guest went pale again. His lips seemed to have been deserted by his blood. He had run out of words.

'For the world, for God, one day I will exhibit that painting in Paris, and in your own country.'

'No need to show it in the Indies, however,' I added in French. Marais looked at me, shook his head and smiled.

'There is no need in the Indies, Monsieur Minke,' he answered. 'No vampire likes to admire another.' Marais's voice rumbled in a low tone, like the far-off thunder. 'Murdering people's children, robbing the fruits of a woman's labour, whom he should in fact be protecting; and a Native woman too, whom he normally would consider a barbarian!' He laughed loudly, insultingly. 'Long live Tuan Engineer Maurits Mellema! Long live murderer and thief.'

'There has been no murder, let alone any theft.'

'What did Tuan Mellema, your father, bring here from the Netherlands?' asked Mama. 'No one knows but me: two sets of underclothes. Not even a shirt. It was only afterwards that, together with me, he began to keep a few dairy cattle in Tulangan. Listen to me, Tuan Engineer Mellema. Everything he owned in the Netherlands – I don't know whether it was a lot or not – he left for your mother and you. If you owned a dog, if you know dogs, you would know it could tell you that there is none of the salt of your sweat spilt on the floor upon which you now stand. Nor on the land that I now occupy.' She coughed and Rono woke up. She rocked him in her arms. 'Everything you see around you here would tell you if it could, it is all salty with the sweat from my body.'

'The woman you consider a barbarian is speaking to you now, Tuan Engineer Maurits Mellema,' said Kommer in Malay. 'Now you'll pretend you don't understand Malay?'

'You understand the meaning of *salt* and *sweat*?' asked Jean Marais in Malay.

'I understand,' he answered weakly.

'You haven't spoken enough,' Mama pressed me.

'Mama, I'm admiring, at the moment, an educated European, civilised and cultured, who has robbed my wife in both life and death. So this is what he is like in reality: a graduate, dashing, handsome, tall and well-built, broad-chested . . .'

Engineer Maurits Mellema turned to me: 'Truly, Tuan, I join you in your sorrow,' he said.

'Even the name of my wife's husband he does not know,' I said. 'Was this the kind of guardian my wife had?'

'Truly, Tuan,' now he began to defend himself, 'I was in South Africa at the time.'

'So you're saying South Africa is to blame?'

'Yes, it's indeed South Africa that's to blame,' said Jean Marais. 'Tuan Mellema doesn't have any business with blame, let alone sin. His only business is profit.'

Engineer Mellema, uninvited, dropped to his seat. His white scabbard got in his way and he shifted it with his left hand. His white cap still sat perched on his head.

Seeing him collapse onto his chair, the others with relief sat down as well.

Maysoroh's eyes popped out as she tried to follow the conversation that was going on in French, Dutch and Malay. She did not understand what was happening, but suspicion shone from her eyes, and it went straight towards the visitor wearing all the gold embroidery.

'Speak, Darsam!' ordered Mama.

In Malay, and with words that he had readied in his mind beforehand, Darsam began: 'So it is Tuan who took Noni Annelies. Since she was little, I have been the one who has guarded over her. Every day I took her to and from school. No one dared worry or touch her. Then you came and took her as if she were some goat's kid. And only now I find out' – he couldn't go on for a moment – 'she died at your hands.'

The visitor took out a kerchief. He wiped away his sweat.

'If you like, Tuan can unsheath your sword, and we will fight like men.'

Engineer Mellema pretended not to hear. He didn't even turn to look at Darsam. Darsam stood up, rubbed his machete, and stepped forward.

'Stay where you are,' ordered Mama.

Darsam's face was red with anger. As he edged back to his place, he growled in fury: 'It was I. I who gave Noni away when she married!' He pointed accusingly, still on his feet. 'You wouldn't recognise it! Legal and right! Legitimate in the eyes of my religion!'

Hearing Darsam's roars, two sailors came in, gave a salute and stood on either side of their superior.

'Good. The three of you can fight me at once.'

'Go!' the visitor ordered his guards, 'and bring that *thing* inside!' he shouted without looking behind him.

They saluted, then went to fetch the *thing*. What kind of weapon was it?

'My job is to guard the security of this family and business. Whoever disturbs it . . . Darsam's machete is ready to cut up anyone who deserves it.'

'That's enough Darsam. You have to understand that the Tuan before you now is going to take over all this business, everything that the business owns, now that he has murdered Annelies.'

'He has killed Noni, and now he wants to take everything?'

'Yes, that's the man.'

'It is he, Nyai? He did that?'

'Yes, Darsam.'

'And I must keep still and do nothing, Nyai?'

'You may only speak. Nothing else.'

'Just speak, Nyai? That's all?'

The guest took no notice of the conversation taking place in Malay. He pretended not to hear, but he was struggling to stay calm and in control of himself and the situation.

'But Darsam is willing and ready to fight with him, Nyai,' Darsam's eyes radiated disgust, 'now, later, whenever he wants.'

One of the sailors came back inside. It wasn't a gun he was carrying, but a large package, not heavy, tied up with silk. He saluted, put the thing down beside his officer's feet, saluted again, then left.

'Sit down, Darsam.' Darsam sat down again, still grumbling.

'You shame Europe before Natives,' Marais began again, 'and in the eyes of Europeans too. If you are the best Europe can produce – a graduate, a scholar – what in heaven's name are its ignorant bandits like?'

'Nyai, Tuan-tuan,' Mellema began to regain his confidence and self-

552

control, 'if need be, if you feel it's necessary, take me to court. I am willing, I would accept that happily.'

'Give me a pencil and paper,' asked Kommer. He had forgotten to bring his weapons of war. I gave him what he wanted and he began taking notes straight away.

'You of all people know better than anyone else that there is no way for a Native to sue a European.'

'You can do it, as a European, Monsieur Marais.'

Jean Marais lost his temper. In rapid French he answered: 'Good. I will paint you and exhibit the painting both in France and in the Netherlands. And I will not paint the vampire with a tail but just as you are now, in an officer's uniform, representing the barbarian who salutes the law.'

'Please, do,' answered Mellema.

'Don't worry, Tuan Mellema,' Kommer started, 'I will publish a special edition in both Dutch and Malay. Don't worry, Tuan Engineer Mellema, I will circulate that special edition among the sailors, so that they too may know who you really are.'

'Please do. That is your right,' he answered, with reviving confidence.

'And to the readers of Surabaya, I will say: Read about Lieutenant-Colonel Engineer Maurits Mellema and find out who he really is. I will tell the newspaper boys to shout out on every street corner: He hated his father, but not his father's property, and now he faces his enemy – a Native woman named Ontosoroh, the person who worked to build the wealth of the father Mellema hated so greatly.'

'Superb!' shouted Marais.

'Don't worry, Tuan Kommer,' I said. 'I will write it all out for you in Dutch: the day I met my wife's murderer; the murderer of his own step-sister.'

'No need for a lawyer, no need for a court,' added Mama enthusiastically. 'Only then will I be happy to leave behind what I have worked for all these years, this building and everything in it, the business and all its wealth.'

For the first time, the guest bowed his head deeply, and wiped away the sweat again with this kerchief.

'So, so,' Maysoroh shrilled in her pure, clear voice, 'Sis Annelies is dead, Nyai?' she asked in Dutch.

'Yes, May, she is dead,' answered Nyai.

'This Tuan, he was the one who took her and killed her?'

'Yes, he's the one, May,' answered Marais.

Maysoroh now realised what this meeting was about. She went silent. Her eyes popped out as they stared at Engineer Maurits Mellema. Suddenly her two hands seized her cheeks, and the cheeks went red. Two tears launched forth across those cheeks.

'Sis Annelies is dead! Dead!' she screamed; she pushed out her lower lip as she groaned and groaned.

Engineer Maurits Mellema rose, moved to her, tried to caress her hair. Sorrow defeated the little girl's fear. 'Murderer!' she screamed, and ran inside. From where I was sitting I could hear Minem's mother ask in Javanese: 'What is it, Noni?'

Rono, still in Mama's arms, struggled to get free, voiceless as always.

'Sis Annelies, Mbok, dead, dead, killed by that man in there – the visitor, Mbok, killed by him.'

I couldn't hear whether Minem's mother said anything; all sound was drowned out by May's protests to heaven and earth.

Everyone in the front parlour was silenced as they listened. Mama turned towards the inner rooms and called to Minem's mother: 'Quiet her, Mbok!' Then she hushed Rono, took the bottle of milk wrapped in one end of the selendang, and gave some to him.

The guest seemed confused, listening for a moment to May's cries as they faded into the distance, then glancing across to the baby in Nyai's arms.

'Even that little child knows how to grieve for her sister,' Kommer went on. 'But you want only to profit from her death.'

Engineer Mellema didn't reply. His eyes focused on the baby.

'Everyone here loved Noni Annelies,' Darsam added. 'Only a devil would have the heart to kill her.'

'Tuan Mellema,' Mama began her accusation, 'Tuan needed to have the guardianship of my daughter in order to gain control over her inheritance. Why did no one even visit her before she died? Even when she was buried, there was no one.'

'Who said so? That is a lie, she was looked after well, and as she should have been.'

'Do I need to bring in witnesses? The person, for example, who escorted and looked after my daughter from when she left Surabaya until Huizen and B.?'

'I've a letter from the Huizen Hospital; she was looked after well.'

'Who doesn't believe that the hospital looked after her well? But what about yourself and your mother? Tell me it's a lie! Or tell me you were in South Africa. It is no other than Tuan yourself who knows. Whatever my faults might have been as her mother, I could look after my own daughter better than a thousand women like Amelia Mellema-Hammers.'

Sitting in the corner, Darsam was listening attentively to all the conversation, even if he could not understand it all. Every now and then he twirled his moustache or rubbed his machete.

'I don't believe you treated Annelies in the way that even European custom dictates that a sister, even a step-sister, should be treated.'

The sound of Minem's mother taking May outside floated in from the back parlour. We could see people trying to peer inside. Perhaps Marjuki had told everyone there was going to be a big party.

554

Maysoroh was still shouting and crying out, calling for Annelies and cursing her murderer.

Some of the people who were peering in through the windows withdrew from view. Perhaps they wanted to hear what May was crying about. Soon the village people began to gather around the front of the house, men and women, children too, swarming around everywhere. Several women were being shooed out of the back parlour by Minem's mother. Maysoroh's crying wasn't as loud as a minute ago. Coming from not far behind us we could hear her weeping, interspersed with Javanese: 'That's him, yes, that's the one, he killed Sis Annelies! That's the one who did it, Mbok, him!'

The women pushed forward, closer to the door that led from the back to the front parlour. Engineer Mellema lifted his head to look at them. He stood up. But before he could go, Nyai quickly spoke again: 'So when do we have to get out of here?'

'I've already appointed someone to manage the business.'

'So when do we have to leave?'

'I've decided on a postponement.'

'Good. A postponement. And what about this child? Rono Mellema?'

Maurits Mellema looked at the baby. His eyes blinked: 'Who is Rono Mellema?'

'You had better take the child with you now. The baby will be easier to kill. If you don't, you'll get a smaller inheritance. You couldn't possibly let him live. This child has never cried. Perhaps he has been mute since birth.'

People began to push closer to the door, both at the front and into the back parlour.

Mama held out the baby to him: 'Take this baby with you, your own nephew, also a Mellema heir.'

Maurits Mellema looked confused.

'Don't think of him as a rival, Tuan Mellema,' said Jean Marais in Malay, in a clear voice so that everyone could understand. 'And don't murder him – for the Netherlands.'

'You can't even bring yourself to touch your own nephew,' added Kommer. 'He too has property, Tuan; you're not going to give up his wealth, are you?'

'Why do you hesitate?' pressed Mama, 'Take the baby. We believe you'll be a good guardian.'

The guest didn't know what to do.

It was then that Maysoroh ran back into the front parlour. Her eyes were red and wet. Crying out, weeping uncontrollably, she lifted her little hand to point at Engineer Mellema: 'Yes, here he is, Engineer Maurits Mellema. He stole Sis Annelies. He killed her!'

May lost control of herself. She ran up to the big marine engineer, and threw her little punches onto his thighs and stomach. 'Give Annelies back! Give her back!'

Some of the women behind us could now also be heard crying and sobbing. Then somebody asked in Javanese: 'Noni Annelies is dead? He killed her?'

'Noni killed her.' Maysoroh pointed accusingly, exhausted from her punching.

'Why is Cak Darsam doing nothing?' someone whispered.

'I will not throw you out, Tuan Mellema, because this house is your property,' said Nyai. 'Go now, before there's a riot. They know how to feel sorrow, they are all sorrowful and angry.'

'Give her back, give her back!' cried Maysoroh, panting.

Engineer Maurits Mellema pointed to the parcel at his feet, but no voice came from his mouth. The tip of his finger trembled. He turned his back to us and strode heavily out of the room. His left hand gripped his scabbard.

We remained seated.

Maysoroh followed him, pulling at his trousers and groaning 'Give back Sis Annelies! Sis Annelies! Sis Annelies!'

Mellema did not look back. His two arms did not swing. His body was stooped as he descended the front steps. He looked like a frog lost among a crowd of humans. He looked small, insignificant.

The crowd parted to make way for him. You could hear them buzzing beneath the shouts of Maysoroh, who was still tugging at him: 'Murderer! Murderer of your own step-sister!'

Darsam jumped up, pulled out his machete and began swinging it about: 'Animal! Evil, filthy animal!' he roared.

'Noni Annelies, oh Nyai, we didn't realise,' the people expressed the sorrow they shared.

Mama didn't answer. She gave Rono to one of the women. She opened the parcel the guest had left behind. In it was an old tin suitcase, dented and rusty. She opened it. There were a few sets of Annelies's clothes.

'Good,' she sighed, and stood up.

For only the second time ever, I saw Mama shed tears. She could not bear the sight of her daughter's clothes, packed in the suitcase she herself had taken with her when first she was sold to Herman Mellema.

She quickly wiped away the tears.

'Just as we will always remember this day, he too will be haunted by it, all his life, and into the grave.'

'Yes, Ma, we fought back, Ma, even though only with our mouths.'

Buru, spoken 1973
written 1975

556

Glossary

Acehnese	the people of Aceh, the northern-most province of Sumatra, well known for its militant Islamic sentiments
aduh	a common exclamation
andong	a traditional horse cart, similar to a buggy
arak	Javanese liquor
Assistant Resident	for each regency there was a Dutch Assistant Resident in whose hands power over local affairs ultimately resided
auction papers	newspapers that publish announcements relating to auctions, and advertisements
Ayoh	an exclamation meaning 'come on!'
azan	the call to prayer at the mosque

babah	a term referring to Chinese shop-owners, which also has connotations of 'boss'
Babad Tanah Jawi	a classical Javanese literary work, claiming to trace the history of the rulers of Java
bahu	a measure of area, equivalent to 7096.5 square metres
Baleo	kinds of 'magistrates' in the period of the Dutch East Indies Company, who had the right to use the Company's own soldiers; *baleo* is from the Dutch *baljuw*

bang	'older brother', 'comrade' – friendly but respectful
Banowati	a character in *Wayang* – She was a queen, and renowned for her beauty
Bapak	literally 'Father', used to indicate respect
Batara Guru	Siva, the greatest of Hindu Gods
Batara Kala	Hindu god of death
batik	a process for decorating cloth by using wax to prevent some areas from absorbing dye
belggol	a 2½-cent coin
Betawi	the Malay name for Batavia, the capital of the Dutch East Indies, now Jakarta
Bharatayuddha	a famous Hindu epic, depicting a great war between two families of nobles
biawak	iguana
blangkon	traditional Javanese head-dress made from *batik* and worn mainly by the nobility, or those with pretensions to an elite status
boerderij	(Dutch) firm, company
Boerderij Buitenzorg	the Buitenzorg Agricultural Company – the name of Nyai Ontosoroh's late husband's firm, which Nyai had always managed
bupati	the title of the Native Javanese official appointed by the Dutch to administer a region; most *bupatis* could lay some claim to noble blood
Buta Ijo	a giant ogre with a rapacious appetite

C

cak	East Javanese term for 'older brother' or 'comrade'
camat	the title of the native official in charge of several villages

candi	traditional Hindu temple
carambol	a kind of billiards
cempor	paraffin wax
'chicken-clawed'	an idiom meaning 'bare-footed'
Chinese Officer	a member of the Chinese community appointed by the colonial government to supervise tax collection within that community
chiu	Chinese wine
Culture System	the system of forced cultivation of certain crops enforced by the colonial authorities; under this system, Javanese peasants had to grow export crops such as coffee and sell them to the Dutch authorities at extremely low prices

D

Daendels	Governor-General of the Netherlands East Indies, 1807-11
dalang	the puppet-master of Javanese shadow puttetry
de Lafste	'the most cowardly'
delman	a kind of horse carriage
destar	an East Javanese form of head-dress; a kind of head-band
dokar	a two-wheeled horse cart
dukun	traditional Javanese magician and/or healer
Dutch East Indies Company (VOC); the Company	*Vereenigde Oost Indische Compagnie*, United (Dutch) East India Company

E

Eighty Years War	a seventeenth-century war between Holland and Spain, ending in the Peace of the Hague in 1648

ELS	Dutch-language primary school
Roorda van Eysinga	a writer (1825-1887), expelled from the Indies in 1864 because his writings were regarded as harmful to the colonial government

F

Factorij	Dutch for 'factory' – refers to a memorial publication on the history of the sugar mills
Forschung and Prefung	a Dutch term for 'research and experiment'
forum privilegiatum	the right to appear before the 'White Court'
Francis, G.	Eurasian author of the early Malay-language novel *Nyai Dasima*

G

gamelan	traditional Javanese percussion orchestra
gapit	the stick, made usually from buffalo horn, that keeps the leather shadow puppet rigid
garuda	the mythical magical bird upon whom the gods rode
Gatotkaca	a character from *wayang* stories who has the ability to fly
grobak	a large carriage sometimes pulled by buffalo or cattle, or even by men
guling	a long cylindrical pillow, also called a 'Dutch wife'
gus	a term of affection used among the families of the Javanese aristocratic elite by parents towards their male children

H

haji	the pilgrimage to Mecca, or the title of someone who has made the pilgrimage itself

halal	permissible according to Islamic law (see *haram*)
Hanchou	a city regarded by the Chinese to be one of the most beautiful in the world
haram	forbidden according to Islamic law, sinful (see *halal*)
harvest-time fever	an illness induced by extreme expectations and hyperactivity prior to harvest
HBS	the prestigious Dutch-language senior high school
hermandad	a neighbourhood night-watchman
hordah	Dutch military slang for 'Who goes there?'
hosee	a cry of excitement, exuberance and enjoyment
Dr Snouck Hurgronje	a Dutch scholar who was an influential adviser on Native Affairs to the colonial government
husy	equivalent to 'hush' or 'shush!'

I

Indisch	the Dutch term for Dutch Indies Eurasians
Indische Bond	founded in 1898, this was an association of Indies Eurasians demanding an end to discrimination against them by the Dutch colonial elite
Indische-Gids	'Manual of the Indies': a series of government reports containing economic, historical and statistical material on the Netherlands Indies
Indo	a term used to refer to Dutch–Indonesian mixed-bloods

J

Japanese Gardens	houses of prostitution

Java Doctor	someone trained in the Dutch-run special medical school set up exclusively for Indies Natives
Java Kade	the 'Java Docks' – the part of Amsterdam harbour where ships from Java docked
jawara	term for a rebellious hero or fighter
joged	a popular Javanese dance, in which the audience often participates

K

kabaya	a Javanese woman's traditional blouse worn always in combination with a *sarong*
kabupaten	the formal local term for the administrative area that an Assistant Resident (through the *bupati*) administers
kain	traditional dress worn by Javanese women; a kind of *sarong* wrapped tightly around the waist and legs
kain wulung	a head-dress usually worn by Moslem students and therefore with additional status
Katasura, Court of	the court of the sultanate of Mataram (in 1740 a rebellion by the Chinese population, backed by a sultan of Madura, attacked Katasura and annihilated the Dutch East Indies Company troops guarding the Court)
kati	a unit of weight (625 grams)
Katipunan	an abbreviated form of '*Kataastaasang Kegalang-galang na Katieunan ng mga Anak ng Bayan*' (Supreme and Venerable Union of Children of the Nation), a Filipino secret association with the goal of achieving national independence
kemban	a long, narrow sash wrapped around the body above the waist
keris	traditional curved-blade Javanese dagger

kliwon	one of the days of the Javanese five-day week
koh or *engkoh*	Chinese for 'father' – the equivalent to *bapak*
kompeni	Dutch soldier, this originally referred to the soldiers of the Dutch East Indies Company
kowe	familiar form of 'you' in low Javanese, considered an insult if used by lower-class person to member of elite
KPM	the Dutch shipping company operating in Netherlands Indies
kretek	a four-wheeled horse-drawn carriage
kris	see *keris*
Kulo-nuwun	polite high Javanese greeting, especially used when visiting somebody's house
kuntow	one of the Chinese martial arts

L

La Solidaridad	a newspaper published by the Filipino community in Spain in the 1870s (although a moderate publication, demanding only the assimilation of the Philippines with Spain, it inspired the formation of the more nationalistic *Katipunan*)
lasting	a kind of plain material
leberan	the festival days at the end of the Moslem fasting month
legi	one of the days of the Javanese five-day week
Lodewijk the Sixteenth	Dutch for Louis XVI of France, who was overthrown during the French Revolution

M

mahjong	a Chinese gambling game

Marechaussee	the elite troops of the colonial army in the Netherlands Indies
mas	Javanese term of address literally meaning 'older brother'; used by a young woman towards a man, it indicates an especially close, respectful affection; it can also be used between men, indicating respectful friendship; by a sister to her older brother; and also by a wife to her husband
Mataram	a Javanese kingdom founded in the late sixteenth century
Max Havelaar	novel by Eduard Douwes Dekker (Multatuli)
mbok	colloquial Javanese for 'mother'
meneer	Dutch for 'Sir' or 'Mr'
'mevrouw, mevrouw	Dutch for 'Madam' or 'Mrs'
mrojol selaning garu	literally 'to escape from the prongs of the rake', an idiom meaning to diverge in behaviour from the usual norm
Multatuli	pseudonym of Eduard Douwes Dekker, an outspoken humanist critic of Dutch colonialism and author of the anti-colonial novel *Max Havelaar*
Mylord	(English) a luxuriously outfitted horse carriage

N

nah!	a common exclamation
ndoro	an honorific used by a lower-class person when speaking to someone in the feudal class or of similar status
nduk	an affectionate way of addressing young girls (from *genduk*, meaning 'young girl')
noni	'miss'
nyai	the Native concubines of Dutch men in the Indies

Nyai Dasima	the heroine of G. Francis' popular Malay-language novel
Nyai Royo Kidul	the powerful goddess of the seas to the south of Java
nyo	abbreviated form of *sinyo*, used to refer to young Dutch boys

O

Onze Koloniale Modderpoel	'The Cesspool of Our Colonical Policies'
Oranje Vrijstaat	small Boer (overseas Dutch) states in South Africa
Oriental status	inhabitants of the Netherlands East Indies were divided into three categories: European, Oriental and Native; European and Oriental status conferred special privileges on those concerned; included in the Oriental category were Chinese, Jews and, for a time, Japanese

P

pak	see *bapak*
Pancatantra	a collection of five stories of Indian origin with animal characters, and with a strong didactic character
Panji stories	a collection of stories of knightly heroism, based on the legendary activities of an eleventh-century Javanese prince
'Pantoen Waktoe Kadatangan Prince Frederick Hendrik di Ambon'	'A Poem on the arrival of Prince Frederick Hendrik in Ambon'
patih	the chief executive assistant of a *bupati*
peci	small black velvet cap, originally a sign of Islam
pendopo	a large roofed verandah or reception area at the front of a Javanese dignitary's residence

perak	a Malay term for one *rupiah* (100 cents)
plikemboh	a nickname slang for 'ugly, disgusting penis'
preng	Dutch military slang for 'friend', a reply to military interrogation: 'Who goes there?'
priyayi	members of the Javanese aristocracy who often became the salaried administrators of the Dutch

R

raden ayu	title for aristocratic Javanese woman, especially the first wife of a *bupati*
raden mas	*'raden'* and *'mas'* are titles held by the mass of the middle-ranking members of the Javanese aristocracy; *raden mas* is the highest
ringgit	2½ *rupiah* or 2½ *perak*
rupiah	basic unit of currency (100 cents)

S

sanggul	a traditional Javanese hairstyle – a bun at the back of the head
satan	an abbreviation of the term 'Assistan Wedara', the powerful assistant to the Native District Head, the *wedara*
sausing	Chinese wine
selendang	a sash worn by Javanese women as part of traditional Javanese costume
S.E.&O.	'Save of Error and Omission Certificates', a statement that accounts have been audited and found without error
SIBA	high school to train Native boys for the civil service
silat	a Malay form of self-defence
Sinar Djawa	'Light of Java'

sinkeh	term used to refer to a Chinese immigrant
sinshe	a traditional Chinese healer
sinyo	form of address for young Dutch and Eurasian men or Europeanised Native young men, from the Portuguese *'senor'*
slametan	a traditional Javanese ceremony where people come together to share a ritual meal to commemorate an auspicious occasion
smaadschrift	the Dutch word for libel
Speceraria	the name of Nyai Ontosoroh's new spice trading business
Sumatra Kade	Sumatra Docks

T

talaq	the Moslem divorce procedure
talen	Indies currency, a quarter of a *rupiah*
tali	a 25-cent coin
tayub	a folk dance in which the male partner is normally chosen by the professional female dancer from among the audience
tetirah	to go away to rest, often to the mountains, in order to recuperate from illness or fatigue
Thong	Chinese secret societies
Transvaal	small Boer (overseas Dutch) state in South Africa
tricolour	the Dutch flag
Trunajaya	a prince of the island of Madura who lead a successful rebellion against the Javanese nobility in the late seventeenth century (the nobles of the Javanese sultanate of Mataram only succeeded in defeating Trunajaya when Dutch military might was against him)

truno	the Javanese word for 'young'
tuan	Malay word meaning 'master' or 'sir'
Tuan Raden Mas	the title of nobility of lesser rank
TVK	abbreviation for Tijdeman and Van Kerchem, the company that owned the sugar mills in Tulangan, Tjandi and Krembong in the Sidoarjo area

U

ulamas	Moslem teachers or learned men

V

Vervolg	a primary school for non-Dutch-speaking Natives
VOC	'Vereenigde Oost Indische Compagnie': Dutch East Indies Company – the major power in the Indies until 1798, when it was taken over by the Dutch government
Vorstenlanden	the region covered by the kingdom of Surakarta and Jogjakarta in central Java
Vrizinnige Democraat	a liberal democratic party, whose members were known as 'radicals' because its first name had been *'Radicale Bond'* ('Radical League')
Vrouwen naar Jacartra	'Women of Jayakarta'

W

wayang	shadow puppets
wedana	the native district officer in the colonial administration

Y

yu	abbreviated form of 'mbakyu', a familiar term meaning 'elder sister'

FOR THE BEST IN PAPERBACKS, LOOK FOR THE PENGUIN

ALSO BY PRAMOEDYA ANANTA TOER

Footsteps

As the world moves into the twentieth century, Minke, one of the few European-educated Javanese, optimistically starts a new life in a new town, Betawi, new studies at medical school and new friends. At last he can leave behind the tragedies of the past.

Minke cannot escape being part of an oppressed people under a foreign power. His world begins to fall apart. But a small and passionate group draws together to fight back against colonial exploitation.

During the struggle, Minke finds love, deep friendship and horrifying deceit. He and the others of this group begin to understand the great personal danger they face from powerful and merciless enemies.

This is the third novel in the Minke series

House of Glass (available 1991)

The nationalist movements are gathering force in the Indies as well as China and the Philippines. Jacques Pangemanann, a police officer, is given the job of containing and crushing the emergent desire for reform of the colonial rule.

Minke is a major leader who needs to be neutralised, but as Pangemanann becomes more successful his conscience becomes more painful.

This is the final novel in the Minke series.

FOR THE BEST IN PAPERBACKS, LOOK FOR THE PENGUIN

BOOKS BY BLANCHE D'ALPUGET IN PENGUIN

Monkeys in the Dark

Young Australian journalist Alexandra Wheatfield takes a job in Djakarta at a time of chaotic change: President Sukarno is about to be overthrown, and he has warned the people that without him they are like 'monkeys in the dark'.

Alexandra is moved by the raw colour and sullen violence of life in the city, and it mirrors her affair with Maruli Hutabarat, poet and party activist. But she is faced with the conflicting demands of two societies – her own and that of her lover – and she is finally betrayed by both.

'Blanche d'Alpuget's novel reveals more about the cultural, social, political and sexual tensions of Australians working – or filling in diplomatic time – in Indonesia than a thousand guarded press releases.'

Financial Review

Turtle Beach

Judith Wilkes, an ambitious journalist, goes to Malaysia to report on an international refugee crisis. Ten years before, Malaysia had provided Judith with her first major career success . . . but also with personal disaster.

Through her encounters with Minou, exotic, young French-Vietnamese wife of a high-ranking diplomat, the ambitious Ralph Hamilton and, ultimately with enigmatic Kanan who tries to liberate her, Judith is thrown into dramatic personal and professional conflicts.

The train of events has a Graham Greene sense of inevitability as the characters move between cultures and the tensions heighten.

It is on the East Malaysian coast, when turtles gather to breed, that the dilemma reaches its tragic, brutal climax.

'The sort of novel one encounters at very rare intervals: broad in scope, ambitious, yet written with a crisp breezy intelligence . . .'

Newsweek

FOR THE BEST IN PAPERBACKS, LOOK FOR THE PENGUIN

High Banks, Heavy Logs Nikom Rayawa

A fascinating novel set in the forest country along the banks of the Yom River in Thailand. Kham Ngai is very attached to his elephant, Phlai Sut. When the elephant is sold to a local businessman, Kham Ngai goes to work as a woodcarver and taxidermist. To recreate his lost love, he tries to carve a life-size wooden elephant for his son. After many years the carving is complete but when Phlai Sut is injured and the businessman offers to trade the ailing old animal for the work of art, Kham Ngai does not hesitate.

This story about man and nature and man and himself set in the Thai rainforest won the South-East Asian Writer's Award.

Lower Latitudes James McQueen

A new collection of short stories from a master of the art which takes the reader on a voyage of the imagination to the tropics. Although many of the settings will be familiar – Tahiti, Thailand, the Philippines, the Cook Islands – James McQueen's delightful (and not so delightful) characters add a new dimension.

'Wonderful feel for relationship between people and place.'

Judith White